The
Agenda

THE TRIBULATION SERIES
Book One

The

Agenda

Ralph D. Curtin

RESOURCE *Publications* • Eugene, Oregon

Resource Publications
A division of Wipf and Stock Publishers
199 W 8th Ave, Suite 3
Eugene, OR 97401

The Agenda
The Tribulation Series Book One
By Curtin, Ralph D.
Copyright©2007 by Curtin, Ralph D.
ISBN 13: 978-1-5326-8777-8
Publication date 4/6/2019
Previously published by Oaktara, 2007

The Agenda is a work of fiction. References to real people, events, establishments, organizations, or locales are intended only to provide a sense of authenticity and are used fictitiously. All other characters, incidents, and dialogue are drawn from the author's imagination.

To the avid student of prophecy
who knows that the Bible
is true and alive.

To Kathy, my helpmate,
and Michael, my son,
who labored to bring this work to fruition.

Acknowledgments

Praise and accolades for OakTara. Their passion for storytelling is an inspiration for authors who long to see their ideas and experiences shaped into a novel, then placed into the hands of readers who demand excellence.

ONE

Bacteria, protozoa, viruses.
About the only genuine sporting proposition
that remains unimpaired by the relentless domestication
of a once free-living human species
is the war against these ferocious little fellow creatures,
which lurk in the dark corners and stalk us,
and waylay us in our food and drink and even in our love.
Hans Zinsser

Caravan Airlines had begun operating their economy flights between Miami and Trinidad nearly two years earlier, and the prospect for continued success appeared very bright. Hauling cargo between the two points, together with the increase in passenger service, enabled the carrier to maintain low fares, even during peak travel periods. *Economy, even for a college professor, must be factored into the expense equation,* Jonathan Keahon thought, as the aircraft circled the small landing strip strategically located on the tiny Caribbean island.

The sea looked especially beautiful in November. The early morning sun smiled low on the horizon, its rays reflecting off the blue and green waters. Johnnie basked in the warm thoughts that Trinidad would always be a tropical waterway between the frigid North and the sunny warm vacationland of the Greater and Lesser Antilles.

Johnnie's gaze panned from the sea over to the minute patch of green that appeared in the aircraft window. He mused that within several hours, he would be walking in that dense foliage looking for butterflies: exotic butterflies. The kind that inhabit jungles and sun-baked fields like this southern outpost, offering ideal conditions for feeding and breeding.

He retrieved his field manual from his attaché case, then pulled out one of the many clear plastic sheets that transported his 35-mm trans-

1

parencies and held it up to the light. He stared at the image of Diaethria aurelia, compared the image to the reference book, and said to himself, *You're a jewel. This time I'm going to get you.*

"What in the world is that?" a pretty stewardess asked, casually glancing at his work as she walked by.

"They're my butterflies—my children, you could say," Keahon replied. Then with a devilish grin he added, "I'm a lepidopterist."

The stewardess did a double take at the handsome middle-aged man. "A what?" she inquired, almost blushing. He might have been a bug collector, but he was still quite dashing with a full head of jet-black hair and a wiry build, accentuated by a thin line moustache reminiscent of David Niven.

"A lepidopterist; I do research on butterflies and moths," he continued while exhibiting the slide sleeve. The stewardess's relief was evident as his explanation continued. "I teach zoology at Miami College, and I'm flying down here for another collecting trip. Actually, I don't really collect them. I just photograph them." Johnnie held the sleeve to the window to see the iridescent colors cascade through the insect's wings.

Shaking her head in astonishment, the stewardess moved to pick up the magically colored card. "That's amazing! You sure have come a long way to get them."

"Well," Johnnie said, "I'm after a special one this time. If the bug won't come to you, you have to go to the bug!"

The stewardess gave Johnnie a glowing smile as the captain announced the tower had cleared their flight for landing.

Johnnie stowed his images, closed his eyes, and relaxed as Ivo Pogorelich hammered out Chopin's "Piano Concerto No. 2" into his earphones.

At the hotel, Johnnie meticulously organized his photography equipment for his tour of the bush. He loved photography and often used it as a form of therapy to disengage himself from his rigorous teaching schedule.

Preparation was of particular importance; his 105 mm macro lens and the TTL flash that sported a portable dome to diffuse the light on the subject at high magnifications were essential. Being the consummate professional, Johnnie had begun to carry two camera bodies some time ago: one he used for chromes or slides, the other for digital. As a teacher in zoology he would show his images to his students. The better images he would sell to butterfly collectors or calendar and greeting card companies. These sales augmented his teaching salary to allow continued forays to increase his growing collection.

The phone rang.

Johnnie quickly recognized the voice of Manny, the hotel's manager. The native's singsong accent made Johnnie smile. England's influence touched everyone here with an individual style.

"Your Jeep is ready, Mr. Keahon, and it looks like weather cooperates with you. Good luck to find da bugs, mon."

Johnnie thanked him and got off the phone, making a mental note to increase the size of Manny's tip when he checked out. He liked a man who took care of things without being told.

The island was small, but the people made up for it in enthusiasm. He double-checked his gear and headed for the lobby. Once outside, Johnnie breathed deeply and agreed with Manny. The weather was beautiful and just right for photographing butterflies. Cool afternoon temperatures meant the sun-powered creatures finally came down on plant leaves for a landing, creating the perfect setting for an ideal shot. On sunny, bright days, the fliers performed aerial zigzags at high speeds, making it extremely difficult to capture them on film. There were those who coaxed butterflies by enticing them with fruit, pollen, or even carrion, but for Johnnie the naturalist, no means of coercion was necessary. He would hunt them down, stalk them—even wait days for them—in order to catch them in their perfect habitat. To him that was more than half the fun.

Johnnie motored along the winding route to the rain forest while the brisk afternoon air swirled through the Jeep's cabin. His heart reveled in anticipation of what lie ahead. Exhilarated by heights, he stopped the Jeep and walked to the El Cerro del Aripo overlook. Rising over three thousand feet above the sea, the observation point afforded a grand view of neighboring Tobago Island, situated only 20 miles north of where he stood. He marveled at the beauty of the Caribbean with its rich blue waters and azure skies. *Despite the encroaching industry,* he thought, *this is still a slice of paradise where I can find peace in a hostile world.* He took a moment to reflect upon his own life, and the serenity began to pervade his thoughts. He forced himself to focus on his trip, and slowly the feeling of peace receded.

Conscious of the fading light, Johnnie jumped back in the Jeep and headed downrange to the rain forest. His thoughts began returning to butterflies and the recent reports from returning guides that told of sightings of the Diaethria aurelia butterfly, native to Trinidad but rare in North and South America. Commonly called the 89 butterfly, this species of the family Nymphalidae had been threatened with extinction since modern development caused the destruction of millions of acres of rain forest each year. Being a graceful solar flier, this species had a wingspan of almost two inches. The upperside of the forewing was dark with a short green band in the center. The underside of the forewing was red, patterned with alternating black and white bands in the discal area. On the hind wings the alternate black and white bands formed a figure 89, giving the species its common name.

Johnnie sniffed the wind as he drove. His keen ability separated the scent of the Trema micrantha, which the 89 butterfly caterpillar feeds on, bringing a surge of confidence. He recalled his pledge and chanted his mantra, "This time I'm gonna get ya," over and over. The forest appeared before him, and he entered in; the outside world withdrew as he was drawn to his prize.

Jean Claude lifted his knee to hold the steering wheel steady while he tightened the bandanna that held his long, black, curly hair in place. He hated sweat dripping into his eyes while he drove. As he sped through the forest in the incessant heat, his thoughts centered on what captured his attention the most: he detested the dirt roads of Trinidad's forest hills during dry periods. Traversing the rough ranges in a car was bad enough, but to drive a step van in these mountains gave him the creeps—especially when he was late for a delivery. But the special pay was good, and he needed it. England's influence had disappeared long ago when it came to the standard of living.

Despite the long working hours to prove himself, he determined in his mind not to upset Larry, Rainbow's crew chief, who handled incoming cargo. He had to keep his options for advancement open. For a man of 35, he had a future to consider. He really didn't care about the cargo itself. He had been around enough to know that petroleum and rubber companies rarely got secret deliveries of unknown cargo. After six months, he still had no idea of what he was delivering, only that the cargo smelled. Yet his curiosity didn't get the best of him. If he was caught inspecting the cargo, he knew his job and career would be over with Rainbow. With the employment problem in Trinidad, he couldn't take any chances.

He was told he had an "entry position"; that's what this delivery job was all about. Greater responsibility was promised within six months. "We will move you inside, supervising cargo shipments," they told him. *Yeah, mon,* Jean Claude thought, *for sure. It's been six months, and I'm still driving this truck. And it still smells!*

Jean Claude reacted to the oncoming vehicle but not fast enough. He hammered the brakes, then veered left to avoid the Jeep that suddenly appeared in the road as the truck slid into a roadside ditch.

"You idiot!" Jean Claude yelled. He jumped from the truck to survey the damage, relieved that it had not flipped over but concerned since one axle hung suspended in the air. "Oh no, mon!" he cried out, throwing his hat to the ground.

"Are you all right, Mac?" the driver of the Jeep inquired, coming from behind him. "Thank God you were going slow, or you could've been hurt," he added while dropping to the ground to inspect under the truck.

"What are you doing here?" retorted Jean Claude. He glanced at the man's photo vest and the dangling cameras. The man's face reminded him of some actor he'd seen on a vintage late-night TV movie. "This is not a nature trail, mon. My truck is in deep trouble. How will I make my delivery?" he lamented as he pointed to the wheels still spinning in the air.

"Your delivery? You almost killed me, *mon*!" The stranger's use of the vernacular was peppered with sarcasm and anger.

Now he'd really be late, Jean Claude realized. It was time to deal with the situation and the possible consequences. "I'm sorry, but please—can you help me? I have to get this truck goin' and get my delivery done on time."

The earnest plea seemed to placate the stranger. His voice softened, and he visibly relaxed. "Okay, okay." He held out his hand. "I'm Johnnie

Keahon."

Jean shook his hand. "I'm Jean Claude."

"I'm sure you were as surprised by me as I was by you," Johnnie said. "I'll connect the cable from my front-end winch to your bumper and pull you out."

Johnnie walked around the other side of the truck toward his Jeep. A branch was piercing the truck's aluminum side. He examined the shredded metal and exclaimed, "What's this?" He looked up. A branch had been severed from the tree and was now protruding through the thin aluminum siding of the truck. The light metal had offered scant protection against the hearty tree when both met during the abrupt collision.

Jean Claude stood gaping at the hole, then glanced nervously down at the liquid dripping from the seams. It was blood!

"What are you carrying in here, anyway?" Johnnie asked. He stepped back to read the writing on the side of the truck. "'Rainbow Petroleum and Rubber?' Since when is oil the same color and smell as blood?" He took off his hat and waved it in the air as if signaling an alert and coolly added, "Okay, open this truck. Right now!"

Jean Claude flew into a panic. He made up his mind to get away quickly without answering any questions. "It can't be blood, mon," he shot back. "It must be some form of transmission fluid or something," he offered lamely. Rotating on one foot, he pointed his finger at Johnnie. "Are you going to help me or not? I've got to get to da plant!"

Johnnie considered Jean Claude, then reached down and poked his finger in the small red pool on the dirt road. Smelling his finger, he looked at Claude and said with a sardonic grin, "Sure. It's transmission fluid." Wiping his finger on his handkerchief, he added, "Okay, let's get you going."

Jean Claude nodded in assent and breathed a sigh of relief.

Johnnie went back to his Jeep and hooked up the winch.

Jean Claude felt like his chest was on fire and had to force himself to breathe. Not until he resumed his journey did the panic begin to subside. He knew the stranger did not believe him and saw that he was smart enough to stay out of something that was not his business. *Americans,* he thought as the plant came into view, *are not as stupid as in da movies.* He actually managed a bright smile, feeling confident the man would forget the incident.

The daylight needed to photograph the butterflies had ebbed away. Johnnie watched Jean Claude as he sped away. His mind reeled over the realization that something more than just an accident happened. But what? *I'm not a reporter. I have no interest here except my photography.* He continued to repeat this in his mind, but he couldn't turn his thoughts away from the imagery of some horrific scene inside the truck. *Why can't I just let it go? But what was he carrying in that truck?*

As his thoughts raced, he realized it was time to return to his hotel. Tomorrow he would return to the bush and look for his prey. Tonight he had some phone calls to make.

After sending an E-mail to his friend Brandon Lane, Johnnie linked his laptop to the Internet. *Thank God for telephone lines and technology.* Johnnie's laptop was his key to modern civilization no matter where he went. With it, even in the bush, contemporary society was only a phone line away.

Brandon didn't understand his penchant for butterflies, but he had a keen interest in Trinidad. Johnnie began to understand why, as he browsed the search engine. He began his online query with the key words: *rainbow petroleum/rubber products.*

The computer whirred while he waited for his answer. Within seconds he had his response:

> *A Subsidiary of the Rainbow Corporation, Rainbow Petroleum is the largest exporter of petroleum products in Trinidad. Through government contracts, Rainbow leases the 12,000-acre tract of land for both research and exploration. See also Rainbow Corporation.*

Johnnie raised his eyebrow slightly. He already knew most of what he had just read. However, he didn't know Rainbow Petroleum was connected to a larger corporate giant. One that he knew little about.

Inquiry: Rainbow Corporation

Johnnie patiently waited for the computer to return to his command and began sipping on his drink in the cool evening air. He moved closer to the window and realized once again that Trinidad was a very quiet and serene place. A place where he would never expect any trouble or intrigue.

Beep, beep, beep! The computer's alarm sounded and prompted him to return to his inquiry.

> *Founded in 1968, Rainbow Corporation has vast holdings in shipping, petroleum, pharmaceuticals, and real estate. While principally grounded in the US, the corporation has extensive interests in Greece, Italy, Trinidad, and Puerto Rico. Family owned since inception, little is available regarding assets and corporate structure. Chief executive and founding officer: Gregory Kavidas. No cross reference available.*

Surprised and dismayed at the lack of information on the company's principals, Johnnie wondered why he hadn't heard of Gregory Kavidas before. The company's diversity and mammoth size astounded him. Surely the head of such a large company would have been in the newspaper or *Forbes?* Privacy didn't usually apply to money.

Inquiry: Gregory Kavidas

Johnnie was uncertain whether to be more surprised from the response or the speed it appeared on his screen:

No information available: Gregory Kavidas

"Hmm. Looks like the data is blocked," he murmured while staring at the screen. Reaching into his pocket, he pulled out the stained handkerchief and held it up to the light. He smelled it once again, then grabbed the phone.

Florida had changed entirely too quickly for David Douglas. When he had first relocated to Miami Beach from Long Island, the family was thrilled. That feeling lasted only two years, ending when his wife, Kathy, fell victim to a bash-n-grab incident while waiting at a traffic light in downtown Miami. From there they migrated north to Coral Springs, a suburb west of Fort Lauderdale.

He adjusted well to the commuting. The hour-long run on the Tri-rail shuttle from Coral Springs to Trinity College in Miami, where he taught, proved essential to him. The inbound trip enabled him to prepare his lectures; the outbound trip allowed him to grade his papers without the hassle of bumper-to-bumper traffic on Interstate 95.

He ran his fingers through his bushy moustache as the phone rang. David was more than mildly surprised by the caller.

"David, this is Johnnie. I'm in Trinidad and I need your help," the voice on the phone said.

"Hello! How's the bug hunt going? I was told you flew down to Trinidad early this morning. What's wrong?" David asked.

"I ran into a snag down here when I went out photographing. I had an auto mishap on a deserted dirt road near the rain forest where I was headed; a local in a truck nearly killed me. Neither of us were hurt, but there was something weird about the truck. There was something inside that has me puzzled, and I need it checked out."

"What did you find?"

"The truck side-swiped me, then ran into a ditch. There was this low-hanging tree branch that penetrated the side, and I think it stuck into something inside the truck. Blood drained out onto the ground."

"Blood?" David gulped. "Are you sure?"

"Something was bleeding," Johnnie insisted. "I took a sample of the fluid on the ground, held it up to the light, then smelled it. The driver was a real wise-guy. He tried to tell me it was transmission fluid. To tell you the truth, it does look like it. Since the truck placard said 'Rainbow Petroleum,' I'm sure he thought it would fly, but I don't believe him. What I need is for you to find out all about Rainbow and what they're doing down here."

"Johnnie, leave it alone; I don't like the sound of this. Why don't you just finish your photography and get out of there? Besides, you're due back here tomorrow night. You have a class Monday," David entreated.

"I know that," Johnnie said, ignoring his plea. "What has me going is the data I received from the Internet. This Rainbow outfit is massive, and I'm curious to find out why some 'petroleum' outfit in the middle of a rain forest has a truck filled with secret cargo. Especially when one of their drivers acted so suspicious."

David sighed. "Johnnie, I'm sure there's nothing to it."

"I E-mailed Brandon some questions about Rainbow. His father has a lot of connections. By the way, do me a favor and call Krissy; tell her I'm fine and that I'll call her tomorrow night."

"She already called me from New York to ask if I had heard from you. I'll pass the message on to her. Don't worry." By now David knew Johnnie had made his mind up. "Okay, super sleuth, call me tomorrow night, and I'll have the information for you. And please be careful. Remember, your students love you." He hung up the phone and rubbed the ache in the calf of his right leg. His battle wound from his tour of duty in Vietnam cost him a piece of flesh that acted up every time he smelled trouble.

Morning came early for Johnnie. At daybreak he went directly to the front desk to see Manny. He needed answers about Rainbow and Jean Claude. "Mr. Keahon, good morning," Manny said casually. "How was your trip into da forest yesterday? Photography good, I hope?"

"Not bad," Johnnie answered. Being a man of few words, he did not wish to lengthen the encounter. "Listen, Manny, what can you tell me about a driver for Rainbow by the name of Jean Claude? I have something of his, and I want to return it." Knowing the natives' affable camaraderie, he expected Manny's cooperation. Johnnie's habit of giving large tips also helped.

"We all know each other here," Manny boasted. "Jean Claude is a family man. He look to get ahead. He work hard. He make da deliveries for da plant." He paused, then waved his hand, adding in his native-styled English, "He pick up shipment at da dock, take to da plant, return to da dock, take to da plant—that's it, mon."

Johnnie raised an eyebrow and nonchalantly continued, "Yeah, okay, I know that, but what does he deliver?"

"I don't know. Some say they do crazy stuff at da plant. Da dock has security all around it. So does da plant. I guess they do oil or rubber research; maybe they afraid somebody steal their ideas." He looked at Johnnie, waiting to see his reaction.

Johnnie smirked. "Yeah, right." He started to leave, then turned and asked, "Do you know where I can find Jean Claude? Where does he hang out?"

"Probably at Salem's. It's da taxi place down on da strip. He works nights and weekends to pick up cash for his family. He work hard, very hard."

"Fine. Fine," Johnnie returned emphatically. "Thanks for taking care of things for me," he added, pushing some cash into the man's hand. Johnnie lumped Manny's good service and the information into one gratuity.

"Thank you, Mr. Keahon. Thank you."

Johnnie waved him off and walked away before hearing the final salute.

Salem's Taxi Company was located only one mile from the airport, so Johnnie knew right where it was. Fortunately, Jean Claude didn't have a fare, so he was easy to find. The taxi depot was a converted soft ice cream stand sporting ceiling-to-floor insulated drapes to shield the make-shift terminal from the tropical sun. Once inside he spotted Jean Claude and saw him do a double take once he recognized Johnnie.

Jean Claude nervously moved away from his group of friends and attempted to leave out the back exit.

Johnnie moved to block his way and dangled the stained handkerchief in the air and inquired in a stage whisper, "Jean Claude, remember this?"

Jean Claude rushed to his side, snatched the handkerchief out of Johnnie's hand, and glared at him. "You crazy, mon. You get rid of this. You ask for trouble." Johnnie noticed Jean Claude's twitching lip and suspected he was scared.

"There already is trouble," Johnnie shot back. "I had this analyzed. It's not transmission fluid," he lied. "Now what was in that truck? Tell me, what are they doing at Rainbow?"

"Nothing. Nothing is going on," Jean Claude murmured miserably.

"Don't lie to me!" Johnnie retorted.

Jean Claude shuddered, as if he knew Johnnie was not about to back off. He rubbed his chin, then ushered Johnnie out the back door.

Moving toward a sheltered alcove, Jean Claude looked around surreptitiously and began to whisper, "This could be serious. Say nothing to no one. I left you on da road, and I go right to da plant. I don't stop because I am late. Da foreman is very upset when he see big gash in da side of da truck. He run to back of da truck, he take out his key—he da only one with da key—and open da door with me there. This is da first time. He open da door, and da smell almost knock me over. Da truck is full of monkeys! Sleeping monkeys! Da tree branch go through da truck and kill da monkey. Da monkey is bleeding. Da foreman, he be upset."

"Monkeys!" *What would a petroleum company want with monkeys?* Johnnie asked himself incredulously.

"Other workers tell me they do tests on monkeys in lab. I say nothing or get fired. Da foreman tell me to get out after I explain da accident. I tell him I hit a bump. He say to forget da accident. Forget da night. This is what I do. You forget, too." He emphasized his point, sticking his finger into Johnnie's chest.

Johnnie's mind whirred with the possibilities. *What kind of research is being done with monkeys and oil?* "I'm going to get into that plant. Can you help me get inside without being seen?" Johnnie looked Jean Claude right in the eye and challenged him.

His unwanted accomplice was snared by fate. His face contorted in fear and anger. "You be crazy," Jean Claude began quietly. "You be killed. Guards are there with guns. They don't want nobody in. I cannot help you. We both *die.*" He ended by thrusting his face directly in front of Johnnie.

Johnnie could see the red rims of Jean Claude's eyes and could read the terror: not just for the native alone but for his family—even his people.

Johnnie knew what that meant and knew that Jean Claude would not help him without knowing that at least his family would be safe. "I can help you get out of Trinidad. I've got connections. We can send your family first. Help me get in."

Jean Claude backed away. "You go home," he said softly, "and let me do da same. I go work and take care of my family. You go back to America.

12

Leave da plant alone."

"Will they do the same to you?" Johnnie asked quietly. He watched as Jean Claude's eyes widened in realization of the truth he had been avoiding since last night. Johnnie felt sympathy well up inside him for this simple man, being drawn into this complicated turn of events by force of circumstance. "You know when they realize what you saw, they will find you and kill you. Maybe your family, too."

The words hit Jean Claude like blows, and his face began to crack with emotion. His eyes welled in tears, and his body convulsed. "No, mon, they cannot hurt my family. We did nothing." He fell to the ground, quietly sobbing. "What could be so bad they would kill me? What can I do?"

Johnnie dropped to one knee, then put his hand on Claude's shoulder. "I don't know what they're doing," Johnnie began, trying to console him, "but we can find out. Then we can get out. But let's move fast, before they do." Johnnie moved the man into action and turned him toward his waiting car. *Brandon,* he thought, *I need you, buddy, and so does Jean Claude.*

Brandon Lane's eyes lit up when he read Johnnie's E-mail. He knew there was something happening in Trinidad, despite his father's optimism. But then again, his father didn't have some of the unsavory connections he had or a friend like Johnnie. "Evelyn," he called to his nearby secretary.

"Yes, Mr. Lane?" the cute petite blonde answered. She disliked working on Saturdays, but because Brandon rarely asked her, this Saturday she had agreed. Besides, his good looks and charm for a man of 35 made it easy to be around him.

"Please contact my father as soon as possible and schedule a meeting with him today. Then call the airlines and try to get me on a flight to Trinidad tomorrow."

"Right away, Mr. Lane," Evelyn promptly replied as she went to leave the room. Knowing Brandon's father, she hesitated before going to book the flight, anticipating that he may want to put a stop to that. Then again, Brandon was her boss, so she complied with his instructions.

Brandon sat down and called the operator. He needed to speak to Johnnie right away. Something told him that Johnnie might need more help than just his arrival tomorrow. Something else told him he was in trouble.

The approach to the south end of the rain forest afforded complete secrecy. Thick, dense foliage blocked the dirt road that was once used by firefighters a decade ago during a dry season fire that ravaged the preserve. The Jeep traversed the road easily.

Despite the emerging tension in Johnnie's mind, his trained eye noticed nature's prolific display. Butterflies, some iridescent blue and red, some clear-winged, were alighting on glossy leaves or hovering at their favorite plants. Great blue herons, red ibises, and great egrets strategically maneuvered around low-lying branches and hanging vines on their way to the inland lake. Several toucans, parrots, and macaws looked on from high altitude perches as Jean Claude directed Johnnie's skillful driving through the winding path leading to the plant.

Estimating the distance from the plant at half a mile, Jean Claude suggested they walk the rest of the way. The moment they stepped out of the vehicle the noisome insect world suddenly became quiet. The droning of the cicadas and locusts would have muffled their approach, but their intrusion into the natural habitat did not go unnoticed by the wary insects. Additional precautions had to be taken, and the two men tread lightly and slowly. Within 20 minutes the compound came into view.

Huge satellite dishes loomed in the background near a large concrete block facility. There were no wires visible, which was not uncommon in a modern structure in a tropical climate; wind and heavy rains could be detrimental to any purposeful activity with aboveground utilities. But why the fence, spotlights, and barbed wire here in the midst of a rain forest, surrounded by wildlife and butterflies? *And why a massive building with no windows? Who or what was meant to be kept out? Or,* thought Johnnie, with a sense of foreboding, *what was meant to be kept in?*

Jean Claude perspired heavily as he neared the front gate of the complex. Crouched down, they watched the activity in total silence. Both men noticed the patterns of the guards, the location of the lighting, and the places they needed to be to accomplish their mission. Jean Claude committed it to memory; Johnnie put it all on film. *Tonight,* Johnnie said to himself. *It has to be tonight before dark.*

The men retreated after an hour and moved back to their hidden Jeep. No words passed as they returned to Johnnie's hotel. They knew what had to be done and planned in their own minds the way they would do it. Johnnie's stomach had butterflies of a sort he didn't photograph as the hotel approached. *This has got to work.*

Brandon was with his father when Johnnie's call came through. He was both relieved and alarmed. His father knew more about Trinidad than he expected and was more than willing to help out. In fact, he was eager to be involved. He just didn't want Brandon to be involved. "Send someone else," his father said. "You're needed here."

Brandon stared into his father's eyes and saw the determined look that had made this man the self-made magnate he was today. He always regretted not having enough of that look, that drive, or that feeling his father used to his advantage. He almost felt intimidated enough to back down, to say, "Okay, I'll stay home." But he knew better; he knew his father well enough to know that he had to take a firm position or lose ground altogether.

This time, however, his father relented. Knowing Johnnie was involved, giving Brandon a personal interest, made it hard to refuse his only son. "Take enough money to loosen tongues and to ensure you get out of there. And, son," he said, his voice softening as he approached Brandon from behind his massive desk, "come back to me. I need you." He embraced Brandon.

Just then Johnnie's call was announced over the speaker. "Brandon, am I glad I got you. Did you get my E-mail?" Johnnie sounded out of breath and a little nervous.

"Of course," said Brandon. "I'm getting ready to leave now."

"Leave?" Johnnie exclaimed. "Where are you going?"

Brandon moved back toward his father's desk and got out his pen.

"Relax, I'm coming to Trinidad. Did you think I was going to let you get all the glory? I'll be there tomorrow." There was no sound, and Brandon thought the line had gone dead. "Johnnie, are you there?"

"Yes, I'm here. I'm glad you're coming. But I have something I have to do tonight, and I can't wait. I have some people I need you to help; they're going to be desperate by tomorrow. Can you help them? I know it won't be easy, but you're all I have."

Brandon smiled and looked at his father. "Well, you have more than me. My dad is involved, and that means the whole company is involved. Don't worry. Just tell me what I have to do."

Thankful that Lawrence the foreman would be off today, Jean Claude nonchalantly walked up to the security guard, waved hello, then presented his pass.

"What you do here today, Jean Claude?" Peter, the uniformed sentry, asked. "Why you no have your truck?"

"I come to da plant to find my watch. Yesterday I lose da good watch Lucinda give me for my birthday." He flashed his vacant wrist, then looked around to locate his truck. "I think it fall on da truck floor when I have da accident yesterday. My truck be here."

Peter eyed Jean up and down. "I did hear about da accident. Go look, mon, but be quick about it."

Jean Claude nodded in appreciation and walked out of view. He checked his other wrist and noted the time; three minutes had elapsed. He was confident that was enough time for Johnnie to get over the rear fence.

Climbing trees, ducking under limbs, and negotiating brush were second nature to Johnnie. He remembered being in Costa Rica to photograph the Atlas moth, having to act like Superman leaping tall trees with a single bound or slinking his body into caves where their chrysalises hung, carrying all his equipment. So for him to climb a tree and lower himself on

16

a rope from an overhanging limb into the compound would be easy.

The difficulty lay in the timing. The entire period for Jean Claude to search for his watch would be no more than 15 minutes, enabling Johnnie to get a good look at Rainbow's mysterious cargo. Maybe even the contents of the bunker that loomed in front.

The inside perimeter of the compound that faced the front gate looked like a loading dock. The remainder of the yard looked different. Petroleum drums and large fueling hoses were conspicuously placed in view, while wooden crates were methodically stacked in quadrants on the obscure side of the building. Next to the wooden crates were numerous large stainless steel medical disposal containers marked *biohazard*.

Johnnie scanned his memory and remembered where he had seen similar boxes before. These containers were the kind found in hospitals. He pulled out his camera from his photo vest and fired off 15 shots of high-speed slide film.

Looking around, he realized the compound lacked surveillance cameras. Knowing the islanders rarely ventured into the rain forest, with their jobs in the tourist areas of the city, there seemed to be no apparent need to videotape the activity. There would be no need for extensive security measures, since most natives knew enough to mind their own business. A barbed-wire fence was enough to keep the natives or the curious out.

But not Johnnie. Moving against time, he dodged behind the disposal vessels until he reached the rear door of the building. *If only there were windows,* Johnnie thought as he listened with his ear to the metal door.

Silence pervaded the area. A peculiar odor drifted upward from under the door. He sniffed in disgust, then changed lenses on his camera. He would need his telephoto lens for this work; he was sure of it. He exchanged his standard lens for the 80-210 mm lens, and in one sweeping motion, tried the door knob. "It's open," he muttered. "Maybe this *is* going to work." He mumbled a silent prayer and pushed his way in.

Jean Claude could feel the sweat rolling toward his eyes. Slowly, carefully, he raised his arm to wipe his forehead. *I am crazy. Why do I listen to that*

mon? He opened the truck door and looked around the floor while he glanced toward the gate. Peter was still there, and Jean Claude was grateful the guard was not watching him too closely.

"Five minutes more," he mumbled to himself. "Johnnie will meet me here; then we go to America." He took a deep breath and continued his search in vain.

Johnnie entered a passageway with large connecting rooms. Blank, white walls, doused with sterile light, reminded him of a medical laboratory. *Where is the smell of crude oil, grease, or gasoline? And what is this smell?* he wondered. A foul odor filled his nostrils.

Clank!

He heard the noise, so he slipped into one of the rooms. A great fear came over him as he stared at rows of bell jars neatly placed on racks. His stomach retched, and he forced the bile down. There were three to five hundred labeled jars, each containing some kind of object dangling from a center rod. The dark purple and blue objects were slightly larger than a walnut, each with what looked like severed veins protruding out from the center.

He gasped and moved reflexively to photograph them. His pulse quickened, and his mind raced. Images blurred before him as he snapped the shutter feverishly. Closing his eyes, he began to change the film and reload the camera. *What would be so secretive about testing monkeys? Scientists have performed tests on lab monkeys for years.* He stared at the jar directly in front of him, and his blood thickened and began to slow. His skin felt cold and clammy, and his brain began to register the unbelievable.

Thymus: Rhesus Sample 27R—HIV Positive
Thymus: Pigtail Macaque Sample 27P —HIV Negative

The organs were suspended in a gelatinous fluid. He began to see why monkeys were being brought in. Testing was going on; that was certain. But still he couldn't understand. *Why the secret?* His gaze ran down the labels, and he hesitantly touched the jars. His hand stopped on one jar different from all the rest. His eyes met up with his hands, and he pushed himself back against the wall. His breath came in shallow gasps as he read the label.

Thymus: Human Sample 39H—HIV Positive

Johnnie squinted at the label, reread it, and repeated the title to himself so he wouldn't forget. He backed off three feet, then zoomed in his telephoto lens for a close-up of the cabinet and its contents. Checking his wristwatch, he saw that only two minutes remained to meet Jean Claude and allow him to distract the guard. He opened the jar with disgust and dipped his empty film canister into the thick, warm fluid. He closed the jar and moved to leave.

He mentally calculated the distance from the voices he heard, then opened the door into the passageway. *Clear*, he thought. *Great!* With the rear door in sight, he inched along the wall and nudged the door open. He knew there was a lot more to this plant—even more than what he'd been able to digest. But he was out of time. Through the crack in the door he saw Jean Claude leaning in the cab of the truck. Glancing toward the guard, he moved in the direction of his waiting accomplice.

Jean Claude saw the door open a crack, and his stomach tightened as Johnnie began to sneak toward him.

Johnnie arrived next to him and wordlessly handed him two film canisters, motioning with his hands toward his two cameras. *Two for you, two for me*, thought Jean Claude. The practical thinking made Jean Claude realize that they were now totally committed; it filled him with hope—and dread. *Now it is real. We can be killed*, went through his mind as Johnnie pointed to his watch. Jean Claude looked at the watch on his left hand, and Johnnie moved away.

Jean Claude waited until he was lost from sight before exclaiming, "Here it is!"

The guard glanced in his direction.

Now we finish, Jean Claude said to himself as he approached the gate.

Johnnie rounded the corner of the building before he came face-to-face with a man carrying a custom-made 45-caliber pistol. "Well, what have we here?" the red-haired man with a New Englander accent asked. He ordered the uniformed guard to seize Johnnie. "Aren't you a little out of your element?" he continued as he scanned Johnnie's photo equipment.

Johnnie's mind went blank. He glared at the two men, looked at his camera, then at the fence.

The New Englander followed his glance. "Forget it. No chance."

Johnnie fought the urge to look toward the front gate, in hopes of alerting Jean Claude. But he didn't know if the men were aware of Jean Claude's presence and didn't want to endanger him.

The man holding the gun must have sensed Johnnie's desperation. "Your friend left. Peter might look stupid, but he is our best security man. He called me when your partner first arrived looking for his watch. We let him go quietly, but we will deal with him later; he's not an immediate threat."

Johnnie stared directly at the man's eyes. He couldn't tell if the man was bluffing. He could only hope.

"Why are you here?" the man asked him.

"I could ask you the same thing," Johnnie said defensively, struggling to break from Peter's hold. "There's no way you're working with oil here. You're doing some kind of illegal experiments in this place!" he blurted out. "You won't get away with it!"

Johnnie continued in his futile attempts to wrest himself free, becoming more savage as he realized he was caught. He allowed himself to be filled with rage, knowing how the animal that is cornered gains strength in their last moments. But it wasn't enough.

Grinding his teeth in contempt, the man simply pulled the cameras from Johnnie's grasp. "You'll have no use for these." He motioned to Peter, who began to escort Johnnie at gunpoint around to the front of the building.

"People know where I am!" Johnnie shouted to the New Englander while Peter locked his grip on him. "Important people who will come to look for me!"

The New Englander gestured to Peter that Johnnie should be silenced, then slipped inside the building.

Johnnie didn't struggle as Peter escorted him. He simply calculated his chances. He judged the distance to the main gate and reasoned that once Peter was overpowered and the New Englander was still inside the building, he could make it easily. He only needed a split-second opportunity to pull it off. He heard the door to the bunker slam and saw Peter glance to his right.

Seizing the chance, Johnnie doubled over and forced his elbow into Peter's groin. They went down, and Peter squirmed like a snake as Johnnie desperately tried to get away. While Peter fumbled with his gun, Johnnie reached into his photo vest and pulled out his flash unit. With one swoop, he slammed it down on Peter's head. Peter moaned, then fell limp on the ground.

Johnnie needed this moment. He looked in vain for the familiar branch that gave him entrance, then ran for the gate. *Freedom is only 20 yards ahead!*

Then the gate began to close, and the guard moved in his direction. "Stop or I'll shoot!" the guard yelled.

A shot was fired in the air, and Johnnie slowed his run, just enough for the gate to close before him. He leaped onto the fence, clutched the galvanized wire, and screamed. His body absorbed the electricity flowing through the fence, and he fell backward onto the pavement.

"God, help me," he whispered. His eyes fluttered as two men bent over him. Johnnie turned to see the blue sky behind them, while clouds suspended majestically over their heads, causing time to slow in his mind.

"Where you goin', mon?" the cabby asked as Brandon jumped into the taxi.

Brandon, surprised at the cabdriver's cooperation, directed him to the hotel. *On to stage two*, he thought. Since his arrival, he had been busy—primarily with Johnnie's plan to take care of a Trinidad family. *Now*, he said to himself, *I want to find out why.*

"Your hotel," the cabby announced, breaking his reverie.

Brandon paid the man handsomely and went directly to the front desk and began his inquiry. "I'm a friend of Jonathan Keahon, one of your guests. I believe he left something for me?"

"Your name?" the desk manager asked.

"Brandon Lane," he replied confidently.

The man handed over a small envelope and motioned to the bellhop.

Mechanically the bellhop reacted, whisking up Brandon's bag. "Are you checking in?"

Brandon nodded and told the bellhop to put everything in his room. After going through the formalities, he strolled around the lobby for several moments before deciding to survey Johnnie's room.

Johnnie was so fastidious that Brandon couldn't imagine what his home looked like if his hotel room was this organized. His laptop was hooked up to the phone jack, and his excess photo equipment was all neatly in place. Looking into the closet, he snickered when he saw the footwear in sequential order while the clothes were in graduated lengths. "Unbelievable," he said, shaking his head, "no wonder he loves bugs."

The electronic sound of the phone alerted him. His first thought was to let it ring, but thinking it could be Johnnie, he answered it.

"Hello, mon, you okay? I thought you be in trouble so I wait. You not meet with me. Why did you leave me alone there?"

"Who is this?" Brandon asked, looking at the mouthpiece.

The silence caused an audible shock; the caller apparently did not hear the voice that he expected. "Jean Claude. Who are you?" he returned.

"This is Brandon Lane. I'm a friend of Johnnie's. Where is he?"

The phone went silent again.

Brandon glared at the phone and considered slamming the receiver down onto the cradle. "Now what?" he mumbled to himself. He breathed deeply to ease the building tension, then started again. "This is Brandon Lane. I'm waiting for my friend Johnnie. Do you know where he is?"

"I know where he was," began Jean Claude.

Fatigue began to overpower Brandon, so he returned to his own room to rest. Despite his athletic build, finding out that Johnnie was missing took the last of his strength. He pushed through Johnnie's camera bag and the other items he had moved into his own room. Jean Claude's revelation was disquieting enough. Brandon knew that Johnnie must have put some of the clues to the puzzle he was encountering among his belongings. *But where?* Considering the careful way that Johnnie had organized his bags, he quickly concluded that neat people hide secret things very carefully.

"Think. Where would Johnnie put something," he ranted as he opened Johnnie's luggage, "so that no one would suspect anything?" *Johnnie was much too meticulous to stash something in any of the obvious places. No, he would have put it where his valuables were,* Brandon concluded and abandoned the luggage.

He opened the camera case and unzipped the film storage area. *Scanproof* was written across the boxed area. He carefully opened the lead-shielded, X-ray-proof container and noticed eight boxes of film inside, all labeled *Trinidad.* He carefully opened them one by one. Two still had film inside, four were empty, one held an exposed roll of film, and the last contained a handkerchief stuffed in the canister. He pulled out the blood-soaked cloth, held it up to the light, and stared in wonder. "This might be it, Johnnie," he said aloud. "This could be all that we need." He took the handkerchief and the exposed roll of film and closed up the cases.

He flopped onto the sofa and began planning his day with Jean Claude tomorrow. Rainbow could be a formidable adversary. He had hoped to find out more information from Jean Claude, but the native seemed too nervous.

"Wait a minute," he yelled, jumping off the sofa. He ran over to the laptop and turned it on. The computer began to whir, and the screen lit with activity. He was sorely disappointed when the screen indicated: Disk Failure Reading In Drive A. He sat back and wondered how Johnnie had communicated with him. Dejected, he began to close the computer when he noticed a faint whirring. He reached around the side, and pressed Eject. A disk popped out. He quickly restarted the computer and waited. He reinserted the disk and typed the display command to scan the disk.

Rainbow.doc appeared on the screen. He removed the disk, placed it carefully into his own valise, and packed up. *Now to find you and get out of here.* He reclined on the bed, and thoughts of Johnnie filled his mind. He closed his eyes and within minutes was fast asleep.

At daybreak Brandon called the desk only to find out that Johnnie had not yet returned. He closed his eyes, then massaged his neck while thinking about his next move. He looked down at his legs and realized his knees were knocking together; he was more worried than he thought. He sighed and headed for the bathroom to shower.

It was 7:30 a.m. when his phone finally rang. "Mr. Lane, this is Manny at da front desk. We have word on Mr. Keahon. Can you please come down?"

Brandon's apprehension was now replaced with foreboding.

A smartly dressed American stood at the desk, waiting.

"Mr. Lane," Manny said, "this is Mr. Leonard Marris from da American Consulate in da Port of Spain. He is very anxious to talk to you."

Mr. Marris escorted Brandon to a lobby sofa before saying anything, which only heightened Brandon's concerns. "Mr. Lane, Manny tells me you are a friend of a Mr. Jonathan Keahon. Is that right?" he asked delicately.

"Yes, I flew in last night to see him. We've been friends for many years. Is there a problem?"

"I'm afraid there is—" Mr. Marris started. "He was found dead early this morning on a dirt road near a wildlife sanctuary. A rain forest, in fact, not far from this town."

Brandon could feel the color drain from his face. He clutched the side of the table as his body convulsed with the staggering revelation. The image of his friend flashed before his eyes, and he could feel his eyelashes getting wet. *I knew,* he thought, *somehow, I already knew.* "How did it happen?"

"No one knows for sure, but it appears that he fell from a tree. We have learned that he was down here on a photography vacation to photo some rare butterflies. Climbing trees and rock ledges to reach them, it's possible he simply lost his grip and landed the wrong way. He had multiple fractures throughout his body."

That was more than Brandon needed to hear. He excused himself and returned to his room. Once inside, he went into a rage, throwing anything he could reach at the walls. After several minutes, his anger vented, he slumped in a chair and cried.

It was the thought of Jean Claude that caused his tears to subside. Knowing that the Trinidad authorities, in conjunction with the American Embassy, would make arrangements to get Johnnie's body back home, he went down to his car.

Once inside Maples Market in the center of town, he began looking for Jean Claude. *What better place for a secret meeting than in the middle of a crowded store?* "You look for me, mon," Jean Claude had said, "one block east of Salem's Taxi at da Maples Market. I wear da red jogging suit."

Great, Brandon thought as he looked around at the vivid displays of red—the clothes, the paint on the walls, the signs—*that will include just about everyone. Apparently red is in.* His strict attention to the matter at hand enabled him to avoid thinking of Johnnie.

Just what I was afraid of, Brandon thought. *No Claude.* He impatiently checked his watch as he patrolled the area. *Twenty minutes late already. Now what?* he asked himself. *Something else is wrong.* He began to walk toward the parking lot and his Jeep when a hand came down on his shoulder.

"How is da family, mon?" asked a native clad in familiar red. "You must tell me everything on da way to dinner. Come on. We are late already."

Brandon noticed everyone returning to their own business—the man had deliberately drawn everyone's attention to them. To his surprise, the man's obvious display had caused little reaction at all. *Reverse psychology?*

"Who are you?" Brandon ventured to the man quietly. "Is it you, Jean Claude?"

"Get in," the man hissed under his breath. "Do not bring attention with questions."

Brandon glanced around again as he got in the Jeep and saw a few watchful eyes turning his way. *How could a question attract attention?* Nevertheless, he did as he was told and drove away without a second look.

"Yes, I am Jean Claude. We are being watched, so be careful. Do not do anything I do not do."

Brandon nodded and waited for the native to speak. When he did not offer information, Brandon began, "Johnnie is dead."

"I know. I heard at the hotel. I am sorry." There was genuine remorse in the native's tone.

"So am I. But now we've got to get out of here. Quickly," Brandon insisted.

"Listen, you don't owe me nothing. My deal was with Johnnie. You did your part with da family. I will stay here. You leave."

Brandon looked at the man in unbelief. "You'll be killed. You know that."

"I know, but with my family safe, I am ready to die. Are you?"

The thought stopped Brandon. He turned the Jeep toward the hotel and home.

"Mr. Lane," Manny called as Brandon entered the lobby. He waved him over to the desk. "There were two men from Rainbow looking for you while you were out."

Brandon's heart began to race. Obviously, concerns about his presence in Trinidad were escalating. "Oh? What did they want?"

"They wanted to talk to you, but I told them I didn't know where you were. They ask to go to Johnnie's room, but I told them no. When they come back, they will not take no for an answer."

Brandon realized that the island natives were well educated when it came to people and the lengths they'd go to get what they wanted. *It won't be long before the island police are all over this place.*

"Thanks for covering, Manny," Brandon returned. "I'm checking out now quietly, so please order me a cab to the airport."

Brandon opened the door to his room and was not surprised to see Jean Claude already there. "I thought you were going to stay and die," he quipped affably. "Change your mind?"

"Mon, you be crazy. I am here for you. You will not get off da island without Jean Claude. They will be watching for you." He walked toward Brandon and opened up his palm. "Besides, I didn't give you these. Johnnie gave them to me the night we were at the factory." Two film canisters were pushed into Brandon's hand.

Brandon looked up at the man with respect. "You didn't have to give me these. You could have bought your way out with Rainbow. You could have bought back your life with these."

"But not your friend's."

Brandon gazed up at Jean Claude and nodded.

The men packed up the bags as fast as they could. Brandon placed the two rolls of film into his jacket pocket and followed Jean Claude from the

26

room. *Now to get out of Trinidad.*

"Rats!" he said, looking down from the window as he waited for the elevator. Just off the hotel property he could see a small panel truck with Rainbow Petroleum lettered on the side and two men sitting in the cab. "I think it's time to go to plan B," he muttered.

Jean Claude said nothing but motioned toward the back of the hallway as the elevator stopped on the third floor. "This way," he indicated.

"What about my bill?" Brandon gestured in the general direction of the lobby.

"Forget it. That is what they are waiting for. They will charge your credit card and don't complain if they pad da bill. It will be worth it. They help us get out...you will see."

Brandon nodded and followed again. He could only feel admiration for this simple worker, whose life had become so complex.

Once outside, Jean Claude headed for a large sanitation truck, whose workers were busy carting away trash from the hotel. "Plan B," he whispered to Brandon as they walked up to workers. Brandon took out a few one-hundred-dollar bills from his wallet, placed them in Jean Claude's waiting hand, and nodded.

"No questions, mon," Jean Claude murmured as he handed the money to the waiting men. "Just get us to the airport now."

Brandon climbed into the cab of the truck as the men took their places in the back. "Jean Claude, come with me!" He grabbed the man's hand and earnestly tried to pull him into the cab.

"No, my place is here. Jean Claude will make sure they do not follow you to da airport." Pulling his hand away, he quickly waved away the cash that Brandon offered. "I will not need it."

The door closed, and the truck drove away. Brandon sat there, numb and dazed by Jean Claude's sacrifice, for he knew that was what it was. The man had only wanted his family safe. That was all.

But through the fog that was in Brandon's mind, one thought pervaded, even plagued him: *Would I have done the same for him?*

TWO

*The AIDS epidemic has rolled back a big rotten log
and revealed all the squirming life underneath it,
since it involves, all at once, the main themes of our existence:
sex, death, power, money, love, hate, disease, and panic.
No American phenomenon has been
so compelling since the Vietnam War.*
Edmond White

Searchers after future knowledge haunt strange, far places. Like the busy labyrinths of the streets of the Lower East Side of New York, the catacombs of ancient Israel, or the sacred shrines found hidden in the peaks of the eternal Himalayas. They linger around sinister occult shops to solicit fragments of their destiny that will enable them to plot their course. For them, fate can be controlled.

Mortimer Stein had suffered no regrets when he'd sold off his stock brokerage firm, for once again, his keen discernment for business proved correct. Heralded as visionary and daring by the press after his assertion that the market was about to tumble came true, Stein quickly moved into the public eye. However, during negotiations with Intrastock, who virtually swooped up his offer to sell the company, he was looked upon as the market idiot; why sell when business was so good?

Yet somehow he knew he was making the right move. Cash in hand, he plunked the profit down on a floundering retail credit bureau. Three years later, every request for credit information in America's East Coast region passed through his company. *Forbes' Review* praised Stein's singular gift of handling Intrastock. Combining the infusion of cash with his ability, he was strategically poised to take his newly acquired credit bureau and gain control of credit-clearing houses on a national and international scale. In Mort's mind, this had all been supernaturally prearranged.

Mort's fanatical beliefs exiled him from the majority of entrepreneurs; his highly focused mind sought continuous revelation from a higher source. Knowledge was power; he knew that. Integrating his knowledge with his determination made the difference between success or failure. Mort Stein's resolve to succeed, regardless of the cost, eliminated the risk of failure.

Redisearch maintained a magnificent office that appeared more than just a building. Located in a prestigious commercial area of Boca Raton, the three-level, two-hundred-thousand-square-feet "city" housed three Cray XMP supercomputers designed to facilitate credit checks for all online retail establishments in the eastern regions of the United States. The firm employed 260 full-time employees and 87 part-timers for evening inquiries.

As he strolled toward his private office library, Mort walked past a wall of mirrors. He stopped and turned to catch his profile. *Not bad for 47.* He rubbed his bald head and shrugged. "It's keen to stay lean," he said as he smiled at his chiseled features. He believed his thin build made up for his lack of hair.

Mort's corporate suite served two purposes: first, to act as command central for his credit gathering operations; second, to provide on-site quarters for his ongoing studies into learning more about his future. Consistent with his demanding, melancholy personality, he personally configured and systematically drew up the blueprints for his headquarters. His suite alone occupied half the third floor of the building; the suite was divided into segments that included a massive library, where he found peace and quiet. Mort possessed a photographic memory and continuously tested himself to ensure the gift would progress.

At his bar mitzvah, where it is customary to chant a prophetic portion of Scripture and give a discourse on a theme from the Talmud, Mort recalled it from memory. At age 13 he had memorized great portions of the books of Deuteronomy, Psalms, and Isaiah. While in college, his adroit mind simply absorbed information at first glance. His companions shrugged and labeled him a variety of names. No one asked about his IQ. Even his friends shuddered at the thought of mincing words or sharing in his wit.

His fingers nimbly navigated through his Jewish theology books looking for the Kabbalah, the Jewish book of mysticism. He walked over to the intercom with the book and rang his secretary. "Donna, please hold my calls for the next hour while I take a break in my library."

"Yes, sir," Donna replied gingerly. For her this was standard routine maintenance.

The thick, time-worn volume, now in the family for the last three generations, represented one of Mort's prized possessions. The book was weighty and bulky, with Hebrew letters hand-carved in the wooden binder. Mort estimated the printing to be in the late 1800s, yet the lettering and pages were remarkably preserved.

Turning to the theosophy section, where the destiny of man and the universe is discussed, Mort sat back in his vintage morris chair and concentrated on the writings of Hayyim Vital. Vital's interest in metaphysics fascinated Mort, who relied on his thinking for guidance. Once again, he would reread the texts, run through a silent diatribe, throw his head back, and close his eyes. He remembered the time from his youth when the authors of the Kabbalah began to guide his future.

Keeping up with the old man had been extremely difficult for Mortimer. *Fatigue is a physical attribute,* the lad had told himself, *and this is a spiritual quest. Therefore, I must press on. I must keep up with him.* They had been climbing a mountain in the Sinai Peninsula when the aged man with the mantle turned around to make sure the lad was still behind him.

"Come along now, Mortimer Stein. We have only a short distance to go," the old man said.

"We have been climbing for hours and hours, and still we have not reached the summit," Mortimer lamented.

"Just a little farther Mortimer," the old man yelled as the distance between them widened.

Mortimer paused long enough to look down. His feet were bleeding through the torn, wet leather of his shoes.

"Just a little farther, Mortimer, and it will be worth the effort," the old man once again assured Mortimer.

After what seemed like another hour, Mortimer reached out and clutched the extended hand of the old man. "I will help you reach your goal in life, Mortimer. You must simply call upon me."

Then, with hands clasped, the two looked out into the expanse before them.

30

Mortimer held his breath as he looked down at the tableland rising to over 2,200 meters above the sea. Patches of snow still remained in the shaded ravines, despite the warm air of summer, while away in the distance he could see the ancient Red Sea. "This is a sacred place, isn't it, Rabbi Vital?" Mortimer asked.

"This is indeed a sacred place, Mortimer," the aged man replied. "This is the site where your forefathers camped after crossing the Red Sea over 3,500 years ago. It is here on Jebel Musa where the prophet Elijah received special revelation from God; it is here where Moses stood." The old man took off his cape and laid it over Mortimer's shoulders. "You too shall do great things, Mortimer."

"This is Mount Sinai? Where Moses received the Ten Commandments?" Mortimer asked incredulously.

The aged man looked into the lad's eyes, held his shoulders squarely, and said, "Moses climbed this mountain and received the tablets of the Law from God, and afterward his face shone from seeing God's glory."

"But I am not like Moses," Mortimer replied.

"No, you are not like Moses, my son, but you are to be a great person. Just trust in me."

Mortimer gazed off into the wilderness while pondering everything Rabbi Vital said. *Yes, make me great.*

Now, Mort thought in his library, *each day that goes by, I am closer.*

"Donna, get Gregory Kavidas on the phone."

The pounding on the front door of David Douglas's home at daybreak roused him and his family to life. David looked at the dresser clock, jumped out of bed, and dashed downstairs to open the door.

It was Brandon. David took one look at his friend's disheveled appearance and exclaimed, "Are you okay? You look terrible."

Brandon eyed David up and down and couldn't stop his involuntary smirk. "I'll be all right, but those shorts have to go."

Despite the resplendent sunlight flowing through the kitchen windows, breakfast afforded few moments of reverie. Both David and Kathy listened in numbed silence as Brandon reviewed the known details of Johnnie's death and the events leading up to Brandon's escape from Trinidad, both painting a dismal cast on the otherwise bright morning.

"How did Krissy take the news?" Brandon asked halfway through his narrative.

David gazed out the window at the distant orchid tree. "Brandon, she took Johnnie's death so badly, I don't know when she'll recover. Her mother called me late last night, within two hours after we heard about it, and said that Krissy is in the hospital; she went into shock." He sighed. "It's all so unbelievable."

Kathy clutched David's hand to console him, then said to Brandon, "We're all very grieved over this, and I'm worried about Krissy. She's wrapped very tightly with such a short fuse. I hope she can get over this— and us too."

After hearing the complete narrative, David pursued Brandon's motive in asking that the film canister containing the gelatinous fluid be examined. "I remember Johnnie calling me regarding blood dripping out of a truck that he collided with while en route to some rain forest. Obviously you believe he was onto something and whatever he uncovered led to his death, right?"

"I'm convinced of it," Brandon asserted. "Before I get the authorities here in the States involved, I'd like to do some checking myself. First things first: Let's find out what's on the disk I found in Johnnie's laptop. My dad should be calling here soon with news on the film and the fluid I dropped off at our lab."

David inserted the disk into his computer, then keyed in the commands to print the contents of the disk.

"What does all this mean, David?" Kathy asked while looking on.

"It's a report off the Internet describing Rainbow Petroleum and Rubber Products, with some person named Kavidas as the main man. I warned Johnnie to leave this business down there alone."

"Brandon, what do you know about Rainbow Pharmaceuticals and this guy Kavidas?" Kathy asked.

"They are really big. Massive, in fact—one of the world's largest drug companies and a competitor of ours. I have only heard of this Kavidas fellow. I've never met him. I saw a few photos of him in trade magazines last year; that's all. My dad probably knows more about him."

David turned to Kathy and suggested, "Why don't we call Louie in

New York and ask him if he's heard about Rainbow? As for me, I guess I'll call school and take the next few days off."

Another sunny day in south Florida, Mort thought. He looked at his watch and remembered how much he hated waiting. Arising from his table in the El Lago Lounge, he walked over to the stone wall, then stood and gazed into the water of the intracoastal waterway flowing before him.

Impatiently turning around, his eyes took in the splendor of the Boca Raton Resort and Club where he frequently lunched. Built in 1926, the elegant hotel is situated on 356 acres in the center of Florida's Gold Coast and is renowned for its architecture. Originally built by the famous designer Addison Mizner, it reflects Spanish-Mediterranean and Gothic influences accented by two 18-hole championship golf courses and a host of other amenities.

"Sorry, Mr. Stein, still no sign of Mr. Kavidas," the messenger said.

Mort grunted, then returned to his table and ordered his meal. In his usual fashion, Mort gulped down his lunch but relaxed over his dessert. Sweets were his downfall. He demanded strict dietary laws for everything except desserts.

Once he had eaten, he glanced across the intracoastal canal to a lavish estate garnished with a white gazebo that overlooked the waterway. The balusters of the gazebo were plain and reminded him of the columns of the Parthenon in Athens. Then his mind filled with thoughts of Gregory and their first encounter....

July is not the time of year to walk up the hill of the Acropolis, Mort thought. But as long as he was in Greece, he had to tour the ancient ruins, despite the heat. *Man, how did the ancient Greeks keep cool during the sweltering summer?* he asked himself. *Well, maybe the offshore breezes coming from the Aegean Sea were cooler then,* he reasoned.

Once he reached the summit, he scanned the horizon and took in the view of the city. *Beautiful.* He walked back off the temple mound to take a photograph of the Parthenon—Temple of Athena—with modern Athens in the background. The peripteral Doric temple was cluttered with tourists and wouldn't make a good picture. Walking back toward the temple, a man in a white linen suit approached him.

"You are an American," the man began, "and I can see that the beauty of the temple ruins has been marred for your photograph by all these sightseers. May I offer another location for you to capture the splendor?"

Mort stepped back, remembering how Americans are frequently accosted by panhandlers and European entrepreneurs scouting for gullible investors in their foreign enterprises. However, he recognized something quite different in this man. Sincerity and compassion just flowed out of him. This man was a Greek gentleman, possibly educated at Oxford or the like, and looking to ingratiate himself to a tourist strictly as a humanitarian gesture. He was somewhat handsome with rugged looks and wavy jet-black hair neatly combed over his ears. His penetrating eyes seemed to invite mystery while his tall, disciplined physique announced a carefully controlled lifestyle. Mort immediately knew he could trust him.

"Why, yes, that would be wonderful," Mort replied. "I really would love to bring home a nice photograph of the Parthenon that I could say I took myself."

The man pointed to the mountainside of the city. "See, above the city, is my home. It is nearly as high as the temple of Athena and boasts of a grand view of both the mount and the sea behind it. You must see it from there. You will be my family's guest. But you must also photograph Sounio and the Temple of Poseidon to give each their due. My home lies between them both."

Mort's curiosity was piqued by the offer. "Sounds great. But before we go any farther—" he extended his hand and broadened his smile—"my name is Mortimer Stein. And yours?"

"Gregory Kavidas. Come along. My chauffeur will drive us home." Mort and Gregory walked off the temple mount and into his waiting car.

Within an hour, Mort stood on the Kavidas estate balcony and viewed the Parthenon from an altogether different perspective at a mile and a half away. The scene was enthralling.

Gregory changed his clothes as Mort casually photographed the scene of the Acropolis. *Somehow,* he mused, *this rendezvous had been prearranged. I plan to take full advantage of the opportunity.* But his goals could not turn to financial or avaricious avenues. This was unique: he could feel a real emotional bonding with Gregory taking place.

"So, what brings you to Greece?" Gregory inquired as he meandered out on the balcony in tropical gym shorts and a T-shirt.

"Please call me Mort," he replied and joined Gregory at the table. "I'm scouting, you might say. I have a dream or vision of establishing a European credit bureau here in Athens."

"Is that what you do back in the States, credit processing?"

"Yes, that's what I do," Mort replied with a smile. "And I have built up a substantial business based in Boca Raton, Florida." He then quickly took a panoramic view of the Kavidas estate with the Parthenon visible in the background and added, "And you, Mr. Kavidas—your line of work?"

A thin smile appeared on Gregory's lips. "Our family is diversified in oil, rubber, and pharmaceuticals. You may find this hard to believe, but the main division of our drug company, Rainbow Pharmaceuticals, is located in Florida also. We have our corporate office and research facility in Palm Beach County in Wellington."

Mort stood up and beamed. "You're kidding! I travel 6,000 miles to an ancient land exploring for new business territories to conquer and run into someone from home? That's unbelievable!" He felt fate taking hold of him once more as a woman approached from inside.

"Oh, excuse me, Mr. Stein. Please meet my mother."

From behind Mort a trim, gray-haired woman in her 70s walked over to join them. She wore a long black evening gown accentuated with an exquisite diamond necklace.

"I thought I would say hello to our guest before your father and I go out for dinner," she said.

"Mr. Stein, this is my mother, Augustina Kavidas." Gregory looked approvingly at her and smiled. "Her roots extend deep into Roman antiquity—my mother is named after an early Roman emperor."

"Ah yes," Mort concurred, "Augustus from the branch of the aristocratic family of Julii..." He looked skyward to gather his thoughts, then added, "27 BC to AD 14, wasn't it?"

"Why, yes, Mr. Stein! You must have a penchant for Roman history," Gregory's mother replied. "I'm sorry I have to rush off. It was so very nice meeting you, and I hope to see you again."

Mort watched Mrs. Kavidas leave and turned to Gregory, astounded. "I'm surprised your mother wasn't named after a Roman goddess instead of a caesar. She is very beautiful. I take it your father is Greek, going by your last name?"

"Yes, my father is Greek, born here in Athens. His family goes way back into the annals of antiquity." Gregory called for his butler, Demitrios, to bring some wine. "We shall have dinner here on the balcony and discuss ways of helping one another. I'm very interested in your business prowess and visionary inventiveness. Perhaps we can discuss future business arrangements."

Mort knew this meeting was no coincidence. Destiny had enabled their paths to cross. With raised glasses, he proposed a toast: "To our friendship and future partnership that was made in heaven."

Gregory nodded.

The present returned quickly when Mort caught sight of Kavidas entering the glass-enclosed portico connecting the hotel with the outdoor patio, escorted by his personal bodyguard, Nickolas, and the hotel manager. *An entourage. Well, his presence is very commanding, isn't it?* Mort's gaze followed Kavidas as he approached the table.

"Mort, very sorry for the delay, but we ran into a minor problem with our research lab in Trinidad. I had to take care of it." Kavidas raised his hand and motioned to the waiter standing behind him. "Edison, bring me the seafood platter and an iced tea."

"Yes, sir, Mr. Kavidas, right away," Edison intoned.

"Anything serious going on in Trinidad?" Mort asked.

Kavidas shook his head. "Not serious. Some fool broke into the lab compound, did some snooping around, and got himself killed."

"Killed?" Mort exclaimed.

Kavidas shot him an exasperated look. "Shhh! Couldn't be helped. He came in through the experimental entrance and photographed all the apparatus and specimens. He was caught by our overseer and tried to escape. He was electrocuted, then fell from our security fence."

"But what about the police? Won't there be an investigation?"

Calmly and resolutely Kavidas replied, "No. We made it look like an accident, and in fact it really was; the American consulate already closed the case. They shipped the body back to his family."

"What about the research? How far has it progressed? Will this affect our plans?"

"Not at all." Kavidas looked up into the sky. "We are very close to developing the vaccine. We will be able to test it within the next 90 days."

"That soon?" Mort replied.

"Mort, don't forget, we've been working on this for the past five years. Only recently have we isolated the virus. If it were not for our recent breakthrough with those monkey glands, we would still be years away from the cure." Kavidas raised his hand in praise. "We've been fortunate; we must be enjoying divine favor."

Mort nodded. "What about approval from the FDA? They won't be looking at us favorably when the world learns human glands are involved as well."

"We're working on that. We hope to begin testing the live virus on volunteers; we already have them lined up. Some of them are prisoners, some terminal patients with nothing to lose. We're confident the FDA will adjust their waiting period—considering the magnitude of the epidemic. As for the human factor, they'll balk. They'll be horrified. But they'll give in. Social and moral pressure, you know."

Mort breathed deeply in exultation and emitted a reverent smile. "I have the gut feeling that everything is going to work out well for us."

"I wouldn't have it any other way," Kavidas affirmed.

Kathy rushed into the study where Brandon and David sat and blurted out, "Your father is here, Brandon. Wait 'til you see these pictures!" Slightly frazzled, she pushed her red hair away from her eyes and spread the photos out on the coffee table as Matthew strolled in.

"Look at this one," Matthew intoned, "the one labeled 'Thymus: Rhesus Sample 27R—HIV Positive.' Makes for an interesting photograph, doesn't it?"

Brandon grimaced while holding another print. "This one says

'Thymus: Human Sample—HIV Positive,' and it's really grotesque. Is it really a human organ?"

David was closely examining the photograph. "Johnnie's photography is unparalleled," he offered in testimony. "If the things in these jars are what the labels state, then this lab is messing with real sensitive stuff."

"A monkey and human organs and HIV? What does that mean?" Kathy asked.

David scratched his cheek. "I can only offer a guess at this point. It looks like someone is experimenting with the HIV virus on monkeys and humans at the same time."

"But what could this have to do with Johnnie's death?" Brandon queried. "Experiments with monkeys and AIDS are not new and certainly not secretive. We've been doing them as well. Dad, what do you think?"

"You're right. Ongoing research on AIDS and the HIV virus is common knowledge. The cure is still not in sight; in fact it's years away. There's a great problem with both isolating the virus and the DNA strand's inability to block the attacking virus." He paced the floor in silence while both Kathy and Brandon continued to study the photographs. "The human thymus gland. Now that's another thing altogether—a very scary thing."

"David, there's obviously a link between Johnnie's death, Rainbow Pharmaceuticals, and now this monkey business. No pun intended," Brandon postulated.

David froze in his steps, pulled the film canister containing the handkerchief out of his pocket, and held it aloft. "What would you say to the possibility that Rainbow Pharmaceuticals isolated the AIDS virus and is looking to corner the market on the vaccine?"

Brandon looked in astonishment at David, then at his father.

Kathy in turn looked up at David. "That possibility gives me the chills. The ramifications of such a thing is beyond belief."

Matthew ran a hand over his creased brow. "I don't think anyone could keep that quiet. We'll know more when the lab results come back from that fluid Brandon brought in."

David walked to the coffee table, opened the film canister, and draped the handkerchief over the photographs. "I'll bet this is blood from some lab monkey and together with the data on the disk, it all adds up to some mighty convincing evidence. Evidence that Johnnie felt strongly enough about that he was willing to die for it."

Kathy brought in Chinese food for dinner, but the cloud of gloom suppressed everyone's appetite. They simply picked through the containers and munched while pondering their findings of the day. Despite her infectious perky personality, Kathy was not able to overcome the pervasive aura of despondency gripping the room.

"Since Louie is now aware of our concerns relating to Rainbow, what is the possibility of him investigating to find out more about Johnnie's death, David?"

"My view, based on that info we retrieved on the disk, is that Rainbow is a very convoluted enterprise, with most of its operation below the surface. If Louie finds out anything, it will probably be just street knowledge anyway. Short of launching an FBI investigation or senate subcommittee search, very little will be revealed. It would probably take someone to infiltrate into the organization before any substantial evidence could be gathered. And besides, at this point, with the inconclusive evidence we have and Johnnie's death being called accidental, there is no case. In fact, case closed."

After David's summation, Brandon announced that he needed a ride, as Matthew had left earlier, promising to meet with them again the following day. David offered to drive Brandon home.

The two hour round-trip drive to West Palm Beach and back enabled David to unwind and collect his thoughts. He found some relief in his sorrow over Johnnie when memories of their college days filtered through the morass that filled his mind. Flashbacks of Johnnie impersonating Brandon brought a tinge of pain and happiness. He thought of all the parties and clubs they'd been to. Then he remembered the night at Ginzo's when they became inseparable friends. It had taken until years afterward to get Brandon's side of the story, too....

Brandon sat back and looked around the bar. Johnnie and David were by his side, as always, but he still seemed to be alone. He looked toward the dance floor and could see his nemesis, Mindy, coming toward him. It was a foregone conclusion that she would ask him to dance, and the guys would pressure him. *How long do I have to put up with this?* he thought as he steeled his mind against the upcoming onslaught.

Sure enough, he wasn't disappointed. She was as consistent as ever. "Brandon, come on. Dance with me," she wheedled.

"Mindy, you know I don't dance."

"Oh, I don't know," put in Johnnie lightly. "You danced pretty well the other night with Sue—wasn't that her name?"

Brandon gave him a look that was almost pleading, but it had no effect.

Johnnie merely winked and pushed them toward the dance floor. "What do you think, Dave? Do they look like a couple?"

"I think he looks uncomfortable," Dave replied, "and I don't think I'd wish her on anyone."

Johnnie snorted a quick laugh and returned to his drink. He had been looking for a girl for himself before Mindy came along. "Well, I don't know, the girls all seem to go for Brandon. You'd think he'd have a different girlfriend every week."

"You'd think so," answered Dave quickly, "but truthfully, he doesn't seem to take much notice of the girls the way they do of him. Either he's modest or he's dead."

Both guys laughed again as they saw Brandon motion to them from the dance floor to come and rescue him. No one moved to help.

After the dance, the guys regrouped around the bar. Mindy, realizing that one dance was the most she was going to extract from Brandon, had moved off to the next victim. Johnnie and David still wanted to give Brandon a hard time, but their attention was turned to the couple now approaching the bar.

"Look at that," Johnnie said, disgusted. "How can those two come out in public?"

Brandon and David turned around and saw two guys sit down

together and order a drink.

"I can't believe they have the nerve to sit next to us. Do you believe that?" he asked, turning to Brandon. "Doesn't that make you sick?"

"Yeah, I guess," Brandon said, somewhat noncommittal. He turned away and looked toward the dance floor.

"What do you mean?" pressed Johnnie.

"Nothing. I don't mean anything."

Johnnie raised his eyebrows. He glanced back at the couple next to them at the bar and then signaled to David. "Let's go."

"Okay, I'm ready."

Brandon looked over toward Johnnie and then looked down. He took the last swallow of his drink and grabbed his coat. "Fine, let's go."

"Man, what is the matter with you?"

"I said there's nothing wrong. Let's just go."

The car ride was quiet, almost uncomfortable. Brandon sat there, almost brooding, while Johnnie shifted in his seat. David knew something was wrong and didn't want to allow himself to dwell on what it was.

Johnnie's personality wouldn't let it go. He pulled into their next stop, another of their usual haunts, and parked.

No one moved.

"Brandon, if there's something wrong, why don't you just tell me? Did I do something? What's up, man?" Johnnie had reached out and put his arm on Brandon's shoulder, trying to bring him out of his melancholy.

Brandon shrugged it off. "What is it you want, Johnnie? You want me to tell you what's really wrong, or do you want me to tell you what you hope is wrong?"

"What's the difference?" asked Johnnie hesitantly.

"I think you know exactly what's wrong. I think you both do. You just don't want to face it." Johnnie and David looked at each other uncomfortably, while Brandon lowered his face onto his chest.

"Look, Brandon," began David, "you don't have to say anything you don't want to. Let's just forget about tonight, okay?"

"Why? Will that make it not true? Maybe it is time to talk about it."

"Talk about what?" cried Johnnie. "You guys lost me. What's going on?" A pause left Johnnie looking from Brandon to David. "You gonna tell me or not?"

"You want to know," said Brandon, "then fine. I'll tell you. I'm gay."

His eyes slowly lifted, and he glanced at Johnnie before looking at David. "Just drop me off. I want to get out of here."

David looked askance, then looked back to see Johnnie's reaction.

"Wait a minute, Dave. You knew?"

David turned away and took a deep breath. "I didn't *know,* but I had a hunch."

"Why didn't you say anything?" asked Johnnie.

Now David stared at Brandon and forced their eyes to meet. "Because," said David quietly, "I didn't want it to be true."

All three men sat quietly, waiting to see where the conversation would go. Finally, Brandon couldn't stand the silence. "Take me home. I've got to get out of here."

Johnnie started the car but didn't move. "Now what do we do?" he asked no one in particular.

"Well," began Brandon angrily, "you can start by castrating me! How's that? Why do you feel there is something you have to do—who do you think you are?"

His attack took both men by surprise, and it took several seconds for Johnnie to respond. "Brandon," he said softly, "I didn't mean what should we do to you. I was speaking about all of us. Now."

"Does anything have to change?" asked David. "We don't have to agree with you, Brandon, and after all, I've known for a while. I think we've all known."

Brandon cleared his throat cautiously. "You guys are my closest friends. I don't want to lose that. If you can live with it, let's leave it alone. Nothing will change."

Johnnie sat back and shook his head. "What do you mean nothing will change? You're attracted to men—you may have slept with one—and you're saying let's forget about it? Are you telling me that you've got a boyfriend? Because I really can't handle that."

Brandon looked at Johnnie, and his lip began to quiver. But he didn't cry; instead, he began to laugh. "I'm sorry, guys. I don't mean to laugh," he said between gasps. "I just can't help it. I mean, you guys do everything with me and really know everything about me or almost everything. I don't have a boyfriend hidden anywhere. I think you would have figured that out before now."

All three seemed to sense that the longetivity of their friendship hinged on whatever happened in the next few minutes. But something wonderful happened. As Brandon continued to laugh, Johnnie and David began to analyze the man in front of them. The same man that they had loved just a few hours before.

"Look, Brandon," Johnnie began, "this is a whole new world. One I'm not comfortable with and one I don't want to know. Can you keep that part to yourself, or do you have to come out of the closet and tell everyone and talk about sex all the time?"

"We always talked about sex before anyway," said Brandon.

"Not that kind of sex," said David quickly. "Let's take it as it goes, okay? Let's not make a pact or anything tonight, please! In fact, I could really use a drink about now. What do you say? Agreed?"

Brandon met each one's eyes briefly and put out his hand. Tentatively, they both reached out to grab it. "Thanks, you guys, for not hating me or being disgusted. It would really devastate me." The weight of the discussion started to set in. "I've seen the looks you've given other people we've run into—like tonight—and I expected the worst."

"Hey, buddy, that look was for *what* they were, not *who* they were. We didn't even know those guys. But you—you I know. So I can look at you differently. Or I can just look away." Johnnie reached over and tousled Brandon's hair, one sure way to get a quick response.

"Hey, watch it!" he yelled and reached for Johnnie's head and began to give him some of the same.

David joined in, and the three of them were quickly panting from the exertion and the relief that things were more normal.

"I've got just one question," said David. "Where does this leave Mindy?"

David remembered nothing of the last 30 miles he had just driven but could remember every detail of that night with his two friends. He pursed his lips as he realized that the evening was a turning point for all three men. In fact, it was the most significant moment in his memory with the exception of the day he met Kathy and the day he'd come to know Jesus....

David counted the minutes as the sermon came to a close. He glanced over toward Matthew Lane and could see the peace and joy the man experienced just by listening to the Bible being read. Then Matthew turned to look at Brandon; his face contorted into a malevolent glare. *So that's what the evil eye is,* David thought to himself.

He was mad enough that he had to overcome the gay factor in Brandon's life and act as if nothing were different. *Now,* David said to himself, *Brandon's father asks me to come to church with him so Brandon can see how important it is. And here, the guy looks a million miles away!* Brandon continued to stare blankly into space as David turned away in disgust. *The least he could do is pay attention since I'm only here because of him!* David's only consolation was the picture in his mind of what he was going to do to Brandon when the service was over. The sight was not a pretty one.

David quickly moved to the church exit as the recessional hymn began. He knew Matthew would be embroiled in church politics after service; running things just seemed to be in Matthew's job description. David learned after his first visit to this church to make himself scarce lest he himself become entangled in planning upcoming events—or worse, become involved with any of the various youth groups. He had almost made it to the car when someone called his name.

"David," a soft voice called, "what's your hurry?"

Skeptical as to the person's motives and intentions, David turned slowly. He was pleasantly surprised. "No hurry, none at all," he almost stuttered. "Have we met?" He eyed the young woman up and down, then quickly looked away, remembering their present location.

"No, but I've heard about you. We've been visiting my grandmother at her beach house in New York. It's in Far Rockaway. We just got back. I'm Kathy Schildt." She extended her hand and smiled. Her broad smile was accentuated by her two dimples that sat atop a field of fading freckles. Her flaming red hair radiated around her face.

David was smitten. He lost track of time until Brandon tapped him on the shoulder and told him it was time to leave. He shrugged and motioned to Kathy that his ride was leaving. He couldn't take his eyes off her as he got in the car, and reveled in the thought that her glance followed the car as it left. David stared at Kathy till she was gone from view.

In the next three months, David stuck to Matthew like glue, and while Brandon declined to participate, David was at every church meeting and suddenly was joining every group. He began to share his life with the church, and Kathy began to tell him about Jesus. The moment that Jesus became real to David, when he actually knew that Jesus had died for him, his life was complete. Jesus was his Lord, and David allowed him to take charge of his life. Soon he and Kathy were inseparable, and the wedding was announced. His hostility toward Brandon for being dragged to church was long since gone.

His gratitude to Matthew was overwhelming, but the man rebutted the praise. "David, it's nothing I did. I only reached out to you. Jesus called you to him. You don't have to thank me." Matthew looked at David with joy.

"Don't worry, Mr. Lane," David quipped, noticing Matthew's faraway look and his sad countenance. "He made me sit and listen to him. He'll hear this message, too. I'll be sure to tell him." Matthew smiled, and David took Kathy by the arm and walked away.

As lightning filled the sky, David's attention returned to the roadway. The rain began to fall and cover Interstate 95 with an impenetrable curtain, as was its usual wont in the humid summer. His exit was fast approaching, and his heart soared as he thought of home. God had blessed him with a wonderful wife, a beautiful family, and faithful friends. His lifestyle had changed, but God had prospered him in his relationships.

He thought of the people in his life who he loved. Their faces passed before him as he drove, and only one caused him pain. Johnnie. The trio was no more. Johnnie was gone. David's mood blackened as he thought of the loss they would all feel. *And someone is going to pay.*

As David walked in the door, Kathy handed the phone to him. "It's Krissy. Johnnie's death was not accidental—he was murdered!"

"What? Johnnie was murdered?" David exclaimed into the phone.

"I'm sure of it, David. The coroner's office performed an autopsy on Johnnie, and they told me his death was the result of electrocution. The multiple fractures from the fall were incidental." She renewed her sobbing into the phone, then blurted out, "I know he was murdered!"

Krissy Kramer's hysteria heightened so that her dialog became sheer gibberish.

"I can't understand what you're saying, Krissy. Slow down. What do you mean some guy who knew Johnnie down in Trinidad turned up dead?" David repeated.

Krissy sighed. "I called the hotel where Johnnie stayed. You know me—I have a very suspicious nature. Well, I told them who I was, and the manager, someone named Manny, volunteered the info that rumor said Johnnie was killed, and the person who helped Brandon get off Trinidad died also. He said they found him at the base of an ocean overlook; it looked like an accident."

David turned from the phone. "Ugh," he muttered. "This whole business is mushrooming like a nuclear bomb."

"David, what should we do?" Krissy asked, now much more calm after her torrent of words had ended.

"I'm not sure yet. I need time to think things out. I'll call you soon; try to get some rest." David hung up the phone, then turned to Kathy. "Put on a pot of coffee. It's going to be a long night."

Krissy crushed her cigarette into the car ashtray, then opened her side window to vent out the smoke. "This is my last pack," she pledged to herself. The nagging habit just would not go away. It seemed as though every time she attempted to give them up, another crisis developed. *Someday, Lord,* she thought.

She turned off the Florida Turnpike at the Wellington exit, turned west, and continued another 12 miles to a remote, undeveloped area near the northern tip of the Loxahatchee National Wildlife Refuge. The single-lane highway cut a wavy line through desolate, unfamiliar territory. Large prairies spotted with saw grass clumps and fresh water sloughs ran as far as her eye could see. Maleluca and cypress trees, along with scrawny scrub pines, randomly studded the roadway. Occasionally a junglelike hardwood hammock would appear and break up the monotonous landscape that was a part of the Everglades ecosystem. The hammocks, containing mostly mahogany trees, formed a natural sanctuary for exotic birds.

Then, 45 minutes after leaving the turnpike, she saw an indication of her destination, a small roadside sign that read Rainbow Corporation, Five miles ahead.

After four miles, Krissy stopped the car when the contour of the landscape abruptly changed to a lush oasis. Royal palm trees with hibiscus and bougainvillea bushes were strategically placed in oval gardens, each with a fountain to accentuate the rolling lawn that extended for nearly half a mile where it met a mansion. Even from this distance, Krissy was overwhelmed with the splendor of the estate. The house resembled the Biltmore House, the palatial estate owned by the Vanderbilts that she toured when visiting friends in North Carolina. There were at least 200 rooms in that building. She shook her head. *This can't be his place of business. This place is a palace!*

Once she reached the summit of a hill, the fence and guard building came into view. The realization of being watched suddenly came over her.

One of the security guards waved her over to his side and asked her as she rolled the car window down, "Can I help you, lady? We've been watching you drive up."

Krissy looked around for the surveillance cameras and saw none. "How did you manage to see me coming?" she asked coquettishly.

The muscular guard with a nicely cropped beard snickered while pointing skyward. "Geosynchronous satellite. No one goes in or out without us knowing."

"Oh, well, I'm looking for Rainbow Industries. Is this the right place, or did I make a wrong turn?" Krissy replied as she stepped out of the car.

The guard swelled with pride and said while pointing to the mansion, "You're in the right place; this is Rainbow. Sort of an unconventional plant, isn't it?"

Krissy looked astonished. "To say the least," she said meekly. She turned around and surveyed the estate in her mind. "I'm seeking a position with Rainbow, and I thought I could simply show up at your personnel office and fill out an application."

The guard scanned Krissy up and down, grinned, and shot a look at her fire-engine-red convertible. "Honey, if it were up to me, you could start today. But it isn't. All of our applicants must submit a résumé through our employment division; then they call you. That's the game plan. Sorry."

He started to leave when Krissy asked, "Is it all right if I look around? This place is so beautiful." She threw her hands into the air and added, "As long as I'm here."

"No problem. Just stay on this side of the fence and no photographs. Security reasons," he admonished. He wrote her license-plate number down on his clipboard and asked, "Your name for the record, miss?"

"Linda Martin," she answered. She opened the car door and with a puzzled look asked, "By the way, who owns all this?"

"Rainbow Industries and its subsidiaries are wholly owned by the Kavidas family. I thought everyone knew that," he replied with a tinge of sarcasm.

"Well, I'm from a small town near Love Canal," she said with a smirk. *That's the second lie,* she thought.

"Thank you, Miss Martin. I hope you have a nice day," the guard replied as he waved her on.

Krissy drove down toward the employee parking lot and noticed at least 50 cars there. The shipping and receiving bays were barely in view, off to the side of the mansion, mostly shielded by decorative panels. She continued until she reached the corporate lot, then carefully looked at each car. At the end of the reserved spaces she spotted it through the fence.

It was a black Rolls-Royce, two years old by her estimate, and exquisite in detail. A custom model, no doubt, with all the trimmings. The license tag read *Kavidas.* She paused to study the vehicle when she heard a man's whistle. When she turned, she saw the guard in the distance motioning for her to move on. She waved back and continued out the exit. She lit up another cigarette and inhaled deeply, as if throwing caution to the wind, and made up her mind what her course of action would be.

An hour later she arrived at David and Kathy's home in Coral Springs.

Kathy met Krissy at the driveway and escorted her onto the screened patio behind the house. "David and I are worried about you. How have you been? You sounded confused over the car phone. Krissy, what's going on?"

She shook her head, then began crying. "It's this Rainbow thing and Johnnie. Something must be done; they just can't get away with this."

Kathy affectionately stroked her hair. "Well, we do have some proof that Johnnie was murdered, but it's all circumstantial."

Krissy looked into Kathy's eyes. "I realize it's risky, but I went to Rainbow's headquarters in Wellington just to see what it's like."

"Are you crazy?" Kathy retorted. "Why didn't you wait to hear from David or something? You can get into deep trouble around there. If this business and Johnnie's murder are linked, we all could be in danger. Did anybody see you?"

"No," she said, "I gave a phony name. Nobody knows who I am. Unfortunately, I was videotaped—by satellite—can you believe that? But I'm not worried." She began pacing the patio while recounting her visit. "This Rainbow and Kavidas family must be powerful. I mean, the headquarters building alone is bigger than any building I've ever seen owned by one family."

"How did you know about Rainbow and Kavidas, Krissy? David and I just found that out from the computer disk Brandon brought back from Trinidad. And in fact we're still checking it out."

"You forgot I'm a New York probation officer. I have friends on the police force who owe me some favors. They accessed the information for me after I found out about Johnnie." Krissy stopped pacing and mused briefly. "I wonder where this guy Kavidas lives."

"Don't you dare even think about Kavidas or anything about him," Kathy warned. "It's much too dangerous; just keep away from him and Rainbow! This thing is too big for one person to take up a personal crusade. Wait until we have more proof and we notify the authorities."

Krissy wasn't sure she could do that, but she didn't want to worry Kathy further. "Let's just see how they make out."

Minutes after Krissy left, Kathy called David on his cell phone. "David, Krissy just left, and I'm afraid she's going to do something stupid. She found out about Rainbow and Kavidas and went to his headquarters up in Wellington."

"Oh, great," David lamented. "Do you think she'll be all right?"

"Well, she seems obsessed with finding out and punishing whoever killed Johnnie."

"Hmm. Did Louie call back yet?" David asked. "Maybe he has some news. He should be able to get a handle on what's going on. This way we can placate Krissy before it's too late."

"No, not yet. I'll call him again," Kathy said.

The Fifth Precinct police station in Queens Village, New York, originally built in the 1940s, resembled a converted armory from World War II. The recent renovations, mostly structural, did little for the dreary look that pervaded the police station. If it were not for the bulletin boards, posters, and calendars covering most of the wall surfaces, visitors could easily tell the rooms were in desperate need of painting.

The redeeming element that elevated the "dungeon," as it was aptly called by the force, was the low rate of recidivism in the area. The tough uniformed police and detectives, under the watchful eye of the commissioner, took such a serious view on drug interdiction that the outcry from the public defender's office over the number of convictions frequently appeared in the newspaper columns. So when it came to the aesthetics of the building, nobody on the force really cared. The real issue with the Fifth was simply to rid the neighborhood of the scum that infected society—regardless of what was needed to accomplish the job.

"Donato! Call for you on 03," squawked the telephone intercom.

His 210 pounds, when hung on a five-foot-seven-inch frame, made him clumsily walk to his desk. Donato snuffed out his cigarette and reached for the phone. "Lieutenant Donato."

"Louie, this is Kathy down in Florida. How are you doing?"

"Busier than a one-armed paper hanger. You know me, always involved. It's great to hear from you! How is the family?" Impulsively, he reached into his desk and grabbed a handful of cashew nuts and stuffed them into his mouth.

"We're all fine," she replied passively.

"Is everything all right? You don't sound good," Donato inquired. Louie, David, and Kathy had been friends for a long time. He could tell when something was up.

"Well, yes and no. David and I and the children are fine, but a problem involving one of David's close friends developed, and we're hoping you can help us with your access to FBI information," she entreated.

"Just name it."

THREE

I go the way
that Providence dictates
with the assurance of a sleepwalker.
Adolf Hitler

Information fascinated the Watchman. He learned early in life that information is a commodity that can be easily converted into cash when you have the right outlets. His ears were always attuned to new vibrations; his nose was always sniffing the wind for the scent of fresh meat. He possessed the extraordinary gift of acquiring valuable information, then finding the right buyer, and fortunately, his career allowed him access to unlimited amounts of information.

"Mr. Kavidas's private line please," the caller said.

"And who shall I say is calling, sir?"

"This is Watchman," he replied.

It only took a second to get his call through Kavidas's private line.

"Kavidas, here," the voice on the other end of the line said.

"Mr. Kavidas, I've become aware of certain inquiries regarding your interests in Trinidad. At this point they are simply inquiring about ownership and holdings. I thought you would like to know." The Watchman paused and waited for the fish to take the bait.

"And just who is making these inquiries?" Kavidas asked.

"Mr. Kavidas, you're a businessman. So am I. I gave you the first piece for free. You can't always expect something for nothing, you know." The Watchman knew that Kavidas was hungry for information. He also knew that dealing with him was dangerous: like trying to feed a hungry lion. Things can go just right, or you could lose an important part of your anatomy. Knowing how far to push was the important part, and the Watchman knew precisely how to balance the equation. "Of course with you I will always throw in a few tidbits on the house. Considering you've been such a good customer in the past, you understand."

"I do indeed. And I also understand that you would like to have me remain a good customer. I can't be a patron to someone who isn't available now, can I?"

"Mr. Kavidas, please," he pleaded in mock offense, "you can't be serious! You're threatening me like a common thug! Trust me. What I have to sell is something you'll want. And you'll want more of it."

"Okay. Until I'm convinced, it's the standard pay. If I want more, we'll talk."

The Watchman passed the information along in his usual way. And he knew that the fee would be paid, as always. Kavidas was not just a good customer; he was one that always paid. "Interested in any more?" he asked as he concluded.

"This is high priority. Let me know the very moment you find out anything else," Kavidas said. "I'll double and triple the fees with your next call."

All in all, Watchman thought to himself, *a very profitable day.* But a shadow of doubt crossed his mind for the first time as he went on his way. *Kavidas will pay a fortune for my next call.*

What could be that important—or need to be kept that secret?

"Louie! I don't believe it! What are you doing here in Florida?" Kathy exclaimed as she answered the call at the front door.

His smile widened as he hung his arms over her shoulders to give her a big kiss. "After your call last week, I decided to take an impromptu vacation with the people I love. Can you put me up?" he said in his gregarious manner.

"You're always welcome, and David will be so pleased to see you. And guess what? You're just in time for lunch."

Louie rolled his eyes while patting the pouch where his stomach should be. "Any homemade chocolate-chip cookies on hand?"

Kathy grinned. "Just so happens I froze a batch I recently baked. I'll take them out of the freezer while you get settled."

A short while later, as they sat around the kitchen table, Kathy quickly surmised that Louie's unexpected visit could only be related to her phone call and not his vacation. "I thought you would call us with the information I asked you for. We never thought you would hop a plane and fly down here—my, what service."

"Well, honestly, after I ran a search on this Rainbow thing, I thought you might be getting in over your heads," he offered.

"Well, you're probably right. I wish that David thought the same. How big are they?"

"*Immense* is the key word. This Rainbow empire, if you will, extends from here in Florida into the Caribbean, then all the way to the Mediterranean, and who knows where else," he advised. "But the scary part is not their oil holdings but their pharmaceutical interests. I found out when I ran their holdings search that a Rainbow subsidiary, a Paris facility called La Femme, did the joint research on the RU-486 abortion pill. It was one of their latest projects. When the pill passed through the FDA here in the States, it was a boon for Rainbow. And that's just one little sliver of the pie. They have numerous dummy corporations, subsidiaries, and facilities. They also have one of the biggest research and development departments of any company in the world." He shook his head and snagged another cookie out of the freezer bag. This time he dunked the thawing cookie into his hot coffee.

Kathy dropped her head back, then rubbed her neck in an effort to release the building tension. "It sounds to me like they have all the money they need at their disposal for whatever cause they choose—whether for good or for evil," she said as she gazed out the window.

"Uncle Louie!" a little girl shouted as she pushed open the kitchen door.

Louie looked down at the child and beamed. "My, my. Aren't you one beautiful little lady?" he said as he held his arms out to grab her. He looked up at Kathy and added, "I haven't seen Hillary for over a year. I can't get over how adorable she is. She is really a prize."

Kathy glowed. "Our gift from God and one of our greatest blessings." She looked down at Hillary. "Go change your school clothes, honey, while

I put some chocolate-chip cookies out for you."

Hillary looked over at Louie and quipped, "If there are any left."

Louie lurched after her, but she scooted into a distant corner. "Uncle Louie, I learned the names of all the books of the Bible. My daddy taught me. Do you want to hear me sing them?" she asked as she fluttered her eyes.

Louie shot a look at the cookie bag, then up at Kathy. "Just the Old Testament for now."

Hillary jumped up on his lap and rattled off the entire list without missing one. The books fit perfectly in her little song. She cocked her head and gave Louie a big kiss and darted off to her room.

A ray of sunshine in a darkening world, her mother thought.

Mort pushed the recliner back as he prepared for the show. The mini-theater at Rainbow in Wellington reminded him of the vintage movie producer with his own private viewing room. Instead of the traditional in-home theater with darkened paneling or drapes and the antiquated lighting apparatus, Gregory's interior decorator went with modern art-deco wallpaper and paint to accentuate the rainbow theme. Mort thought the motif to be radical for Gregory's temperament but considered it to be one of his therapy rooms—a place to unwind while still at the office, so to speak.

The electronics and lighting were state-of-the-art, and once Gregory loaded the DVD into the player, he sat in his own personal recliner. Attuned to his voice commands, the drapes closed automatically, the lights dimmed, and two wall-to-wall bookshelves parted, revealing a 10-by-12-foot rear-projection screen.

Gregory smiled at Mort. "Brace yourself for an incredible excursion." He then turned toward the screen and raised his voice slightly to order, "Run film."

The screen illuminated with the Rainbow logo dominating, then diminished as dramatic classical music thundered through the omni-audio system. Mort looked over at Gregory in expectation.

The music subsided as Gregory appeared on the screen in his library at

Rainbow. Dressed in a white medical smock over a blue suit and tie, he warmly greeted the viewers. "Dear friends, we at Rainbow Pharmaceuticals have an important announcement to make—one that will change the scope of science and the future of the world." He walked to his heavy antique desk and sat on its corner, picking up a manila folder. "For the past five years, we at Rainbow have personally undertaken the 'mission,' if you will, of developing the vaccine for AIDS, and we are pleased to report that we have not only isolated the AIDS virus but have found the vaccine."

Suddenly the background shifted. Gregory appeared in the same outfit, but now he was walking through one of his laboratories. The camera zoomed in on the cages containing rhesus monkeys as Gregory walked into the scene. He motioned toward the cages. "These monkeys furnished us with important data on how the HIV virus reacts, and we thank them for their early contribution to our war on the plague. But the real contribution toward our cure came from here—" His voice broke off abruptly, and the scene changed to an undisclosed hospital corridor. Gregory again greeted the viewers as he opened the door leading into a ward.

The camera panned the ward where 275 men were staring at Gregory as he walked in. The patients were fully clothed, sitting on their beds as if waiting to be discharged.

Gregory raised his hands in applause. "These gallant men have endured great risk and sacrifice in volunteering to test this vaccine. These valiant soldiers entered our program only six months ago when they were bed-ridden, HIV-positive, and waiting to die. They have been introduced to our new vaccine, and they are no longer at risk to develop full-blown AIDS; they are ready to go home." The camera panned the smiling faces as the view faded.

Gregory reappeared in his office wearing his clinical apron as the violin in the classical piece softly played toward its conclusion. "We at Rainbow are very confident that the FDA will approve our vaccine for public development very shortly, and we encourage you to support our ongoing research to rid the earth of this dreaded disease as the vaccine enters its final distribution phase."

The screen filled with thousands of shoppers walking down New York City's streets: an ocean of humanity. The Rainbow logo reappeared, slowly displacing the human collage. "Rainbow, working toward a better world and a better you," the narrator concluded.

"Video off. Lights on," Gregory said. As the room condition returned to normal, he looked over at Mort. "Well, what do you think of it?"

"It's sensational!" Mort replied. "Are we—?"

A knock at the door interrupted Mort as Sydelle Swain, an exacting brunette, and another woman walked in.

"I waited until the video monitor light went out before knocking, Mr. Kavidas," Sydelle began.

"That's fine. What is it?" Gregory asked as he looked at the woman accompanying Sydelle.

"Well, I'm leaving on my maternity furlough in two months, and I wanted to introduce you to my temporary replacement before we left for lunch. She is well equipped and comes to us from our administrative branch in New York."

"Well equipped is right," Mort remarked as he scanned the new assistant.

Gregory made a face at Mort. "With things moving so fast around here, despite your condition, I forgot about you leaving." He scratched his head and said to the recent transferee, "Some mighty big shoes to fill, Ms.—?"

"Ms. Martin. Linda Martin," she said, completing his hopeful statement.

"Stay close to Sydelle so she can bring you up to speed on our southern operation down here, Ms. Martin," Gregory replied. He turned toward Mort as the ladies departed, then abruptly rotated on one foot and added, "Oh, and have a nice lunch—on me. I insist. It's the least I could do."

"Thank you, Mr. Kavidas," they replied in unison.

Mort alighted from the recliner and wandered over by the window. "I'm amazed at the progression here. Are we that far along that we are preparing DVDs for the public?" He gazed out the window and caught sight of the two girls getting into what appeared to be Linda's car, then asked Gregory, "What about those patients? Where did you take that video?"

Gregory pointed westward. "Right here at Wellington in our research wing. We had temporarily converted it into a hospital ward some time ago, envisioning this day. The beautiful part is that we were, and still are, able to control the environment at our own facility. Makes it easier, if you know what I mean."

"You mean as far as controlling public and official inquiries is concerned?"

"Something like that," Gregory replied. "Our plan is to use this video as a sort of promotional thing. To gather support in political and severe geographic areas where there is a high demand for the vaccine. This should bolster our chances with getting market approval sooner than the required time. As far as the patients in the video are concerned, their cases are all documented and ready for any scrutiny. We made sure of that."

"It sounds to me like you already have a target date for marketing the vaccine," Mort observed.

"We're looking at this Christmas as the 'advent' of the vaccine, if all goes well." Gregory said it as if it were an official announcement.

Swept up by the news, Mort shot his two fists into the air in triumph. "Yes! That gives us almost 11 months to prepare the world for one of the greatest accomplishments ever achieved by mankind." He looked reverently at Gregory. "You will be credited for being some kind of savior of the world."

Gregory gave Mort a long, silent stare, then abruptly said, "We have a lot of work to do before then. In the coming weeks you and I will discuss how we will transform *Redisearch* into a network that will enable us to expedite and control distribution of the vaccine and ultimately something else that will help our purpose."

"What would that 'something else' be?" Mort queried.

"Well, let's just say for now that with your expanding access to credit information, we may be able to diversify into other ventures. After all, once the inoculation program is complete and we relinquish certain distribution rights for humanitarian purposes, where do we go? Should we wait for another 'bug' to emerge or do we set out now to conquer other frontiers?"

"Sounds like good long-range planning to me," Mort concurred.

"I need you to prepare *Redisearch* in the next 11 months to go international. Now that you are this nation's leading credit-search clearinghouse, I think it is prudent to send some of your VPs and liaisons to sell *Redisearch* overseas. The time is right, businesses are already wired, the public is prepped, and we will need the global networking." He turned to look out the window as two wood storks flew by, then added, "Take some time off. Go to your place in Cozumel for two weeks and think out a plan for the future. Bring me back the ideas you come up with to carry it out. You know what an important role you play in this."

Mort joined him at the window. "Ah yes, the future."

Kathy enjoyed working at Logos International part-time as a software distribution consultant, despite her inward desire to be home. Her aspirations for a career in computer technology were not the same as they were when she first graduated college; her love life had changed all that. Once she married David, the driving force that propelled her through college became diverted toward building her home and raising her children. She agreed with David's philosophy that a trade-off between being home when the children returned from school or keeping a new car in the driveway each year was worth it.

Lenny Helman walked over to Kathy's desk. "A Louie Donato is on the phone for you. You asked him to check into something?"

"Oh yes, thanks, Len," Kathy replied. She looked around for unfriendly ears, and seeing none, picked up the phone. "Hello, Louie."

"I have been having a devil of a time getting any good data on this Rainbow outfit. I did check with the American consulate in Trinidad, and they simply confirmed the death of Johnnie back in November, but they didn't have any other details. Then I ran an FBI check on Rainbow and its subsidiaries, and they appear to be clean," he concluded glumly.

Slightly disappointed in the report Kathy asked, "Were you able to find out anything about their laboratory in Trinidad, or what they're working on? We have some information, but it's all circumstantial, nothing concrete."

"Well, I found out that Rainbow has a 50-year property lease in Trinidad for petroleum exploration and pharmaceutical research. But there isn't much more to know apart from Rainbow having legitimate worldwide financial interests. I know you're disappointed at the lack of data available, but I wanted you to know as soon as possible."

"Thanks. I'll see you at home."

Miami's Bayside, a bulk-headed shopping mall on the Atlantic Ocean north of Key Biscayne, attracted thousands of tourists each week. Sailboats, yachts, and touring water craft filled the harbor, connecting the inlet to the ocean every day. In the distance cruise ships made their way through the waterways on their way to Bahamian and Caribbean ports.

Bayside represented a special place for Louie whenever he visited Florida. He loved to meander through the crowds on the boardwalks, then onto the sidewalks that crisscrossed the giant department store. He enjoyed haggling with the merchants to make a deal and rarely missed an opportunity to look for something for his mother back home in New York. Normally he sat and watched Bayside's famed outdoor street theater before moving on.

But today, five days into his Florida visit, his mind was consumed with David and Kathy. He reminded himself that they were his purpose in being in Florida.

He checked his watch to confirm the rendezvous time and made his way up to the food court to meet David and Brandon. When atop the second floor, the aroma from all the food artisans enraptured him. He checked the time again. *I still have 10 minutes,* he thought. Surveying the vast selection of international food vendors, he made a snap decision.

Entranced by the scent of tomato sauce, he approached the Napoli Grill counter. "One sausage roll, with plenty of sauce, please." Pointing to the soda fountain he added, "And one small diet cola, no ice." Looking around, then back at the counter girl he said, "Can you hurry it up?" Compensating for his New York behavior, he left a hearty tip, to which the girl returned a voluptuous smile.

He dashed over to the adjoining portico, sat at one of the tables, and proceeded to devour the sausage roll, dipping the uneaten portion into the sauce at each bite. While guzzling the cola, he looked at the clock. *Not bad,* he said to himself. He surveyed the empty paper plate. *Only five minutes.*

He walked around the food court to the Hispanic section and waved to David and another man sitting at a table.

As Louie approached, David stood up. "Louie, this is Brandon Lane.

Brandon, Louie Donato, the famous detective from New York."

"David has told me a lot about you, Brandon," Louie said cordially. "I'm looking forward to working with you on the Rainbow matter."

"Likewise," Brandon said. "I've heard a lot about you also." He glanced at the wall clock. "We have to meet my father at one o'clock, so we better get lunch out of the way." He looked at David, then back to Louie. "You guys hungry?"

Louie smirked. "Sure. I'm always hungry."

From Bayside they walked the short distance to Miami Avenue, the headquarters for Lane Pharmaceutical. Built in 1946, the three-floor building had endured three face-lifts and two structural renovations to bring it up to present-day safety codes. The surrounding area, under the auspicious ideal of attracting tourism from the Northeast, was similarly upgraded with modern tropical colors.

Exiting from the elevator on the third floor, Louie was surprised at the unpretentious look of Matthew's office. Considering Matthew to be the CEO of such a huge corporation, he expected expensive medieval furniture and elaborate gold furnishings to match his title. Instead, he saw a modest decor that was functional and one that on the whole generated a rather unofficial atmosphere. In fact, he felt more like he was in a den than an office. They walked into the waiting lobby and sat down.

One of the secretaries approached them. "Mr. Lane, your father asks for you and your associates to join him now."

"Thank you, Millie," Brandon replied as they filed into the office.

Matthew Lane walked around his desk and hugged Brandon. "Good to see you again, Son." Turning to David, he said, "You're looking well. Family okay? Is teaching treating you good?"

David smiled. "Thank God. We're all doing fine."

"And you must be Louie, David's policeman friend from New York."

Louie shook his hand, then retired to the rear of the room.

With a deep, spirited voice, Matthew added, "Please sit down, gentlemen. Care for any soft drinks?"

One by one they waved him off. Then Brandon spoke up. "Just had

61

lunch over at Bayside—and you?"

"Once a week I work through lunch to catch up, as if you didn't know. It might not be a bad habit for you, Brandon," he said, smiling. He walked to the large picture window with the view of downtown Miami in the background, then turned to the three men and asked, "Gentlemen, what do you propose we do about Rainbow?"

Louie sat quietly and observed the towering man before him that David had spoken so highly of. Looking like 55 when he was 64 counted for something. Together his robust build, his full head of hair, and gripping handshake signaled virility while his history of personal sacrifice told of humility.

Reputation dictated that he represented some kind of an icon to the drug industry. In a world of compromise and corruption, maintaining corporate integrity for nearly five decades deserved great accolades. His unprecedented desire to create a fair and challenging workplace for his 7,000 nationwide employees, instead of trying to win public approval, frequently annoyed fault-finding critics who looked for ammunition. Always one to do his homework, Louie could see the man earned his success.

Matthew watched Louie with almost equal interest. He couldn't quite figure Louie out and wasn't sure why the man was so eager to help. Civil duty, being a public servant—that was all well and good. But he knew it had its limits. Climbing the corporate ladder is never an easy task, and Matthew had already had his share of difficult times. *It's a lot easier when you get to the top and don't have anyone else to answer to. On the way up, however, you're always working for someone.* Matthew wondered who Louie answered to. Was it David?

From his earliest memories, Matthew thought that the person he'd answer to would always be himself. It wasn't until his college years that he'd realized there was a grander scheme than just his corporate goals. It was then he'd discovered that Jesus had plans for his life, and he would be answerable to not just himself but also to God. He remembered the time fondly....

Matthew arrived at his college dorm on time to hear his roommate, Scott, complain to Deidre on the phone. "He always says he'll be here by 7:00, and he never is...don't take it out on me. He's your boyfriend. He's just my roommate." He smiled as Matthew walked in. "Hold it, Deidre. Mr. Wonderful just arrived." He handed the phone to Matthew, who was grinning effusively.

"You're so good at being a secretary," Matthew whispered with his hand over the mouthpiece. "I'll make sure I keep a place for you in my company."

Scott rolled his eyes in exasperation. "Promises, promises. You and your company. What about Deidre? Is she going to hold forever?"

Matthew put the phone to his ear with a jerk. "Honey, I'm sorry to keep you holding."

"Holding? I've been waiting 40 minutes! What's another few moments? When are you picking me up?" Deidre shouted into the phone.

Matthew grimaced as he steeled himself to the task at hand. "Deidre, I don't think I can make it." Silence greeted him, and he couldn't help holding his breath. "Deidre, don't you want to know why?"

"No, Matt, I really don't. I'll call you tomorrow." She hung up, and Matthew reluctantly put the receiver down.

"Matt, you're driving yourself too hard. You don't have to build your company this year. Finish school. There's plenty of time."

"That's just it, Scott. That's the one thing we don't have. The world needs help. There's too much suffering. And I'm going to change that. You'll see. I am. I'm going to help heal the sick, just like Jesus did." Matthew looked at the charts and graphs before him. What had begun as his senior project was fast becoming a real part of his life. Maybe even part of his dream. He didn't know why, and he never asked himself. He just knew—had always known—that he wanted to help people. And he knew he would.

"Scott," he called out to his roommate, who was already changing to go out, "what do you think of Lane Laboratories?" Matthew smiled when he heard Scott sigh.

"I think it's as good as the last six names. Why?"

"I don't want it to be a tongue twister."

"Well, let's see. It's better than Matthew's Medicine," Scott said with a grin as he finished putting on his belt. "I still think it's better when you take Lane out of it. Like last month's winner. Business Linked Technologies." He covered his mouth as he laughed. "I'll take the BLT to go." He stood up and laughed out loud, holding his mouth closed. The result was a stifled snort that left Matthew frowning.

Scott slapped Matt on the back as he went to the door, which made Matt chuckle inwardly at Scott's attempt to make fun of him.

Scott grabbed his keys and waved good-bye. "Don't give up, Einstein. You'll come up with a winner."

Matthew was alone when he finally realized he had to not only name his fictional company but think of a reason why he canceled his date with Deidre. She didn't want to know the reason now, but tomorrow would be another story.

When nothing came to mind he did the only thing available: he prayed. The legacy his father had left him was simple. When in doubt—pray. He smiled as he remembered his father's example and moved over to his bed. He physically kneeled down and sought the Lord. "Father, you know I want to serve you and build a company that will make a difference. One that will take a stand when things get difficult." He paused to reflect on the choices he'd already been forced to make. *Peer pressure notwithstanding, being 21 years old is hard work! So many people want you to be someone else, to do something.* He'd always dared to be different. But I can't keep it up without your help."

He finished his prayer silently and returned to his desk. The papers in front of him cried out to him. *Use us!* The name Lane Laboratories was scribbled on the front page. He crossed it out. "Reminds me of Lex Luthor," he said aloud, as was his wont, and threw the paper into the garbage can. He reached for the newspaper, and the business section seemed to draw his attention as he scanned the headlines. His answer jumped out at him.

Pharmaceutical Companies Show Recent Decline, read the article. He didn't see any more. *Lane Pharmaceutical*—it just seemed right. It fit his goals, his objectives, and his name requirements. Alliteration just wasn't working. *Lane Pharmaceutical will be my dream,* he thought. *With my dream, I will fulfill God's goals.* The fact that some of his goals would overlap with Matthew's only crossed his mind for an instant. He knew what was more important. He didn't want to just make a mark. He didn't want to just make a stand. He wanted to make a difference. *And now, Lord, you've shown me how.*

Matthew broke from his reverie and returned to his desk, holding up a large accordion file. "Men, I'm concerned about our suspicions regarding Rainbow's secret experimentation. Of course our critics may accuse us of industrial espionage, but I am placing all of our liquid assets at Brandon's disposal to discover what Rainbow's real motive is."

He opened up the file and spread numerous documents across his desk. Reaching into his desk drawer, he lifted out a flash drive, several photographs, and laid them on top of the pile. "If the data here is a microcosm of their designs, we haven't any time to lose."

"But, Mr. Lane," David said, "shouldn't you be concerned with discovering a vaccine, rather than getting involved with this detective work?"

Mr. Lane nodded toward Louie. "I have a very high regard for what you call detective work. But believe me, it is not my primary concern. While you three make inquiries, we here at Lane are working very close with the FDA and national medical foundations to share information—hoping to find a cure for this disease. The right way. I have a hunch that Rainbow is avoiding any governmental agencies that could possibly hamper their marketing and public approval, while we are asking for their help. There's a big difference. Don't you agree, Louie?" Matthew turned toward Louie with anticipation. The fact that Louie was studying him did not go unnoticed, and Matthew wasn't sure he liked it.

"Mr. Lane, I've had a lot of experience dealing with crime," Louie said. "I've observed firsthand how people operate when the stakes are small...but we're talking about something that would make any criminal act in history pale into insignificance." He rose from his chair and addressed the room as if he were at a trial summation. "Financially, Rainbow would make billions upon billions—exclusively. But the sociological and moral ramifications are beyond my comprehension."

"To say the least," Brandon concurred.

Talking into the air, Louie appeared to reenact a scene from some

New York drug bust when he theorized, "Suppose someone penetrated Rainbow undercover, then fed the information back to someone here. Would that work?"

"That's crazy, Louie!" David blurted out. "If we wanted to take that approach, we would simply contact the FBI and apprise them of our hunches and let them handle it."

"The problem here, David, is just what you said. You have only hunches, nothing really conclusive. The evidence brought back from Trinidad is still insufficient to launch an official investigation into a conglomerate that's as powerful and successful as Rainbow. Don't forget they have friends in high places." Louie looked down at the floor and concluded, "Believe me, I know my business, and infiltration is the only way you'll get anywhere."

Several days after his meeting with Gregory, Mort's flight on Aero-Mexico from Miami landed in Mérida on the west coast of the Yucatán Peninsula. He rented a car and drove to the ruins at Chichén Itzá 75 miles away. He rarely indulged in vacations but sensed his life would soon be restructured by Gregory's plans. Accordingly, he forced himself to enjoy this hiatus by touring an area of Mexico he neglected on his previous trips to his condominium on Cozumel.

Ancient civilizations held Mort's interest. He related to former empires that emerged from nothing, flourished for eons of time, then faded away. The Mayan people of Chichén Itzá reminded him of other historic cultures that impacted on society to this day. He admired the Babylonian, the Medo-Persian, the Greek-Macedonian, and Roman empires with astonishment. Even his own heritage of Judaism had left an indelible mark on the world. In times of meditation he often wondered what really went wrong with these mega-cultures. Some were conquered and displaced, while others slowly corrupted themselves from within and crumbled.

After checking in at the Hacienda Chichén, he grabbed his camera, a plastic bottle of drinking water, and headed for the sacred ruins.

He amazed himself by the ease in which he climbed the 91 steps of the Castle or Pyramid of Kukulkan. *Still can handle the hurdles, can't you,*

Mort? he said to himself. But when he reached the top, he sat down to rest.

Of the 30 buildings still visible of the Mayan people, the Pyramid seemed to be dominate. He scanned the horizon from the lofty tower and took in the spectacular view of the ancient city with the jungle background. He shook his head in bewilderment. Completing his picture-taking, he descended on the north side and crossed the connecting courtyard to the Temple of the Warriors. This 27-foot-high pyramid without a roof had a sculptured statue of the deity Chac-mool guarding the entrance. Mort reverently sat upon it and asked a passing tourist to snap his picture.

Carefully negotiating the crumbling staircase, he paused at the Group of the Thousand Columns at the foot of the temple. Meandering in and out of the standing columns and pillars of the colonnade reminded Mort of his trip to Greece and the Parthenon.

The temperature by midday hovered in the 80s this time of the year, so Mort paused at the Tzompantli for a drink of his water. He ran his fingers into the carved relief of a skull on the wall panel, then stepped back for a better look. As he did, he recalled reading about this strange edifice on the flight from Miami. The rectangular platform monument depicted skulls placed on poles, alternating with scenes showing eagles in the act of eating human hearts or showing feathered serpents and warriors.

The Tzompantli, or wall of skulls, built in Chichén Itzá during the Toltec period, was used regularly when human sacrifices played a very important role in their religion.

Mort began to feel something—something that he had felt before. He sensed a part of him reaching out to the ruins around him, becoming part of the history, the fervor, the madness. He felt as if it would consume him if he didn't move. He pressed on and moved away from the skulls and the dais.

He passed a hand over his head and continued his tour for the next hour, forcing himself to go on, then continued his drive on to Playa del Carmen on the Caribbean where he took the ferry to Isle de Cozumel. He sat there alone. For some reason, he didn't want to go right to sleep.

Watching Sydelle and monitoring her conversations became second nature to Krissy after one week's time. Under the guise of recording her job routine, she secretly documented Sydelle's actions in an encrypted document on her PalmOne PDA. She did not want any paper trail of her surveillance.

Not knowing what to look for, she relied upon her instincts and experiences when working in the probation department of law enforcement. *Listening to alibis and excuses all day long from "clients" sharpens up one's discernment,* she reminded herself. If there was to be any job satisfaction at all from working for the county, it was learning how to outsmart your clients since their mission in life invariably included eluding their probation officer.

Sydelle jumped up from her desk and waddled her way into Mr. Kavidas's office.

Krissy scanned the hallway, then casually strolled past Sydelle's desk, hoping to catch sight of anything of importance. She lifted two files and saw nothing of any consequence. Then she noticed in the vertical file a manila folder entitled Haiti. Piquing her curiosity, she turned the file corner down while listening for oncoming footsteps and watching Mr. Kavidas's door. Only three words were visible: *Voluntary Testing Program.* She paused, concentrated on its possible value, then pulled the file halfway out.

She spotted among the contents three stapled sheets of paper appearing to be a roster of names. She went to write some of the names down when her senses told her to flee. She quickly burned two names into her mind and rushed back to her desk. Sydelle reappeared within seconds after she arrived back in her seat, and she sat there with her heart pounding furiously.

"Can you cover my phone, Sydelle, while I run to the ladies' room?" Krissy asked.

"Sure, take your time, Linda," Sydelle replied.

Once in the ladies' room, Krissy positioned herself in a stall, removed her PDA from her purse, and typed in her password. She keyed in the two names and finally breathed a sigh of relief. *That was real close,* she thought. *Be careful and be alert,* she warned herself. *But now, at least, I have a place to start!*

Mort adjusted his sombrero, kicked off his shoes, and dug his feet into the hot sand. After making sure the umbrella fully covered him, he fell back into the lounge chair. "Ah, now we're relaxing, Mort," he said aloud to himself. While his eyes were transfixed on a passing freighter out on the horizon, he suddenly felt sleepy and began to nod off. *I can take it easy today, but tomorrow I need to get some work done,* he pledged to himself.

Images began floating into his consciousness, images of the past that coalesced into recognizable shapes. Two men were walking along a mountainous winding path heading for the summit. The aged man with the cape put his arm around Mortimer and said, "The time for greater understanding has arrived, Mortimer. Now you are ready to talk about future things."

"Rabbi Vital!" Mort heard himself utter imperceptibly. They walked to the next peak and stood on the precipice overlooking what appeared to be a great city.

"This city represents the world, Mortimer, and it will be yours. You need only this key to unlock the door leading into the city." Rabbi Vital handed Mortimer a rolled parchment tied with a leather cord.

Mortimer looked into the face of Rabbi Vital. "Are you a prophet? Is this an omen?"

With a suppressed smile he said, "You shall perform great things; now go."

Mortimer grasped the parchment and walked down the path alone. At the foot of the mountain, he found a small rise in the terrain and sat down. He untied the cord and opened the parchment. Inscribed on the parchment were three horizontal rows of Hebrew alphabet characters.

He studied them for several minutes and fell backward onto the ground.

The salt air blew Mort's sombrero off his head, awakening him from his nap. Checking his wristwatch he realized it was nearing the time to contact Gregory back in Florida.

He walked the short distance back to his beachfront condo, sat in his living room sofa, and picked up the phone. As he keyed in the number, he noticed his book of the Kabbalah in his open attaché case. He put the phone down and dashed over to get the book. He turned to the section of Gematria, then recalled the inscription on the parchment. Assigning each letter its numerical equivalent and place value, he then transcribed the numbers into English.

Within 20 minutes he deciphered the characters. He grinned, looked heavenward, and said, "Great minds think alike." In his heart he knew this to be divine confirmation. He decided to postpone his call to Gregory until he put together the plan. Suddenly his trip to Mexico seemed more than just a vacation. Somehow he had a feeling Gregory knew it would be.

That same night at her apartment Krissy prepared to make some phone calls. Retrieving the two names on her PDA, she gave her law enforcement ID code to her Haitian counterpart, with the Port-au-Prince public authorities. "This is Krissy Kramer of the Fort Lauderdale Police Department. We have a medical crisis involving two Haitian nationals, and we must contact their nearest relatives."

The sergeant cooperated without hesitation, though she was having a difficult time with the accent. Krissy was just grateful she found someone to speak English at all. "I am trying to reach Toussaint Ramcharitar and Milton Davielir, who have their city of residence listed as Port de Paix. Can you help me?"

"We have one listing only: Mr. T. Ramcharitar," the man reported. "We have nothing on Davielir."

Krissy curled her lip in disappointment. "Fine, that will help."

The man read the listing and quickly hung up.

So much for the long arm of the law, Krissy thought as she dialed the number.

"*Oui,*" the voice answered.

"*Parlez vous Anglais?*" Krissy asked tentatively. She waited, expecting the usual no. Her fear expanded with each phone call. The last thing she wanted was a translator who could report what she was doing.

"Non. *Une* moment."

Krissy waited patiently and hopefully.

"*Oui,* hello? I speak English."

Krissy breathed again and made a mental note. *I've got to remember to do some deep breathing during this spy stuff—it's killing me.* "My name is Krissy Kramer, with the American Department of Health, and I am trying to reach Toussaint Ramcharitar."

"I am sorry, but he is not here," the woman replied.

Disappointed but determined to get information, Krissy pressed on. "This is an emergency; I must talk with him. Do you know where he is?"

"Yes," the woman replied.

"Are you related to this man?" Krissy asked.

"Yes," the woman replied again.

Great, Krissy thought, *now I'll have to drag every piece of information out of her.* "How?" she asked impatiently.

After a long pause, the woman said, "He is my husband. What do you want?"

"Well, we at the Department of Health are following up on tests taken on your husband at a hospital two years ago. We must have current information." Krissy despised lying but justified it in her heart when she thought of Johnnie. Besides, *test* and *hospital* were the only words she saw in the file before Sydelle came back.

"He is in the hospital again," the woman lamented. "A private hospital outside the city of Cap Haitian."

"Oh? Is he ill?" Krissy began, then remembered to get more facts. "What is the name of the hospital?"

Krissy could hear the woman break down and begin to cry on the phone. "He has been sick on and off since they did the tests two years ago. This last time it turned serious so they take him to Clarion Clinic," his wife said while trying to compose herself.

"Do you think the testing is related to his illness?" Krissy probed.

"I am not sure. The whole thing is very secret. No doctor or nurse will tell me anything, no matter how many times I ask. And then I can only visit him once a month, and each time he looks worse," she added while stifling a sob.

Passionately Krissy pledged, "We will try to get more information to help you. I will call you again. Thank you."

Krissy quickly hung up before the woman could ask any more questions and phoned telephone information for the name of Clarion Clinic near Cap Haitian. Reverting back to her probation officer's commanding voice, she acquired the hospital's switchboard number at Clarion, then paused to rehearse what she planned to say.

The switchboard operator connected her to an English speaking nurses' station on the floor. "Bebbe Lowtow, can I help you?" the nurse asked.

"This is Ms. Kramer with the American Red Cross in Miami. One of your patients, a Mr. Toussaint Ramcharitar, is listed as 'friend' to a homeless patient dying of AIDS here in Florida. Since we do not expect our patient to live through the week, we wanted to contact someone who may be able to encourage him. That's why we are calling Mr. Ramcharitar. Can I speak with him?" Krissy raised her eyebrow in hopes that the story would work.

"He is not doing well, and there are no phones in the patients' rooms," the nurse said lamely.

"How serious is Mr. Ramcharitar's condition?" Krissy asked covertly.

Swept up into the story the nurse said, "Well, his condition is guarded. We are about to—" Then suddenly as if someone warned her, she blurted out, "I am sorry, but that is all the information I am authorized to release." In an attempt to satisfy the caller, the nurse repeated, "His condition is guarded. What did you say your name was?"

Krissy surmised someone got to her and flagged her off. To avoid suspicion, she backed off. "Well, thank you very much. We will convey the information back to our patient."

Click.

Krissy walked slowly into her bedroom and fell on the bed. Her mind reeled. Rainbow's convoluted structure and its involvement in her life frightened her.

David reached for his driver, walked onto the mound at the first hole, and placed his golf ball high on the wooden tee. Louie cocked his head to scrutinize his approach and watched how he performed his practice swing. David looked over at him, but Louie said nothing. David could feel Louie's eyes riveted on him and paused to remember that it was only a game.

"Beaut-i-ful!" Louie yelled as David's ball soared heavenward.

David stooped to follow the ball's flight, watching it drop in the middle of the fairway, nearly 175 yards from the tee.

"I'll take it," David offered. Louie ascended the mound while David walked over to the motorized cart to put his club away.

Louie appeared to measure the distance to the green by celestial navigation as he patiently waited until all distracting noises subsided. He took a practice swing, then turned to David. "Whenever you're ready, Dave."

David shook his head and waved at him.

Louie pulled back on his club and hit the ball with all the ability he could muster up. "Wowee!" Louie shouted as the ball disappeared into space. The ball landed some 55 yards ahead of David's drive. Louie's victory strut off the mound made David smile. Then Louie motioned for David to drive him away as if he were the chauffeur.

Seconds after leaving the mound, Louie turned to David. "I booked my flight back to New York for tomorrow. I called my office, and they need my help on a murder case."

David stopped the cart momentarily. "But we were just beginning to redeem some fun out of your vacation. With all this business about Rainbow, it hasn't been very entertaining for you. Couldn't you get your partner to cover for you until next week?"

Louie pointed to David's ball lying in the grass just ahead of them. "Can't do it. This is a special case where I was involved in the arrest. We're preparing our pretrial presentation. Trial schedule moved up." He threw his hands into the air and added, "Can't be helped. Sorry, buddy."

David frowned. "You'll be missed." He looked up ahead to Lou's ball and added, "That's why I let you win this hole."

The drive from the West Palm Beach airport to Wellington enabled Mort to crystallize the details on what he had newly dubbed Project Renaissance. His revelation made it clear to him that Rainbow needed an innocuous medium to assist in the vaccine distribution. One that would link him to vast amounts of information and link Rainbow to the world. Experience told him that Gregory's plan to expand into international markets was more than just foresight. *It's obvious he had it in mind when he sent me to Mexico,* he realized—to integrate Renaissance into his framework before the AIDS epidemic subsided. Now he wondered if Gregory already knew the name—or was that part of his assignment and a task that only he could fulfill?

Renaissance would expedite the financial end of the vaccine distribution, while at the same time acquainting the public with the concept of centralizing their personal credit devices. Using the crisis as a vehicle to catapult Renaissance into the monetary mainstream would also position Rainbow for what Mort deemed the checkmate. The ultimate position in society where mankind could go to only one place for help: Rainbow.

Visionary people make their presence known in the world, Mort told himself, and he prided himself with the gift of vision, although he had to admit it was "assisted vision" at times.

He stopped for security outside Rainbow, then parked his Lexus next to Gregory's Rolls-Royce. He ascended the three staircases to the executive offices in record speed, then went directly to Gregory's office. He decided that waiting for the elevator would be too long.

"Mr. Stein, how nice to see you. Did you enjoy your vacation in Mexico?" Sydelle queried.

The new assistant, whatever her name was—Mort couldn't remember—sat next to her.

Slightly winded, Mort responded effusively, "Exhilarating! Totally relaxing yet fulfilling. Very meaningful."

He quickly walked to the water cooler, filled his cup, and asked Sydelle, "Are you hoping for a boy or a girl?"

"My husband wants a boy; I'm hoping it's a girl," she said, smiling. "Is anybody with Mr. Kavidas?" He looked down at his watch, then back to Sydelle. "Pretty early. Is he free? I need to see him ASAP."

"He's expecting you, but he just received a phone call. Would you care for a cup of coffee while you wait?" Sydelle entreated.

"Coffee, at this time of the morning? Are you kidding? That stuff will kill you." He looked over at the closed cabinet next to Gregory's door and said, "How about a bourbon?"

Sydelle raised her eyebrows and shot him a look. "Mr. Stein, what's come over you? I never remember you acting so flippant before. Are you feeling all right?"

"Time for celebration, Sydelle. Rainbow is going to embark on a wonderful program that will benefit the world, and I can't contain the excitement." He glanced at the telephone on her desk and saw Gregory's line light go out. "See you later, girls." He ceremonially strolled past their desks swinging his attaché case, then stood at Gregory's door, turning the knob and opening it as if he were about to announce the arrival of a king.

Gregory arose from his chair to greet him exuberantly. "Mort! Great to see you; how was Cozumel?"

Somewhat muted by Gregory's overpowering presence, Mort approached him, embraced him in friendship, and said, "Have I got a plan for you!"

Gregory put his arm around him and escorted him over to a seat at his conference room table. Sitting across from him in expectation, he stared him in the eyes. "What's the plan?"

Mort opened his case, removed his laptop, and set it before Gregory. Mort's eyes twinkled as he switched the laptop on and began his rehearsed presentation.

"The great Carthaginian conqueror, Hannibal, once said, 'I find a way or I make one.' Well, at Cozumel, an inspiration showing me the way to your *Redisearch* challenge came to me." He pressed the paging key to show Project Renaissance. The title was superimposed over a sculpture of Michelangelo.

"Impressive opening," Gregory observed.

"Project Renaissance is a four-stage program that will ultimately 'renovate' the entire medical and financial information world." Mort keyed the next page showing the *Redisearch* logo with subheadings underneath: Commercial and individual credit clearance; Commercial and individual background clearance.

"Renaissance will utilize *Redisearch*'s data files, soon to be totally international in scope, together with…" Mort paused for dramatic effect, then pressed the paging key again. This time the screen filled with the Medlink logo. He pointed to the screen on the laptop as if he were making a sales presentation and continued, "Medlink will be introduced within the next 90 days. Medlink is the natural successor to *Redisearch* since we need the background information to implement control *of the vaccine*. The public will assume it is a necessary step to gain access *to the vaccine*.

75

Medlink will add to the *Redisearch* system all new subscribers who utilize the vaccine and those slated for the vaccine protection program.

"The vaccine protection program (VPP) will attract those who fear being infected with AIDS but do not presently have it. So Medlink will contain all the information from *Redisearch*, the subscriber's personal description, together with any emergency information, and all their medical history. For example, if an ambulance arrives at the scene of an accident and finds an unconscious man bleeding profusely, rather than dealing with his possible contaminated blood or typing him, the technician simply waves the electronic wand over the Medlink ID, and within three seconds all the information needed to save his life is available. Any surgical or prescription history will be automatically updated as performed."

Mort noted that Gregory seemed enthralled with the plan. Mort then keyed the next page on the laptop. Infolink appeared on the screen, with a small window depicting a supercomputer with a file flying out of it. "This is phase three, Infolink! This will be installed 90 days after Medlink is launched. We will need six months to draw in our international market. This phase differs from its predecessors by including credit availability. In other words, a subscriber will have all the privileges of Infolink, with the additional feature of being able to charge all purchases."

"Purpose? To swallow up all competition? To centralize all credit devices?" Gregory asked.

Mort nodded. "All of the above, and at three points below prevailing interest rates. What's more, Infolink will deter crime since it is nontransferable. It cannot be stolen." His smile faded as he touched the *Enter* key to unveil the final phase.

Holding his breath, Mort looked over at Gregory, then exhaled and said, "Phase four. The final stage of Project Renaissance." He pointed to the screen that read *Masterlink*. "*Masterlink* will be the culmination of phases one through three that enables the implementation of the most sophisticated information system ever developed. This level of the Renaissance Project will also include personal asset info along with political and religious affiliations."

Mort reached into his attaché case, pulling out a sheet of paper with a tiny spot in the center. He pointed to the pinhead-sized spot. "This is *Masterlink*. It is a microprocessor chip in the form of a dot that contains everything we talked about, with a capacity of 15 megabytes of data." He touched a key on the laptop displaying a pull-down menu, then clicked on *Masterlink* ID.

The command initiated a graphics program that demonstrated the ability and mechanics of the *Masterlink* ID dot. First a wand passed over the dot; then the computer program added graphic boxes with captions inside. The captions defined the information contained on the dot. Graphics box one read: Personal Description. Then the graphics box blinked, showing a unisex symbol with a physical profile inside. Box two read: Commercial/Individual Background Updates. The third box read: Credit Availability/History. Number four box blinked red and contained all emergency and medical information. This included relatives to third cousins, kin with power of attorney, and phone numbers updated monthly, as well as blood type, allergies, drug interaction statistics, and medical history since birth.

Mort typed in another command. "The rest of the information requires a special password that must come from *Masterlink* directly. No one can access this information out in the field. Authorization must come from here." He keyed in the password, and three other boxes emerged on the screen. Labeled AI for Asset Information, it would disclose the individual's asset information that included real estate, bank accounts, pension funds, insurance policy values, and tax return data.

"Now watch this," Mort said, pointing to the screen. He typed in another password, and a diagram that resembled a tree appeared. "We can trace all assets, even if hidden in bogus or in pseudonym accounts, regardless of where they are. Domestic or foreign. The other boxes will store political and religious affiliations, which can be developed later."

"What kind of a device will hold the dot?" Gregory asked inquisitively.

Mort held the outside of his right hand in front of Gregory's face and said, "What do you think of my new freckle? Can't lose or forget it—it's always with me."

Gregory held his hand and inspected the dot. "How is it attached?" he asked.

"Takes two seconds to implant it." He pulled a Band-Aid from his attaché case, removed the dot from the sheet of paper, then placed the dot on Gregory's hand. "This is all the data I have on you—right here in your dot." He pulled out of his pocket a small tube of ointment, rubbed a tiny portion over the dot, then covered it with the Band-Aid.

Gregory looked stunned. He turned to Mort and said, "Is that it?"

Mort chuckled and said, "That's it. The ointment is like an emollient; it softens the first two layers of skin, absorbing the dot. Takes 48 hours. Perfectly harmless." He held out his hand again. "Behold, my freckle."

Gregory looked astounded. "Mort, this is superb! That 'inspiration' you mentioned will turn the world around for us." He walked to his desk. "What do we need to implement this?"

"We'll need some front money to graduate Renaissance from *Redisearch* to Medlink. Funds to advertise, secure personnel to make the transition, card issuance, and monthly maintenance. Right now we'll stick with the plastic card with the security hologram, replacing it with the dot within six months." He placed a printed ledger in front of Gregory. "I've allocated $750,000 dollars from *Redisearch* but will need at least another seven million to place this in the market so quickly."

"Done," Gregory stated. He reached for the pad on his desk and made a note. "We do have one small problem that just developed. Before you came in, Watchman called me, advising me of a leak."

"A leak?" Mort exclaimed. Watchman always fascinated him. As close as he was to Gregory and the operation, he had no idea who Watchman was—or where he was. And he didn't particularly like it.

"Someone is making calls from here in Florida to Haiti about the vaccine tests. Watchman received a call from the hospital where one of our patients is now being treated. Seems some minor side effects occurred, so he is being watched. If this problem doesn't go away, I will need you to get involved."

Mort watched Gregory grind his teeth and perceived his alarm. "Are you concerned about this?"

"Nothing we can't handle. Just be aware and be careful," Gregory warned. "Now that you're about to start this project, nothing can go wrong."

David's house was becoming a meeting place of sorts as he, Kathy, Brandon, and Matthew struggled to unravel the mystery of Rainbow

Pharmaceuticals. The familiar surroundings did not lend themselves to anything sinister and may not have contributed to their recent success in gathering information; to Brandon, it was feeling like home.

Sitting around the house was an exercise in patience today as they waited for Matthew Lane to arrive with the news of the contents from the last of Johnnie's film canisters. At last they'd know what was in that fluid that Johnnie had traded his life for.

When Matthew came to the door, they knew the answer was not good. "Dave, Kathy, hello. I wish I could be bringing better news." He crossed over to his son and embraced him.

His father's presence, Brandon thought, was always one that added both character and integrity to any room. An aura surrounded the man that could not be ignored. Today it was particularly noticeable, as it was colored with both anger and excitement.

"Brandon, I have the results. You won't believe it without seeing them." Matthew passed the documents from his briefcase into his son's waiting hands. "I had our research doctors check the results twice. They are accurate, but I'm afraid we don't have all the answers yet."

Brandon started looking at the results as David came to his side.

"Would you like something to drink, Matthew?" Kathy asked.

"No thanks. I have to get going shortly. I just wanted to bring the news over in person."

Brandon's mind whirred as he ingested the lab report. His mind entertained the various possibilities the data presented. It seemed incredible and horrific at the same time. He passed the sheet to David as he finished it. "Dad, do you really think they're using humans to cultivate a vaccine? It sounds like something from a horror movie."

"Brandon," Kathy asked with concern, "what do you mean? Using humans for what?"

"Kathy, how much do you know about the AIDS virus and the race for the cure? Do you know what we are trying to do to cure it?" Brandon looked at his father, and Matthew nodded. The time had come to share not only what Lane Pharmaceutical was attempting but the rest of the scientific world.

"Well, I know that monkeys have been involved, and they have been coming up with some drugs that have been helping. Like that AZT, right?" She looked toward David for confirmation, but he was staring in morbid fascination at the document in front of him.

"AZT acts as an immune enhancer or even as a symptomology block. But it does not slow or arrest the disease," added Matthew as he turned to Brandon and motioned to him to continue.

"What we've done," Brandon said as he gestured with his hands, "is to get things to a cellular level. We're trying to find something that stops the virus or kills it. Then we use that thing to make a vaccine."

"It seems as if that is awfully simplified," put in David, joining the conversation for the first time since he had read the research report.

"It is," Brandon said, putting his arm around his friend, "because most cures are actually simple, once you've narrowed the possibility down to a feasible live or dead virus to act as your vaccine facilitator. Live virus creates a live vaccine—similar to what they use with smallpox. They put in a small amount of the virus, and your body creates its own method of resistance: antigens. These are permanent, and you are always immune to the disease. Then there are dead vaccines."

He picked up a glass of iced tea from the counter and swallowed long and hard before continuing. "Dead vaccines make the body immune, but it is not permanent. It needs to have a booster, or the body may lose its immunity. Like the measles. Kids often go for boosters in high school to protect them for their early adulthood. That's why pregnant mothers are so fearful. They've been immunized against measles, but there is always the chance that their immunity has worn off."

"Where does that leave us with the AIDS virus?" David interjected. "Are you using a dead or live virus to come up with the vaccine?"

Brandon's eyes met his father's for an instant, and he saw encouragement as he made his way toward the center of the group. "So far, we have been afraid to use live virus in any vaccine or test, since we don't know if we can halt the mutation or the longevity of the virus itself. In short, we've been afraid that even if our bodies allegedly kill it, it may not be dead."

"You mean it would appear to be stopped and then restart again later?" asked Kathy, aghast. "How can you fight something that you are not sure will ever die?"

"Well," Matthew lectured, "most scientists have been trying to come up with a vaccine that uses portions of the virus, so that the body will effectively create a defense, but they leave off the part that allows the virus to replicate. In essence, you inject a live virus and allow the body to react, then make sure that the virus cannot reproduce. You have the benefit of a permanent immunity and the surety that the virus cannot kill the person receiving the vaccine." He sat down after his oration and glanced at his son, in a way to apologize for stealing the floor.

Brandon merely nodded, giving Matthew the clear sign that this was a joint venture and one in which he was an active participant.

"That sounds simple enough. What's taking the world so long, then, to come up with a cure?" Kathy asked simply. "There are enough people that have it. Don't they want to at least try it?"

"Kathy, it's not that simple!" Brandon exclaimed. "At least not for people who do things the proper way and go through the proper channels. The FDA does not allow you to take volunteers, willing or not, and just pump them with drugs. Think of the ethical and morality issues! We could be sending people to their graves without even thinking about them. What would stop us from just using everyone with AIDS as personal guinea pigs if there were no serious consequences?"

Realizing his voice had been rising in indignation, Brandon said, "I'm sorry, Kathy. I didn't mean to grandstand. It's just that people often think that we simply come up with a cure like pulling a rabbit from a hat, and it doesn't work that way. Often it takes years just to get approval to do the testing for a drug you know works and has no side effects." Slightly deflated, he sat down.

David took over. "Where are you in the research stage? It seems this fluid took both of you by surprise."

Brandon shrugged, and Matthew nodded to confirm his son's chagrin.

"It's not that it took us by surprise," Brandon started. "It's just so incredible that Rainbow is going in this direction and leaving out the 'middle' section that we all go through—FDA approval and the years of monitored testing and trials. They seem to be attempting to supersede all the system's checks and balances. And it appears that it's working."

"Brandon, I think we're assuming too much," his father pointed out. "We have only a theory or two to work with after this data. We don't actually know what they are doing."

"Dad, I don't think so. I think we know exactly what they are doing. We just don't know how, where, or when. The rest is fairly obvious."

"None of this is obvious to me," Kathy said, looking embarrassed.

"What exactly did the fluid contain?"

This time Matthew answered. "Virus cells that had been genetically altered. It appears to be combinations of human-simian viral cells that are not progressing in the disease state. The fluid is what we would call the precursor to a vaccine—the DNA building blocks of the necessary altered virus to enable the body to react and protect itself."

"Is that good?" asked Kathy tentatively. "It sounds as if it might be what everyone is looking for."

"Good!" shouted Matthew, getting upset for the first time. "Of course it's good if it works, if it's safe, *and* if it is approved by the FDA. Good for Rainbow. Terrible for Lane. Terrible for the rest of the world, if this outfit didn't do everything according to Hoyle. You cannot fool around with a vaccine of this magnitude. There are too many lives at stake!"

Brandon could see that Kathy and David were taken aback but still did not understand. "Most research facilities do not use humans in order to get results," he offered casually, "for obvious reasons. The risks are incalculable, and we'd be using so many people that over-population would never be a problem." He tried to throw them a wry smile before continuing. "We've been trying insects, monkeys, rats, cats, *anything* that will bring us closer. Except humans. Humans have not shown any promise in staying the disease. Only a certain species of monkey has shown an immunity, and only one has shown symptomology from human HIV virus. We've been pursuing that aspect."

"A rhesus monkey," David offered. He'd come around and put his arm around his wife for protection and support. "No, actually a pigtail macaque. The pigtail reacts to the virus, similar to a human reaction. The rhesus acts as a carrier. They have no reaction to the human aspect of the disease."

"Well," began Kathy, "wouldn't that mean that the combination of the two would enable a cure? One can have it without a problem, and one is affected. The difference should give us an answer."

Brandon shook his head.

Matthew gave her a quick smile before he told her of the irony. "There are thousands of DNA combinations, and finding the right one could take well, lifetimes. That's the problem."

Realization set in, and Kathy could only nod.

"Rainbow must have found a connection," began David, "or they wouldn't even try to be so secretive. They must have a bridge."

"Dave, that's a good way of putting it," said Brandon, beginning to get excited again. "That's always been a big problem. Bridging the gap between the monkeys and the humans. They're not as compatible as evolutionists would have us believe." Another one of his wry smiles escaped. "This fluid is both exciting and puzzling. How did they bridge the gap? They have come up with a combination of viral cells that will produce an effect in the monkeys and arrest the disease. The problem is, how can we give that to humans? How can we benefit from the monkey's natural immunity?"

"Didn't the same thing happen with syphilis?" Dave asked. "Didn't the sheep have a natural immunity that we lacked that protected them from the disease?"

"Exactly!" shouted Matthew triumphantly. "The sheep had an antigen in their blood that protected them from contracting the disease. But we couldn't use their blood. It was too foreign. So we grew penicillin in the form of a mold right on the sheep's liver. The mold extracted the necessary antigens from the sheep's body and gave us the cure. That's what we need for AIDS."

"Don't you see," Brandon said with animation, "we can extract some of the monkey's blood, and we know that it is immune. But we can't use it! If we plant human virus into pigtail macaque, it reacts and a simian monkey can then take this virus and carry it with no adverse effects. Like a carrier. But the problem is, how do we get it back to humans? How do we benefit from their immunity?" Brandon's excitement gave way to resignation as he crossed into the area of uncertainty.

Kathy was quick to ask, "Why can't we find something similar to the sheep's liver? Something that could grow the virus into a vaccine for humans? Just like it was done with the cure for syphilis."

Brandon's blood quickened and his body stiffened. He looked at his father, seeing a mirror reflection in his father's face.

"Kathy," Matthew answered, "Rainbow may have found such a thing. The question is, what are they using to grow the virus on? What atrocities are they committing in trying to bring this virus to fruition before it is ready? And who is paying the price of their impatience?"

The room seemed to get visibly darker as the four of them exchanged worried and excited glances.

Brandon felt a surge of panic as he studied each face. *Where are you doing it, and how?*

FOUR

I learned early in life
that you get places
by having the right enemies.
Bishop John Spong

For native Floridians, tropical weather in February demanded little bodily adjustment. They were raised in the environment of Christmas Day in the backyard swimming pool or surfing on New Year's Day at the Fort Lauderdale beach. But for ex-New Yorkers like Krissy, for her to journey outdoors without a coat when the Northeast is blanketed with snow required getting used to. She delighted in not having to drive in northern hazardous weather and welcomed the spring wardrobe that allowed her to shed unnecessary insulating apparel.

She adjusted her makeup and zipped up her short white skirt, then glanced over at the wall calendar. *Monday, President's Day,* she reminded herself. *My mission is to penetrate, to probe.* Sydelle's imminent maternity leave made it easy for her to suggest working the holiday. The premise: preparing for the temporary takeover of Sydelle's job. Her confidence was high that, today, security at Wellington would be minimal.

Weeds and briers dominated the north or back entrance to Rainbow at Wellington. Busy wild things rustled in the dry brush along the driveway as Krissy drove in off Route 441. To Krissy, the contrast was very apparent. She recalled the dreamy, flora-laden south entrance she traveled two months ago when exploring Rainbow, then compared it to the north entrance. This neglected entranceway reminded her of the double standard

Rainbow stood for. They kept the public driveway beautifully landscaped, while the employee service entrance consisted of broad dried-out expanses and leafless bushes that smacked of desolation and ruin.

Extending the analogy, she substituted the driveways for Rainbow. To the public, Rainbow represented a beautiful public servant, duly assigned to benefit mankind through drug research and development, while at the same time, their furtive actions and intentions were like the rear entrance, a pathway to a strange laboratory that was inhabited by strange creatures.

To avoid being recognized by the security guard, Krissy used the north entrance, requiring only her employee badge to gain access to Rainbow. The high-tech badge displayed photo, thumbprint, and an encoded description of the employee that included their position in the company, protected with a rainbow hologram. Once inserted, the barbed-wire gate opened. Krissy would rather negotiate these safeguards than risk exposure by a guard with a good memory for faces.

As she drove up to the gate, she noticed a disheveled man lying on the pavement. At first he looked dead with his face to the ground. She watched his chest rise, then instinctively darted to the man's aid. She turned him over. "Are you okay? Are you hurt? Do you need a doctor?"

When the wizened old man fluttered his eyes and opened his mouth to speak, Krissy nearly fell over. His breath carried with it a stench that reminded her of the drunks that hung out around Central Park in New York. Taking a second whiff, she identified the smell of booze and knew he had passed out. With his gnarled fingers he reached for his neck and groaned. Krissy pulled back the collar on the heavily soiled flannel shirt, exposing a surgical incision approximately two inches in length at the base of his neck. The stitches closing the cut were dangling wildly, and Krissy surmised the man had been unwittingly pawing the raw wound.

"It burns," he whispered from sun-beaten cracked lips. "It burns."

Krissy inspected the wound again. "This thing looks infected. You need medical attention." She reached down and pulled him up, making him sit against the fence.

"I mizzed da bus. I furget it's a holiday." His voice trailed off as he started falling over. Then he muttered, "Thought I cud walk it. Need to see da doctor at Rainbow." With that he slumped over again.

Krissy lifted one of his eyelids and thought he'd passed out a second time.

Then without warning he regained some strength, reached for the fence behind him, and pulled himself up. Reaching into his ripped pants pocket, he pulled the liner out and said, "Need ta git paid for last week's treatment so I can git sum food."

"I'll be right back," Krissy said. She ran to her car and punched in 911 on her cell phone. Just before pressing the Send button, she stopped and thought about what was happening. "If I call the police or Rainbow security, there goes my mission," she said aloud. She looked at the man and thought, *But I just can't leave him here.* Deeply inhaling gave her time to think. Instead of dialing 911 she grabbed her lunch bag and pulled out her sandwich. She ran and offered it to the man.

He gaped at the sandwich. "Tanks, lady. May Gud bless ya." After putting half the sandwich in his pants pocket, he slowly fed the other half into his mouth.

Krissy called a roaming cab company to advise them of her crisis.

Within 10 minutes a cab pulled up.

"Take this poor man to the nearest hospital." She reached into her purse, pulled out three 20-dollar bills and gave two to the driver. The other 20 she stuffed into the old man's shirt pocket.

Staggering to the cab, the man reached in to feel the bill in his pocket, then waved at Krissy. "You're an angel of mercy, ma'am. My name is George, and I won't forgit ya."

When the cab departed, Krissy returned to her car and sat quietly for half an hour before entering the gate.

Against her will Krissy drove slowly down the driveway, mulling over the new pieces of the puzzle. *Is Rainbow busing in and experimenting on these homeless people—then paying and feeding them to keep them quiet?* "How ghastly," she said aloud.

Somebody had to stop them.

Krissy glanced into Mr. Kavidas's office to ensure her privacy, then resolutely went to her desk, retrieving her chart of Rainbow's building directory to study it. From there she took the staircase to the first floor cafeteria. Being a holiday the cafeteria would not be functioning, but for the few security guards and special task workers, a complimentary coffee and cake refreshment section had been set up.

Casually enjoying her cup of coffee, Krissy took notice of all the trash cans in the room. She targeted the large one standing adjacent to the fire alarm system. She lit up a cigarette, simulated two puffs, then slipped the lit cigarette into a full book of matches. Carefully placing the cigarette to extend one and a half inches from the match heads and closing the cover, she estimated seven minutes before the matches would ignite. At the trash can she dumped the empty coffee container in, then slipped in the matchbook with the lit cigarette after it.

Avoiding the elevator and keeping to the shadows, she descended the staircase to the lower level. From there, she carefully passed the restricted zone and hid in the ladies' room. Monitoring her time, she waited three, four, five, six minutes. At seven minutes, Krissy peeked out the door toward the lab in the restricted zone, and waited again. Nothing.

At eight minutes, the fire alarm sounded. A loud siren echoed down the corridors while red lights flashed and white spotlights illuminated the staircases. Then a prerecorded woman's voice came over the loudspeakers saying, "This is not a drill. Evacuate the premises immediately. This is not a drill. Evacuate the premises immediately."

Krissy held her breath and looked out down the hall as one man wearing a doctor's coat rushed out of the lab and scaled the stairs.

Pausing for 15 seconds seemed like an interminable period of time for Krissy, but she had to be sure all personnel left the lab. As hoped for, the lab tech left the door ajar, allowing her access into the laboratory.

Once inside, she scanned the room for her objective. One wall housed a bank of refrigerators with glass doors, another shelved specimen bottles, and the third was a library filled with medical journals. She ran to the refrigerators where the vials were stored. Trays of blood samples, along with beakers containing bizarre-colored liquids, occupied several coolers. In one refrigerator/cooler there were rows of small bottles. The bottles, sealed with rubber stoppers, looked like vaccine bottles.

Krissy opened the door of the cooler and read the labels: Toi-VAX. Concluding the vaccine bottles to be important she reached into the cooler and took a bottle from the rear of the top shelf. Stuffing the bottle into her handbag, she then turned to the apparatus tables situated in the center of the room.

Slate-top tables laden with flasks, blowpipes, capillary tubes, graduated cylinders, and other chemical and drug paraphernalia occupied every flat surface. Watching her time, she was drawn to the table where the Bunsen burner flamed. Next to the burner were dozens of small labeled jars in a rack. Two of them had the lids off, and one had the contents lying in a glass dish. Inside the dish, surrounded by gelatin, was a pinkish-colored mass of flesh with a tiny wedge cut out. To the right of the dish Krissy saw the wedge on a glass slide under a microscope.

She started to move on when she caught sight of the labels. Suddenly she glared at one label and staggered back against one of the tables. She looked again to confirm her sighting and whispered it to herself, "Sixty-eight-year-old male Caucasian, HIV-positive thymus: George Arnstead."

She picked up the jar, held it in her hand for several seconds, thinking of the homeless man she helped this morning.

Returning the jar, her right ring finger caught on a sheet metal screw protruding out of the rack. As she started to leave, she noticed drops of blood on her finger so she stuck it quickly in her mouth, ran for the door, then scurried up the stairs.

Safely reaching her desk on the third floor, Krissy entered all the pertinent data she observed in the lab into her PDA, then called security to learn the status of the small cafeteria fire. With the crisis over, she busied herself for several hours before leaving for the day.

Krissy awoke the following morning with a pounding headache. Acquiring and accumulating information about Rainbow these last several weeks, along with the ordeal of breaking into the lab yesterday, kept her in a constant state of stress and anxiety. At first she planned to call in sick but reconsidered and simply called in late. Despite her condition, she had to show up at work today to avoid suspicions.

Sydelle's usual daily greeting carried with it the news of the fire and then the countdown announcement. Once her delivery date dropped below the 40-day mark, Sydelle regularly proclaimed a calendar check-off to keep the office posted.

When Krissy simply waved to her, Sydelle dutifully went to her side to entreat her. "Linda, why did you come in today if you were sick? Believe me, after I leave to have the baby, things will be racing around here, and you won't be able to squeeze 15 minutes for a smoke break without permission. So why come in today?"

Rubbing the back of her neck to soothe the tension Krissy said, "I haven't been here that long, and I wouldn't want to give the impression of abusing my freedom." Changing the subject she asked, "Did security determine the cause of yesterday's cafeteria fire? I was here but left shortly after the all-clear signal came over the PA system."

"Really nothing. Some garbage can fire lit off the wallpaper, then shorted out a ceiling light fixture."

Krissy shrugged. "I enjoyed the half-hour walk outside while security did their thing. What's going on here today?"

Sydelle brought her pad over to Krissy's desk. "I spoke with Mr. Kavidas early this morning, and we must start preparing documents for a new program called Project Renaissance." She glowed and wistfully added, "I'd love to be here to help you launch this; it sounds terribly exciting."

She looked back at Kavidas's door. "Some of this is still pretty hush-hush, but I can tell you this—" she pulled out a chart from the folder in her hand—"a colossal innovation in medical information is about to occur. *Redisearch*, owned by Mr. Kavidas's partner, Mr. Stein, is going to underwrite and create an international organization known as Medlink. This is going to help with our drug and vaccine distribution in the future. That's all I've been told, and based on my experience here at Rainbow, we're looking at mega-bucks come bonus time. Not to mention the impact on the Stock Exchange."

Krissy's mind reeled when she coupled what she'd discovered with such an enterprise. She started to ask more when Mr. Kavidas's door opened, and a man wearing a doctor's coat walked out. She fell back into her chair as a wave of anxiety swept over her. Her heart raced uncontrollably. Her voice stammered slightly when she asked Sydelle, "Who was that?"

"Oh, that's one of the research doctors from the lab downstairs. He came to speak with Mr. Kavidas before you came in," Sydelle replied.

Krissy reached into her purse, picked out her mirror, and looked behind her as the man walked away. She also looked at herself and recognized fear in her eyes.

Thirty minutes later, Mort walked into the office, circled Krissy's desk, and sat on one corner. "Mort Stein to see Mr. Kavidas, as ordered," he reported. He looked over at Sydelle, then back at Krissy. "What's happening?"

The women shrugged simultaneously.

"Damage report on the fire, I guess," he concluded while throwing his hands up in the air. Reaching over the desk, he grabbed Krissy's hand. "Your hand is shaking. Are you all right? Is anything wrong?"

Disguising her feelings she replied, "Just tired, I guess."

Mort gestured toward Kavidas's office with his thumb and said facetiously, "He's a slave driver, isn't he? No wonder Sydelle got pregnant; so she could get away from here for a while." He snickered and walked over to blow Sydelle a kiss.

Krissy's intercom buzzed.

"Mr. Kavidas will see you now, Mr. Stein," Krissy announced.

Mort snapped to mock attention and saluted Kavidas's office. On the way in, he stopped at Krissy's desk and whispered, "Is there a chance you might have dinner with me sometime?"

Suppressing her apprehension, she giggled. Sydelle looked at her funny, and Mort said, "Is that a yes?" She looked into his eyes, feigned a smile, and nodded. Mort turned on his heel and marched into Kavidas's office.

Mort quietly closed the door behind him and stood patiently as Gregory finished up another phone call. Gregory rotated on his swivel chair and motioned for him to walk over and sit down. Mort couldn't help but observe Gregory's somber look, as if he had received some bad news. Rising to the occasion, Mort changed to a more serious countenance.

Gregory set the phone down. "We have a problem—the leak just became worse."

"The fire?" Mort asked. "The lab doctor? A break-in? What?"

Gregory nodded. "After the fire marshal declared the all clear, Dr.

Morris, one of our research consultants, returned to the lab and noticed the specimens he had been working on were out of order."

Mort's eyes were transfixed on Gregory's face.

"He passed it off as nothing until he noticed drops of blood—one drop by the specimen rack, the other on the floor. Knowing they weren't his, he suspected someone tampered with his specimens. From there he took inventory of the vaccine supplies and found one vial missing."

Mort shook his head in disbelief. "Someone stole some of the vaccine? Was it someone from inside or outside?"

"I suspect from the inside and probably during the fire. The person or persons waited for a holiday when security would be light, then staged a fire as a diversionary tactic to gain access to our restricted zone. It won't happen again; we're moving the vaccine to the vault until we're ready for distribution. As far as the lab is concerned, we'll post double security outside the lab from now on."

"Did Morris test the blood for a lead on the culprit?" Mort inquired.

"Running the tests as we speak. When he's finished, I need you to take care of this for me. The vaccine cannot be analyzed by another lab before we receive our patent or approval from FDA, or we're in big trouble."

"No problem," Mort said. "I'll clear my schedule until this is corrected."

"Work with security, find out where the problem is, and eradicate it," Kavidas pronounced.

"You give me authority to handle this however I see fit?"

Gregory cracked his knuckles. "Rainbow will stand behind you. Just take care of it."

Mort assented and began to leave when Gregory added, "Oh, regarding our advertising program. I have strategically placed bits of information of our vaccine development and marketing dates into certain responsible parties that are influential with the media. Rumors about our December advent should be forthcoming. Be prepared."

Mort walked out of Gregory's office and straight to Krissy's desk. "Have you thought any more about going out with me?" he asked confidently.

Suspecting exposure, she hesitated and studied his facial expression. "Maybe."

Mort grinned. "You're weakening, aren't you?"

Krissy turned to Sydelle for rescue and said to Mort, "I'll let you know."

Sydelle called over to her, "Linda, call for you on 05."

Krissy picked up the dead phone, winked at Sydelle, and waved Mort off. Mort bowed away gracefully. Krissy followed his every move until he left the room. Once he was outside, she realized her heart was pounding. *Could he know it was me?*

From Gregory's office Mort headed to Wellington's personnel department and asked to see the employment roster. He asked the manager for the list of those employees who actually worked on President's Day, learning that twelve women and six men were scheduled, not including the research staff doctor. On Gregory's authority, he photocopied the files and departed for the security office.

Located on the east wing of the first floor, Wellington's security division consisted of both men and machine. The protective agency enlisted 25 full-time guards and 10 part-timers, all with extensive police or military backgrounds. The office contained an elaborate array of electronic surveillance equipment, together with data-gathering linking devices through *Redisearch* and local police files, enabling quick identifications.

Randy, the middle-aged pugnacious chief of security, waved to Mort as he walked in holding the personnel file. "Mr. Stein, how can I help you?" he solicited.

Mort looked at the three security guards having coffee at the dispensing machine and said to Randy, "Can I speak to you in private?"

"Sure, no problem." Randy motioned to the three men, and within seconds the room was vacated.

Mort pulled the roster from his personnel file and laid it on Randy's desk. "We have a security leak that must be plugged. The fire on Monday appears to have been staged as a diversionary tactic to steal vital research records from our laboratory downstairs."

Randy wiped his brow. "Whew, I'm glad it wasn't on my watch."

"That might be, but we are holding *you* responsible until we catch the culprit. One of your functions is to continually check all personnel files for integrity and compromise. Is that correct?"

Randy's countenance abruptly changed before Mort's eyes. "Yes, sir, that's my job."

"Well, you haven't been doing your job," Mort said as he pointed to the roster, "because we believe somebody has phony ID and probably is on the payroll. So, each name is to be confirmed with photo ID from our corporate office in New York, along with any other source you can access." He stopped, looked Randy in the eye, and added, "The report is to come straight to me, nobody else. Clear?"

Randy stood erect. "Yes, sir, I'll get right on it."

"Report your progress to me tomorrow."

Krissy's headache returned that night. Rainbow's stratagem and the fear of exposure consumed her. The pressure needed to be vented. Certain that the escalating stress would continue, she placated herself by thinking of contacting Kathy Douglas. Reason dictated that she couldn't hold on to the information about Rainbow or the vial she possessed; it wasn't safe, and it wasn't practical. Information can be dangerous, and she knew she was only one person against a monster conglomerate like Rainbow. She needed advice and protection quickly. Then meandering thoughts about how and when she would exit from Rainbow filled her mind. The prospect of Mort coming on to her heightened her trepidation.

She finished off a bottle of sherry to calm her nerves, then reached for the phone to call Kathy. "No, you idiot!" she said to herself. "It's too soon, and I can't endanger anybody else. Just a few more weeks, then we can bail out with all the ammunition we need to hang these parasites."

She turned and opened the refrigerator door and spotted the Skippy peanut butter jar. Impulsively she unscrewed the lid and peered into the hollowed-out contents, revealing the vaccine vial she hid there. "Just making sure," she said to the vial. "You're my insurance."

Mort emerged from his library at *Redisearch* as the phone was ringing. "Mort Stein."

"Mr. Stein, this is Dr. Morris in the research lab over at Rainbow. I have the results of the blood analysis."

"Let's have it," Mort replied impatiently.

"The blood type is O-positive, pretty common; of a woman who was menstruating and a nonsmoker."

"Can't you narrow it down more than that?" Mort said.

"We can do a DNA scan, which takes a couple of days, but unless we have a means of comparison, it wouldn't really help."

"Yes, I understand. Well, at least we have something to go on. Go ahead and do a DNA scan and advise me of your findings." Mort hung up the phone, then went to his desk file to retrieve the roster of the employees who were working during the lab break-in. He skimmed over the names, focusing on the women on the list.

Krissy loved Sundays. Sunday afforded her the opportunity to sleep late and catch up on her chores around her apartment, but today would be different. Awakening early, she searched the telephone directory for a Christian church, wrote the address and time of service down, then prepared to leave.

She looked in the mirror and shuddered. "Wrong way, Krissy," she muttered. "You're going the wrong way with this." Massaging her temples and eye sockets, she realized her indulgence with the sherry the night before had taken its toll. The puffiness would subside, she knew that, but the ache in her heart for Johnnie and the tension in her mind over Rainbow would not.

Resolute, she went to the service, pledging to cast her troubles on the Lord.

"Linda, this is Mort," the caller announced. "How's your Sunday afternoon going? I thought I'd give you a ring and follow up on my request."

Krissy squeezed her eyes shut and shot a silent prayer up to God. She vacillated for a second on how to respond. "I thought it over and decided to risk going out with one of the bosses."

"Smart girl. We'll have a good time. I'll book us for dinner tonight at the *La Reserve* in Fort Lauderdale. Sound good?"

Krissy bit her lip and said warmly, "Enchanting." She gave him directions to her apartment, then ran into the bathroom. When she looked in the mirror this time, she saw only terror.

Mort behaved like a country gentleman. Greeting Krissy with a bouquet of roses and a box of miniature chocolates suspended her apprehension. He escorted her to his car, then graciously opened the car door for her, bowed in mock obeisance as she entered, and proceeded to charm her as they drove off.

"I've been smitten by you, you know," he began, "and I can tell that you like me."

"What gives you that idea?" she said demurely.

"Because every time I come near you, you seem nervous. I believe physical attraction is at work here. Besides, if you didn't care, I wouldn't have any effect on you. Right?"

Feeling relieved by his affection and the fervor of the moment, she replied, "You may be right."

"Thought you might like a preview," he said as he handed her the dinner menu. "I frequent this restaurant; I'm on their mailing list."

"That's neat," she said while leafing through the pages. She stopped at the seafood section and asked, "How is their blackened tuna steak?"

"I never had it; I'm strictly a lobster man, but everything they serve is superb. Trust me."

"Lobster?" Krissy said.

"Oh. I know what you're thinking, being Jewish and all that. Well, I sort of believe in Jewish mysticism, but I don't practice all that dietary stuff. Stuffy, you know," he offered in apology.

Krissy simply shrugged in mute assent and studied the dessert section.

"Sydelle tells me your record from our New York office is exemplary. Magna Cum Laude graduate of Hofstra business college, 15 years with Standard Oil, then on to executive secretary at Rainbow. Impressive."

Krissy crammed the menu above the sun visor, looked over at Mort and said, "My, my, you've been doing your homework. What else have you uncovered? Have you put me through your *Redisearch* system?"

Mort's facial expression changed. "Didn't mean to pry into your life, but every employee at Rainbow and *Redisearch* is screened each year; you know that. Sought of like an annual drug testing, if you know what I mean. Staves off employee problems with bankruptcy, credit abuses, and drugs, among other things."

He accelerated deliberately around a curve, moving her body toward him and added, "Don't you remember signing the authorization when you joined up with Rainbow?"

"Sure, I remember." She snickered, then remained silent the rest of the drive while staring out her window at the night scape.

"To you!" Mort announced to Krissy at the champagne toast over dinner, "the brightest color in the spectrum at Rainbow." After touching glasses, he said, "Forgive my inquisitive nature, Linda, but how come a beautiful girl like you is unmarried?"

Krissy weighed the question, then replied, "My fiancé was killed last year in an accident." Turning her head in repose she watched a yacht pass by on its way through the intracoastal waterway toward the Atlantic Ocean.

"I'm truly sorry," Mort replied. "I promise not to ask any more questions tonight." He reached over the table and patted her hand in consolation just as the waiter came to take their order.

Krissy snapped out of her reflection and decided to use the occasion. "Tell me about yourself. How did you start *Redisearch* and get involved with Mr. Kavidas?"

Mort beamed and spent the next hour recounting his life history for the past 20 years, unwittingly paying homage to his friend and business partner, Gregory Kavidas, as some great mastermind who possessed the singular gifts necessary to save the world.

In Krissy's mind, the evening simply represented an extension of her mission.

Young Alan Douglas lumbered down the driveway to pick up the newspaper rolled in a plastic sleeve, lying on the ground. Then he wandered into the kitchen. After glancing at the sports page, he quickly abandoned the newspaper on the table.

Kathy walked over to set up for breakfast, caught a look at the front page, and yelled out, "David! Come here right away."

He quickly appeared, with shaving cream dangling from his half-shaven beard and looked around for the crisis. "What is it, babe?"

"Look at this article on page one!"

David read it aloud as he held the shaving cream from dripping off his face. "'AIDS Vaccine in Sight; Rainbow Pharmaceuticals Expects Government Approval of Vaccine Soon. Researchers Plan Distribution by December.'" He turned and looked out the window and acted out a soliloquy. "Now the spider spins his web and waits to draw the unsuspecting fly unto its death."

"David!" Kathy exclaimed. "What does this mean?"

David gestured to Kathy to pour the coffee as he wiped the cream off his face. "Obviously Rainbow plans to circumvent safety standards, disguised in public demands, and is going to market the vaccine." He shook his head in disbelief and with a cracked voice added, "We haven't much time left if we are to stop this madness."

"We need to meet with Brandon immediately," Kathy insisted,

stroking Hillary's hair gently. "I had a dream about Krissy two days ago, so I called her in New York and I kept getting her answering machine. So I called Louie to look in on her." She paused and looked directly at David.

"And?" David said.

"His partner said he is still vacationing down here in Florida."

"What? How can that be when he told us he had to get back to New York on a pressing murder case?"

"I didn't want to worry you, but with this newspaper business, I sense real danger here. Somehow I believe it's all connected."

David gulped down his coffee. "I'm skipping breakfast. I'm going down to Miami to meet with Brandon right away."

In Rainbow's lunchroom, discussions of the news leak occupied the majority of conversations. Both Sydelle and Krissy discussed the advent at length, reveling in the fact that they had some preview of the event.

After lunch, Mort scooted past Sydelle's desk, waved the newspaper at Krissy, and walked into Gregory's office. "Nice," Mort said as he opened the newspaper on Gregory's desk, pointing to the article.

"It pays to know people," Gregory replied. "This advance notice will pave the way for us in December. If there are any rats out there, this fire will bring them out now so we can clobber them before our marketing schedule nears."

"Speaking of rats, I'm meeting with your security chief, Randy, after I leave you. I expect he will find the varmint who broke in very soon," Mort declared as he exited.

He paused at Krissy's desk and pointed the newspaper in his hand toward Gregory's office. "He's a genius. Knows just when to ignite the fire to maximize the burn."

Krissy looked over at Sydelle, then back to Mort. "We know he's a genius. But what does 'the burn' mean?"

Mort smiled and explained, "Mr. Kavidas's timing with this press release will place us in the perfect position to secure our place in the market." He quickly placed his hand over his mouth and added, "Oops. I guess I should keep my mouth shut, but when something this big enters the arena, it's hard to keep the spotlight off it."

"That's what we are hoping for, right, an early vaccine release?" Krissy asked.

"Yes!" Mort replied. "And I'm also hoping to drop over to your apartment tonight on my way home. Just for a cup of coffee, mind you." He smiled after entrapping her.

Krissy looked up at him, shot Sydelle a look, and repeated, "Just for a cup of coffee."

As Mort opened the door at the security office, Randy held up a CD and said, "Mr. Stein, they FedEx'd it overnight, arrived here at nine this morning."

"Would you excuse me while I access this, Randy?"

"Time I made my rounds anyway, Mr. Stein," Randy said as he walked out.

After inserting the disk into the CD drive, Mort entered his password to open the confidential files on the Florida Rainbow employees. The CD contained a full description and history of each employee, along with 45 seconds of sound video where the employee recited a portion of the constitution for voice identification. Mort keyed in the 12 female employee badge numbers of those working during the break-in, then watched the monitor as the files came up in review.

As each of the women appeared on the monitor, Mort examined their pictures and descriptions very carefully, writing down blood types and significant body marks and features in his file. When he came to the file on Linda, he studied it closely and printed the records for his report.

Then he called Randy on his portable phone and asked him to return. "I need you to scan the satellite surveillance videotapes for the past three months for anything unusual. Get with your crews and ask them to check them also. This is a serious matter requiring speed to enable us to acquire the needed proof."

"Mr. Stein," Randy said, "I've cleared my schedule to give this top priority."

Mort cracked a thin smile. "Good. Get right on it."

"For the last three hours we've been brainstorming about Rainbow, and still nothing," Brandon lamented. He threw the newspaper with Rainbow's announcement in the trash can, then turned to his father and David. "Let's go with what we have so far. I'll call the newspapers anonymously and suggest that Rainbow has developed a harmful vaccine and let nature take its course. That will ruin them."

"No, it won't, Brandon," David retorted. "We haven't sufficient evidence to cry foul yet. The media will immediately suspect treachery from a rival drug company with something as big as the AIDS vaccine. No, we must wait until we have proof that their drug is dangerous; then we can blow the whistle."

"You're so practical—it makes me sick," Brandon shot back.

"You're being too emotional, Brandon," his father interjected. "We're all getting hyped up prematurely over this. Let's just wait another 10 days. If something doesn't break by then, I'll contact the surgeon general with our suspicions."

"And with that you can kiss Lane Pharmaceutical good-bye," Brandon said. "Believe me, Rainbow will bury any evidence implicating them with a faulty vaccine, and we'll be the laughingstock of the pharmaceutical world. Remember, their drug must work initially, or they will never be able to get it marketed. So whatever evidence we uncover must be able to show the long-term ramifications. We need to find one of their victims who was inoculated a few years ago and take a sample of their blood today and study the results."

"Brandon's right, Matt. We'll have to tough it out until something turns up," David summarized. While cracking his knuckles he added, "Meanwhile, Brandon, if we don't hear from Krissy or Louie within the same period, 10 days, we'll have to report them as missing."

Matthew Lane dropped back into his desk chair in despair and simply shook his head.

Brandon went to his side and said, "All is not lost, Dad. Something will show up."

Lane nodded but didn't look like he believed that.

From her second floor balcony, Krissy could see far into the Everglades. Her Boca Raton apartment faced west, enabling her to enjoy many spectacular sunsets over the wildlife sanctuary.

After 30 minutes of meditation, the doorbell sounded. Looking through the peephole, she saw Mort, carrying two containers of coffee and a bag of donuts.

"Guess who?" he said as she opened the door. He held up the coffee containers and donuts and reminded her, "I said I would stop over for coffee." Grinning, he whispered, "But I didn't want to put you out, so I brought it with me. Is it okay?"

"Sure, come in," she answered. "I was enjoying the sunset this evening."

Mort grabbed her arm and said softly, "I love sunsets." He walked her out to the balcony and pointed toward the horizon. "This reminds me of my condo overlooking the Atlantic at Cozumel." He embraced her and asked, "Would you go there with me for a vacation?"

Krissy backed off. "Whoa, there, big guy. Aren't you driving a little too fast?"

He relaxed and yawned. "Just testing the waters."

Krissy's intuition told her to maintain her defenses at all times, exercising caution not to disarm Mort prematurely. She whistled a stanza of the tune "Winchester Cathedral" and said, "Maybe sometime in the future."

Mort studied her face for a few seconds, opened the bag, and put the coffee containers on the patio table. "The waitress forgot the creamers," he said as he walked to the refrigerator.

Krissy froze for a few seconds, then blurted out, "I take it black."

Mort pivoted on his heel. "Oh? So do I."

"Any further developments on that laboratory break-in?" Krissy asked

101

glibly.

"Still working on it. I asked security to look into it; we're not really concerned about it."

"I can't imagine who would want to burglarize a drug laboratory. Unless the person is an addict, what would be the point of it? All the drug vials have registered lot numbers, so no one could legally administer any of our drugs without our permission. So what's the purpose?"

"The problem here, Linda, is illegal drug use. If someone stole one of our drug vials, they could injure themselves if they used it improperly. Then there is the issue of industrial espionage. One of our competitors could snatch up our drug formulas before we had a chance to patent it." Impatiently he added, "There are many advantages to burglarizing our drug lab; that's certain."

"No one knew at the office, but were any drugs taken at the break-in?" she asked methodically.

"No. We suspect the intruder was looking for narcotics, and we don't keep any at this facility."

"Case closed?"

"All but the paperwork," he said nonchalantly.

Krissy knew he had to be lying.

Mort looked at his wristwatch. "It's still early. Why not go out to a movie?"

"If you promise not to talk shop about Rainbow," she replied.

Mort beamed. "Done."

She dashed toward her bedroom. "I'll just change this outfit and be right with you."

Mort watched Linda walk away, then went to the kitchen, looked around, and opened the refrigerator. He quickly took inventory of the contents, rearranging the vegetables and the dairy products, then looked in the freezer. From there he returned to the cooler section and scanned the condiment shelf. *Now, who keeps peanut butter in the refrigerator?* he asked himself. He reached for the jar, opened the lid, and looked in. *Nice*

touch, Linda.

Swiftly restoring the refrigerator's contents to their original positions, he turned and scooted out of the kitchen before she returned. Seconds later she emerged from her bedroom in a shorts outfit, grabbed her purse, and walked to the door, waiting for Mort.

Mort walked up to her. "Do you want to stop and buy a bottle of wine for after the movie?"

"Sure, why not."

Mort nodded in assent and walked her to his car.

As they were walking to the car, Mort dropped behind three paces as she strolled in her short-short skirt. "That's a cute little birthmark on your thigh."

"Thank you." Taking the remark as a compliment she smiled at first, then realized the implications. He had been studying her employment profile; she was sure of it. Then the moments where Mort was alone while she dressed loomed in her mind.

At the theater mall, Mort stopped in front of the liquor store. He looked over at Krissy for approval.

"I've changed my mind. Not tonight," she said, her heart pounding. "I feel a sinus headache coming on."

Mort shrugged and looked away at the movie marquee, then back to Krissy. "Want to pass on the show?"

She nodded, then fished in her purse for her compact to freshen up.

Mort turned the car around and drove her home without saying another word.

Sydelle was surprised when she arrived early in the morning and found a man waiting to see Gregory Kavidas. She extended the amenities, then went to her desk in silence.

Her eyes were riveted on Kimsley's face as he sat reading Immanuel

Kant. His long wavy red hair was pulled back in a ponytail, which only accentuated his massive nose and lips. His features were unlike anyone she had seen outside of horror movies. To brighten his appearance, he wore a diamond stud in his left ear and an exotic-colored shirt. When he stood up to stretch after one hour of waiting, he looked like a giant. She estimated he was over six feet five inches tall.

When Krissy returned from picking up the mail and saw Kimsley, she went right over to Sydelle's desk. "Who in the world is that? Godzilla's brother?"

"I never met him before. I had a note on my desk this morning from Mr. Kavidas advising me that a Mr. Kimsley from our operation in Trinidad is to be expected. That's all I know."

Krissy repeated, "Trinidad?" With that she turned and walked over to the extremely muscular man. Up close, she estimated his age to be in the mid-40s. "Hello, I'm Linda Martin, Rainbow's special project manager, temporarily assigned to Mr. Kavidas."

The towering man arose and extended his hand. "Jerry Kimsley, very nice to meet you."

"Sydelle said you're from our Trinidad location. How is everything going down there?"

He hesitated as his gaze shifted back and forth between Sydelle and Krissy; then he coughed nervously, "Real quiet."

Krissy pressed a little harder. "What is your position with Rainbow down there, if I may ask?"

Kimsley sat back down again and groped for words. "I guess you could say I handle security there and at our other facilities."

Deciding not to overdo the questioning, Krissy changed the subject. "You have an accent. You sound like you're from the Northeast. I'm originally from New York. And you?"

"Grantham, Massachusetts."

Sydelle's phone beeped. "Mr. Kavidas will see you now, Mr. Kimsley," she said.

He tightened his tie and dusted his lapels, then walked into Kavidas's office.

"Strange-looking fellow, don't you think?" Sydelle said, gawking at Kavidas's door.

Krissy's mind exploded with the possibilities of Kimsley's job and his sudden visit to see Kavidas. She didn't even hear Sydelle talking to her.

Ten minutes later, Mort walked into the office with Randy, chief of security. Krissy looked at him with consternation when she saw his demeanor noticeable altered. He simply saluted the two ladies, then went directly into Kavidas's office.

"Oh, oh. Something's going down," Sydelle said.

I hope it's not me, Krissy thought. A sharp pain stabbed her in the stomach followed by pangs of indigestion. "Need to use the ladies' room," she announced to Sydelle. Inside the restroom Krissy speed-dialed Kathy Douglas on her cell phone. Kathy answered on the first ring.

"Kathy, this is Krissy, and I'm in trouble."

"Where are you? We're worried sick about you!"

"Shut up and listen! I've infiltrated Rainbow, and I have a vial of their vaccine and other documentation of their testing that can really hurt them. But I think I've been found out."

"Get out right away!" Kathy broke in. "We tried to reach you but your phone—"

"I'm here in Florida, in Boca Raton, not New York. That why. I've got to go."

"Krissy, wait!" Kathy implored. "I'll send David and Brandon to get you."

"I'm in too deep. I'll call you later tonight."

The phone went silent. Kathy burst into tears and called David.

Gregory studied the satellite surveillance video, expertly zoning and enlarging on the red sports car and its driver. The computer-enhanced imaging reproduced a remarkable representation of Linda. "Did you compare the records with the DNA and the blood droplets found in the lab?" Gregory asked Mort.

Mort nodded with his face to the floor. "Yes, it's her all right. No question. I even know where the missing vial of Toi-VAX is. She hid it in her refrigerator."

"Do you think she told anyone or has other evidence that could hurt us?" Randy asked Mort.

Mort bit his lip. "Don't think so, but can't be sure."

"Sorry about this, Mort, considering you have an interest in her," Gregory offered officially.

"I'll see that this is remedied quickly before there are further problems," Mort assured Gregory.

Gregory looked at Mort with a glint of concern, raised an eyebrow, and said, "Mort, remember the future. Our plan must be protected, regardless of cost." He nodded to Randy and Kimsley, who excused themselves and marched out.

"I can't do this by myself. I'm afraid I got a little too close to her," Mort lamented.

Gregory put his arm around him. "Fine, I understand. Put Kimsley on her; he's the best."

Mort turned in reflexive obedience and departed. He couldn't say a word to Linda as he passed her on the way out.

Kathy's task of finding a dress for Hillary to attend a friend's birthday party snowballed into a major project. Starting out in the Coral Springs Mall proved fruitless. Meandering through the Fashion Mall in Plantation offered possibilities, but the Sawgrass Mills Mall solved the problem. Despite its remote location in western Fort Lauderdale, the mall boasted a busy labyrinth of hundreds of small shops, fairs, and bargain haunts for the adventurous shopper. Located off the Sawgrass Expressway in a reclaimed section of the Everglades swampland, shoppers traveled from distant counties just to say they visited the place. It was not unusual to shop for many hours and never see the same store twice. Usually a person would shop there so they wouldn't have to worry about being seen.

Within 15 minutes, Hillary lost interest in the escapade. The cry began. "Mommy, I'm hungry." She squirmed to free herself from Kathy's grip and heightened her wail. "I'm hungry, Mommy."

Kathy checked her watch and realized it was lunchtime. Her unsuccessful quest to find Hillary a dress only frustrated her more. "Okay, we'll go to the food court for a sandwich, and if you're good, an ice cream."

"I'll be good," Hillary pledged repeatedly as her mother rushed her through the busy promenade toward the restaurants. Then, just as they entered the spacious atrium, Hillary yelled, "Mommy, look, there's Uncle Louie!"

"Where?"

Hillary pointed to a concession stand. "Over there, eating a big ice cream!"

Pushing her way through the crowd, Kathy came up behind Louie and placed her arms around his neck. "Where have you been? We've been worried sick about you."

Louie nearly gagged on the ice cream.

"Uncle Louie, buy me an ice cream, too," Hillary whined.

"After lunch," her mother interjected. She looked Louie straight on and said, "What's going on with you? I called your partner last week, and he said you were still down in Florida, when you told us you were returning to New York."

Louie dumped the half-eaten ice cream into the trash can as Hillary's eyes widened to a glare. He walked them over to a table, then reached and held Kathy's hand. "My department has been working with Florida police on this business with Rainbow. Covert operation. I couldn't tell anybody. We're watching both their Trinidad and Wellington facilities carefully."

"I don't get it. Why would New York police be interested in the affairs of a Florida-based pharmaceutical company?"

"Because Rainbow Pharmaceuticals is incorporated in the State of New York, NYPD has a stake in this murder case. I've been on it from day one, the day you first called me."

Taken aback, she asked, "What have you found out?"

"Progress is very slow. We're working with the FBI to see if there are any anti-trust laws being broken, or if this vaccine falls under federal statutes once it's released. But that's about the size of it."

Kathy closed her eyes and shook her head. "This is unbelievable. You're a professional detective involved in some underground network struggling to uncover Rainbow's subversive activities, while Krissy, the fiancée of a murdered college professor, in two months works her way into the organization and sits next to the number one man, a Gregory Kavidas. Now you figure that one out."

Louie's eyes were transfixed on Kathy. "What do you mean?"

"We received a frantic call from Krissy a few days ago telling us she infiltrated Rainbow's Wellington facility and has tangible proof of their experiments, stuff to really hurt them." She cocked her head and asked, "How come your detective work hasn't turned up some evidence?"

Louie said nothing for several seconds. Then his words were measured. "These people have powerful people protecting them against probes, unless you're on the inside. Are you telling me Krissy is inside Rainbow?"

"That's right, and we're terribly concerned for her safety."

"Kathy, we must do something to get her out before it's too late," Louie implored.

"Great idea, but how? She can't be reached, and if anybody makes an inquiry at Rainbow, she would be exposed and her identity compromised."

Louie gazed off into the mall promenade. "Let me make some phone calls. Some people down here in Florida owe me some tribute. Don't trouble yourself over this. I'm sure she's fine," he soothed.

"Louie, we can't let anything happen to her," Kathy said as her eyes began to tear. "But we just don't know what to do. We're stumped. All of us."

Louie moved toward her, as if to comfort her. "We? Who else is helping out *now?*" He raised his eyebrow.

"What are you talking about *now?*" she answered, almost agitated. "The same people who have been from the beginning. David and I, along with Brandon and his father. They're coming over to the house so we can discuss what to do with what we know. Oh, Lou, can you come, too? I know you're busy here with your own investigation, but it would really help. We'd all feel so much better." Her tears flowed now in earnest.

"Now, now, don't start that." Louie reached over and hugged Hillary now in an effort to divert Kathy's tears. "Of course I'll come; you know that. Don't give it another thought. We'll work it out together." He motioned toward the far side of the wall. "How about that ice cream, princess?"

Hillary jumped up and down and smirked at her mother as Louie towed her toward the refreshment stand.

It wasn't until after Louie left and Hillary's dress was purchased that Kathy realized Louie didn't give her his Florida address or phone number. But she felt more at ease, knowing he was nearby and would be at their next meeting.

Kathy, thought Louie as he walked away from their surprise encounter in the mall, *that is one meeting I will not miss—and one that none of us will forget.*

It was just as well that Sydelle didn't know the Watchman's real name. In two weeks, she would be going on maternity leave, and her life would be forever changed. She might even decide to stay home and care for the baby rather than return to work. Time would tell. But for now, the Watchman's call disturbed her once again.

"Do you wish to continue to hold, Mr. Watchman, while Mr. Kavidas finishes up his call?" Sydelle asked.

The caller said he would wait.

Seven minutes later Sydelle returned to the caller. "I can put you through now, Mr. Watchman." She watched the phone line light transfer to Mr. Kavidas's private line as she held the phone in her hand.

"Mr. Kavidas, this is Watchman again. There are many developments since I've talked to you last."

"Yes, I know. Tell me something I don't know," Gregory replied impatiently.

"I found out where your leak is. It's coming from within your organization, quite close to you."

"How did you find this out?" Gregory asked. Confirmation of Mort's findings would only reinforce his responsibility to settle this problem promptly.

"My reliable sources advise me that a Krissy Kramer has been working in your facility for over six weeks now, acquiring information about your operation and has documented proof that can hurt you."

Gregory dwelled on the name. "Your sources know her name to be Krissy Kramer?"

Click.

"What was that?" the Watchman asked. "Is this a secure line?"

"Yes, this conversation is private," Gregory assured. "It must be on your end." He thought of the implications of Linda Martin having an alias and wondered who else might be involved. "Listen, Watchman, I need you to track this Krissy Kramer's family and friends. Find out who she may have divulged any information to. Get back to me." He hung up the phone.

Once Gregory's line indicator went out, Sydelle walked over to Krissy's desk, grabbed her hand, and pulled her out into the hallway, away from Gregory's hearing. Sydelle's frantic physiognomy couldn't be concealed.

"What's wrong?" Krissy asked. "Is your baby all right?"

Sydelle's face grew red with rage. "I'm fine. It's *you* that's in serious trouble. They know who *you* are. I just overheard a call from a Watchman who calls Mr. Kavidas regularly. I never eavesdropped before, but this Watchman person gives me the creeps, so I decided not to hang up the phone this time. I heard them talking about you being some kind of informer. What are they talking about?"

Krissy turned to the wall and clutched it in despair. "They killed my Johnnie." She sobbed. "And I don't care what happens to me as long as I get them back!" She turned and bolted down the corridor, then out the exit.

By the time Sydelle returned to her desk, Gregory was standing at his door, beckoning her to his side. "Where is Ms. Martin, Sydelle?"

Instinct dictated that she should keep her mouth shut. "She had an emergency, something about one of her sisters having an accident." Pointing to the doorway, she shrugged and added, "She just left."

Sydelle returned to her desk as Gregory closed his door behind him.

Seconds later his private phone line lit up.

In the parking lot, Krissy sat calmly in her car, collecting her thoughts for several moments, then called Kathy Douglas on her cell phone. *Thank God for this gadget,* she thought. On the fourth ring, the voice mail came on. "Lord, help!" she said aloud. "Where are you, Kathy? I need you desperately." Resigned, she simply reported, "Kathy, this is Krissy. I need to talk to you immediately. Please call me on my cell phone. I'll be waiting. Hurry!"

Krissy waited five minutes, then departed.

Heading southbound on Route 441, Krissy raced, weaving in and out of traffic, to place as much distance between her and Rainbow as possible. After 15 minutes, the realization that the evidence she possessed represented security so she slowed down and obeyed the speed limit. *What am I worried about? They can't risk killing me when I might have injurious evidence.*

Crossing into Broward County once again, she pulled into a fast-food store for coffee. Just as she opened her car door, her cell phone rang. "Are you all right? Where are you?" Kathy said.

Krissy slammed the door closed, started her engine, and pulled out into traffic again. "I'm in trouble. They know about me."

"Come to our house. We'll hide you until the police are brought in."

"No, I can't do that. My presence will jeopardize your whole family. No. Meet me somewhere." As she looked to the side, she saw a road sign that read Loxahatchee Wildlife Sanctuary of Boynton Beach. She quickly turned into the preserve and came to a stop a hundred yards before the ticket booth. "Meet me at the Loxahatchee Wildlife Sanctuary on Route 441 in Boynton Beach. I'm running home to get that vial. By the time I return, you'll be here. Hurry."

Kathy checked the time, called David at work to advise him of the events, then left Hillary with a neighbor and departed to meet Krissy.

Fifteen minutes later, Krissy arrived at her apartment. She could hear her phone ringing as she opened her door. Intuition told her not to answer. Rainbow would be looking for her. If Kathy were to change the rendezvous point, she would call Krissy's cell phone.

Frantically she gathered her files on Rainbow, including Haiti, her computer files, and the vial of Toi-VAX. As she turned to leave, an ominous feeling came over her. She closed the door and slowly walked through each room of her apartment, reminiscing and touching her valuables. At her bedroom, she opened her dresser drawer and pulled out a framed picture of Johnnie. Anger surged within her as she squeezed the vial in her hand, nearly to the breaking point, before tossing it and Johnny's picture into her handbag.

Retracing her drive, Krissy paced herself in order to plan her strategy. Noticing the farmlands and irrigation canals somehow brought solace and peace to her. A wave of confidence swept over her as she forced herself to relax.

Her cell chirped out a tune. She couldn't read the number while she drove, but in the frenetic moment took a chance. "Hello, Kathy?" she said. She heard a pause and background music but no voice. "Kathy, is that you?" she repeated.

Click.

Suddenly Krissy's heart fluttered as renewed fear took over. "The dirty dogs tracked my cell number," she said aloud. Checking her distance at five miles from the Loxahatchee meeting place, she abandoned caution and passed the fruit-laden rack truck in front of her.

Route 441 scaled down from two to one lane in each direction, with random passing zones. Signal devices at major intersections appeared frequently. Krissy hoped for all green lights, but that proved improbable. She retightened her seat belt and calculated her risk factor, then pushed her sports car to 95 mph. She was running out of time. The sportster' s suspension system proved highly effective in the turns, and its low center of gravity reduced swerve. But commercial trucking on Route 441 moves very slowly in and out of the orange groves adjacent to the road, especially in late February, when tourists clog the main traffic arteries. At high speeds it would be almost impossible to avoid a collision.

The Boynton fresh-water canal, dug by the Army Corps of Engineers in the 1940s, withstood the test of time. Not only did it provide a continuing source for irrigation since then, but the crisscross network of secondary canals attracted all the neighborhood fisherman. Fisherman with their parked cars frequently lined the canal bulkheads, paying little or no attention to passing motorists. Dallying pedestrians meandered throughout.

Concentrating on meeting Kathy as she played leap-frog on the roadway, Krissy didn't see the little boy running with his fishing pole behind two parked cars. He darted out to cross Route 441 but failed to look for oncoming traffic. Realization of his presence came to Krissy within 100 feet of the boy, but she knew it was too late.

She slammed on her brakes just as the boy froze in his steps, then yanked the steering wheel to the left as her car began to fishtail out of control. "Lord, help," she cried out. In an instant, a man from behind grabbed the boy and pulled him out of the roadway as Krissy took her foot off the brake to allow her car to straighten out of the skid. She shook her head and looked in the rearview mirror as the man scolded the boy. "That was close." She sighed as she brought her speed down to the limit.

Passing through the entranceway and the visitors' center, Krissy drove up to one of the levees and parked her car to wait for Kathy. Moments later her eyes fell on the prolific display of wild birds that abound at the Everglades sanctuary. Taken in, she wandered out to the shoreline and walked out on the observer's boardwalk that juts out into the slough to watch nature continue in its course as man busied himself with plans of destruction.

Ten minutes later the honking of Kathy's car horn alerted Krissy to her arrival. When they met, they silently held each other for several moments until their anxieties subsided.

They walked to Krissy's car while stifling their sobs as Krissy explained, "My life is in danger. I know that. Rainbow must have triangulated on my cell phone. They know where I am. After I meet with you, I'm going to leave the phone somewhere to divert them." She reached in her handbag and pulled out the evidence against Rainbow. "Here is the vial of Toi-VAX that I took from Rainbow's vaccine cooler. Guard it carefully. It is vital in our case." Handing her the PDA she added, "The password is 777. In this you will find my notes on Rainbow's clinic in Haiti, where a vaccine volunteer is dying, and also notations about a George Arnstead, an HIV-positive old man they have been testing their drugs on—"

"They're experimenting on old men? How ghastly."

Krissy nodded. "It gets worse. If they have their way, Rainbow will introduce and implement a program they call Project Renaissance that will revolutionize the entire medical information storage system. Their goal is to control all medical services, and someone must stop them before it's too late. Once their vaccine is distributed and they receive world acclaim, it will be almost impossible to stand against the founders, Kavidas and Stein."

Kathy was visibly shaken. "This is a nightmare. You must come with me—never mind the danger. David, Brandon, and Louie will take you to the police; they'll protect you."

"No. I've thought this out. I put myself in this predicament, and I cannot involve or endanger your family. I'm going to fly back to New York tonight and resume my real life as Krissy Kramer, probation officer. No more Linda Martin. My investigative work is over."

Kathy held her hand. "We love you and want you to be safe."

"I'll be fine. Don't worry." She started to leave when she remembered something. "Rainbow has an informer who goes by the name Watchman. He must be close to us since he knew about me from some unidentified source. Be alert. He is a dangerous person who will probably play Rainbow against anybody who will offer him the right price. He's like a double agent." She kissed Kathy good-bye and added, "God bless you."

Kathy stood and watched a great blue heron gracefully fly over the dirt road as Krissy sped away.

At the congested intersection of Route 441 and Wiles Road, Krissy pulled over and put her emergency flashers on. She walked behind her car with her cell phone, dialed 911, and waited for the operator to answer. Then she placed the phone on the ground by the roadway and drove away.

Relief and accomplishment pervaded Krissy's thoughts as she drove to her apartment. *Don't look back. Just look ahead*, she thought. *A new life is emerging back in New York.*

She darted from her car, then scrambled up the staircase to her second floor apartment. Ironically, she turned the handle before inserting the key. When she realized the door wasn't locked, she froze. *Did I accidentally leave this open on my way out to meet Kathy?* She slowly opened the door, stuck her head in, and saw that all was quiet. Breathing easy, she entered her kitchen, checked her time, then reached into the cabinet and stuffed some potato chips in her mouth. She glanced around to decide what had to be packed, then walked into the bedroom.

"Hello, Ms. Kramer. I've been waiting for you," Kimsley said as he walked away from the window toward her.

Krissy jumped, then instinctively grabbed her dusting powder can from her dresser and threw it at him, hitting him square in the head. She rotated and ran for the front door, only to be met by a black man pointing a gun and walking toward her.

"Where is the vial, Ms. Kramer?" Kimsley demanded.

"You're too late, you two-bit thugs! Any evidence I had is safely in the hands of those who can close down Rainbow."

"Who did you deliver the vial to, Ms. Kramer?" Kimsley pressed.

"You red-haired worm! As if I would tell you," Krissy sneered. Her eyes darted toward the door. She had left it open. She reflexively kicked the black man in the groin, toppling him to the floor. The gun flew into the corner as she made her move.

"Stay where you are!" Kimsley demanded.

Without looking back she ran out the door and vaulted the railing, but Kimsley's trained killer instinct caught up with her just as she was about to jump to the ground below.

"Help!" she screamed.

No one heard it.

Before she could utter another word, he muffled her mouth and dragged her back into the apartment. "Our conversation is over," Kimsley said as he nodded to Lester, the black man, who grabbed her by the head and twisted it sharply until he heard a crack.

She gasped as she fell to the floor....

Kimsley and Lester carried Krissy to her bed. "Torch the place. I'll meet you in the car." Lester nodded, then methodically stuffed old newspapers in the sofa cushions and set them on fire. He walked to the kitchen stove, blew out the pilot light, and turned the gas jets on full before leaving.

In slightly over a half hour, the explosion ripped through the apartment complex.

When Sydelle read about Krissy's death in the newspaper the next morning, she typed her resignation to Mr. Kavidas and mailed it to Rainbow.

FIVE

Forsake not an old friend;
for the new is not comparable to him:
a new friend is as new wine;
when it is old, thou shalt drink it with pleasure.
Apocrypha Ecclesiasticus 9:10

Brandon's entrance to his father's office was interrupted by the sound of his father's laughing. It wasn't so much that he didn't hear it often. He just didn't hear it in the presence of Sam Barrett. The last time Brandon had spoken to Dr. Barrett, he was digging around the Dead Sea. The time before that, he'd been unearthing a startling discovery in ancient Canaan. Now he was supposed to be dazzling the world from Pompeii. It was hard to keep up with him, and as successful as his own father was, he always felt awed in the presence of Sam Barrett. Unfortunately, his appearances rarely meant good news.

Walking through the door stopped the laughter, but he was still greeted with big smiles. Brandon walked over and clasped his dad's arm as Dr. Barrett put his arm around his shoulder. The wiry little man made up in character what he lacked in stature.

"Can't believe it's really you, son. It's been too long." Dr. Barrett looked at Brandon with remorse. He'd told Matthew many times that Brandon was the son he would never have. Never could have. *You can't serve two masters,* was the line Matthew would always feed him. And Sam knew he was right. His love for history and archaeology had captivated him long ago and became his only love. But seeing Brandon always brought joy. And regret.

"It's only been too long if you have good news," Brandon began jokingly. "I'm starting to think of you as the raven. Every visit is like an omen." His smile faded as he saw the serious look pass between Sam and

117

his father. He realized quickly that his feeble attempt at humor had struck too close to home. He motioned to have them both sit and quickly put his briefcase down. "Dad, what is it?"

"Brandon, you know that Sam has been working over in Pompeii for some time, don't you?"

"Of course. Everyone knows it. The whole world has been following his progress. What could you discover in Pompeii that's so bad? The place is so old, and there's been digging going on there for...well, it seems like forever." Brandon's thoughts jumbled, something that had been happening quite a lot lately, and he realized that he may in fact be out of touch with what was happening in the world. His focus had been so intensely placed close to home.

"You're right," Dr. Barrett answered. "People have been digging there for years. But until recently, some of the findings have been meaningless because we had no frame of reference. Now we do."

"I'm not sure I understand," Brandon said.

"Well, say you were living in the 17th century and found a can opener. What would you think of it?" The doctor's eyes lifted.

Brandon ran with the thought. "I imagine I would not know what it was, since there were no cans at the time."

"Precisely. That's exactly what we've experienced. Many of the writings and the pictures that have been discovered have been neatly catalogued and put away. Because no one really knew what they were talking about. I think I do."

A grand pause filled the air, and Brandon's mind raced with possibilities. Who could limit the outcome of a man that discovers new treasures from the past every day?

No one spoke, and Brandon looked at his father for help. For a change, his father did not offer anything that would make it easier for him. Brandon looked back to Barrett and shook his head. "Well, are you going to tell me or keep me in suspense with the rest of the world? I assume they don't know either."

"They do not, and I am here for that reason. To discuss with your father the possibility of telling them. Or not. There are strong arguments either way. The impact could be severe. The evidence is quite overwhelming."

"Sam, let's not make a movie. What is it?" Brandon squirmed in his seat. Nerves always brought out a subtle and dry humor.

"Brandon, I have reason to believe that the population of Pompeii was dying before the volcano ever erupted. In fact, they were dying horrible, painful deaths. We've always known that the state of affairs was chaotic before Vesuvius put the place on the map. Now it looks like we've figured out why. They were sick, they were dying, and the rest of the world was keeping away from them."

Brandon was listening intently, his mental prowess kicking into high gear. "I still don't see what the big secret is. They were lepers? It was fairly common in those days. Why the big decision? Most people don't think of leprosy as a real threat today."

"It's not leprosy," Matthew said as he came over to his son's side. "The people were dying of AIDS." A hand came down on Brandon's shoulder as he took in the shock.

"It's impossible. How could they have had AIDS then? Everything we've heard. Everything we've read. It all says it's new. Brand new. That's why it's so hard to beat. It's…" He trailed off, then blurted, "I just can't believe it!"

The two older men drew back as Brandon absorbed this latest development. Matthew turned to Barrett and nodded gravely. "Sam, it's too risky. I think it's too early to spring this on the world at large. There's too much at stake and—"

"Matthew, it goes beyond that," Barrett inserted. "What about the world's right to know? What about all the people that are punishing themselves today for what is happening? Do we have the right to make that decision?" His expression revealed his pain and grief.

Brandon quickly recovered from his personal shock when he saw that these two men were contemplating releasing this knowledge to the people at large. It overwhelmed him.

"My dear old friend," Matthew started, "we live in perilous times. All I know is that we are accountable for what we do and for what we say. Before we unleash this on the world, I want us to have proof—beyond a shadow of a doubt—and a reasonable theory as to why or how it happened. Don't we have the same responsibility to avoid a panic in the populace that will be fueled by wild speculation and creative attempts to reinvent history? Listen to me, Sam. You came here to ask my advice. Here it is. Wait a little while longer." Sam was looking at Matthew, and Brandon noticed he hadn't even blinked the entire time his father spoke.

Sam broke contact first and walked toward the window that overlooked the street below. "You don't understand. I'm scared, and I'm nervous. Knowledge is a powerful and dangerous weapon." He took a quarter out of his pocket and aimlessly tossed it in his left hand. "I came here to ask you, but I don't know if I really want to listen. I know too much, and I'm afraid to learn any more." He absently replaced the coin in his pocket and turned back to Matthew as Brandon looked on in fascination.

"You mean there's more?" asked Matthew, a little surprised.

"I don't know. But I think there may be. Now that I know what we found in Pompeii, I started to think back on some of the unexplained things we've found in the past. I think there may be a connection." He scratched his beard in frustration.

Brandon started to squirm again. "What do you mean a connection? With the disease or Pompeii in general? What do you remember?" He stood up and moved to the other side of the room and turned around to face the men again.

"Sam, we've come this far together," Matthew said gently. "Tell us what you mean."

The doctor gave Matthew a wan smile and turned back to the window. "Now that I know they were talking about AIDS, I realized something else." He took a deep breath. "This isn't the first time I've seen it. I've come across it before." He waited for the information to settle. Then he turned and faced his audience, as bravely as he could muster.

"Are you sure?" Matthew whispered, looking startled for the first time.

"Yes, about seeing it before, and no about being sure. I'd have to go back and research it. Dig around, verify my facts and my suspicions. I never pursued it before. It didn't seem important."

"Well, it does now," Matthew said firmly. "Don't you see? That confirms what I said before. We need more facts, more proof. More research! Go back and verify what you suspect. Then maybe you'll be in a position for an announcement when you are sure about everything."

Barrett narrowed his eyes and looked at Matthew, as if waiting for the rest of the plan. Was this a maneuvering tactic to make him stall the announcement?

But, clearly, Matthew was speaking earnestly. He meant what he said, and he would back it up.

"All right then," the doctor said with composure, "I'll do just that. I'll go back and verify my suspicions and weigh the facts—with your support, of course."

The tension broke and Matthew smiled. Now it was just a matter of closing the deal.

"You sly fox! Has all this been a ploy for me to finance another dig?" Matthew went to his friend and grabbed his hand. "You know I'll always support you."

"I know. Of course. And I wish it was just that. Another way to prolong my work and further my career." A hint of sadness was added to his voice as he turned back to Brandon. "Tell me, young man, what do you have to say? Do you agree with your father? Should I go back and verify my thoughts?"

Brandon thought hard but quick before he answered. He knew better than to speak a thought off the top of his head with these two old sages. "Of course I agree with him. He's my father. You need to go right away. All I want to know is what the climate is at this time of year. Is it very hot?"

Sam looked at Matthew and shrugged, as if to say that every time the generation gap seemed to disappear, a new gap would make itself known.

"For heaven's sake, Brandon, what difference does that make? Haven't you listened to what Sam has been saying?"

"Of course, Dad. I've listened to every word. That's why I want to know."

"Why?" asked Sam with curiosity. "Why do you want to know the climate? Do you think it might be related?"

Matthew, arms folded across his chest, waited for the answer.

"No, not at all. I wanted to know the climate so I know how to pack."

"Pack what?" Sam asked.

Matthew groaned as if he didn't feel well and turned away.

"My suitcase. What did you think? I'm going with you."

Sam looked askance at Matthew. Then he turned back to Brandon. "Are you sure?"

"I'm very sure. I have a personal stake in the matter." Brandon stared at Sam, refusing to give in. His father wouldn't object—couldn't object. He was going.

"All right then. We'll find out together."

Brandon sighed and got ready to leave. There was no time to waste, and there was a lot to do. He looked at this father, knowing he would object later, but it wouldn't affect his decision or the outcome. When Brandon turned to say good-bye, he realized that his question had still not been answered. "So, how is the climate? Where are we going?"

"You mean you haven't figured it out?" Barrett began. "You better pack for warm weather. And bring good shoes for hard work. This is not going to be easy."

Brandon nodded and made a mental note. "But where are we going?"

"Oh, of course. You have a right to know. We're going to the Dead Sea."

Normally Mort felt confident about his meetings with Gregory and didn't feel the slightest apprehension. Not so today.

Wanting every advantage, he had asked Gregory to come to his house to discuss his proposal and to make any last-minute changes to Project Renaissance. The need for urgency was increasing, and with it, the need for accuracy and timing. Mort just hoped that Gregory would agree.

While Mort used his natural ability to influence people to get where he was, he knew Gregory climbed an entirely different ladder to the top. Bringing home his point was not easy when the man it was directed to was born with an innate genius to succeed. But he knew it was essential that they followed his plan. And he knew that the idea didn't come just from within himself.

"Mr. Kavidas here to see you, Mr. Stein," the butler announced, forcing him to abandon his attempt to plan his strategy. He knew it was pointless anyway. Gregory may put up a fight, but he always *knew* what should happen. And he did it right.

"Gregory, come in. Come in. It's been too long since you've taken advantage of my hospitality." Mort noticed immediately that Gregory was traveling alone. A prospect he often found courageous but alarming.

"Mort, you are too kind. What do you have in mind that we have to meet tonight? We could've discussed it at the office today or at worst tomorrow." Gregory moved toward the bar and motioned to the valet waiting to pour his usual drink.

"I wanted to discuss this with you away from the office. This is important."

Gregory took a sip of his drink and smiled. "And what we normally do is not important? Come, tell me. What urgent message do you bring me that we need to discuss it here? I trust you've had the room tested to verify that we are not being bugged?"

Mort smiled since he knew that nothing could compare with the security that existed around the office. Rainbow had state-of-the-art security that only big money could buy. It was times like this that he appreciated Gregory's humor and his propensity for making a situation lighter than it was.

"I'm through with tests," Mort announced, "and I'm ready to move on to the real thing. It's time we got involved with a group that will bring us some national recognition and the audience we need to complete our plan." He watched as Gregory scowled. The words *group* and *audience* were enough to bring on a dose of the hives. But he knew when to come through and how to captivate a crowd.

"I don't know. I think it may be too early to affiliate ourselves with any one group." Suddenly he looked so miserable.

"One group!" Mort yelled. "One group! Who's talking about one group? I'm talking about a dozen or maybe two. What is this one group stuff? Honestly, Gregory, what are you thinking? You know we need to get ourselves into the public eye as much as possible." He looked at Kavidas incredulously and turned away. But he smiled. This was just what he had hoped for.

"Well, what do you suggest? You want me to sponsor a group and see what happens?" He seemed contrite, and Mort knew he meant it.

"I mean, we should support and sponsor a group that will be bigger than itself in the next few years. You need to be recognized. So that everyone knows who you are." *There, I've said it,* he thought. *Now the worst he can do is yell and object.*

"You're right about that," he countered.

Mort couldn't believe it. He thought, *Would it be this easy?* "Well, then, let's get you involved with something high profile. You can associate with G-Men or GLAAD."

Gregory looked at him confusedly and shook his head. "Why those two? They aren't the only ones. Why does it have to be a gay and lesbian association?" He looked at Mort with such pleading that Mort almost felt sorry for him and gave in. Almost. But he knew it was time to begin, and the queasy stomach need not apply.

"Why? Have you given any thought as to who is mostly affected by the disease?"

Realization that this was the only choice settled on Gregory's face. "Of course I am aware, and that's fine. Let's do as you say and start being a support group. Just let me know how the reaction is."

"The time is ripe now. This is when we win—when the ball is in our court. Let's not stop here. Push on, be the senator, run for office." Mort's enthusiasm was only interrupted by Gregory's laugh.

"Mort, you're getting carried away again. I have a different idea."

The phone rang.

"The office." Mort grimaced as he handed him the receiver.

Gregory smiled as he answered.

"Mr. Kavidas, I think a foreign country is on the other line," his secretary, Marion, announced. "I can't understand what the operator is saying. They won't hang up. I don't know what to do. Do you want me to put you on a conference call?"

"Yes, thank you," Gregory replied, then shot a look at Mort. "Gregory Kavidas," he announced.

"*Kalemera, kyrie,*" the caller responded.

"Greece," he mouthed to Mort as he listened to the operator's whining voice.

Mort walked over to the window as Gregory chatted in the background. Most people have trouble speaking their own language, but Gregory spoke six with ease.

After several minutes, a somber Gregory replaced the phone. "Mort, we'll have to postpone any more conversation on politics, groups, and whatnot. I've got some calls to make."

"What happened? Family crisis?"

"Larger than that I'm afraid. That was the prime minister. He wants me to loan the Bank of Greece several million British pounds."

Mort looked astonished. "The government borrows from you?"

"In a way. Really, I'm just protecting my own interests. If the government collapses, so do all my holdings. And I've had to put some of the more delicate Middle Eastern holdings into a more governmental setting. The government works with me, and I return the favor."

Gregory took a number from the book in his vest pocket and grabbed the phone. "Marion, get me this number in Italy and let me know as soon as someone answers the line. They may answer in Italian; just say *moment, graci* and put me on conference again." He gave her the number and turned back to Mort.

"You look rather pensive. Is it just a matter of money, or does this go deeper?" Mort realized that his own world, complicated as it seemed, apparently didn't have the gravity attached to it the way Gregory's did.

"You might say that it involves a network I began setting up years ago. By placing major deposits in foreign banks, purchasing real estate in various areas, I've managed to put my fingers very deep into some big pies. Now the time has come to go in up to my elbow." His usual smile was not visible, and for the first time Mort thought he saw doubt in Gregory's mind.

"It seems like the most logical next step. You can't very well back out."

"Precisely," Gregory intoned, "and that's what I'm concerned with now. At this point, if I pull out I lose a finger, maybe two. Now I'm starting to risk my arm. It's a little different. The web is starting to get a little sticky."

Mort was unable to ask his next question. Marion's voice came over the phone rather confidently. "Italy, sir."

"Good job, *Marion*," he said quickly, emphasizing the name.

"*Bonjourno, Tonio.*" Gregory's face remained serious as he listened to the response. Mort was surprised when he continued in English. "I   need you to transfer enough lira to the Bank of England so I can have my man there wire some money."

Mort was fascinated and listened carefully but with a handicap. He only heard Gregory's responses. "Yes, that's right. Enough for eight million pounds...yes, you do the conversions and send me a confirmation...no, no, it must be done today. You have him call me if that's a problem." Gregory paused and began to look through his Rolodex again. "Just mention that incident with the sheik from Omar and he'll quiet down...you bet. Okay,

125

Tonio. I knew I could count on you." He put down the phone.

"That's it?" Mort asked. "You saved the country—with one call?"

"Except to tell my man in England about the transfer, yes." He looked somewhat surprised at Mort's astonishment.

"Why did you talk in English?"

"I always talk to my people abroad in a language that is not native when I give special instructions. It's part of my code."

"What about the man in England?"

"I'll talk to him in French, of course."

Of course, thought Mort, *how did I miss that? What else would you speak to an Englishman when rescuing a whole nation?* "Does this affect our plans? Should we curtail our progress on Project Renaissance for a while?" Mort asked.

A look of annoyance flickered across Gregory's face. "Mort, we're not running a department store. Don't be absurd. Continue full speed. This is just a minor inconvenience—which may just be the catalyst I was waiting for to pull in some markers in Europe." He picked up the phone and started to dial again. "Don't worry. This will push us along only quicker."

Mort smiled wanly. *One decision, one phone call to rescue an entire country?* He listened to Gregory instruct Marion to put a call through to England. *Why do I feel surprised after all I've seen? After all we've done?*

After the calls, Gregory excused himself and left for his office.

The real question is, thought Mort anxiously, *what will he do next?*

Matthew sat in his den, gazing at the portrait of his deceased wife while Sam Barrett fixed them each a brandy. Matthew thought about what Deidre would say to him if he could tell her Brandon was going across the world with Sam. He smiled. Fond memories went through his head as he gazed at his good friend. The man who was taking his son to chase an idea. Perhaps a dream. He sighed and placed his hand lovingly on the ornate frame of the large portrait and thought back to the day Deidre told him she would never trust Sam again....

They were sitting in church, the three of them thick as thieves, quietly waiting for the sermon to be over. "Matt," Sam asked quietly, looking slyly at Deidre, "do you know what I heard yesterday?"

Matt looked at him nervously, knowing his father would be angry if they got caught talking in church. But Sam had whispered his question, so no one else heard. Except Deidre. She looked quickly at Sam, and Matt blanched. Deidre was beautiful, and Matt had always known it. But what a look she could give when she was mad!

"You be quiet, Sam Barrett," Deidre hissed quietly, "or I'll never talk to you again!"

This caused Sam to smile even broader, and his smug look quickly showed he had won this round. Now he knew that Matt hadn't heard. A complete victory.

"It seems our partner has developed an interest in boys," Sam whispered, his eyes straight ahead.

Matt never turned to look at his best friend but could see from the corner of his eye that he was gloating. From the other corner he had seen Deidre's mouth drop open. Her face grew red as she glared at Sam in shocked outrage. The boys kept looking ahead, never taking their eyes off the pastor.

Matt choked as he tried to suppress his laughing. Sam probably knew that Matt wouldn't be upset by this news—surprised maybe but not angry. Deidre seemed more upset about Matt finding out than he did. Matt was starting to find the whole episode amusing. Sitting in the middle of the two of them, Matt was caught in the crossfire.

"You shut up, Sam Barrett! You don't know what you're talking about." Deidre's eyes pleaded with Sam, and Matt could see her looking at him next, trying to see what his reaction was.

This only egged Sam on further. "Well, I'm only talking about what I saw," he muttered, smartly keeping his voice down.

Matt gave a perfunctory look around to see if there was anyone taking notice of the small conversation taking place in the seventh pew. So far, no one was paying them any attention.

"You say one more word, and I'll never trust you again," Deidre said, this time a little louder than before.

Mrs. Duncan turned around from the row in front of them and gave them a shush with her finger over her mouth.

Deidre turned back to face the front and look directly at the pastor.

Matt threw a hazardous glance at Deidre, like he was taking a great risk by turning his head away from the direction of the podium. Their eyes briefly met, and he could see a tear forming in her eye. His heart string pulled, and he regretted allowing Sam to go on. Especially since Sam had already told him about the kiss. In fact, Sam had run all the way to his house last night just to let him know. At 13, a kiss is a big thing, but Matt thought it could have waited till the morning. Now he wished he had never heard about it. Besides, it didn't seem as if Deidre was allowing it to affect their trio. She met them outside church this morning like she always did. Everything seemed the same.

"Deidre," Matt began, "don't worry about it." He saw her close her eyes and turn away from him. *What did that mean?* He was hoping that would make her feel better.

"Yeah, Dee," Sam smirked, as he did the unthinkable and leaned over Matt to whisper at Deidre, "it was only a little kiss."

Matt heard Deidre gasp, and then she jumped up. "Sam Barrett, you're a liar. You promised! I'll never trust you again!"

That did it. Both boys slumped down immediately to avoid attention. But it could not be helped. Matt saw his parents look at him, and he knew he was going to have some explaining to do. The pastor paused in his homily, and the eyes of the whole church slowly panned to the trio, one of which was now making a quick exit, rather in a dramatic state of an elaborate huff.

To Matt's chagrin, Deidre tripped as she left the pew, almost falling over Mr. O'Brien's big feet. It was the last straw. The nervous tension was too much for the boys, and they couldn't help but laugh. They began to giggle uncontrollably, almost falling out of their seats as they clutched their sides.

Matt knew that later he would pay for this, but for now the moment was too funny to ignore. There was always time to make up with his parents and with Deidre. It was Sam that Matt was worried about. His chances of being forgiven were a little slim. But maybe someday Deidre would trust him again. He just knew it would take a long time....

"Come on, Matthew. Don't get melancholy."

He smiled as he remembered his friend's prank. He put his hand out as Sam passed him a crystal goblet filled with steaming coffee and heavy cream. Another reminder of Deidre's presence and her continual elegance.

"Not a chance, my friend," he replied as he softened his smile and raised his glass in salute. "To a successful and informative trip."

"I'll drink to that."

The men settled by the large sitting area and faced the crackling hearth. Minutes passed as they rested in the quiet and enjoyed the fact that no one had to speak. That kind of friendship was far too rare.

"Sam," Matthew began almost hesitantly, "do you really think you'll find a clue? Is it too much to hope for?"

Sam took another sip and exhaled with a grand sigh. "You know, I'd like to say it will be easy. But it won't. The Dead Sea has been picked over many times. But that's not where I'm placing my bet." For the first time a twinkle hit Sam's eye, and Matthew pounced on it.

"Where do you think your best answer is? If it's not the Dead Sea, then where?" All melancholy aside, Matthew began to forget about the hectic pace and the fast moving chain of events that comprised his life. Now he wanted answers.

"Well, most people go to the Dead Sea and look for Sodom and Gomorrah. They are, after all, the most famous of the cities that were in the area."

"What for? Going out with a bang?"

Sam laughed softly, then evidently caught Matthew's serious, apprehensive tone. "Famous historically. You know, the Bible stories, the tales we're told as kids, the movies. No one ever talks about the other cities of the day. There were several, you know."

Matthew gave him a look of consternation and dropped his shoulders. "Of course I know there were others. What's your point?"

"My point is simple. In the mad rush to uncover Sodom, many historians and archaeologists have overlooked the fact that other cities existed of equal importance. Or significance. I'm looking for a reference to one of those. I want to uncover something of the Canaanites that will link me to Sodom. I want to work in reverse."

Matthew nodded and digested the information. "I understand the link, but why do you have an interest in the Canaanites? If Sodom is the ticket, why not go after that first?"

"First! How can I be first when hundreds have looked for the city and never actually found it? I've seen information, which I've discounted in the past, which may lead me to Canaan. Then I may find out some information that is worthwhile. It may even point to Sodom. But Sodom itself," he said as he raised his glass, "that's almost impossible to get to. It's under the sea. And no one has been able to get to it. So far, no one has had the reason to really try." He took another sip of his drink.

"What's so interesting about the Canaanites that you feel it will relate to your findings in Pompeii?"

Sam smiled at Matthew's attempt to bring the conversation back to the issue at hand and his uncanny ability to zero in on the problem. *Now I know why he gets so much done.*

"The Canaanites were known for their perverse lifestyle. The Bible refers to them several times and indicates that they were reprobate and would do just about anything to satisfy their lust. Kind of like it is today."

The slight humor appeared to catch Matthew by surprise. "I know the Bible is important to archaeologists, helping you find cities and landmarks. But the lust and perverse lifestyle? What does that have to do with it? Seems like the reference is a little out of character dealing with an archaeological dig."

"Are you kidding?" Sam almost choked as he tried to answer Matthew calmly. "You've been supporting my expeditions for years and don't know that we use the Bible for a reference?"

"I know," Matthew said simply, "but do you really need to use it to zero in on the reprobate cultures of the day? Can't anyone unearth a city that was filled with people that were just normal or not completely perverted?"

"Well, as you know there isn't much mention of the cities that housed the good people. It describes the areas and gives landmarks, and it's always right. Unfortunately, most of the ancient cities were evil, and they were destroyed. I'm not trying to uncover the sins of the cities. Just the cities themselves! So we look in the Bible. You can't ask for more than that unless you call Rand & McNally."

"What are you thinking?" Matthew asked. "That the lifestyle of the Canaanites caused their destruction? Similar to the way it destroyed Sodom and Gomorrah? You think they're related?"

"I'm not sure. But I think we will find some link. And when we do, we'll be tracking it down. We'll have some answers. I just hope the world will be ready for them."

"Me too," Matthew said quickly, "but more important is my son. Take care of him and make sure that he comes home soon. With or without the information you want to find." Matthew smiled and raised his glass in final salute.

Sam returned the gesture and swallowed hard. "Matthew, we've been friends for a long time."

"Yes, we have. And?"

"Well, I just want you to know something. You know I love you and your family. We've all loved each other since we were kids."

"I know, Sam. You've been there for us through everything. I could never have gotten through Deidre's death without you."

Sam paused and debated whether or not to continue. He took another sip of his coffee and went on. "Matt, I think it's time you confront Brandon. You can't ignore what he feels. We might disagree with it, but you have to face it." Sam saw Matthew turn away and look back over toward the portrait on the wall. This was the only time Sam ever saw Matthew look defeated—when he talked about Brandon and the fact that he was a homosexual.

"I can't, Sam. You know I can't." It was that simple. A resigned statement that seemed to have no need for further discussion.

Sam saw the raw emotion that rippled across Matthew's forehead. Having had this discussion with Matthew before, Sam was inclined to disengage. However, he knew he had to persevere and press forward. This trip was going to be a long and arduous one. He knew he had to say these things. If not for Brandon and for Matthew, then for Deidre. As if he owed her. Before she died she had entrusted them to his care. He had failed her once with her trust, and she had finally forgiven him. He had resolved never to do it again.

"Matt," he said, "you can't blame yourself. You didn't do anything. And neither has he. He's just a sinner like the rest of us. He's no different. Only lost. You've got to help him find his way. You're his father. You're his friend."

Matthew turned back to his friend and nodded. "I know you're right. I just need time."

"I've been doing some studying, and I really feel that things are happening in the world today at a rapid pace. Matt, this is something you already know." He paused to gauge the reaction in Matthew's face before continuing. "I think it's all part of a plan—God's plan—and I think that he is bringing things about to show us that we are nearing the beginning of the end. We just have to read the signs."

"'The beginning of the end,'" Matthew repeated.

"The end of what we know—the world as we know it," Sam said seriously. "The beginning of the time where God calls the shots—and they are all big hits. No more little stuff. This is the end."

When Matthew looked away, Sam felt he better not say anymore for now. Matthew would search his own self and see the truth in his friend's words.

"You may be right, Sam. You may be wrong. Right now I can't think beyond tomorrow. And I know I need some answers, and you're the man to find them for me. Bring them back to me—with my son—and let me know where we stand. Then place God in his rightful perspective, and we'll talk."

"Good enough, old friend. And don't worry. I'll look out for Brandon. He'll be safe. And he'll be back." Sam winked at Matthew and moved toward the door. "Time to call it a night."

Matthew moved to do the same and paused once more in front of Deidre's portrait. He looked at her as if she'd been listening and would now enter her opinion on the subject. "I know you would be more cautious, Dee. But we're living in scary times, and I'm afraid to take it slow. And for that, I miss you terribly." He smiled at the painting and closed the screen on the open fireplace to go upstairs to his room. He passed Brandon's suite of rooms on the way to his own and couldn't help pausing at the door.

Go with God, my son, and may he be the one to show you and Sam what we need to know. Without his help, I'm afraid you'll be gone for a long time. Too long.

David stood motionless and stared at the screen of Krissy's PDA for a long time.

Kathy sat rigid at his side. She had cried all the tears that she could and had played the scene in her mind over and over. But nothing would bring Krissy back. And that was what bothered her and David the most. Nothing they could do would change the past. And at the moment the future was not looking bright.

"Go over with me again, Kathy, what Krissy told you about this Watchman character. How did they find out about her?"

Kathy wiped her eyes again, then covered her forehead with her damp palm. "David, I just can't! She only said the Watchman was dangerous and that he knew about her. She had no clue as to who he was or what he was going to do. Please, I just can't go over it again. Not now." She broke down again.

David knew that it was pointless to continue. In truth, he didn't have the heart to ask any more questions. He was relieved when the door bell rang, and Hillary came running in.

"Daddy, it's Uncle Brandon."

Brandon rushed over to David, took him in a big bear hug, and walked over to Kathy. "I'm so sorry. I don't know what to say."

Kathy just nodded and allowed Brandon to console her as best he could. "It's just so unbelievable," Kathy blurted out. "Not long ago we were all together. First Johnnie and now Krissy. And," she said as she started sobbing, "I'm afraid. What if one of us is next?"

David took her by the arm and led her out of the room.

Brandon gathered Hillary onto his lap as David and Kathy left the room. He could see the little girl's fear and confusion and lightly stroked her hair. "Don't worry, sweetie. Mommy will be all right. Daddy will take her and let her have a nap, and she will feel better."

Hillary's big brown eyes widened as she considered Brandon. "Is it because Aunt Krissy isn't coming back?"

Brandon just smiled and wondered at the simplistic way children view life—and death. He questioned how adults so totally screwed things up that they couldn't take it for what it was. A passing to a better world. *God knows anything is better than right here, right now.* "Yes, honey. It's because Mommy will miss Aunt Krissy. But she knows that now she is in heaven, and she is happy about that. She's just sad she won't see her for a while."

Hillary nodded, as if in complete understanding, and patted Brandon's arm. She got up and went back to her room to play and to be a kid.

Suddenly, Brandon felt strangely comforted. *And to think I was trying to console her.*

Just then David reentered the room. "It's been tough on Hillary, Bran. And Kathy is beside herself."

Brandon moved toward his friend and put his arm around his shoulder. "I see that Kathy is taking it very hard. But you don't have to worry about Hillary. She's tougher than you might think. And maybe smarter, too." He smiled, and David smiled back as he settled in on the couch.

"Are you here about the test results?" David asked. "Has the lab finished with the sample?"

Brandon's smile vanished. "David, only the preliminary work is done. It seems to be what we thought, a primary viral vaccine. Rainbow has done that much. They crossed the species' barrier and have come up with an inoculant that will prevent the spread of the disease. For now."

"I'm sorry, Brandon. I know you had hoped Lane would come up with a cure first." He reached over to Brandon who pulled his arm back—almost too sharply.

Brandon's words rushed out. "Cure? Lane? This has nothing to do with competition! Don't you see what's happened? They have a vaccine. It is not a cure. Don't you know what that means?"

David paused. "I guess I don't. What's so bad about the vaccine? Think of the people that will live because of it."

"That's just it," Brandon cried. "You're not thinking of all the people that are going to die." He grabbed David's arm. "Rainbow is not interested in a cure or they would be continuing with their research and not looking to go public with this find. Think of all the people that have AIDS now. What is going to happen to them?"

Silence reigned for a moment, then David said, "I still don't understand. The ones that have AIDS—can't they take the vaccine? What's the difference?"

Brandon shook his head. "No, no, *no*. The vaccine is just a *preventative*. The people with AIDS will continue with it. They'll die and that will be the end of them."

"Well, isn't that what you expected?" David asked hesitantly.

"No, we didn't want to doom them to die! We wanted to develop a serum, to arrest and reverse the disease. We didn't just want a vaccine. That's just the first step."

"So why not keep going?" Dave asked casually. "What's to stop you from proceeding to stage two?"

Brandon shook his head. "You just don't get it. This disease is not like typhoid; it's not like cholera or TB. The populace doesn't care about the people with AIDS. They only want to prevent it from spreading. Now that there is a vaccine, the public will want to stop fighting the AIDS problem. They won't want to carry it through to its conclusion. In short, they don't care about the people who have it. They'd just as soon let them die. They feel *those people* deserve it."

"All of us don't want them to die just because they're homosexual, Brandon. Some of us love them, too. That includes you, too."

The last-minute correction and the love and compassion on David's face was just enough to make Brandon smile and throw back his head in relief. "Thanks. Sometimes I just need to hear you say that." He stood up, grabbed two drinks from the counter, and offered one to David. When David accepted he took both glasses back to the couch and sat down.

"What do we do now?" David asked. "Do we go public?"

Brandon almost choked on his iced tea. "Public? Absolutely not. That would only make things worse and may even play into their hands."

"I don't see how," David stated, "when they're going to go public themselves anyway. Why not expose them?"

"As what," Brandon said, "the heroes of the decade? It will only make them look better to the world! We don't have any evidence linking them to Johnnie's death—at least nothing that would stand up—so the authorities would only laugh. Aside from that, it will take even more time away from us, while we're looking for a cure, a serum—anything to help all the afflicted. The government will stop funding universities, and the pressure will subside. No, we have to wait."

David ingested this information. "What does your father say?" he asked after a moment's reflection. "Does he think we should wait?"

"Yes," Brandon said with animation, "for the very reasons he stated in the beginning of this nightmare. Rainbow is trying to avoid the FDA, the normal channels, and giving them the means to run to the press with their discovery will only hasten the distribution of their vaccine, and put the brakes on everything else."

"But we can't just sit by and wait and see. We just can't. There must be something we can do."

"There is," said Brandon guardedly, "but it is going to take everything we've got. And I need your help."

David moved closer as he felt the need for secrecy arising. "You've got it, of course," he whispered. "What should I do?"

"For now, nothing," Brandon whispered back. "The ball is in my court, and I've got to play or give it back. And I want to play. You've got to stay here and lay low. Don't let anyone know what's happened. And I mean no one."

"But why?" David asked curiously. "Why do I have to hide out? We've only told Louie and your father what's happened so far."

"Exactly," Brandon said, looking uncomfortable. "But we don't know who Krissy told. It appears she didn't tell anyone. But she's still dead."

David's eyes widened. His mouth moved into the shape of an O, and he nodded.

"I think we should confine our strategy to no one but ourselves and Louie. You tell Kathy and Louie. I'll tell my father. But that's it, Dave. I mean it. We're putting everything on the line now. We can't take chances on anyone or anything."

"You're right, Bran. No chances. I can't afford them."

The men shook hands and stood up.

"But can you tell me what *you* are doing with the ball?"

Brandon smiled. "Fair enough. I'm leaving for Canaan. My father and Sam Barrett think we may find something of importance that will link us to the disease."

"Barrett—the archaeologist? What does that have to do with this situation?"

Brandon used his hand to motion to David to keep his voice down. "Not so loud. I don't want anyone to know where I'm going." He moved closer to Dave and whispered, "Dr. Barrett has found a link that may tell us where AIDS originated. If we find that out, we may be able to discover how they got rid of it. It may be the thing we need to conquer this thing— the right way. But we need time." He grabbed David's hand and shook it firmly. "Give me the time, and maybe we'll have something to tell the public that won't play into Rainbow's hands. We could use a good break where they're concerned."

"Be careful and keep me posted."

"I wouldn't have it any other way." Brandon moved to go and opened the door. "I won't be leaving for a day or so, and by then the lab should have finished isolating the sample. I'll call you when they do."

David nodded and waved as Brandon moved out toward his car. He thought of Kathy and his children, and his fears mounted. So much was on the line. He thought of the hymn he had heard so many times in church. It gave him comfort as he walked into the bedroom to check on Kathy. *No turning back. No turning back.*

Mort was excited as he entered the lab room beneath Rainbow's corporate facility. The link from *Redisearch* to Rainbow was complete. Everything was ready. *Today Project Renaissance will move toward its next step.* He stopped at the last door, which had no guard or sentry. He placed his palm on the glass to the left of the door and waited while the computer scanned it.

"Prepare for retinal scan," a metallic voice intoned.

Hardly able to contain himself, Mort turned toward the scanner and braced himself for the intrusion. It wasn't so much a feeling as it was a sensation. It caused him to tingle all over as the laser traced his optical pathways to verify his identity.

"Identification confirmed. Stein, Mortimer. Stand clear to enter the classified area." The doors gave way with a hiss and a groan as the great steel giants swung outward.

He entered the lab area and could see the many eyes turned to him, waiting for a sign. "It's magnificent," he cried as the staff cheered his arrival.

Gregory approached him gladly and led him toward a group of anxious men. "I knew you'd be intrigued by the scan. Coupled with your *Masterlink* dot, there will be no way to falsify identification of any kind. Just the kind of proof we needed for our nervous board of directors. The dot alone scared them, thinking people could encode them falsely to impersonate others. With this state-of-the-art retinal scanner, there is no way to beat the system. It keeps getting better and better."

Mort just smiled as Gregory led him toward the waiting men. To see his dream becoming reality so quickly was more than he could absorb. He allowed Gregory to acknowledge the patronage of his partners in this latest venture.

With the latest in technology at their fingertips, the rest of the afternoon was a mere technicality. The board of directors unanimously approved the continuation of Project Renaissance.

Gregory ascended the hastily erected platform to address the small crowd. "Gentleman, we've reached a critical stage in the joining of the world financial and credit market. I have invited the heads of all the European Banks and credit clearing houses to assemble at my estate on Mykonos. With only three weeks to prepare, the island is already busy to accommodate our guests every whim." A sly wink escaped to the crowd, and a light banter could be heard as they discussed the news among themselves.

Gregory gave them a few minutes before continuing; the crowd sensed there was more and no gavel was needed. "We are poised on the brink of our greatest achievement: the AIDS vaccine. Watch as we change the world."

This time the furor was uncontrollable as the board of directors, along with select scientists and Rainbow's chief executives heard the news.

Mort was waiting to find out the one piece of information he lacked. When was it going to be announced?

"I know that all of you are excited," Gregory went on, this time motioning for quiet with his arms, "and you want to know when the news will be made public. We will decide that issue collectively when we are on Mykonos in the presence of the world's financial elite." He stepped off the dais and began to make his rounds as the room congratulated him and offered endless praise.

Except for one man. *Will I be able to tell anyone before we leave for Greece?* he thought. *And more importantly, who will I tell?*

Eddie, Sydelle's husband, was busy doing insurance claims paperwork when she came into his office and sat down. He smiled at her and keyed in the command to print the estimate he was working on so he could give her his full attention.

"So, how are *we* feeling?" His grin widened as he looked at her belly: swollen, distended, and round. He didn't envy her.

"Like I'm going to explode," she replied congenially. "*You* wouldn't understand." She patted her stomach and looked back at Eddie, who took it somewhat as a challenge.

"About the belly or the part about exploding?"

"Neither," said Sydelle, starting to pout when she didn't get the response she expected.

"Well, the pregnancy part I have to agree with you. But the exploding part, well, lately it seems I'm beginning to be an expert." He heard the printer cycle off and turned to remove his completed estimate from the tray. "I've just finished adjusting another explosion not too far from here. Take a look. Total loss to the whole place." He handed the report to Sydelle.

She sighed. "Oh, Eddie, it's not another one of those propane tanks, is it? I'm afraid to barbecue—you've had so many claims like that. What are they making them out of, cheap tin?"

"No, no, no," he said quickly, "it wasn't a propane tank. The fire marshal thinks it was the stove. The knobs were left on. After that, spontaneous combustion. That's why we got the electric range, remember?"

Realizing she could still barbecue in relative safety left Sydelle less interested, so she glanced at the report only casually.

Eddie turned back to his computer screen and turned around quickly when he heard a sharp gasp.

"Eddie, do you realize who this is?" she cried. "This estimate is for Krissy Kramer's apartment!"

"Yeah, so? I have 275 claims. Should Krissy Kramer stick out in my mind as someone special?"

Sydelle shook her head and waved him off. Krissy's name caused her to scan the estimate in earnest. She quickly looked up. "Is that it? No report?" She handed it back and looked in expectation to the computer; the cursor blinked methodically but with no reply.

"Yes, I have a report. Why are you so interested in it? Did you know her?" His hands were already flying around the keys to print out his full report.

"Yes, I knew her. She was the one that was supposed to replace me at the office. The one that just…"

"Died," Eddie put in, finishing her thought.

Sydelle nodded and grabbed Eddie's hand urgently. "You've got to look into this for me. There is nothing regular about this claim; I can tell you that. Please send someone to find out what happened."

"Syd, I check out every claim—that's my job. I'm a life and casualty adjuster, remember? But there is nothing suspicious about this claim; believe me. The gas was left on in the stove. Simple as that. I have a cause and origin guy checking it out for sure, but I have a good idea what he's going to tell me."

"Well, you just listen to what I have to tell you for a minute, and then you look a little closer at the facts of this claim. I'm telling you: Krissy was murdered, and the fact that her home exploded at the same time is not a coincidence. And I'm going to do something about it." She looked at him smugly.

He almost started to laugh. "You! Have you gone mad? You are going to do no such thing, my dear. You are going to rest and relax until you have this baby. Then you can go back to playing with your friends and plotting intrigue. Till then, you are out of this loop. If there is something to find, my cause and origin guy will find it. Leave the investigating to the professionals. I'm sure he will be happy to leave the childbirth to you." When Sydelle's eyes narrowed, he realized he'd made a mistake.

"Oh? Is that so? Well, you can take your sexist remarks and go back to your other 274 claims. It's obvious you're missing the boat on this one. I'm telling you there is more than just a leaky knob on a stove." With that, she rose to go but not before a tear sprung from her eye.

"Syd, what are you going to do? Where are you going?" Eddie felt guilty, seeing the tear and knowing that emotions were high toward the end of any pregnancy. And no wonder.

"It looks like nothing and nowhere. Except maybe to the kitchen to do up a few dishes while I leave all the *real work* to you men." She walked away.

Eddie knew she was mad but knew her well enough to know that she was mad about the situation and not really angry with him. He returned to his work and resolved to apologize later. Much later, when she'd cooled off and her thoughts returned again to the big event that was ever more eminent as each hour went by.

When Sydelle reached the kitchen she dabbed her eyes once more for good measure, then turned around to see if she was followed. *Good,* she thought, *he'll think I'm all caught up with that sexist remark, and he'll leave me alone for a few hours. Works every time.* She reached into the closet and took out the recycling bag and quickly found yesterday's paper. She pulled out the obituary section and located Krissy's name. *Yes! Just what I thought!*

She tore off the section she needed and folded everything back up neatly before putting it away. She moved toward the phone and dialed the number for directory assistance. No family members were listed, but the names of the funeral parlor appeared, which would lead her to friends who just might like to know that Krissy's apartment was blown to bits the same time she died. And people that just *might* be able to answer a few of *her* questions as well.

She took the number from the operator, wrote it down, then clutched the paper to her chest. She could feel the baby moving beneath her with the added excitement, and for a moment she felt panic and doubt. But she took a deep breath, which she had trained to do for labor, and began to exorcize her fear.

When she began to feel it was conquered she stared at the number and slowly lifted the phone. *I owe it to you, Krissy—and to my friend Linda.*

The receptionist was friendly and consoling when she asked for the name of the minister who conducted the service or the person who arranged for the funeral. Arrangement information was confidential, but she was able to get the name of the church where the service was conducted, along with the pastor's name.

She stared at the phone a long time, her heart aflutter, and tried to think of the words she would need. Finally, with a look of reservation toward Eddie's office, she picked up the phone and dialed the number. She only realized she'd been holding her breath when someone answered. She quickly exhaled and took a breath so she could speak. "Can I speak with the pastor, please?" she asked weakly, her voice raspy and hoarse with fear.

"Who's calling please?" the girl inquired pleasantly.

"A friend of Ms. Kramer." Sydelle closed her eyes and willed her lungs to expand as she waited for a reply.

The silence pervaded her thoughts. She began to give way to the anxiety and moved toward the phone. *I'll just hang up. No one will know it was me.* With her finger poised on the hook, she slowly inched the receiver away from her ear.

"Hold on please." The voice startled her, and she yanked her hand back from the hook. She gasped and shook slightly as she waited. It wasn't until she heard a man's voice that she began to lose her fears.

"Pastor Jack. How can I help you?"

Listening to tapes with conversation on it was mildly interesting to Mort as he scanned the activity and callers to the Douglas home. For the price he was paying, he hoped he would see results. His source told him that tapping phone lines was very illegal and very expensive. Judging by what he was being charged, this was apparently so.

Trying to hear the caller's words over the television or background noise made him feel like he was going crazy. He thought he would enjoy screening the various callers, but he soon came to realize that the people he was monitoring received phone calls that were, well, just not interesting. By the third day he knew all the voices by name, and by the fourth he was able to listen and work on something else at the same time.

It wasn't until the fifth day that his attention was suddenly drawn to the Douglas home. It wasn't the conversation or the commotion. It was the voice.

"Kathy, it's Louie. I just wanted to confirm the time for the big meeting. Is it still on for tomorrow?"

"Yes, it's still on. Same time. Same place. I told David you were coming. We all feel better about it."

"Good enough. Catch you tomorrow."

Short and sweet, the kind of phone call Mort liked. But something irked him, and he tried to put a face to the voice. And he couldn't. Aside from the fact that something was going on tomorrow that sounded important, Mort knew that the voice was familiar and that he had to do something about it. The fact that he was getting the information from the tape was in itself only mildly rewarding. He needed to turn the information into something useful.

That's it, he thought as he snapped his fingers. *Information! That's how I know the voice.* He quickly dialed Gregory's private line and began to gather his things to leave in a hurry. *Gregory will know how to contact him. These tapes may have been worth it after all.*

Gregory sensed the urgent need for a meeting with Mort. He opened his daily planner and penciled in a note for tomorrow. *Gratuity: investigator— early morning shift.*

SIX

Gregory reached into the mail bins and held up a handful of letters from the thousands Rainbow received after he released the laboratory video to the media. "*Reciprocity* is the key word here, Mort. These gay groups, especially the G-Men organization, have substantial clout in the media, and at the polls. The feedback from our video amply proves that. It's vital that we maintain reciprocity with them in order to meet our objectives. We'll work with them in perfecting the vaccine once it's available, and in exchange they'll help fend off any negative press and expedite launching the inoculation program."

"Together with the public's favorable reaction from the press leak, we should be in a good position," Mort concurred. "Did you expect this kind of a deluge from your advertising?"

"Yes, and that's why we needed the lead time. We've received positive public acceptance of the pending advent of the vaccine, and frankly, we couldn't have asked for a better method of transmission than to have the homosexual community spread the news for us. Free publicity if you will."

They walked from the mail room to Kavidas's office where Gregory led Mort over to the window overlooking the main entrance of Rainbow and pointed at the crowd of protesters carrying posters. "Although I'm delighted at the favorable response from the gay sector, the people down there may be a problem. Right now, they're quiet while they're getting organized. They're waiting for someone to lead them against us."

"Who are they?" Mort asked.

"They're protesting the vaccine's potential of giving license to the homosexual community. Rainbow has also received hundreds of letters since the vaccine's advertisements, mostly from private sources defending the claim that AIDS is a judgment from God to punish gays, maintaining that the vaccine would only promote that lifestyle."

Mort peered off into the distance to take another look at the group parading by the entranceway. There were several hundred dissidents, with cars and vans continuously rolling in to add to their ranks.

Mort assessed the situation quickly. "I've seen protests like this before. They get out of hand very quickly. This could get serious." He took a second look, then said, "There's only one television station covering this. I'm really surprised. Why hasn't there been more newsmen down there?"

"Well, right now publicity isn't a problem, since our connections with the gay network will squelch any bad press for the time being. There is one Christian station down there that's out of Fort Lauderdale, and they barely squeak by, so they're not a major threat. But if this continues to mount, we'll have to reevaluate our strategy and take appropriate action to suppress them."

Mort nodded, walked out of Gregory's office, and waved to Laurie and Leslie, the new girls that had replaced Linda and Sydelle. On the way to the elevator he couldn't help but wonder what action would be necessary to stop the forces mounting to fight the soon-to-be-released vaccine.

The town of Tamarac, a suburb of Fort Lauderdale, is a retirement haven for thousands of Floridans, boasting affordable housing, suitable roadways, close-by shopping, and a vast array of recreation facilities. The town is known for its secure and peaceful environment. Family Foods, part of a south Florida supermarket chain that offers membership bulk discounts, attracts many bargain shoppers with growing families.

Sydelle looked forward to her first day outside with her new baby. "Mommy's taking baby Julie shopping," she said in nursery rhyme. She transferred Julie in the car carrier to a shopping cart, then headed for the entrance.

Suddenly from behind her came a middle-aged homeless man in a soiled suit and tie who grabbed her handbag out of the shopping cart and ran off.

"Help! Police! I've been robbed!" She took little Julie out of the shopping cart and clutched her tightly until a patrolling guard heard her.

"Some man just stole my purse!" she yelled to the guard as she pointed to the parking lot.

The guard spoke into his cell phone as Sydelle broke into hysterics.

"He took the food money for my baby," she cried as a small crowd assembled around her.

An elderly woman put her arm around her and said, "Don't be frightened. The store manager has promised to have armed guards patrolling the parking lot next week, so it will be safe to shop again."

Tamarac's Congregational Church started out as a Bible study group in Jack Hammond's home five years ago and progressed to a double storefront in a shopping strip mall in Tamarac's northwest quadrant. The church not only ministered to the regular families that attended but served as a mission to the homeless and unwed mothers in the area.

Pastor Jack, an austere graduate of Trinity Bible College in 1973, was dubbed "scary Jack" because of his propensity to connect current events with Bible prophecy. Denouncing increasing social wrongs as apocalyptic, his reputation quickly spread to the community as being a radical fundamentalist. On numerous occasions Pastor Jack would read articles from the daily newspaper, then compare passages in the Bible to prove the fulfillment of the event. Labeled dogmatic and legalistic by some members, Pastor Jack maintained his resolve not to compromise the Bible's doctrine under any circumstances. In his mind there were few preachers left in society who would agree with his position, but he attributed that problem to the times in which he lived. He called it the Laodicean period—when church leaders would be lukewarm, claiming neutrality and indifference toward the issues that were continuing to invade his homeland.

But this generated unpopularity with certain factions that opposed his theology and brought fear into some of the worshippers who were bothered by the ongoing harassing and warnings toward the church membership. Receiving daily threats either by phone or letter was becoming normal.

Arriving early at the church on Saturdays enabled Pastor Jack to work on his Sunday sermon with little interruptions. He cherished this time where he could sit down with his Bible, his computer software support programs, and his God, to hammer out a message for his congregation.

This morning, he not only had to complete his sermon but also had two unexpected counseling appointments that couldn't be postponed. Hopefully, he would have enough quiet time to meditate on his message before his counseling sessions.

"Pastor Jack!" a woman yelled from a parked car as he opened the front door of the church.

He looked suspiciously at the woman, then waited as she climbed out of her car. As the woman approached, he recognized her. "Well, hello, Sydelle. So good to see you again. How is your husband, Eddie, and your new baby?"

She held the baby aloft. "Julie is fine, and Eddie is busy settling life and property insurance claims as usual."

Quick to discern difficulty, Pastor Jack invited Sydelle in to talk and then looked up to heaven when he thought about the preparation of his Sunday sermon. "You look distressed. Is everything all right?"

"Well, sort of." She appeared to grope for the right words to say. "I guess you could say I'm troubled about a few things."

Pastor Jack escorted her over to a chair and then plugged in the coffeemaker. He had a sudden pain in his stomach. *Getting hungry,* he thought. It was times like this—when tension mounted—that his aggressive appetite reminded him of its need for food. He looked up at the box of donuts next to the coffeemaker and curled his lip. *Have to wait,* he commanded himself. "Go ahead, Sydelle. Tell me what's troubling you."

She fussed with Julie for several seconds. "Last week I was accosted at the supermarket, and my handbag was stolen by a man who didn't even look like a thief."

"I'm so sorry to hear of it," Pastor Jack entreated.

"Things in my life are accelerating too fast. I haven't been the same since Krissy died. I'm always on edge, even with God's precious gift of Julie. I'm really troubled about the whole thing. Then the purse snatching incident just triggered in me a reaction that makes me keep searching for answers."

Pastor Jack reached for her hand. "Take your time and let it out."

"Well, I couldn't say anything to anybody at the funeral parlor about what I know, but I guess I can tell you."

"Go on."

She fumbled with her car keys, then adjusted Julie's blanket. "I used to work at Rainbow Pharmaceuticals in Wellington before I had Julie. I was the owner's personal secretary. There was this girl that worked with me, Linda Martin, who I later found out was Krissy Kramer, who told me that Rainbow killed her fiancé and that she had evidence that could really hurt them. It must have been true because I overheard a phone call to the owner, who must have ordered her murder. I read in the newspaper that she died in a suspicious gas explosion the same day. Of course it was called accidental."

"Does this have anything to do with the AIDS vaccine that Rainbow developed? I've read newspaper articles about their drug discovery," Pastor Jack said.

"Somehow they're all linked together." She began to whimper, then muttered, "Rainbow, Linda, her fiancé."

"Hmm. Who else knows about this?" Pastor Jack asked.

"Only my husband."

"Why didn't you go to the police?"

"Because I'm afraid for my family. The owner, a Mr. Kavidas, is a very powerful man with many connections. His phone call instructed a person by the name of Watchman to look for Krissy's friends, and I can't handle any more problems."

Pastor Jack pondered the ramifications. He strolled over to get two cups of coffee. "I can see how that ordeal and the purse snatching would frighten you. Tell me, what do you think became of the evidence Krissy referred to?"

"Knowing her resolve, she probably handed it off to somebody before they killed her."

Hearing a commotion in the parking lot, Pastor Jack casually walked to the front window, pulled back the drapes slightly, and saw a crowd forming. He calmly returned to his seat next to Sydelle. "Do you suspect they know about you? I mean, if they're aware of what you know?"

"It's not likely. At the office I didn't spend much time with Linda. Besides, Kavidas really trusted me; I'm sure they simply assumed I didn't

148

return to work because I opted to stay home with Julie."

Crash. A rock burst through the front window, hitting the drapes, falling to the floor.

"What in the world was that?" Sydelle covered her mouth.

Racing to the front door, Pastor Jack watched as the sizeable crowd began marching with signs proclaiming Gay Pride, jabbing their clenched fists into the air. He turned to Sydelle. "I think you better be going. This looks like it could get ugly."

Sydelle carried little Julie with her to the door and peeked out. "Who are they?"

"It's a radical gay men's group called the G-Men. I've had encounters with them before but never at my church. I've protested at their rallies, and I guess this is retaliation. They must have found out where my ministry is located."

Thud. Thud.

Pastor Jack looked up to see eggs splattered all over the windows and door. He turned to Sydelle. "Call your husband on the phone and have him come get you right away. Leave by the back door and wait in the rear alley for him. You can return for your car later."

Sydelle grabbed his arm. "You're not going out there, are you? They might do something to harm you."

"Don't worry. I'm a veteran of this kind of combat," he said bravely. He opened the door and quickly closed it behind him as Sydelle retreated to the rear of the church.

"Who gives you the right to judge us!" they screamed in unison as Pastor Jack emerged.

Then without warning, a man ran up to him and threw a red liquid at him, splashing over his face and draining on his suit. "Have some HIV-positive blood!" the man yelled, then returned to his ranks.

Pastor Jack wiped his face with his handkerchief and cried out, "Christ can forgive you of your sin by covering you with his blood—just come to him in repentance!" He held up the blood-drenched handkerchief and continued, "His blood will cleanse you of the disease that is ravaging you. Just turn from your sin—"

At the back door, Sydelle suddenly realized Pastor Jack had stopped yelling into the crowd, so she set Julie in a stuffed chair near the exit. Then she ran to the front door only to see Pastor Jack lying on the ground with a rock next to his head.

"They killed him!" she screamed. She looked back at Julie and started to open the door, then thought better of it. She quickly closed it, ran to the phone, and punched in the emergency number. "Send the police to the Tamarac Congregational Church. A riot has broken out—" She slammed down the phone, then burst through the front door onto the sidewalk.

Pastor Jack lay stunned with his eyes fluttering. "Get inside," he moaned.

"No! I won't leave you here." She dragged him inside as the throng moved menacingly toward her.

He reached for his head. "What hit me?"

Sydelle locked the door. "A rock." She shook her head. "And they claim to be non-confrontational. That's a joke."

"Don't hate them. Jesus loves them as much as he loves us. They are still in darkness; that's the only difference."

Sydelle looked into Pastor Jack's eyes as he lay on the floor reeling from the injury and marveled at his love for God.

Fifteen minutes passed and still, there was no police response. The crowd outside broke up into small groups; some chanted vicious epithets about the church, while many couples simulated sexual acts.

Sydelle held a cold compress on Pastor Jack's head while he lay on the floor in a semi-conscious state. "You must see a doctor right away. We can't wait for the police. I'm calling my husband at work."

Twenty minutes later Pastor Jack was being treated at University Medical Hospital. Eddie stood by his side as the emergency room doctor advised Pastor Jack that he had been doused with chicken blood and that he had a minor concussion.

Relieved, Eddie went to the waiting room to report Pastor Jack's condition to Sydelle and to hold his daughter. As he turned to take Julie, a young black woman ran out from the emergency room.

"No, it can't be! It can't be!" she wailed. "He's only a baby!" She thrashed her arms about, then ran to a vacant gurney and pushed it through the closed glass door, shattering the glass.

Within seconds two security guards subdued her and escorted her away.

When Eddie returned, Pastor Jack's head was bandaged and his eyes tightly closed, leaning to hear the conversation in the next bed behind the white linen drape.

"You won't believe what I just heard," Pastor Jack whispered as he pointed to the next bed. "The little boy just had a blood test that showed him HIV-positive."

Eddie groaned. "How awful. I saw his poor mother flip out in the waiting room."

Pastor Jack gestured for Eddie to come closer, whispering, "It had nothing to do with the boy. He was bit by a mosquito carrying HIV-positive blood."

Eddie was aghast. "What?" He gulped. "A mosquito?"

"Shush! I heard the doctor tell his mother."

Eddie walked out, shaking his head, hoping Sydelle wouldn't ask him any questions.

When Sydelle checked with the police late in the afternoon, they insisted they weren't able to find the church since she'd neglected to give them the address.

The supercomputers at *Redisearch* updated the progress on Project Renaissance every 60 minutes. Mort scanned the status boards and compared them with his population census provided by the Bureau of Records. The data association task of combining *Redisearch's* global credit clearance membership with the new subscribers coming in on Medlink was almost 80 percent complete.

Historically, the public's reaction to remedial health reform was always met with enthusiasm when the potential for lower consumer cost was dangled in front of their eyes, regardless of long-range effects. Mort's advertising genius coupled Medlink with the pending AIDS vaccine release, requiring pre-registration by those desiring the drug. His marketing division carefully worded the advertisements to remind potential subscribers that Medlink's confidential system would guarantee immediate medical attention and ongoing access to the AIDS vaccine.

In effect, he was establishing his own insurance company since enrolled members would benefit by a 60 percent discount on the vaccine and medical services. The capital deposited by Rainbow into the Medlink trust fund would be used to pay member medical expenses until the fees for the vaccine from both government and private sources replenished it.

Independent statisticians, financed by Rainbow, projected that the government would save 18 billion dollars in 10 years by inoculating the public before they contracted AIDS, based on projected figures of 25 million potential AIDS patients nationwide. Existing HIV-positive persons would have to wait until a serum was perfected from the vaccine. Rainbow promised that within two years both the vaccine and the serum would stamp out the epidemic. Mort's strategy would ultimately swallow all other health insurance plans and enroll every person on earth wanting protection from AIDS.

Bringing detail work home after spending a full day on the phone aggravated Eddie. Someday he hoped to have a career where he left the job at the office at five o'clock and enjoyed the rest of the day with his family. Until then, especially now that Julie came along, he would tough it out.

Fastidiously he piled his claim work on one side of his desk, the prospects to call on the other, and his diary in the center. He reached for the phone to begin his evening calls when Sydelle walked into his study.

"Keep an eye on Julie while I run down to the grocery store to get some diapers. She's in her crib. I'll be right back."

"Sure, no problem."

Sydelle glanced at the stacks of work on his desk. "Don't you hate

Mondays?"

Eddie nodded and pulled a piece of paper from the pile and handed it to Sydelle. "The Krissy Kramer life claim just came in."

Sydelle read aloud from the death certificate attached to the claim's loss notice. "'Compound fracture of the spinal cord at the neck...asphyxiation by smoke inhalation...'" She stifled a whimper and continued, "'...Kathleen Douglas, friend.'" She fell back into the sofa and cried.

Eddie read the status sheet on the policy. "The beneficiary was recently amended to this Kathleen Douglas of Coral Springs from a Jonathan Keahon."

Sydelle waved him to silence while she remembered Krissy Kramer as Linda Martin, the warrior who stood up against Rainbow.

Pastor Jack and Sydelle pulled up to the modest house on Riverside Drive in Coral Springs and discussed strategy before leaving the car. Pastor Jack looked in the visor mirror and hummed the hymn "Redeemed" as he adjusted the bandage on his forehead.

Sydelle squeezed her eyes shut as if silently praying, then opened the door. As they walked to the front door, a sensor signaled an alarm with a recorded voice that advised them that they were being videotaped. As they stood motionless, someone peeked through the curtain, then addressed the visitors through the intercom.

"Who is it?" the metallic voice asked.

Pastor Jack took the lead, cleared his throat, and said, "This is Pastor Jack Hammond with Sydelle Swain. We're looking for Kathleen Douglas."

The door opened, then abruptly stopped as the chain check held. "I'm her husband. Can I help you?"

A little girl shot her face through the opening. The man pulled her back. "Who are you?"

Pastor Jack took a deep breath, then put his arm around Sydelle. "Mr. Douglas, this woman used to work with a friend of your wife, a Krissy Kramer, and we would like to talk to you about a few things. We thought the information too sensitive to discuss over the phone, so we agreed to risk a visit instead. We hope you don't mind."

"How did you manage to locate us?" David said.

Pastor Jack nodded toward Sydelle. "Mrs. Swain's husband is the insurance adjuster who is processing Ms. Kramer's apartment fire and death claim. Your wife is listed as the beneficiary."

David released the chain and opened the door.

The security measures, he explained, had been installed after Krissy's death. Video surveillance and a central station alarm system would bring the police to his home within five minutes. This helped their peace of mind, but, David lamented, probably wouldn't withstand an armed intruder determined to harm them. Alarms and protection devices only acted as a deterrent to keep honest people from breaking the law.

Bonding between the four lives brought together by Krissy Kramer's death took place immediately. Sydelle, in retrospect, detailed her relationship with Krissy at Rainbow, focusing on the phone call she overheard with Kavidas and the Watchman that signaled the threat on Krissy's life. Being supported by Pastor Jack helped her recount her final moments back at Rainbow.

"Pastor Jack," David began, "we believe we have uncovered a colossal plot to really damage humanity. However, this is all relatively new to both of you." He hesitated, loosened his collar, then continued. "Your lives could be in jeopardy and perhaps your family's if you get any deeper into this."

"The information we have gathered about Rainbow over the last several months has resulted in two deaths so far. Johnnie and now Krissy," Kathy put in.

"I'm curious, Kathy," Sydelle said. "Did Krissy meet you the day she died and hand off the proof she was holding?"

Kathy nodded. "Just before she was killed."

Sydelle winced. "Speaking for me and my family, we're already in this. I've discussed this with my Eddie, and the cost to remain silent is too great. As for me and my house, we're in."

David turned to Pastor Jack.

"From the day of my ordination as a pastor, I took an oath before God to speak up wherever the truth of God was being compromised or his people were being threatened. In this case, I see both scenarios. I'm in."

"Fine," David said. He asked Pastor Jack to lead the group in a brief

154

prayer, then opened up the discussion. "The hard evidence we're holding is photographs of their Trinidad laboratory specimens, a blood sample from one of their test monkeys, names and locations of their experimental stations in Haiti, and a vial of their vaccine."

"We also have the name of a vagrant whom Rainbow performed surgery on, where they removed and experimented on his thymus gland, but that in itself could be circumstantial," Kathy added.

"Well, isn't that enough to hang them?" Sydelle flared.

"Hold on." David soothed. "We're not the only ones involved in this. Lane Pharmaceutical and a New York policeman is helping us develop a case against them, and we all decided that we cannot blow the whistle just yet. We must wait until we have conclusive evidence that cannot be disputed. To go to court with them now would be suicide for us."

"So are we supposed to just sit here and do nothing?" Kathy demanded.

David bit his lip. "No. We wait for them to make the next move."

The lightning strikes were so intense, more so than Kathy could remember in all her living in South Florida, that she pulled off the road to wait for the storm to move on. Checking the time, she used her cell phone to call home and alert the children of her delay from work.

The phone rang 12 times and then the answering machine kicked in. "Okay, where are you, Alan and Paul?" she said aloud. *Hillary is bused home at four-thirty,* she thought, *but you guys should be home by now.*

The electrical storm heightened with the rain obscuring all vision, blowing branches and debris on the windshield. After 10 minutes, the traffic signals and the power in the nearby development went out.

She tried calling home again but no answer. The downpour flooded the street, snarling the traffic to a standstill. Kathy picked up the phone again and hit the speed-dial button.

"David Douglas's office," the girl said.

"This is Kathy. Can I speak to my husband right away, please?"

"Of course, Mrs. Douglas. I'll page him right now. Please hold."

Kathy looked into the phone when the background music began and suddenly felt cut off from the outside world.

Within five seconds, the phone clicked, "Hi, babe, are you all right?" David asked.

"No! I'm stranded on Sample Road in a mini-hurricane and I can't get through to the house and no one answers the phone. The boys should be home by now."

"I'm sure they're okay, honey. They probably waited the storm out at school. They'll be fine."

Kathy felt the tension subsiding. "I didn't think of that. I just imagined them getting caught in this storm, and with all the people getting hit by lightning, I guess I just—"

Kathy saw lightning strike, then heard an electronic beeping. Her cell phone went dead. She threw the phone on the floor, grabbed the steering wheel, and grunted, "I'm really getting to hate this Florida weather."

The storm's fury persisted for over an hour.

David left the college early and rushed home. When he opened the front door, Kathy met him and hurriedly escorted him to the living room where Alan and Paul sat rigid on the sofa. Hillary tugged at his arm for attention and didn't stop until he reached down and lifted her up.

"Tell your father what you told me," Kathy said, fighting back the tears and motioning for Hillary to leave the room.

Alan, the eldest, looked at Paul. "A car with two men inside followed us as we walked home from school. When we noticed it, we ran through the short cut on Riverside, but when we came out, the car found us again."

"Did you recognize the men or the car?" David asked.

Both boys shook their head in unison. Then Alan added, "One of the men in the car had red hair in a ponytail."

David looked up at Kathy, scratched his moustache, then covered his mouth and muttered something under his breath. "Go on, Alan," he instructed as Kathy raised her eyebrow and took a deep breath.

"We got caught in the storm, so we ran behind Josh's house and waited there till it let up. Then we looked, and the car was gone. So we walked the rest of the way back to the house."

156

"That was smart," David affirmed.

"You haven't heard the rest," Kathy said impatiently.

Paul shot his hands up in the air and yelled, "The car was waiting outside our house when we walked up."

Alan calmed his brother and finished the statement as David's face contorted with anger. "But it pulled away when we spotted it."

David forced a smile. "Okay, boys, good work. Now run along while I speak to your mother."

"Rainbow is watching our family. I just know it!" Kathy paced the floor angrily as Hillary strolled back in the room. "They're probably monitoring all of us who know anything about Rainbow. None of us will be safe!" She swept Hillary up into her arms and said, "If they touch one of my kids . . ." She broke into sobs and carried Hillary upstairs to her bedroom.

David went to his study and phoned Pastor Jack.

The concrete had set and the anchor fasteners were holding tight. Pastor Jack drilled a hole in the two-by-four, then bolted it to the foundation of his extension. This would be his sanctuary at home. Gifted with his hands from his youth, he enjoyed small building projects that acted as diversions which took his mind off his ministry and his problems. Actually, they gave him perspective. He recalled the many sermons the Lord gave him while making bookshelves for his library room or when repairing his lawn mower.

He reached for his nailing gun as his wife, Doreen, stuck her head out the window. "Jack, phone for you. David Douglas."

He stamped his feet on the door mat to loosen the sawdust, then walked inside and picked up the phone. "Hello, David. When are you going to use that great mind of yours and help me with my extension?" he chided jokingly.

"Pastor Jack, my sons were followed by two unknown men in a car on their way home from school today. Kathy freaked out. We believe it's Rainbow watching our house."

A long pause ensued. "I was afraid of this."

"We need to talk. Can you get over here right away?"

"I'm leaving now."

By the time Pastor Jack arrived at David's, Eddie, Sydelle, and Louie were already there, rehashing the day's events.

David was appointed as the chairman. "The last time we met, I suggested that any action on our part would be premature. That we would wait until Rainbow made the next move. Well, I've conferred with Matthew Lane, who as you know is deeply involved in this investigation, and we are of the same mind. We believe this threat of intimidation on our family is only the tip of the iceberg. We need to take action now to let them know we are prepared to stand up for what is right. We are going to move on Rainbow."

Louie shook his head. "Could be dangerous. Why not allow me to call in the police and the FBI?"

David looked at him in disbelief. "Louie, you know we decided not to involve the police, so why bring that up?"

"Are you sure that this incident with your boys concerns Rainbow? I mean, we need solid proof," Louie argued.

Kathy whispered as she pointed to Sydelle, "If there is any doubt in anybody's mind as to Rainbow's involvement, listen to this—"

Sydelle picked up the cue. "Kathy recounted the incident where her sons were being followed on their way home from school today. Well, Alan remarked that the man driving the car had long red hair in a ponytail, and I remembered such a person by the name of Kimsley who came to visit Gregory Kavidas at Rainbow while I was still working there."

Louie sat speechless.

"Oh, brother." Pastor Jack sighed. "The spiders are casting their webs."

"Yeah, well, we're not going to make it easy for them, Pastor," David assured. Turning to Eddie, he said, "Tell Pastor Jack about your phone listener."

"Last night, while on my way home from the office, I called Sydelle from my cell phone, and halfway during the call a funny signal could be heard, sort of like when you go out of the range of the relay antennas or your cell phone goes near high voltage wires. But this was different. There was a click and a pulsating tone; then I could hear background music coming from a speaker near the phone. It was as if the person listening to my conversation didn't realize the music could be heard."

"Not that it helps, but what was the music?" Pastor Jack said.

"It was classical music. I heard it before on a beer commercial, but I don't remember the name of it."

"What was the name of the beer?" Sydelle asked sarcastically.

He looked at her and grinned. "It was Smugglers."

Sydelle gave him a dirty look. "Big help you are."

"Seriously, I have no doubt that our phones are being monitored, so try to use public phones or phones from work," Kathy suggested.

"So what's the plan?" Pastor Jack asked.

"We're going to gather support from a group that has been protesting out at Rainbow Pharmaceuticals for the last month or so. Matthew Lane has been videotaping the newscast coverage of the dissenters who object to Rainbow's production of their abortion pill, the RU-486, and their AIDS vaccine. I met with Matthew and viewed the tapes, and we agree that this nonviolent group would make a good nucleus for us to join with. In many ways, they believe the way we do. They just lack direction, and we purpose to finance them and give them the direction needed. Looking down the road, we hope to form a formidable coalition to help us combat Rainbow. For now, that's our plan."

Louie looked David in the eyes. "I hope you don't regret this plan."

David's children crept down the stairs and wondered why everybody seemed to be whispering.

The Watchman hung up the phone, then smashed his fist into the nearest wall. "You rat dogs!" he yelled. He walked into the bathroom, looked into the mirror, and said in disgust, 'That's what I get for selling my soul to the devil."

After he shaved, he walked down the street to Finnigan's Pub, ordered a bottle of Jack Daniel's bourbon, and a pitcher of water. He stayed until the bottle was empty.

Miami's elevated Metrorail circled the city, pausing at convenient locations, including Bayside, the wharfs, and Trinity College. The indigent frequented the stations while the panhandlers marched in their sectors. In the afternoons, after class, David would see the homeless carrying their cardboard beds and shopping bags to their designated quarters. There they would spend the night, only to awake and renew the cycle.

While he enjoyed walking to the Cuban restaurants and lunching on paella, he often bought two lunches, one for a homeless person, one for himself. He would walk into the courthouse pavilion, sit down, and wave to a passing vagrant, hoping to bait one to feed and engage in conversation. He often wondered if he had a time machine and took a homeless person back 10 or 20 years and showed them what the future held for them, what their reaction would be. Would they try to circumvent the acts and decisions that would sentence them to the streets for the rest of their lives, or would they simple shrug and succumb to the whims of destiny?

As David stepped off the Metrorail staircase, a bearded man with a shopping cart filled with discarded plastic bottles and aluminum cans pushed his way through the crowd. As the man passed, the commuters turned and sniffed in disgust as he walked by. It seemed apparent the stench was coming from the street beggar. He wore a baseball cap and a brown hooded parka with holes in the sleeves and food stains on the front. The plaid shorts were sagging as his belly flopped over the belt. He wore sneakers with holes that let his toes peek out. His beard looked oily, knotted, and filthy with spittle dried on it.

Meandering through the flow of commuters, he took off his cap and held it out like a basket. "Help a homeless man," he said in a feeble whisper.

"At least he doesn't carry those phony signs that say Will Work for Food," one passing contributor remarked.

160

"Help a homeless man, will ya, brother?" he repeated in a cracked voice as he neared David.

David saw him from a distance and reached into his canvas sack and took out the extra lunch. For a moment, he thought he knew the man.

While he was still a good 10 feet away, the man peered at David, then suddenly reached into his jacket pocket and pulled out a pistol and shot him.

David fell to the ground while the screaming crowd dispersed, providing a diversion for the assailant to flee.

The Jackson Memorial Hospital emergency room was accustomed to gunshot wounds. With Miami ranking in the top five highest crime cities in the nation, a street shooting was almost an everyday occurrence. The rarity here, the police argued, was that the shooter was a homeless person. Homeless people just don't carry guns.

When David's eyes opened, the first thing he saw was his family, his pastor, and a doctor. Kathy, escorted by Pastor Jack, had driven into Miami with the children as soon as the police notified her of the shooting.

"The bullet went through the muscle in the left shoulder, with a clear exit. There will not be any serious damage, Mr. Douglas," Doctor Beatty, the surgeon, advised. "You will be able to leave in two days, but you won't be able to use that arm for several weeks." He smiled at Kathy and Pastor Jack, waved to the children, and walked out.

A nurse popped her head inside the room. "There's a detective Lewis waiting to see you, Mr. Douglas."

Pastor Jack motioned to the children to follow him out. "What do you say we check out the cafeteria? We'll go for some ice cream. Good idea?"

The children all nodded, then marched after him as if he were the pied piper.

The detective looked at the police field report, then said, "Mr. Douglas, we've interviewed several witnesses and a dozen street people in the vicinity where you were shot, and no one has ever seen this assailant before. In fact, this is the first incident where a homeless person ever shot someone." He looked at Kathy, then back to his report. "What do you think could be the motive for this kind of thing? Surely it wasn't robbery with such a crowd nearby. Besides, two witnesses said all you were doing was sitting there, with a lunch bag…" The detective scratched his head.

"Detective Lewis, don't you think it strange that he shot him in the shoulder, of all places?" Kathy asked. "One would think he would aim for a different target." She shook her head as if nothing made sense at all.

"Have you ever given these homeless people money before? Could this man have thought you were carrying a large amount of cash?" the detective speculated.

David shook his head. "Hardly a place for a mugging. In broad daylight, amidst a crowd?"

Detective Lewis nodded.

David squeezed Kathy's hand as he postulated, "Somehow I got the impression by the way this guy looked at me that he was out to kill me. Then at the last minute he changed his mind."

"The grace of God," Kathy interjected.

Detective Lewis picked up on David's hunch. "Although our preliminary investigation shows none of the witnesses ever saw this person before, have you ever seen him before? Ever given him a lunch in a different place while walking in town, while shopping? Seen him on the college grounds, etcetera, etcetera?"

David winced as he moved his wounded shoulder. He shot Kathy a look. "No."

"Have you or any of your family members received any threats or encountered suspicious activities recently?"

Kathy opened her mouth to speak as David shook his head to warn her off.

"Here's my card, Mr. Douglas," Detective Lewis said. "If you think of any more details, give me a call. I'll be in touch if our investigation warrants it." He tipped his hat toward Kathy and walked out.

"Why didn't you want me to tell him about the activities? Shouldn't we report the car following Alan and Paul? We just can't ignore this assault on our family."

David's eyes slowly closed. He reached to adjust the shoulder sling and tears ran down his face. "Are you in pain, honey? Shall I call the nurse to give you a sedative or something?"

His eyes opened to a stare. "It's not the pain." He turned his face into the pillow.

Kathy touched his face gently. "What is it then, darling?"

His face contorted, and his mouth went dry. His voice quavered as he said, "I sorted the face out in my mind. I know who shot me."

Kathy glared at him. "You do? Who?"

"It was Louie."

The Watchman's hand hovered over the phone; then on the seventh ring he picked it up.

"Thought you wouldn't answer," the caller said.

"Thought about it," the Watchman replied.

"We have a problem. Someone didn't follow orders this morning," the caller said in a singsong voice.

The Watchman stuffed his suitcase and surveyed his apartment as he talked on the portable phone. "So sue me."

"You act like you lost your nerve, but you sound like you have a lot of it. Which is it?"

"I'm done. I'm clearing out tonight, end of story." He slammed down the phone and walked out.

Fifteen minutes later, as darkness cloaked his actions, the Watchman drove slowly by David Douglas's home. It was his way of saying good-bye.

The Watchman chose Interstate 75 to travel to the Fort Lauderdale airport. Interstate 75, known as Route I-595 where it intersects with Route 441, has an overpass that is exceedingly high. Rising to 62 feet above the ground and often used by state troopers as a post to watch for speeders on the roadway below, it is protected by four-foot-high concrete sidewalls to deflect runaway vehicles. It's almost impossible to break through.

Checking his watch, he reckoned he had only 20 minutes left to drop the rented car, check in, and board the flight to New York. Instinct dictated that danger would befall him if he missed the plane.

As he neared the overpass, thoughts of David and Hillary surged into his mind, bringing pangs of guilt and ushering tears to his eyes. Yet the flashbacks quickly assuaged when he remembered the financial security he had established in a St. Thomas, Virgin Islands bank account. All that remained was to clear out of New York, then begin a new life.

Crash!

Suddenly, out of nowhere, a speeding car slammed into his vehicle, causing it to careen against the concrete barrier. The Watchman recognized Kimsley at the wheel so he pulled out his gun and fired, missing him.

The attack continued. The Watchman accelerated to 85 to escape, but the aggressor easily kept pace. Again he rammed the Watchman's car against the cement wall, ripping off his right fender and front bumper.

The Watchman then slowed considerably and waited for Kimsley to come alongside to take another shot, but Kimsley seemed to lag far behind. The Watchman believed he purposed to stay out of the line of fire, but he was wrong.

Within sight of the overpass, Kimsley brought his vehicle up to over 100 miles per hour and plowed into the left rear of the Watchman's car, catapulting it over the concrete barrier, where it burst into flames, tumbling and crashing onto Route 441 below.

Kimsley resumed the legal speed limit, then made an unauthorized U-turn to connect with I-95 North to Wellington.

The Fort Lauderdale Police would later list Louis Donato's death as accidental.

Skywatch traffic circled the crash site from the air, beaming vivid pictures of the smoldering car to viewers in all of Broward county. Even in Dade County, some 20 miles south, the news media televised such a spectacular crash. Rarely did a vehicle and driver jump a barrier and plummet over 60 feet to their death. It became big news quickly.

The early morning hours were best for Kathy to visit David in the hospital. When she arrived David lay in bed, watching the television with a blank stare.

She pointed up at the TV rerun of the sensational I-595 traffic fatality dubbed the "fire ball" by the media. "That's why I'm late—rubber-neckers like crazy; it's still a traffic jam."

David reached out with his good arm for her to come to his side. In a

164

faint monotone he said, "After two hours of sifting through the crash debris, charred bones and teeth, they just announced the identity of the driver."

She sensed disaster before he even uttered the name. Her instincts signaled that she must reject any further heartache, and yet, shaking her head, she lip-synched David's words, "It was Louis Donato." He paused, then recited the rest of the official newscast. "A Queens, New York, policeman on leave of absence here in Florida. On his way back home."

"Oh no!" she cried, burying her face in David's embrace.

Somehow, David thought, *Louie was involved in something that possessed him to turn on his friend.* "I just pray that God will avenge his death," he whispered in Kathy's ear.

The early morning dew on the sprawling lawn at Wellington's Rainbow facility had burned off by the time David and his friends arrived. Pastor Jack's passenger van provided an excellent mode of transportation, allowing David room to nurse his wounded shoulder, while Sydelle and Julie could occupy the rear bench and still leave adequate room for equipment and boxes of leaflets they planned to distribute. Their frontal attack plan was to form a coalition.

The slow trickle of protestors soon gave rise to a steady flow of dissidents. Within an hour a large crowd had assembled at the main gate.

Pastor Jack erected a podium and two folding tables, while Sydelle, carrying Julie in a back harness, handed out pamphlets. David walked amidst the people, listening and noting their complaints about Rainbow's soon-to-be-released AIDS vaccine.

After nearly an hour of gathering testimony, David went to the podium to address the crowd. He turned toward the Rainbow building and sniffed in disgust as the warm humid air carried with it a medicinal odor that reminded him of his recent stay in the hospital.

"My friends and fellow laborers," he began, "you have had an opportunity to read the flyers and talk with Pastor Jack, Sydelle, and myself about what is going on here at Rainbow. We believe their production of the oral contraceptive was the precursor to their RU-486 abortion pill that makes it all too easy to dispose of human life. With these two drugs, Rainbow has been making a statement. A drug company's role in society is to alleviate, not elevate, human suffering through pharmaceuticals. And yet the preponderance of proof points to their pernicious intent to capitalize on destroying life. And if their AIDS vaccine is marketed, we will see another holocaust, one that will bring an end to our society as we know it.

"I remind you: the AIDS vaccine is urgently needed, but how the vaccine is developed and dispensed needs to be brought under strict regulation before it is released. We cannot afford to release an unproven vaccine that appears to be a panacea to end the crisis." Sydelle handed him several photocopies, which he held in the air. "We have proof that Rainbow is testing their vaccine on unsuspecting victims and that a clinic in Haiti has a patient who is still testing positive to HIV, despite his inoculation with Toi-VAX."

In the corporate office, Gregory motioned to Mort and Kimsley to come to the window that looked down toward the main gate. "Have the satellite imaging focus and enlarge on the guy who's yelling out there, Mort."

Mort walked to the security panel and maneuvered the satellite's resolution and magnification so that David's face filled the monitor. "I know that man," Mort said. "Isn't that the one we sent Watchman to dispose of?"

Kimsley nodded. "David Douglas. We now have a complete file on him through *Redisearch*. A Christian college professor who lives in Coral Springs. Friend of Krissy Kramer, *aka* Linda Martin, whichever you prefer. Has other connections to Lane Pharmaceutical. Probably knows everything and probably holds evidence to hurt us."

"Have the satellite pan the crowd for a moment." Mort made the adjustment.

"Hold it right there." Gregory pointed to the woman with the baby in the carrier. "Isn't that Sydelle Swain, who used to work here?"

Mort peered at the screen. "Yes, that's her." He flicked his finger at the monitor in contempt. "I suppose she's joined alliances with Douglas, and undoubtedly they're mounting a campaign against us."

Gregory walked into a corner, turned around, and said, "You two go down to the fence line and scare them off before any media arrives."

Pastor Jack, now at the speaker's platform, had the crowd in a frenzy as he pounded the podium while preaching from his Bible. "...in my view, unless there is a change in the heart of man, this AIDS vaccine will only encourage drug abuse and homosexuality, giving them false hope that the vaccine will arrest the disease so they can continue in their sinful lifestyle without consequence. And I stand before you to remind you that my God will not let that happen."

He turned to the back of the Bible and held it up. "I read the last chapter of this book, and they don't win!" He wiped his brow, looked over at the two Rainbow officials that just arrived at the fence, then raised his voice to a fever pitch as he pointed to them. "If we don't unite and stand up against evil, God will hold each one of us accountable—"

"Move out! Move out!" one of the officials bellowed through a megaphone. "The police have been called, and you will all be arrested for trespassing, disorderly conduct, and unauthorized assembly. So if you don't want to spend the night in the slammer, you better get out of here right now!"

David walked boldly to the wire fence. "You pretend to be angels of mercy helping the sick when you are all devils in disguise."

The massive official curled his lip and hissed at David, then turned to speak to Mort, allowing David to see his profile. Suddenly David placed the man from his son Alan's description. His face contorted with rage. He shook the fence and shouted, "If you ever come near my family again, you red-tailed snake, I'll make it my personal mission in life to see you suffer a slow, painful death behind bars!"

Kimsley gestured to the crowd to scatter and dissipate while David looked over at the other official. This man, arms folded on his chest, silently observed David and his newly formed allies. David clutched the fence again as a wave of oppression swept over him while an inner voice whispered danger to his heart. He silently returned the icy stare, recognizing that the message was clear. The battle lines had been drawn.

Mort returned to Gregory's office and spent the next two hours deciding what their next move would be.

Emotions ran high as David, Pastor Jack, and Sydelle broke out into song on their drive home. They were singing of spiritual victory, for in David's mind, he interpreted the rally to be a huge success. A group had been formed that brought concern to Rainbow, and that was his intent—to worry them.

After 20 minutes on the Florida Turnpike, the drone of Pastor Jack's engine lulled David to sleep.

At the Sample Road exit, David awakened. "Pastor Jack, have you always had a storefront church? The thought occurred to me while you were preaching at Rainbow, and I meant to ask you about it. You possess homiletic gifts that endear large audiences, so why such a small church?"

Pastor Jack looked into his side view mirror. "I lost my church three years ago."

"You lost your church?" David said, astonished. "How?"

"Well, I don't want to frighten you, David, but these are very difficult times for Christian churches and dangerous times for pastors."

"You mean physically, like the incident with you and Sydelle, where the protesters assaulted you?"

"Well, there is that form of peril, but there is a greater enemy lurking around in the inner recesses of men's hearts that is determined to destroy us, and that's through our judicial system."

"How so?"

"By using the law as a way to entrap the church. You see, three and a half years ago, an out-of-state abortion protest group called me at my 'large' church and asked if I would simply rent them my church as a base of operation. From there they staged a sit-in—a sit-in mind you—at a nearby clinic. The nature of the rally was to pray to end abortion; that's all. There was no hurling of names at doctors, no throwing of eggs, no physical action, just a quiet group praying in front of the clinic."

"So what's wrong with that?" Sydelle chirped in.

Pastor Jack shook his head in dismay. "In my mind, there was nothing wrong with it. I certainly don't approve of violence such as shooting a doctor at a woman's clinic, but I wholeheartedly support praying as a silent protest, especially when through the years minority groups have gained approval through violence. But not with this issue. So a lawsuit was filed against the church citing we violated the RICO statute, which is the Racketeer Influenced Corrupt Organizations law written in 1970. The women's groups claimed the protestors had violated women's constitutional rights to abortion by blocking the clinic."

"You're not serious," David moaned. "What about your constitutional right for free speech?"

He laughed. "It gets better. The RICO act defines 41 offenses as racketeering activities, among which federal attorneys clamp down on organized crime bosses known for their exploits in child pornography, drug dealing, money laundering, extortion, and fraud. Imagine being lumped together with them."

"So how did you lose the church?" Sydelle asked.

"The judge awarded the women's group $325,000 thousand dollars, so we had to close our bank accounts, sell our building, sell off our furniture and books to meet the settlement. In fact, federal marshals were poised and ready to padlock our doors and auction everything off to the highest bidder if we didn't sell it first."

"Sure, you can have sex with your girlfriend in the local neighborhood park in front of little children, provided you use a condom, or you can watch a leading female vocalist have relations with a goat on a music video, but don't dare infringe on people's rights by praying in public," Sydelle lamented.

David's face flushed with rage. "Curse them!" was all he could say.

Kimsley stroked his ponytail and fiddled with the diamond stud in his ear as he listened intently to Mort's assessment of the potential threat of David's group.

Mort made his position clear: Both he and Gregory were consonant about disarming any subversive movements, especially prior to the release of the vaccine. After the release, the plethora of praise from the elated population would suppress any propaganda. They would be home free, and rewards would be handsomely distributed.

From Kimsley's viewpoint, Mort's personality was changing rapidly, and he recognized that Mort's leadership role in Rainbow's affairs was intensifying. It appeared he was allowing Gregory time to design strategy. His gut feeling was that in the next year, Rainbow and *Redisearch* would form a giant conglomerate, with Mort in charge of everything. Kimsley, being an opportunist, wanted to remain an integral part of the operation.

With a sardonic grin, Mort advised, "What I had in mind, Jerry, is for you to secretly infiltrate this David Douglas-Jack Hammond alliance and discredit them. I don't want to know how you do it, just take care of it. Let me know the evening before the newspaper announces their demise that you've disposed of the problem."

Kimsley thrived on challenge and intrigue. "Don't concern yourself with this, Mr. Stein," Kimsley assured, then inhaled deeply and thrust forth his chest. "The problem is as good as solved."

Mort's grin changed to a smile as he patted Kimsley on the back. "Good man."

After the recessional hymn, Ronnie Baker, one of the church elders, escorted the fashionable young woman up to the pulpit to meet Pastor Jack. "Pastor," he said cordially, "this is Maggie Clark, a visitor who said she attended your rally at Rainbow last week. She told me she wants to be a part of our ministry."

Jack Hammond welcomed her. He spent several minutes discussing his excursion to Rainbow, then clasped her arm in friendship as he introduced her to his wife.

Doreen hugged the newcomer and invited her over to the coffee and donut table to meet other congregants. When Doreen looked back at

170

Ronnie Baker, she caught him admiring Maggie's shapely figure from afar and frowned at him.

Embarrassed to be caught in the act, Ronnie quickly returned to his conversation with his wife.

"We're so delighted to have you with us today. Is it Ms. or Mrs. Clark?"

"Ms. Clark, but do call me Maggie," she insisted.

Doreen Hammond was struck by Maggie's stylish blonde hair, short skirt, and glamorous profile. She gauged her age at 32 to 35. "We have a women's Bible study each Sunday morning before our service in case you're interested," Doreen entreated.

"Oh, I'm already a Christian," Maggie volunteered.

Slightly flustered, Doreen smiled and added, "I didn't mean to imply anything. I only wanted to invite you since it's a class for new and mature Christians alike." She turned to several persons talking in a corner and said, "Come, I'd like you to meet other recent newcomers."

Doreen gracefully walked Maggie over to the small cluster of members gathered in the vestibule. "Maggie, this is David and Kathy Douglas." She pointed to the rear of the church. "And those are their three children: Alan, Paul, and Hillary." Putting her arm on Sydelle's shoulder she continued, "And this is Eddie and Sydelle Swain, with their new baby, Julie."

The group wished her well.

Maggie beamed from all the attention. "How very nice to meet all of you." She looked around as the congregation filed out the exit. "Everything seems so homey here, and the people appear to be quite friendly. It's not like you're a conventional church or something like that."

"We take that as a compliment. We try to make everyone feel loved here," Doreen said.

Kathy motioned for her children to follow her and said to Maggie, "It was nice meeting you, and I hope to see you again."

Maggie nodded as Kathy hailed Hillary out from playing behind the pulpit.

Doreen noticed that Maggie seemed to be studying David as he walked out.

Sydelle made her 12 calls to engage the telephone chain, then called David to apprise him of the group's readiness for the rally.

David in turn called a colleague who promised full news coverage.

As soon as Mort turned into the driveway at *Redisearch*, he recognized trouble. Three step vans with satellite dishes erected on their roofs stood out amidst the multitude of protestors carrying posters. The demonstrators marched in circles at the front entrance, with the TV cameras concentrated on three women burning a Rainbow-colored dummy in effigy.

Mort pulled his Lexus into the employee parking lot, then walked over to his security chief, who was arguing with David Douglas. Sydelle stepped out of the crowd with Julie in her arms, blocking his path to David.

Mort recognized her. "Can I thank you for disclosing my whereabouts, Mrs. Swain?"

Sydelle glared at him. "I just want you to know, Mr. Stein, that we—" she gestured to the throng behind her—"are not ignorant of your devices and what steps you and Rainbow will take to get your own way. We will continue to mount our offensive until Rainbow, and if necessary, *Redisearch*, is shut down."

Mort silently looked at her with disdain, then waved her aside to excoriate David. "Call your people off right now, Mr. Douglas, or I shall have the police here in 20 minutes to arrest every one of you. Then we'll slap you with a lawsuit that will ruin your life. This is private property, and this gathering is illegal. I want—"

Suddenly a microphone was pushed in front of Mort's face. "Mr. Stein, care to make a comment to our TV audience about this protest?" the newsman asked. He turned to David and repeated the question.

Mort momentarily looked skyward, as if awaiting divine instructions, then grasped the microphone and focused his gaze directly into the

172

cameras pointing at him. "We are not enemies waging war on one another. We simply have experienced a breakdown in communication. We at Rainbow need a little more time and tolerance to meet the public's needs." He extended an open hand to David. "We really want the same things—to meet the needs of humanity. Your watchdog group is looking out for people, and so are we. Medically through Rainbow Pharmaceuticals, financially through *Redisearch*. Can't we work together?"

David scanned the crowd to measure the effect of Mort's words. He suddenly realized how adept his adversary really was. He had disarmed the fury of the protest. With the microphone at his lips, David calculated that any disparaging rebuttal would only make him look like the villain. "I wish it were otherwise, but I don't trust Rainbow or *Redisearch*. May I suggest an open discussion where you assure us of your trustworthiness toward the public?"

Mort, capturing the moment of victory, smiled into the camera. "I'll have my secretary set up a meeting for next week." He nodded to David and entered his building.

The cameraman followed the news reporter into a clearing as he gave the epilogue, "Wouldn't it be refreshing to see our international issues settled this way?" The commentary continued for several minutes as the crowd lost its cohesiveness and began dispersing.

David called Pastor Jack and Sydelle to his side and shook his head. "You have just experienced a subtle display of group psychotherapy disguised as aplomb, resulting in a reversal of public opinion." He threw his hands up and lamented, "We lost this round."

From Mort's executive suite he watched the crowd disband. Time eluded him for the better part of an hour; then he methodically walked into his library where he could meditate. One thing he was sure of—there would be no meeting with Douglas.

SEVEN

We often discover what will do,
by finding out what will not do;
and probably he who never made a mistake
never made a discovery.
Samuel Smiles

The ubiquitous rain finally stopped. For seven long weeks the incessant rain fell, saturating the soil of south Florida until a cool front moved the low pressure system off into the Atlantic Ocean. Meteorologists call it the rainy season. A season where the copious amount of precipitation enables one to hear the grass grow and the mosquitos breed.

To David, it seemed like an interminable dreary period. Dealing with the deaths of his two friends, teaching at the college, developing an infrastructure with the anti-Rainbow people, writing to inquire as to Brandon's progress, trying to maintain some semblance of a family life while still working on restoring his personal health. At times the temptation to abandon the fight against Rainbow and get on with this life seemed unbearable.

He looked out his dining room window in the early September afternoon, just in time to see a spectacular Florida sunset. The red solar ball momentarily hovered above the Everglades while distant water birds streaked across its glowing face, reminding him that there are places on earth where peace does exist. *Lord, how long will you look on? How long will you allow this Rainbow system to continue their crimes without doing something?*

He recalled the Rainbow official, a person named Mort Stein, who promised to call him for a meeting but never did, renewing his disdain for the drug company with their inimical view toward helping humanity. In

David's mind, Rainbow had no intentions of admitting any wrongdoing and was forging onward to seize control of the AIDS vaccine market.

He glanced heavenward, sighed, then forced himself to dwell on happy thoughts until the doldrums passed.

"You look engrossed in deep thought," Kathy entreated, breaking into his concentration. "Are you all right?"

"Just thinking." His countenance lifted as she stroked his arm.

"Pastor Jack is showing a prophecy film down at the church tonight. Why don't you take the boys to see the movie, while Hillary and I make some cookies for you men."

David's eyes lit up. "Sold!" he said, then yelled to his sons to get ready and meet him by the front door in 15 minutes. Turning to Kathy for a reassuring hug he quipped, "Do you think the way to a man's heart is through his stomach?"

She smiled and pecked him on the cheek. "It happens to be one way to get a man's attention."

Eschatology films attract attention, and Pastor Jack expressed delight as he remarked to David that the announcements placed in the neighborhood supermarkets had paid off. This was one of the largest turnouts he'd seen in a long time.

After the film, Pastor Jack gave a brief but stirring invitation to any member of the audience to come to Christ as their Savior. David was surprised that his message was somewhat fiery for a Saturday night movie. Several visitors responded to the pastor's call, bolstering up David's faith, reminding him that there are other concerns in the world besides Rainbow. David's spirit was refreshed.

As Pastor Jack stepped off the dais, David greeted him. "My, my, that was a wonderful corollary you made over Israel's place in history during the end times."

The pastor graciously accepted the compliment, then drew David away into a corner. "David, I will need you to give some sermons for me while I'm away."

"Where are you going?"

"I've been invited to Jerusalem to speak at a prophecy conference sponsored by the Friends of Israel. Both Doreen and I will be leaving in a few weeks. We'll only be gone for 10 days, and I thought I could depend on you to be the interim pastor until I return."

David's eyes filled with tears as he once again mentally thanked God for using him. "It will be an honor."

Just then Maggie approached them, then stood motionless just out of earshot.

Pastor Jack motioned for her to come forward. "How did you like the film?" he solicited.

She smiled coquettishly at David. "Prophecy is all so confusing to me. Maybe one of you could help me study it sometime."

Pastor Jack put his arm around David. "Here's the man to help you. Not only is he educated in the Bible, but while I'm away in Israel, he will be in charge and he can teach you about eschatology." He grinned and added, "That's a theological term for Bible prophecy of the end times."

Maggie nodded, then said, "You're going to Israel?"

Pastor Jack's face lit up as Doreen came over to him. He put his arm around her waist. "It's only for 10 days. Conference and vacation. We'll make the official announcement tomorrow at the worship service."

"That's wonderful, Pastor," Maggie said. She looked at Doreen and added, "If there is anything I can do while you're away, just let me know." She looked at David before walking away.

"She really has blended in here," Pastor Jack remarked as Maggie reached the other side of the room. "Always volunteering for the trench work yet never complains."

"Everybody likes her," Doreen put in.

After the accolades, David looked over at Maggie and saw her glancing back at him. "That's nice," he said.

The oatmeal-raisin cookies looked delicious. David slapped Alan's hand as he grabbed three off the plate. "Not so fast, buddy! RHIP."

"What does RHIP mean, Dad?" Hillary asked with a puzzled look as Alan's countenance fell.

"Rank has its privileges, honey. That means Dad gets first pick on the cookies." He smiled, then placed the plate in front of her.

She politely lifted two off the plate and set them on top of her napkin, then waved her two brothers on.

Kathy sipped her tea and nibbled on a cookie. "Tell me how the movie and the pastor's message went."

In between bites, David related the events and the wonderful response that transpired at the church. "Pastor and Doreen were invited to speak at a conference in Israel. They're leaving in two weeks," he announced in summation.

"Really? That's wonderful!"

"Yes, and he asked me to give the sermons and handle any counseling while he's away."

"Well, you need this to take your mind off everything that's been going on around here for the past 10 months. It will be good for you."

David nodded. "What's that letter in your hand?"

Kathy handed him the letter with the Logos International trademark embossed on the top. "It's a letter from our group medical insurance department at work that I've been meaning to ask you about. It seems our regular carrier was taken over by a firm called Medlink, and we were all issued a new ID card. Everyone is very excited about it since they reduced the co-payment and opened up the enrollment for you and the children. This way we can cut out the medical plan you have at school and just keep this one which will save us 250 dollars a month."

"If it saves us that kind of money, I'm all for it."

"We were also advised that within a short period of time, the ID card would be replaced by a state-of-the-art identification system for the entire family. Sounds cool, doesn't it?"

David reached over and gently lifted the letter from her hand, then scanned the four paragraphs. "Medlink, huh? I never heard of them. I wonder who is underwriting them. Let me borrow this letter while I do some checking." Pensively he folded the letter and slipped it into his shirt pocket, then ate the rest of the cookies while his children glared at him.

He held his breath as he stood before the darkened escarpment, awestruck by the dimension of the rocks that seemed to glow in the fading daylight. Gazing briefly at the sky, he saw the moon in waning gibbous. *I know this place,* he thought. *I've seen it before.*

He fell to his knees in prayer and whispered, "How manifold are thy works." His heart pounded as the cool air from the abyss below arose and crept over the precipice and encircled him. He shivered, then embraced himself to keep warm as he continued to invoke divine guidance.

His heart raced out of fear as he cried out, "Help me, Elijah!" He dropped backward onto the ground while beating his chest. He reached down to clutch the dry earth, then poured dirt on his head in self-flagellation.

After an interminable period, he stood erect once again, looking into the vast expanse. A unification with divinity occurred. He believed it possible to leap into the abyss to the other side of life as the Zaddiks of old did during their deep periods of meditation. He felt holy.

A voice called to him from the air before him.

Startled, he listened again. "Bath kol," he said. "This is a heavenly voice." Then suddenly a hand rested on his shoulder, pushing him to the ground. He looked up and said, "Rabbi Vital, my heart is frightened from the voice and darkness that envelopes me."

"It is the voice of Elijah, my son," Rabbi Vital replied. "Look again."

Mortimer peered into the air before him that had turned to blackness. He reached for the tiny ray of light that emanated from a central point in the middle of the night and felt his feet begin to slip precariously.

"Not so far, my son," Rabbi Vital warned from behind as he grabbed his shoulders.

"But I want that light," Mortimer cried.

"You will be rewarded for your quest for light. Behold…" Rabbi Vital waved his hand into the void where the needle hole of light radiated, and suddenly the cloak of night lifted and it was daylight once again.

Mortimer lifted his hands to shield his eyes. "It's so bright."

"Yes, it is an angel of light," Rabbi Vital advised. "Open your eyes."

Mortimer opened his eyes to see an aged man clad in a loin cloth and a leather belt around his waist, suspended in the air.

"I have a message for you to give the world," a figure resembling Elijah boomed.

178

Mortimer stood still as if he were a pillar of stone.

Elijah raised his arm, then in one gesture, brought his arm down in a slicing motion. The earth's crust beneath Mortimer began to shake violently as he clutched a nearby bush to hold on to while he squeezed his eyes shut.

"Look, my son!" Rabbi Vital commanded.

Mortimer squinted as he dared to look at the brilliant light before him, then cast his gaze into the valley below that once was the abyss to see a huge earthen crack that ran for miles. "Earthquake!" Mortimer mouthed in horror.

He sensed other subterranean forces exerting pressure on the earth, and then the giant rock formation ahead of him began to rise before his eyes until it ruptured and cleaved in two. The titanic energy release lasted only 12 seconds, but to Mortimer it was like a lifetime....

Mort pushed the recliner footrest down, catapulting him out of the chair. He felt his hands, then his face. *Where am I?* he wondered. He couldn't remember ever having such a vivid, frightening dream before. Looking around at his library brought some semblance of normalcy, but images from the dream drifted in and out of his mind until he reached over and held on to the bookshelves. His hands migrated toward his reference section as intrusive thoughts of the rock formations from his dream began to drive him uncontrollably.

Within minutes his fingers pulled out the National Geographic atlas on America's national parks, then flipped the pages until he matched the photograph with the image in his mind. He perused the article, then swiftly walked to his phone and pressed the buttons for California information.

"Fault and Fold Tectonics Institute," the receptionist answered.

"I'd like to get some information about an earthquake," Mort said.

"Sir, can you be a little more specific? Earthquake history, research, cite investigation, prediction?"

"That's it," Mort broke in. "Prediction. Earthquake prediction. Connect me with someone in that department."

"Right away, sir," the woman said.

"Earthquake prediction. Jane speaking," a deep raspy voice answered. "Can I help you?"

Mort decided to remain anonymous. "I'm doing a research paper on earthquake predictions and would appreciate it if you could answer some questions."

"Fire away! Magma flows slowly this time of the year so we're not too busy." She chuckled.

Mort curled his lip. "What do you do there at the Institute?"

"We interpret seismic shock activity in connection with known geological patterns in an attempt to predict and warn the populace about the approach of an earthquake."

"I see. Well, what is the possibility of an earthquake of major magnitude occurring at Tenaya Canyon in Yosemite?"

Pausing for a millisecond, she responded, "A thousand to one."

"Well, what if the North American Plate under the Sierra Nevada range, on the outskirts of the Calaveras fault zone, built up enough velocity at the transform plate boundary to cause a strike-slip that ruptured?"

"Nearly impossible," the scientist postulated. "The crust beneath that range is composed of mostly granite up to 40 miles thick; it's unmovable."

"Just play along with me. What would happen?"

After several seconds of silence, Jane cleared her throat and said, "A big problem. The velocity between the two adjoining plates would be tremendous at the convergent plate boundary. The thrust fault that would be generated at this site of collision would dip at a very low angle through the lithosphere, forming a fault plane with a huge surface area. The linking of high velocity and a large fault plane would result in a large earthquake, probably over 8.5 on the Richter scale."

"Enough to split Half Dome?"

"Split Half Dome? Are you serious? That rock is over 8,000 feet high, made of solid granite. It's not going anywhere," the scientist concluded.

"Oh, really? Well, how do you think it split in half to begin with? 'Half' Dome, remember?"

"What did you say your name was?" Jane said.

Click.

Mort pressed Gregory's number on the speed dial and told his secretary to schedule an emergency meeting. Then he returned to his recliner for a 15-minute power nap.

Matthew Lane escorted David into his office, then gestured for his secretary to bring them some coffee. "Good to see you this morning, David. I heard from Brandon last night. He's acclimating himself to the rocky terrain of Israel real well, and he loves working with Dr. Barrett. He said he would be speaking to you soon."

"I miss him." David expelled a sigh. "Seems like he's been gone for such a long time."

"How is your campaign against Rainbow going?" Matthew inquired.

"Slow these last two months. We suffered a setback when Rainbow's executive made that phony display of friendship on TV; it took a lot of fire out of our cause." He reached into his jacket pocket, pulling out Kathy's insurance notification letter, handing it to Matthew. "That reminds me. What do you think of this?"

Matthew read the first sentence of each paragraph, then reread the letterhead. He reached into his desk and pulled out a file labeled Rainbow Pharmaceuticals. He leafed through the file, then handed David a document from the Florida Department of Commerce. He quoted a highlighted portion of the document, "'Medlink is a wholly owned subsidiary, operating under joint enterprise with *Redisearch* and Rainbow Pharmaceuticals, incorporated in both Broward and West Palm Beach Counties in Florida...'"

David shook his head. "They're swallowing up everything they touch!"

"'Under license granted to Gregory Kavidas and Mortimer Stein, residents, etc., etc.,'" Matthew added. "My field liaisons advised me of this venture when *Redisearch* first penetrated the medical arena. Frankly, we've been expecting it. Rumor has it that this Medlink plan will expedite the distribution of their AIDS vaccine, and who knows what else they're capable of throwing at us."

"Yes, that's the million-dollar question. What else are they planning to throw at humanity?" David stood up to retrieve the letter, tapping it against his hand. "For a long time I've been getting the feeling that the owners over there at Rainbow are up to something really big, and that this business of the AIDS vaccine is only a smoke screen. A means to an end, so to speak. A way for them to achieve power by controlling the masses or something."

Matthew walked around his desk and sat next to David. "I agree with you. But remember this, God is on our side, and we're racing to find a cure for this AIDS plague. If we do, their vaccine discovery will be greatly overshadowed by the cure. Remember, Brandon and my old friend Dr. Barrett are tirelessly combing ancient Israel examining civilizations that may have the link we need to take the lead here. We just have to wait."

David grunted. "Waiting has never been one of my gifts." He stood and extended an embrace to Matthew who warmly returned the hug.

"Stay well and keep in touch with me," Matthew entreated.

David smiled and departed.

Brandon scaled the face of the cliff and looked up in wonder at the barrenness of the Dead Sea region. The disappointment he'd experienced in not finding any evidentiary clues did nothing to discourage him in his appreciation of the natural beauty. Even his latest assignment was proving to be fruitless. The rock climbing seemed his only vice, and he took advantage whenever possible.

On initial arrival he was exuberant and ready to go. When nothing was found on the outskirts of the Essene ruins or at Masada, he wasn't even phased. Hopefully, digging around the ancient Canaanite ruins would prove more exciting, especially since they were more remote and less studied.

Back at his hotel, his power nap was interrupted by a welcome call. "Brandon, it's good to hear your voice. I miss you, buddy," the voice on the phone said.

David. Brandon smiled to himself. "I miss you even more. I don't have the entourage you keep to stop me from being lonely."

"Anytime you're ready to start one, let me know," David put in quickly.

"There isn't much to pick from over here, friend, when you are looking to start a club. But you'll be the first to know, pal. What's new in the States?" Brandon sobered himself and steeled for the worst. American papers notwithstanding, news traveled entirely too slow. "I appreciate you returning my call."

"It's the least I could do. After all, I was waiting for it to come for almost three weeks."

"All right, all right." Brandon chuckled, sufficiently chastened. "Quit the remarks and make with the news. What's happening? Is there anything I need to know?"

"Two things actually," David began. "The first is plain good news. Gregory Kavidas is leaving the country. And as he goes...so goes Rainbow Pharmaceuticals. I hope it's a nice long trip."

Brandon sensed a grand pause before David continued. "The second part is actually part of the first. Mr. Kavidas is going to Greece, and we have no idea what he is going to be doing there. His press agent announced he was taking a holiday to his ancestral home on one of the Greek islands."

"That could present a problem." Brandon groaned. "Why don't we send someone over to keep an eye on him?" It seemed like the obvious thing to do.

"Actually," David replied slowly, "that's what we had in mind. And we have just the guy to do it. He's fluent in Greek, and he's not too far away."

"Great. Who is it?"

"Well, it's you. You're the perfect man for the job."

"Me?" cried Brandon. He turned around quickly to see if he had attracted attention and continued. "Why do you think I should go? I'm in the middle of a dig. This is important. They need me." He waited while the silence grew louder. "David, are you there?"

"Sure, I'm here. Where are you with that story? I've heard the news. The dig is not going well, and from what I hear you could use a few days out in the field. As vital as you are to the project, I think they can spare you for a few days. What do you say?"

Brandon began conjuring up images of the Greek islands—warm blue water and plenty of sandy beaches. It started to look good in his mind's eye, and the thought of climbing for another week or two began to look much less attractive. "Well, if you really need me, I'll go. They were starting to get off track here anyway."

"Great, my friend. The meeting is on Mykonos. That's all we know. Do you know the place?"

"David, of course I know the place. I've been to Greece before. And I've been to Mykonos. As for finding Gregory, well, I'm sort of connected to the home boy network on the island. I'm sure I'll find him."

"Just make sure he doesn't find you."

Brandon smiled as he replaced the phone. He stared toward the mountain in the distance and geared his mind toward the last climb he would take in a while.

Preparations for the trip notwithstanding, Brandon was on the slope near the Canaanite ruins within an hour. With his flight booked and his bag packed, he deviated from his predetermined plan and took off on instinct. Normally Dr. Barrett planned all the climbing activity to conform with his master excavation plan. But not today—at least not for Brandon. Something about this certain cave had caught his eye. It wasn't as high as the ones he normally climbed.

When he reached the summit, he climbed into the small cave mouth and was forced to crawl in on his stomach, using his hands to pull him in. It was not his first choice; nothing created a feeling of claustrophobia like crawling into a cave whose opening was smaller than you.

The cave soon expanded, and he could move into a sitting position. Unlike most of the caves he explored, this one seemed to have some light emanating from a higher vantage point. Brandon tried to locate the source when he saw the tiny opening in the zenith of the cave. It projected a thin ray of light toward the opposite wall. He moved over to it in a semi-sitting position and tried to gaze around. As his eyes adjusted he inspected the rock wall's surface. He was surprised and awestruck to find traces of lettering in the rock itself.

He carefully pulled out his magnifying glass and flashlight to boost the light and his viewing area. The rock face was worn with the weather and time. But he could still make out portions of lettering that he knew so well: Greek in all its ancient glory. He began copying down portions of whatever he could read and noticed that the light was beginning to dwindle. He looked at his watch and was alarmed to see that several hours had passed.

He hastily sketched the few pictures on the wall without thinking and scrambled back toward the opening. *I may not be seasoned, but I know enough not to climb in the dark!* He reached the opening and began his descent.

When he reached the bottom, he was careful to place a marker. After doing so he tried to inspect the evidence he had just harvested from his newest source. He could see from his traced relief that there was a hidden room behind the area that he had just visited. There was obviously a reason for the light in the cave. *Could it be an air shaft?* Brandon translated the inscription he had traced from the rock:

Εδω ειναι την πορτα τησ ζωησ. Τα βιβλια θα δωσουνε Ζωη αν μβορεισ να βρεισ το κλαιδι
Here is the door to life. The books will give life, if you can find the key.

Brandon could only sit for a minute and wonder. Not just a possible historic find but a mystery! To Brandon it was better than finding a treasure trove. A mystery that would give life. It excited him even more— an elixir, the fountain of youth—the possibilities were endless. If only he had more time to explore it before going to Greece. He felt like cursing his timing but instead decided to be thankful for the first find that was of significance to him. *I don't know exactly what is in here, but it has to be important. Whatever it is, I'm going to be the one to uncover it.*

He set off to leave, but he didn't despair. He knew he'd be back.

With the doors closed behind them, Mort and Gregory quietly exchanged fraternal embraces. Then Mort walked him over to the window, the site of many of their discussions, to view the panorama from his executive office.

"What's the emergency, Mort?" Gregory unwittingly asked before Mort could speak his mind.

Mort stood silent, as if he were invoking divine guidance, then reached out and held Gregory's hand.

"What's going on, Mort? You feeling okay?"

Mort tightened his grip.

Suddenly Gregory reckoned with Mort's reverent look and added, "Mort, I'm getting concerned."

Mort set his other hand on Gregory's shoulder. "This morning I had a dream that could change everything in the world."

"We've talked about your dreams before, and I know that your spiritual awareness is very acute. But..."

Mort waved him silent. "This dream involves you."

Gregory walked over to his desk chair and sat down to brace himself. "Uh-oh."

"I had a dream about an imminent earthquake in Yosemite National Park, making it clear to me that the time has come for you to increase your public exposure. I believe this has supernatural origin that is designed to bring you to prominence. We must not shrink back from our responsibilities to mankind. You are destined for greatness."

Gregory massaged his face to ease the tension while he contemplated the implications. "How *imminent* is imminent?"

Mort reached over Gregory's desk for his calendar. "The moon will be in the waning gibbous phase. That's the 26th. Next Thursday."

Gregory gulped. "That soon?"

"Things are occurring according to schedule; need I remind you?" Mort asserted. "This is the impetus needed to launch your political career." He turned stone-faced. "You have no choice but to take credit for the warning."

Rising from his chair, Gregory walked to his personal bathroom to look into the mirror and said, "You're right. I have no choice."

Mort nodded, then walked to the phone to call Channel Seven Eyewitness News in Fort Lauderdale. The switchboard operator connected him with the general information desk. "This is Mort Stein of *Redisearch*. Mr. Kavidas of Rainbow Pharmaceuticals has an important message for the news desk. Kindly transfer this call."

"I'll see what I can do, Mr. Stein," the accommodating person replied.

Mort checked his watch to see how long it would take to cut through the nonsense to reach a responsible party. After only five seconds, Mort heard a voice. "Mr. Stein, this is Philip Wilton, news director here at Channel Seven. I've heard a lot about you and Mr. Kavidas of Rainbow and especially your commitment to ease the struggle of my people."

Mort looked into the phone. "Your people? I don't understand."

"Many of my friends are HIV positive and are waiting for the vaccine to be released; even if it doesn't help them, it will help our cause. So how can *I* help you?"

Mort cleared his throat, carefully choosing his words. "Mr. Wilton, since time evolved, there has only been a select few that have changed the course of history, and Mr. Kavidas is one of those great personalities. He would like to arrange an interview and press conference to announce a future earthquake that—"

"Excuse me, Mr. Stein," he snuffled. "Did you say *earthquake?*"

"That's right, an earthquake. Mr. Kavidas will explain the details at the conference."

"I'm on my way to Rainbow right now, just do me one favor."

"Yes?"

"Don't call any other TV stations just yet. Please give us a lead on this."

"No problem," Mort replied calmly.

"Oh, one more thing, Mr. Stein—"

"Go on."

"Can you just tell where the earthquake takes place so I can square this with my news editor and station manager? I mean, does it happen in China, Japan, or Alaska? As it is he'll probably accuse me of smoking funny grass or something."

"Here in the States. California."

"I was afraid you were going to say that," Philip Wilton said into the phone. "We'll see you right away," he told Mortimer Stein. "And thank you." He hung up the phone and looked around in amazement. The palms of his hands were clammy; how he hated that. His temples began to pound as he picked up the phone again to verify some information.

After 20 minutes of calling his associates throughout California, he finally hit upon the one organization that could help him—the Fault and Fold Tectonics Institute. "This is Philip Wilton of the Channel Seven News team in Fort Lauderdale. I'd like to speak to somebody about an earthquake."

The telephone receptionist replied, "Sir, can you be a little more specific? Earthquake history, research, cite investigation, prediction, or cost to rebuild after . . ."

"Prediction, I guess."

The phone clicked several times; then a woman answered. "Bernice Sawyer, can I help you?"

"Bernice, this is Philip Wilton of Channel Seven News in Fort Lauderdale. I'm calling to verify some information about an earthquake."

"Mr. Wilton, we don't verify information here. That would be in our research or investigation division. We're involved with prediction."

Philip squirmed in his seat as his face contorted. "Well, I know that," he struggled to get the words out, "and that's why I'm calling, to verify an earthquake that hasn't happened yet."

"Mr. Wilton, is this a prank call? Because if it is, we're pretty busy here, and earthquake prediction is a delicate science that hasn't arrived yet. Your call doesn't strike me as funny."

Philip attempted to justify his madness. "You see, I'm a newscast director, and I received a phone call from someone who predicted an earthquake in California."

He heard the woman snicker. "Is this person a clairvoyant, psychic, prophet of God, or just plain crazy? No one can accurately predict earthquakes." Just then Philip heard a voice in the background. "Hold on a minute," the woman said, "somebody heard my conversation and wants to talk to you."

"Hello, this is Jane. Who are you?"

Philip rolled his eyes as he identified himself once again. "As I told your fellow scientist, I'm calling from Florida's Channel Seven News team to verify information about an earthquake prediction."

"Strangely enough, several hours ago some kook called here asking all sorts of questions about the possibility of a quake in Yosemite National Park. I normally don't give any credence to such a call, but this guy knew a lot about outer shell movements, seismic activity, and plate spreading. Frankly, he gave me a stir when he pinpointed the area where the fracture could occur, and since the call, I've been studying the possibilities."

"Is it possible?" Philip demanded.

"Mister, when you deal with the earth's unstable internal heating and cooling system, anything can happen."

188

"That's all I wanted to know. Thank you." He slammed the phone down and ran past seven astonished columnists and reporters on his way into the station manager's office.

Mort welcomed Philip, his two news reporters, and a cameraman into Gregory's office. Assuming a commanding pose, Gregory stood in front of his desk, while Mort yielded a wave and said, "Gentlemen, Mr. Gregory Kavidas." Mort then quietly retired to the rear of the room.

As the videotaping began, the two reporters looked at Philip to see who would be first. Philip nodded to them and asked suspiciously, "Mr. Kavidas, can you explain the nature of this prediction? Was this a revelation from God, a message from a dead ancestor, or did you receive this information from outer space?"

"I believe it was from God," Gregory replied resolutely.

One of the reporters jumped up and said, "Mr. Kavidas, was this a apparition, a vision, a dream, some kind of mechanical drawing, or just a voice?"

Gregory shot a look at Mort. "A dream."

"Can you disclose any details about the vision? Eh, I mean, dream," Philip asked.

Gregory looked askance at Mort, who concealed a tight smile. "Yes." He walked over to a ceiling mounted atlas, then pulled down one of the tabs. It was a contour map showing the elevations and mountain ranges of California's east coast. Then he used a pointer on the insert of Yosemite. He placed the pointer on Mirror Lake Meadow, by the Merced River, that separates the Washington Column formation from Half Dome. "There will be a cataclysmic earthquake of at least 8.5 on the Richter scale right here, next Thursday, when the moon is in the waning gibbous phase."

Mort looked at the reporters as their mouths dropped open. He couldn't believe the authority Gregory's voice carried. They looked at him as if he just came down from Mount Sinai with the Ten Commandments.

"The Hayward fault will displace the Calaveras fault, causing a slip that will build enormous, even titanic pressure right here." He put his finger at the foot of Half Dome. "The fissure will extend from the base of

189

Glacier Point, radiating out to Tuolumne Meadows. The displacement will cause a rift sufficient to shift the underlying granite base so Half Dome will fracture. The crevasse in the valley should measure at its widest point, 36 meters—"

"How could you know all this?" One of the reporters blurted out, visibly shaken by the revelation.

"I told you; it was a dream."

"Mr. Kavidas, how come our scientific experts and our geologists aren't aware of this?" the cameraman yelled out.

Gregory glared at the camera with a foreboding look. "Because I'm the only one who knows about it."

Beep. Beep. Beep.

Philip excused himself, walked to the rear of the room next to Mort, and answered his cell phone call. He then turned to Mort and said, "The station manager is monitoring this; he wants to go live. Will it be okay with Mr. Kavidas?"

Mort grinned. "He would be disappointed if you didn't."

The intercom squawked, "Phone call for you, Mr. Douglas. Your wife on 03. Sounds urgent."

David looked up at the clock. It was unusual for Kathy to call during his lunch hour. "Hello, sweetheart. How's your day going?"

"David, turn your office TV on right away! Put on channel seven!"

He reached over to his seven-inch portable TV, flicked the station to channel seven, then set his half-eaten sandwich down as Kavidas's office at Rainbow filled the screen.

The cameraman then zoomed in on a reporter later identified as Philip. "We are still bringing this news-breaking story to you live from Rainbow Pharmaceuticals, here in Wellington, Florida. The president, Mr. Gregory Kavidas, has just made a startling announcement—a prophecy, if you will. You will remember that his firm pioneered the discovery of the soon-to-be-released AIDS vaccine, and if that weren't enough of a gift, we now have a revelation from Mr. Kavidas that further authenticates his value to humanity."

Philip motioned for his cameraman to focus on Gregory.

Gregory sat with his hands clasped on top of his desk. "I have been entrusted with a great truth that I should like to share with you all. By special revelation, I have been shown that an earthquake of great magnitude will occur next Thursday at Yosemite National Park in eastern California....The wonderful thing about this premonition is that it showed me very clearly that not one soul or animal will be harmed—"

The camera turned toward Mort, who was clapping vigorously.

"There will be property damage and a reconfiguration of the park's layout and ecosystem, but the important thing is—" Gregory paused to emphasize this—"not one vital life will be lost."

"Mr. Kavidas, your account sounds like it has already happened," Philip broke in.

Before any more questions could be asked, the network returned to its newsroom, announcing that a complete report would be forthcoming on the hour.

David turned the set off and looked out his window, shaking his head in bewilderment.

"Are you still there, David?" Kathy asked.

"Yes. Just trying to piece this together. Either this Kavidas has a severe case of dementia, or he's on the rise as a greater demagogue than Adolph Hitler."

"Do you think it's true? Could he actually foresee an earthquake?"

"It's clear Kavidas is no evanescent personality but a force to be reckoned with. Further, he's not going away; that's for sure. When you connect his discovery of the vaccine, his vast assets, the development of Medlink, and now this. Only God can stop him now."

"David, can you come home now? I'm frightened."

He rolled up the rest of his sandwich and threw it in the trash basket. "Yes, I'll leave early today."

Doreen ushered David into Pastor Jack's study, then cordially invited him to stay for dinner. He accepted.

Since the time of the Kavidas prediction, both David and Pastor Jack met each evening to discuss their change in strategy, keeping an eye on the calendar as Pastor Jack's departure to Israel neared. Heightening news coverage brought immediate popularity and worldwide notoriety to Kavidas, Mort Stein, and their affiliates, both Rainbow and *Redisearch*. Pastor Jack assessed the atmosphere quickly: Any attempt to discredit either Kavidas or Stein would be considered hostile and un-American. David reckoned that both Gregory and Mort would be deemed national heroes before the year was over.

Pastor Jack sat watching news clips glamorizing the development of Rainbow and *Redisearch*, along with their founders, enlarging on their respective humanitarian contributions to society. David heard Pastor Jack mumble as the screen filled with head shots of both Gregory and Mort.

"Sickening, isn't it?" David lamented. "Do you have any idea what the likelihood is of predicting, even pinpointing with that degree of accuracy, where an earthquake will occur?"

"Unbelievable," Pastor Jack agreed. He pressed the Mute button as the TV scanned Yosemite Park, showing the valley floor from high atop Glacier Point. The cameras panned the observation post, crammed with tents and trailers housing scientists in readiness to view the earthquake below.

"David, I've been thinking since you left last night. I believe the reason the Lord hasn't given us a plan just yet is because he wants us to suspend our activities for now. At least until I return from Israel. Due to what's going on with this earthquake business and the world's reaction, let's just hold off on any rallies or protests until we see which way the Lord is leading."

"Naturally I'll do as you say." David sighed. "But I hate to let up on them."

"Have you spoken to Matt Lane today?" Pastor Jack asked. "What's his thinking on the announcement?"

"Since the time of Kavidas's newscast, Lane refused to make a statement. Now after several days, he has."

"And?"

David pointed to the TV screen for reference. "He thinks the whole thing is satanic. A colossal scheme being perpetrated on mankind to ensnare them into the web of deception. Kavidas being the chief spider."

"And I thought I was the only one who had these notions," Pastor

Jack postulated. He switched off the television, then walked over and stood next to David, who rocked nervously back and forth. He put his hand on David's shoulder. "Don't despair. God is still on his throne. We still must wait. I have a strong leading that there are answers over in Israel and that Dr. Barrett and Brandon are going to uncover them. Lord willing, my trip there will allow me to visit with them; we'll see."·

Inconsolable, David sighed as he walked to the sofa and sat down. He put the TV back on and turned on the football game.

On Thursday, at 6:23 a.m. Pacific time, the groundwater level in the Tenaya Canyon fell. Then a tilt and bulge in the earth's crust was visibly noticeable seconds before the first tremors were felt at the seismic gaps stations. The audience, perched high above the valley floor at Glacier Point, braced itself as these signals alerted everyone along the proposed fault line.

Within 40 seconds, the earth shook violently beneath the geologists' feet, knocking them to the ground. Despite their alleged safe location, a mask of horror came over their faces as the mosaic of trees, rivers, and rock formations changed before their eyes. Eyewitness TV coverage recorded man's ineptitude when faced with the titanic force of nature. Overcome with fear, several scientists simply neglected to monitor their equipment when the quake actually occurred. When the valley floor began to divide, one geologist ventured to the overhang at Glacier Point for a closer look, became disoriented at the chaos below, lost his footing and fell over, not before he managed to grab a shrub embedded under a rock. He screamed for 10 minutes as he dangled in the air before help arrived.

Then the sounds from the depths of the earth were heard. The dragging sound of gigantic subterranean rock strata being compressed and folded by mighty forces enraptured the onlookers so when the earth's crust opened, allowing the Merced River to pour in, a great hissing was heard as the water cascaded into the fiery chasm that led to the earth's core. Not a soul dared to move.

At Lehamite and Vernal Falls, waves of water flowed over the precipices as if the rivers and lakes that fed them suddenly were inverted, pressurizing and spewing their contents as the beds and basins convulsed. Then Half Dome began to lift.

One earth scientist looked aghast at the magnetic field on his P and S-wave recorder when it peaked, warning him of the jolt to follow. He looked around at his fellow scientists, jumped up in the air, and yelled, "Everybody on the ground!"

Seized with fear, every person within hearing range grabbed onto a bolder or fell to the ground as the massive rock monument continued to rise.

"Oh no!" the geologist cried out. He checked his laser transit and estimated that Half Dome lifted seven meters before it stopped. Not a human sound could be heard.

Then without warning, the facade of Half Dome began to crack. At first the fissure seemed only inches, but the boundless energy being exerted by the internal engines deep in the earth refused to abate. Cameras and equipment resumed their operations as man feebly attempted to capture on film and device what man rarely witnessed: the movement of a giant stone sentinel.

Centimeters grew to meters as the immense rock continued to divide. Ear-shattering cracking noises echoed through the canyon as the granite monolith that had stood since primordial times yielded to the tremendous power of subterranean pressure.

After 45 seconds, the great stone succumbed and cracked down the middle, leaving a gaping cleavage to disfigure forever the beautiful formation.

What seemed like a lifetime had lasted only four minutes. Then a supernatural quiet blanketed the valley, marking the end of the enormous spasm.

When it was all over, the newsmen and scientists compared their reports with Gregory's detailed prediction. They were amazed when the description matched the event perfectly.

Five minutes after Sydelle placed Julie in her crib for her afternoon nap, the phone rang. She hurried to the phone and almost collided with Julie's playpen, placed strategically in the path between the living room and kitchen where the phone was.

"Hello, is this Sydelle Swain?" the male caller asked.

"Yes," she answered without thinking.

"The same Sydelle Swain who used to work at Rainbow?" the caller inquired.

Sydelle felt her muscles in her neck begin to tighten up. "Who's calling?"

"My name is unimportant, but suffice it to say that I hold a position at Rainbow that keeps me close to Kavidas and Stein, and I have information that will help your cause."

"Is this a put-on or something, mister? Since when did Rainbow care a flying goose about our cause?" She reached over to break the connection but heard a plea coming through the earpiece.

"In the name of God, please hear me out."

She decided to listen. "Go on."

Sydelle heard a sigh of relief. "Thank you for not hanging up. You don't know me, but I was present at the rally where Stein made a fool out of your leader, David Douglas. I've been summoned on official business. Since that time things have been eating at me. I just want it said that there are certain persons at Rainbow who do not agree with everything that's going on."

"It's refreshing to hear there are people of conscience still around," she said sarcastically. "So what made you see the light?"

"I, eh, got scared after the introduction of Medlink. Then after the earthquake, I became seriously worried. I decided to try to strike a balance between the needs of Rainbow and the needs of the public, so I'm giving your group some information to try to correct any wrongdoing on our part."

"Such as?"

"There is going to be an important meeting next week on the Greek island of Mykonos at Kavidas's estate. All of Rainbow and *Redisearch*'s corporate executives will be there. In addition, Kavidas has invited respected scientists and those dignitaries with great financial power—"

"Funny, he didn't invite anybody I know," she inserted. "What's the meeting about, world domination?"

"He invited only those who will advance his cause and kept the agenda secret. No one knows what he has in mind."

"That reminds me. Just what is his cause, anyway?"

"My advice is for your group to send someone to the island to find out what Kavidas is up to. Good-bye." The line went dead.

Sydelle flopped into the nearest chair and dropped her head against the wall in mere exhaustion. When Julie awoke, Sydelle bundled her up and drove over to see David and Kathy.

The encouraging phone call couldn't have come at a better time, Kathy confided in Sydelle. She added that David had been very discouraged since the earthquake prediction catapulted Kavidas into stardom. This appeared to be good news. Kathy celebrated by making a batch of David's favorite cupcakes.

"Very interesting development, even a breakthrough," David remarked as he scribbled some thoughts on a napkin. He reached for his fourth cupcake and asked, "Could I have some more hot in this coffee, doll?"

Kathy recognized David's spirit rebounded minute by minute as he reviewed the potential of the anonymous phone call. "What do you plan to do?"

David reached for the phone, then flipped through their personal phone directory. "I'm going to call Brandon. We already knew Kavidas was in Greece; we just didn't know why or with whom. Brandon is on Mykonos now to figure it out. It may interest him to know that the world's biggest financiers are attending." He turned to Sydelle and clasped her hand warmly. "Thank you for your help. You've confirmed something that could be a breakthrough for us. Do you have any idea who called you?"

Sydelle shook her head. "I only know one thing. He sounded tormented. And I know just how he feels."

"Oh, nuts!" David griped as he pulled off the Florida Turnpike onto the southbound lane of Interstate 95 heading toward Miami. "You would think there would be some relief from this traffic on a Sunday night, but no, that's when they decide to re-pave the road." He looked at his watch. "The flight leaves at 9:20, right?"

"Don't worry, David. We'll make it on time," Doreen reassured. "Just take it easy."

David scratched his head in frustration. "Let's review the plan."

Pastor Jack smiled at Kathy since this was the third time they reviewed the plan that night.

"When you first arrive in Tel Aviv, you'll call Dr. Barrett who is either at Beth Shan or Megiddo. Once you locate him, he'll contact Brandon; then they'll come to visit you at your hotel where the conference is."

Pastor Jack nodded, and as David concluded, they said in unison, "Then I call you." They both laughed.

Tuesday evening after dinner, David ran some errands, then stopped off at the church to collect the mail and to prepare his Sunday sermon.

As he walked into Pastor Jack's study, he was overwhelmed with the numerous volumes of Bible commentaries, lexicons, and devotional aids lining the bookshelves. On the south wall were several ancient maps of the Holy Land depicting the journeys of the patriarchs and apostles. Other maps graphically illustrated great battle scenes where the Lord delivered Israel out of the hands of the Philistines, the Ammonites, and the Canaanites. Then in the corner, the modern pastoral aid, the computer, with all the resource software needed to embellish on and dress up any Bible study. He walked to the pastor's desk, opened his own Bible, and began to develop his homily.

Ten minutes later, Maggie walked into the office and softly knocked several times on the door. "Surprise," she said demurely.

David jumped up and greeted her. "Maggie, it's good to see you."

"I was hoping you would be here. I took a chance and drove past the parking lot, praying you might stop in. Have you heard from Pastor Jack yet?"

"He's supposed to call me by tomorrow after he catches up with some of our friends."

"That's great!" she replied happily.

Puzzled, David asked, "Was there something that you needed help on?"

"I'm having trouble with my Sunday school lesson; that's all," she said with a nervous titter. She walked to the far corner and sat down.

The way she moved provoked David, and he scanned her as she walked. He noticed how high and tight her skirt was.

"I'll just sit here and wait for you, if that's all right," she added with an amorous look.

He closed his Bible. "I'll get to this later. What kind of trouble are you having?"

She pulled her chair over to the desk and set her lesson book in front of him. "I don't understand the passage in the Gospels where Christ quotes Psalm 110, written by King David, as referring to himself. I don't get it."

"Oh, that's easy."

"Easy for you," she replied artfully, "because you're a scholar, but for us little people, it's difficult."

David thumbed through his own Bible, then read his marginal notes to refresh his thinking. "Psalm 110:1 is a messianic prophecy written by King David, at least one thousand BC, foretelling the event of Christ's resurrection and subsequent appointment to the right hand of God. It also advises of the deity of Christ, since David, under the inspiration of the Holy Spirit, equated Christ with God by placing him at his right hand."

"How does that apply to the deity of Christ?"

"Because in the ancient East, when royalty was sitting on the right side of the throne where the king sat, that person was considered the king's equal. So God was telling David—and us—that Christ is God's equal. And besides, Christ referred to this prophecy in Matthew 22 and declared that it was talking about himself." He looked into her eyes to see if the explanation sunk in, but she only smiled at him and let her pen roll toward his hand.

Reaching over to fetch the pen, she grabbed his hand. "How did you learn all this?"

Opening his Bible again and placing his hand back on the page, he said, "By reading and studying God's Word. My college education only augmented what the Lord taught me."

Maggie withdrew her hand. "Well, I'll let you get back to your sermon. Thanks for helping me tonight." She began to leave, then added, "Would you be able to help me next week, too?"

David hesitated. "Sure, just remind me on Sunday since my available night to come here may change."

She paused at the doorway before scooting back to him. "Thanks again, and God bless you," she said as she kissed him on the cheek.

While his heart raced, he watched her walk out.

The six-hour time differential meant that David received the phone call from Israel slightly after midnight, Eastern time. In the short period he had known Pastor Jack, he couldn't recall him being as effusive as tonight.

"David, it's really wonderful to be back in Palestine again," he began. "Our flight was smooth, and the first few conferences were exciting as ever."

"Where are you calling from?"

"We rented a car, and I drove here to Beth Shan to meet up with Dr. Barrett; Doreen is with her friends back at the hotel in Tel Aviv."

Beth Shan, a city at the junction of the Jezreel and Jordan valleys, attracted huge amounts of tourists and archaeologists each year. The waning daylight still afforded Pastor Jack a spectacular view of the great Tell and the ruins of the Roman amphitheater as he spoke to David on the phone from the visitors' building adjacent to the site. "Is Dr. Barrett there?"

"No. Dr. Barrett is at Megiddo. He ran into a snag while at the Dead Sea so he moved on to Megiddo. Brandon was there with him before he left for Mykonos."

"I wonder what Dr. Barrett thought of the earthquake prediction by Kavidas."

"I spoke with him briefly. He has some very interesting theories. In a way, he kind of expected something like this."

"He did?" David replied incredulously. "Like what?"

"Apparently he and Brandon are acquiring information and facts that will tie together a lot of what's going on. But I couldn't get all that information. Maybe Brandon knows more."

"Too bad. What's this about a snag at the Dead Sea?"

"I think you should get that from Dr. Barrett directly. It seems very involved. We'd be on the phone for an hour. I trust all is well with the congregation?"

"Everything is fine, and we all miss you and Doreen. Enjoy yourselves."

"That's wonderful, David. I don't want to run up the church's phone card, so we'll talk to you in a few days."

The congregation's eyes were riveted on David as he expounded on a scriptural passage that was dear to him. He loved the encouraging text in Matthew 14, where Christ asks Peter to keep his focus on him, enabling Peter to walk on water.

Afterward, Kathy put her arms around him as Hillary latched onto his leg. "That was wonderful. You really have a gift for both teaching and preaching."

"Mommy said you love getting excited about God," Hillary chimed in.

"Nice preaching, Dad," his son, Paul, announced as he patted Hillary on the head and ran off.

David looked to the rear of the church where Maggie nonchalantly paced back and forth while waiting for him. He turned to Kathy and said, "Excuse me, honey, while I see what Maggie wants."

Remembering his commitment, David pulled out his electronic pocket diary. "We can meet next Wednesday for a little while, Maggie."

She glanced over at Kathy. "About eight o'clock?"

"Yes, that's fine. I should be finished with my sermon by then and able to help you," he said officially and headed back to Kathy.

"Is everything all right with Maggie?" Kathy asked.

David gave Kathy a reassuring smile. "She's okay. She just needs a little coaching with her Sunday school lessons; that's all." He put his arm around her and escorted her to their car.

Lunch, consisting of bagels and tuna fish salad, continued to be the standard fare for Sunday afternoons at the Douglases.

David stuffed himself, then shuffled over to the recliner for a nap. Content for the present and reveling in spiritual fulfillment, he quickly fell asleep.

"Dad, I found an interesting bug. I think it's a mosquito. I found it on the flowers in the backyard," Paul said, waking his father from his five-minute nap. "Look how big it is," he added as he rotated the plastic jar containing the insect in his father's face.

David squinted at his son, then at the jar. "Holy cow! Where did you get that monster from?" He grimaced at the insect. "That's about five to six centimeters long."

"I found a whole bunch of them on the flowers," he repeated as he pointed to backyard.

David peered into the jar. "It looks like a crane fly, but it has a proboscis to suck blood. Huh. Let's look at this sucker a little closer."

They marched into the den, then looked at the insect in the window light under a magnifying glass. David walked over to his PC and keyed in the commands to retrieve information from an online encyclopedia.

Within 20 seconds he was looking at a picture of a tiger mosquito that matched the one in the jar. "Oh, oh. Looks like we have something here."

"I told you I found something interesting!" Paul exclaimed.

"You have indeed," he mumbled. "Go ask your mother to come in here."

Seconds later Kathy entered, still holding a dish towel. "What is it?" she said, examining the insect in the jar. "Paul said he discovered a new bug."

"Well, it's not new, but it sure is different. Look at the monitor and see what a normal tiger mosquito is supposed to be, then compare it with the one in the jar."

"It's three times bigger!" Kathy replied.

David turned to Paul and said, "Go into the garage and get me some more of these plastic bottles." When he was out of hearing he said, "Read what it says about the tiger mosquito."

"'Unlike other American mosquitoes, the tiger mosquito is capable of carrying many disease-causing viruses...'"

Massaging his neck in a vain effort to ease his anxiety he continued, "Remember when Pastor Jack told us of the little boy in the hospital who tested HIV positive from a mosquito bite?"

"Don't say it!" Kathy warned. "It's too scary. I don't want to think about it."

"Well, until I have this sucker tested at my school lab, the backyard and any area where mosquitoes frequent is off limits for the children."

"Do you think repellent will work?"

"I'm sure it will." He held the insect up again. "But for how long, who knows? If these things are mutating, we're in big trouble. We won't be able to go outside. No repellent will be effective." He shook his head as Paul entered the room carrying the empty jars. "Just one more thing to worry about."

Holding up the plastic jar as he entered Matthew Lane's office, David said, "My son found this interesting bug in our backyard yesterday, and rather than have my school lab examine it, I thought I'd take the opportunity to visit with you."

"Is that what's bugging you?" Matthew replied jokingly.

They laughed, embraced, and caught up on Brandon and Dr. Barrett's progress in Israel.

Then Matthew's attitude turned serious. "This may surprise you," he said as he turned the insect jar, "but I've seen this mosquito before. In our lab. We've been monitoring the migration of this dastardly member of the Anopheles family all the way from Brazil where it was originally found back in 1986. Frankly, we're a little afraid of this thing since it has mutated twice since we first started keeping records on it."

"You mean it mutated and got bigger?"

"Not only did it get bigger, but its feeding capacity got bigger as well. That means its blood reservoir enlarged. Our concern is that this species is an ideal vector to transport the HIV virus." He reached over and pulled out a manual of disease-carrying insects, turning to the tiger mosquito.

Pointing to a photo of the insect he said, "Excessive rains must have been the necessary catalyst to catapult this thing."

"Seems like all the necessary ingredients for a cataclysm are coming together," David observed glumly.

"Could be. The time seems to be right." He held up the specimen. "You see this gal—only the female sucks blood—she has the ideal body to carry the HIV virus. It has the normal elements in the mouthparts, but they're larger than the regular American mosquitoes. It has two pairs of needlelike maxillae and mandibles, a food channel, which sucks up the blood, a saliva channel, and a sheath. Because the mouthparts are bigger, the food channel in particular, when the mosquito's itchy saliva, containing anticoagulants to stop the blood from clotting, is injected into the skin, the host's blood is somehow integrated indefinitely. I propose because of the enlarged apparatus, if she draws contaminated blood, it will be partially excreted during her next blood-sucking dinner."

"Spreading the virus to the next person," David deduced.

"This form of transmission is very indiscriminate. This mosquito will bite anybody it lands on, whether or not they use drugs or whether or not they're homosexual. Therefore, the infection can easily spread to every level in society. And of course, mosquitoes also bite animals. Now we know that animals presently carry the HIV virus, but this will accelerate the spread of it."

"We won't be safe anywhere."

"That's why the cure is imperative. Spraying and draining their habitats has contained them up until now." He tapped the plastic specimen bottle. "But nobody has foreseen a mutation taking place. This heightens the dilemma."

"Why?"

He shook his head. "Because they will probably develop immunities to our insecticides and maybe taste horrible to their natural enemies, like the mosquito fish. Then we'll really be in for trouble since their natural enemy won't eat them."

"This kind of thing makes me crazy. Somehow, I believe the Lord will provide a panoply for his people."

"May it be so. We will need a coat of armor as the epidemic worsens. But for now, I have a duty to alert the Centers for Disease Control about this." Matthew picked up the phone and waved good-bye to David.

The following day newscasts in South Florida reminded the public of the encephalitis-carrying mosquito scare of 1991, then warned residents to avoid foliage, standing pools of water, and staying outdoors after dark, citing that this mosquito carried a much deadlier virus. Persons required to work outdoors were encouraged to wear long, heavy clothes and use generous doses of repellant until the CDC declared conditions safe.

Maggie waited in the parking lot for David to arrive, with the car's windows tightly shut and the air conditioner on maximum. She hated mosquitoes, and despite the cooler temperatures, would not dare open a window to invite any of the parasites in to feed on her.

When the skin on her right leg suddenly started itching, she immediately turned on the car's dome light and frantically searched for any kind of bug that flew. Then she turned on the radio, hopeful of an announcement that the mosquito crisis had subsided.

Tap. Tap. Tap.

She turned to see David peering in her window, waving her to follow him into the church. She sighed as if her assignment had finally come to fruition, then leaped out of the car to catch up to him.

David turned to see Maggie running toward him. He watched the way the wind caught her long hair and opened her blouse. "My, my! Why did you run?"

She hastily brushed herself off. "I'm skittish about those tiger mosquitoes the radio warned us about."

David opened the door to the church. "I can understand why. I'm the one who helped form the alert. My son found a whole bunch of those things in our backyard."

"Man, what is this world coming to? Now the insect world has gone crazy."

David closed the door behind them. "The world is coming to an end; that's what. If things continue the way they're going, Jesus will be back soon."

She stopped. "You really think so?"

"I know so." He patted his Bible. "It's all in here. There's a prophecy in Revelation predicting that insects would mutate, but it cites locusts as an example. Maybe the mosquitoes are just the beginning of the process."

Maggie shivered. "You're scaring me."

They walked to the pastor's office.

After an hour of intense Bible study, Maggie set her pen down. She looked into his eyes, then walked around the pastor's desk. "You look tired," she began as she put her hands on his shoulders. "Your schedule must be a bear. You need to relax more."

"You're right," David replied as he closed his eyes, rolling his neck in response to the massage. "My work is catching up to me."

Her soothing hands meandered to his neck, then found their way to his collar. Nimbly she untied his necktie, then unbuttoned the top buttons of his shirt, slipping her hands under his shirt to rub his chest. "I've had this thing about you from the first day," she whispered in his ear, "and it won't go away. I've got to be with you—"

"No!" David jerked, awaking from what had felt like a trance. He turned to her as she slowly dropped her hands to her side. "This is not right. I'm a happily married Christian man, and there's no future in this."

Taking the defensive, Maggie said, "David, I'm not asking you to give up your marriage. I'm simply drawn to you. I find you very interesting, warm, and handsome, I might add. I enjoy being with you; that's all."

Closing up her Bible for her he replied, "I want you to go now. I'll see you Sunday morning." He escorted her to the front door and simply said, "Good night," as he re-buttoned his shirt and adjusted his tie.

With a sparkle in her eye, Maggie replied flippantly, "Thanks for the help," and hurriedly walked out the door.

When David returned to the pastor's study, he realized Maggie had never apologized for her behavior.

As soon as Maggie arrived home, she called her fiancé, Kimsley, giving him an encouraging progress report.

EIGHT

There is no arguing with the pretenders
to a divine knowledge and to a divine mission.
They are possessed with the sin of pride,
they have yielded to the perennial temptation.
Walter Lippmann

As an omniscient observer he watched every move the group made. Their target: the structure's internal lifeline, known but to a few technicians; the outside of the structure, known to the world. Their furtive entrance, prearranged by partisan employees, placed them in the basement of the building where the greatest destruction would occur before extending upward throughout the 1472-foot-high skyscraper. A predawn installation would ensure against any interference.

Experience dictated where to place the puttylike substances composed of nitroglycerine and nitrocellulose: on the outside wall stanchions and the motors controlling the elevators proved to be most effective. The massive charges would be electrically detonated by a timing device during peak daylight hours to inflict the necessary damage and injury. Human life would be expendable for the cause.

The observer then found himself next to the assault team as they hurriedly set the explosives in place, silently concentrating on their mission, when one of the accomplices dropped the igniter coil of wire behind one of the main steam lines. The expletive he uttered gave him away.

The scene shifted to a street hawker holding up a newspaper with the headline: "Empire State Building Bombed...."

Mort awakened in a cold sweat and looked at the clock on his night table. He still had five hours remaining.

"This was different than the vision I saw of the earthquake," Mort explained to Gregory at his house. "This was a dream, and the outcome is changeable."

"Changeable? You mean you have the ability to change the future?" Gregory asked.

"Why do you doubt? Sometimes the future can be amended, yes. Remember in the Bible when the Assyrian king Sennacherib threatened Jerusalem with annihilation and the king of Judah, Hezekiah, prayed, bringing an angel to execute them all? The future changed. And what about when Hezekiah prayed to God for his fatal illness, and the Lord healed him and extended his life 15 years? Yes, we can change it. Besides changing it, we need to make it serve our purpose." Mort then orchestrated a plan.

Special Agent Reynolds received the call from Florida.

"Mr. Reynolds, the information desk tells me you're the nighttime duty agent assigned to terrorism. Is that correct?" a man said authoritatively.

"Yes. Can I have your name, sir?" Agent Reynolds countered as he reached for the standard CIA profile form.

"Gregory Kavidas of West Palm Beach, Florida."

"The same Gregory Kavidas of Rainbow Pharmaceuticals and the one who predicted the earthquake at Yosemite?" the astute agent asked.

"The same."

"How can I help you, Mr. Kavidas?"

"Brace yourself for this, son."

"Yes, sir." The polite agent responded in readiness as if to take dictation.

"It has been revealed to me that high energy explosives have been planted in the basement of the Empire State Building by members of the IDF, Israeli Defense Force, set to explode in three hours. They are going to strike at one of our symbols of freedom, enterprise, and democracy, for their God-given right of sovereignty and solidarity against the Arabs."

"Are you serious, Mr. Kavidas?"

"I'm dead serious, and you need to move on this right away."

The agent frantically wrote notes on the profile form, then paused and asked innocently, "Mr. Kavidas, why would the Israelis want to hurt the U.S.? We're their ally."

"Because American political and public affection for Israel has once again soured, and they've worried about defense since the time of the Lebanon-Israeli war. They purpose to call the media to take responsibility after the explosion, posing as an Iranian fundamentalist group. Their plan is to pin the rap on the Iranians in retaliation for their arms support of the Hezbollah in Lebanon. They believe Americans will buy it easily."

"Those rotten Jews."

"Excuse me, Mr. Reynolds?"

"Oh, nothing, Mr. Kavidas. I will contact the night director immediately and take the necessary steps to protect life and property."

"Very good, Agent Reynolds."

"Sir, my director will want to confirm all of this. Please stay at your residence until further notice. We will have a field agent stop by within the next hour. Meanwhile, we will alert the authorities." The line disconnected.

Gregory hung up the phone and nodded at Mort. "That plan to flip-flop the blame is going to work."

Mort returned the nod, completely confident that things would get really interesting from this time on.

Personally directing the investigation, CIA Eastern operations Deputy Adrian Rayles, based out of Manhattan, appeared at the landmark slightly over one hour after the initial call from Kavidas. Local police were instructed to evacuate a four-block containment area and cordon off one square mile where all traffic was diverted to provide a buffer zone. Deputy Rayles's memory still troubled him after the bombing of the World Trade Center. The terrorists had cared little for human life. But this time, suggested by some to be divine intervention, they were warned in advance.

In the building's basement, Deputy Rayles examined the plastique, then instructed his technician to disconnect the timer. Carefully dismantling and scrutinizing the mechanism, he remembered seeing this type of device before when working in the Mideast. The curious thing, however, was the stamping on the digital clock circuitry that few people know about. It was not Israeli but Arabic. He stuffed the timer into his athletic bag and walked out of the building. He was elated that a news blackout had been ordered; he hated TV cameras.

Thirty minutes later, the research lab checked the manufacturer's code to confirm his hunch. In turn they performed a search and found the timer was made in Iran, then shipped to Beirut, a known terrorist hub, where it was assembled into a detonator and smuggled to the Palestine Liberation Organization in the West Bank, Israel. He then requested an immediate audience with his director.

Waiting outside the branch director's office, Deputy Rayles continued to examine the timer when the district's public TV flashed a news bulletin coming live from the Empire State Building area. The cameras panned the police barricades and switched to an aerial view coming from an airborne helicopter, hovering within one mile of the skyscraper.

The narrator said that an anonymous tip came into a Fort Lauderdale TV station stating that an Israeli right wing commando group had taken responsibility for the planting of the bomb. However, the CIA at Langley was alerted hours before the bomb could explode by Gregory Kavidas, the same pharmaceutical magnate that predicted the earthquake in Yosemite National Park only a few short weeks earlier. The newscast heralded Kavidas as a welcomed modern psychic, raised up to protect lives from catastrophic events. So far, no official word had been received from the Israeli ambassador's office.

Storming into the director's office, Deputy Rayles placed the documentation and the timer on his desk while he continued to talk on the phone. Seconds later the director excused himself, saying he would return the call.

"Sir, this is a mistake," Deputy Rayles flared. "This bomb was planted by the PLO, who are working with the Iranians, not Israel. Who authorized the media to imply this was set by Israel? You need to make a public retraction correcting that lie."

The director inhaled deeply. "Mr. Rayles, I just hung up the phone after speaking to our bureau chief, Edward Keller in Washington, and this thing has already blown up in our face. In our interest for political correctness, we're not about to accuse the PLO or the Iranians when we haven't adequate proof to substantiate such a claim. We already walk a delicate tightrope in the Mideast, and a little writing on a digital timer doesn't cut it without an investigation. Besides, the volatile situation in Israel with the PLO will go ballistic within three hours if we announced that this was indeed a hoax to implicate and frame Israel. No, we will let it stand for now and take our chances."

Deputy Rayles turned on his heels and silently walked out, leaving the evidence on the director's desk. He walked up to the director's secretary and said, "By my calendar's reckoning, I have only 18 more months until I retire from this menagerie." He turned toward the director's office and added, "And it won't be a moment too soon."

She shrugged and frowned as he walked off to the elevator.

The Israeli government categorically denied any affiliation with the bomb planting, claiming the accusation to be apocryphal in nature. The Israeli ambassador later filed an official complaint with the State Department but recognized the public was predisposed to believing the media's report. Once again, Gregory Kavidas was right.

The recent expansion and merging of Alligator Alley into I-75 allowed Gregory and Mort to cross the 90 miles of Everglades quickly. Then they slowly drove through the town of Sanibel, arriving in Captiva in less than three hours after departing West Palm Beach.

Captiva Island's reputation for a friendly, quaint, relaxed living was just what Gregory and Mort needed after the Empire State Building incident. Gregory's altruistic label and rise to fame brought with it a commensurate loss of privacy. Something that required getting used to. A deluge of news reporters dogged Gregory for interviews, while palm readers, astrologers, and self-proclaimed faith healers sent a steady barrage of mail asking him for special tips and confirmations of their forecasts. With the heightened level of notoriety, Mort intervened whenever possible to fend off the queries, leaving Gregory to the more important matters of orchestrating his entrance into the political domain. Captiva-Sanibel would be the catharsis Gregory needed before going to Mykonos for his planning session.

Registering under a pseudonym at the South Seas Plantation resort overlooking the Gulf of Mexico, Mort hoped for complete seclusion during their weekend away.

Once the hideaway of sixteenth-century pirates and modern-day seashell collectors, Captiva Island hosts many of Florida's west coast premier resorts. Miles of white beaches invite tranquility while the countless marinas provide a fair haven for the seafarer anxious to dock on the tropical getaway island. A myriad of shops on adjacent Sanibel Island provide an endless variety of wares and artifacts to fill any and all souvenir bags.

As they walked along the beach, Mort sporadically stopped to pick up interesting shells, examining their convolutions, then holding them up to his ear to listen to the sounds of the seashore. Impulsively he stuffed them into his canvas bag to be sorted out at a later time.

Casting his gaze into the Gulf he saw what looked like two sharks, with their dorsal fins cutting through the water, swimming parallel with the shoreline. Then the unmistakable beaklike snouts surfaced as the sleek and smooth dolphins performed their vertical oscillations. Explosive exaltations through their blow holes caused him to nudge Gregory to acknowledge their presence.

Breaking out of his concentration, Gregory nodded, then reached down for a handful of sand, allowing it to sift through his fingers.

"Our lives are like this sand, Mort. We quickly pass through time, and before we know it, our time is up." He inverted his palm to show the sand had vanished. "I remember reading Victor Frankl, embedding in my mind his words, 'The basic need for life is for each of us to have a purpose; a meaning for life, a reason to live.' It's obvious to me that we have a purpose, even a destiny to fulfill, which includes dominance in the public and political arena."

Mort stood still. "Does that mean we're going to run for office in the EC? You have many upper echelon friends and public awareness, and what's more, the people see you as a Samaritan, a divine benefactor if you will, sent to help humanity. You will quickly make the transition from corporate leadership to political leadership. For you it will be a natural—" he corrected himself—"make that a *supernatural* stepping stone."

"Of course I would have to disenfranchise myself from Rainbow and Project Renaissance. I'm not sure the European Community is where I should be. If I had the time, I might seek a greater office."

Renewing their walk along the beach, Mort patted Gregory on the back. "Fear not. That will be my mission, to take Rainbow's commitment to the AIDS problem and Project Renaissance all the way through to fruition, leaving you free to concentrate on your office."

Gregory snuffled the salt air. He reached down for another handful of sand, throwing it against the soft blowing wind. "We'll be going against a strong tide and heavy wind," he shouted to the sky, then ducked to avoid the sand blowing back into his face. "But it will be exciting to see this divine plan unfolding before our eyes."

"And I'm going with you all the way," Mort rejoined as he mimicked him.

The King's Crown Restaurant at the Plantation boasted of a scenic view of the marina, secluded booths, and white-glove service, just the right atmosphere to finalize the next stage of Project Renaissance. Mort handsomely tipped the maître d' to ensure a quiet dinner.

With their dinner ordered, Mort lifted his glass aloft and proposed a toast. "To the next president of the European Community and who knows what after that."

Gregory smiled and followed his lead. "Do you think my predictions will help my popularity in winning the office?"

"Having a man who knows the future as their president will have its advantages in the marketplace." Mort chuckled. "I'll start making preparations."

With a wave of his hand, Gregory dismissed the details into Mort's care, then mentally wandered off to strategic ruminations.

Moments later, as Mort finished his salad, Gregory announced, "We need to engage the Infolink phase of Project Renaissance before the election. I don't want Infolink, or Renaissance for that matter, used as a political football of sorts, despite my divestiture, so we'll have to push the date up."

"Everything is in place, waiting for you to give the go-ahead," Mort reminded him.

"Our last discussion on Renaissance touched on one area of Infolink that I would now like to enlarge on."

Mort turned his head to give him his full attention. "Listening."

"With Medlink we have the personal profile, confidential information, and all emergency medical data on the subscriber."

"Right," Mort agreed, munching on a flatbread.

"Infolink would be all of Medlink with the added feature of credit accessibility, right?"

Mort nodded.

"Well, to accelerate subscriber acceptance, we need to emphasize our unique security system with the retinal scanner and microdot, and to captivate the market, I want to capitalize on the 'smart card' concept. Everything that a person needs to make purchases or to receive medical treatment will be on their person at all times—right on our microdot, safely implanted in their hand. The subscriber will only need our services, an advanced successor to the hologram credit card."

"Again, the timing is perfect. Consumer spending has been down for the past six months—a depressed economy—I guess mainly due to the instability in the Mideast along with the devaluation of the dollar, so this should really generate sales on our system and inject money into the marketplace." He closed his eyes and speculated, "Maybe we can unlock some of the billions stuffed away in investment and retirement accounts of the elderly for consumer spending since they're reaping the benefits of Medlink right now…"

Gregory didn't comment; he only absorbed the information while working on his lobster tails, allowing Mort to rant on.

Two days later, Gregory boarded Olympic Airlines for his flight to Mykonos, leaving Mort to set in motion the plan he had engineered at Cozumel, ratified by Gregory at Captiva.

Breakfast at the Douglas household was an important meal. Divergent schedules restricted the quality time the family could spend together, so breakfast was a time to reaffirm family values and to get a pulse on her children's attitudes and behaviors.

Reaching over for a second portion of cereal, Alan looked first at his father, then said, "Mom, Sal is having a party in a few weeks. Can I go?"

Kathy sipped her coffee, sensing a loaded question. "What kind of party?"

Carefully watching his parents, he said, "He's having a few kids over for a Halloween party."

When Kathy looked over at David, Alan added, "His mother will be there."

With conflict stirring within, Kathy sighed. "I'll see."

"No," David declared.

"I knew you would say no, Dad. How come?" Alan begged.

"Why not, David?" Kathy entreated. "They've been cooped up in the house with the rain, then the mosquitoes, and then with the added tension of all this Rainbow and Kavidas stuff. I think it will be all right."

"No one is going to any Halloween party," David said emphatically, putting a stop to the dialog.

Kathy jumped up from the table and, throwing her hands in the air, shouted at David, "I thought we discussed things here, instead of just laying down the law."

"Kathy, you know as Christians we don't celebrate Halloween. So why would it be okay for Alan to attend a party?" he asked calmly.

"Because it can't hurt anything; that's why," she insisted. "After all, what's the harm in a small party with some of his friends, chaperoned by the boy's mother? They're not going to dig up a corpse at a nearby graveyard, if that's what you're afraid of," she added sarcastically.

"I thought we were in agreement over this last year," David reminded her.

With fury in her voice Kathy blasted David. "Last year was totally different than this year! Didn't we lose two dear friends—Johnnie and Krissy—to some insane drug company? Were you not shot by who you thought was your friend from New York last year? Didn't we have our sons followed by some sleazy nuts from Rainbow last year? Didn't we have our whole world turned upside down by earthquakes and bomb scares last year?" Turning and holding onto the sink, she broke out into tears.

David stood up to embrace her, but she walked to the other side of the kitchen to avoid him. "C'mon, now. You're just upset by everything that's been happening." He looked over at the spellbound children, whose eyes followed their every move. "We'll talk about it tonight after work."

"You're going to church tonight to prepare your sermon, aren't you?" Kathy reminded him in a muffled sob.

Something flashed through his mind. "I'll make it an early night." He looked up at the clock. "I'll be late for my class. Can we postpone this discussion until then?"

Kathy replied, "Have a nice day, and we'll settle this tonight."

On his way into Miami, David suddenly remembered that the family had neglected their daily prayer time that morning.

David looked at the clock on Pastor Jack's desk, secretly wondering if Maggie would show up as she did for the past two weeks. He struggled with his sermon as distracting thoughts meandered through his mind, often taking him down the road of immorality, which he knew could only lead to a dead end or destroy his marriage. After battling with the forces of evil that would have him compromise his faith, he settled down to prepare his homily about God's love out of the epistle of First John.

Thirty minutes later, Maggie walked in. Dressed in a tailored suit and high heels, garnished with a diamond lapel pin, she looked stunning. She had let her hair down so that it flowed over her shoulders, giving occasional glimpses to the matching diamond studs in her ears. David looked at her and began to feel himself slip out of control.

"I thought we ended last week's study on a bad note, so since this is the last week before Pastor Jack returns, we would make amends."

David stood up and extended his hand. "It was just as much my fault. Won't you sit down?"

Maggie sat down, then crossed her legs and pulled her skirt up to reveal her thigh.

Despite his forceful attempt to study his notes, he found himself glancing at her legs while she opened her Sunday school booklet.

She stared him down for several minutes, then said trenchantly, "Is everything okay at home?"

Surprised at her intuitiveness, he replied sheepishly, "Today wasn't such a great day. What made you ask?"

"A woman can tell when a man is admiring her."

"Now, Maggie, just hold on," he fired back in lame defense.

Slowly rising as she closed the booklet, she reached over the desk and grabbed his hand to offer him a way out. "David, let's get out of here. Let's go to a diner or someplace."

Torn between desperately trying to remember some biblical principle or precedence and releasing the building tension in his life, he hesitated.

Maggie tugged at his hand. "David, it's all right. We're only going for coffee."

He looked down at his Bible, then up into her eyes. "Well..." He glanced at his wristwatch. "Just for a cup of coffee."

Maggie turned to pick up her handbag. Maintaining the lead as they approached their cars, she darted to hers and said, "Let's take mine."

Mechanically, David sat in the passenger's side, feeling somewhat detached from his spirit as Maggie turned on her CD player to allow erotic music to permeate the air. David just closed his eyes and allowed himself

216

to be transported to a foreign land where values and rules were mere abstracts with floating pieces of reality encircling them.

Suddenly he realized the car had stopped, and it was not at a diner. He looked at her quizzically. "Where are we?"

"My place. I thought you might object to being seen in public with a woman other than your wife. Shall we have our coffee?"

"Thought of everything, didn't you," he gabbled.

"What are you worried about? Take it easy. Relax."

He looked around nervously, then dropped his head back on the headrest. His eyes slowly opened, and he caught sight of Maggie's legs once more. "Fine, let's have our coffee."

Ephemeral pangs of conscience quickly succumbed to sensual anesthesia as David followed Maggie up to her second floor condominium. She paused at the entrance and looked into David's eyes. David reached over and opened the door.

Taking David by the hand, Maggie escorted him across the room, then kicked off her shoes as they both flopped onto the sofa. "Would you prefer a glass of wine over coffee?" she asked.

He rubbed the back of his neck as he pondered the ramifications of the question. In his mind he wanted to say no, but it came out, "Yes, I'll have the wine."

"So will I."

The conversation revolved around Maggie's childhood traveling and David's teaching career, with little said about his involvement in the campaign against Rainbow.

After the first glass of wine, David noticed he was laughing and having a good time. "Put on some of that music you played in the car," he said, patting her knee.

Springing off the sofa, she walked to the center console, pressed several buttons to activate the music, and said, "Be right back," as she continued to walk into her bedroom.

David looked out the window and said to himself, *What am I doing here?* Then a picture of Kathy drifted into his mind, followed by a voice reminding him of his past faithfulness. His guilt began to assuage.

"What do you think?" Maggie asked as she strolled out in a long silk bathrobe. "I just bought it last weekend. Do you like it?"

David scanned her up and down, then sniffed the refreshed perfume.

217

"It looks great on you."

After refilling the wineglasses, she sat down next to David and reached over to loosen his tie. "Let's dance," she said softly.

Obediently, he walked with her to the tiled section of the floor. Seconds later, her arms were around him as they gracefully swayed to the music.

She broke away from him momentarily, rushing back to take another sip of wine, then returned to his side. "I must have you," she whispered in his ear nd on her thigh.

His heart raced uncontrollably as his eyes looked down her robe and on into her bedroom. He said nothing.

Maggie put his head down on her shoulder and kissed his ear, slowly working around to kiss him on the mouth.

David tasted the wine on her lips and wanted more of her, but his spirit cried out in torment. Mentally embedded Scripture began to fill his thoughts as he felt his heart begin to slow and his spirit take control. "No, I can't do this!" he shouted as he broke from her embrace. He turned and focused on the front door, refusing to look at her. "I cannot dishonor my Savior."

"Look at me, David!" Maggie looked herself up and down. "Am I all that terrible to look at? What's wrong with you, anyway? You can't be normal."

David turned and looked at Maggie ruefully. "I'm to blame for this. I'll take a cab back to my car. Good night."

When the door slammed, Maggie ran to her bed and punched the pillows until her fury was spent. Knowing she had failed was one thing. Thinking about telling Kimsley—that was another.

At the breakfast table the following morning, when Alan asked his father for the decision about the Halloween party, he told him he could go.

George Douglas's check usually came on the third of the month, but this month was different. It didn't come until the seventh of the month, and when you're retired, that can be a long time between paychecks. David recommended direct deposit to avoid delays, but George preferred receiving the actual check so he could maintain physical control of his banking. After he opened the envelope, he called his son.

"Kathy, this is Dad. Is David nearby? I need to ask him a question about this month's Social Security check."

Kathy turned to David as he finished reading the newspaper. "It's your dad. Something about his Social Security check."

"Hello, Dad. You and Mom all right?"

"We're fine, David, but I'm a little confused about something that came with my check this month."

"Like what?"

"It's a computer readout on all our finances and medical history, with a small black dot fastened to a computer card. The letter that came with it said that a new system has been installed that will assist Social Security recipients by centralizing their money transactions and medical treatments by inscribing them on this computer chip called a microdot. What do you make of it? Is it safe?"

"What's the name on the microdot or on the computer card?" David asked, suspicious.

George fumbled for his glasses, then read the name on the bottom of the accompanying computer card. "It says 'Infolink, a subsidiary of *Redisearch*.' That's all."

"That's all? That's enough!"

"Is something wrong? It looks okay and sounds really modern. It will make it much simpler for us since we won't have to worry about carrying cash, credit, or medical insurance cards or any ID for that matter. And with my eyes bothering me, I won't have to drive to the bank so often."

Not wanting to alarm his parents, David discreetly replied, "Don't worry about it now. Just follow the instructions for you and Mom and send back the reply card."

George thanked his son for the advice and promised to stop by the following Sunday for a visit.

David hung up the phone and said, "Lord, help."

"What is it?" Kathy asked.

"My dad said he received a microdot from an outfit called Infolink, an offshoot of *Redisearch*, included in his Social Security check."

"Oh no! They're moving right along."

"This is incredible. At first this *Redisearch* takes over your medical plan, and now they're seizing control of the finances of the retired and elderly on Social Security by managing their money for them under the guise of safety and convenience."

"Is it really all that terrible?" Kathy observed. "Won't it solve one of the elderly's problems? They're often robbed or mugged for the money they carry with them."

David had expected his dad to be compliant but not his wife. "Are you serious? This is one more step toward government control—only this is under the corporate banner, approved by the government. Before long, we won't be able to buy or sell anything without *Redisearch*'s permission. It's going too far! After the government pensions and retirement checks are accounted for, they'll go after the corporate and private sector to get them to swing over to this system." He scratched his head. "This just stinks."

"Well, if that's the way society is going, what can you do?" Kathy asked helplessly.

David mused for several seconds, then said, "I don't know yet—this is just one more thing—but something must be done."

He paced the living room floor for 15 minutes before he finally sat down on the sofa, totally frustrated once again. Relief came only when he remembered Pastor Jack was returning tomorrow.

Surprisingly, Pastor Jack didn't help Doreen unpack but immediately called David upon his return to Florida. There were certain issues that couldn't wait.

Doreen escorted David through the house to the incomplete extension where Pastor Jack sat on his plastic chaise longue, writing notes and gazing out at his fruit-laden orange trees.

David looked about and said in the form of a greeting, "Good to have you home again. Think you'll ever finish this project?"

Pastor Jack stood and gave David a hug. "Good to be back home again." He walked over to one of the framed-out doorways and ran his hand across the transom. "David, since I've been away, many things have happened, and I believe the Lord has revealed many things to me. I think I'm going to be too busy to work on this project."

David's mouth went dry, and his palms began to sweat. "Like what?"

As if he had summarized everything in his mind Pastor Jack began, "Well, we must be in what the Bible calls the end times, because many of the parts of this puzzle that we have faced with Rainbow are coming together." He returned to his chair, then opened his personal notebook. "While I was away in Israel, I began to correlate many of the patterns that have transpired over the last year, and in view of what is happening in the Mideast, I've put together a gestalt. The clincher was this business with Kavidas and his visions."

David pulled up a folding chair and sat next to him. "I've been doing the same thing myself. Let's figuratively build a conceptual model and work our way up."

"Excuse me. Doreen, honey!" he called. "Can you bring us two cups of coffee, please?"

Doreen came to the doorway. "I'd be happy to," she said and departed.

"To begin with, on the political scene, when I was in Israel, an aura of serious concern is building within the people over this bombing accusation. Israel is claiming that this is a hoax being perpetrated by an Arab-bloc country to turn away American favor. I heard them call it a frame-up. Then, with the PLO now controlling the West Bank, their latest bargaining chip is a cessation of terrorism at the holy sites if Jerusalem is sectioned off to give them the land they feel entitled to. And that item alone will ignite a war. The kicker here is that the Jews have finally resumed, after many years of negotiations with the Islamic Council, unearthing the rabbi's tunnel. This prophetic piece of the puzzle, allegedly the place where the Ark of the Covenant is hidden, could pave the way for the rebuilding of the Temple. Again, a portent of Christ's return. This has many prophetic implications. And frankly, I see the West capitulating to prevailing world sentiment over the Jews so that the difference between political censuring and anti-Semitism is becoming harder and harder to detect."

"Hmm. Reminds me of the '74 oil crisis, with the 'We need oil, not Jews' bumper stickers," David commented.

"I'm afraid that is only the cusp of the problem."

Slap.

He looked up into the air. "Are you getting bitten out here?"

David stood up and brushed off his clothes. "Mosquitoes have become a big problem. I think we should go indoors."

Pastor Jack led the way into the kitchen. "By the way, how is Maggie doing?" he mentioned as he sat at the table.

David grimaced. "She's fine."

Pastor Jack turned to page two of his notebook. "It gets better," he began flippantly, as he nodded to thank Doreen for the coffee. "When we try to fit Kavidas and his gang into this hypothetical paradigm—whether retroductively or deductively—it renders the phenomena intelligible."

David began to get the picture, building on the hypothesis. "Let's face it. Kavidas' meteoric rise to stardom as a result of both the AIDS vaccine and his forecasts about the earthquake and bombing has got to rank up there with..." He hesitated, groping for words.

"A person having supernatural powers," Pastor Jack said, finishing his sentence.

"Something like that. And then there's the control. The way Rainbow and its subsidiary *Redisearch* has begun to infiltrate into the mainstream of the economy, first through credit reporting, and now they're all the way up to microdot IDs to Social Security recipients."

Pastor Jack gulped. "Since when?"

"Since you've been gone. Their pioneer program was set up to assist the elderly with managing their medical and banking needs, and you can be sure that within a year, it will permeate every aspect of finance." He shook his head. "My parents already received theirs in the mail. It's supposed to be permanently affixed through absorption onto the hand."

"Did you say affixed onto the hand?" Pastor Jack asked.

"Yes, it's a tiny computer chip that identifies the person and gives the scanner all their medical history and credit information." David glared at Pastor Jack as his own words rebounded. He looked down at his own hand.

"The right hand? David, do you realize what you are saying? You know the prophecy about the monetary/credit system predicted in the Bible—this is getting pretty close to it."

Extending his arm over to Pastor Jack, David put his hand on his shoulder. "If we add to the hypotheses that this AIDS vaccine could be a potential bogus vaccine that gives AIDS victims hope, a false hope that is drawing the world, then we are one step closer to solving the equation."

"Do you think that Kavidas and Stein are biblical characters?" Pastor Jack asked.

"I'm afraid to speculate at this point. Let's leave it unsaid until we've had a chance to discuss our theories with Matthew and Brandon. Together we should be able to formulate a workable theorem where people will listen to us."

With his mind whirring, Pastor Jack reluctantly agreed, then mentally designed a back-up plan.

"Mr. Kavidas, this is Darrell down at the guard shack."

"Yes, Darrell?"

"I hate to disturb you, but there's a Pastor Jack Hammond here requesting to see you. Should I let him in?"

When it came to names and faces, Gregory had a photographic memory. He paused to place the person, Jack Hammond, then said, "Let him in, but call down to Randy and have him send an escort."

"Right away, Mr. Kavidas," Darrell answered, then called the security chief.

The Rainbow estate reminded Pastor Jack of the ancient fortress at Jericho, destroyed by God under the command of Joshua in the seventh millennia BC. In his field of view, the massive brick building seemed impenetrable, with Kavidas remaining untouchable, much like the Old Testament city before the Israelites encircled and brought the walls tumbling down. He wondered if he would be used of God like the patriarch Joshua.

When he was politely led into Mr. Kavidas's office, oppression gripped him. The cool air gave him chills as sinister thoughts engulfed him. His spirit sensed an evil presence that reminded him of the days when he facilitated a counseling group of persons deeply involved in the occult. He shot a silent prayer to the Lord for protection from demonic forces.

The overhead lights were unlit, and the drapes were drawn tightly closed, leaving only a desk lamp illuminating the area directly in front of Kavidas. His face was hardly perceivable.

"Nice to see you again, Pastor Hammond," Kavidas said cordially.

"Again? Did I ever meet you?" he replied cautiously.

"Not exactly. I saw you from my window when you were speaking during the anti-Rainbow rally a few months ago."

Pastor Jack nodded while it occurred to him that Kavidas must have ample information at his disposal on people who don't agree with him. He looked around the room, anxiously searching for clues as to why his heart seemed to be racing. He renewed his silent prayer before making any statements. "We might as well dispense with the amenities, since there is no love lost between us. I came to cut a deal with you."

"A deal?" Kavidas scoffed. "What makes you think I need to make a deal with you or your group?"

Pastor Jack sucked in a deep breath to assist his mounting courage. "Because we can ruin you."

Kavidas smirked. "Mr. Hammond, there isn't anything this side of heaven that you could do to ruin me."

With a broadening smile, Pastor Jack said, "Well, as long as you brought in heaven, the Lord has revealed to me who you really are, and I plan to stop you."

Kavidas's right index finger began thumping on the desk, obviously keeping time to his mental calculations. Hereached over to the desk lamp and brought it closer to his face. His eyes bored holes into Pastor Jack. "And who do you say that I am?"

Calling on powers far beyond himself, Pastor Jack stepped forward and placed his hands on the desk, starring directly into Kavidas's eyes. His tongue stuck to the roof of his dry mouth and his legs began to wobble, but he refused to back down. He raised his head toward the ceiling to call for added strength from above and boldly shouted in Kavidas's face, "You're the Antichrist, the son of Satan!"

Kavidas remained motionless.

A knock at the door sounded. "Are you all right, Mr. Kavidas?" one of his secretaries asked.

"We're fine." Kavidas rose from his chair, walking slowly and deliberately into the subdued light by the drawn drapes. "What's your deal?"

Triumphantly, Pastor Jack replied, "You must withdraw from marketing your unsafe AIDS vaccine and call off your master plan of conquest. I will in turn see that the evidence we possess is buried, and you can make a new life. If you don't, then I will make a public statement as to who you are, producing our evidence to the authorities. Of course, your vaccine distribution wouldn't have a chance after that, and the world will be warned."

Kavidas walked behind Pastor Jack, then softly put his hand on his shoulder. Pastor Jack's body tilted from the touch as if it were a tremendous weight. "Jack Hammond, what makes you think people will believe you? You are only a half-rate pastor with a small storefront church, who, I might add, lost your church over a civil suit because you couldn't keep your mouth shut. Over the years your ministry has had only small victories, leaving you with a small operation, continuously on the verge of bankruptcy. Despite your faith, your ministry has little effectiveness. Then, while you were away in Israel, one of your congregants had an affair with your interim pastor, your friend David. This will be the death blow to your work."

"You lie!" Pastor Jack retorted, then hurled back at him, "Your whole life is a lie!"

Kavidas ignored the charge. "Look around you. Look at who I am and the empire that I have built. Do you think you could bring any accusation against me that would hold up? You have no proof, only circumstantial evidence, which would evaporate in public. Especially after the notable base we have just established. You're wasting your time."

Pastor Jack felt momentarily abandoned and defenseless. "Your *Redisearch* is really paying off. You know quite a bit about me—" he squeezed his eyes shut for a second and shot another prayer to God for protection—"and I know about you, so I refuse to get into a verbal confrontation with you. Knowing your deceptive devices, I would lose.

But you will not win against the Lord!"

"You already have lost the battle, Mr. Hammond," Kavidas said trenchantly. "Look over at my video screen." Gregory pulled a hand remote unit out of his pocket, then pressed a button that opened the doors on his video cabinet.

Seconds later the screen filled with a distant view of Pastor Jack's church. As the camera zoomed in for a close-up, he saw David talking to newsmen at the front door with many of the congregants huddled behind him. Suddenly he realized David was crying, but he could not hear his words.

Then the scene changed to Pastor Jack's home with his wife, Doreen, beckoning to him from the kitchen door. He saw himself running in his backyard, through the lawn, up through the unfinished extension, into her arms. Then the screen went blank.

Pastor Jack stood erect, with his eyes riveted to the screen. "What kind of parlor magic is this? If you think you can scare me off with a concocted, manipulated video, you're crazy."

"Mr. Hammond, you are looking at the final scene in your life and that of your church. What's more, your friend David will be disgraced in front of his family." He clicked the button again, and the screen lit up showing Gregory and Mort being welcomed into the White House, surrounded by foreign dignitaries. They were escorted to the Oval Office to receive personal congratulations from the president. "This is what will be happening within the next 12 months after you're gone."

Clutching his chest, Pastor Jack stumbled backward, falling against the bookshelves, then fell, faint, on the floor.

Moments later Kavidas said calmly, "Get up, Mr. Hammond. You must leave now."

Mechanically obeying the command, he struggled to his feet and sheepishly rushed out the door.

On the way home the feeling of defeat overwhelmed Pastor Jack. Staggering out of the car, he managed to walk into his backyard and sit on one of the folding chairs on the unfinished extension.

Doreen walked out and stood over him. "Are you okay? You look terrible." She reached over and felt his forehead, then clutched his wrist to check his pulse.

He sat mute in the chair.

"I'm calling a doctor," she said and dashed into the house.

Pastor Jack turned his head, thinking he heard a car door slam, then got up and walked toward one of his orange trees. Somehow the visit with Kavidas was just a blur, and the urgency of his mission drained out of him on the ride home. He touched and turned an orange to reveal a scab on the rind, then gouged it out with his fingernail and whispered, "The Lord will cut you out like this scab, Kavidas."

"Jack! Help!" Doreen screamed from behind.

Pastor Jack spun around and saw two men, one with a red ponytail seizing his wife, the other lunging for him. He darted to her defense.

"Who—?" Pastor Jack felt something hit him on the head; then he crumpled to the ground. His eyes rolled several times. He saw Doreen lying next to him. He clutched her hand.

Whack! Whack! Whack!

The sudden whacking of a hammer hitting nails overpowered his senses.

As he turned and looked up at the sky he envisioned Christ on the cross at Calvary saying to his Father, "Forgive them, for they know not what they do." Then Jack saw an opening in the clouds that led to the heavens and Jesus standing, beckoning to him. He couldn't say no.

David gagged as he stared down at Pastor Jack and his wife, then looked up at the detective assigned to the murder. "What kind of sick mind would do something like this?"

Detective Menzler held up the nailing gun with the police label attached to it. "It wasn't a burglary, so I guess someone wanted them silenced. Did this belong to him?"

David pointed to the frame. "Yes, he was using it to build this room."

He reluctantly looked down again at the two bodies, nailed to the unfinished floor. "Who found them?"

Menzler nodded toward a neighbor's house. "Teenage girl next door, chasing after her dog. The dog stood barking for something like 10 minutes until the girl came to fetch him."

He shook his head. "Too bad, the girl needed sedation. Really shook her up."

As the crime lab photographers arrived, David walked into the kitchen where Kathy waited, sobbing over the loss of her pastor. He bent over and kissed her, then walked into the living room and sat down in Pastor Jack's recliner. He looked out into the backyard as the police pried the nails up and loaded his pastor and wife into body bags. His heart just broke for his comrade in arms who fell in the line of duty.

He pushed the recliner back and noticed Pastor Jack's notebook. Looking about, he quickly reached for the book and opened it up. All the notes were ripped out. In his mind, he knew who the murderers were; this only undergirded his presumption.

David and Kathy stayed for several hours while the detectives pored over their statements, then drove home and went straight to bed.

The following morning, David went to the church, where he was met by a flock of news reporters. When they questioned him about the double murder, he found himself crying through most of the narrative.

NINE

He said, "Next time can I bring my friend?"
and I thought, "Does he mean friend?"
and I thought, "Yes, he does mean friend."
Which was quite bold in those days.
It was the Dark Ages. Men and men.
And they could still put you in prison for it. And did, dear.
Alan Bennett

Brandon arrived on schedule, thinking Mykonos looked as beautiful as ever. From the air, he could see the whole island in all its splendor, and as the aircraft descended, the unique architecture of the buildings became visible. Each whitewashed roof shone in contrast to the deep blue sea. The ancient monuments of past ages were peppered throughout the island, giving him a glimpse of a heritage that was both rich and majestic. Columns and pillars surrounded the island as reminders of the temples that had once stood as proud centers of worship. The sea provided the perfect background for these monolithic memorials that once held throngs of admirers. Only the sea with its foaming waves, timelessly hitting this eternal shore, could overshadow the elegance of the island.

Still, he was glad he had flown from Athens. With no direct flight from Israel to the island, Athens was the logical place for a layover. From there, it was a short plane ride or a long boat trip. He had thought of taking the ferry over but reconsidered when he remembered his last experience with the Greek ferry system.

On his last trip to Greece he'd wanted to go to Rhodes. In truth, he just wanted to be by himself for a few days since the family was vacationing together. It was getting a little tiresome getting up each day for a group sightseeing tour. But that wasn't the only reason he'd wanted to go. The fact that one of the Seven Wonders of the Ancient World had

229

stood there for centuries was enough to draw him. The Colossus of Rhodes was long gone before he arrived, but it had made a permanent impression on the island.

Trying to look like a native when he bought his ticket, he requested standard passage from Pireus to Rhodes City. When he inquired about the departure and arrival times, he was told the ferry left at 11:00 a.m. and arrived in Rhodes at 3:15 p.m. When they asked if he wanted a cabin, he declined. What sense was there in taking a cabin for a four-hour trip? He never dreamed they meant 3:15 p.m. the next day.

By 6:00 p.m. it was fairly obvious that they were not coming to port anytime soon, as there was no land in sight. The other passengers who had purchased standard passage were quite comfortable. In fact, when he boarded he wondered why so many families had quilts or blankets and were toting pillows. The deck chairs were taken long before he thought to reserve one. He was relegated to external quarters: the cold steel deck.

The hum of the engines, the slap of the sea against the hull, and the beautiful stars glittering in the night seemed to offset the inconvenience. Although sleeping on a throbbing steel deck was an experience, it wasn't one he wanted to repeat.

When Brandon arrived in Rhodes, his first order of business was to book a flight back to Athens. There was no way he wanted to take the trip back to the mainland by sea. Olympic Airlines whisked him to Athens in a mere 20 minutes. Although Mykonos was only half the distance, even a 12-hour ferry ride was too long.

As the jet began its descent, Brandon wondered at the way the island was built. The mere fact they could fit an airport on each of the Greek islands amazed him. But Mykonos fascinated him with its white buildings. Somehow it made the entire island look like a city of sky and clouds. He had no idea where the Kavidas estate was located. But it was understandable. From the sky, and even from the road, each home looked the same. They were all white with a little blue accent. A perfect place to hide or to blend in.

Mykonos was his favorite hot spot in Greece with Plaka, the old town district in the heart of Athens, coming in second. The similarities between the two are few, but their unique flavor gave each one its own mystique and allure. Plaka was in the heart of a city, and Mykonos was in the open sea. But both were amenable to alternative lifestyles, and the nightlife in

Plaka was unequaled in Athens. Mykonos was becoming renowned for its gay activities, and Brandon was more than happy to visit the island—alone. Traveling with the family was not conducive to his meeting anyone of interest.

He arrived at his hotel, the Esperides, and he took note that he chose this particular hotel again. Its sister hotel in Rhodes was known for its quality, and for its lounge. Greek hospitality was usually second to none. However, the hotel standard was not quite American. This five-star hotel was very nice to look at, but the rooms were a little warm until the air conditioning came on, and the decor was definitely not like the Athens Marriott.

He was sure he would achieve his principal goal, which was to relax first and then worry about finding Gregory's estate. Generously tipping the locals usually yielded information to spare, and his skill in the Greek language let him blend in. He didn't know if he would be considered a native, but he knew he'd pass as a resident.

"Kalemera kyrie," the attendant announced as he picked up his towel at the pool.

Good day to you, too, thought Brandon as he carefully gave the man the once over. Their eyes met and held just long enough for Brandon to know that he met one of the *family* and that information might come his way a lot easier than he thought. He even thought he might enjoy getting it.

"Ti kaneis,"" he replied as he grabbed the towel and walked to his chair. He felt eyes following him as he sat down and tried to preoccupy himself with sunbathing.

As he looked around he saw that there were quite an array of guests at the hotel. Expecting to find a predominantly gay clientele, he was surprised to see many families and even older couples around the pool. In contrast, he realized that Americans have few places where gay and straight couples could meet so openly. But therein lay the attraction that brought people to Greece. Their extreme tolerance and understanding attitudes were welcome to him. Homosexuality was something that was still uncomfortable to him in the States. But not here. *Why, for that matter,* he thought, *the Greeks practically invented it.*

Knowing the bar list to be limited, he ordered a beer when the waitress came around. He knew it would be cold, so he didn't care what it tasted like. He just wanted to sit and look at the amazing sky and breathe in the air coming off the Aegean Sea. He watched as people got in and out of the pool and noticed the white rings that dried on the skin. He smiled and realized the pool was not fresh water. The people exited the pool and quickly showered to remove the salt.

He laughed to himself as he remembered his first dive into the ocean outside Glyfada, the beach that the wealthy Athenians frequented. He exited the water and panicked as the white rings of salt stained his skin. He saw the people floating around him, and he knew that salt added to buoyancy, but he never made the connection. The shock of the saline content made itself known, however, when his eyes and mouth begin to sting. In fact, that first day his mouth and lips were raw from the salt. He could see why there wasn't a lot of horsing around in the water. It was bad enough having it touch your skin, but you didn't want to swallow it.

His reverie was broken when the waiter brought his beer. He was surprised, however, when the man who had handed him the towel was the man who brought him the drink. *"Oriste,"* the man said in a rich baritone voice. *Here it is.*

Brandon took the beer and looked up. *"Ev-charistò poh-lee,"* he said with a smile. *Thank you very much.*

The waiter smiled back and walked toward his booth.

Brandon's eyes followed him with interest. When he'd had enough sun, he sat there thinking about how he could introduce himself to this man and not let the man know he was a tourist. Knowing the language was one thing; using it without an accent was another. Being a guest in the hotel also didn't help him fit into the native environment.

Brandon returned to his room. He was surprised to see that there was a tray of cake and coffee waiting for him. Knowing that he did not order anything, he ignored the food and went to shower. He was not surprised when someone knocked on his door. The man with the towel and the drink was walking in before he could argue.

"Mou llenen Pano." *My name is Pano.*

Brandon realized that either Pano didn't speak English, or Pano actually thought he was Greek. He switched to Greek himself with ease and began to converse.

"My name is Brandon. How are you?" Brandon extended his hand, and Pano quickly took it and shook it vigorously. His strong handshake, together with the looks of an Adonis, immediately arrested Brandon's attention.

"I am fine. You are alone?" Brandon was somewhat taken back by the direct approach that Pano took. But he knew where the conversation was going, so he couldn't blame the man for being blunt.

"I am alone," he started almost without regret, "but I am supposed to be working. I'm not supposed to play." He tried to smile and saw that his last remark only fazed the man to the point that he was obviously encouraged. "I'm supposed to be looking for someone. Someone I have to find."

"Pano will help you. Who are you looking for? Pano knows everyone on the island."

Seeing the way the man looked, Brandon only smiled. *I'll bet you do!* "I'm looking for a man named Kavidas. Do you know him?"

For the first time the man's face darkened, and he turned away.

But Brandon was encouraged. He'd obviously struck a nerve and didn't want to let it go. "You know of him? You obviously heard the name—you turned your head away."

"You must forget about this man," Pano said. "He is not who he seems. He is bad."

Brandon stared at him curiously. "I know he is not what he seems. But I must find him. Will you help me?"

Pano didn't answer in words. But Brandon knew from the look in his eyes that he had help.

David's conscience was at war. Should he tell his wife what happened or not? He knew that he was able to stop himself with Maggie (even though he knew he had received divine help) before anything happened that would be very hard to forgive. But he knew Kathy would still be hurt and want an answer to the question, *What were you doing there in the first place?*

Since he had no credible answer, that side of his conscience won out. He wouldn't tell. He hated keeping secrets but knew the disclosure would only hurt his wife's feelings. As long as no one got hurt, and nothing happened, save a brief kiss, he would let the incident go where it belonged—his distant memory. But this did nothing to eradicate the anxiety he felt in his heart. After all, there was still another important question that still remained unanswered. *What was Maggie going to do now, and who was she going to tell?* All he could do was hope that her resolve was the same as his and that she would remain quiet.

Whether it was the incident itself or just his own sense of foreboding, things appeared strained between him and Kathy. She didn't say anything, but that didn't make him feel any better. He almost wished she would talk—about anything.

He returned to his routine without hearing from Maggie. He wondered if she was going to show up on Sunday. He almost wished it was his last Sunday to preach. Then the thought hit him: *The incident has robbed me of my joy to preach the Word. How weak I am and how humble I should be.* He asked for God's forgiveness and prayed for a repentant heart. *How can I be thinking these thoughts, with Jack lying dead in the funeral parlor?* His mind began to stir in anger again: for Jack's death, for how it was changing his life, and for the loneliness they brought. He needed Jack now. He needed to be strong. *If only I could get the incident out of my mind!* Confirmation that Gregory had left for Mykonos arrived. *Need to call Brandon,* David thought, but he knew he needed some time for a breakthrough and even some time for a break.

Still, he felt helpless. Brandon was in Greece, and Matthew was fighting the cause from the laboratory. Jack was dead. He knew it was time for him to take over and continue the fight, but he felt powerless. *Lord, what should I do?*

Sunday morning brought them back to church. Kathy grabbed his arm as he headed for the pastoral office and turned him to face her. "David, is something wrong? I don't want you to have to preach if there is something on your mind or on your heart."

David felt himself start to choke up and forced it down. He couldn't go into this now and wasn't sure he wanted to. "Sweetheart, believe me it's nothing. I'm fine. Everything is okay."

"And us?" she asked as she looked into his face. "Are we okay?"

David smiled. Nothing happened in his life that his wife didn't know about or sense in her spirit. A hidden gift the kids affectionately called *radar* was part of Kathy's discernment network. A gift he knew should not be discounted. "Fine. As a matter of fact, we are fine." He gently kissed her, and she smiled back as he went to give his message the final preparations. *Jack, I wish you were here. I need you!*

Maggie's sister, Rikki, entered the church in a whirlwind, exhibiting a countenance of a force to be reckoned with. David had met her only once before, when she was with Maggie at one of the Bible studies, but the resemblance was keen enough that he didn't forget her. The reacquaintance, however, did not bring on any feelings of joy. With the service about to start, David felt an icy finger grab him around the heart and begin to squeeze. His breathing slowed until he had to remind himself to take in air. She came right up to him.

"You hypocrite!" she began loudly. "I hope you're not going to get up there and give a sermon."

The display had its intended effect, and a crowd quickly gathered around the man now being accused.

Kathy was by his side in a moment.

"I'm sorry, but I don't know what you mean. Would you like to go to my office and talk for a minute?" He attempted to take her by the arm and escort her away from the scrutiny of the entire church crowd, but she pulled away violently.

The feisty woman stood firm with her lip curled up. "Don't you touch me, you pig. I know about you. My sister told me how you took advantage of her. You make me sick!" She spat the venomous words out.

Shock, fear, and panic welled up within him. "That's absurd," he began lamely. "I did no such thing! I have never taken advantage of your sister or anyone else."

The words lacked conviction, and Kathy's expression of utter disappointment devastated him.

"Do you deny that you went to my sister's apartment Wednesday night after your little counseling session?"

The crowd, Christian or no, reacted with enthusiasm as they listened to the account of the sordid affair unfold.

David knew that his next answers would be his condemnation or his vindication. "We were going to get a cup of coffee after studying." David's mind raced, but no explanation seemed plausible and that question flashed again before his mind. *What were you doing there?* "Maggie suggested going to her apartment for coffee, so we did." He could see the heads turning and the whispers begin.

Kathy's head lowered.

"Well, it's really cute," Rikki said, dripping with sarcasm, "that you went there for coffee and started having wine. I suppose Maggie suggested that, too?"

"Yes, she did," David answered simply.

"And you say that nothing happened?"

"Nothing happened," David replied emphatically.

"That's not what I heard. My sister is in shock, and I can't get her out of bed. Her story is very different. She says you got her drunk and took her to bed—and I believe her." She turned to walk away, then pivoted back. She hauled off and slapped him across the face.

"I'm telling you that is not true!" He groaned.

"Yeah, well, maybe you shouldn't have been in a woman's apartment drinking wine instead of coffee. If you want people to believe you, you should try and avoid being in such a compromising position—don't you think so, *Preacher?*" She sneered and walked out.

David stood there stunned, stung more by her last remark than by her slap. The church was completely quiet until he heard the sound of heels walking away. It was Kathy, walking out the side door. He knew that he finally had the answer to the question: *What were you doing there?* And it didn't make him feel good to know.

The congregation stood resolutely behind him, knowing that at the moment he was alone and unapproachable. He could see the women begin to lean over toward the closest person and whisper in their ear. He could see the reaction on some of the men's faces, and he knew that he had to be resolute in his denial of any wrongdoing if he was ever to be vindicated.

His heart welled up in grief as he scanned the crowd again. He could see that they were still suffering tremendously from the loss of Pastor Jack. He could see disdain in some of the men's faces. After all, he'd stepped up to take Jack's place—and had filled it so miserably with this apparent failure and breach of trust. The difficulty of succeeding a man like Jack was hard enough. The congregation, however, looked at him as a replacement, which he knew he could never be.

Some of the stares were becoming cold, and some looked at him compassionately. Many, however, simply shook their heads and walked away. Other cold stares followed him until he broke away and moved toward his office. The looks continued to haunt him as he thought about how he would resolve his inner conflict and redeem himself in the eyes of this church.

Brandon walked along the beach and smiled at Pano, thinking that the last 10 days had been the best he had experienced in his life. He believed that he loved the man next to him, and he knew that he had changed by knowing him. Sure, people would think it ridiculous to love someone in such a short time, but in his heart, he did.

His assignment was going well; he knew that. He had pinpointed the area of the estate, and he was ready to begin the operation. He just couldn't figure out why he didn't want to call home or talk to David. Was it still that feeling of guilt, of doing something wrong? *I'm an adult; I can do what I want.* But the sentence lacked conviction, and he knew it. Here, on Mykonos, it was different. Here he could be what he wanted with no one to tell him it was wrong.

Besides, he said to himself, *I did what they wanted. I found him.* He had located the Kavidas compound with Pano, staked it out for five days, confirming that Kavidas indeed had arrived on the island, followed by an endless flow of dignitaries entering his estate.

The compound itself seemed to stretch from the center of the island, extending into the southeast corner to the Aegean Sea. In the distance he could see the nearby island of Delos shining in the afternoon sun. Known as the mythical home of Apollo and Artemis, his twin sister, Brandon had to smile at the symbolism. Where else would Kavidas situate his Greek seat but overlooking the godlike palace of Apollo in the form of modern-day Delos? The island was completely uninhabited and looked serene and majestic. Brandon wondered how often Kavidas would venture to the island and walk its shores, thinking of the gods and the power they wielded—not unlike the puissant power he himself commanded.

The mansion and the estate grounds were not visible from any distance. It was secluded and heavily guarded, but Pano was undaunted; he knew a way to get Brandon in. Pano had friends all over the island and was able to connect with many of the staff and concessionaires that were servicing the conference. This afternoon they would go in to learn what called the meeting of so many powerful people together.

Brandon looked into the mirror and tried to adjust his bow tie.

Pano came up behind him and reached over to pull it into place. He smiled at Brandon's reflection. "You are beautiful," Pano said as Brandon tilted his head back onto Pano's shoulder. "We must be careful. You must fit like a glove and not stand out. You must not be recognized."

Brandon grimaced as the realization of what Pano was saying set in. "You're spoiling the mood," he said playfully as he squirmed away.

"I would rather spoil the mood than lose you tonight," Pano said seriously. "Kavidas does not fool around. You must take this seriously."

"I will," Brandon said. "You're right. I'm just so happy; it's hard to be so serious. I know that I owe this all to you. I don't know how I would have done anything without you."

"Do not thank me now, *paidi mou*. We are not safe yet. Are you certain you know how to do this?" The man looked quizzically at Brandon as he raised his arm with an imaginary tray.

"Do what?" Brandon inquired. "Carry a tray and serve hors d'oeuvres? I should think I could do that easily, in spite of your warning that it is harder than it looks." He slapped Pano's back and began to walk out toward the waiting cab. "Greeks don't have a monopoly on hospitality, you know. We entertain in America, too."

"Yes, but paying the bill and doing the work are two different things."

Until that point in time, Brandon felt that he had lived a life of privilege. He had seen the great cities of the world, he lived in a mansion, though a modest one, and was accustomed to luxury. There was no comparison in his experience for the opulence of the Kavidas estate. It was vast, elegant, and regal. But there was something more. It added to the character of the place and created an atmosphere.

Brandon stared at the furnishings of gold and silver, the tapestries of historic events that surrounded and draped the walls. It went beyond wealth as he knew it. He had been to the homes of some of the wealthiest people in the world. It just wasn't the same. It was as if there was a presence or driving force that guided the people around the house. Something, or someone, had carefully controlled the estate through the centuries and preserved a long-gone era. The fixtures cried out with history; each one held a story Brandon longed to hear. But he didn't have the time. He was there to do a job and to gain information.

Something spoke out to him as he surveyed the room. Antiquity, that was it. Ancient beyond all that he had ever known. He was puzzled. The place was carefully preserved with every item in sight in good repair as if it was brand new. The candelabra on the mantel was heavy, made of antique gold and ornately fashioned to resemble an ancient lamp. The piano was shaped like an old-fashioned harpsichord, and Brandon could just imagine that it had been there during the time of Mozart or Bach. Everything he looked at or touched gave him the feeling of time. The place itself was an anachronism in every detail. It both fascinated and terrified him.

Scanning the crowd seemed relatively safe as the guest of honor, or host, had not yet made an appearance. Brandon shot a peek into a wall mirror and realized that a week in the Greek sun had done wonders to darken his complexion to an olive brown, and he hoped that he would be fairly unrecognizable. He almost felt as if he was flattering himself as he looked around the room. Some of the world's richest, most powerful and influential people were in attendance. *How would they know me?* he thought with chagrin. His family influence had not yet spread to the European Community.

When he learned that Gregory had been elected president of the EC, he was stunned. Not because of the election. It was hardly unprecedented for a celebrity with his status to gain political office. His strides in the war against AIDS as well as his philanthropic offerings certainly qualified him. What made Brandon curious was how Kavidas knew to invite the EC to his home. He had already invited the group before the election. The semiannual meeting of the EC was held in various places. It was not unheard of for a member to host the gathering. *Could he have known he was going to win?*

Despite Pano's concern, Brandon quickly adjusted to the job of being a server at the gala party quite easily. He had to concentrate so much on what was being served that he had little time to concern himself with the activities of the party itself. However, he made sure that both he and Pano were on the team that served the meals. Then he would be able to hear more of what was going on.

The first day was basically fruitless, with the exception of his becoming accustomed to the house, his coworkers, and the job. He also noticed that there was a section of the house that was even more mysterious than the rest—the basement.

He discovered it by accident.

"Basili," Stelio, the maître d', called out to him, "go down and get two more cases of the good red wine for the afternoon."

Brandon nodded to the man and went in search of the basement door. He knew that there was one off the kitchen, so he headed in that direction. He laughed as he thought about his name, since *Brandon* was not exactly a Greek name, and there was no real translation. *Basili* was a fairly common name, but the word meant king, so he couldn't argue when Pano told him to use it. It also was the closest one that resembled Brandon, and he needed to condition himself to answer to it as soon as someone called it.

The basement was very well lit, and he could see the foundation of the house. Huge stones, each the size of a small room, were carefully placed in line to form the smooth walls of the lower basement. The cracks that separated the stones were very thin and smooth. As you looked at each surface, it was as if you were staring at a sheer, hard, and solid cliff wall. He ran his fingers along the crack and imagined the age of the building. He imagined that it was very old. What bothered him was that he felt something else. The house seemed almost too perfect in its antiquity.

Curiously he poked around and saw several doors leading to several staircases for various parts of the house as well as several large storerooms. He found food and supplies that could feed a large amount of people for months with ease. He also came upon an ornate door with engraved markings depicting various parts of marine life, sea shells, and beach fare.

He saw the word *thalassa* engraved in the center and deduced the door led to the ocean. It appeared as if it was no longer used, and he reasoned it was in use before the large swimming pool was put in. However, it was a long distance to the water, and the basement was fairly deep. Looking closer, he saw that the door was padlocked and felt disappointed. He really wanted to see how it led out to the water. A subterranean tunnel was just the sort of surprise he'd expect in this house, which was turning out to be full of wonders.

He attempted to locate the wine cellar, realizing they would come looking for him soon, and looked through several doors before finding the storeroom. Multiple rows of bottles were before him, and he could smell and see that there was a fortune in rare vintage wines. He began moving several cases out into the open.

He shifted around several cases until his curiosity piqued. He noticed a crest out of the corner of his eye and picked up a bottle before leaving. *Rothschild Bordeaux 1908* was imprinted on the label. He was unable to calculate how much the bottle was worth and carefully began putting it back in place when someone came up behind him. Startled, he gasped in surprise and dropped the bottle on the floor.

"Pano!" he exclaimed as he turned around and saw his companion.

Pano looked just as surprised as the bottle exploded and splattered wine all over the floor. "*Panayia mou!*" he cried as the wine bubbled and started to settle in the cracks.

Brandon leaned against the wall, then panicked as he looked to see what was behind him. "Now what?" he asked Pano nervously. "That bottle was worth thousands—and look at the mess! They'll discharge us for sure! And what are you doing here, anyway?" His voice took on an angry tone, both from the surprise and shock of the accident.

"Stelio told me you were getting the wine. I came to help you carry it. I'm sorry, *paidi mou.* I didn't mean to frighten you."

Brandon started to shake with worry. "I know. I'm just not used to this spy routine. What should we do?" He quickly realized that they had no time for regrets and had to salvage the situation as best they could.

"Calm down, *Basilimou.* We must act as if nothing has happened. Kavidas will not miss this wine; he will not know it is gone. We will clean up and go about our business. No one will know it happened when we were here. Bottles crack when they are old. It is not as unexpected as you might think."

Brandon could see that Pano was serious and not alarmed, so he forced himself to calm down and began to scramble to find something to clean the wine up off the floor. He just wanted to get out of here.

"You're right. Help me move this rack out of the way so we can clean up the glass and most of the wine. It's running toward the wall." The men moved the rack from the corner and began to collect the shards of glass. As they finished, Pano grabbed a cloth from the storeroom and began to wipe up the wine.

"Basili, there is very little wine here," he observed as he mopped the floor.

Brandon crouched and ran his finger along the floor. It was damp, but there was no puddle. He moved toward the wall and pressed his finger into the crack between the floor and the wood wall causing it to move.

"Pano, there is something behind this wall! There is a crack in the floor. The wine is going into it and behind it." He gestured by pressing against the wall itself. The wood moved. Brandon stood up, and Pano leaned against the wall until they heard a click. Both men moved back as the door swung outward. They scrambled to move the rack out of the way to open the door completely.

The doorway was completely dark, and an acrid smell wafted up toward them, mingled with the now puissant smell of the spilled wine. The only thing visible was a step. Brandon saw what looked like fog begin to roll into the wine cellar. He momentarily recoiled from the vitriolic spew that was now rolling onto his feet, but he pressed on.

"Come on," said Brandon. "Let's go down and take a look." His concern and caution rapidly gave way to inquisitiveness as his adrenaline pumped wildly with this new discovery.

"No, Basili!" Pano exclaimed. "We will be missed; they will come looking for us. We cannot be caught down there. Kavidas is a powerful man. Two men disappearing will not be strange to the government if he is involved. He has many connections, and whatever is down there must be secret. That is obvious to me."

Brandon moved to close the door as Pano dragged the rack back into place to restore the cellar's appearance. The wisps of fog disappeared from the air, leaving only a vile stench behind which began to mix with the smell of the wine.

"Pano," Brandon began, his voice now a whisper, "that's why I'm here! To see what is going on."

"No, *paidi mou,* you are here to see why they are having this conference, and we will find that out. To go down there is to invite trouble. We do not care what he does down there. He may not even know it is there. It smells old and bad. Leave it alone."

Brandon escorted Pano out and closed the outer door to the cellar.

"Pano, I can't just leave it," Brandon pleaded. "I need to know what is down there. If you don't want to help me, I will do it alone." He could see the man stiffen as he turned his back.

Pano turned him around to face him and looked at him squarely. "Basili, *Brandon,*" he started, "I don't know why you want to do this. But you do not have to do it alone. You just cannot do it now. The conference will last for a few days. An opportunity will come where we can slip away unnoticed. But now we must go. You must listen to me. You are not in America where it is safe and where you have rights. Here on this island no one will question Kavidas, not even the government. Come on." Pano grabbed a case of wine and moved toward the basement steps. He paused at the steps.

Brandon begrudgingly followed Pano's example and grabbed a case of wine.

An opportunity did not present itself again that first day, and by the second day Brandon was convinced that he would have to do something drastic to get information.

However, by midafternoon of the second day, the conference was getting serious, and he could tell by the tone of the speakers and the guests that the real purpose was about to be unveiled. Both he and Pano were making themselves conspicuously present and busy to be around the delegates. Brandon's only concern was to stay clear of Kavidas and his immediate entourage to avoid detection. He didn't know if they knew him or not, but he wouldn't take a chance.

When Kavidas finally called the ensemble together to speak, Brandon could feel his heart skip a beat. Being in a hostile territory and spying on someone was not as glamorous or as easy as he had thought it would be. In fact, it was not only work; it was dangerous and sometimes terrifying. *It sure doesn't look this way in the movies,* he thought as his heart raced and his anxiety heightened.

Brandon scanned the room. He could see the relaxed look on all the members' faces. It was obvious that the combination of good food, wine, and elegant surroundings had softened the group for Kavidas's latest revelation.

The room was decorated in the style of an old Italian palazzo. Brandon could see several paintings that could only be described as priceless hanging on the walls between the tapestries. The vaulted ceiling was lined with splendid beams of fine cedar that still gave off a faint scent of the outdoors. The marble fireplaces, one at each end of the room, were works of art in their own right. The carved relief depicted angels coming down to assist men in various worldly pursuits. The mantels were lined in shiny gold and silver, and the warmth helped to add to the ambiance of the room.

The members all seemed comfortable enough to casually debate but exuded an energy that surrounded the room in an aura. It was almost tangible enough to see it. Brandon could feel it well enough to know that it was coming not just from the members or from Kavidas. Part of it was coming from the house.

"Friends, the time has come to discuss the culmination of our grand purpose for being here this weekend. We are living in truly momentous times."

Brandon was trying to look busy but was feeling strangely obvious in his forced but contrived behavior. He was startled to hear English again. Kavidas was addressing the crowd in a language that was apparently a common denominator for all of them. He had heard several languages being used consistently the last 36 hours. English hadn't been one of them.

"I have gathered us all together to renew and bind old ties and to offer you and your governments the one thing that has eluded all of the scientific world. The AIDS vaccine."

The room immediately began to buzz with conversation, and Brandon himself felt an immediate alarm. He looked around and saw nothing but excitement. For him, it was more of a feeling of dread.

"I realize our agenda was supposed to be more succinct: the first meeting of my presidency of the EC, and I called for it here on Mykonos. Let me preface this speech by saying that I am honored to represent the EC in all its endeavors. And I thank you all for electing me to this grand post. We have discussed many subjects relative to common interest. However, we are here today for an entirely different purpose. One that will affect each one of your countries. A purpose that will assist you in ironing out a dreaded killer. A disease of pestilence. A disease of hatred that is full of vigor. We are here today to iron out the details that will be necessary to facilitate the transfer of the necessary vaccine in sufficient quantities to those of you whose people are in desperate need. However, I have some news that will undoubtedly be considered ill-fated for those of you who have waited for so long."

The fervor that had erupted in the room was vanquished as the crowd waited in anticipation for the next step. Brandon, being more cynical than the invited guests, waited for "the catch."

"Our facilities are insufficient to provide adequate quantities of the vaccine for global distribution at this time. Naturally, to protect our discovery and our considerable investment we must safeguard our product and its manufacture. In order to be fair in the distribution, we have developed an information system that will enable us to identify the most desperate needs in your respective countries and fulfill them with the utmost urgency. By graduating through several different levels, our system will enable us to inoculate the global population within one to two years. Standard distribution would take three years to reach some of the more obscure areas that you represent." Kavidas stopped to allow the group to digest the information.

"Signore," began an Italian delegate, "your proposal is most intriguing. Tell us what we must do to implement this system. What is the cost and what is your criteria?"

The crowd nodded as the question was raised.

Kavidas waited till there was relative quiet before answering. "In order for the information network to be successful, the only requirement is that everyone participate. As for the cost, it will be spread equally among the members according to their population and participation in the inoculation scheme. The implementation will be taken care of through Rainbow's corporate structure, which will be organized and conducted by this man." He paused and turned to Mort, then added, "Ladies and gentlemen, my right hand, Mr. Mort Stein."

Mort stepped into full view, and Brandon turned around to face the serving table.

"With my pressing commitments in the political arena, I must retire from some of my corporate efforts for now. I'll monitor everything from a distance while Mr. Stein has control of the hands-on operation. It's only fair to the European Community, which has sought to place me in this position of honor."

Brandon's face flushed with frustration. He realized that he was involving himself in a scheme that would affect the entire world while he also knew that his presence would present some problems to not only Kavidas but his own friends and associates. His feeling of wanting to disappear became more acute, and he moved toward the other servers who were preparing coffee and drinks. In his peripheral vision he could see the throng of people coming up to meet and ingratiate themselves to Mort Stein, who would be the conduit for not only the precious vaccine but obviously other information and technological advances as well. Brandon could see Kavidas begin to fade into the background as he pushed Mort into the spotlight.

Something bothered him, however. Why would a man whose achievements just catapulted him to worldwide notoriety then take a backseat to his second-in-command? Brandon couldn't help but think that something else was in the works. After all, the AIDS vaccine was enough to bring anyone to a worldwide meteoric rise. Add Kavidas's power of prediction, and it seemed hard to keep him out of the media. The job as president of the EC seemed an easy victory. He only wondered if Kavidas was truly setting his sights that low. Brandon could see that there was a grand scheme being orchestrated. He just couldn't figure out all the players.

The next few hours kept the serving crew busy as they ministered to the needs of the delegates and provided them with every comfort they could provide.

When Brandon and Pano finally left for home, Brandon having forsaken the hotel for the comforts of Pano's small house, Brandon breathed a sigh of relief.

"You must be glad, *paidi mou,* that you have found out what you wanted to know. You are finished here."

Brandon sensed Pano's discomfort in speaking about the subject that apparently spelled Brandon's upcoming departure.

"I am not done," Brandon insisted. "I have something else I have to do, and I want your—no, I *need* your help. But in any case, I want you with me. Here and now and then when I leave, I want you to come with me to America. I've been alone for so long, and I can't bear to think of going back without you."

Brandon closed his eyes as he pictured the road before him. It made him hold on that much tighter to that which was precious to him, knowing that he might lose everything before he gained anything else. He knew that the time was coming where he would have to make a choice: leave Pano behind or take him and introduce him to his family, his friends, and his life. He could easily weave him into his life and believed his family would understand, but it was his father and his Christian ethic that worried him. The ramifications were sure to be of a significant magnitude. His standing in the corporation, his position in the office, in his family: all things that haven't been addressed as of yet, since not one of his *friends* had ever made it past this point. No one had ever been brought home...*until now.*

In reflection, Brandon remembered when he first addressed the issue with his father. It was during his dating with Michelle. *Yes, that was it,* he recalled....

Brandon took a deep breath before he walked into the house after a night at the movies with his girlfriend, Michelle. *Hiding my lifestyle in high school was bad enough,* he thought, *but coming home to tell Dad about my love life is even worse. How am I going to tell my dad I broke up with Michelle?*

Brandon silently asked himself why he even bothered with the question. Breaking up with Michelle was the easy part. It was *why* he was breaking up with Michelle that would bother his father. *Getting Dad to understand me; that's the trick,* Brandon thought as he finally turned the key. Brandon's father had always been generous, and growing up in a setting of wealth and privilege had been part of Brandon's life since he could remember. But his father had always reminded him that with those privileges came responsibility. "To whom much is given, much is required," his dad used to say. Brandon had no doubts he'd be disappointing his father today.

Telling his friends he was gay had been one thing. They got over it and they understood. Living this lie for his father's sake was another. He didn't want to date Michelle, and he didn't want to get involved with another girl. He had avoided this confrontation and argument long enough. Now it was time to tell his dad. In fact, he was afraid not to tell him. He knew that if he didn't come clean soon enough, someone else would tell his father. He knew how that would wound his dad, so he resolved to at least spare him the humiliation of being the last to know. *Small comfort that will be tonight,* he thought sadly as he entered the house.

Having to plan a strategy was difficult but no more difficult than when he had told his friends. In fact, telling his friends, while it had been rehearsed, was more of a spontaneous act than telling his dad. This had taken careful planning. While each reaction was anticipated, Brandon knew that the element of surprise would play a key factor in his father's response. It was impossible to plan in its entirety. He had to trust that he had calculated each detail as best as he knew how.

Matthew Lane, a man of discipline and composure, spent much of his leisure time in his library. The very place Brandon found him. As always, Matthew jumped up to greet him.

"How was the movie?" Matthew asked as he embraced his son warmly. He put his book down and motioned for Brandon to have a seat.

"Great, Dad," Brandon replied as he sat down. "It was fine."

A pause filled the air as Brandon decided what to say next. "Dad, I don't know quite how to tell you, but Michelle and I broke up tonight." He lifted his head to meet his father's gaze. He could see the instant look of anguish in his father's face as he responded.

"I'm sorry to hear that," he replied with empathy. "What happened?"

"Nothing actually happened," Brandon said coolly. "I just felt it was better that we break up." He stopped to let his father digest the information before continuing.

"Is there someone else?" Matthew inquired.

"No one in particular," Brandon responded quickly. One thing he wanted to avoid was being set up with someone else. Another girl he would be forced to hurt.

"Is Michelle all right?" Matthew asked kindly.

"She's fine. I think she expected it."

Matthew said nothing as he studied his son's face. Brandon knew that Matthew was trying to read his emotions and possibly even read his mind.

"What happened? She's just not the one?"

Brandon felt ashamed as his dad innocently asked questions, knowing that his father sincerely wanted the best for him and only asked out of love.

"Dad, there's something I've been meaning to tell you. I don't quite know how to say it." Brandon stared at his father and directly met his eyes. "I think it has a lot to do with the breakup."

Brandon saw his dad rearrange his chair as if he was preparing himself for this latest update on Brandon's life. *Somehow,* Brandon thought, *my father is not going to be ready, regardless of his preparation.*

"What is it, Brandon?" his father politely asked.

Brandon felt a momentary panic and silently debated whether or not this was the time and place he should enlighten his father. He glanced around the room at the familiar mementoes and questioned whether or not his father suspected. *Surely he has an idea,* Brandon thought as he mustered his courage.

"Dad, I've been doing a lot of thinking. I find that I'm different from most young men my age. I don't find myself having the same feelings that they do." *There,* he thought, *I've said it. It may not be clear, but I've started the ball rolling.* Brandon looked to see if his father had taken his meaning.

Matthew just continued to look at Brandon, seemingly unaware that a life changing statement had just been uttered. "Brandon, you've always been different. You're smart and mature. You never really felt the way other boys do."

Brandon thought he almost detected a hint of pride in his father's voice, and his heart sank. *How do I tell him now? He's expecting something great. I can't imagine this will make him happy.* Brandon quickly thought of an alternative to the present conversation but was reminded of the fact that he had already told his friends. The day of reckoning seemed at hand.

"I mean, about women, Dad. I don't feel the same way about them that other men do." With this, Brandon looked to the floor, unable to meet his father's glance.

Matthew said nothing as Brandon fidgeted with his hands. He waited patiently as Matthew absorbed the news. Or so he hoped. He didn't want to explain any further.

Fortunately he didn't have to. The silence led to Matthew's realization. As the truth dawned, Matthew's face drained of color. The muscles sagged, and suddenly he looked haggard.

"I see." Matthew pursed his lips as he nodded in reply. "This is some revelation. How long have you been keeping this from me?"

Brandon could hear the disappointment and anger in his father's voice but knew that he could not back down now.

"I don't even know how long I've known," Brandon replied honestly, "so I can't say how long it's been that I haven't told you." He ventured a glance at his father's face, then forced his stare back to the floor.

"Am I supposed to be glad you're finally telling me?" Matthew said incredulously. "Should I be impressed by your progressive thinking or your grasp of the avant-garde?"

Brandon heard the pain in his father's voice. Whenever his father started using French, Brandon knew he was in trouble.

"Dad, it isn't as if I planned it or made it happen. It's just who I am." He hung his head, waiting for his father's response. It wasn't long in coming.

"Oh, it's just what you are! I see. So God is responsible. Is that what you're trying to say? That God made you this way so I should just accept it?" Matthew stood up and moved away toward the center of the room.

Brandon followed with his eyes and tried to gather his defenses. Things were unfolding just as he had expected. "Dad, I didn't expect you to understand. I just hoped you would try to support me. Even if you don't agree." Brandon knew this was a mistake even before he had completed his statement.

"Agree? Support? How can you even think that! I don't agree or support it, and I won't understand *this!* I'll do everything I can to change your mind. I'll do everything I can to show you the truth." He walked over to Brandon and began to put his arm around him. As if a fatherly gesture would bring him around. Help him back to the road he should be on.

250

"What truth?" Brandon shouted as he pushed Matthew away. "I don't want your truth. I don't want your support if it means changing who I am." Brandon's defiance was met with Matthew's stern disapproval.

"Brandon, you don't even know who you are. You just admitted that. If this is a phase, I'll help you through it." Matthew tried to be conciliatory, but Brandon knew he was going to be steadfast in his conviction. He always was.

"Dad, it's not a phase. You can't help me. For once, you can't help me." Brandon felt the anger well up inside him, knowing that his father would not accept him. Not like this. But it dissipated quickly. He never expected anything else. His father had always been faithful to what he believed. Brandon knew there was no reason he would change that now. In fact, he always admired his father for the way he stood by what he believed. It just made it hard now, since Brandon didn't feel the same way. The fact that Matthew couldn't help, couldn't make things right—that was what Brandon knew would hurt his father most. With his mother gone, his father had always tried to be everything—and he had! Brandon could see in his father's face that the agony of being helpless was starting to become real.

"So that's it," Matthew said flatly. "There's nothing I can do? Nothing I can say?"

Brandon felt a knot in his throat as he realized he was causing this pain in his father and knew that he could not take it away any more than his father could help him. "You could tell me that you love me." The dam burst, and Brandon cried.

Matthew didn't hesitate to take him in his arms and console him. The anger was gone for both of them, and what was left was a father and son.

"Brandon, you're my son. My only son. But I can never accept this part of you. I won't because I don't believe it's God's best for you." He patted Brandon's head as his son cried on his shoulder. Then he lifted Brandon's face and looked into his eyes. "But I will never stop loving you. No matter what you do, I will always love you. I can't say I will support you, and if you insist with this lifestyle, I'll have no choice but to oppose you in it. But that will never change how I love you."

Brandon nodded and tried to wipe the tears from his face. "I always knew that, Dad." He walked over to the bookshelf and casually wiped the dust off a book as a distraction.

Matthew Lane watched his son carefully. Questions assailed Matthew about how deeply Brandon felt, whether he really had chosen to be gay, or if he was involved with someone now. Questions that Matthew wanted to ask but didn't. Either because he didn't want to know the answers yet or because he wasn't ready. He avoided the issue and concentrated on what he should do next.

Neither of them seemed to know.

"Should I be preparing myself to meet someone?" Matthew finally ventured to say.

"No," Brandon replied, almost shocked. "There isn't anyone right now. Why?"

"I just want to be ready when the time comes."

"Why?" Brandon asked guardedly. "Is something going to happen? Something I should know?"

Matthew paused before answering. It was a good question, one to which he didn't currently have the answer. "I'm not sure. I guess we'll have to cross that bridge when we come to it. *If* we come to it."

Brandon looked up and saw his father giving a wry smile. It was just enough to bridge the gap that had widened between them. "Okay, Dad. I'm willing to wait and see if you are."

"Sounds good to me. I've seen and heard enough tonight to last me a while."

Brandon said good night and walked back up to his own suite of rooms. For better or for worse, he was glad it was all over.

The only thing that gnawed at him was the fact that someday he would have to confront his father again. Only then, he wouldn't be alone. He went to bed wondering what that would be like. *I don't see why I'd have to face him with this—I could just not tell him. Then I only have to worry about how I would hide it.* The thought brought him no comfort, however, and made him question why he even told his father in the first place. *After all,* he said to himself as he drifted off to sleep, *it might never be an issue. I might never have someone to bring home. Then all this will have been for nothing.*

Kathy Douglas turned onto 119th Terrace with anticipation and determination. She was a woman whose mission was simple: discover the truth and deal with it. Knowing that her family was in jeopardy, she knew it was up to her to stand up and fight. *And I won't give up, not unless I'm absolutely forced to,* she told herself as she pulled into Maggie's driveway and steeled her mind and heart for the worst. *If David made a mistake, I will find out why. And if he didn't...*

She knocked confidently on the door and waited for an answer. She knew David would be angry if he knew she was here, but she didn't have time to think about that now. She had her own road to follow, one in which she felt a divine presence pushing her along. How else could she face this woman? How else could she even begin to believe David, who adamantly opposed the accusations against him? It was so easy to believe that the world was in the period known as the end times. *But how do I believe that we, David and I, are caught up in the scheme of things? Who are we?* To answer this question, Kathy knew she had to confront the accuser. The only one who could let her know if God had decided upon her and David as divine instruments.

She knew Pastor Jack would have had an answer. He would have helped them through this crisis and helped her to discern what the truth was. Now she was on her own. She choked back the tears that came involuntarily to her throat. *No, I've cried enough. Compose yourself,* she demanded.

The questions in her mind continued, and no answers seemed to be in sight. She knew that she should trust the Lord, but she could not see the purpose in Jack's senseless death. David tried to make her understand God's purpose and told her to think of the various martyrs in Scripture. Thinking of Stephen, however, and how he was stoned while he looked blissfully into heaven, did nothing to ease the burden or the loss when she thought of Jack.

Moments passed before she realized no one was home. Kathy knew she had come too far to go back. In fact, she knew she had to confront Maggie now, before anyone had the chance to tell her she was doing the wrong thing. *I know that this is right. I can feel it.*

She attempted to open the door and found it locked. She peered in the window and saw the villa in a state of disarray. She looked for signs that someone was home and could see the kitchen and the family room were empty. She tried the side door, which was also locked, so she looked in the living room window to find it deserted.

From there she went around to the adjoining porch. The bedroom was partially concealed by the vertical blinds, but she could just see in by looking between them and noticed someone lying in bed fully clothed, moving around as if in pain. She tried to see if it was Maggie but couldn't make out who it was. The ceiling fan was blowing through the room, and the curtains were extending in the breeze like streamers that threatened to cover the bed entirely. It looked as if the person on the bed was shivering.

"Maggie!" she called as she banged on the glass door. "Maggie, is that you? It's Kathy Douglas. I want to talk to you. Let me in."

The body continued to writhe but did not move to let her in or even acknowledge that she had detected Kathy's presence.

"Maggie, can you hear me? Open the door!" Kathy's insistence brought no response so she muffled the impact and broke through the window. Once inside she could see that it was Maggie.

"Maggie," she started softly as she grabbed her shoulders, "is that you? It's Kathy Douglas. Can you hear me?" She saw that Maggie had undergone a horrifying transformation. There was terror in the woman's eyes, and her countenance gave only a blank stare.

Kathy tried to shake her to get her attention. "Maggie," she pleaded, "snap out of it! Wake up! I've got to talk to you."

Not being prepared for this unexpected sight, Kathy felt her resolve and determination begin to waver. *What am I doing here?* Seeing Maggie before her, however, caused Kathy to continue her efforts. She ran to the bathroom and grabbed a glass of water. She tossed it on Maggie's face and shook her shoulders again. "Can you hear me? Are you in there?" In desperation Kathy began slapping her face until she saw some degree of recognition return.

Maggie's head rolled back; then she started to cough.

"Maggie, what's going on? What happened?" She went back to the bathroom and got another glass of water. This time she handed it to Maggie and pressed it to her lips. "Tell me why you're sitting here with the house locked and you almost in a coma." She waited as Maggie gulped down the water and began to straighten her mussed hair. Kathy sat back and watched as Maggie began to take in her surroundings once again. Kathy noticed with alarm that Maggie was still terrified and was looking around as if to make sure it was safe. Her eyes continued to dart back and forth as she visibly calmed down.

Satisfied she was not in danger at the moment, Maggie looked Kathy in the eyes. "He didn't do it. That's why you're here, isn't it? Save yourself the trouble of asking. He didn't touch me."

Kathy closed her eyes in a silent prayer of thanks but quickly returned to the subject at hand. "I did come to ask you about it, but it hardly seemed to be the most pressing subject as I came in through the window." She tried to make her laugh, and she did elicit a thin smile, but apparently Maggie had been through something more serious; it wasn't enough to make her laugh.

"Tell me something. If you were so quick to tell me the truth, why did you bother to concoct the whole story in the first place?" Kathy was still genuinely puzzled as to why the girl would accuse her husband, but her maternal instinct was also emerging.

"Truthfully, things have changed so much since then that it didn't seem to matter," Maggie replied. "The whole point of the lie doesn't exist for me anymore. And in all actuality, I don't think I have too much longer to live, so I wanted you to know the truth. It's that simple."

"*Simple* isn't a word that comes to mind, honey," Kathy replied as she wrapped some more blankets around Maggie. For some reason she still seemed to be shivering. "Why would you think you don't have long to live? Are you sick? Are you in trouble?" Kathy's concern was giving way to curiosity as she wondered just how this woman seemingly walked into their lives, caused such a ripple in the fabric of her family, and now was checking herself out early without so much as an explanation. It wasn't something Kathy could let go easily. "Why are you so afraid?"

"Because my boyfriend is coming over to kill me." The statement was simple but cold and effective. It took Kathy by surprise, though she couldn't think why.

"Well, then, what are you doing here? Go and hide someplace else. Go someplace where he won't find you."

"You don't understand," Maggie added, almost disgusted. "He works for people that will find me. They won't let me get away. Believe me I know. I've seen them work—a little too close to home." She got up and began to cry and walked over toward the door.

Kathy let her go and cry it out before she pushed her any further.

"Who does he work for, Maggie? The mob? The CIA? What kind of group can go around killing people so indiscriminately?" She waited for Maggie to answer.

Slowly, she turned around, but before she spoke, Kathy knew, and the feeling in both her arms went numb as she heard Maggie say it. "He works for Rainbow."

Kathy's mouth just opened and hung there. The silence was heavy in the room until Kathy moved over toward Maggie and the window. "You're right. You're not safe here. I don't know where you, or any of us for that matter, are safe from Rainbow." She put her arm around Maggie's shoulders and pulled her back toward the bed. "But I do know this—you've got to come with me. Let's go and find David; he'll know what to do. We'll find a way to protect you."

Maggie jumped up and moved away. "David? No. I couldn't possibly face him! After what Rikki did in church the other day? He must hate me! No, I couldn't see him. I just couldn't."

"Maggie, he doesn't hate you, and he will help. Now come on. I won't take no for an answer. You will come with me, and you will confront David. Worry about what he is feeling later." Kathy grabbed her and railroaded her through the doorway to gather a few items before dragging her out to the car.

Maggie looked back at the house as they left. "You know this is not safe. You're putting yourself in danger by helping me."

Kathy gave her a wan smile. "Jesus is watching over me and my family, Maggie. You watch and see what he does to protect us. Now that you're with me, he'll be watching over you too." Kathy offered up another silent prayer and headed toward Coral Springs and home.

Brandon spent most of the night planning on how he could best utilize the last day of the conference and therefore his last day with access to Kavidas or the house. *That house, that house,* he repeated in his mind. *Why can't I get that house out of my head?*

Pano had provided him with a little more information about the estate itself. There just wasn't anyone who remembered being inside recently or who could remember who lived there before Kavidas. Apparently Kavidas, and perhaps even the previous owners, wanted their privacy—and they got it. With very little time, Brandon couldn't go to see if there were any plans on file at the government center (Pano told him this was a waste of time anyway, as the house was hundreds of years old) so he had to use his own limited knowledge to formulate a plan. Getting in again was going to be easy; it was getting out that worried him.

They arrived on schedule to continue in their duties to wrap up the conference and give the delegates whatever their whims fancied. Brandon still could not believe the amount of money being spent on food and drink for the weekend but could easily see the reason why. *Why spare expense when you're trying to captivate the entire world?* By this point Brandon knew Kavidas's intention and even the means. He just didn't know the motive. With all that Kavidas already had, Brandon couldn't figure out why.

Little was said in the form of meetings, but Brandon stayed in the main areas to listen anyway. When Kavidas walked over to him with Mort Stein, Brandon nearly fainted dead with fright. He could see Pano panic out of the corner of his eye as the two men approached. Unfortunately, Pano was too far away to rescue him without being obvious.

"Young man," Mort began in English, "I've seen you around quite a bit, but we haven't met. What is your name?"

Brandon feigned ignorance and looked bewildered. His mind was reeling.

"Sig-nó-mai, kyrie," he stammered. *"Allá den miló an-gli-ká."* He prayed that his Greek would hold with Kavidas. He was counting on his apparent nervousness to cover up for any trace of an alien accent.

"He doesn't speak English, Mort. I told you as much from across the room. Whatever you need to know I'll ask him."

He could feel Mort looking him over and was glad that Kavidas himself was not scrutinizing him. His presence alone was daunting enough. He glanced furtively at Kavidas and could see that his attention was obviously diverted elsewhere. He looked at Kavidas's eyes, and a strange feeling crept over him. It was as if the eyes, the man, and the house all belonged together. Something was tying them all in. It was that feeling of antiquity again. It struck him like a blow, as if it was radiating from Kavidas, or perhaps to Kavidas from all that surrounded him. There was definitely an aura surrounding the man—or was it both men? Whenever they moved together he thought he could see a palpable nimbus of evil beginning to form. He could see it trying to take form or shape as it attempted to coalesce.

"Tell him that the Italian minister has taken a liking to him and that he wishes to meet with him upstairs after the conference. Tell him he will be paid an additional 20,000 drachmas." Mort motioned to Kavidas to pass it along.

Kavidas was not amused. "Really, Mort, why are you involving yourself—and me—in this sordid type of affair? You know how I find it distasteful," he added sourly. "Find one of the boys to translate for you—I have no time for such nonsense," he concluded and began to walk away.

"Gregory," Mort began exasperated, "I wouldn't ask you if it wasn't important! I'm not running a brothel on the side, you know! The minister has informed me that he is not persuaded by our argument. I don't have to remind you of the influence he wields, not only with the Italian State and the Vatican but with the surrounding countries as well. I don't want to involve the local boys, but I've heard he likes this one. I could use a little finesse in getting him to the minister's room."

Kavidas rolled his eyes and came back to quickly translate for Mort.

Brandon, though dumbfounded, knew that his answer could only be yes, since no local would dream of turning down 20,000 drachmas, regardless of the request.

"There, are you happy? He has agreed to go. Can I be dismissed as well?"

Mort smiled at the rhetorical question and both men walked off, leaving Brandon a little shaken. Pano was there in moments and so were some of the other workers. An audience with Kavidas was no small feat.

"What happened, Basili? What did he say?"

Brandon turned to Pano and closed his eyes. "They wanted to pay me to go and visit with the Italian minister after the conference. I am to go to his room at nine o'clock, after dinner. Apparently I am going to be the dessert."

Several of the other young men clapped him on the back heartily and wished him well before returning to work. Some even looked at him with envy. They no doubt assumed that money was to be involved, and they were jealous in a good-natured way.

Pano, however, knew the ramifications all too well. Their plan was quickly crumbling. "What will we do? He will expect you to stay the night with him. What now?"

Brandon was taken aback, assuming that Pano would try to stop him from going. He was forgetting that Pano was a native like the rest of the waiters and thought nothing of providing this extra *service* to the clientele. Brandon was having a hard time concentrating on the plan, thinking about his impending rendezvous.

"What about the plan? What about me? What am I going to do, Pano? I don't want to go to the Italian minister's room. How can I get out of it?" He pulled himself together and looked at Pano to get the answer.

"Get you out of it? Out of what? You'll have a hard time leaving this house if you try to get out of the meeting in the minister's room. There is no way out. You agreed to go. You will have to go. Our plan will have to wait."

"How can it wait? This is the last night of the conference. Tomorrow everyone will be gone. Some are leaving tonight." Brandon was trying to control his panic. Everything was going well until Kavidas came over; now everything was going wrong. "We won't have another chance. We won't get back in."

"So you will get him drunk. He will fall asleep right away, and then we will follow the plan. I will wait for you. No one will know I am here." Pano seemed resigned to the fact that the plan would continue but just as resigned that Brandon should go to the minister's room and take care of his needs.

"I know you do no want to go, *paidi mou,*" Pano said softly, "but there is no way to avoid it. You are on Mykonos, and the men are friendly here.

The delegates all know it. You should feel fortunate no one approached you before now. I am surprised. I thought you were going to be very popular with the crowd."

"Lucky for me they were so busy with Kavidas's proposals—his Christmas gift to the world." He couldn't help but have some bite to his remarks, though he knew it wasn't Pano's fault that he was being forced to go to the minister's room. He suddenly felt very ashamed.

"I will meet you at our spot, *paidi mou*. I will wait for you till you come there." He squeezed Brandon's arm before returning to duty.

Brandon's mind was not on work as the last few hours passed by.

With a bottle of good cognac and red wine Brandon made it up to the Italian minister's suite. Kavidas's house was larger than any hotel he had seen on the island. It still seemed hard to believe that the delegates and their respective staffs were all housed on the grounds.

His heels hit the rose-colored marble as he walked down the corridor toward the room. He could hear the echo of his feet against the walls, slightly muffled by the impressive tapestry hanging against the cool, smooth stone. He recognized it as Wagner's *Ride of the Valkyrie* and wished he had time to stop and admire it. It was beyond a work of art; it was rather like looking at a play in suspended animation. Each character, if you stared at it long enough, seemed to come to life.

The door stood before him, and he waited there for a minute before knocking. He reflected on his life, and what he saw he didn't like. This wasn't what he wanted, and when he decided to be gay, it didn't mean for him that he would lend himself to casual affairs or sexual encounters. And he didn't. This just wasn't him. *This just isn't me.*

Yet here he was. As if to perform a duty, with all the implications of the word. It didn't matter if he wanted to or not. He was being told to do it, even though he was paid, and therefore he had to do it. It made him realize how little people argue when it comes to doing what they are told.

He did it. He knocked and waited. The door opened, and a handsome man stood in the opening. Brandon had seen him during the conference and knew that the man had been staring at him. Now he knew why. *"Mou llenen Basili,"* he offered. *My name is Basili.* "

"*Ela,*" the man responded graciously, "*Ela*—come."

Brandon walked in. He heard the door shut behind him, and he wondered again at the splendor and beauty of the room. It took his breath away.

"I don't speak Greek," the man began in English, "and I was told you don't speak English. We're in for a rough time."

He smiled so Brandon smiled back, knowing he could not respond. He could feel the sweat starting to drip down his back, and he knew that he looked uncomfortable.

The man sensed it also. "Take off your jacket and your shirt if you like. I want you to be comfortable." He gestured with his hands and pretended to take off his imaginary jacket and shirt for Brandon's benefit. Brandon began to unbutton his clothes. The man pointed at himself and then gestured back to Brandon. "You, Basili. Me," he said, pointing a finger at this own chest, "Antonio."

When Brandon had his shirt off, Antonio came up behind him and began to knead his shoulders. "You've had a hard day. Relax. Just relax."

Brandon couldn't help but close his eyes and enjoy the massage. He was tense but not from the work. The day was unfolding unlike he'd expected, and he had no idea where it was going.

Antonio brought his mouth close to Brandon's ear. "I know who you are. And I know why you are here."

Brandon didn't know if he should ignore the man's English or be alarmed. His body, however, didn't have such qualms and stiffened involuntarily as the words were spoken.

"So, you do speak a little English, don't you? What other surprises are you going to give me tonight?"

Brandon looked skeptically at him and made no response.

"You're very quiet, Basili. Or can I call you Brandon?"

The shock registered with such a start that Brandon flinched. "How did you know who I was, and what do you want?" Brandon took on an attitude of defiance as he looked at Antonio to gauge the man's response.

"As to what I want, that should seem fairly obvious. As to whether or not you're offering remains to be seen." He smiled briefly. "How did I know you? It's very easy. In addition to my position as minister, I sit on the board of directors for Rainbow Pharmaceuticals. You're very familiar to me, Brandon Lane. I noticed you some time ago. It was only my good fortune that I recognized you here. I must say, your disguise is nearly perfect. The native dress, the local color—and that Greek accent! However did you manage it? The Greek god that is by your side all day helps you blend in as well. If I hadn't marked you some time ago, I would never have recognized you. But I did. You and your father have been around, and so have I. I'm surprised no one else figured it out. I would think you would be in high demand."

"So I've been told. Now that you know, what's your plan?"

"For you? Like what? Have you burned at the stake? I assure you I'm much more civilized. I may just have to take it out on your body, though, being as you were spying on my colleagues and myself. It really was very naughty." Antonio's attempt at humor did nothing to endear Brandon.

"Enough," Brandon said. "Why did you ask to see me if you knew who I was? You know I'm not here as a guest. What do you want from me?"

Antonio's expression turned very grave as he picked up Brandon's shirt, then threw it at him. He gestured for Brandon to put it on, and he complied immediately.

"I want to trust you, because I am desperate, and I have no choice. There is no one else for me to tell." He picked up a glass of cognac and offered one to Brandon.

"No, thank you. Why do you need my trust? Why would you want it?"

"I am not entirely happy with the arrangements that are being made by Kavidas, and I have made it known. But that is not the real reason. When I recognized you, I saw an opportunity to meet with you here and see if I could trust you. When I realized you would give yourself to me to keep your cover, I knew I could. I arranged for Stein to have you brought here, so that I could be *persuaded* to follow his lead, which I will. But my conscience is beginning to bother me. I have seen some terrible things— things that should be known, things I want you to tell."

Brandon was trying to assimilate all this information as quickly as possible. The waters were moving fast, and the tide had already changed since he'd walked into the room.

"What have you seen, and why do you want to tell anyone? If you are on the board of directors, surely you have some say as to what takes place?

Why not change it?"

"Machinery is in motion now; gears are rotating that cannot be slowed down. I can only do so much without raising suspicion. In reality, we are only there to legitimize the corporate structure. Kavidas makes all the decisions. We have to live by them. It's made me very rich, but I'm beginning to see beyond the dollar and worry about my soul. The people, the experiments...it's been so awful."

The man seemed racked with pain and guilt. "The labs—there's one in Rainbow's office in Wellington, and there's one in Trinidad and one in Haiti. All of them have been experimenting with people and animals. Unspeakable things have been going on. And I can't stop it. I don't know if you can either. But help me try. This race for the vaccine has caused them to break all moral barriers, and now I don't know what to do. You're my only hope. I wanted to tell someone before I lost the chance."

He walked over to his suitcase. "Here is some evidence of what I'm talking about. Take this with you and have it examined. I'm afraid you won't be happy with the results." He handed Brandon a small vial.

"Where did you get it?" Brandon asked quietly, no longer suspicious.

"I picked it up at my last corporate inspection. The board of directors had it at the Florida lab."

Brandon understood immediately since his hopes were that he would do the same thing here tonight. He put the vial in his pocket. "I will do what I can. I wish there was more I could do for you." He moved toward the door. "I should go. There is something else I need to do tonight. Something I have to check out. It has to do with this house. Do you know anything about it? There is something very odd about the way it feels."

Antonio was silent. He finished his cognac, then shook his head. "No, there is nothing I've been told or heard about this house. I only know it is very old. Do not stay in it too long. Leave quickly while you can. It is important you get this evidence out. I need to know that I did something that was worthwhile. Something to check the atrocities that they are committing."

Brandon did not want to press for details and thought it best to move on. Still, he felt bad leaving the man in such a state of flux. "Are you going to be all right? I feel funny leaving you this way."

"I will be fine. Take this and go." He handed Brandon an envelope with his name, *Basili,* marked on the front.

"I can't take this money—"

"You must. It will look wrong if you don't. People will want to know why you don't have it, and you will not be able to answer. You must not do anything to arouse suspicion. Take it and go, and I will try and contact you some other time. Maybe someday we will meet again." He nodded at Brandon and pushed him out the door.

Brandon headed off toward the kitchen and the last stage of his plan. Only now, he was more uncertain than ever.

"Gregory, I'm telling you it is even better than we could have expected. Not only are all the countries going to be bringing their governments on line with Project Renaissance, as their newly elected president it will be only natural that you influence them to achieve your goals. It couldn't be better." Mort's exuberance was obvious but not contagious.

Gregory seemed preoccupied. "Merely another stepping stone."

"Yes, and the time is ripe—the world is ready. They want you! They see the power you have. We can't disappoint them." Mort was hoping he could inflame Gregory's enthusiasm. The servant brought coffee in on a silver tray.

"Ev-charistó-poh-lee," Gregory offered graciously to the man serving. *Thank you.* "Mort, we are of the same mind in this area. We are serving a higher purpose than our own, so there is no such thing as rushing. But that doesn't mean we don't have to safeguard against mistakes. You know how costly they are. And the penalty is usually severe when the stakes are this high."

Mort nodded and waved off the cream and sugar. "I just hate to miss an opportunity; that's all. It's the same as when the vegetables are ready to be picked from a garden or a flower from its stem. You know you'll have them again next year. Who wants to wait?"

"No one," Gregory replied as he approached Mort's chair, "is as anxious as I am. But that does not mean we can rush. We will stay with the timetable. As for the EC, well, that is another matter. I am inclined to agree with you. That is an important first step. It is a step that will bring us closer to the governments of Europe and the men that run them."

"One which is being worked on right now," said Mort with a sly grin. "You know Antonio, the Italian minister I asked you to speak to today? He's with that young Greek man, being persuaded to join our cause completely. And if you recall, the Italian minister is one of the principals in the EC committee. Tonight may be the night the next phase of our plan is implemented."

"Fine, fine. Let's just make sure nothing goes wrong. The conference will be over tomorrow, officially that is, and we can say good-bye to all the delegates. Then we'll—"

"Mr. Kavidas," the intercom cried, "there is a motion detection alarm in section 001. Would you like us to investigate?"

Gregory jumped up to speak into the intercom. "Under no circumstances are you or anyone else to enter that sector—*is that clear?*" he boomed.

Mort was surprised at the tone of Gregory's voice. He was even more surprised at the interruption. *There is still so much I don't know about this man,* Mort thought as Gregory started to go. "Do you want me to come with you?" he offered hopefully.

He was disappointed but not affronted when Gregory declined. "Please stay here, Mort. Hold down this part of the fort." He was out the door, and Mort could only watch as he moved toward the main stairwell. He had never seen Gregory jump like that, and it unnerved him. But not the physical aspect of the jump itself. It was something else. Something he sensed in Gregory that he had never seen before: fear. *What is he hiding in there?*

David was very surprised when Kathy pulled up with Maggie. He didn't know if he should be nervous, happy, scared, or excited. His first reaction was to be sick, wondering what else could happen that would destroy what he was trying to build. Then he remembered that he was not in control and that a higher power was guiding his destiny.

"David, help me get Maggie inside." Kathy took charge in her efficient manner.

David was only too happy to comply. He reached over and helped take the bundled woman into the house and sat her on the sofa. Kathy was already headed toward the kitchen, and it left him feeling slightly awkward. He glanced at Maggie and could see that she was in a very depressed and vulnerable state. *Did I do this to her—even inadvertently?* He went to ask her if there was anything he could do when he heard Kathy's voice.

"David, can you help me, please?"

He motioned with his hand that he had to go and realized that Maggie was oblivious to his presence. He moved over toward Kathy and saw that she was boiling some water on the stove and was already filling a pot for coffee.

"Give her a few minutes," Kathy advised as she worked, "and let her settle down. She's been through some ordeal."

David, bewildered, could only look at his wife. "Kathy, what's going on? What are you doing with Maggie?" His natural inclination to go over and put his arms around his wife was purposely suppressed. He had to know what she was thinking and where they stood.

"I'll be honest with you. I went to see Maggie to see what was going on with my own eyes. Now I know."

David felt an icy finger crawl toward his heart as dread set in with the expectation of what was to follow. It left him speechless, knowing that there was nothing he could say to alter what Kathy was going to say or what she was thinking. He grimaced as he prepared for the blow that would alter his world forever.

"I know there was nothing going on between you."

He was shocked when Kathy's words registered in his mind. "I don't know what to say. How did you know?"

"A woman knows, David, and I knew I had to go and see Maggie and find out. So I did. Now I'm glad. I was anxious before—probably feeling the way you were a few seconds ago. Seeing Maggie allowed me to see that you had been faithful. But I still expect an explanation as to why you were at her apartment."

David had begun to relax and felt himself stiffen again as Kathy asked him the one question for which he still had no concrete answer.

Before he could stammer and try to tell his wife something that was not entirely true, she came to his rescue. "Let's make a deal," she began as she walked to David's side and put a finger against his lips. "You can give me an answer in a few days as long as you promise to stay away from apartments late at night."

David sighed and put his arms around Kathy as he had wanted to do since she had arrived. "You have a deal. And I pray nothing will ever happen again that could potentially come between us." He put his head down on Kathy's shoulder and took a deep breath. "Thank you for having the wisdom and discernment of your own to be able to see between the lines and know that God had a greater plan in mind."

Kathy stroked David's head and whispered in his ear, "Don't thank me, David. Thank the Lord. He's responsible."

"So where do we go from here?" He looked sheepishly at Kathy. "Let's go back into the living room and see what we can do with Maggie. We have a death threat from her ex-boyfriend to diffuse, and we have to figure out a way to get her sister into church so we can tell her what happened and explain to her the way of salvation. After what Jesus did in Maggie's life, I have no doubt that he will be using her mightily. And I think we should be doing everything in our power to allow that to happen."

David could do nothing but smile. He leaned over and kissed his wife as he triumphed in this round with the devourer, who wanted to split them up and make them ineffective. David couldn't help repeating to himself the words that were becoming not only his confidence and his strength but his credo: *"I can do all things through Christ, which strengthens me."*

Brandon left to meet Pano as soon as he exited Antonio's quarters. Finding him would be easy enough, as he was well liked among the kitchen staff and knew he could find an excuse to go looking.

It was only the interim time period he was worried about. Most of the staff knew he was the Italian minister's entertainment for the evening. He needed a plausible excuse to be out of his company. All he had to do was pretend he was here to get some nourishment for the Italian minister. "Exercise can make one very hungry," he told the crowd, all of whom were eager to hear details.

Within ten minutes he saw an opening by the door leading to the cellar, and he took it. Once inside, he could feel Pano's reassuring presence and knew also that he was no longer alone.

"*Panayia mou.*" Pano sighed with relief. "You are safe and here with me again. What happened?"

"Surprisingly little," Brandon replied with chagrin. "He is an ally. I'll fill you in later. Let's finish this job and get out of here." He saw Pano nod as they moved down the stairs.

As they made their way toward the wine cellar, Brandon stopped and took in the fresh air. There was something different about it. The smell of it was familiar but unlike his previous trip to the basement. He tried to pinpoint it when he recognized the scent. It was ordinary brine, and the smell of the sea was now seemingly strong since he had made the connection. He turned to Pano and gave him a puzzled look.

"I took the time to make sure we had an escape," Pano whispered to the bewildered Brandon. "I noticed the door marked *thalassa* when we were here; I went down and opened it up so we have an alternate route out of the house."

"How did you know where it went?"

"Well, *thalassa* seemed explicit enough. It means *the sea*."

"I know it means *sea*," Brandon whispered back, "But how did you know that it was a door that went to the sea? It was locked and bolted, and we're a long way away from the water."

"Many of the old houses were built with an access to the ocean. This was a fishing town. People were always in the water. As for the locks and bolts, I had plenty of time while you were attending to the Italian minister. I removed them."

When they approached the door, Pano leaned over and said in Brandon's ear, "We have to be careful. There may be listening devices or sensors. Once we've opened the door, we won't be able to talk."

Brandon nodded, and they went inside. It was much easier to open the hidden door, having already gone through the experience. The passage down was only faintly illuminated, and Brandon did not recognize the light source. He couldn't see any kind of fixture; an eerie glow permeated the rock and gently lit their way. Slowly and carefully they eased their way down the steps. The same luminescent fog that surrounded the stairs clung to several of the room's fixtures. The light switches, the lights themselves, and even the walls seemed to reflect the moonlight. Only there was no moon. And there were no windows.

Brandon held on to the rail as his eyes adjusted to the dim surroundings. He couldn't see any evidence of a motion detector—or any security visible to the naked eye. They continued.

Brandon first encountered a desk while Pano stayed by the stairs. In the phosphorescent glow he could see vague shapes cluttering the surface. None seemed overly significant. He made his way toward the next object of intrigue and noted that it was an altar. His first instinct was to back away. He could sense some force at work, pulling him closer and pushing him away at the same time—yet it was strangely attractive in its conflict. He felt drawn to it but knew that this was not the item he was here to see. He could just feel it.

He continued down the corridor and was surrounded by an even greater plethora of art than what he had seen in the main living areas. Representatives of all the major artists seemed present, with a significant emphasis on Monet. Each painting glowed in the ghostly light. He couldn't begin to calculate the values, but a thought hit him. Perhaps he had uncovered a vast treasure chamber or vault of sorts? There certainly seemed as if there were enough valuables to start a first-rate museum. What if this was nothing more than a rich man's fantasy to have a secret hiding place for his finery?

There was no apparent evidence to the contrary. And then he saw it. Plain as day and as lit up as the morning sky. In what seemed a hallowed corner stood an ornate topographical map, perfect in every detail. The entire world was spread out in all the colors of the rainbow. Each area was specifically lit to represent a different region.

But that was not the point of his concern. What drew him were the unique markers that were strewn over the map's ornate face. Since the map was mounted to the wall, the markers were deeply embedded to keep them in place. What caught his attention were the shapes. At first they appeared to be nothing more than ordinary arrows in the shape of thunderbolts. His mind whirred with imagery of the king of the gods, Zeus himself, and how his thunderbolts from heaven were feared by all mortals of the earth. However, when he looked closer, he realized they were each shaped like a small Lambda, the Greek letter L and one of the universal symbols for gay men. It was not the shape that made his blood run cold. It was the location that chilled his heart and left him bereft of feeling.

The largest bolt was marked Alpha and was situated by the location of the ancient cities of Sodom and Gomorrah. The second arrow was located in the center of Canaan and was slightly smaller than the first. It was labeled with the Greek letter Beta. The third arrow was embedded in the heart of the extinct city of Pompeii and was marked Gamma. The fourth bolt was labeled Delta and was centered over Germany but had several tendrils that crept out over the surrounding countries.

Brandon froze as he realized that each arrow corresponded with disaster. His eyes closed in despair when he noticed the final group of arrows that were strewn over the United States. The last arrows were marked *Omega—ton Telon*. Omega—the Last. They were located on the West Coast of the United States—in the heart of San Francisco with similar sized arrows scattered throughout the Americas—New York, Miami, Chicago, Dallas, Puerto Rico, and Port-au-Prince. They were distinct in their unique shape and size. Together they gave the map an almost global perspective on afflicted or affected areas. Those that had been touched by the arrows had also been touched by catastrophic disasters of previously unparalleled proportion.

Brandon was stunned as he realized that someone or something had been tracking the spread of the disease and the effects it had on the world. He reached over toward the largest arrow and tried to pull it out. He needed documentation to show to his friends and colleagues so they would know it was real and it was planned. By whom and for whom was still a mystery. Brandon hoped to resolve at least the meaning of placing the board here in this house before the night was over.

He called to Pano above a whisper, "I need help!" He couldn't get the arrow out, and he so desperately wanted Pano to see the map and experience the terror he felt by looking at this cold and calculating plan of destruction—to see that there was something more than paranoia involved in his crusade—to see some evidence that someone was working toward: what?

Pano was not in the doorway as he expected. Brandon turned back to the board and could see that the map was shrouded in the same fog that had encased the steps. The fog was moving toward him! His legs were no longer visible, and the air was becoming difficult to breathe. He reached out and grabbed one of the smaller arrows and pulled as hard as he could. He could feel it begin to give way, and he thrust his foot against the wall for leverage.

When the arrow came loose, he lunged backward and fell against the floor. He was completely covered in the menacing fog, and his heart felt constricted in his chest. An overpowering terror gripped his soul. In his mind he began to scream, and he could hear moaning from deep in the bowels of the earth. He couldn't believe it was possible—but he couldn't think. He didn't know what to do. He clutched the arrow in his hand and could not focus on anything but the moaning, which was beginning to rise in pitch and was approaching a scream. He threw his hands to his temples and could feel the arrow cut his forehead as the blood streamed into his eyes. But there was nothing he could do to stop it. He only wanted to block out the noise. He tried to stand and move but couldn't rise above kneeling. His head came above the fog, and he tried to breathe to clear his mind. He began to fall backward until he heard Pano.

"Basili! Where are you?" he heard faintly. Then Pano grabbed his arm. "What are you doing? What happened? Come on. Someone is coming. I heard the outer door to the basement open. We've got to go. Come on, Basili!" Pano dragged Brandon by the arm toward the stairs, which were almost completely obliterated by the fog.

Brandon himself was in a fog. Pano must have realized it, for he draped his arm over Brandon's shoulder and steered him up the stairs. There were footsteps overhead, but they didn't seem to move closer.

Brandon clutched the object in his hand to his chest. His hand was now bleeding from his tight grip.

As they moved them toward the door marked *thalassa*, they could see the men in the outer area of the basement. Yet for some reason the men were not still not coming any closer. He heard some activity around the basement door and what sounded like instructions being given. Pano opened the door and pushed Brandon through.

Pano closed the door and scrambled with his other hand for something to keep the door closed—a hasp to put on the padlock on the door, or anything. But there was nothing.

Now the men came closer. Had they seen Brandon and Pano exit? Some men passed the door. It was obvious someone was going to inspect the wine cellar. Pano stood on the tip of his toes and felt along the edge of the door. He almost collapsed when he heard a click and a small bolt fell into place. Whomever had made the door had planned for the possibility of wanting to lock it from this side. He reached down and pushed Brandon back into motion, and they continued along the tunnel toward the sea.

Within 10 minutes Brandon began to shake with cold and terror. Pano stripped off his jacket and his shirt and put them on Brandon. They continued to move along in the dark. The only light was the faint glow of the moon at the end of the tunnel. It seemed miles away. Pano listened for any sounds of pursuit but heard only the padding of their tired feet moving them toward freedom.

Brandon had felt Pano put the shirt on and then the jacket. He'd wanted to talk but could not. He could feel the words form in his mouth, but he heard no sound. He could feel the strength coming from Pano, and he tried to awaken out of his stupor. He knew it would not take long for Kavidas's men to figure out where they went and then have someone waiting at the end of the tunnel. Which he knew was still some distance.

He tried to relax his grip on the arrow but couldn't. His fingers were stiff and would not open, or they would not respond to the mental commands that he was giving. He kept walking along next to Pano and blankly stared ahead toward the light and the sea. His body moved and worked, but he seemed to have no control over it, no matter how hard he fought. His eyes wandered, and he tried to see if there was anything visible on the walls of the tunnel. Any clue as to what had happened and where they really were. But it was too dark and he couldn't focus.

Suddenly salt air blasted his face. It was like being hit with a wave of water, and it made him sputter and cough. It assaulted his nostrils and entered his lungs like liquid fire. He doubled over as he choked over the pungent air. Then it was done. His hand moved to the floor, and he realized that he had willed it to happen. His knees bent, and he noted that he had told them to do so. He turned his head toward Pano and could see only the glint from the man's eyes to know that he was still there. He reached out and tried to touch the man responsible for his rescue. "Pano," he groaned, his throat dry and raspy, "take my hand."

"Basili, you are back!" I didn't know what to do. You were gone, and I heard a noise. When I came back you were in the fog. I just knew we had to leave. It happened so fast." He choked on the words.

"It seemed like forever to me," Brandon said. "I can't believe it happened so quick. But let's go. I can move faster now. We've got to get out of here before they come to the tunnel's end. There isn't much time; it may be too late already."

Brandon moved again with Pano, stumbling at first, then more sure of himself. He repeated over and over in his mind that they had to make it to the end, to get free. The oppressed feeling passed, but he would not forget it. He knew there was some power at work behind him, and he wanted nothing more than to get away from it.

He wiped the blood from his face as they ran and tried to stow the arrow in his pants. He could feel his hand throb with pain from the lacerations of the arrow. He had no attention to spare and concentrated on escape. His mind fixated on the entrance that was growing before him on the horizon. Pano's hand held his forearm tightly, and he knew that they would not be separated.

When the tunnel ended, Brandon wanted to jump out onto the beach. But Pano held him back. He made them sit for several minutes just listening to the surf and checking for signs of pursuit. "I do not understand it. Basili. Where are they? They must have figured out where we went by now."

"They let us go. It is the only answer. I only hope that they do not discover what I took with me. If they knew, I do not think they would have been so quick to dismiss us. As it stands, they probably think it was just some locals looking for money. What I took would be meaningless to most. It is only because I was there to find something that has significance. They cannot be worried about a minor break-in. They didn't have the advantage of knowing who was in their midst." He paused. "Let's go. Let's go home."

He allowed Pano to lift him up, and they moved out on the beach. They continued to look over their shoulders but moved slower now. Brandon tapped his pocket and sighed, knowing that the arrow would provide some answers to a larger riddle. Then he felt for the vial he had received from Antonio and wondered what mysteries would be found inside.

He closed his eyes as he walked. *Time to go home. Together—to see my father and sort out this mess: my own life along with the information from Kavidas. My father has got to know about Antonio! He'll know what to do. At last some sort of ally in the enemy camp. Time to see if we can do anything to stop this man. And this disease. If there is, I think I have the key.* He held the arrow up to the sky. He knew it wouldn't mean anything to anyone, and he didn't expect an answer from any supernatural power. He did it for himself; after all that had happened, it just felt good.

Christmastime seemed unusually busy this year. In addition to the normal hustle and bustle in the commercialized holiday, the advertising blitz surrounded by the release of Toi-VAX by Rainbow Pharmaceuticals gave everyone something to wish for. Suddenly peace and goodwill toward men were all important virtues once again. It was almost as if the vaccine was being presented as the world's biggest and best Christmas present. Not only did everyone want it for Christmas; it was something that everyone could have. Something everyone could share. It couldn't have been more perfect if it had been planned that way. But no one stopped to think that perhaps it had.

You could tell Rainbow had done well by the happy, grateful looks people expressed whenever the subject was discussed. In fact, no one had anything bad to say about Rainbow. And if they did, they weren't saying it, because no one wanted to hear it.

Christmas morning dawned, and the vaccine was injected into people in hospitals, clinics, and wherever else Rainbow had arranged for the initial release. The vaccine cost 1,200 dollars per person, while the government subsidized the opportunity for those who couldn't pay.

Children complained that they weren't getting the toys and games they were used to. Christmas didn't seem as commercial this year as it had in the past. The emphasis wasn't on buying; it was on living. It was on Toi-VAX. It was on Rainbow. It was on Kavidas. It was even on Mortimer Stein and his new and wonderful way to link people together with a huge information net that would help distribute the vaccine and eventually make health care easier, faster, and cheaper.

There was only one thing that wasn't emphasized. It was Jesus. And no one seemed to notice.

TEN

Here I swear, and as I break my oath may eternity blast me,
here I swear that never will I forgive Christianity!
It is the only point on which I allow myself to encourage revenge.
Oh, how I wish I were the Antichrist,
that it were mine to crush the Demon;
to hurl him to his native Hell never to rise again.
Percy Bysshe Shelley

The Very Large Array (VLA) telescope, located on the plains of San Agustin, about 95 miles southwest of Albuquerque, New Mexico, is the world's largest aperture-synthesis radio telescope, consisting of 27 identical 25-meter reflector antennas that are located on railroad tracks stretched out in a Y pattern. The northern arm is 19 kilometers long, and the other two arms are each 21 kilometers long. With greater resolution and sensitivity than any other single radio telescope, the radio waves from space are converted to electrical signals by electronic correlation and compared to stored images for analysis. Only radio signals emitted from celestial bodies are received; there is no visual image.

At 0325 GMT at the Observatorio del Roque de los Muchachos on the island of La Palma in the Canary Islands, John Weldon of the Royal Greenwich Observatory (RGO) peered into the powerful telescope and noticed a change in the angular velocity of a extragalactic gaseous nebula located near the star Metallah in the constellation Triangulum. He immediately checked the celestial coordinates to calculate the movement, then sent a fax transmission for confirmation to San Agustin.

When Ira Goldstein, the director of the VLA, with a doctorate in celestial mechanics and astrophysics, received the fax transmission he reconfigured the radio telescope's bowl-shaped reflectors to an area of the sky between the constellation Andromeda and Aries, focusing on Metallah, the southern-most star with a visual magnitude of 3.60, 57.2 light years away. Included in the constellation is a large spiral galaxy, M33, that seemed to be incurring a chaotic rotation. It appeared to him that together with the gaseous nebula, the spiral galaxy, while enjoying a fixed rotation and orbit in space for an infinite period, had suddenly shifted its position in the universe.

Using a spectro analyzer to calibrate the Red Shift, where the wavelength of light in the spectra of types of stars are known, he concluded that an earthward movement could be possible. Recognizing a potential violation of the Hubble Constant equation theory, he noted the change in his log and dismissed the phenomenon, since 57 years from now he would no longer be around.

Floating fragments of reality mixed with mental blockage as he tried to free his mind of whatever was gripping it. As he slept, he saw the immense fiery lake approaching. He tried to scream, but only a thunderous silence was heard. It was a bizarre happening that was only beginning to take shape, causing him to yell out in the darkness to attempt some form of sane-mindedness from the dreadful vision that engulfed him.

The fiery lake had detached itself from the gaseous nebula in the outer regions of the universe and progressed unrelenting toward earth. As it neared, he found himself suddenly transported above it to a fixed point in space where he was held captive by an angelic guardian. He gasped and writhed in anguish as the divine restrainer held him firmly while a six-winged creature flew toward him carrying another mortal who had also deceived the world.

Together they stood suspended above the lake, now a flaming inferno that spewed sulphurous gases for thousands of miles into space. As far as they could see, only fire existed—engulfing flames that splashed and swashed over their bodies, burning for all eternity, yet not consuming them. A place where mind and soul would acknowledge the loss of salvation for all time. A place where death and hell would be imprisoned and sentenced to a remote location far from heaven, where they would remain forever.

For a brief period the prisoners were allowed to look at each other as episodes of their time on earth flashed through their minds. They remembered each other and how they deceived the whole world, then in a vain attempt to strike a bargain, pleaded with Michael the angelic chief sentry, arguing that they too were deceived by Satan. With a dismissive wave of the hand, Michael gave the command, and the keepers released the two men into the vortex of fire that awaited them. Horrible screams echoed as they fell into the fiery lake, and it began to recede to a location where only God knew its destination—where he would recall it at a later time....

Mort awakened when the sweat from his face soaked his pillow, then sat at the end of his bed for 10 minutes before taking a shower.

Worth Avenue in West Palm Beach is known for its elegant shops and extravagant cubby holes where a shopper can find anything imaginable to buy. From life-size bronze boy and dolphin sculptures to pig-shaped salt and pepper shakers to 1,000 dollar price tags on designer dresses. The luxury car enthusiast would be in his glory as he walked the avenue while taking inventory of the various breeds of vehicles. Restaurant valets stand watch on the sidewalks, waiting to park a prospective patron's automobile as the celebrities prepare to dine on five-course meals in one of the many popular haunts. Boasting of attracting presidents' wives and other VIPs who love to shop, Worth Avenue continues to charm tourists as well as Florida residents.

Just south of Worth Avenue, Kavidas's estate on Route A1A stands on a promontory overlooking the Atlantic, commanding a spectacular view of the glistening body of water. Mort always looked forward to visiting Gregory and his mansion.

The wrought-iron fence surrounding Kavidas's estate made a statement. While Kavidas enjoyed notoriety and fame, he still relished his privacy at home. Security guards, a contingent from Rainbow, patrolled the estate every hour to ward off potential criminals and onlookers.

As Mort arrived, he stopped his car at the main gate and announced his arrival into the intercom. While waiting for clearance he looked at Kavidas's home in the distance and thought, *Someday we'll have to leave our homes here in the U.S., but we'll be back at an appointed time, and when that time arrives, we will be ruling!* The gate electrically opened, and he continued up the treed driveway that led to the front door of the house.

"It's a little early in the morning, Mort," Gregory grumped as he opened the front door.

"I thought it important that I see you," Mort replied nervously. "I didn't want to see you about this down at Rainbow." He stepped in and walked onto Gregory's spacious patio overlooking his T-shaped swimming pool.

When the servant peeked in, Gregory waved him off and asked Mort to sit down. "What's troubling you, Mort? You look like you're carrying the weight of the world."

Mort tittered, "I had this crazy dream last night—"

"Uh-oh, another one so soon?"

"This was very different from all the rest. This concerned you and I and some wretched place..." He gazed off into space and started to grimace as if reenacting the dream. "It was terrifying. I really saw you and myself being thrown into—"

"Mort, ease up!" Gregory ordered as if to awaken him from a trance. "You're working too hard on the vaccine distribution, and it's taking its toll on you."

Mort jumped up and seized Gregory by the shoulders, shouting at him, "It was you and I! They threw us into a lake of fire where you keep burning forever." He fell limp into Gregory's arms.

Moments later Gregory held a wet washcloth on Mort's face to revive him from the faint. When he regained consciousness, he reached and held Gregory's hand. "Tell me there's nothing to worry about, Gregory. You know about such things. Tell me!"

"You had a *normal* nightmare; that's all," Gregory assured as he massaged his hands to soothe his anxiety. "Not all of your dreams are prophetic. You simply had a *dream* like the rest of us get—dismiss it from your mind."

Visibly shaken, yet resting in the assurance that a child would receive from a parent while experiencing a frightening dream, Mort slowly regained his composure. He stood up, walked over to a mirror, and proceeded to comb his hair and freshen up. "I'm okay now. As they say, letting the job get to me."

He started for the front door when Gregory put his arm around him. "You need not worry about your future; it's secure with me." He looked him in the eyes and added, "You can trust me on this."

Mort took a deep breath as he strengthened his resolve. "I'm putting my whole life in your hands to show my trust."

Mort had no way of knowing that it was a lie.

Vacant stores in strip malls provided the perfect registration centers for Rainbow's AIDS vaccine. Every clinic and doctor's office in the nation had received their own limited supply for emergency cases, but the hypertrophied epidemic required staggering quantities of the preventative medicine, which would not be available to the general public for quite some time.

Meanwhile, the Centers for Disease Control rented available space wherever possible and set up stations to preregister applicants for distribution once the vaccine was available. The lines at the centers were often blocks long, where haggard and impatient sufferers argued and fought constantly over their rights to sign up first. Food vendors and newspaper hawkers found the lines at the stations to be a lucrative place for business. At some locations, clothing merchants paraded their wares up and down the line as captive waiting patients negotiated for bargains to loll away the hours until their turn came up.

David stopped at a traffic signal on his way to the church and caught sight of a vaccine registration station with an extended line meandering for nearly half a mile. He pondered the ramifications of the program with its effectiveness and incalculable cost, deducing that the taxpayer would inevitably pay for the inoculations and in effect finance the continuance of the behavior that brought on the plague to begin with. But rather than let his mind think globally, invariably replaying the negative tapes that heightened his discouragement and ultimately crippled his ability to function, he resolved to concentrate on his own local arena of concerns: teaching, defeating Rainbow, and now his newly acquired pastorate. At this level, he could see measurable victories. Victory over the forces of Kavidas and Stein were not measurable.

David's first task as interim pastor would be to settle and unite the church that was still reeling from the shock of their pastor's untimely death and the scandalous behavior that Maggie's sister accused him of. With Maggie being sheltered by Kathy, the congregation had little skepticism as to his innocence: *A wife always knows* was whispered around the church, and he had to smile. Sometimes an old adage, Christian or not, has its place. It certainly was helping him now.

His plan was to use the church as a staging area for the idle anti-Rainbow group he planned to inject with renewed hope now that the public was becoming aware of their battle. By keeping the congregation and the coalition busy fighting Rainbow, they would feel productive and useful in their Christian service. It was a strategem that always worked for him personally.

Winter break provided a hiatus from school, enabling him to focus on ministerial duties, which included being a tactician to lead the revitalized offensive against Rainbow. He marveled at the workings of God: just one month ago his marriage was in serious jeopardy, while now he reveled in the joy of the Lord when he saw both Kathy and Maggie working together, along with Sydelle and Rikki as committee persons, united in purpose to triumph over a common enemy.

Kathy had been right about Rikki. When she saw that Maggie was in trouble and had been threatened by her boyfriend, she was quick to join the throng at the church in their cause. David sometimes wondered if Rikki didn't have her own agenda when it came to discussing the still unresolved issue of Maggie's menacing boyfriend. But she wasn't talking about it, and he didn't feel it was his place to continue to ask.

"Hello, Pastor David," Maggie yelled with a friendly wave as she emerged from the church with a box of tracts under her arm, destined for hand distribution at the Rainbow facility.

"Good to see you ladies serving the Lord," David rejoined with a tight smile. He paused to reflect on how far Maggie had come since her salvation through Christ experience. Being overwhelmed in his forgiveness, she immediately shared her liberation with her sister, Rikki, but with disappointing results. Rikki was happy to be involved, but she was not ready to commit to Jesus. Obviously, David thought, it wasn't God's time for Rikki yet, but he knew Maggie would continue to share her newly found faith with her, looking to the day when Rikki would respond to God's calling.

As a veritable hub of activity, the church not only provided a safe haven for wayward souls but also served as a command center for the assembling troops arming themselves against the amassing forces of evil.

Kathy whisked Maggie into the pastor's office as David arrived and proffered, "David, Maggie and I have been talking about her ex—"

"You mean Kimsley?" he blurted.

They both nodded at the same time.

"Maggie feels compelled to try to witness to him about Christ."

David grew concerned. "I don't think that's such a good idea, in the circumstances...he's a murderer."

"So were Moses and Paul," Maggie countered sheepishly.

"They were different."

"How were they different?" she asked innocently.

"They didn't kill my friends!" he retorted and showed them out the door. He walked over to his desk, fell into his chair, and cried out, *Lord, you are a God of judgment. Why aren't these people being brought to justice?*

And then it hit him. He couldn't bear the thought that Maggie could share Christ with Kimsley, only to have him acknowledge Christ and be forgiven his sins. The whole concept turned his stomach. He wanted the man to die a slow, painful death, and then go straight to Gehenna for his ultimate reward.

But fragments of a past discussion began to drift into his mind. He suddenly remembered an exercise he did in graduate school when Professor Cohen presented a scenario before the class in which Adolph Hitler came to receive Christ moments before he died. Would he be saved? Would he go to heaven? Everyone laughed at the prof until he reminded them of the penitent thief on the cross next to Christ at his crucifixion. Christ announced, after the thief acknowledged Christ's personage, that today the forgiven sinner would be in heaven. The prof went on to prove his point with systematic theology—much to the chagrin of the class—that up to the last minute of death, one could be saved, regardless of their previous atrocities.

As David remembered that incident, he shook his head and resolved not to interfere in Maggie's scheme, even if he did have concerns about her safety, but to let God's divine plan unfold.

In Maggie's mind, the decision had already been made.

Over one year had passed since she worked on the Haitian Experiment file, and she needed to confirm the information for Lane to legally document their case. Sydelle had discussed the situation with Matthew, and both had agreed to use a Haitian native to translate and get information. Knowing that the Haitian people were very close-mouthed to outsiders, they were doubly happy when Marie-Clarisse and her family joined David's church. When she heard about what was happening to some of her country-folk, she was more than happy to help out. Working with Krissy's PDA, Sydelle retrieved the information she had forgotten about since she left Rainbow. As she looked at the data in Krissy's notes a remnant of times past drifted through her mind. She recalled how important the vaccine project was to her while working at Rainbow—being an important part of the drug that would benefit mankind. Now it represented a weapon in the hands of an artful adversary. In fact, her whole world had changed in that one year.

Picking up where Krissy left off, Sydelle sat in a back room of the church with its newly added phone line and telephoned Haiti. She switched on the speaker phone, then handed the phone to Marie-Clarisse.

"Oui," the soft-spoken woman answered.

"Mr. Toussaint Ramcharitar, please," Marie-Clarisse asked in perfect Creole.

"Who's calling, please?"

"This is Marie-Clarisse representing a research group in Florida checking on the progress of certain vaccine recipients. Can you help me?"

"Yes, he was my husband."

"Was?" Marie-Clarisse blurted out unexpectedly. "What happened to him?"

"Who are you?" the woman demanded. "Why would I talk to you?" The woman stifled a sob. "I don't know you. You could be the same sick people that did it to him in the first place."

Sydelle sensed that things were not going well, and she could do nothing but trust in the Lord and in Marie-Clarisse to say the right thing and let the woman open up.

"You don't know me, but I know you—or I know people like you. My people are from the Port-au-Prince Delta area. We know what you have gone through. If you don't want to talk, I will understand."

Sydelle listened quietly as she tried to understand the accented and animated conversation.

Marie-Clarisse put her hand over the phone and motioned to Sydelle. "I don't think it is going to work; she isn't talking."

Sydelle put up her hands, both to shrug off that they could do nothing about it—and to signify that maybe God could.

Marie-Clarisse turned back to the phone and continued her monologue. "Thank you for listening to me, ma'am. I will leave you alone now. God bless you, ma'am...." She shook her head at Sydelle and went to hang up.

Then Sydelle heard loud, almost frantic, pleading words through the speaker from the woman at the other end of the phone.

"Wait! I could use a friend. Your people have been good to me, and I know that you will be different than the ones calling to give me trouble. I will tell you what you want to know. But my heart is broken."

Marie-Clarisse turned to Sydelle in triumph and motioned for Sydelle to give her the pad and pen.

"Tell me, Mrs. Ramcharitar, what happened to your husband? What went wrong?"

"He died six months ago of AIDS, and it's only by God's grace that he didn't give it to me. If he hadn't been in the hospital for over two years, I would probably have it too."

As Sydelle knew, Marie-Clarisse would be sympathetic to the caller. So many of Marie-Clarisse's own people had died of or contracted the disease. "It was horrible," the woman continued, almost incoherently. "It was last summer, when the Clarion Clinic called me and said I had to come get him, that there wasn't anything more they could do for him. So I borrowed a car and drove down to Cap Haitian. Then when I saw him, I couldn't believe my eyes; he looked like a corpse, only barely alive. He was so emaciated and frail, I was able to lift and carry him to the car myself, and I'm not a big woman." She paused to sniffle woefully and gather her thoughts.

"Were you with him when he died?"

"I held him in my arms as he took his last breath."

"I know this is painful, but can you describe his appearance to me for our records?"

She paused, then started up again. "I suppose it's all right. The first thing that bothered me was his eyes. They were glassy and sunken in his head. When I looked into them, he wasn't there. Who knows where his mind was. Then there were oozing blisters on his face and in his mouth, along with purple and black welts all over his body."

"What about his hair?"

"Most of it fell out when he was in the hospital."

"And how would you describe his frame of mind? Normally a state of depression sets in before death halts life."

A long silence, followed by continued crying.

Sydelle's heart broke as Marie-Clarisse's face told the tale of this poor woman who was so desperate for consolation that she would unburden her problems to strangers, hoping for some small measure of comfort.

"That was the strange part. The doctor said he would be very despondent, then just slowly deteriorate until he died, but he went into a state of fantasy or delusion instead. He kept saying he would be fine in a few weeks. He kept saying it over and over."

"What do you mean by a state of fantasy?"

"One day he imagined himself as a healthy person back to work at his old job of working down at the docks where the ships come in."

"Go on, I'm listening," Marie-Clarisse entreated.

"Once he talked in his sleep. Something about going fishing with his best friend, Reggie, as soon as daylight came. Then one time he grabbed me when I was bathing him and started to kiss me and call me by his girlfriend's name, Aida, the girl that gave him the AIDS...Another time he somehow believed he had a new strong body, climbed out of bed, and for 15 minutes rearranged the furniture in the room, then gasped and fell flat on the floor. I didn't go back in the room for the rest of the day. I was too nervous."

284

"Oh, my. That must have been hard for you."

"Yes, that was hard but not as hard as when he screamed about the demons."

"What? Did you say demons?" Marie-Clarisse replied and shot a bewildered look toward Sydelle.

"Yes. When he wasn't fantasizing, he would go through periods of torment and tear at the sores on his body, yelling that the demons were dragging him off his bed. Once he cried out that he was in hell and wanted water to pour on his feet—screaming his feet were on fire."

"Was he on any medication that could have induced these dreams or fantasies?"

"No, the doctors said there was no medicine that could help him anymore."

"No tranquilizers of any kind?"

"Nothing."

Marie-Clarisse did what she could to offer sympathy and encouragement, indicating that perhaps her help would assist them in their cause and allow them to help some future person similarly afflicted. She wished the woman well and told her of some friends in the Delta District who would be able to talk to her from experience and said good-bye.

Sydelle left her office, drove to the Coral Springs library, and consulted several medical journal reviews, then returned and went to see David in his office. "Something strange is going on," she began. "I just came back from the library after getting off the phone with a woman in Haiti whose husband was on Rainbow's experimental vaccine list. She said that before he died, he alternated between bizarre delusions and weird behaviorism."

"That's interesting, like what?" David asked.

"Like fantasizing that he was getting healthy, then exhibiting unusual physical strength, living in a false reality. Like he were reliving his life over again."

"Probably just the final stages of death, going through phases of nostalgia or imagining your getting well; a state of euphoria is not too unusual for terminal patients," David observed.

"I suppose," Sydelle mused. "But then his wife recounted some crazy events where he claimed demons were dragging him off the bed and crying our for water to pour on his feet that were on fire in hell—that's a little much, don't you think?"

"Run that by me again—the part about the demons," David returned.

She reviewed the events, then handed him some photocopies of the medical journals.

"There's nothing in current AIDS research that even hints of these kinds of—" she waved her hands in the air—"hallucinations or whatever you would call them. Something is different here. When I was at Rainbow, I read all the lab and research reports regarding the side effects of their vaccine. Up to that time frame, there was no such documentation of this kind of thing. Do you think they could be related?"

"Something you just said strikes a nerve. 'Up to that time frame.' I'm wondering if there could be some emotional, even mental side effects from their vaccine that required over a year for incubation, manifesting itself after you left, which seeps in and affects the mind." David looked over at the clock hanging on the wall, threw the papers he was working on in his attaché case, and added, "I'm going to see Matt Lane. I'll talk to you tomorrow." He dashed out the door.

Matthew Lane sat in his swivel chair, oscillating a quarter circle as he listened to David propound his theory on Sydelle's phone call to Haiti. Scary thoughts drifted through his mind when the suggestion of demonic involvement suddenly became part of the mushrooming vaccine equation that became more complicated with each new day.

David suggested they try to find a living person who had received Rainbow's trial vaccine so they could observe the behavior for themselves. But Rainbow Pharmaceuticals would never permit such an inspection—of that he was sure. Matthew mulled the circumstances over in his mind for several minutes after David stopped talking, then opened his desk drawer to retrieve his personal phone directory. He spotted the roll of evergreen Life Savers and popped one in his mouth as he pressed a sequence of numbers on the telephone. "Antonio, please."

David looked at him strangely and mouthed, *Who is Antonio?*

Matthew covered the mouthpiece of the phone. "Brandon's contact at

Rainbow."

"Antonio, this is Matthew Lane. I need a favor. Naturally everything between you and me is top secret." He nodded, then continued, "I know it's dangerous for me to call you at work, but this is urgent. We're onto something that requires some substantiation, and I need the present location of the vaccine volunteers."

A monologue ensued, followed by Matthew's insistence. Then Matthew winked at David while reaching for scrap paper. He quickly wrote down addresses, thanked Antonio, and hung up the phone.

"He gave me two."

"That's something," David said optimistically.

"He didn't know about the rest—only the ones that were in nearby hospitals. One in Key West, the other in Miami."

"Big drug problem areas," David observed.

"How much time do you have?"

"I know what you're thinking. I'll just call Kathy to tell her I'll be home late tonight."

Matthew grabbed the rest of his Life Savers from his drawer. "I'll meet you in the lobby."

Brandon was nervous as he picked up the phone to talk to Dr. Barrett. He knew that Sam would be calling him back, but he was uncertain as to when the call would come through. Until now, he hadn't shared the arrow with anyone, not even his father. The vial was something else—that had been tested. Now he needed the help of an expert who would give him the information he needed.

"Sam, it's good of you to call so quickly. It's important, or I wouldn't have bothered you."

"Brandon, don't be ridiculous. Nothing you could do would be a bother. Why the urgency? And when are you coming back to join the dig—or are you caught up in something else altogether?"

Brandon closed his eyes as he let the air escape and thought of his next words. "Sam, I'm not sure what I'm involved in anymore. What I do know is I need your help. I've come across an artifact that I can only describe as ancient and cryptic. Sounds right up your alley, don't you think?" He could hear Sam's laughter in the background as he mentally reviewed the arrow.

"Well, that could encompass just about anything under the sun, Brandon. You're going to have to be a little more specific. Where did you find it and what period is it from?"

"I found it on Mykonos, and it doesn't conform to any known period that I'm familiar with. The inscription is all in Greek. Other than that, I have no idea what time is associated with it or what civilization. It doesn't seem to match. I need your help."

"Well, I'd be only too happy to help you. What does the inscription say, and when can I see it?"

"Well, I can fax you a photograph of it, and I can fax over the transcription and the translation. That would be the best way to start. After that, you tell me."

"You certainly seem all riled up about this—it seems like a big detour from where you were headed the last time I saw you. What happened?"

"Sam, I think they may be related. If you knew where I got the artifact, you might agree. But I think I'd like to leave that out of it for now. Let me fax this over to you; then you call me back. How does that sound?"

"Sounds good to me—except be prepared. I'm calling collect." His father's oldest friend chuckled as he hung up.

Brandon smiled. He went to get the materials to fax and reviewed the inscription again.

Σπαθια και αν βρεξεισ σε ουρανε
Μαιχαιρια και αν χιονειζεισ
Αλλα την κατσικα του θανατου
θα ειναι το κλειδι τησ νικησ.
Το ματι θα ειναι την πορτα.
Η κατσικα -φιλη και εχθρη μαζι.

Swords will come as rain from heaven
Knives will be like snow.
But the she-goat of death
Will be the key to victory.
The eye will be the door.
The she-goat—friend and foe together.

Brandon had looked at it for hours after he translated it and wondered what it could be talking about. He knew there weren't any goats on Mykonos or even in the area. *If only I knew which arrow I pulled out—that would tell me which area to look in.* He could only wait.

He felt guilty about not telling his father, but there was still a lot that had been left unsaid. For now, it seemed easier to leave the arrow out and concentrate on the vial. That was enough to keep him busy in the crusade. *Yes, for now,* he thought, *I will let this arrow be my own crusade—for me, for Pano, and for those who have been the target of this vendetta that has gone back centuries.* He didn't even think that Pano understood how he felt. He didn't even know himself. It seemed absurd, and it seemed oblique. But he had to press on.

He put the papers into the fax machine and pressed Send. It was on its way—there was no turning back.

"Looks familiar, doesn't it?" Matthew asked David as they arrived at the reception desk at Jackson Memorial Hospital.

David looked around the room, then felt his arm. Only a slight pain from the bullet wound remained. He remembered being wheeled in through the emergency room in the hospital's east wing after the attack at the Metrorail station; then his heart ached once again for Louie. "Yeah, sure does." He shook his head and reminded himself of his abhorrence for hospitals.

"I'd like to visit with Franklin Nesbitt, please," Matthew asked.

The volunteer keyed in the name, then looked at the monitor and up at Matthew. "This patient is in isolation on the fourth floor. You'll need to check in at the nurses' station before visiting." She handed him two passes without a smile.

"Are you sure you want to go in?" Nurse Lenton asked.

Matthew looked at David, then back to the nurse. "We have to."

"Okay, then follow me." She escorted them to a clean room where they were instructed to don rubber gloves, surgical masks, and hospital suits and slippers. "Remember not to touch the patient or any of his body fluids," she warned as they neared the isolation ward.

The room was located at the end of the corridor near the fire exit door, where the lack of sunlight cast a dismal group of shadows in the hallway. Dirty linen lay in the corner by the adjacent exit door. David twitched his nose to signal Matthew of an odor coming from the room, and both of them rolled their eyes and braced themselves as nurse Lenton opened the door for them and announced, "This is Franklin's room." With that she turned and departed, leaving them alone with the patient.

Despite the hospital's effort to maintain an antiseptic, comfortable environment, the air was cold and dank with a pervasive peculiar odor. David quickly looked around the room in a vain attempt to spot the cause of the smell, then turned to see the patient. His stomach began to heave as he viewed the deformed head of a man. The skull looked enlarged, while the cheeks and neck were gaunt, almost skeletal, with tight shiny skin pulled over it. Nearly completely bald with sunken eyes, now closed in sleep, his tongue almost fully extended, he gave off a deep rapid wheeze when he breathed.

Matthew pointed to the yellow-brown color of his skin and raised an eyebrow.

David walked around the foot of the bed and noticed leather straps partially concealed by the blankets and sheets. He lifted them and saw that Franklin's ankles were securely tethered to the bed frame. He motioned to Matthew, who watched at the door, then began to lift the covers to see the rest of his body. Large purple and brown boils and welts extended as high up as he could see. Franklin's hands were fastened with Velcro strips to a bar beneath the sheets. On the other side of the bed, a neglected catheter and colectomy bag hung perilously. David shook his head and sniffed in disgust at the scene. He turned to relieve Matt at the door and heard a low rumbling voice call him from behind.

He turned and looked at Franklin, but he was sound asleep. "Did you hear that, Matt?" David said.

Matt nodded. "Sure did. He called your name out."

"Funny. He's still asleep," he said dryly.

David proceeded to move the covers away from Franklin's face when his eyes fluttered. Franklin then forcefully lifted his head off the pillow and looked David in the eyes. David immediately recognized that Franklin was not in control.

"Oh no," David muttered.

Carefully articulating with a deep throaty voice, Franklin said, "Why have you come, David? Have you come to torment me? Leave me alone!" Suddenly he convulsed several times, then tore one of the hand restraints and lunged for David, knocking him back against the wall.

David grabbed the hand, looking at his forearm, holding it until it fell limp.

"I've seen this before, David," Matthew whispered, pulling David away from Franklin's bed, "and this stuff can get nasty."

"Hang on—," David started, then went to the door to look out. The hallway was clear. "What do you make of it?"

"I studied occult and demonic activity." He pointed to the restraining straps and to Franklin's distorted face. "This is more than AIDS. This could be a case of possession as well."

A face popped in the nearly closed door. "Everything all right, gentlemen?" Nurse Lenton asked as she scanned the figure in the bed.

David stepped forward. "What does the doctor say about his condition?"

"He has AIDS. What do you expect? He'll probably live this way for another few weeks and just die," she noted officially.

"We know he has AIDS, Ms. Lenton," Matthew said impatiently, "but why are you restraining him?"

Nurse Lenton's face tightened. She stepped inside the room and closed the door behind her. "We have only three living AIDS patients at this time, and Franklin is the only one in isolation who received the vaccine. We're not worried about him spreading the AIDS virus; we're scared stiff about him killing one of us!"

"What do you mean?" David asked.

Nurse Lenton hesitated, then turned and unlocked a nearby apparatus table drawer and pulled out a clipboard with Franklin's charts. "Last week Franklin pulled out all his life support tubes during a nightmare, then managed to run up and down the hallway like a maniac yelling in a strange language. Then he grabbed the fire extinguisher off the wall and began spraying it all over himself until we called for two orderlies to subdue him." She pointed to the straps and added, "The doctor ordered him to be tied down until further notice."

David looked at Matthew, then asked Nurse Lenton, "Was anybody able to interpret the strange language?"

She pointed toward the nurses' station. "One of the nurses is Jamaican, and she said she thought Franklin kept yelling, 'I am burning, burning, burning!' but wasn't sure since it was an obscure dialect." She shook her head and concluded glumly, "We all feel so helpless."

"What about your other two patients?" Matthew said.

"If you can use the term 'normal,' they're normal."

David scratched his head. "Thank you, Miss Lenton. You've really helped us, but we're still trying to find a common denominator here. Do you know how Franklin contracted AIDS?"

"He was a heroin addict."

"I suspected as much. I saw needle marks on his arms. Did he have any homosexual partners?"

"No, we questioned him; he was straight."

"Just curious. And the other two?"

"They were gay but not drug users."

David nodded. "Now if you'll excuse us for a few minutes longer we plan to help Franklin in prayer."

She smiled in compliance, then closed the door.

Both David and Matthew walked over and placed their hands on Franklin's forehead, then cried out in unison to petition the Lord to free Franklin from his demonic captivity. But when they looked down, his eyes were wide open and his pupils were fixed and dilated.

Halfway down the Florida Turnpike, en route to Key West, few words were exchanged. David mentally reexamined the events involving Franklin, feeling concerned for the man's lost soul, while Matthew only briefly mentioned he was pondering the ramifications of a vaccine that was enabling a virus to dangerously mutate.

Traveling south on US-1, they reached Key Largo, where they stopped to rest and refuel. Renewing their journey and feeling refreshed, David began the conversation. "Matthew, I'm convinced that demonic infiltration is taking place in random AIDS patients, and the window must be drugs."

Matthew nodded. "That makes sense. The evil spirit would take control of the mind where their drug abuse left off."

"Yes, drug abuse is key." He shut his eyes to concentrate. Hold it!" David exclaimed. "Pull over to the side of the road for a moment. I just thought of something." He reached in his jacket and pulled out a pocket New Testament. He fumbled through the back of the Bible and paused to recall the location. "I know there's a verse in Revelation 9 that speaks of—" he looked carefully at the pages—"sure enough, listen to this: 'Neither did they change their mind and attitude about all their murders and witchcraft and immorality.'" He shut his eyes and reached for information. "I remember doing a word study on this once. The word *witchcraft* also means 'pharmakea,' the root word to pharmacy or drugs. Certainly the margin here can be applied to this vaccine from the devil."

"You must be right," Matthew said. "Just as there was a catalyst somewhere along the chain enabling the HIV virus to cross and jump the species barrier to humans, likewise the vaccine must be acting as a catalyst to enable demonic activity among drug users."

Turning toward the ocean, David grimaced. "And God only knows what will happen when it mutates and jumps into the homosexual sector."

Matthew then pulled out onto US-1, heading south to Key West.

Unlike Jackson Memorial, the Monroe County clinic on Truman Street had seven living AIDS vaccine recipients, all in a separate wing, of which two were former drug addicts. Interviewing the gay, non-drug users proved David's hunch: They showed no symptoms of demonic involvement.

Noting their findings, they hurriedly proceeded to the two AIDS patients listed as substance abusers. Surprisingly, the duty nurse simply smiled and pointed to the location of the patients' room.

Convivial laughter and jocular conversation rebounded off the walls and into the hallway as they approached the room. Matthew shot a look at David and shrugged, as if to say, "Are they having a party?" David compared the pass with the names on the door to confirm their identity.

He nodded to Matthew, then walked in the door.

Silence.

The younger looking one, a man David estimated to be in his 30s, was sitting up in his bed, dressed in street clothes. He slowly turned and glared at David. "Hello, David. Franklin said you might drop by to see us."

David noticed an absence of vital support apparatus at his bed.

"And you too, Matthew," the other sickly looking man said with a broad smile.

Matthew froze in his steps and grabbed David's hand. "How did they know–?"

"Shush!" David commanded Matthew. Surveying the room, David sensed an evil influence but saw no signs of it. Obviously they were both hyperaesthesia, capable of sensing invasive spiritual prowess. Calculating their every move, David and Matthew moved toward them, while David extended his rubber-gloved hand in guarded friendship to the younger one. "I don't recall having the pleasure of meeting you—" he quickly looked at his index card—"uh...Richard Clendon, right?"

"Very good, David," Richard replied acidly.

David was astonished at his appearance. The man looked very healthy, yet was terminal with AIDS. The older one, a Malcolm Ritter, appeared frail, with the AIDS mask that belied his facade.

"Why have you come?" Richard added, his eyes suspicious.

"I suspect you already know," David replied. He remembered reading about demonic encounters and the paranormal ability that evil spirits are capable of manufacturing.

"You're right. I do know," a raspy, quavering voice (definitely not Richard's) answered from under his bed.

Then from Richard's sneering mouth came these words: "You've come to talk to us about Christ."

Without warning, Malcolm began blabbing incoherently, then sat up in his bed and pointed to David and laughed hysterically.

David shot a prayer up to heaven, asking for divine protection, then yelled at Malcolm, "Be still!"

With that Malcolm fell backward into the pillow, remaining motionless.

Fully conscious of Richard's acute awareness, David turned to him and said, "Well, not exactly. We've come to discuss your condition—your physical appearance is remarkably good—despite your medical records. We are documenting the vaccine's effects on those AIDS patients who have had past experience with drugs."

"Why, so you can build a case against Rainbow?" Richard snarled.

"No, not against Rainbow," Matthew cut in. "We suspect a deviation in the vaccine's ability to prevent the replication of the virus, and we want to correct it to minimize any side effects."

"Very noble of you," he said in a muzzy whisper, then slowly dropped down on the bed as if commands to move were temporarily suspended.

Matthew seized the moment and reached for Richard's hand to feel the flesh but immediately flinched. The hand was ice cold, despite its appearance, and slowly began to take on a putrefaction.

"Uh-oh," Matthew uttered. As he stared at the hand, the hand and arm passed through the sheets and mattress and dangled under the bed momentarily.

David walked over and placed his hand where Richard's arm was, but the solid arm, still attached at the shoulder, had simply dematerialized and reappeared under the bed. After several seconds, it reappeared on top of the bed once again, with whole, normal flesh.

"I get the picture now," David said to Matthew. They both withdrew to the open window and briefly conversed in whispers. Then they separately walked to the beds. David stood at Richard's side; Matthew at Malcolm's.

Suddenly images of Kathy and Hillary flashed like a strobe in David's mind. Screaming and thrashing in water, they were trapped inside her car after driving through a canal guard rail. The water was rising, suffocating them. Aware of demons' abilities to project false realities, David backed off from Richard's bed to lean on the sink for several seconds, then cried out, "In the name of Jesus, I cast you out!"

Richard let out a shrill yowl and jumped off the bed. He stood poised to attack, growling like an animal. "Malcolm, get up!" he wailed.

Malcolm bolted upward in his bed, then seized hold of Matthew and held him firmly. All at once two nurses appeared in the doorway, aghast at the scene.

"Call the police!" Matthew screamed.

With that they both ran back to the nurses' station.

Matthew elbowed Malcolm in the face, freeing his hands, then stepped back and shouted, "Christ's blood will cover you, Malcolm. Call upon him!"

Malcolm pointed to a toy unicorn placed at the foot of his bed, causing it to animate and spring upward onto Matthew's face, goring him at the right temple. Matthew flung the creature clear across the room, then held Malcolm down, fervently praying for his deliverance.

At the same time, Richard's facial features began to distort; his face and arms began to erupt into sores and gashes.

"Now will the real Richard please stand up," David quipped, bracing himself for a fight.

Richard's whole body jerked uncontrollably and began to dehydrate and shrivel up. Within seconds his tissue did shrink tightly against his skeleton. Dazed, he began to teeter, then caught a glimpse of himself in the bathroom mirror. "Argh!" he clamored and convulsed violently.

"David, he's having a seizure!" Matthew yelled. "Hold him down before he harms himself!"

But the warning came too late. Richard regained his stability and dashed out into the hallway, screaming for help, followed by David who leaped and tackled him, both of them crashing down on the hallway floor.

Able onlookers from the adjoining rooms spilled out into the hallway and gathered around the melee unfolding before their eyes.

Straddling Richard's body, David slapped his face until his eyes focused. "In the name of Jesus, I cast you out!" he ordered.

The crowd gasped and ran for their rooms, slamming their doors.

Richard's body went limp; then he blinked in recognition of the command.

David suddenly felt dizzy while his heart began to palpitate in his chest. He relaxed his grip on Richard and swayed perilously.

Richard squirmed to free himself.

"Matt, help me!" David shouted.

Within seconds Matthew fell to his knees next to David and cried out, "Jesus' blood is covering you, Richard! Call upon him to deliver you!"

Again Richard's body fell limp. As Matthew helped David to his feet, Richard's eyes searched the hallway for an escape route.

But Matthew was watching him. "It's not over," he warned.

From behind, Malcolm's arms clutched Matthew in a choke hold as Richard renewed his strength, jumped to his feet, and ran for the open window in his room.

David, reeling from the dizzy spell, temporarily became disoriented and staggered off the other way.

"David, get him!" Matthew yelled in a muffled gag to redirect him.

By the time David reached Richard, he had climbed on the window ledge, threatening to jump. David slowed his pursuit and calmly said, "Don't do it, Richard. Suicide is not the answer." David extended his hand toward him while racking his brain for something spiritual to say. But in the frenzy, his mind went blank. "Lord, help," he muttered.

Hanging precariously with one arm, Richard glared at David and shouted, "It's over! My life is over—I want out!"

"You'll burn forever in hell, Richard. Is that what you want? Die a wasted death, then spend eternity in the lake of fire?" David pleaded.

"He's not going to hell," a metallic voice announced from somewhere inside the room.

David rotated in place but saw nothing.

"I want to go to heaven!" a tender voice from within Richard cried out.

"You can; you can," David entreated with his eyes riveted on the hand holding on to the window frame. "Just hold my hand and I'll show you how."

"You can let go and you'll be in heaven," the voice in the room thundered.

From behind, Matthew started reciting Bible verses from John's gospel. As Richard turned to hear toward the words, he unwittingly relaxed his grip on the window.

David gulped as his heart leaped in fear. He lunged for the hand, clasping it, pulling Richard to the floor.

Richard's eyes began to flutter as he groped to find David's hand. "I want to go to heaven," he whispered.

"You will," David assured. "Just say this prayer after me." He recited the sinner's prayer, and the mysterious voice faded.

As Richard repeated it, a beautiful, peaceful smile came over his face. David carefully picked him up and laid him on the bed.

When he turned around, two police officers with short staving poles were holding Malcolm on the floor as his body twitched violently with spittle flowing from his mouth to the floor. Matthew was on his knees, praying.

"Matt, look!" David exclaimed, pointing to Richard. Richard was sleeping as if nothing had happened.

As they raced to the hallway, one of the policemen named Alan said, "This guy's nuts," then dropped to one knee and reached for his handcuffs. The other officer, Rooney, a brute of a man, refused to look at Malcolm; he just placed his foot and held it on Malcolm's neck as he dropped the staving poles.

"He's not an animal!" David flared.

"They are to us," Officer Rooney replied coldly.

"Take your foot off his neck, Officer," Matthew demanded.

Rooney grunted under protest and slowly withdrew his foot.

In a split second, Malcolm thrust himself upward to pull on Officer Alan's holster as he fumbled for the cuffs, releasing the safety strap. He grabbed the officer's gun and pointed it at Rooney and fired one round. The shot grazed Rooney's right thigh, knocking him to the floor.

"Don't shoot, Malcolm!" David yelled.

Malcolm turned to David with sorrow in his eyes, then pointed the gun at Officer Alan, cocking the hammer.

Thwack! Officer Rooney slammed a staving pole on Malcolm's head, crushing his skull. Malcolm collapsed on the floor, dead.

It would be the better part of another two hours to complete the police department paperwork before David and Matthew would be on their way home.

ELEVEN

The moral immune system of this country
has been weakened and attacked,
and the AIDS virus is the perfect metaphor for it.
The malignant neglect of the last twelve years
has led to the breakdown
of our country's immune system,
environmentally, culturally, politically,
spiritually and physically.
Barbra Streisand

Brandon arrived at the lab in time to talk with his father's secretary only to find he was out with David. It was almost a relief as he wanted to sort things out for himself. He had catalogued the evidence they had accumulated since Johnnie was first killed and assembled it all together. He hoped that this vial filled in a link or at least pointed him in the right direction. He wanted to close this case quickly so he was free enough to pursue his own quest with Sam Barrett. He only hoped Sam would be willing to break away from his dig long enough to give Brandon the help and attention he needed.

As he had requested, the lab's top security worked on the vial and its contents, and he found the results in the corporate safe in his father's office, where he was told they would be. He was surprised to find them unopened; he thought his father would be more anxious to read the results. He could only surmise that something equally pressing had come up that he would put the matter aside till he could give it his full attention.

With no small trepidation he opened the envelope and began to scan its contents. The gelatinous contents were no surprise, so he quickly moved to the specimen area to see what exactly it was that Antonio felt so compelled to transmit to him.

Specimen sample:

Interferon: *Class unknown*

Consistency: *Recombinant DNA strands*

Makeup: *Sufficient live HIV virus present within an opsonin matrix*

Opsonin origin: *Evidence of human opsonin in suspension of green rhesus and pigtail macaque thymus cells*

Clinical and evidentiary correlation: *Using evidence previously examined which showed a suspension of human thymus gland as harvesting ground for green rhesus recombinant DNA, it is theorized that live viral cells were injected into a neutral carrier (hypothesis: pigtail macaque) and were then engorged within the thymus gland by the animal's opsonin. These opsonin ingested the HIV viral cells, allowing the animal to be a carrier breed. These opsonin were then placed within the green rhesus for a simian HIV reaction. The cultivation of these cells were then embedded within the human thymus to produce human interferon for harvest and cloning.*

Suggested Purpose: *Theoretically, this matrix would allow for the injection of the live virus and the charged opsonin cells to provide the current host with a Viral Blockade. The specimen would be the precursor to an HIV-assimilated vaccine.*

Prognosis: *The genetic material of the HIV viral cell is unstable and subject to mutation. Therefore, while this Viral Blockade could be seen as a temporary cessation to an HIV infection, the results and the effectiveness should be classified as such.*

Recommendations: *While this line of reasoning is valid, the chain is not direct enough to pattern the viral strain and avoid replication failure due to mutation. Suggested strategy would be to identify the direct cause of the HIV strain rather than splice and harvest HIV-infected opsonin for human vaccination.*

Brandon put his head down on his hands as he digested the report. He was glad his father put it aside and allowed him to read it first.

It's a lie, he thought at first, as he allowed himself to breathe again. *It's not a vaccine. It's a temporary medication. It's all a rotten lie!* He couldn't stop his hand from crashing down on the desk as he vented his frustration. He had to fight the feeling that they had been defeated. In the back of his mind he hoped that the cure would spring out at him after the evidence and specimens were all completely analyzed. Now his most brilliant research team could only tell him that a cure would be more easily found if they could isolate the original source of HIV infection. *Oh, is that all?* he thought with derision. *The one question everyone has been asking since HIV was first heard of: Where did it come from?* To think he was back at square one.

He sealed the folder and the reports back in the envelope and carefully replaced them in the safe. His father would read them and be more discouraged. Matthew's principal opposition to Rainbow stemmed from the fact that a cure was vital and that a vaccine was not the answer. Especially one that would not be readily available and one that would not eradicate the disease. Now to find out that the existing vaccine was nothing more than a glorified form of AZT, well, he knew his father was going to react accordingly. What he was going to do...that Brandon didn't know. And didn't want to know.

His only vindication was in knowing that Rainbow hadn't done what they said. He knew they were liars, and he knew they had an agenda beyond the AIDS vaccine. Now he knew that they hadn't done humanity any favor at all. In fact, they had done the worst thing of all: produce a false hope by heightening the world's expectations with a vaccine that was doomed to fail.

Somehow the rivalry he had been feeling toward Rainbow seemed strangely unimportant.

Matthew waved into David's home security camera as he held up a bag of bagels as a morning peace offering, then spoke into the intercom, "Good morning, Mr. and Mrs. Douglas."

Moments later the security latches were released, allowing Matthew entrance into their home.

"Get any rest?" Matthew said as he plopped into a kitchen chair.

"A little," David replied through a yawn, scratching his scalp in an effort to wake up.

"David stayed up for two hours explaining everything to me," Kathy added while pouring coffee into their cups.

Matthew opened up a folder and laid it on the table. "Early this morning I made a number of phone calls to my colleagues throughout the country, asking them for their input on this demonic affiliation with drugs thing, and I've compiled a makeshift chart based on my findings. Of course it's not conclusive, but at least it gives us an idea of the patterns being made."

"That should help," David noted as he scanned the chart.

"Random calls to known heavy drug-use states revealed that an average of one out of four ex-drug users who were treated with Toi-VAX showed signs of demonic harassment or involvement. Of course, the other three may not even be aware yet that they're acting as vessels." He paused to butter his bagel, handing off the chart to Kathy.

"Did your colleagues make the connection?" Kathy asked.

"Not at first. Naturally they have been monitoring Rainbow's vaccine and its effects, but they didn't know about their early experiments like we did. When I told them about the case in Haiti and then our encounter with the three cases here in Florida, they quickly correlated their recent reports and complaints. They're ready to go to the CDC and the FDA when we are."

David slapped the file shut. "That sounds great, but what do we say? That with every other injection, Rainbow passes along a demon with their vaccine as a free bonus? And what are we supposed to do then? Perform some global exorcism to rid the earth of all the demons dwelling in the ex-addicts with AIDS?"

"David, don't be such a cynic," Kathy scolded. "Remember, this is a winnable war. Once the battle with Rainbow crossed over into the spiritual realm, as Christians with the power of Christ, we can lick them."

"Amen!" Matthew concurred in support as he reached for his second bagel. He winked at David, then glanced at Kathy. "There's another problem too. The problem that we're aware of that has quantitatively multiplied."

David returned the wink with a grimace. "The mosquito, right?"

Matthew nodded. "You hit it. Only now there's another blood-sucking bug in the soup, the chigger. These two AIDS virus carriers are becoming very serious, even in the states that don't regularly have a bug problem. At this point the baneful bugs are being somewhat contained by

302

insecticides, but I fear they're building immunities. One of my associates in Minneapolis advised me that they're on alert."

"They've traveled that far north already?" Kathy wondered.

"And have adapted to colder climates as well," Matthew continued. "There's no doubt that the insect world is undergoing some kind of metamorphosis."

David silently rose from the table and walked in the adjoining room as Matthew looked at Kathy. "Was it something I said, David?" he remarked with a grin.

A moment later David returned with an open Bible. "Yes, it *was* something you said," he rejoined. "There's a prophecy in Revelation chapter 9 that describes insect mutations that would befall mankind in the latter days. I think this could be the start of it."

Kathy pulled the Bible from his hands and read it for herself. David looked at her suspiciously, expecting a reaction. "Reading the Bible has become like reading the daily newspapers. Now what? Are we supposed to stay indoors for the rest of our lives?" she lamented.

Assuming the pillar of courage, Matthew stood up and put his arm around her. "We've got to trust in the Lord to supernaturally protect his believers. These dilemmas have become much too complex for us to solve."

Kathy sniffed to stifle her tears, then ruefully set the folder on the table and momentarily stepped away. An instant later, her courage had rebounded. "If it weren't for that hope," she said, "I'd seriously think about packing it all in."

"That's my girl!" David cheered.

"Speaking of hope, Kathy," Matthew stated. "David and I agreed last night that the time has come to fight Rainbow officially. I hope to convince the CDC to issue an immediate recall of Toi-VAX. I'm leaving for Atlanta this afternoon."

Kathy's eyes blazed. "Let's hit them with everything we've got!"

"Well, not everything," David interjected. "We're still hoping and waiting for the missing ingredient to find the cure and win the war."

"And Brandon brought some interesting things home with him from Greece. I have the lab inspecting them now. They may be the things that we have been looking for. Until then, we can only hope to win a battle here and there."

"Small victories can keep a person going," Kathy said.

David smiled at Matthew while pointing to Kathy. "Now you see why I wouldn't be where I am today if it weren't for her."

"Don't you blame me," Kathy teased.

At the Atlanta Marriott Hotel, Matthew noted that his sinus condition, which often led to serious sinus infections, had temporarily abated. With the elevation over 1,000 feet above sea level, the little menacing microbes and pollen pests, as he called them, left him alone.

Looking out his hotel window to the horizon, he saw the rolling foothills of the Blue Ridge Mountains, which often acted as a shield against bitter northern waves. Matthew found himself bewildered by the huge change in the city since his first visit 20 years ago...especially in the area of transportation. Now with MARTA, Atlanta's rapid rail transit system, traveling from place to place would be much easier.

The CDC, the Centers for Disease Control, was originally established in 1946 as the Communicable Disease Center—a part of the United States Public Health Service. In 1970, the name was changed to the CDC. Among the main divisions of the CDC are these widely known ones: Epidemiology, Prevention, Environmental and Occupational Safety, and Education Center for Infectious Diseases.

The Center for Infectious Diseases conducts extensive research on cause, prevention, and control, while training doctors and providing public health information in ways to combat disease. Additionally, the center provides immunization services with state and local agencies and establishes standards in conjunction with the FDA for the distribution of vaccines. This was the place where Matthew would bring his case against Rainbow.

His background in the manufacture and legal distribution of drugs qualified him to petition the CDC to hear his argument and see the documented proof of Rainbow's deception. Historically, the CDC was credited with determining the nature of Legionnaires' disease and the diagnosis of toxic shock syndrome, a modern-day malady affecting countless middle-aged women. Their ongoing research into AIDS was unparalleled in Matthew's mind.

Going to the FDA was another matter. Overseeing the safety of foods, medical devices, and cosmetics as well as drugs, is an awesome responsibility for any government agency. Averting disaster in 1962 by delaying approval of thalidomide, the FDA issued new regulations that made drug testing and distribution considerably more stringent—in many cases up to three years.

It was the "fast-track" approval handed down to Rainbow that worried him.

The phone rang. It was the secretary to Dr. Noreen Dillion, the director of the CDC, returning his call and advising him that she consented to see him at one o'clock this afternoon.

He agreed and replaced the phone. What did she mean by "consented"? he wondered. Gathering his evidence, he left the hotel with enough time to enjoy the renowned railway system and prepare his notes.

Escorted into a waiting room, reminiscent of a doctor's office, Matthew glanced at the wide array of framed diplomas that sometimes impressed observers, intimidated others, and outright annoyed still others who questioned their legitimacy. Michigan State University, Magna Cum Laude, Harvard Medical School, etc. He certainly couldn't argue with her credentials.

"Dr. Dillion will see you now, Mr. Lane," her secretary announced.

He looked at his watch. Only 15 minutes of waiting. *Keeps a tight schedule, too,* he noted with a chuckle.

Tall and shapely with long, flowing blonde hair and a chic two-piece suit, the woman commanded attention. He shot a look to a family portrait on her desk of what must have been her husband and daughter. Unwittingly he shrugged in misjudgment and fumbled with his attaché case containing the files and exhibits.

"Thank you for seeing me, Dr. Dillion," he began with a nod.

She returned the nod. "I've heard many good things about Lane Pharmaceutical and your pioneer spirit to help the needy." She turned and glanced out the window while musing, "A much-needed ingredient today in our fight against AIDS." Refocusing on Matthew, she added, "Well, how can I help you?"

Matthew took a long swallow, wondering how he could present his case without coming across as having sour grapes against Rainbow, his alleged competitor. On the other hand, he recognized the great mushrooming political and financial power that Rainbow wielded and its potential tenacity to extend into the domain of the CDC.

"Over the past year, we have acquired certain evidence that points to Rainbow Pharmaceuticals operating in a highly unethical way, and unfortunately, we now have what I consider ample proof to warrant an investigation and recall of their Toi-VAX vaccine. In the interest of public welfare, I strongly advise you to issue a stop order of all distribution before you have a disaster on your hands."

"Need more than that to shut this down, Mr. Lane," she replied suspiciously.

Matthew opened his briefcase and displayed the various items like table-top ornaments on the edge of her desk. Pointing to each one, he built his case systematically. "This is a handkerchief containing the blood stains of a rhesus monkey obtained by a nature photographer at Rainbow's Trinidad research lab before he died in a so-called accident at their plant last year. These are photographs of a human thymus gland, taken by the same photographer, the same day, the same place. And here is a vial of fluid taken from that lab that turned out to be a sample of a hybrid DNA we think was used to synthesize the vaccine.

"I also have a statement regarding human experimentation taking place at Rainbow's Wellington facility, where they performed surgery on homeless people in exchange for money. These point to unorthodox, unethical, illegal, if not barbaric, human testing taking place." Checking her reaction, Matthew noted the lack of concern.

"Inconclusive," she noted, folding her arms and shaking her head. "Animal testing and volunteer human testing is perfectly legal and within the bounds of accepted medical practice."

"Listen, Dr. Dillion," Matthew replied, with a slight edge of impatience, "their vaccine is corrupt and is going to harm people." He paused and questioned if the rest of his evidences would be considered inconclusive as well.

"What else do you have?" she asked dryly as she glanced at the photographs, then at her wristwatch.

"Our latest research shows that the vaccine is unstable. It is nothing more than a viral blockade that will only last as long as the virus does not mutate. We both know that it is mutating. A new vaccine will be needed almost immediately. Toi-VAX is not going to work."

He took a deep breath to regroup. His trained spiritual gift of discernment alerted him to the possibility that this woman was predisposed not to believe him. "As you know," he continued, "I have an extensive background in drug research, reactions, predictions, and longevity. In my professional opinion, there is something wrong with this vaccine. I'm sure the FDA will agree with me. Unfortunately and miraculously, Rainbow Pharmaceuticals has managed to bypass this most stringent step."

He could see he was beginning to step on the woman's toes and they both were starting to feel uncomfortable. He knew he either had to back off or take it to the next level.

"Give me some medical data on your observations and findings," Dr. Dillion said very coolly.

Matthew could see she was attempting to placate him, and he knew he needed something to grab her attention. He knew he had to take the next step. "I'll be happy to leave this package with you for your perusal. I'm sure you'll agree with our findings."

"I see," she responded as she picked up the voluminous material. "Is there anything else, Mr. Lane? I'm sure you appreciate how busy we are around here."

Matthew paused and gauged to see how far this woman would go to seek scientific rewards and how quickly she would shut him out in search of money and notoriety.

"I think there may be a problem with mosquitoes as well," he blurted out.

She nodded. "I've had several field reports of problems with mosquito migration," she conceded reluctantly.

He cleared his throat. "I'm talking about mutating mosquitoes, not just migration."

She looked at him with disdain. "Oh, so you also want to throw in monster mosquitoes, do you? Of course it's Rainbow Pharmaceuticals that's growing them." She set her palms down on her desk and leaned over to scold him. "You know, Mr. Lane, you must be suffering from some form of myopia. We have a board of directors here who makes decisions. If I went to them with everything you've told me and showed them this so-called evidence, they would laugh at me. Your evidence is flimsy and circumstantial, at least on the surface. Considering the magnitude and prestige of your target, Mr. Kavidas of Rainbow Pharmaceuticals, and the fact that his vaccine *is working,* you must do better than this."

"But, Dr. Dillion, people have died trying to preserve and secure this information." He stood up, controlling the frustration and fury building within him. *Why can't she see that this is wrong?* he questioned himself. "Do you require the death of thousands of people before you order a withdrawal?"

"Mr. Lane, kindly dispense with the sarcasm," she demanded. He watched her grind her teeth momentarily while in deep thought. "Out of deference to you, I'm willing to retest the vaccine and look into your allegations by reviewing your materials. We will interview some HIV patients and advise you of our findings." She pointed to the exhibits on her desk. "You can leave them with me. Contrary to your opinion, we *are* concerned with the public's welfare. We protect the public trust. In that vein, I will make sure your research is thoroughly checked out."

For a split second Matthew thought otherwise but relented. "Sure." He handed her his business card. "Please call me as soon as possible with the results."

Dr. Dillion lifted her phone and asked her secretary to escort Mr. Lane to the elevator; then they exchanged good-byes.

Looking back at the CDC as the cab took him away, he wondered how convincing he really was.

"Why didn't you call me instead of sending this letter? You know how I hate things in writing," Kimsley grumped as he slammed his car door holding her letter.

Maggie clutched his hand to soothe his foul mood. "Because I wanted to see you face-to-face, and I knew the letter would get you here." They walked up to her villa and closed the door.

"I've missed you, babe," he said as he grabbed her and started kissing her. "How's my girl doing down at the little churchie-poo?" Holding her shoulders, he looked at her squarely and seriously. "I've been worried. No calls or reports for over two weeks."

Breaking away from his embrace she replied, "Well, that's one of the reasons I needed to see you. Will you have lunch? I made some salads for us."

When he nodded, they headed toward the kitchen.

He sat down at the table. "This David fellow and his followers along with this Matthew Lane are giving us a real cramp, you know. Mr. Kavidas and Mr. Stein are always watching their moves. I've been instructed to look for ways to bring them down."

Maggie braced herself for a tirade, hoping to somehow turn it around to soften his heart. "I've tried to understand David Douglas better so as to identify his weaknesses, and in doing so, I'm wondering why we just don't leave them alone; they're not a threat." She knew that was a lie but justified her duplicity. "Rainbow is so big—a giant, in fact—why worry about those little people?"

"Look, honey," he flared, "maybe being away from me this past month or so has caused you to take leave of your senses; you're not thinking right. They *are* hurting us, and Kavidas is not going away. So we have a conflict of interest here, and my assignment is to remove the conflict, if you follow me."

"You mean like killing off his whole church or something like that, you idiot? You already have more blood on your hands than a slaughterhouse hatchet man! When does it stop, Jerry?" she retorted. The second the words left her lips, she regretted them. She promised herself not to revert to her old ways, but this slipped out.

He jumped up from the table and slapped her across the face. Then he clutched her against himself and whispered, "What's gotten into you, Maggie? You know who I am and how I work. It never bothered you before. What's changed?"

She started to cry in his arms. "*I've* changed. I can't be a part of this anymore. It's evil, Jerry, and it must stop. There are great forces exerting pressure on Kavidas to see that his scheme is thwarted."

Kimsley's grip tightened. "They won you over to their side, haven't they?" he uttered with a snort as his hands slowly traveled up to her neck. "How much have you told Douglas about me, Kavidas, and Stein?"

She shook her head. "Nothing. They don't even know about us." *I'll tell him the truth next time*, she thought.

"Yeah, right!" he scoffed. "And I suppose you now have religion. Am I right?"

She looked into his eyes with compassion for his soul, dismissing in her mind the evil deeds he'd committed. "No, not religion but Jesus. I have Jesus, and my sins are forgiven, and yours can be, too."

He exploded with anger and shoved her against the electric range. "What kind of nonsense are you handing me? Do you take me for a fool? You've seen enough to see me hang—"

She shook her head and pleaded through tears. "I wouldn't betray you."

Kimsley sat back down and began biting his nails in silence, as if pondering his options.

The phone rang.

His gaze darted to the phone. He nodded to Maggie, who picked the phone up.

"Hello, David," she answered in a lame attempt to conceal her crying. She listened for several seconds, then replied, "I'm fine, just tired and feeling a little melancholy......"

Kimsley gestured for her to get off the phone quickly.

A pause ensued. She cracked a thin smile. "Yes, I'll read Psalm 34 and then get some rest. I hope to see you Sunday, too." She replaced the phone.

"Now ain't that special?" Kimsley mocked. He gnashed his teeth and mimicked her. "I hope to see you Sunday." He seized her arm. "Are you two getting it on together? Is that it?"

"Our relationship is strictly spiritual," she countered. A flashback of Kimsley beating her up after she refused to experiment on some hallucinogen last year stirred fear in her heart. *Lord, help*, she prayed.

His eyes bored into hers. Searching and calculating. For a moment she believed he saw something within her that arrested his soul, changing his heart. He turned away in a rage and overturned the table, then raced out the front door.

Maggie looked toward heaven and yelled out, "Thank you, Lord!"

Moments later he returned.

Summoned early in the morning to Gregory's office, Mort looked at the parking lot and thought, *It's jammed.* The release of Toi-VAX to the public created such an amelioration in their drug firm that over 100 new employees were hired to handle the additional volume of distribution.

Gregory handed Mort four sheets of paper as he walked in. "Mort, read this fax that came in on our secured line two hours ago."

Mort sensed tension in Gregory's voice and simply obeyed his request without comment. He read the first sentence of each paragraph on two pages, then scanned the rest, looking to Gregory to interpret the fine print. "Lane went to CDC in Atlanta with this?" *That's what I get for thinking everything is fine*, he thought.

Gregory nodded. "I know some people up there; they keep me informed."

"Are we in trouble?"

"No, not yet. To curry favor with the CDC, Lane postulated a theory about our development of Toi-VAX, suggesting corruption and unscrupulous testing techniques, then among other things, expounded to include cases where ex-drug HIV patients reacted and went into fits of demonic possession."

"This could be serious," Mort noted as he pondered the ramifications. "What about FDA?"

Gregory shrugged. "Nothing yet."

"What do you suggest?"

"You and I are going to spend the morning together to hammer out a solution to prevent any recall. It's as simple as that."

Mort rested in the confidence that Gregory never made an idle threat.

Sunday after lunch, the Douglas's phone rang. "Kathy, this is Rikki. Is Maggie still staying with you?"

"Well, yes, but she went to her villa for the weekend, thinking she was coming down with the flu. Didn't want to spread any germs, you know."

"I called there first, let it ring nine times—no answer—and her answering machine is off."

"She missed church this morning, too, but I'm sure she's fine. This strain of influenza is a brute. Do you want me to drive over and check up on her?" Kathy solicited.

"Yes, would you?"

"No problem. I was about to take Hillary out to get shoes, so I'll stop over there first and call you from Maggie's. Okay?"

"Thanks, I sure appreciate it."

As Kathy turned into the parking lot, an ominous feeling overwhelmed her. She turned to Hillary and said, "You stay in the car. I'll be right back."

Knocking led to pounding on the door until finally she reached into the hanging plant and retrieved the spare key. The second she opened the door, her sense of trouble heightened. Calling out to Maggie proved futile, so she walked into the kitchen, only to find last night's dirty dishes piled in the sink.

"Something's wrong here," she mouthed. She called out to Maggie again.

No response.

Kathy dashed to the front door to check on Hillary, then decided to look in the bedroom. She cried out again to Maggie when she saw the empty, unmade bed.

Again, no response.

She flopped on the bed and glanced into the dresser mirror, then gasped. A bare foot extended out the bathroom door wedged between the door and the jamb.

"Lord, let her be all right," she repeated as she pushed the door open. Immediately she grabbed Maggie's wrist. Feeling no pulse, Kathy opened Maggie's eyelids. Her pupils were fixed.

Lord, no, please. She squeezed her bluish legs and felt their cool rigidity, then spotted a small plastic container in her hand. She pulled it loose and ran to the phone and punched in 911.

"My friend overdosed!" she yelled into the phone to the police department dispatcher.

"Is your friend alive? Is she breathing? Did you check her eyes?" the dispatcher asked.

"No, she's not breathing! Please hurry."

"Her eyes?"

"The pupils are dilated."

The dispatcher automatically asked for vital information to send a patrol car and ambulance immediately, then continued, "Is there any evidence of the drug she took? Sleeping pills, aspirins, barbiturates?"

"She was holding a drug container," Kathy replied.

"Read me the label," the dispatcher said.

"There is no label, only two pills left."

"Describe the pills."

Kathy read off the markings and color.

"Sounds like Nembutal. I'll advise the paramedics, who should reach you in two more minutes."

"Mommy, are you okay?" Hillary shouted from the front door.

"Don't come in here! Stay where you are. I'll be there in a few minutes," she yelled back. She suddenly realized that Maggie was only half dressed. Her skirt was off, but her blouse and jacket were still on.

Puzzled, she returned to the bed and probed the covers, finding nothing. Looking under the bed revealed nothing. Would Maggie decide to take her life while she was undressing? The picture was wrong. Even in death, Maggie would be organized; Kathy knew that. The dishes in the kitchen and the general disarray of the villa was unsettling.

Then she spotted a letter. It was not the expected suicide note but an opened letter addressed to Jerry Kimsley, placed under the table centerpiece. She quickly read it as the police car arrived 30 seconds before the paramedics. The letter confirmed her hunch. Maggie could never commit suicide; it was now clearly a murder.

Late that same Sunday afternoon Matt Lane's phone rang. When Matt heard Noreen Dillion's voice, he knew that the eight-day study and investigation, which was only a preliminary inquiry at this juncture, had been completed.

"We at CDC first want to thank you for your salubrious spirit in bringing to our attention what you considered to be potential problems," she began softly, "but our findings do not corroborate your allegations, and therefore I find no basis to warrant a recall of Toi-VAX."

"But what about the dastardly way Rainbow went about developing Toi-VAX? Don't you and your colleagues understand they're using humans as guinea pigs to experiment on?"

"We've already established, Mr. Lane, that there is no substantive proof or misconduct on that issue," she defended.

"You mean to say that performing surgery on homeless people for money—cutting out their glands and injecting them with monkey's blood, then reinserting them—has now become acceptable operating procedure in the medical profession?" he asked in staccato voice. "And what about the statements and my personal testimony about the vaccine mutating and causing—" he paused to carefully substitute key words—"*emotional behavioral changes?*"

"If you are referring to your absurd conjecture that the vaccine is causing demonic activity to increase in drug addicts, we are pleased to report we looked into that as well. We have performed psychological tests on our in-house HIV patients with historical drug abuse, and there are no unusual results to report," she said emphatically.

He bit his lip in frustration, recalling his original thought about corruption extending to the CDC and how 20 years ago his pristine, American ideology would have immediately rejected such a theory. But not now. With impropriety like human atrophy slowly debilitating the once wholesome American body from the White House down to the local mayor, he questioned the very fabric of the political society. Was any public office beyond temptation or reproach?

"Nothing," he murmured. "You've basically found nothing." He quickly surmised there was no real point in pursuing this crusade with Dillion. "And what about the mosquitoes—are you going to tell me you have *no basis* for that problem either?" he added with stinging resignation.

"Well, we have tested area mosquitoes, together with national samples, and we found some irregularities. Nothing alarming, only that some insects were found carrying HIV-positive blood, and I've alerted the department that acts as the watchdog for any airborne or insect-vector viruses. Of course we've had previous problems in Florida and elsewhere, where the encephalitis-carrying mosquito, the Culex pipiens, had to be dealt with. By spraying, draining, and applying oil slicks to ponds, we feel we've brought it under control."

"But those mosquitoes didn't build up resistance to the insecticides and mutate like the tiger; that's the glitch here," he replied acidly.

"Calm down, Mr. Lane," she warned. "It's people like you that create hysteria in the world. We'll take care of it. Don't worry about it."

"Fine," he said in perspicacity, knowing now his visit to the CDC was in vain.

"We'll send you a hard copy on our findings, along with the articles you left with us, so you needn't make another trip up here."

"That's very kind of you," he appeased.

"Oh, one more thing. I've taken the liberty of sending our findings on those articles you left with me to Jack Moran, over at the FDA, and I'm sure he'll contact you and discuss your concerns. Thank you." The phone clicked off.

Yeah, right, Lane theorized. *Being warned by Dillion, the FDA would naturally side with the CDC. Lord, no one is listening.*

As he waited for David to arrive at his home, Matthew went into his garage to work out on his exercise equipment. Jumping rope for 15 minutes, along with other forms of calisthenics, provided a refreshing diversion, plus time to think from a different perspective.

Running spiritual and drug interdiction against confluent evil forces on a global scale is a task well beyond human ability, he thought. History proved that in order to bring about societal change, society's moral values needed transformation; force or education had limited impact. It was axiomatic that in order for society to be cleansed of this scourge of AIDS, the value system needed to be changed since force and education had proven impotent. Therefore, appealing to the CDC to withdraw the Toi-VAX, heralded as the ultimate prophylaxis, in the midst of the AIDS epidemic, without converting moral values would only be a waste of time…especially when the CDC really didn't think anything was wrong.

"It's a sure bet the CDC buries your reports," David growled a short time later in disgust after Matthew related Dr. Dillion's early morning phone call.

"And any findings they may have uncovered after my meeting with Dillion," Matthew concurred.

The thought of receiving financial or political remuneration from such a giant as Rainbow became increasingly more plausible.

"I hate to say it, but we have no way of knowing whether Kavidas or Stein have any connections with the CDC or Dillion. It just seems strange to me that she would act so uncooperative with Lane Pharmaceutical, considering our substantial share in the marketplace, then make a statement denying any link between Toi-VAX and demonic influence when I handed her documents that supported my theory."

"Let's face it. We represent a big thorn in the side to Rainbow and the CDC when we shake the bushes of drug research and distribution. Not to mention the flak the CDC would get from all the groups pushing for the AIDS vaccine. With their clout, in 1991 a congressional subcommittee killed a proposed bill mandating that HIV-positive patients and health-care workers disclose their status, thus circumventing an attempt to stave off the mushrooming epidemic," David observed. "No, we'll have to beat this adversary a different way—"

Matthew's phone rang.

"Phone's for you, David. It's Kathy. Sounds urgent," Mrs. Lane announced.

David rushed to the phone. Five minutes later, he returned to Matthew in deep distress. "Kathy found a girl from our church dead an hour ago." He slumped down in the chair and spoke through tears. "A new believer who wanted to share her new-found faith with everybody—including her ex-boyfriend. It was made to look like a drug overdose, but it appears to be murder. The police are hunting her ex-boyfriend now."

"How horrible! I'm terribly sorry."

"I have to go to Kathy, but I'll talk to you soon," David said as he dashed out the door.

Matthew stood, speechless, shaking his head in disbelief. *Lord, when does this killing stop?*

Forty-eight hours later, Kathy received a phone call from Detective Menzler of the Fort Lauderdale-Tamarac Police as she started to leave for work.

"Mrs. Douglas, this case is out of my jurisdiction, but we're reciprocal with Margate PD, and they called me on this one. We have a confession by a Jerry Kimsley on the Maggie Clark murder. Can you come down to our precinct in Margate to answer a few questions and give us a statement?"

"I'll leave right now," she replied. After she hung up, she shouted upstairs to David, who threw on a jogging outfit to accompany her.

"She's been here since they brought him in for questioning," the desk sergeant advised David and Kathy, pointing to Maggie's sister, Rikki. "Pacing up and down—she looks strung-out from all that coffee—hasn't eaten anything either."

They walked into the room, waving their hands to circulate the cloud of stale cigarette smoke. Stacked upon the corner table were empty Styrofoam cups with doused cigarettes in the residue.

There was vengeance in Rikki's eyes. "He killed my sister, and they better not let him out or I'll kill him myself!"

David walked to her side and hugged her. "We're sorry that her life had to end in tragedy," he offered in sympathy.

She cried on his shoulder as Kathy patted her back and whispered, "Let it out. Let it out."

Detective Menzler stuck his head into the room and gestured for David to follow him.

David nodded to Kathy, then walked out.

The antechamber of the interrogation room had a TV wired to a concealed video camera focused on Kimsley as he sat sleeping with his head on a table.

"Nice guy, this Kimsley," Menzler said fleetingly as he pointed to the TV screen. "Your ministry is saving people; his *ministry* is *killing* them."

"My wife said he confessed."

Menzler nodded as he opened a file to recall the salient facts. "This Maggie, his ex-girlfriend, must have somehow touched the only tender part in his heart. He kept repeating how sorry he was for his crimes—very remorseful. After only 30 minutes of questioning, despite counsel advising him otherwise, he just broke down and unloaded everything he ever did."

He held up a signed statement. "He listed the people he's killed or had executed over the years. For the past two years he's been working protection for Rainbow, but we don't have any evidence to connect Rainbow with the murders. He claims he's an independent contractor."

"That figures," David rasped.

Menzler straightened his tie, disjointed after his extended duration of questioning. "Your friends—Johnnie Keahon, Krissy Kramer, Louis Donato, and Pastor Jack Hammond and his wife, among others—were all on his list."

David cringed, then reached for the nearest wall to hold himself up. "I just knew Rainbow was involved somehow." He groaned.

"We have nothing to link them," Menzler repeated.

"He worked for them!"

"A court of law will have to establish that. He'll be arraigned tomorrow. Once again, I'm sorry."

Menzler escorted him into the waiting room where Kathy and Rikki were seated. "I hate to say this," he advised them, "but Kimsley has given us a confession of a string of murders he's been involved in...many of your friends are included. I'm awfully sorry." He reached out and touched Rikki's hand, then nodded to both David and Kathy as he walked out.

Kathy and Rikki burst into tears and fell into each other's arms as David gathered them into a huddle and joined them in sorrow.

CNN carried the news piece, along with the commentary that Kimsley, although working at Rainbow Pharmaceuticals, was simply an employee with no ties to the corporate head.

A brief background cameo showed earlier photos of Kimsley with his mother and father as a boy in Chicago. A video clip panned the Wellington facility exterior, then highlighted the important service Rainbow afforded the nation with their recent development of Toi-VAX.

Rikki looked at the TV with utter abhorrence. "With the money you guys have, I'll bet everything I own that he gets off," she said in disgust. "With the media playing up how he's been deprived as a boy, together with his fool lawyers—always finding a *loophole*—sure, he'll serve five years and be out."

The newscaster completed the story announcing the district where his arraignment would take place. Rikki reached for a pen and pad to write the name down.

The third district court in downtown Fort Lauderdale services over one-third of the felony cases in Broward County, producing a staggering volume of cases each day. Today was no exception. Traffic congestion and an ocean of people flowing from the parking building to the courthouse steps would be normal.

Rikki sat waiting in her car with the engine running, across from the rear security entrance where suspects were transported to the courthouse for arraignment. After 30 minutes, the vehicle carrying Kimsley arrived under armed guard.

"Sir! Oh, sir!" she yelled to the guards escorting Kimsley toward the electrically operated gate.

The guards paused.

She waved a piece of paper in one hand with a clutch purse in the other as she approached them. "Can you help me find the Broward County courtroom?" She feigned confusion to gain their help. "I can't seem to find…"

The senior guard motioned to the other to stay with Kimsley while he walked the short distance to the fence.

Rikki held the paper in the fence webbing so the guard would reach for it. "I think it's—" she said as he pulled it through to read it—"near…" With her eye on the guard with Kimsley, she slipped her other hand into the clutch bag to retrieve her revolver, dropping the bag on the ground, distracting the senior guard next to her.

At that instant she yelled, "You're dead, Kimsley!" and pointed the gun straight at him, sequently pulling the trigger until the chambers emptied.

Both Kimsley and the guard with him fell to the ground as she started to run back toward her car.

The senior guard next to the fence brandished his service revolver at her as she ran and shouted, "Stop or I'll shoot!"

She turned to confirm the kill while opening the car door and saw Kimsley twitching on the ground. With unabated rancor she yelled back, "That's one slug for my sister and one for each of her friends."

Despite the second warning, she jumped into the car and rammed the gearshift lever into Drive, then floored the gas pedal. The car lunged forward nearly five yards as the senior guard followed her path with his gun, then fired off a burst of three shots. Two penetrated the door, striking her in the side and chest; the third pierced her left temple. Her body fell limp on the seat as the car careened off the fence, colliding with a Dumpster and flipping over.

A montage of her teenage years with Maggie floated through her mind until the unceasing headache became unbearable.

Mobile news vans continuously traverse the streets in search of breaking stories to transmit crimes and misfortunes instantaneously to the waiting television and radio audience. Monitoring police and ambulance radio and telephone frequencies often enables them to arrive on the scene as the event unfolds, giving homeviewers the added pleasure of a live telecast.

WSVN's video van picked up the call while traveling south on Andrew's Avenue, only two miles away. In seven minutes, they had uplinked their onboard satellite dish and were feeding live back to the station even before the police could light flares or string yellow tape around the courthouse area.

Several seconds after WSVN arrived, two ambulances pulled up with paramedics fanning out to diagnose the victims.

Showing the rear wheel turning on Rikki's car and the police covering Kimsley and Rikki's body as a backdrop, the newswoman brought the public current by announcing the guard on Kimsley only suffered a wound to the shoulder, while the brave, senior officer emerged unscathed from the shootout.

By the time Detective Menzler contacted Kathy an hour later, it was old news.

Pano sat on the lounge chair by the expansive pool in the Lane backyard. Brandon was sitting next to him, but it was distracting Pano to the point that he could not even lay in the sun. Brandon kept getting up and sitting down and was obviously anxious: his leg was moving up and down like a piston, and Pano felt as if he'd had enough.

"Basili—*para-ka-lo! Please!* Can you sit still? It will do no good to worry and jump around. He will call you after he has information. What do you expect?"

Brandon glared at him. A retort sprang to his lips. Then his eyes softened. "You're right, of course. I just feel guilty. I feel as if there is something I should or perhaps could...well, do! It's been two days. He didn't even call to say he got it. What could be the problem?"

"You said he would do some research first. Maybe he can pinpoint where it came from. Maybe he knows someone that knows someone..."

"All right." Brandon laughed as he stood up again. "I get the point. I'll try to calm down." He walked over to the edge of the pool and sat down. The air was warm, but the water felt slightly cold, even for Florida. He stared at his reflection and could see the beautiful sky overhead behind his face. He smiled and tried to relax.

"We almost didn't make it, you know." He turned around and faced Pano who sat up and considered Brandon skeptically.

"You didn't want to talk about it. What changed your mind?"

"I don't know," said Brandon quietly. "I guess now is just the right time. I never really thanked you for what you did. I don't even think we both know what really happened. I think it was more than just a cellar. I know what we found was more than just a marker on a map. Of that much I am sure."

"As for there being more to that house than meets the eye—I agree.

The arrow or the Lambda, I don't know. It's like a poem. It means nothing to me, but it must be important to someone. They certainly were guarding it well enough," Pano replied.

"And this wasn't even the largest one. I couldn't get that one out of the wall." Brandon raised his hand as if to prove that his efforts had failed.

Pano quickly saw what was now the red, swollen remains of several deep and nasty lacerations.

"Pano, where do we go from here?" The question remained unanswered as the portable phone rang, and Brandon grabbed it. "Hello?"

"Sir, it's Dr. Barrett calling in for you. He's calling collect from Europe."

"Accept immediately and send the call back to me, please," he responded hurriedly.

"Very good, sir."

"Sam, is that you?" Brandon was not one to stand on ceremony under the best of circumstances. Here, with this level of excitement, he could hardly maintain the standard courtesies.

"Brandon, I found something! Something you may want to see."

"See, how? What is it?" Brandon and Pano exchanged equally bewildered looks.

"It's a fragment of an old scroll. At least that's what we think. Have you ever heard of the *Genesis Apocryphon*? It's a very large and sometimes enigmatic work. It is not completely catalogued, and it is believed that there are pieces still missing."

Taken aback by the new, Brandon tried to regain his composure. "I've never heard of it, if you want me to be totally honest. What makes you think it is from that? Is it a passage from it?"

"We're not sure, but one of the books we came across had a reference that seemed very similar to the verse you sent over. But that isn't what prompted me to call. If that was the only thing I'd found, I would have waited. There's something else."

Brandon could feel his skin start to crawl. "So what is it? Tell me."

"I think I know where the inscription is from. The region and perhaps the time period. I've checked it with some other artifacts. It looks like a match."

Brandon couldn't believe what he was hearing. "Where? Tell me where."

"Get ready for this. I think it's from Canaan. Very near to where we were digging when you left." Dr. Barrett paused."And there's one thing more. We were able to match one other thing to the *Genesis Apocryphon* when we were doing that research. Guess what else is linked to that mystical and elusive commentary?"

Brandon could hardly think, let alone answer.

"The writing you found in that cave you explored before you left is a direct quote from one of the other writings we found. It looks like wherever you were, some writings were kept or left. We don't know which. We aren't really sure where you were when you found the small cave. The wall you traced is apparently some kind of credo for the *Genesis Apocryphon*. It may be unrelated, but I thought you should know." Dr. Barrett finished his recitation.

Brandon sat there with his mind whirring and his hand tightening on Pano's palm.

"Brandon, are you there? What are you doing?"

"I'm going to pack. We're coming to Canaan as soon as possible. Whatever it is, my answer lies there." He hung up the phone without any further information. He didn't care. He knew Sam would call back. All he could think of now was that something was at work. He didn't know what, and he didn't want to think about who. He just knew he had to get back to Israel and see what else was in that cave.

*As to it being related...*who could draw the line when everything in his life was running together?

With Pano in tow, he raced back toward the house and told the first person he encountered to get his father and his secretary on the line. He needed to make travel plans and talk to his dad. The second person he met was told to go to the library. He needed books. Everything that could be found about the *Genesis Apocryphon*. He wanted them all—and he needed them fast. *One thing for certain, I intend to know everything I can before I go back.* His mind was preoccupied with his vision, and the pressures of reality that seemed only too vivid a few moments ago were driven back into the seclusion of his inner brain.

Pano, several steps behind Brandon, only hoped he was to remain in the forefront as he followed Brandon up the steps toward what was apparently their approaching destiny.

David signaled Matthew Lane's secretary and walked right into his office. Matthew sat at his desk, studying his Bible.

Matthew rose and walked to David. "My heart goes out to both you and Kathy over this ordeal with her friend Maggie and her sister," he began. "The Lord's ways are mysterious to us, and his way of dealing with Maggie, Rikki, and Kimsley is difficult to understand."

"We lost a good soldier for the Lord when Maggie died," David replied ruefully. He shook his head and clenched his teeth. "Kimsley got just what he deserved. He lived by the sword and died by the sword. Good riddance."

Moments of silence passed after David had vented his frustrations. Then Matthew said, "Of course Mrs. Lane is very grieved over all this, and she asked me to invite you and your family over this Saturday for dinner."

David nodded. "Thank you, we'd love to."

Matthew returned to his seat. "There's something very peculiar about this report from CDC about their not finding any demonic activity among any of the drug users they tested," he observed as he leafed through several pages in his Bible.

"In my off minutes I've been thinking about that, too," David remarked brightly, making a concerted effort to lift himself out of the mental quagmire he'd descended into.

"I've called an old college roommate of mine, now a practicing MD over in Dania, and asked him if he had any ex-drug addict patients with AIDS who might have been involved with Rainbow's early testing program of Toi-VAX. It was a breach of confidentiality, but we're of the same mind. When it comes to a disastrous plague like AIDS, the rights of the innocent and uninfected must be protected."

"Interesting. And?" David replied.

"He gave me the address of a home-ridden patient and said he would accompany us to introduce the patient and her mother to us. Otherwise, I doubt we could even get in the door." He glanced at his wristwatch and said, "I told Dr. Lansing we would pick him up at 11:00, so let's get going."

David's eyes brightened at the prospect of getting closer to the problem.

Raymond's mother warmly greeted the three men at the door, then insisted they sit and have homemade cupcakes and tea before visiting her son. A dowdy woman whose life clearly revolved around her son, she gave Dr. Lansing a flowery report on the amazing change in Raymond's attitude within the past two days.

Temporarily regressing to contrast the alteration in his behavior, she recalled how just last week his mental deterioration dipped to its nadir where he talked suicide and frequently searched the house for matches where he proceeded to burn himself on various parts of his body to somehow either purge or punish himself. Often he stood mute in a corner for hours, then cried out for his former lover. Afterward he would refuse to cooperate with his mother. This routine often necessitated her threatening to leave him alone for the rest of his life unless he participated in his therapy.

Now things were different. Not only did his demeanor change, but his attitude toward the future took on an incredible outlook. He was cheery and optimistic as if he were cured.

David exchanged suspicious glances with Matthew while Dr. Lansing wrote notes in Raymond's file.

"May we visit with him now?" Matthew suggested.

"Of course," his mother said proudly.

With that they all rose from the table and filed into the converted garage (now a special bedroom equipped with a hospital bed, a small table with two chairs, a recliner, an entertainment center with a stereo, a TV, and a DVD player, and a treadmill). Raymond sat watching a music video, clapping and laughing. He bounced out of the recliner, wrapped his arms around Dr. Lansing, and said, "How good to see you again."

"My, you're looking terrific, Raymond," Dr. Lansing marveled, appearing astonished.

"And feeling good," he blurted as he did a pirouette to display his form. He then skirted around David and Matthew to his mother and gave her a hug and kissed her several times on the face. "Mom," he said, while rubbing her shoulders, "you've been a saint through all this."

His mother blushed and sighed in bewilderment at the amazing recovery her son apparently underwent.

He then asked the doctor to sit with him at the table to discuss his progress while using Toi-VAX.

David shrugged, then gestured to Matthew that Raymond never acknowledged their presence.

"Raymond," Dr. Lansing said as he cleared his throat, "this is Matthew Lane, a colleague and college pal of mine, and his friend David Douglas. They're doing research on AIDS patients who have been inoculated with Toi-VAX."

Matthew and David extended their hands to greet Raymond, but he ignored them. David suddenly turned his ear to Raymond, thinking he heard him say, "I know who you are," but he couldn't be sure, so he simply nodded toward him. It was then that an alarm went off in David's mind.

With Doctor Lansing and Raymond discussing his progress, his mother sat down in the recliner to watch the video while David and Matthew stood looking at each other, wondering what to do next.

"Is it me, or is this one crazy house?" David, somewhat perplexed, whispered to Matthew.

Matthew scanned the room, then whispered back, "I want to try something." While closing his eyes he began to whisper Bible verses. David joined him until they heard the conversation between Raymond and Doctor Lansing come to an abrupt halt.

Raymond turned his head almost mechanically and glared at them. "What are you doing over there?"

Matthew slowly walked toward Raymond with his eyes fixed on his, saying, "The blood of Christ covers you; the blood of Christ covers you."

"Why are you doing this?" Raymond protested, "I'm a Christian and take offense at your insinuation, so kindly step back." Frigid air dropped from nowhere and suddenly enveloped the table.

The doctor shivered,

David joined Matthew as he advanced toward Raymond while Doctor Lansing pushed himself back from the table, grabbing Raymond's mother and fleeing to the doorway.

"It's an evil spirit imitating a good spirit!" Matthew shouted as a howling sound started up.

Raymond's mother screamed as her son's features began to change before their eyes.

Raymond fell to the floor and convulsed violently as his face began to assume grotesque expressions.

Doctor Lansing's mouth hung open and then he yelled out, "He's having an epileptic fit!" He started toward Raymond.

"Stay where you are, Doctor," David warned. "It's not epilepsy—it's possession!"

Raymond's eyes met David's; then he pointed at him as flames shot up from the floor, encircling David.

David shouted, "Lord, protect me!"

Standing erect, poised to attack, Raymond cried out, "Stand back or you'll be killed!"

A whirlwind erupted in a corner, picking up the table and chairs, hurling them at David through the circle of fire.

David ducked and fell to the floor. "You have no power over me as a child of Christ," he cried, then stood up again.

Turning around and looking behind him, as if peering through a porthole in the wall, Raymond nodded and appeared to wave on reinforcements.

"Oh no!" Matthew gulped from behind. "David, back off. Quick!"

Dozens of shadowy disembodied figures passed through the wall, then crouched as if ready to spring.

Raymond stood gloating with a fiendish expression as he pointed to David. "Take him," he commanded.

David's mind locked as the host of damned spirits with their hands clasped together began forming an outer ring around the fiery circle, chanting in an unknown tongue. The circle grew tighter and tighter until they let out a squeal.

With that, Raymond's mother jumped out of the room, pulling Doctor Lansing with her.

David cupped his ears and held his position. He shot a look over at Matthew through the ring of fire and yelled, "Pray!" He squeezed his eyes shut for a second and mouthed, "Lord, deliver me."

From behind, Matthew's arm reached in through the flames and pulled David backward before the menacing demons closed in on him. "You're safe!" Matthew exclaimed.

"We're not out of this yet," David replied as he wiped his brow, preparing for another bout. He latched onto Matthew's hand. "Repeat after me as we go back in."

Matthew's face turned pale as he followed obediently.

With mounting courage they thrashed violently and broke through the line of the denizens from hell, then stood before the flames.

David cried out, "In the name of Jesus I order you to stop!" In unison they continuously repeated the command until the flames began to die out. Filling with power David shouted, "In the name of Jesus I order you all to leave!"

Suddenly a great calm came over the room. All the noises and flames disappeared, leaving only the legion of fallen angels cowering in the corner. "Where shall we go?" a raspy voice pleaded.

David looked around the room to assess his position. Dr. Lansing, still in the doorway with Raymond's mom, glanced at her with terror-stricken eyes, then back at David and Matthew, then ran out of the house.

"Return to the abode of torment where you came from," David instructed.

A spiraling mist appeared in the center of the floor followed by a loud sound of suction.

David and Matthew jumped clear of the widening hole in the floor, standing by Raymond as he lay motionless. "Watch out!" David warned as the evil messengers from Sheol were inescapably drawn downward. The vortex increased speed until the whirling funnel sucked the ungodly garrison back into the netherworld.

David turned Raymond over to find him panting uncontrollably with his eyes glazed, whispering, "Save me. Save me."

"Believe on Jesus Christ of Nazareth, and you will be saved," Matthew instructed.

David stroked Raymond's head to calm and soothe him while adding, "You're clean now. Just open your heart and let Jesus come in."

His mother ran to his side and kissed him. A peaceful smile came over his face.

"He'll rest comfortably now," David advised his mother as he nodded to Matthew to help lift Raymond to his bed. When they walked out of the house, Doctor Lansing was waiting inside Matthew's car.

The drive back to Doctor Lansing's office proved to be very enlightening for Matthew and David. Regarded as a luminary in immunology, Doctor Lansing recognized Raymond's case to be beyond the scope of his practice, attributing his patient's behavior to the supernatural.

Matthew described his previous encounters with other victims of Toi-VAX to Lansing, then asked, "Will you report this to AMA or the CDC?"

"I'm not sure," he temporized.

Matthew exchanged a glance with David. "Lansing, we need to alert the public that many ex-addict AIDS victims treated with Toi-VAX may have serious potential problems. You saw with your own eyes what we're talking about."

"Yes, I know, but—"

David's mind drifted off when he realized the problem. Considering Lansing's professional reputation, crying foul in the game of medical ethics was not popular or profitable. Sprinkle into the doctor's mortar a few grains of fear from bodily injury and potential lawsuits from family members, then grind them with the pestle of incredulity and disbelief, and what would the compound be good for? Perhaps a prescription for the ruination of a good physician.

Giving him a way out of the dilemma, Matthew suggested, "Will you contact us if any other patients of yours in this category show signs of emotional imbalance?"

Relieved, the doctor nodded in consent, then resumed his pleasant manner for the rest of the drive.

A secluded table in the south corner in the Fountain's Restaurant in Pembroke Pines provided the perfect setting to sort things out. "Why would these evil spirits change their tactics with these ex-addicts?" Matthew wondered aloud as he ordered a toasted bran muffin. "At first they were brazen and open; then with Raymond, they were disguised and covert."

David ordered a toasted bagel, then replied, "I'm convinced that with the present decline in the spiritual life of this nation, there is a corresponding increase in demonic activity. Add drug addiction and Toi-VAX to the problem, and you have—" he waved his arm to indicate the current scenario. "Then, on the other side, Satan in all his craftiness has implemented a master plan of delusion. Under the cover of darkness, he and his forces are concealing his purpose, his true nature, and his presence. Since you went to the CDC they have gone underground, to avoid detection so to speak. For them to openly display possession would arouse suspicion and reveal Satan's real plan and character and bring on opposition."

The waitress brought their food.

"Are you suggesting that somebody has *alerted* these evil beings?"

"Putting certainty aside, it's a safe assumption. Of course, from Dillion to around the nation, few will get the show we got because we're aware and informed. The masses are not."

"Since people today regard the existence of Satan and his army of cohorts with weak superstition, to propose the concept of demonic possession will be met with contempt," Matthew concurred, then asked, "Do you think Dillion is involved?"

"Certainly a prime suspect." He shook his head, slightly bewildered, and added, "I wouldn't be surprised if Kavidas and Stein were somehow informed and they—" he stopped himself short.

"They made a phone call and conferred with the devil. Is that what you were going to say?" Matthew replied half seriously.

David's eyes met his. "Something like that."

While David and Matthew made numerous phone calls, Kathy and Sydelle used their mailing lists to send E-mails to the area church pastors and leaders. Doctors who Matthew calculated would have interest in the subject were included in the listing.

The focus of the symposium—agreed upon by David and Matthew as the only viable alternative to notifying the CDC and FDA—would be to alert the public through area churches of the pervasive diabolical powers unleashed upon the world and. of the dangers they posed to mankind. Whether or not to attack Rainbow by suggesting their vaccine was corrupt was still undecided. To avoid initial confrontation through offensive titles, David suggested a theme of ecumenism. In reality, the subject of unity in the church was really at stake and therefore truthful.

The Deike auditorium in Plantation was rented to act as a non-sectarian, neutral environment meeting place. David busied himself setting up the video projector while Matthew and Kathy greeted the 200-plus respondents who turned out.

David walked to the lectern to lead the invocation, then introduced his speakers. Matthew Lane would discuss the pharmaceutical industry, Doctor Barrett would voice his concerns over the history of plagues via a prerecorded DVD, David the spiritual upheaval that is taking place nationally, and finally Kathy would appeal to the women in the audience to engender support for the protection of the nation's children.

Matthew generated an aurora that quickly embraced and unified the audience with his prologue of Christ's love for humanity. He cited himself as a nondeserving sinner, clutched from the jaws of sin to salvation at an early age, who had been in God's service ever since. He had dedicated his drug company as a healing ministry, and it had been used of God to alleviate pain and suffering worldwide.

Affirming the integrity of the drug industry and its oath to protect human life inevitably ignited in him a fire that smoldered until it burst into flames. In his mind, the unnamed conspirators who were determined to maim society by bungling vaccine development and misleading the public down a path of destruction could no longer be protected. "I believe it improper to divulge names or sources, but we're aware that many crimes have been committed during the development of the vaccine being used today. Even our watchdog agencies, namely the CDC and the FDA, may very well have been compromised, placing the population at great risk."

A hand went up in the audience, and Matthew felt compelled to recognize it after his last statement.

"Mr. Lane, are you suggesting complicity between Rainbow and the *government-run* CDC?"

"Anything is possible today. Remember Watergate and Whitewater?"

He left the inference right there, without adding further comment.

The crowd murmured after that statement.

"We at Lane," he continued, "are dedicated to solving the AIDS epidemic the right way and believe we are close to finding the cure through a serum that will not have any side effects. And let me add unequivocally that this meeting is not about a race for a cure or competition between drug companies but a concerted effort on our part to alert the clergy and some of the medical profession about our plan to unite and form a coalition. We must do this to protect the rights of the innocent." He nodded toward David, then walked off the speaker's platform as the applause began.

After David related a brief biography and list of accomplishments of Doctor Samuel Barrett, he waved to the technician operating the DVD projector. Seconds later the lights dimmed, followed by a screen dropping down from the ceiling. The screen filled with Doctor Barrett welcoming the audience as he held a scroll of obvious antiquity. The camera backed off, revealing an arid mountainscape behind him with laborers carrying digging equipment while others were kneeling and sifting the soil.

Maurice Ryder, of the *Miami Star*, was listening intently. He had been invited to the symposium by Nick Lanter, the pastor of Miami Congregational church. Pastor Lanter held to different views than the "radical churches," as he called them, and seized the opportunity to see firsthand whether the rumors he had heard about side effects from Toi-VAX had any credence and what this church meeting planned to do about it.

It was of particular importance because many of his congregants were AIDS victims with homosexual and drug backgrounds who had started Toi-VAX treatment. The purpose in inviting reporter Ryder was to document the agenda and provide an official unbiased opinion of the symposium's findings. His goal was to strike a balance between the fundamentalists and the mainline churches in his area, feeling confident that no violation of ethics had taken place by bringing a newsman.

Looking around at the gathering, David could only recognize a small segment of the pastors and medical personnel who had been invited. Most of these people were complete strangers. Standing in front of a roomful of people with the intentions of speaking to them about volatile spiritual subjects didn't help his jittery nerves. Yet despite his anxiety, his duty to proclaim truth had to be served.

Repeating the welcome lessened the tension he detected in the air, but he sensed a rising hostility in the crowd. He nodded to Matthew and Kathy for confidence, then said, "Many of you are unaware of what has been happening over the past year, and we believe it's imperative to apprise you pastors of potential difficulties you may encounter in your ministries. You in the medical profession should also be aware that the problem we have uncovered will impact your practice.

"We have identified two destructive enemies that will endanger all of us unless we, the spiritual and medical fiber of this land, do something about it. Appeals to our governing agency are useless. Therefore we are compelled to turn inward to treat the patient with a different kind of medicine, namely the Word of God, since our number one enemy is unbelief."

His voice bellowed over the applause, "We are not believing what we read in our Bibles! When do we get the message that we must be living in end times? Look around and see what is happening! The very events that have come upon us—an AIDS epidemic, mutating mosquitoes, a man going around making bizarre predictions that come true, and this" he held up the letter his dad received, notifying him of his conscript into Infolink— "represents another step closer to a central worldwide credit and medical bureau that will control your spending and medical treatment and who knows what else in the future. For those of you unfamiliar with Bible prophecy, the Book of Revelation chapter 13 advises us of just such a monetary system to be installed and functioning before Christ returns." He gestured for the murmuring to subside and to recognize a waving hand in the audience. "You have a question, sir?"

"Pastor Douglas," Pastor Lanter objected, "aren't you going a little too far with this? I mean, there are *other* biblical scholars who would disagree with you on every point you've raised if we look at those prophetic passages symbolically. It almost sounds like you're saying that these passages should be taken literally as absolutes when we in the ministry find that hard to accept."

"Oh, really?" David shot back with just a tinge of sarcasm. "Maybe you've been away for the last year or so and haven't taken notice of these things, but applying them to a good exegetical study of the Bible like myself and my other colleagues have done should change your mind. That could be your problem. What's more, we see a threatening infrastructure in place that might very well be the final system that catapults us into the Tribulation period! So don't throw any existentialism stuff at me—this is real."

With that, Pastor Lanter waved him off in contempt, got up, and walked to the back of the room. Ryder frantically wrote notes and remained quiet as several other pastors and guests followed Lanter.

"Let's discuss the second enemy now," David continued after looking askance at Matthew for a sign of encouragement, who held two thumbs up and gestured to continue the assault. "Both Matthew and I have personally encountered demonic possession in three individuals, who were ex-drug addicts treated with Toi-VAX early in its development. It may not be conclusive, but I don't consider them isolated incidents either. Random field reports from other pastors and physicians treating these certain AIDS victims have confirmed our findings and agree that this is a serious problem emerging on the horizon. Of course, there have been so-called exorcisms to rid those victims of evil spirits, but that only occurs when they are biblically challenged.Otherwise, they are remaining covert.

"May I add here, with caution, that we have no way of knowing whether the AIDS virus has mutated, thus enabling this, or whether the demonic influence could cross over barriers into the realm of the non-drug victims of AIDS or even into the heterosexual sector or beyond." He threw his hands up in dismay and added, "Maybe this is the start of one of the Seal judgments to come upon the world. Who can say for sure? But we do know this: evil men are seizing control, and we must draw the line in the sand and arm ourselves now before it's too late."

David quoted Second Chronicles 7:14, then briefly expounded on how the verse instructs humanity to rid itself of the AIDS plague. But until that happened, he warned, the world was being put on notice to prepare itself for a cataclysm. When he looked up, many of the guests were filing out the door as the remaining audience stood and applauded.

Kathy ascended the platform as David walked over to Matthew and shrugged in disappointment over the dissenters who walked out. "They're pooh-poohing this away, but they'll be sorry," he whispered to him.

Scanning the audience, Kathy decided on her course of action. While Matthew, Doctor Barrett, and David focused on the pulpit and medical ministry, she would concentrate on the ministry of the women. "I would like to speak to the ladies involved in ministry and medicine," she began, "who are an essential part of our church structure. I consider myself a veridical, a truthful person who does not live in a world of fantasy, or who claims to be so spiritual that I'm no earthly good, and therefore do not intend to curry favor by watering down what you've already heard this morning.

"I speak from experience since my family has been personally attacked over the past year, and therefore I give you all a warning: We must reinforce a godly value system in our homes as our society apparently enters its final phase. If we do not, our families will split over current political and social issues such as the AIDS epidemic, the rights of certain so-called special groups, and the dramatic changes in our monetary-economic system. Your children and relatives will disagree with your beliefs and endanger your households because of what they're being taught in public learning institutions, and we shall be divided and conquered by the encroaching army of subtle compromise and domestic violence. It is vital that you defend unity in your homes and that you support your husband when he takes a biblical stand.

"We are entering an unprecedented historical period that is rapidly going beyond the limits of reason and will ultimately tax every one of us to the breaking point. Unless we bind together and ask the Lord to guide us, we shall fail." Her last sentence hung in the air like a black cloud, about to drop an alien form of rain upon the land.

Seconds of silence passed until one lone person started to clap in agreement, igniting the rest of the crowd.

In the forming of a consensus, David, Matthew, and Kathy agreed that two separate parties were formed this morning.

For the *Miami Star*, Maurice Ryder would write the story from his point of view.

TWELVE

You must not fight too often with one enemy,
or you will teach him all your art of war.
Napoleon Bonaparte

Maurice Ryder considered the symposium newsworthy to a point but felt it lacked the luster to attract the volume of readers he needed to reach as an aspiring columnist on the *Miami Star*. He needed a following like the big guys. Perhaps the twist of a church protesting the use of Toi-VAX may warrant a spot in the magazine section, but it certainly wasn't a news grabber that would even make second page. Religious issues were not popular or flashy enough to hold the public's interest unless accompanied by a scandal. *And bad news sells papers*, he thought.

He sheepishly looked up at his journalism degree from Northwestern and recalled a quote from one of his term papers: "Journalism, the collecting, the evaluating, and the dissemination of facts of current interest..." Then he put a call into Rainbow Pharmaceuticals.

"Mr. Stein, there's a newspaperman on the phone, a Maurice Ryder, who would like a quote regarding a church symposium that took place last Saturday. He said it was about Toi-VAX. Do you want to talk to him or should I defer him to somebody else?" Mort's secretary reported as she stood at Kavidas's office door.

Mort shot a look to Gregory, who nodded for him to take the call. "Make us look good," he said with a serious wink.

Gregory knew any church synod discussing Toi-VAX would have to

336

be negative press, and he was getting tired of the Christians assailing his company and character. He slammed his fist down on his desk in frustration and demanded of himself, *Why am I allowing these Christians to harass and bother me? I must put an end to it before they ruin my entire operation.*

The time has come, he thought, *to move into the next phase of his Renaissance plan.* He had to squash any opposition now to ensure the completion of the project. *I have enough power to stomp them out: socially, financially, and politically, so why not apply the pressure now to silence them?*

Gregory's mind took a quantum leap backward in time to Nero Claudius Caesar, the profligate and decadent Roman emperor of the first century. Out of his determination to raze the Roman architecture he grew tired of and rebuild according to his flamboyant taste, public disfavor emerged. His senate and many of the citizens were content with the city the way it was and were opposed to his extravagant lifestyle. Self-seeking, he devised a scheme to torch the city and blame it on the Christians, leading to global persecutions.

"Mort, let me talk to him," Gregory interjected as Mort was finishing the phone call.

Mort hit the Mute button. "This guy is looking to land a story with lots of follow-up material. He sounds new and suggested that he could help us since he didn't agree with the nonsense at the church meeting," he added with a nod.

"Interesting," Gregory said dryly.

Mort then alerted Ryder and handed the phone to Gregory.

Ryder thanked him beforehand for the telephone interview.

"You're very welcome," Gregory said. "Now I need you to pay attention to what I'm about to tell you, and although you don't know me personally, that will change. I do want you to meet with Mr. Stein next week so he can advise you of the kind of news coverage we need, but until then, your report should contain the truth and not from the perspective of the Christians.

"It has become apparent that there is a movement being carefully organized to create and maintain hysteria in our country, using the Toi-VAX vaccine as a springboard to embrace other sociological and economical—even spiritual problems—in this world and to put the blame for such dilemmas on the doorstep of Rainbow Pharmaceuticals. My data-gathering networks tell me that the nucleus for the trouble is centered in a Mr. David Douglas of Coral Springs and a Mr. Matthew Lane, the president of Lane Pharmaceutical. Their meetings generate contempt for my firm and family name, not to mention other endeavors that I am involved in, namely the EC, and I cannot tolerate any further disparaging remarks."

"So you want me to fix that, right?" Ryder replied.

"That would be a nice base for our relationship," Gregory added as he slowly replaced the phone.

Ryder looked up again at his diploma, making a fist and gesturing in triumph, "Yes! Mr. Kavidas!"

David stormed into Matthew Lane's office, throwing a copy of the *Miami Star* on his desk. "Matt, you won't believe this newspaper," he fumed with blazing eyes. "They totally distorted the truth. Look at these headlines—"

Standing up and turning the paper to read it, Matthew's eyes turned into saucers as he repeated the headline, "'Christians Split on Use of Toi-VAX.'" He plopped back into his chair. "Lord, help," he grunted, then sputtered off some of the highlights. "'Churches divided over issues as leaders claim vaccine promotes homosexuality. Lane Pharmaceutical, a rival drug company, believes witchcraft involved. Continued protests could bring suspension of Rainbow's vaccine. Distribution centers fear terrorist attacks by Christian radicals.'"

He closed his eyes and remained silent for several minutes, then said, "What are they trying to do to us? The media is crucifying us! This will blow up in our faces!"

"People will link us with the abortion clinic doctor killings—lumping us together and branding us a public enemy," David added in disgust.

Throwing the newspaper back onto his desk, Matthew reached for the phone intercom. "Lilly, get me the *Miami Star* on the phone." He retrieved the paper to check the reporter's name, "Tell them Matthew Lane wants to speak to Maurice Ryder." He replaced the phone and sat silently with his arms crossed across his chest.

A little over three minutes latter, Lilly announced over the intercom,

"Mr. Lane, Mr. Ryder on 02."

Matthew lifted the phone as he bit his lower lip to remind him to control his tongue.

Ryder extended his greetings with a flowery dissertation on his defensive position over Toi-VAX until Lane finally interrupted his dialog. "Mr. Ryder, I didn't call you to hear you throw accolades at Rainbow but to protest your outrageous journalism and demand a retraction."

"Can't do that, Mr. Lane," he countered. "We reported the truth as I saw it."

"Well, I don't know who the snake was that brought you in, but you've pressed your role too far and better be prepared to fully explain yourself to a press council for irresponsibly distorting the truth," Matthew snarled back.

"We are," he replied smugly. "What's more, we as a news agency intend to follow up this story to protect the public."

Suddenly Matthew recognized a driving force within this news monger that told of an ulterior motive. "You know, Mr. Ryder, I believe this issue to be beyond your purview. Let me ask you something." He paused for emphasis. "Did Kavidas or Stein get to you?"

"This conversation is over, Mr. Lane!" Ryder ended sharply. Then the line went dead.

Matthew hung up the phone and turned to David. "Another creep on Rainbow's payroll. Rats!"

By 8 a.m., the CNN news room dedicated 12 minutes to embellishing on the newspaper article, citing the Christian Fundamentalists as inciting trouble in South Florida with their sanctimonious denunciation of the AIDS vaccine destined to save millions of lives. The report continued to excoriate David Douglas and Matthew Lane, along with Dr. Samuel Barrett in absentia, as miscreants determined to undermine the drug's use by fabricating stories of AIDS victims with bizarre behavior.

The report included an interview with Kavidas and Stein and on-location testimonies of outraged recipients.

By the time Wendell Kline reached his church, only the south wall remained standing. The Coral Springs police chief called him at 3 a.m. to tell him his house of worship was engulfed in flames and fire department apparatus were on their way. He lamented that by the time the emergency call came into the station and a car had reached the scene, three-quarters of the sanctuary had been consumed.

Fortunately, he reminded the pastor, the school wasn't attached to the church, and he should consider himself and his ministry lucky. He suggested to Pastor Kline that perhaps the cause was spontaneous combustion or neglected electrical wiring and only mentioned briefly as he was leaving about the possibility of arson.

On Fort Lauderdale's Galt Ocean Mile, angry residents staged a demonstration where they constructed a makeshift gallows, then proceeded to hang a Baptist minister in effigy. An anonymous tip to the media yielded maximum news coverage as protesters throughout the day paraded past the crude representation, chanting and throwing animal blood in its face. The cameras recorded at least six dissidents walking with sandwich-board signs demanding a moratorium of Lane Pharmaceutical.

Spreading to Jacksonville, the fervor of protest emerged at the Provident Insurance Company's corporate office, where hostile complainers accosted the company executives as they arrived for work. The enraged public denounced Provident's support of Lane Pharmaceutical's AIDS research and threatened to embark on a nationwide policy cancellation campaign if their support continued. They claimed Provident supported and funded sexual behavior guideline agendas, disguised as civic rehabilitation programs.

340

By early afternoon, Matthew Lane had all six of his secretaries reassigned to answering phone calls and monitoring the fax machine.

Reports from associated churches telling tales of despicable treatment of volunteers on their way to ministry inundated Lane's switchboard. Complaints and pleas from pastors needing advice were put on voice mail until Matthew had a chance to call them back personally.

By late afternoon, he had David in his office, handling many of the phone calls from major stockholders who threatened to sell off their portfolios unless Lane did something to assuage public sentiment. By day's end, Matthew agreed to hold an emergency board of director's meeting to review their strategy.

Brandon climbed the rocks with his team in tow behind him. Pano came along in spite of Dr. Barrett's objections. Brandon was able to rationalize the man's presence simply because they expected to find some Greek artifacts and his assistance would be of significant importance. However, his inexperience in climbing was slowing the entire expedition down. The men didn't seem too happy about it, and Brandon was doing his best to help Pano along.

Dr. Barrett knew the importance of making sure the proper channels were followed in obtaining a permit with the Israeli Antiquity Authorities. Part of that process mandated that someone stay behind and oversee the exploration. He also felt the climb to find artifacts was a little beyond his mettle. A time for slowing down comes to every creature under the sun, and he knew his time was drawing near. He didn't mind letting Brandon take the credit and receive the glory, either, as it was Brandon who discovered the cave. He just hoped they did what they were told with the contents so nothing was destroyed in the excavation process.

Dr. Barrett could hardly see the men as they continued the climb up the sheer rock wall of the mountain. It was not only the distance that kept them from sight; it was the early morning sun.

They began their expedition at 4 a.m. so they had enough daylight to uncover the cave and remove the precious contents. On the horizon he could see the mountains that surrounded Jerusalem and felt a profound sense of awe, realizing they were in the most holy of lands. After these many thousands of years, the earth was still giving up its treasures and its secrets. It was a feeling beyond excitement, and Sam Barrett was only too happy to be a minor part in the grander scheme of God's design.

As Brandon neared the opening, he began to wonder what they would all do when they attained their goal. He was relatively sure that the entire group would fit in the cave. However, he was equally certain that they would not fit in the cave's outer cavity. Somehow he was sure that he would be digging out the first section to make way for the rest of the party.

He was not looking forward to the claustrophobic feelings he had felt the first time he entered the cave. However, there was nothing that could have deterred him from entering. He hoped Pano would be able to squeeze in beside him as the other men moved around the mountainside and attempted to unearth part of the cave by the area where Brandon had seen a shaft of light streaming through on his last visit. He was unable to tell them if it was an air hole or just a break in the cave's integrity. However, the other men would certainly find that out soon enough.

Brandon was glad they were more experienced than he was, since he most assuredly would have blundered into the cave in the most undignified manner if he was looking for access along the top. These men would carefully mount the cave's zenith and test for structural integrity before attempting to go any farther. Brandon didn't have the patience for that; therefore, he was somewhat glad his job would involve more manual labor. It took a little longer and was a little harder. However, it was a lot safer for him and for the contents that they were trying to protect.

Brandon's meeting with Sam Barrett had gone extremely well, and both men were excited when Dr. Barrett was able to confirm that the inscription on the arrow matched the tracing Brandon had taken from the cave. The fact they both appeared to belong to what was mysteriously being called the *Genesis Apocryphon* was both encouraging and disheartening at the same time. In one fell swoop they would either uncover evidence that would enlighten the world as to the contents of the *Apocryphon*, or they would find some more of the obscure and mystical writings that to date had not yielded any concrete information or evidence from its alleged era that could be substantiated or verified.

His hopes that it would somehow be tied in with the entire mess that was happening as a result of Rainbow Pharmaceuticals made him realize that his usual optimism was working overtime. There was only so much that one could expect from a single find of any significant importance.

He was trying to steel himself for disappointment, but he was not having any luck. He was too exhilarated to be back and pursuing this potential link in their puzzle that he stopped trying to analyze the situation beyond what was happening at that moment. Which, due to the presence of one untrained and untried climber, was more than enough to keep him busy.

"Basili, help me!" Pano cried out in alarm.

Brandon had just reached the summit that acted as a small ledge below the cave's mouth. He began to formulate that the cave itself must have been bigger than he originally anticipated since the shelf was overly large. He knew the cave was meant to be unobtrusive, so he had no choice but to surmise that the cave was built or hollowed for a sizable amount of people. He grabbed Pano by the arm and pulled him onto the ledge.

Brandon entered the cave again and felt the immediate momentary panic that ensued during the last visit. He crawled in on his hands and knees and could feel the rocks scraping and tearing at this back and stomach as he tried to enter. *It's as if it was built to keep people out, or at least make them feel unwelcome,* he thought as he waited for the rest of the group.

Pano's cry had interrupted his reverie, so now he resumed the position of nursemaid as he helped Pano through the final plateau.

As David drove into a service station on the way to Lane's emergency board meeting, he noticed four men wearing G-Men T-shirts sitting in a

Jeep in front of the convenience store.

By the time he removed the filler cap, they were at his side. "Aren't you David Douglas, the crusader who hates gays?" the tall blond man asked with a snort.

David said nothing as he continued to pump the gas.

"Sure you are. Your face is all over the TV and tabloids, friend," sneered the bodybuilder with the large frame.

The other two circled his car, kicking the tires and fiddling with the radio antenna.

When David looked again, one of them had broken the antenna off in his hand. He stood there grinning while the other ran a key down the side of David's car, leaving a seven-foot gash in the enamel.

David held his tongue and prayed for protection to avoid a scene.

Suddenly one jumped on the hood of David's car, jerking his head wildly in a mock seizure, then stomped his heel into the hood, yelling, "The devil made me do it! The devil made me do it!"

From behind, the driver of the Jeep seized David's arms and held him firmly while the other two inflated two condoms and started to force them into David's mouth. David gagged and attempted to kick himself free.

Without warning, two young men ran out of the convenience store, one swinging a baseball bat, the other a bag of ice. The man on the hood was the first target. With one swat, the bat hit him square in the knees, knocking him off the car onto the pavement, while the man who held David crashed against the gas pump after being hit in the face with the ice. Within minutes, they all fled to their vehicle.

The rescuers stood vigilant by David until the four drove off. "We couldn't let them abuse you like that, Pastor Douglas. It wasn't right," the older teen declared.

David looked at the two adolescent Samaritans with dismay. Here were two strapping members of his congregation, sons of long-standing believers, resorting to violence to defend their pastor. The incident challenged the underlying precepts of his faith, yet he couldn't scold them for coming to his aid.

"They're going too far!" the other teen observed as he held his fist up anger.

David shook his head. "I appreciate you helping me, fellas, but violence is not the answer. We have to find another way."

344

Assuming the chairperson's position, Matthew paused for the conversation to subside, then proceeded to stand and address his board of directors. "Ladies and gentlemen, we have called this emergency meeting to discuss the perilous position we find ourselves in because of enemy fire. While we are committed to serve the public with their prescription drug needs, the public has turned against us." He wiped his brow, then added bleakly, "Frankly, I expect it to continue until we find the AIDS cure."

"How far away, Matthew?" an elderly board member interjected.

He raised his eyes to heaven. "Soon, very soon, I hope." Looking at each board member in succession he continued, "I cannot help but think that powerful forces are at work here, not only spiritual but political and economic as well, attempting to besmirch the integrity of our company by deliberately distorting the facts. Interests sympathetic with Rainbow Pharmaceuticals, such as the *Miami Star*, are mounting campaigns to destroy the Christian ethic that we have supported, and accordingly, will use that as a economic weapon against us.

"We have now been linked with the fundamental Christians who are opposed to homosexuality as an alternative lifestyle, and despite our claims of the corruption or side effects of the Toi-VAX vaccine, the public has come up with a verdict that we are the guilty ones, not Rainbow." As he sat down he motioned to David to stand and pick up the discussion. *Many of these people believe as I do*, Matthew thought, *yet they are naturally fearful of public reprisals. I can't blame them. But this position is needed if we are to make a difference—we can't knuckle under to Rainbow.*

"As board members," David began, "you are naturally concerned with Lane Pharmaceutical's reputation and the return on stockholder's investments, but Mr. Lane asked me to appeal to your moral values to stand by him despite public disfavor." He nodded to Matthew. "Mr. Lane has modestly advised me that he will personally exhaust his own assets and plow them back into Lane Pharmaceutical to keep you afloat as long as possible, projecting that by trimming the fat and curtailing purchases, Lane could stay open for the next six months. After that, only God knows. Of course, discovery of the AIDS cure would change everything for you.

"I urge you to persevere and support Mr. Lane since I believe that great supernatural forces are protecting, controlling, and driving Kavidas and Stein." Raising his voice an octave, he added, "But as long as we honor the Lord, we shall prevail—maybe not right away, but we shall have the victory."

While studying the faces of the members during David's appeal, Matthew surmised that the decision was about 60-40 in their favor. *Enough,* he thought. *We can operate with that until the tide changes.*

He thanked David for his support, then stood. "Many of you have been on this board for over 10 years and know by experience how I think and what you can expect from me. I believe we are right in this! Of course, many of you may encounter scurrilous attacks or public ridicule by remaining on the board, but I assure you, your labors will not be in vain. I hope your benefits will be both spiritual and monetary, but I cannot guarantee a financial return—there will be many risks. But if you defend our position and beliefs, I am confident we will emerge a better company. By way of a show of hands, I would like a vote of confidence to reinforce our strategy for the future."

As he sat down, 11 out of 12 hands went up.

"Here are four new faxes from around the state regarding attacks on Christian clergy and laity, Mr. Lane," his petite secretary said somberly as she laid them on his desk and tiptoed out the room.

Matthew groaned in his spirit as he read the reports. The first report, from Tallahassee, told of a Christian elementary school classroom invasion by a group of gay activists. After storming the isolated temporary trailer-type classroom, three members gagged and held the teacher in her chair, while the others drew phallic symbols on the blackboards and distributed pro-pedophilia materials to the children. Then they quietly distributed condoms to each of the students and ran out. Before they could reach their van and escape, the teacher screamed for help, and the nearby physical education teacher and two other middle-aged custodians pursued and overpowered the attackers. A melee ensued, only to be broken up by the police who arrested them all. The judge was presently in deliberation on this one.

The second, from Coral Gables, chronicled the stalking of two teenage girls by members of a partisan Christian church as they left their homes to wait on the Toi-VAX distribution lines. Once they reached the clinic, the youths assaulted the girls, spraying them down with red aerosol paint and splashing on them what they labeled holy water, then fleeing into the neighborhood.

The others clashes were symptomatic of the catharsis induced by the media, proliferating in the state of Florida and beyond. Matthew reached for the phone and asked his secretary to call the attorney general's office.

Forty-seven miles north of Miami, Gregory keyed in the command for his *Redisearch* supercomputer to access Project Renaissance. *Redisearch*'s data harnessing capabilities now included all the collective information in both private and commercial sectors nationwide with an international thrust. The goal to use the EC to launch *Redisearch* abroad was quickly becoming a reality.

His system progressed from the fundamental stage of credit processing to the Medlink stage, where all personal and emergency medical data was compiled. Buying out the Equifax, Experian, and TransUnion credit-clearing network greatly accelerated his program. Medlink, fortunately, helped to expedite the vaccine distribution, enabling a natural successor, Infolink, to be introduced. Infolink connected the credit and medical information on to one file for each person.

Now with *Masterlink* in operation, Gregory and Mort could easily retrieve any piece of information, including political, ethnic, and religious preferences, formally held confidential, on anybody they chose to.

Gregory had a special plan for those stubborn *Redisearch* subscribers still not on the *Masterlink* system. He scrolled through several pages of selected *Redisearch* and Infolink subscribers, noting their picture (retrieved through motor vehicle and passport records), along with their religious and financial profiles, tagging the ones he would start with.

Eddie inspected the prospective crib for its sturdiness and versatility while Sydelle studied its charm. Moving Julie from the bassinet into a crib was a celebratory occasion since their bedroom would now be their own once again. Surprisingly, they agreed on the style and price after only 45 minutes of comparison shopping. Considering the large President's Day crowds, they were fortunate.

Eddie drove their car around to the loading platform to pick up the disassembled crib while Sydelle waited on the cashier's line, fishing for her VERA credit card. Finding it, she looked behind her and was quite surprised to see over 20 people waiting behind her.

The cashier slipped the credit card into the scanner and waited for the green signal, but it didn't happen. Instead, the LCD blinked the words *Call for instructions*. She quickly picked up the phone and dialed the number as Sydelle started to blush.

"I'm sorry, Mrs. Swain, but this account is restricted," the cashier announced so half the line could hear her.

"That's impossible!" Sydelle retorted as she bounced Julie up and down to keep the one-year-old quiet. "I know that VERA card is paid and way under my limit."

The cashier shrugged. "They don't make mistakes with this new *Masterlink* system. If you want to pay by cash or check or have another card, fine. Otherwise you'll have to see the store manager," she replied officially.

Sydelle fumed and tapped her fingers on the top of the register and grunted, "We're trying to cut our credit. That's the only card we own, and we just sent out the mortgage payment."

"Move the line, lady!" some elderly gentleman yelled from behind.

She turned with eyes blazing, to tell him off. Instead, she held her tongue. Her eyes started to fill up with tears instead.

"Cancel the sale," she said with a dismissive wave of the hand and walked out. Once outside, the idea of a bad credit rating brought on rage.

Two hours and six phone calls later, Eddie and Sydelle learned that the VERA Group had been taken over by *Masterlink* and that they were encouraged to make the transition to *Masterlink* or forfeit their future credit line.

After the Sunday worship service, the aged congregant, Myron Cohen, walked up to Pastor David with his last checking account statement in his hand. "David, did you know that my bank is discouraging me from making contributions to this church?"

"What?" David replied. "That's ridiculous."

"Here, look at this," he said and unfolded the monthly statement, showing him copies of the canceled checks.

David studied the statement with the notes on the bottom that explained the tax advantages of putting the same amount of his weekly offerings into a tax-deferred retirement fund. An insert graphically illustrated annual growth in the fund compared to making religious donations. The comparative trend line showed an 8.5 increase in 10 years over the religious contributions. David flipped the statement over and saw on the lower left corner a *Masterlink* Network logotype.

"What do you make of it?" Myron asked curiously.

David bit his lip while pondering the ramifications of such an intrusive proposition. "If I were you, I would continue to contribute to the Lord's work. As for this *financial advisory*, I'll have to look into it."

Myron agreed to give David a copy to research.

Kathy walked into David's office and saw him reading Myron's statement. "The name *Masterlink* is very popular today," she said after noticing the logo on the statement.

"What do you mean?" David replied.

"I was just talking to Sydelle and listen to this one. She attempted to buy a crib yesterday and was advised at the checkout that her credit card was restricted. Not because of a limit or back payments, but because they want her to change over from VERA to *Masterlink*.

"When she made some phone calls, she came to find out that the *Redisearch* group holds *Masterlink* and that it's gobbling up all the competition around. *Masterlink's* interest is one to two points under prime, depending on your balance, and everyone we know is going for it."

"I smell a rat," David noted dryly, "and we're not going for it until I run some questions through the Consumer Credit Bureau tomorrow."

Kathy departed, leaving David to his ruminations.

"I demand to know what information this *Masterlink* outfit has on me!" David snarled into the phone. He began his inquiries at the *Masterlink* level through the subsidiary *Redisearch*.

"Mr. Douglas, we are permitted to provide credit and medical status reports for the past five years if you like," the congenial phone person responded.

"I know I'm entitled to that," he returned sharply, "but I want to know what other information you have on me, such as any personal family information, or for that matter, any ethnic or religious affiliations as well." *Or other pervasive inquiries to watch over me,* he didn't say.

"I'm sorry, Mr. Douglas, but that's all the information we carry," she insisted.

Knowing it to be a lie, he agreed to the hard copy and replaced the phone. He immediately called telephone information to locate the Consumer Credit Bureau for Broward County. Soon he was talking with an advisory person.

"I understand your sentiments, Mr. Douglas," the woman replied tersely, "but every time you apply for credit, you authorize the lender to search your financial history, and whenever you submit a medical claim, you also authorize the provider to search your medical history to evaluate your eligibility."

"Okay, fine, I realize that," David conceded, "but I'm talking about this *Masterlink* network that is spilling over into the banking business, having information that I consider confidential."

"Mr. Douglas, perhaps you're not up to date, because all one has to do is key in your phone number and they can access just about any and all information about you. Whether you agree to it or not is another matter. That information is considered confidential, true, but it's readily traded, just like your telephone number and home address is readily traded for solicitors and mailing lists. Off the record, that's the real truth."

That *was* the real truth, David realized. Extrapolating on that information, he could easily understand how *Masterlink* would monitor asset transfer through credit and banking vehicles. And who knows what else?

As Matthew leafed through the ream of paper he had received from the attorney general's office, he looked up at David and winced. Filing a petition for a Supreme Court hearing on the grounds of religious persecution appeared to be tantamount to rewriting the constitution.

"They give me the run-around on the phone and then sent me a deluge of papers to file—it's a joke," Matthew grumped. "I want legislation to see the clergy, the laity, and all us Christians have the same protection afforded other citizens, including pro-abortionists. It's a shame that Christians are being mistreated the way they are." He set the papers aside temporarily. "Fill me in on that incident at your church."

"More documentation on the continuing saga of troubles coming down the pike from Kavidas-Stein, aka Rainbow-*Redisearch* et al," he began as he handed Matthew the copy of Myron Cohen's bank statement. "This new network *Masterlink*, owned and controlled by Kavidas-Stein, is expanding so rapidly, you won't believe it. I've done some investigating, and as usual, little information is available. I suspect there's some kind of block to avoid procuring information about this system. *Redisearch* has progressed to *Masterlink*, and their design is to create a credit vacuum to suck in every subscriber in America and probably beyond.

"Sydelle was stopped at a department store checkout and later advised that her VERA card should be replaced by *Masterlink* for various benefits. Then when I think about my parents and all Social Security benefit payments being funneled through *Masterlink*, I think about one colossal network designed to seize control of the economy."

Putting his arms across his chest he contemplated for a moment. "I'm convinced that this system is prophetic in scope and incorporates monitoring devices that includes religious and ethnic backgrounds that will be used for methods of selection in the future."

"Darn!" Matthew snapped when the picture David conjured up in his mind materialized. "Sorting out the Christians and ethnic classes, along with any other undesirables to make the world a better place," he added with a wry expression.

"Including Jews," David added, "and the public at large will welcome the day. In the public's mind, to be rid of Christians that bring conviction of sin and Jews that they believe have been the scourge of mankind will be a relief."

"And with that, eschatology moves on," Matthew observed.

"Yeah, regrettably, once our society turns its back on Israel, we're almost at the end," David concluded.

After nearly seven hours in the air to Switzerland, Gregory Kavidas and Mortimer Stein welcomed the limo service to their hotel near Lake Geneva. Mort detested air turbulence, and despite their altitude of 39,000 feet, the shaking of the jumbo jet on the last stretch into Europe unnerved him. Once more, he swore he would never fly again.

With over 70 percent of its area covered by the Alps, Switzerland is one of the most mountainous countries of Europe, accented by many streams, often interlaced with picturesque lakes and waterfalls. Much of the precipitation occurs during the winter in the form of snow—the mountain peaks, most over 9,000 feet above sea level, are snow-covered throughout the year. Many hydroelectric plants are powered by the runoff provided by the melting snow, reducing dependency on fossil or nuclear fuel.

Passing by the UN and the International Labor Organization's library, Gregory mentioned to Mort that Geneva hosted a great Christian during the fifteenth century. John Calvin, the French theologian, settled in Geneva and revolted against the authority of the Roman Catholic bishop serving there. Organizing his church democratically in Geneva in 1541 to 1564, Calvin incorporated ideas representing government and set up Geneva as the stronghold of the Calvinist brand of Protestantism.

Mort snorted and waved off the piece of trivia as inconsequential.

Resting atop the Swiss plateau that rises to nearly 395 meters above sea level, the Liechtenstein Hotel on Lake Geneva affords a spectacular view of the southwest of Switzerland that borders on France. The 50-degree temperature sent a chill through Mort when they arrived, who in turn whistled for the attendant to hurry and take their bags inside the hotel.

"Sure is cold here," Mort said as he clutched his sides and hopped up and down to generate body heat.

"You should be here in the winter," Gregory replied with a chuckle. "The cold air arrests your breathing."

"I'll pass," Mort said with a wink.

Soon they were unpacked and standing on their balcony, overlooking a cavernous gorge, flanked by majestic mountain ranges that beckoned for the snow to fall upon them to whiten and fill their time-etched wrinkles.

Maintaining neutrality since 1815, Switzerland is the seat of many international agencies, including the EC, the European Community. As a world banking center, Switzerland's stability of the currency, along with banking secrecy, has encouraged foreign investors from many parts of the globe. In 1992, responding to international pressures, the nation relaxed its traditional insistence on secrecy and phased out the famed accounts and allowed investigators access to financial records where illegal acquisitions or use of funds was suspected.

In Gregory's mind, his plan was not illegal. He knew within himself that the funds he would deposit for the purchase of armaments would ultimately accomplish one of his goals, and therefore, it was not a matter of legalities but rather of morality. The people receiving the monies were entitled to the land, and since God had enabled him to provide the funds for that purpose, he had a moral right to ensure they got them.

After lunch, Mort called down for a limo to take them to the Geneva branch of the Bank of Zurich, where Gregory signed over his draft of 75 million American dollars to open an account titled *Euro-Rainbow*. Officially, the account was established to finance the European distribution of Toi-VAX, but unofficially, the funds would be drawn out by the duly appointed agent of the militant arm of the PLO and the Hezbollah to advance their ideology and fight against Israel.

Yes, Gregory recognized America's ambivalent attitude toward Israel, fully believing that would change. While there were pockets of partisans scattered around the nation, an increasing amount of adversaries viewed Israel as a faraway political burden that continued to wage war with its Arab neighbors, retarding the peace process in the Mideast. The Jewish population in the U.S. presently carried substantial clout to protest any overtures to bolster the Arab league, but he would be patient, friendly, and tolerant toward the Jewish nation, for in time, he knew public opinion in America and around the world would be in his favor.

At the Hotel Liechtenstein, Kavidas and Stein dined with Omar Sidmaj, the emir representing Hezbollah, and after the pleasantries were exchanged and dessert was served, Mort handed him an envelope containing the deposit slip from the Bank of Zurich.

Gregory immediately took control of the conversation. "One of my primary functions as the president of the EC is to take whatever steps I deem necessary to perpetuate the existence of the alliance. If that includes radical surgery to excise potential cancerous lesions that could impair our growth, then it must be done."

"Agreed," the emir replied as he shot a look at the envelope.

"In time, we will suggest to member nations that they implement certain trade and tourist restrictions that will slowly strangle off the flow of money to Israel. This will greatly impair their ability to arm themselves and force them to acquiesce to the demands of the Hezbollah in Lebanon and the PLO in Israel, your compatriots. I have projected that this will take five years to engage fully, and by that time, your government and its allies will have sufficient capital reserves to seize the control you need while at the same time enabling the EC to embrace the world of Islam."

"We are willing to wait," the emir replied gratefully, "but I am curious to find out why are you doing this. What is in this for you and the EC?"

"The EC is nothing more than a group of international businessmen that have pooled resources to further commercial enterprise between member nations. As their president, I am committed to financially strengthen the group and recognize that—" Gregory paused to select his words—"your relatives are all petrol rich, and let's face it, the country that controls the oil controls the destiny of the oil-dependent world. This will further our cause, and I believe we will have an equitable, reciprocal agreement."

"So in other words," the emir replied with a grin, "you're in it for the money!" With that he stifled a laugh, then let out with a devilish guffaw and slapped Kavidas on the back.

Gregory masked his feelings as he glanced at Mort and replied unobtrusively, "I guess you could say that."

The emir dispassionately shrugged as he stuffed the envelope in his jacket pocket, never knowing or caring that the acceptance of the money would forever alter the destiny of Israel and all mankind.

When they all shook hands, Gregory and Mort secretly celebrated another victory that they would not share with the members of the confederation.

On their way to Brussels to address the confederate members of the parliament, Gregory directed Mort to urge the abandonment of the EC's plan for a common currency and install the Euro-*Masterlink* system (knowing he would utilize and integrate this with the American-based system), which would coincide with their plans to create a central bank anyway.

To facilitate the plan, Gregory invited the member nation representatives to Florida for their next meeting to see firsthand how the system operated.

It happened by accident one night as Kathy sat at her PC, paying her bills through Paymaster, the online computer bank network. The cursor stopped blinking for almost 15 seconds; then the keyboard locked up as she punched in her bank account password.

When an uploading icon ghosting in one corner of the monitor occurred, she decided to check her equipment. She rebooted the computer, went through a detailed diagnostic check of the operating system, then ran a trial exam on her modem and found no internal conflicts.

Curious, she proceeded to retrieve her bank statement for the last 30 days over the Internet. She noticed that after one of her checks had cleared the bank a subscript character appeared like an exponent after the entry. "David, could you come in here for a moment!" she called to another room.

As David walked in, Kathy pointed to the monitor. "I think somebody is accessing our account and reading files through a computer net. Look at this character after the entry labeled 'Tamarac Congregational Church.' That's the donation we give to the Lord each month."

"Can't be," David remarked as he pressed the scrolling key. "Who would dare infiltrate our private banking records?"

Peering at the ledger, Kathy announced, "There's another one after the check payable to our VERA card."

With that they exchanged looks. David pulled up a chair and started pointing and clicking to pull-down menus to initiate a search command. Twenty-five minutes later, they had their answer.

David tapped the monitor when the tree tracing the character back to its origin matched the symbol on their statement. "It's a *Masterlink* trademark! Curse them!"

"You mean *Masterlink* is monitoring our account? Can they do that?"

"Apparently they are able to do a great many things, with or without our permission," he postulated.

"I'm worried. What does all this mean? This Rainbow/*Masterlink* is so invasive there are few things left that they can't penetrate."

"Yeah, right," David replied after a minute or so. "I want you to go down to the bank tomorrow and ask them about this."

"What do you think it means?" she repeated with rising concern.

"I shudder to speculate."

"You mean prophetically speaking, don't you?" she discerned with an edge of alarm.

David nodded solemnly. "It could be the foundation of the structure known as the final economic system, where everything that is bought or sold is funneled through one financial network."

"And no one will be authorized unless they have the okay of the architect..." She paused and gestured to pull something out of the air. "And let me guess who that is. Bingo—Kavidas and Stein, the dynamic duo from the bottomless pit!" She fell back into her chair and began to cry. "I'm afraid for us," she whispered through whimpers. "I'm afraid for the world."

To Kathy's surprise, the line to see the assistant manager at American Federal Savings and Loan on Commercial Boulevard in Tamarac was relatively short for 9 a.m. After a 10-minute wait, the assistant manager waved Kathy over to her desk.

Dispensing with the amenities, Kathy sat down and opened the manila folder containing the checking account printouts. "Would you be kind enough to explain these remarks next to these entries?" she began with a tinge of hostility while placing them before the woman.

The assistant manager studied the ledger for a few minutes. "Hmm, yes. Well, we started a pilot program—I guess you could call it a new system—here at American Federal just three weeks ago through *Masterlink*. The system is quite unique. It enables a preferred customer to draw on any check, local or otherwise, immediately. It works like an electronic transfer, making the money available so you can collect and pay right away—no holding. Those *Masterlink* codes simply mean that those checks were paid the moment they were presented by the payee; that's all." She held up her hands in the air and added with a dismissive tone, "Nothing to worry about."

Her impudence touched a nerve. Kathy suddenly set aside her Christian virtues and said loudly, "You empirical witch! Don't hand me that! This bank, along with *Masterlink*, is engaged in a scheme to control everybody's finances under the guise of so-called 'benefits,' when in reality you're snooping into everybody's pocketbooks!"

The stunned woman's mouth hung open as the bank patrons gaped to watch the unfolding skirmish. "Mrs. Douglas, please," she pleaded while looking obliquely at the customers, "there's no need for alarm. We can take *Masterlink* off your account if you like."

Her attempt to diffuse Kathy didn't work. "I want to know who authorized *Masterlink* into my account in the first place," she demanded.

The woman picked up the phone and pressed a speed-dial button while gesturing to Kathy to calm down. After several minutes, she replaced the phone. "Our central office advises me that there was a request to engage *Masterlink* on your account last week. The request came in over our E-mail network."

Kathy shook her head in disbelief. "We never authorized such a request."

"Well, Mrs. Douglas, since we have your signature on file when you opened your checking and savings accounts three years ago, we would only need an E-mail or fax with your account numbers to activate

Masterlink. We are trying to reduce the red tape to expedite this system. Why, with the amount of retirees receiving pension and social security benefits down here in Florida, it's especially convenient to implement this without requiring current signatures, etc."

On the whole, it struck Kathy as an infringement, bordering on invasion, and totally unacceptable. *Why would the banking industry allow such a practice? What would be their gain? There had to be more to it than just rapid check-cashing advantages.* She reached over and rotated the monitor on the assistant manager's desk.

"Mrs. Douglas, please, this information is confidential," the woman complained, as she tried to persuade Kathy from transgressing bank procedures.

"Don't you talk to me about confidentiality," Kathy retorted, "when your bank is tapping into my computer at home!" Kathy scrolled through the data on the monitor as the woman waved the manager over.

"This is interesting," Kathy reported as she spotted the *Masterlink* network encoded designation in apolitical and religious data window. "Since when did a bank need to know what religious persuasion I am before they process my checks?"

Flustered, the woman looked up as the manager arrived and said, "Perhaps Mr. Lansing can explain this encoding to you, Mrs. Douglas." With that, she walked off into the restroom.

Mr. Lansing occupied the woman's seat. "Mrs. Douglas, this system is still experimental right now because American Federal has lost millions in bad loans to poorly qualified customers who really were not suitable to begin with. This new system will lower our lending rates to preferred customers because it will virtually cut our recovery costs on bad loans to almost nothing."

With her eyes blazing, she replied, "What you really mean is that you can apply banking pressure to those you or *Masterlink* consider unfavorable, because of religious affiliations or ethnic backgrounds." She reached over and grabbed his tie, pulling his body forward, and added, "For your information, Mr. Lansing, I've already seen this in action with a member of my church, and it really stinks to high heaven—it's nothing short of Nazism—and you're not going to get away with it!" She flipped the tie into his face, stood up, and marched out the front door.

As she drove to work, she knew that the public probably wouldn't

358

care that their privacy was compromised if their banking benefits were enlarged and costs reduced, and to those who objected, what could they do to stop the encroaching system from taking root and branching out into the entire economy? If the whole banking industry adopts this procedure, there is no other place to go unless you pay cash for everything, and with the credit card dependent world that we live in, that option was quickly diminishing.

Sitting around the campfire was more than just a ritual for Brandon and Sam Barrett. Tonight it was the beginning of a new journey. Brandon was beginning to feel that someone *was* watching over them. The afternoon couldn't have gone better, and the find was more than an archaeologist's treasure trove. It was a historian's coffer. Scroll after scroll containing the mysterious glyph of the *Genesis Apocryphon* was found in carefully sealed earthen jars. Each scroll was wrapped in a well-oiled leather jacket that had kept the fragile documents almost completely intact. Brandon couldn't believe their luck.

"Sam, do you think it's as big as Qumran and the Dead Sea Scrolls?" Brandon's excitement was like that of a little child as Sam tried to carefully undo some of the bindings.

"I don't know yet, Brandon. *Big* is a relative term. It certainly has enough scrolls to make it a major historical find. However, it is their content that will determine the stature of the find. You might say that if it contains what you wanted to find, it is a big score, right?" Sam smirked as he looked briefly at Brandon, whose eyes would not leave the scroll Dr. Barrett was currently working on.

"You're right. If..."

"Basili, I will go and begin reading some of the scrolls," Pano began in Greek, "and I will let you know if there is anything of interest in them."

Brandon smiled as Pano went over to the table that already had several scrolls spread out all over it. Dr. Barrett insisted that he unroll each and every scroll. With the care and meticulous handling that Dr. Barrett was extending to each one, Brandon had to agree it was a good idea.

"Brandon, look at this!" Dr. Barrett had just picked up a new scroll and removed the outer leathers. Inside, the scroll was wrapped again in a multicolored leather skin that depicted a scene of a large city. The scroll emphasized one building in the city that was drawn apart from the rest. It was a majestic-looking palazzo that clearly stood above the rest of the city, both in importance and in decor. Dr. Barrett began to unroll it.

These large Greek letters were stenciled on the skin:

Η ηστορια τησ Κανανησ
Προσευχει ολοι οποιοσ βλεπουνε εδω
The History of Canaan. Beware all who look here.

Brandon translated the cover immediately and called Pano over.

<Πανω, ριξατε τα ματια σου εδω> "Pano, look over here," he cried.

Pano came over quickly to see Brandon's progress and appeared astounded by what he saw. He didn't even stop to read the inscription.

<το σπιτι> "The house," he cried.

Brandon looked at Pano, and their eyes met in fear.

"Dr. Barrett," Pano began in broken English, "this house—I am too surprised to see it here."

"Brandon, I'm not sure I understand. What is your friend trying to say?" Dr. Barrett asked, puzzled.

Brandon took a deep breath and tried to swallow. "It's this house. The scroll says it is the history of Canaan. So what is Gregory Kavidas's house doing there?" Brandon looked at the scroll again, and the picture played in his mind of the Mykonos estate.

"Pano, what do you think? Is it the same house?"

Pano's eyes portrayed exactly what he was thinking and what he felt were the consequences of his conclusions.

"Basili, it cannot be, but it is. It is the same house. How?"

Brandon shrugged and turned to Dr. Barrett. "I don't know how yet, but I know one thing. I've found the scroll I was looking for."

Pano ran his hand through his hair and sighed. He had read the first 25 pages of the scroll seven times and still could not see anything that related to their cause or their quest. Brandon had actually read the scroll to him, since he was having some trouble reading the actual writing. Brandon, surprisingly enough, was more literate in the written sense of the language. He read it to Pano, and then they would discuss the actual meaning. So far, there was nothing that looked hopeful.

Dr. Barrett was snoring soundly on a cot next to the two men who were all too glad to burn the midnight oil. However, frustration was setting in, and Pano just wanted to go on. Brandon wanted to read the beginning again.

"Just how are you so good at reading Greek anyway?" Pano asked, slightly irritated.

"It's a hobby." Brandon was not any happier than his counterpart.

"What is a 'hobby'?" Pano asked reluctantly.

At that, Brandon couldn't help but smile. "It's something you do for fun, when you want to relax or have spare time," he said in Greek to allow Pano to fully understand.

"Basili, let us keep going. It will make sense. We have a lot more to go in the scroll."

"Pano, we are missing something; I know it. The history so far is nothing but a description of daily life. What is so dangerous about that? There must be a hidden meaning."

"I think you are looking too far into it. There are at least 10 more pages to go. Let's at least finish reading the scroll. The next part is about their mating rituals. That's daily life too, but at least it will be more fun to read. It may even be considered dangerous. These people were pretty wild."

Brandon shrugged and conceded. "Perhaps you are right. It can't hurt to finish the scroll and see what else they've left behind for us. So far it's nothing that couldn't be found in a textbook, I'd imagine. Sounds like the routine life of a bedouin. Dull, boring, and dull again."

"Well, all the more reason to move on. This could be the best part."

Brandon smiled and picked up where he left off. Four pages later, they both stopped and stared at each other.

"Pano, what does it sound like to you?"

The men exchanged dubious glances.

Pano motioned to Brandon again. "Read that again, Basili. The last page."

Brandon nodded and searched again for the spot that caused them to shrink in alarm. They had translated it four times, and each time they agreed on the same meaning.

All the animals give us pleasure but none so much as the goat that is called ibex. You can see it jump around on the rocks on any day, and so it will behave when it is mounted. You must hold on tight, for it is not docile as the sheep nor is it big as the llama. It is tight, like unto a man, and must be taken unawares. It is not easy prey but worth the trouble!

Its likeness to our god makes it special, and so we couple with it in gladness to be close to our god and to pleasure him. But the goodness is at times only for a season—woe to him that takes the plague from this godly animal! First he gets sick, and then he is covered with sores. Naught can be done to assist him, and nary a person wishes to try, as it is very contagious. Little can be done to soothe him, and he longs to die.

If the sores begin to cover the face, he is lost. However, if the gods are merciful, and if one of the creatures is killed or dies (we will not touch the beast—whose likeness is our god!) we will roast the entrails and give the man of them to eat. This food of the gods will sometimes bring him back health, if he is not too sick, and he will live again. And so, the creature which begot the disease in the man's pleasure can offer him life. This man, thus cured, can pleasure himself ever and anon and not fear the sickness. Such is the whim and pleasure of the gods, who give life and who take it away.

Brandon's heart constricted in his chest as he looked again to Pano. *Could it really be true?*

The men looked at each other again. Brandon knew what Pano was thinking; it took each of them a moment to register the feeling in their private thoughts. Brandon cocked his head toward Sam Barrett.

Pano nodded. "It must be. It can only be one thing."

"Pano, they say it is new and that it has mutated. How can it be as old as the Canaanites? And how did they cure it? It's ridiculous! They talk of this goat as if it were a god, and in their worship they contracted the disease and died. It's…well, it's absurd."

362

Pano continued to stare at the book.

Who am I trying to convince, Brandon asked himself, *Pano or me?*

"Basili, maybe we should wake up Dr. Barrett. He should know this."

"Know *what?*" Brandon said, almost laughing. "That AIDS may have started with a jumping goat? And that the people knew it—the high priest encouraged it—and they were willing to die for their god? I don't think we have quite the handle on it yet, Pano. This story is not ready for publication." He sat down, disgusted, and grabbed the scroll.

Pano said nothing as Brandon quickly read the remaining pages.

"Nothing. No other mention of the disease. Only that the god will never die and that their worship will endure forever. Great, just what we needed. A cult to resurface that worships goats and then eats their insides, hoping for a cure."

"What part talks about their worship lasting forever? Read me that part."

"It's not very interesting, Pano. It mostly talks about the man who will bring it back. Their priest. We were trying to find something out about Kavidas. He may be evil, but I have a hard time believing he is behind a cult that eats and has sex with goats."

"Read it to me anyway. Indulge me." Pano gave Brandon a stern look, and Brandon only rolled his eyes and turned to the portion in the scroll.

Αυτοσ που ειναι το αερασ θα ερθει παλι
Το ονομα του ειναι στο τουτο βιβλιο, με το αριθμο του.
Αν μβορειτε να το διαβασετε, θα το βρειτε το αριθμο του κ'
το ονομα του. Διπλα, θα εινια τα ιδια.

Brandon finished the recitation and looked over at Pano. "Satisfied? It hardly gives any clues that will blow the lid off our mystery. If anything, it either makes it worse or just talks nonsense about an ancient religion."

"And what about the house? Is that a coincidence?" Pano seemed surprised that Brandon was giving up so easily.

"What about it? I'm tired. I'm frustrated. So what? The house looks like Kavidas's. For all we know, it is a famous design handed down for centuries. He liked it, had it built. Sound good to you? I'm going to bed."

"Five more minutes. Something isn't right about that passage. I don't think we are getting it right."

Brandon groaned and moved back to the scroll. "What do you mean? It's simple.

He who is the priest shall come again.
His name is in this book and his number.
If you can read it, you will find it, his name and his
number. Together, they are the same.

"So what do you make of that? The priest will rise from the dead. His name is in the book. Where? They never mention it. His age or when he is coming again, they never say. Together they are the same? It's silly. There's no reference to him in the scroll again."

"Let me see the scroll for a minute. Point out that passage."

Brandon lifted the scroll and pointed to the section he had just read from. "See, it looks very ordinary. Nothing different about it." Brandon sat down heavily. All this effort, and they were getting nowhere.

"Basili, look. There is something different. Look at the letters. Look at the words *onoma* and *arithmo*. What do you see?" Pano pointed excitedly.

Brandon saw one thing only. "They are capitalized. So are a lot of words. What do you mean?"

"Look," Pano said, almost breathless, "they are capitalized in the middle of the sentence. See?"

Brandon looked again and looked up. "So what? They're like proper nouns. That can be capitalized without creating a big deal."

"Look, Basili! The first 25 pages we read so many times. Nothing was capitalized except the first letter of every line. And now these. No other names or proper nouns were capitalized. It must mean something. It must!" Pano's excitement and assurance were beginning to melt Brandon's resistance. He decided to look a little harder and with more of an open mind.

"So what do you think? A message? A secret?" He could feel the blood begin to pump again, and his fatigue disappeared in an instant.

"Let's see. Get me some paper and a pen. You read the letters off, and I'll write them down."

The men scrambled to find the materials and began again in earnest to glean some information between the lines of the ancient text. Brandon read the letters off, and Pano hurriedly wrote them out.

Το ονομα του ανθροπου θα ειναι το αριθμο του διαβλου εξικοσια εξιντα εξι

The name of the man shall be the devil's number six hundred sixty-six.

The men stared at each other. Brandon knew that the Greek alphabet had a numerical equivalent, but he didn't know what it was.

"Pano, do you know which letters stand for which numbers?" Brandon stood breathless for the answer.

"Of course I do. I'm Greek, you *vlaka*. We all know the numbers. Who should I try first?"

"Try a few names of some people you know. Then we'll get around to the ones that are more prominently known. Do you know what I mean? This way, we'll have something to compare it to." He moved away and walked over to the cot where Dr. Barrett lay.

"What are you doing?"

"I'm waking him up. If we're right, and we let him sleep through this, he'd never forgive me." He nudged the man's shoulder, and Pano started to add.

Mikalis Kourtsounis
Dimitrios Poulos
Aristotle Onassis

He had a long list of names to try. Somehow, though, he had a feeling only one was going to fit. And he had a feeling he knew which one.

THIRTEEN

Silence, indifference and inaction
were Hitler's principal allies.
Lord Jakobovits

D avid insisted on an urgent prayer meeting to petition God for answers and to discuss the latest developments in the war against Kavidas and Stein. *Redisearch/Masterlink* rumors that bantered about in the Christian community at large, together with the persecution many were undergoing, necessitated the amalgamating of Christians to find a common strength.

Despite the confining size of the Tamarac Congregational Church building, it was agreed the premises provided security from outside interference and lended itself to the reverence of the occasion. The church could seat 130 persons, but over 200 showed up. Standing in the aisles and crammed into the corners, the congregation along with the remnant of the Rainbow protesters and the newly persuaded pastors from the symposium, filled the sanctuary to hear from David and Matthew about their destiny. Exchanging experiences and postulating theories, the crowd hummed with conversation as they waited for David and Matthew to appear.

Inside the pastor's office for the past two hours, David, Matthew, and Eddie Swain labored on their knees, begging the Lord for guidance and direction. Warring against discouraging supernatural principalities and powers brought tears to their eyes as they held hands and collectively envisioned Christ as their redeemer and protectorate who would lead them in battle.

God's Spirit encouraged and inspired them as they knelt on the floor, and after another 15 minutes of fervent prayer, they proceeded to search the Bible for instruction. Confidence ran high as they believed God would give them the truth and assurance they needed.

Soon they filed out and walked to the pulpit as the noise of the anxious assembly diminished to silence. Both David and Matthew remained at the pulpit as Swain took a seat in the audience.

"Dear brothers and sisters," Matthew began passionately, "David and I, along with Eddie Swain, have just come from the Throne of Grace, where we have invoked God's Spirit to intervene and show us the path we should take. Although God has not revealed any details to us, we believe the Scriptures contain enough information to instruct us accordingly.

"Many of you have experienced trials over the past few weeks or have heard reports about how our faith has been challenged, raising many questions in your minds. Well, we believe this is an indication, together with other evidences, of what is to come upon the world in the future.

"I would like to bring you up to speed on several careful observations we have recently made regarding what we have dubbed the Kavidas-Stein/*Masterlink* Network. It is apparent that a wave of harassment, both socially and financially, is taking place today. Now, if we link these events with what is going on around us in the supernatural or spiritual world, together with the advent of the Toi-VAX vaccine, we may be able to piece together a mosaic that fits squarely with certain prophecies in the Bible. From there, we hope to plan our future accordingly. Now listen very carefully—" As he looked around, every eye was riveted on him.

"Until recently, the human race has not needed a remedy for such a devastating and all-encompassing plague as AIDS. Sure, there have been ravaging diseases down through the ages, but this is the worst form of disease to ever hit the planet! Many Bible scholars point to Old and New Testament verses that hint of such diseases because of unchecked immorality.

"There isn't a person alive today who hasn't heard about it, fears getting it, or somehow has been affected by it. Scientists and laboratories around the world have been working feverishly to isolate and control HIV to no avail. Billions of dollars in research and many lives have been sacrificed to find a vaccine to stave off the decimation of mankind and—" he paused to glare at the crowd—"*no one* has been able to do it until suddenly *one man* appears out of *nowhere* and claims credit for it." He stepped up to the microphone and blared, "The man, *Gregory Kavidas!*" then stepped back to allow David to speak.

David took up the pitch and tone as he continued, "Until the emergence of the silicon chip and the state-of-the-art electronic surveillance and monitoring devices, financial networks were limited to pen, paper, and the post office. But now with EFT, the Internet, AOL, the search engines of Google, etc., and now the latest, *Masterlink*, the hardware is in place to seize and control the world's economy, enabling one man to decide who buys or sell what and when—and that man could be *Gregory Kavidas*!"

He paused to reach for a chart and added, "The number one treatment for AIDS, Toi-VAX, has generated billions of dollars in revenue for the Kavidas-Stein partnership that has been used to fund and expand their empire through *Redisearch*, etc., enabling him to reach a position of world notoriety where he tenaciously stretched across the globe and landed on the EC. Then shortly afterward, *Masterlink* was born."

As he cleared his throat, he welled up with tears. "We have other proofs, such as his Roman-Greek ancestry and vast wealth, but the most compelling evidence so far is his prophecies. Who, except a supernatural person, could predict tomorrow's news before it happens?" David paused to allow the people to absorb the statement.

Interestingly, David thought, *the human mind either blocks out or conveniently forgets events that either numbs or confuses it.* He saw people nod in recognition of his reminder.

"Pastor Dave!" a voice yelled, followed by a waving hand. "If you're saying these men are really criminals, why aren't they jailed?"

"We believe we are faced with a diabolical being, perhaps two, who are capable of predicting the future and exploiting the phenomenon to achieve their goals. We also believe they have supernatural protection that only God can countermand and bring to justice."

"Does that mean we are powerless to do anything?" a young pastor asked.

"No! We plan to do everything that is possible to deny them their goals. The impossible we leave up to God," David replied.

Heads turned and voices hushed as a well-known senior pastor stood up amidst the crowd. "Pastor David and Mr. Lane, just who do you believe these characters are who are yielding so much power?"

Of course it was unavoidable that the question would be asked. But answering it would raise another 10,000 questions that only speculation could resolve at this point in time. David turned to Matthew. "I'm going to let Mr. Lane field that one."

Lane unfolded a letter and then opened his Bible. "Friends, you should brace yourself for this. Many of you will have a difficult time accepting this truth, but it must be said. We have here a letter from Dr. Samuel Barrett that explains his interpretation of a complex study he completed on Gregory Kavidas. This letter is accompanied by a translation from the original Greek language that still must be verified, but the preliminary report indicates the name *Gregory Kavidas* has an numerical equivalency that is 666." He indexed the verse in Revelation chapter 13. "'If anyone has insight, let him calculate the number of the beast, for it is man's number. His number is 666.'"

As the words left his lips, gasps and sobs broke out. He gulped a mouthful of water from the nearby glass, then forced himself to utter the unmentionable, "He does fit the profile—it is possible he is the Antichrist."

David stepped to the microphone and motioned for the audience to come to order. "Remember, the Bible dictates we are only in the initial stages of prophetic fulfillment at present. Much of Kavidas's character and purpose haven't been disclosed as yet. The machinery is simply being put in place to be used after we are all removed at the Rapture of the church. We still have time to organize and resist this takeover before God takes us home."

Detecting a wave of despair coming over the people David cried out, "God has promised us victories, and we shall overcome this evil, despite the cost!" No sooner did he mouth those words when a chill came over him. *Lord, give me the courage to stand and the grace to fall when you ordain it.*

Introducing Eddie and Sydelle to the platform seemed anticlimatic at this time, but David hoped it would have a soothing effect on the troubled hearts. "Eddie will now speak to you about a plan that he has developed called *Koinonos.*"

With a broad smile that projected assurance and safety, Eddie waited for the audience to quiet down. "Fellow brothers and sisters, Sydelle and I have worked on this project for several weeks now, and we are confident that we can build a working system that will enable us to begin to separate and maintain some element of independence from the Kavidas/Stein *Masterlink* Network. If we plan carefully now, we can work toward the day when we will be self-sufficient, requiring little if any reliance upon the outside world that has been beguiled by Kavidas/Stein and hurtling the planet headlong into his tenacious grasp."

He signaled for his assistants to hand out individual booklets, then continued, "We have compiled a so-called member directory, listing their services, and alongside you'll find what they need in trade to complete a purchase. As long as cash is used for currency, we must exhaust this medium first. But the day will come when all purchases will be done with the *Masterlink* system, and cash will be a thing of the past. By then, the member directory should be complete so that our so-called bartering system will be in full swing, and we will not need to use any form of credit device.

"Of course, there are many things we will have to do without since we will not have suitable items or services to trade, but until we devise a better alternative, this is the way we need to go. *Koinonos* means 'companions,' our organization's name, which undergirds the purpose of our group: to be companions one for another during this time of difficulty.

"You need to get accustomed to the fact that our society is unalterably changing, and we must adapt to this change under our own terms, not those of the Kavidas/Stein network."

And so it went, with Sydelle following Eddie with a framing out of instructions to guide the men and women to begin to catalog their crafts, abilities, and strengths that would enable *Koinonos* to organize a society free from the influence of *Masterlink*.

Rarely did Kavidas show up at *Redisearch*, and if he did, it was a matter of grave concern. When Mort saw his car arrive unannounced, he paused to reflect on the progress of *Masterlink*. Satisfied, he wondered what crisis unfolded to warrant such a visit.

As Gregory walked past Mort's service staff, an awe-inspiring hush came over them as they momentarily interrupted their work or even stopped talking with their eyes transfixed on his every movement.

Once inside Mort's spacious office, he paced in front of his desk for several minutes before speaking, elevating Mort's concern even more. Finally, after coming to a halt he said, "We're in trouble with these

Christian groups. I received a report that they are banding together to fight *Masterlink* and everything it stands for, and our plans may be jeopardized unless we stop them."

"But surely you're not worried about Douglas's church group or several pockets of Christians here and there, are you?" Mort countered. "I mean, with our resources, control, and clout, we can snuff them out in no time."

"This is different," Gregory replied tersely. "They have a plan that potentially could weaken our position, requiring us to shift our emphasis out of this country and into Europe. Strength in numbers and unification of purpose can present a major threat to our overall strategy. I've seen this before. They become an army of resistors, digging and burrowing in, making tunnels in the earth, fortifying storehouses, making ready to engage the enemy, gaining triumph by wearing their invaders down over a long siege—like what happened at Masada, Vietnam, Afghanistan, and Iraq—souring and spoiling the challenge of conquest."

Mort looked at Gregory, and for a moment, he saw weakness. "You do believe we can win, don't you?"

"Our victory," Gregory temporized, "is contingent on time." He shot his eyes skyward. "The sooner we act within the time allotted, the better our chances of success will be. *Time* is our enemy because in *time* our diplomacy will be revealed, lessening our chances to win—and we're in this to win. So we are going to take steps to remedy this problem."

Nodding with a tight smile, Mort knew that Gregory towered over humanity in times like this. There were no obstacles he couldn't hurdle while drawing on the inexhaustible power that lie within him. Together they were unbeatable. "What do you want done?"

Matthew parked his car in the employee parking lot, then walked around the front of his building to buy a newspaper from one of the many street hawkers. When he looked at the front page, his face reddened with rage. He rolled the paper up and shoved it under his arm as he marched up to his office.

His secretaries merely waved to him as he walked by, knowing about the report, not knowing what to say. "Coffee, Mr. Lane?" Cheryl, his administrative secretary, asked.

He snorted and forced a smile to acknowledge her. Once in his office, he pressed David's number on the phone's speed dial as he thumped his hand on his desk.

"David, did you see the morning paper?" he began with a grunt.

"Yes, I was going to call you about it."

"This creep Ryder is getting on my nerves. Where does he get off writing about Dr. Barrett like this? This part about him 'traipsing around Israel, looking at the site of Sodom and Gomorrah in a futile search for an AIDS vaccine written on a cave wall' is nothing but ridicule. I think we should tell Ryder we're going to sue him. They're trying to discredit Barrett's credentials and in turn discredit his authority to uncover any connection with Kavidas and AIDS in antiquity. If they do, any cure that comes out of Lane Pharmacueticals will be suspect since the public links him with us. They're trying to get back at us for the way we exposed them. Threatening to sue *is* an exercise in futility as far as I'm concerned. They bought Ryder, pure and simple." He groaned, then added, "Did you see page two?"

Matthew turned the page and his lip began to quiver as his anger surged again. Ryder authored another disparaging article equating the *Koinonos* movement with the early church's underground opposition to avoid persecution from the Roman legions. It included remarks warning the public that fanatical groups have historically hurt society and recommended that readers contact their congressmen to enact legislation to protect the public from such hazards.

"Do you believe it?" Matthew complained after he glanced over the article. "The very protection *we* need from anti-Christian groups, Ryder is claiming for his side. It's media hype reverse psychology once again." He put David on conference call, then pressed his intercom button. "Cheryl, get that attorney general's office on the line again."

"What became of that petition?" David asked.

"I forwarded it to our attorney for review, and he in turn sent it along to the AG's office. But like everything else, that'll get bogged down in bureaucratic red tape for the next decade or so. We need to have our rights as citizens defended! Lord, who is going to fight for us?" he lamented.

David begged off the line as Matthew renewed his vain attempt to reach the attorney general through the maze of voice mail options and secretaries. It was becoming more apparent to David with each passing episode of conflict that they should expect resistance and not cooperation from a national system that buoyed up the Kavidas/Stein *Masterlink* Network. Further, it was increasingly apparent that *Koinonos* make the transition to an organization apart from *Masterlink* as soon as possible.

Mort was content with the media's treatment of the problem with Douglas and Lane for the present, yet two tasks remained on his agenda. The next item would be easy to implement; the last would take a little longer.

Anastasios Kokkoris of the Athinai Bank in Athens hated Americans but loved their money. His father emigrated to New York at the end of World War II, carrying all the family's wealth on his back. Determined to make a name for himself, he took a job as a custodian at the Chase Manhattan Bank in Rockefeller Plaza and went to night school to get his degree in finance. After five long and arduous years and counting on a pledge from the branch manager, he applied to Chase for a position as a teller. When the big day came, he was told the job had been filled. Unemployment in the banking industry was at an all-time high, the manager advised him, so the position would be absorbed. In humiliation, he begged for his old job as custodian back, and when he returned to work, he discovered the teller's position had been given to a returning war veteran. Broken in spirit, he stayed on as custodian for three more years, then returned to Athens where his people accepted him quickly into the world of finance. His abhorrence for Americans was readily transferred to his son.

Anastasios opened the EFT order, and his eyes widened as he read the sum of 1,500,000 American dollars to be deposited into a new account under the name of Demitrius Dimakos Enterprises, presently operating in the state of Florida, with just a simple post office box as a return address. He ran a check on the validity of the applicant, being confirmed through the Social Security number and genealogy records, and learned that the name showed up as having ties to the Kavidas family. He immediately realized the magnitude of such a client and resolved to keep his discovery secret. As far as he was concerned, every dollar siphoned off Americans and deposited into a Greek bank was worth double.

He quickly sent a confirmation letter back to the post office address in America. Once the letter was received, a return letter to Mr. Kokkoris advised him the same amount would be sent each month in the future.

Struggling to free himself from sleep, Mort bolted upright in his bed, then fell backward onto his pillow as a collage of images gradually took shape and formed a motion picture in his mind.

The lion galloped toward the ancient serpent, who stood as a man on the edge of an escarpment, where flaming fires spiralled upward continuously. Like hands reaching for the heavens, the flames frantically clutched the air above, in hopes of finding relief from eternal torment. From the depths an eerie dragging that sounded like the opening of a gigantic stone door from the very bowels of the earth rebounded off the surrounding mountains. Massive rumblings echoed off the escarpment's wall; then gusts of smoke pushed out from the shaftway below, swirling about in the expanse, beckoning to the serpent that stood chained at the precipice.

The serpent looked at the oncoming lion and trembled. When he tried in vain to free himself from the shackles that held him fast, the realization of his destiny came upon him. "No! Not the bottomless pit!" he cried out. He sobbed as he stood at the edge of the great abyss, that blasphemous canyon where time no longer mattered and hidden horrors were forever being unveiled. He dared not look into the vast chasm that lay before him, but cast his eyes afar to the divine being who changed from a lion to God in the form of a man, now standing suspended above the gulf, from whom glorious light radiated majestically as angelic creatures stood ministering at his side.

"Help me!" he screamed.

Only silence came in reply.

The serpent gave off a guttural yowl, then raised his arms to plead for mercy as the lion signaled the guardian with the keys to the abyss, who watched over the denizens of the wretched place, to bring the new arrival down. Then sounds, millions of distinct humans wailing or metallic-sounding voices, came from that lower place—the abode of the doomed—crying out in agony and despair over their master's defeat.

The serpent listened intently and heard what sounded like an inhabitant of the deep climbing up the wall of the crevasse, seeking temporary freedom from the damned place. Then a hand reached out from the abyss and latched onto the serpent's ankle, pulling at the chains, yanking him toward the pit. "No!" he bellowed as he jumped backward. The escort from the deep possessed hollow sockets for eyes;they penetrated the body in search of the soul.

The serpent sensed a presence below of a busy network leading to an unknown region of horrible groaning and dreadful dirges. Sounds that no mortals would ever utter. Ascending slowly out of the pit, the powerful gnome let out a series of muffled squeals, then extended his arm once again to grab hold of the new arrival's legs, pulling him ever toward the edge. "No! This cannot be! I am too powerful!" the victim screamed out. A guardian suddenly appeared to assist. Then when the serpent succumbed, he released him into the custody of the hairless gnome once again.

Falling to the ground and groveling in the ash-covered rock, the serpent dug his fingernails into the crevices to secure himself. A low-lying mist engulfed him as he lay there for an interminable period; then the stench of burning flesh filled his nostrils. He squirmed and writhed in fear as worms and maggots slowly covered his body. He let out a wail, but no sound was heard, so he wept and gnashed his teeth in desperation as the realization of the inevitable came over him. His fate would be to spend a thousand years with the lost souls and wicked denizens who dwell in the corridors and chambers of hell. Never again would he have free course of the heavens.

As the vermin crept over him, he slithered away from the ragged edge of the fiery netherworld, preferring the blackness of death to the torture of being eaten by worms that never died in a bottomless pit. The shriveled little creature from the pit resumed his task and began dragging him once again toward the ledge of the abyss. With contemptible resignation, he slipped over the edge, only to find himself falling and falling without end.

FOURTEEN

The real Antichrist is
he who turns the wine of an original idea
into the water of mediocrity.
Eric Hoffer

Mort sat in his office and began to open up the channels of his mind that would put him in a meditative state. He wanted to open up his consciousness so he would be receptive to those around him as well as any of the dark powers that wanted to communicate with him.

His recent practice with meditation and altered states of consciousness had opened up a whole new world of power that he never knew existed. He could see shadows that were never there before. He could sense life and energy coming from sources previously unavailable to him.

He began to cast out with his mind and could feel those around him in the office. His mind could lightly brush against those entities in the building so he would get a vague impression of what they were thinking or what was happening around them. He reveled in the knowledge and drank in the power like wine when it drives a man to lust. His only distraction was the people who remained closed to him. Those few whose thoughts and minds remained closed. He didn't know why.

Some people exhibited a natural shielding, and he could not penetrate their minds. This puzzled and annoyed him but just briefly as there was so much information to read and absorb. He could also feel the strength that varied from person to person. Some of those around him had auras surrounding them that warned him to stay away. Those minds, like Gregory's, remained untouched. There were more than enough people with minds to invade without attempting to conquer the thoughts of such formidable and challenging adversaries. He was surprised to see just how many people's minds were weak and controllable.

Mort's casting out was becoming more and more frequent, and his reach was beginning to extend way beyond his physical confines. The taste of this power made him hungry for more, giving him an exhilarating rush of adrenaline that allowed his mind to soar far and wide. He could feel the energy draining out of him as he let his mind wander abroad, and it wasn't until he was exhausted that he would return to his body.

There he would see himself sitting with an eerie green glow surrounding his head, like an evil nimbus of cabalistic power crackling with supercharged energy. He knew, though he didn't know how, that this aura was his own shield against harm and against other intrusive minds such as his. He had felt the presence of other minds pressing against him, trying to penetrate his inner self. Being attuned to the power, he could detect it in others and deter them from probing him. His only question now was how far could he go? To what end?

His ascent into reality was almost complete when it was interrupted with a psychic shock. An internal scream shuddered through his alter-ego, and he could see his actual body buckle from the strain. The green haze glowed wickedly and struggled to maintain its shape around Mort's head. He recognized the voice, telepathic as it was, and knew it was demonic. He sensed the strength and power emanating from the vision, and he knew Gregory was in trouble.

Mort! Help me! Someone is trying to kill me—I need you! The voice rang out in Mort's mind as clear as if Gregory himself had spoken while in the same room. He scanned the area and found the mind with Gregory's distinct signature. The building complex was huge, and Gregory was not in his own office. He made note of the location and quickly rejoined his body and ran in the direction made known by this ever-present familiar. The spirit creature that was once a servant was increasingly becoming the master.

The scene around Gregory's office was not pleasant as Mort saw bodies strewn throughout the hallway in a state of death or close to it. *Mass killings?* he thought. He rushed in and saved his questions for later. How this had happened with all the security they had was beyond his comprehension. His only thoughts were to protect Gregory and save his life.

Mort yanked the door open and saw a man strangling the life out of Gregory. The man looked deranged and as if he were on drugs. Mort grabbed the surprised man and felt a presence of extreme evil, one that he had not experienced at such a close range.

The man turned to glare at Mort, as if surmising that his time was running out to finish the job. His hands tightened around Gregory.

Mort could see Gregory's eyes begin to bulge as foam formed around his mouth. He fought to gain control and to remove the man's hands from Gregory's body. His hold was locked. The man's fervor had given him an almost supernatural strength that Mort could not overcome. He grabbed the man by the shoulder and pulled him back, trying to snap his spine. He could feel the energies within him begin to work, and he saw the man slowly being enveloped by the green nimbus that apparently still surrounded him. Having rejoined his physical body, he was not aware of the ghostly glow that was beginning to take on a malevolent humor. "Let go!" he yelled at the man as he tried to cut off the assassin's airflow. "Let go, or I will break your neck!" Mort jerked the man's head, causing his neck to twist horribly out of shape.

This man is so strong, thought Mort. *Too strong.*

Mort bent his newly acquired energies on the assailant's arms and hands and focused his will. Both men were encased in the cloudlike haze, and as Mort concentrated, tendrils of electricity formed like sparks and began to shower onto the assailant's extremities. The acrid smell of burning flesh filled the room, and the man screamed and released his death grip on Gregory's neck.

Mort took one look at Gregory and feared it was too late. He thrust the man into the corner and grabbed a table lamp and smashed it over the man's head. The man crumpled to the floor, and Mort ran to Gregory's side. The man's plight already forgotten, Mort assessed Gregory's condition.

"Gregory," he began as he gently stroked his face. Saliva was falling from Kavidas's mouth, and Mort could see that he was hardly breathing. "No!" he shouted to the ceiling in an attempt at rage. "He cannot die!"

He thrust his hands over Gregory's chest and could see the green nimbus began to cover Gregory's body like a shroud. Reaching out with his mind, Mort cast his essence into Gregory's body, searching for some sign of life—*anything at all* that would give him hope or direction. His mind was fascinated at the intricate workings of the body, and the mind—*the mind!* Even with his last breaths of life the force of Gregory's consciousness was staggering.

Mort instinctively pulled away from the incumbent force and felt as if he were physically being thrust back inside. Someone—or something—was telling him that his job was not done. *But what should I do?*

Mort continued to scan the body for signs of life and focused on the area that was so badly damaged. The windpipe was crushed, and he could sense the injury itself in his mind. He could see the lifeless trachea spilling precious blood and air into the body cavity instead of sending it to the lungs. He could see the body's reaction and noticed the body's immune system responding—sending thousands upon thousands of cells to repair the wound and stop the bleeding. And he knew it would not be enough.

Without another thought he reached out and grasped Gregory's still and swelling throat. He closed his eyes and forced his mind into the area and slowly, piece by piece, used his energy to pull the trachea back into position. He could feel the warmth of his own body's energy flow into the area of the wound and repair the damaged vessels. Using his own body as a model, he slowly and surely opened the blocked airway and smoothed the area with his thoughts.

Blood vessels began to flow again, precious, life-giving air began to travel to Gregory's lungs, while injured parts and damaged areas were restored to their healthy and vital positions.

Collapsing onto Gregory's chest, Mort was spent. He could feel the last vestiges of his energy being absorbed by Gregory as the man's chest began to rise and fall with regular rhythm. The air around them seemed electrically charged. It crackled, lit up, and then went out as Mort's body could no longer sustain it. He could feel his own body getting cold, and he recoiled as his senses told him to disengage, lest he deplete his own levels beyond their tolerance.

Mort fell to the floor exhausted but knew that he was not finished. He noticed again the man that was in the corner and knew that something had to be done with him. Gregory was already beginning to stir, and so he knew that he had to act quickly. He walked over to the man and put his hand against his chest and thrust out over the man's heart. The overwhelming feeling of evil pervaded, and Mort was repulsed. He tried to tighten his grip around the man's heart and tell the great muscle to slow down and finally stop.

But something was interfering with his plan. He turned around and could see that Gregory was getting up and coming over to him. *Was the great mind interfering with my own sense of justice?*

Gregory walked over and put his hand on Mort's shoulder. The touch alone was thanks enough for Mort, and he could see a thousand words in Gregory's eyes—words that he knew they would share as soon as they were able. But Mort saw anger in Gregory's eyes, anger that was directed not toward him but toward this man. This useless man that almost destroyed all of their plans.

"Who are you? And how dare you rise against me!" Gregory's tone was more than commanding.

Even Mort felt himself shrink back. *And to think, less than five minutes ago he was near death!*

"You have no power over me, Kavidas. I am older than you and stronger. My purpose was not to harm you—that was the idea of this hapless fool you see before you," the voice from the man uttered.

Mort's flesh began to crawl as he realized that the speaker was not really the man sitting before him but a being not of this earth, whose presence appalled him. He felt dizzy and looked at Gregory. Kavidas, however, was undaunted.

"You are the fool," Kavidas said as he lifted the man like a piece of balsa wood and held him before his eyes. "You will be punished for this. You allowed this idiot of a man to interfere in my plans and almost destroy everything. You will answer for it, not this moronic piece of flesh that has no meaning to me at all!" Mort could see the cords in Gregory's neck bulging with his ire, though the man seemed unconcerned.

"What would you do to punish me?" mocked the spirit. "Condemn me? Ha! I was condemned ages before you were born. Don't presume to toy with me. I have apologized for the inconvenience. I will do no more."

Mort was aghast at the scene unfolding in front of him. He saw that Gregory's eyes still blazed, and he could feel the heat being generated from the man's body. The demoniac's rampage had left several people dead in its wake as it tried to approach Kavidas. He was glad of the security and hated to see any of these loyal employees die.

"Who is this idiot you are helping to thwart our plans?" Mort could see control being forced back into Gregory's character as his mind began to whirl anew and turn things to his advantage.

"His brother was an addict that was HIV positive," began the demon. "He has been using your vaccine, and I'm sorry to report it has made matters worse. I've done all I can with that burnt-out corpse. This moron you refer to was the closest and most readily available receptacle for me. I like to think it was a symbiotic relationship. You apparently disagree."

Mort knew Gregory enough to see that he was boiling inside but was once again the master of his own emotions. Mort sat there, thinking to himself that he felt as if he was dead, physically and emotionally. He was anxious and hopeful that Gregory would soon get rid of this nuisance.

"Leave this man immediately. You have used him to bring near disaster on us, but I will use him to further our cause." He paused and brought the man's face close to his own so that the man's nose touched his. "And be aware that I know you, and I know who you are. Do not come near me again. You would be surprised at how I can make things even more unbearable for you. This is my only warning. I think you know I am serious. Don't be stupid a second time."

The man's face contorted in rage, and Mort could see a retort begin to form.

Gregory's nostril's flared, and when he opened his mouth to breathe, the man's face went limp, along with his body. Gregory threw the husk of a body into the corner and smiled.

"Smart move," he announced to the surrounding area, looking to locate the fleeing spirit. Satisfied the presence was in fact gone, he moved over to Mort and helped him up. "Mort, let me give back to you some of the strength you loaned me." He leaned over and breathed on Mort's mouth, almost as if he was giving CPR, and the air flooded into Mort's lungs, filling him and instantly giving him vigor and strength. "I knew you would hear me, Mort. I knew you had been expanding your telepathic abilities. I had no idea you were this far along." Gregory smiled and moved back toward his desk and began putting things back in their proper place.

"We have a lot of work to do to use this man to our advantage," Kavidas added. "Somehow I have a feeling he was part of the rabble that is following Douglas, don't you?" He smiled at Mort, who smiled back wanly.

He told his legs to get him up, and they obeyed. He didn't know how, since he was still reeling with the information and events of the last hour. He knew he would be processing the information for the next day or so and wasn't worried about assimilating it all. What troubled him was the way that Gregory so quickly returned to the business at hand as if nothing had happened. And did he know about the bodies outside his office that lay dying in their own blood? His campaign continued, and Mort expected nothing less. But shouldn't they call the police or do something?

"Uh, Gregory, a few people were hurt or killed outside. Should I call someone? The police, the hospital—who?"

Gregory smiled back and continued straightening his desk. "Mort, you are so thoroughly enchanting when you worry so about such things. Of course, call the police. But call the newspapers first. Let them get here before the police. It's always easier that way."

Mort nodded and shuffled away toward the outer office and began to mindlessly make the calls. He just sat there after that and didn't really hear as the press arrived and the police came to investigate and clear the bodies.

The only thing he heard was the voice in his mind. The voice that kept asking him, *How? How can this man command spirits and make them afraid?* The answer didn't come to him. But something else did. For the first time in their association together Mort felt something he never felt before. It had to do with Gregory, his partner, his mentor, his *everything*. He felt something that made him embarrassed to admit, if only to himself, and something that he knew was ridiculous for a man in his position. But he felt it nonetheless, and the feeling began to grow as the carnage was swept away and he was left alone with Kavidas. The feeling was simple, but it was strong. He felt weak, yes, and tired, certainly. But those he could deal with.

The feeling that bothered him was one he had to hide. One that even Gregory could not know about. A feeling he just couldn't shake. He felt *fear.*

Matthew sat at his desk and put his head into his hands. The paperwork was always overwhelming. Now it was almost unbearable. Every interruption was devastating, inasmuch as it took him further away from his goal in clearing the stack off his desk. However, when his secretary told him he had a visitor, and the visitor was Sam Barrett, it was a welcome relief.

"Sam, come in," he said as he clapped Dr. Barrett on the shoulder. "I was hoping I'd hear from you. Did you finish the research on the name? Did it turn out to be Kavidas? Have you confirmed it?" The questions poured out of Matthew's mouth before Dr. Barrett could utter a single answer. Matthew's excitement had been continually growing since their minor breakthroughs had started to yield some information.

"Matthew, I wish I had good news. But I don't. The name doesn't match. It's off by one—his name has an equivalent of 665. So close. I really thought we had it."

Each letter of the Greek alphabet had a numerical equivalent. Their constant testing of prominent names had given them the number of 666 several times. However, those people were all dead. To be so close—only off by one number! That was rare. Usually it was hit or miss.

"There must be some mistake! I know we're right. You have to check it again!" Matthew was dumbfounded and could only shake his head.

"We've checked it, Matt, and rechecked it. It equals 665. There's no doubt about that."

"But we were so sure. It had to be."

"We wanted it to be so," Sam said sadly, "so in our minds we made it so. Gregory Kavidas is just one small number short of the Antichrist. I'm sorry, Matt."

"Sorry, don't be ridiculous. We were just looking for someone to blame. He seemed the most likely target. He was fitting the profile, too."

"I know. What do the reports look like?" Sam gestured with his hand in a sweeping motion to encompass the entire executive area. "You seem to be inundated with them."

For the first time since he'd heard the news, Matthew smiled. "That's putting it mildly. Sam, things are worsening. The vaccine distribution is increasing exponentially. But there's just one problem. The disease is spreading just as fast or even faster than before!"

"Matthew," Sam chided gently, "that's impossible. How can that be true when the vaccine, at the very least, slows down the replication of the virus?"

Matthew went through a stack of papers on his desk and pulled out some statistical information. "Sam, look at this. Look at these numbers. The number of infected mosquitoes is increasing. There are reports of demonic possession and activity all over the country. Homosexuality is increasing again for the first time in 10 years. It seemed like a hiatus, since everyone was afraid of the disease. Now, with the *vaccine*, they aren't afraid anymore. It's fueling the very activity it was meant to abate instead of slowing it down." He had to fight from slamming his hand on the table to emphasize his point.

"Well, we certainly knew that this was going to happen. We just didn't know when." Dr. Barrett reached out and tried to bring Matthew back to reality in his own way. "Besides, your noble goals of bringing a vaccine to the market place to slow the disease or even eradicate it may not be the same as your esteemed colleagues. In fact, you yourself should know that only sick people need drugs." His sardonic smile was not lost on Matthew, who only shook his head.

"Thanks for the perspective. Not that I can forget for a minute that our friendly competitors are all out to profit, as are we, from the sale of drugs. It's just hard to believe that anyone would be so incalculably inhuman as to watch people suffer when they know they could save them. Just to make money? I don't believe that. It's too horrible."

"Matthew," Sam replied soberly, "that's exactly the attitude the world had when Hitler was burning Jews in ovens, roasting them alive. Remember the motto: 'Never again.' Don't be an ostrich. People would watch others rot for money. It's nothing new. And most certainly they would do it for these stakes. It would be hard for anyone to turn down this situation. Win-win. It's almost a no-brainer."

Matthew looked at his friend very carefully and closed his mouth without speaking. Relaying thoughts and ideas to each other without speaking was a common event for both Matthew and Sam. Knowing what the other was thinking had kept them close for years.

"Matthew, there is one thing I want you to do."

Matthew glanced up quickly at the tone of the request, then swiftly turned away. "If it is about Brandon, I know what you're going to say. And I can't do it. I just can't get used to the fact that this man at his side is...well, what would you call it? His boyfriend? The whole thing is taking its toll on me. Sam—"

"Matthew, I wasn't talking about Brandon's lifestyle. You know I've never interfered or commented about that at all. That is something you take up with him. I'm talking about Brandon, the man, the son. The one you've been avoiding at all costs. This man is about to give us the breakthrough we need to uncover a mystery that is plaguing the entire globe. What the man beside him is doing is up to God to remedy. I only know he's helping us, and you're not."

"Me? Not helping? What?" sputtered Matthew indignantly. "Just because I'm not by Brandon's side doesn't mean I'm not doing my part! I'm providing all the help necessary by making Lane Pharmaceutical available and giving—"

"Matt," Sam interrupted, his tone now almost like a father, "I know you're giving everything you have. Everything except yourself. And that's the part Brandon needs right now. He needs you. And even though you are not stopping him from doing his job and playing his part, your distance is hindering his work. You've got to come and see him. See what he's doing! Him and Pano. It's amazing. The things we've learned and the treasure we're uncovering in this writing. How can you stay away?"

Matthew could see the wonder on Sam's face, and his heart yearned to follow him and allow Sam to take him wherever necessary to experience this feeling. But his feet remained rooted to the floor.

"You want me to listen, and I'm too tired. You want me to change, and I tell you I'm too old. You want me to understand, and I'm only confused. I don't even know *where* to go, Sam. Let alone who to see."

Sam took the man's hand in a good-bye gesture and moved toward the door. "You're wrong, Matt. I only want you to *feel*—and you're never too old or too tired for that. Remember how you feel about Brandon. Think about that. And come down to the lab and see the miracle that's being wrought. If you haven't sorted out how you feel by then, maybe the sight of it will make you young again or less tired. But I guarantee you it will make you *feel*." Sam smiled once and left with a tilt of his hat in Matthew's direction.

Several minutes passed before Matthew moved. But when he did, he searched his soul. And for a minute he felt *something*. He didn't know what, and he didn't know how. He just knew it wasn't the numbness that paralyzed him so much lately. The cold feeling of apathy when you fight a war you can't win.

But Sam's talk had left him with one more important thought. Even if you can't win, you can die trying. And that alone will *feel* good.

David looked up from the study he was doing when he heard a noise. Things being as they were, it was increasingly harder to concentrate. Working on sermons was something he used to enjoy and be able to do in the middle of his house or even on the sofa. Now he needed the quiet of his office in the church to shield him from the outside and from distractions. Not only to make him feel safe but to allow the spirit to speak to him and minister to him. To let him know that he wasn't in it alone and that the Lord was on his side.

The door opened quietly, but nevertheless it created a stir. David fought with the muscles in his face and forced them to remain calm. The last thing he wanted was to show fear and alarm every time something moved or he met someone new. He tried to remember the old David, the one who would have been careful to make a good impression and consider this life in front of him precious. *Why, oh, why did I take those times for granted?*

"Preacher, I need help, " the stranger said. The man was shabbily dressed in what looked like terribly worn beach attire. David could smell the brine that still clung to the man, sensing the ocean was the man's only means of bathing. From the thin and gaunt look in the man's eyes, he considered the possibility that the water was also his only means of nourishment.

David's body involuntarily tensed as his mind resented the intrusion of his sanctum. Again, almost mechanically, he ordered his brain to command his muscles into action. He could see his hand being extended and saw the man's relief in that David was not immediately sending him away. David's anger quickly vented as he saw that this man was perhaps tormented or consumed with a problem and he needed help. He was ashamed that he had at first considered asking the man to leave, if only for a split second, because of the man's ragged appearance. Now he could only see the pain, the outward shell that made up this man was suddenly less important than his soul.

386

"What can I do for you, uh, Mr.—?"

"Andrew Williamson, but just call me Andy. Please just call me Andy."

David studied the man's face and could see worry lines and anxiety written all over it. As their hands clasped, David could see Andy intently studying him and felt compelled to return the favor. His eyes, however, could not leave Andy's face. David could see that his appearance was that of a young man—almost a boy—but there was something about the eyes. Something that gave him a feeling of age, or maturity. David felt as if he were being pulled in, and he could see stars and clouds within the calmness he saw in his eyes. The image flashed before his eyes and was gone, and he could sense Andy shaking his hand vigorously. He just couldn't look down or take his eyes away from the man's face.

"I needed a safe place to go, so I came to you," Andy said. "You were the only person I could trust to help me."

The man's speech drifted over to David as he tried to focus on the words. He had heard him say he needed something and waited to see if he wanted food, help, shelter, or money before continuing.

But he was interrupted again by another frightening vision. He saw a large rock formation in an arid climate and could see hundreds or maybe even thousands of men and women entering the cavelike building. He recognized it and tried to remember where it was when the last whispers of the image faded and disappeared. He blinked, and he could feel the cobwebs dissolve and noticed Andy was talking to him again. He tried to remember the details of the place in his vision, but he couldn't. He saw the man looking at him and knew it was his turn for a response.

"You can trust me, friend," David assured as Andy seemed to relax.

"I saw you on TV when they tried to beat you. I felt very bad. I just wanted you to know that before I say anything else." He tried to give David a wan smile, but it was not very effective.

David could only ask himself, *When is the man going to let go of my hand?*

As if in answer, Andy let go of David and looked away. "I just felt you needed some help. I wish I could have given it to you."

David smiled, realizing that to the average person, his encounter would be considered dangerous. "I appreciate your concern, Andy. But I wasn't alone. I'm sure of that. And you should know it, too. I seem to have an invisible bodyguard. God's children are protected, and he is never far away from them." David looked into the young man's eyes again and could see a spark of light, as if the young man recognized and was acknowledging what David referred to.

Andy nodded and took a seat. He looked at David.

Here it comes. Now he'll ask for a place to stay or some money. David tried to stop these thoughts from forming in his mind but knew that his experience would prove him right. What else did they come in and ask for? Advice maybe? He should be so lucky as to get off that easy.

"Pastor, can you keep this for me? It will just be for a little while." Andy pulled out what looked like a ledger, a small book bound in black and sealed with wax. David had never seen anything quite like it before.

"What kind of book is that? How can you read it if the pages are all sealed together? It looks like you had it bound on all sides." His curiosity got the better of him, and he instinctively reached out to grab the tiny volume. The entire thing fit almost in the palm of his hand.

"People are chasing me. You've got to keep this book for me—keep it safe! I will return for it as soon as I can." The young man's plea sounded urgent.

David had to swallow a smile. *Imagine that,* he thought. *This guy lives like he's homeless and certainly smells like he lives outdoors, and he has himself being chased for a book.* David sat back and waited for what he felt would be the only logical explanation. It must involve the organized crime or the mafia. It had just the right clandestine feeling, mixed with a heart-wrenching hard-luck story that made the mob so infamous.

He decided he was going about things all wrong. He should have just started off by offering the man a meal. Then he would have been spared the hard-luck story, one that was becoming more unbelievable with each passing moment.

"How about a bite to eat?" David asked kindly. "You look as if you might be hungry." He gestured with his hand and moved toward the door that led to the church kitchen.

The young man looked over his shoulder as if he was being chased and went in the opposite direction. "I know it sounds hard to believe, but it isn't organized crime who is after me. It's something or someone much worse. They don't want me here, and I can't stay too long. Just say you'll watch over my book and keep it safe until I come back."

"When will that be?" asked David guardedly. The last thing he needed was more trouble. Whoever was after this book, if someone was actually trying to get it, they were certainly having a profound impact on Andy.

"I don't know. You may see me before I need it—you may not. But when I am ready for the book, I'll let you know. Keep it with you until then. Never let go of it, please!" Andy moved to go and found himself looking once more at David, meeting his eyes. "I have demons of my own chasing me."

David wanted to stop the young man from saying anything else and wanted to let him know that he had no intention of keeping the book in his pocket for an indeterminate period of time.

But Andy didn't give him the chance. With his last words he was quickly out the door...before David even saw him leave. David could only contemplate the last words the young man had uttered before he disappeared. *"I have demons of my own chasing me."*

David sat back in his chair and pondered the bizarre encounter. A homeless person with a priceless relic? Demons chasing him? That much David was too familiar with. Drug addicts and other bedfellows had been pushed together with the horror of Toi-VAX. Stranger things had happened before; that much he knew.

With a sigh he resolved to carry the book around, at least for a while, and see if the man came back. "So I'll wait a week," he said aloud, "and if he doesn't come back, maybe I'll open it up. After all, he didn't say I couldn't read it."

He raised his eyebrows as he stuck the book into his pocket and chided himself for being foolish enough to say such a thing out loud. *Now you're going to open up his book—the one you think involves a silly story about being chased?*

David moved back to resume his study. Before he continued, however, he looked up a verse from Romans and read it several times: "All things work together for good, to those who love God, to those who are called according to his purpose." Now he was ready to continue with his sermon. He smiled again. When would he learn that with God there are no coincidences?

David arrived at the Lane warehouse laboratory that had been converted into their temporary headquarters. Pano and Brandon had been conducting their research here, and the rest of the lab was partitioned off in anticipation of some miracle or breakthrough that would necessitate its use.

Security was tight, and even though the guards knew David by sight and knew that he was a close friend of both Brandon and Matthew, he was still required to show his badge and go through the drill. Though he was normally in a hurry and was bothered by such menial chores, he was glad to go through the procedure. He knew it was necessary.

Seeing the infiltration of *Masterlink* and similar controls being placed into society, David was formulating a plan for their own secret police force and underground network. It was becoming increasingly obvious that an alternative currency was going to be necessary, and strongholds or safe houses were going to have to be strategically located to house those who opposed the wave of change that was being forced upon the confused globe. Frequently thought of as an alarmist, David had to refrain from crying out to those around him as he observed the indicators that led him to believe that soon Christians would no longer be safe or protected by humanity, morality, or even the good old U.S. Constitution.

But the changes that were being wrought around him were the most insidious and damaging type possible inasmuch as they were slow, logical to most, and virtually undetectable to an apathetic world that thought only of today. Lately, even for David looking beyond tomorrow was no easy task.

Brandon and Pano looked like they had slept in their clothes, and both of the young men showed serious signs of facial stubble. They barely noticed David's arrival, so engrossed were they in their scrolls, parchments, and computer terminals. It was almost anachronistic as David looked at technology's finest laser printers and computer screens amidst the writings of an ancient world.

"What news have you found today? Anything new that will help us understand our mystery man Kavidas?"

Both men visibly jumped as they heard David's voice, and they smiled as they recognized him and his presence registered.

"Ti kaneis, file mou," Pano said in greeting as he went back to his work. *What's happening, my friend?*

Brandon took a break long enough to shake David's hand before looking back to his screen. "I'm afraid we haven't had time to think of Kavidas, David. We're onto something else that's astounding and monumental. We can't even sleep!"

Brandon's tone belied his own words as David tried to understand. He could see the fatigue and assumed that sleep deprivation would account for the lack of enthusiasm Brandon was showing. But his words were intriguing David enough to know that Brandon was excited; he was just too tired to show it.

"What have you found? Something else for Barrett to look up—or should I say dig up?" David smiled as he waited for one of the men's attention. He could see that they were not only engrossed but consumed with the materials before them.

"David, I don't mean to be rude, but we're trying to piece things together here. Look at this, and then we'll talk." He could hear Brandon's fingers clicking rapidly on the keys as the printer whirred to life.

He walked over and helped himself to the printout and moved over toward the sofa that obviously had doubled as someone's bed. He glanced over to see if anyone would mind and realized that no one was thinking of him, so he sat down and began to read.

Brandon's log: We've made an extraordinary find, and Sam is beside himself as we tell him about these people. Canaan was one swinging place! No rules, no laws that we can see—anything goes! People complain that the sexual revolution changed the world. They should read some of these stories! They put romance novels and pornography to shame. My father has often quoted Solomon saying, "There is nothing new under the sun," and these writings confirm it. What we see around us today was more than widespread in the past. It was commonplace. People are sleeping with everyone and everything they come across. It almost makes me blush.

Sam wants us to push for some information that will make the world take notice—information that will make all the other scrolls found in the past make sense. If we find this—okay. But it is not what we're looking for. I feel there is something here that is of real significance and consequence. I only hope we can find it.

David looked up at Brandon and raised his eyebrow in consternation. The log was not only personal; it was informative. He could see the men were still busy with their scrolls so he read on.

Today we found out that the Canaanites had a propensity for both sheep and goats. They had a very advanced society. If the scroll wasn't so old, you would think it was today—they had credit, bartering—even loans secured by goods. If it wasn't barbaric in some ways, you would think it was an advanced culture.

We're somewhat confused with this section on home remedies. It seems to be an old wives' tale version of how to get rid of common problems. We were waiting to see if any of the problems of that day are still here today. We wanted to skip this section and move on. But something made us read through it and take note. Not that we were interested in curing the "vapors" or getting rid of warts. It's just that the culture was fascinating and apparently plagued with many of the same problems that we have today. One specifically that is hounding our world even now...we are so excited to have found it that we can hardly sleep. It's almost as if it is a miracle—we would have skipped right over it! But Pano and I are certain of one thing: AIDS was alive and well in the Canaanite society. The symptoms are all there—down to the most significant detail! What's more—I think they developed a primitive cure!

David stopped reading as if his eyes hit a brick wall. A cure? His heart leaped, and he looked back over toward the two men. Like mad scientists working away, they scribbled and wrote notes as they worked on their computers. David had no idea what Pano's background was, but he knew that Brandon knew his way around a laboratory and was certainly familiar with serology and toxicology due to his father's background and being an integral part of the business. But what could inspire the devotion that they were giving to their research? He knew that Brandon wasn't a chemist and couldn't be working on a vaccine or a *cure!* He wanted to jump up and ask a million questions, but his thoughts and his eyes were riveted to this personal log.

We've finally sorted through the remedy section. It almost sounds as if the disease was considered an honor—or a gift to their god. They've linked the disease to a native goat that was in the area, which we've concluded can only be the ibex goat. The writings have some pictures that show this noble-looking creature but not in the context of the disease. They worshiped the image as a god and apparently used it in many of their rituals. If the script is to be believed, and if it is accurate (and we have no doubt that it is) the animal transmitted the disease to the people during sexual intercourse. They developed symptomology in an identical fashion to our modern-day AIDS. The only difference is, the people didn't die! They were looked upon as "touched" by the god and were revered and even cared for as royalty.

The most interesting part is how they effected what they call the χουρα or the cure. It almost sounds the same as what we know about the Toi-VAX vaccine from Rainbow. Isn't it uncanny that Kavidas would know this ancient remedy? Almost as if he had knowledge from some historical source? Can it be there are other scrolls or documents that have been unearthed with this information? It is possible, but it has never been made known. Pano is even now reviewing what we have translated to see if it is correct, and if so, we are ready to test this animal, which has been overlooked in the crusade against AIDS, to see if we may have a serological donor to end this plague.

David had to catch his breath and physically force himself to relax. He felt as if he were running up and down the halls of the building. He was perspiring, and his heart was racing. The information he had just read could change the course of the world. And to think that it was stumbled on by accident. *Correction, Lord, we know that there are no accidents here, and if Brandon has discovered a potential cure, we know it is from you and that you have directed his path.*

He walked over to Brandon and handed the sheets back. Now he understood their tireless efforts to uncover this mystery.

"Brandon, you and Pano do need to sleep. You can't keep this up forever."

Brandon smiled at David and walked over to Pano and put his arm around his avid helper. "Once we finish our work here, we will pass it on to others who can continue our work. But till then, we won't waste any time sleeping. Each time we close our eyes, we know that thousands die. We are in a race, and we want to win."

David smiled back and quietly left the room so they could finish their work. He closed the door behind him and looked out at the world with a different gleam in his eye. He felt renewed. He had once again been given hope by his redeemer. With what he read today, he could face tomorrow, knowing that the battle was not his alone.

Deanna left the church office and went directly to the furniture store. The pastor had given her permission to leave for lunch early, make the deposit, and then try to buy her furnishings on sale. She'd read about the sale that morning, but knew that Mondays were the busiest day in the church office, sorting out the offerings from the day before.

She arrived at the warehouse and was glad she came when she did. It seemed like hundreds of people were all converging to take advantage of an actual bonafide sale. She was even more surprised and pleased to find a selection that she liked and could afford.

Making it to the cashier was no small effort, and the line was extraordinarily long. Still, she was pleased the pastor was understanding about her missing work for longer than usual, and she was happy to finally have the sofa she wanted. She took out her credit card and handed it pleasantly to the girl at the register.

The girl looked worn and somewhat irritated, but Deanna could understand. With these kinds of lines, anyone would be frazzled. Several seconds passed as the girl rang up the sale from the ticket Deanna received in the warehouse.

Deanna searched her purse for a pen and looked up to see the girl picking up the phone to call the manager.

"Is there a problem?" she asked.

"Just one moment, Mrs. McKinney. I'm having my supervisor check your credit card."

Deanna felt herself getting annoyed but tried to control her temper. The girl was just doing her job. Deanna knew her credit was impeccable, so it had to be the volume of the transactions. Perhaps the phone line was down or the computer off-line. She knew these things happened.

"Is it going to take long?" she asked pointedly. "I've already been here for too long. Look at these lines."

"I know, ma'am. It should be just a minute." The girl took the time to clear some of the odds and ends from her register and stack up her blank receipts.

The phone rang, and Deanna sighed in frustration. "Well, it's about time!"

The girl ignored the remark and answered the phone mechanically. She nodded several times, picked up the credit card, and confirmed some of the information, then looked over at Deanna as if she were scrutinizing her. She nodded again and then hung up the phone.

"Well?" Deanna asked quickly, starting to get embarrassed by the groans and moans of the line behind her.

"I'm sorry, ma'am, but this credit card is no good. I'm afraid I have to confiscate it."

"Confiscate it? That's ridiculous!" Deanna reached behind the counter and tried to grab the card.

The girl was quicker and snatched it out of reach. "Security!" the girl called loudly. "Security at register three!"

Deanna felt her face begin to turn deep red as she saw security coming toward her. She had never been so humiliated and still didn't know why.

"Ma'am, do you have another credit card, or would you like to pay cash?" The girl's voice was threatening and was backed up by two men who now stood beside her.

"I want my credit card back right now, young lady! What is wrong with it? You have no right to take it."

The girl looked over at the security guard and motioned for him to take over. "Ma'am, it is nothing personal. This has been happening a lot lately. This card is no longer valid because it isn't registered with *Masterlink*. We are instructed by the bank to take possession of the card. If you like, you can use the phone over at the manager's desk and apply for *Masterlink* now."

"You mean that since I'm not connected to that horrible organization I can no longer use my credit card?" Deanna was astonished. She looked behind her to see if there was any support from the crowd in line. She was disappointed to see that there was not.

"If you have another card, lady, or if you want to pay by cash or check, we'll be glad to help you. Otherwise, go to the manager's office and connect your card to the *Masterlink* system. It's the only way."

"No, I will not join up with *Masterlink*. I have no intention of ever doing so!" She turned to the customer behind her and tried to plead for help. "You don't have that *Masterlink* card, do you? Tell these people how ridiculous it is!"

The man sneered at her and looked as if he was ready to push her aside. "Come on, lady. You're holding up the line. *Masterlink* has been coming for a long time. It's not something new. It's been in the papers, and all the banks have told us that you have to register. You're wasting time. Pay up or get lost." He crossed his arms and looked up into the air as if disgusted.

"Don't you know what that *Masterlink* stands for?" Deanna argued. "It's a terrible group and it's anti-Christian. How could any Christian join it with any conscience at all?" She felt ready to cry, but the tears welling up in her eyes did nothing to move the man behind her to pity.

"It's easy, lady. You want to eat; you join this group. You Christians with all your principles. Let's see how long you hold out when you're hungry." He pushed her aside.

She was aghast when the girl behind the register voided her transaction and proceeded to help the rude man. The two security guards walked away, and she was left there alone, as if she didn't matter. No one bothered her any longer, but they dismissed her as if she wasn't there. She wanted to scream at them and tell them that she counted and that she was important. But she knew no one would listen, and it would make no difference.

She walked out of the store dejected and depressed and couldn't help but wonder if it were possible that any one person or group could make a difference.

When she got home she told her husband what had happened. Without any hesitation and against her wishes, he dialed the toll-free number and immediately linked them to *Masterlink*'s main database. They were only too happy to advise him that they would reissue cards immediately to him and his wife, and they regretted the inconvenience of the day's incident.

Brandon sat back as he waited for the results of the initial testing that was being done using the ibex goat and the information they had gleaned from the *Genesis Apocryphon*. The chemists and the science team had worked around the clock much like Brandon and Pano had done to see what they could discover in a relatively short period of time. Brandon felt as if they were all working on a revised version of the Manhattan Project. Racing against time and working around the clock to beat the enemy to the right formula.

He just wasn't sure who the enemy was—AIDS or Kavidas. *Or,* he thought, with a shudder of revulsion, *are the two of them intertwined?*

Matthew listened to the opening arguments from several of the scientists from the lab and looked over to Brandon and smiled. Matthew had been quick to praise Brandon for the work he and Pano had accomplished, and Brandon knew that regardless of the outcome, Matthew was proud of the efforts he had made. He only hoped it would be enough.

"And in conclusion," the man reported, "the ibex contains a unique inducer that inhibits production of the HIV virus. In our test so far, it is possible that we could harvest some of the inducer, which we've labeled Zeta-Opsonin, and effectively create an inoculant."

"Will it reverse the effects on someone already ravaged by the disease?" Brandon knew from his reading of the scroll that they had fed parts of the ibex's thymus gland to an affected person, and it triggered an autonomic response that affected the symptomology. He knew, however, that there was hardly enough thymus gland to go around and inoculate a waiting world.

"We are currently attempting to implant the harvested Zeta-Opsonin into a host cell that will generate a response in humans similar to the one described in your medical brief. In answer to your question, we think that it will."

Brandon nodded and turned toward his father as the men regrouped in their presentation.

"Dad, it seems to me that Kavidas knew all along that the Opsonin had to be implanted into a thymus host to cultivate the cure. Why would he have used the simian harvest when he would have known that the ibex would have averted the vaccine altogether? He could have come up with the cure himself." Brandon shook his head and looked down at his hands, grappling with the enormity of what they had just accomplished.

"Brandon, you are assuming that your goals and those of our inestimable Mr. Kavidas are the same. I can assure you, they are not. You are also assuming that he knew about the information in the scrolls. That is also something derived entirely from supposition. In any case, Mr. Kavidas used the AIDS crisis to catapult him to power. I really don't think money was his motivating factor; he seems to have plenty of that. Humanity and the end of suffering were not on his agenda."

Brandon pushed his head back and allowed it to hit the couch with a thud. He couldn't comprehend that anyone would have access to this type of information and willingly conceal it to the detriment of an entire race— or an entire world.

"Mr. Lane, we are ready to finish the presentation?" the scientist said to Matthew, interrupting Brandon's thoughts.

"Thank you, Mark. We're ready." The men assembled around a large easel while Mark, clearly the leader of the science team, went back to the computer to illustrate his point.

"You will see in this model that the Zeta-Opsonin harvested from the ibex can be germinated in a human host medium, as displayed here, and the result is the release of the cascading endorphin that creates the symptomology change. The result is so fantastic that it reverts to a complete change in the recipient's RNA. This creates a ripple effect, as you can see here, that causes the DNA to restabilize."

The computer-generated simulation was not only fascinating to Brandon as a scientist but also as a participant in what he now knew to be a miracle.

Mark leaned over and had his colleagues demonstrate the various stages in prints on the easel so that the process could be more slowly introduced.

"What actually causes the effect, Mark," interjected Matthew, "the Zeta-Opsonin or the cascading endorphin?"

Brandon nodded at the question but realized that things were beginning to pass into the realm of the scientific mind and areas that he had never gone to before.

"Actually, Mr. Lane, we've tested them both separately, and for some reason they do not work independently. The endorphin is latent in the human host, but if it is not activated by the Zeta-Opsonin, it has no effect. So in truth, the Zeta-Opsonin Endorphin as a whole is necessary for any real change to take place."

Matthew nodded, and Brandon turned his head toward the easel in shock. He repeated the words in his mind and read them on the board in disbelief.

"Doctor," he called out to Mark excitedly, "what made you call the Opsonin a Zeta-Opsonin as opposed to anything else?"

Matthew looked at him perplexed. The question was hardly scientific and seemed relatively innocuous for such an occasion.

"Well, in our research, we'd exhausted several opsonin possibilities. We started with Alpha, and when we began researching this new one, we were up to Zeta. It's simple really. No specific reason. Why do you ask?"

Matthew looked as if he was about to ask the very same question when Brandon moved over to the easel. He motioned for a marker and received one from one of the technicians who were looking on.

"Dad, don't you see it! Look!" He moved over to the chart, which had the words *Zeta-Opsonin Endorphin* clearly marked. He took the marker and underlined the first letter of each. "Don't you see what it means?"

His excitement would have been contagious…except that the men in the room clearly didn't comprehend what he was saying. They turned, puzzled, to each other.

Finally Matthew broke the silence. "Brandon, what are we supposed to be seeing? What are you trying to say?"

Brandon didn't reply but wrote the letters for himself. "Look—look at the letters." He waved his hand to illustrate his point and then underlined his work. "See—ZOE—that's it!" He put the marker down and brushed his hands as if he had just completed a major discovery.

"That's what?" Mark asked tentatively, looking at Matthew to see if recognition was dawning on his boss's face.

Frustrated, Brandon took the marker again. Ζωη "Zoé. The letters of the cure spell the Greek word *zoé*." He smiled happily and turned back to the men with confidence.

"Is that good?" asked Mark hesitantly.

Brandon came over and put his hand on the man's arm and smiled. "It is very good, Doctor. Something that you may have done by accident but obviously was meant on purpose. You see, the word *zoé* means *life*. And that is just what this will bring. We will bring life to a dying world."

Matthew nodded and smiled to himself. *Yes, my son, we will bring life. But not just for the bodies of this dying world but for their spirits also. This zoe, as you call it, will be the name of our version of Toi-VAX. And you are right. There are no accidents.*

FIFTEEN

Any containment strategy relying upon
the eventuality of a cure for AIDS
is delusional.
Zidovudine

Scholars place the first recorded plague brought upon man during the XVIII-XX Dynasties of the Egyptian Kings of either Amenhotep II or Ramses I-II, reigning from 1570-1150 BC. The plague was a visitation of God on the various gods of the Egyptians to break the will of the Pharaoh and to bring about the release from slavery of God's people, Israel. The Greek word for *plague* literally means a blow or a lash, implying punishment or chastisement for sin or disobedience. The number of deaths was never recorded.

Epidemics have been recorded in China since 224 BC and have destroyed entire populations throughout the ages. One such epidemic killed an estimated 100 million people in the Middle East, Europe, and Asia during the sixth century. The Bubonic plague, or Black Death, an infectious disease brought on by fleas hosting on rodents, turns the flesh purple during the victim's last hours due to respiratory failure, precipitated by inflamed lymph nodes (buboes) that spill in and infect the lymphatic system and the bloodstream. The victim always dies within a day that the symptoms develop. In the Middle Ages, the Black Death claimed the lives of 75 million people.

In 1987 there were up to 10 million people infected with HIV worldwide. The World Health Organization accurately predicted the infection to extend to 200 million by 2001, and according to the surgeon general, the pandemic conservatively annihilated well over 100 million persons by that date. Capable of continuous mutation, the AIDS virus is certainly the worst plague of all time.

Rainbow's capitulation over the AIDS vaccine market was so easy that it came as a shock to the public. The conservative Florida newspaper, the *Southern Sentinel*, claimed that Rainbow's Toi-VAX, with its skyrocketing, tenacious grip on the world's AIDS drug market, suddenly gave way to Lane's ZOÉ serum with few objections. The newspaper cited Toi-VAX as an innocuous, corrupt vaccine with bizarre side effects that clearly outweighed any clinical remedy, while heralding Lane's ZOÉ as the cure for the epidemic.

The paper's rival, the *Miami Star*, considered by conservatives as friendly toward Rainbow, construed the coverage by the *Southern Sentinel* to be malicious and vindictive, labeling it retaliation for the recent bad press given the Christian church. Rumors persisted, however, that numerous lawsuits against Rainbow were being settled out of court, and Rainbow's interest in halting the spread of disease was waning while they reviewed their corporate purpose and restructured their assets.

By mid-summer, more than six months after the drug's release, all of the world's Toi-VAX supplies were recalled, fueling the nagging rumor that Rainbow Pharmaceuticals was about to be sold.

Matthew and Brandon held a victory banquet at their home for every employee and research associate connected with the discovery of ZOÉ. Over 230 guests, including many of the *Koinonos* movement, rejoiced in the hallmark occasion.

Only Dr. Barrett's absence marred the feeling of perfection they all felt about the evening. But even Brandon, who was against Sam's leaving, saw the significance of what he was doing. With the continued harassment of Christians and those who refused to follow in the wave of *Masterlink*, Matthew knew how important it was to establish a safe house, one where believers could flee to for protection and peace in the coming times. To this end, Dr. Barrett was negotiating from Israel to move his archaeological team into Jordan. With Matthew's financial backing, a large-scale restoration was to be done under the guise of a dig so that Jordan's government would not refuse entry of supplies, materials, and laborers. They were hoping that Jordan would be so busy counting the money that was coming in that they would not notice many of the workers were not leaving.

Matthew knew that there would be opposition to this plan, and he knew that the ancient fortress at Petra was not impregnable. Still, it was a place of refuge that was entirely defensible due to the sheer geography of its location. And the name meant so much. *Petra*—"rock." What better place to make a stand during a crisis than on a rock, whose foundation, by virtue of the people that would be harbored there, was Jesus?

As for the early preparation, Matthew would not be dissuaded. Anyone who argued was given a quick lesson in history and was reminded of what Hitler did to the Jewish people of Germany and the surrounding countries. This time, Matthew knew, the Christians would be the target. Even with all the Holocaust memorials and the remembrance of the atrocities committed by the Nazis, Matthew knew that the phrase *Never again* was not entirely true. History has a way of repeating itself. He was going to make sure some of the people were safe.

But I can't think about that tonight, Matthew thought. *As much as I miss Sam being here, we have a lot to celebrate and even more to be thankful for.*

Lane's caterers stood on the sidelines and observed the festivities as the service staff joyfully distributed the food and soft drinks to the guests. Earlier Matthew announced that it would be a celebration despite the fact that sociological changes were occurring all around them that signaled a great challenge to the Christian. He knew that the guests would take this as nothing more than just a token speech, but he said it nonetheless. His job was going to be done, regardless of who listened. *Let him who has ears to hear, hear!*

After dinner, Matthew directed his butler to discreetly summon Brandon, David, and Pano to his library for a brief discussion. Matthew nodded to David to open the casual meeting with a short word of prayer, then motioned for the small group to relax on the sofas.

Matthew opened the conversation. "Brandon, David and myself are in agreement that the Lord has enabled us to discover ZOÉ to combat the evil forces of Satan that are using Rainbow to manipulate and dupe the masses into a false hope or security with their alleged cure. Their first line of defense was Toi-VAX, which, thank God, has been recalled, but keep in mind it has served them well. It provided the medium to achieve world recognition and power. We estimate that Rainbow's profits were over 9.5 billion dollars, while any malpractice claim settlements will be borne by their insurance carriers, resulting in a windfall accumulation of assets.

"Further, the profits from the installation of the *Masterlink* system are incalculable. Simple extrapolation dictates that those assets are now being redirected to another theater of operation. And so, here we are. The battle isn't over, and we're now on the offensive again." He smiled as the men nodded to concur with his military analogy.

"Any ideas as to where Kavidas will be going?" Brandon interjected.

Matthew shook his head. "Only conjecture at this point. Perhaps one of the member nations of the EC in Europe."

"Makes sense," Brandon conceded.

"If I may," David inserted sarcastically. "What I consider to be their *finest* legacy is the opening of the door to the demonic through their vaccine program. They'll probably sell off Rainbow to transfer their assets and move on, thereby fading from the public eye. But to think that the untold thousands, if not millions, who have received Toi-VAX that could potentially host members of the demonic world is tantamount to methodically placing little time bombs throughout the earth. Or maybe I should say 'methodically placing eggs' that will later hatch into monsters. We're talking about a serious matter here."

"David, not so heavy," Brandon warned. "This is a night of celebration, remember? We're obviously here to plan for the future, not to predict it."

David nodded. "You're right. We'll continue to trust the Lord to direct us. Meanwhile, we need to go full tilt on implementing our *Koinonos* system—we cannot chance any regression just because Kavidas and Stein have temporarily suspended their operation at Rainbow. They cannot be trusted."

"Agreed," Matthew said with a smile. "The only question is, do we follow them and continue the fight or try and oppose them from here? Or—" he began hesitantly, gazing at Pano and Brandon—"do we rest on our laurels, market our new ZOÉ, and pass the mantel on to others? Are we ready to relax and get on with our own lives?"

"Dad, it isn't as if we've been shouldering the entire weight of the world," Brandon began. "We've only done what we had to do. And what we will have to continue to do. How can we do less?"

"I am ready to go," Pano said in his increasingly better English.

"Dad, we want to go over and help Sam. We've done what we can here. We want to go together and be where the action is."

The men looked each other in the eye as Brandon raised his glass.

Clink!

The glass struck Pano's and he smiled. Matthew paused as the scene was exchanged. Clearly Brandon and Pano's recent collaboration was not at an end. He could never get used to his son's lifestyle, nor could he agree with it. Yet somehow life went on.

"You realize the area is not just where the action will be," Matthew warned, "but also where the danger will be. We aren't redecorating a condo, you know!"

David cracked a smile at that and winked conspiratorially at Matthew. Matthew knew David understood why he was upset— at the prospect of Brandon's departure as well as the company he was taking along.

"Of course there will be danger, but there will be danger here, too," Brandon said. "What we will try and accomplish in secret, someone has to organize here. We need to develop refuge areas in our own country as well. We aren't going to fit everyone in Petra. Besides, Dad, you know how I feel about the Middle East—why else do you think I bothered to learn Greek and Hebrew? My heart is there. I don't know why yet, but I know that I should be there, too. While Pano helps in the restoration, I'm going to begin storing food and other tradeable goods. We all know that very soon we won't be able to use money the way we used to. All of that is coming to an end."

He chuckled at the irony as he realized that Kavidas made 9.5 billion on Toi-VAX and then instituted a system which you had to subscribe to in order to use credit—and it appeared that it would be eliminating the need for cash. So what do they do with the profits from ZOÉ?

"So what's so funny?" David asked curiously.

"I guess I was wondering," Brandon said, "how we were going to spend all the money we're going to make from ZOÉ if we don't subscribe to *Masterlink*?"

Matthew laughed and walked over to his son and put his arm around his shoulder. "Brandon, in spite of how you think I feel at times, you—and Pano—have made me very proud with your accomplishments. Let's not worry about how we're going to spend money we didn't earn yet. We have plenty to do setting up the refuge centers. That will keep a lot of cash going out. But in the meantime—let's rejoin our guests, shall we," he suggested while gesturing to Brandon to lead the way out. "We've talked enough about the world's problems tonight. I want us to shout and glorify God in how he blessed us with the wonderful gift of ZOÉ. And how he has given us another beautiful gift. Each other."

Three hours later, David sat in the pastor's office, preparing his sermon for Sunday. Focusing on homiletics late at night was difficult for any preacher and even more so for David. Battling the forces of Rainbow, when added to the uncertainty of the future, raised his anxiety level to a new height.

At times like this, his memory played the negative tapes that brought sorrow. He thought of Krissy's death and Louie's betrayal once again. A corrupt vaccine and the advent of *Redisearch* progressing to *Masterlink*. Then images of Kavidas and Stein laughing at his feeble attempts to unmask them.

Who are you kidding, David? he thought. *These evil personalities cannot be beat. At best, you've won a battle, but you'll lose the war.* He folded his arms on top of his desk, then laid his head down to ease the tension in his mind and repeated aloud, "At best, we'll win a battle, but we'll lose the war."

"David."

Lifting his head and opening his eyes, David looked at the young man standing in front of him. "Oh, hello, Andy." David looked over at the clock and noticed it was just a little past midnight. At the same time his hand went involuntarily to his pocket to check on the book he had been given. "How did you get in? I thought I locked the—"

"Don't trouble yourself, David. I've come to encourage you."

"I can use it, Andy, but don't you think it's rather late in the evening?" David grumped. He struggled not to scold the young man for barging in unannounced like this, especially when his soul was so overtaxed with worry, but he decided to withhold any criticism until a more convenient time.

He recalled several reports about the newcomer and wondered how such a person could purport to be so spiritual and encouraging when he projected the image of being aimlessly irresponsible. He had no job. He had no home. He had no car. He dressed shabbily and appeared unkempt with no family ties whatsoever. He was a drifter who mysteriously plopped himself into David's ministry to mooch off the congregation, pure and simple. David scratched his head and suddenly realized, *This is a mission ministry. People like this are drawn to your church. It is not a mega-church that offers a superstructure that attracts professionals; it is a mission church that reaches out to street people and the downcast.* "Thanks for the reminder, Lord," he whispered with a chuckle.

"Have a seat, Andy," he added in contrition. "Don't tell me that you're here to collect your book. What happened? They give up the chase?"

"I know you're troubled about so many things," he began softly as he sat in a chair, "but you should not be. The Lord is going to protect you." He seemed unconcerned about David's remark and ignored the question completely.

David suppressed a snicker, then once again willfully commanded himself to show respect to Andy as a person and as a person who needs Christ. "I know that, and I'm glad that you're such an exhorter—I can use your support and prayers." He walked around his desk and set his hand on Andy's shoulder. "I didn't mean to neglect your needs. How can I help you? Do you have enough money to meet your expenses? Are you eating regularly? Do you need any medical attention?"

The man smiled in such a way that caught David by surprise. "David, this isn't about me. This is about you. I've been sent to help you."

David's knees weakened, and a jolt of fear came over him. He returned to his chair. "What do you mean you've been sent, Andy? Sent by whom?"

With a dismissive wave of the hand, Andy signaled David to silence. He reached over and picked up David's Bible, then turned to the Book of Daniel. "Here in chapters 9 and 11..." Then he flipped to the Gospel of Matthew. "And in chapter 24, the prophecy is written. It is beginning to unfold before your eyes. Kavidas and Stein are the people you suspect them to be, and they are described here. John's Revelation discloses their destiny, but until that time, the earth will go through a great transformation under their control."

Disbelief swept over David. He wiped the beads of perspiration on his brow. "You speak with such authority, Andy. Who are you, anyway?" David stared again at the young man's eyes, telling himself that there was something different about this man. That much he had always known. But to look at him! He looked as if he would be happier on a surfboard, riding on the waves instead of being here now. Was that part of the act?

The man walked over to David. "Let's just say I'm a messenger. One who is always being chased but one who is sent to give you a better understanding of what is happening now—and a glimpse of the future."

"The future? You know about such things?" David asked incredulously.

"These are perilous times when God is going to raise up gifted people to discern the course of events and to warn his people. As for you, the Lord has chosen you for a special purpose."

"Now I'm really getting scared. I haven't the strength to fight against these things."

"You need not be troubled, for the Lord your God will be with you and your family wherever you go," Andy assured. He placed his hand on David's temples to allow his suppressed emotions to rise to the surface then revealed to David the key to many of the mysteries that had been troubling him.

Overcome with a mixture of anxiety and fear, coupled with doubts, David dropped his head into his hands and started sobbing. Seconds later, he felt the oppression vanish as if by divine intervention. He lifted his head and saw the man standing in front of him, praying. David's heart raced as he suddenly realized the presence of a supernatural being. Here was a being that radiated light, whose very presence brought peace and joy.

He looked again at Andy's eyes and could see in them the mixture of antiquity and eternity, forever balanced and intertwined. How did he not see it before? Was it because he only noticed the outside of this man? Could those ragged beach clothes have masked the attributes of this creature that was in the form of a man, right before his very eyes? He sat there gaping as his mind readied itself to receive a revelation, while his senses basked in the light that the angel now cast off.

Twenty minutes later, the mystical person walked out of David's office as mysteriously as he came in.

Another hour elapsed before David sorted the visit out in his head. He reached into his pocket and withdrew the gift Andy had left behind. Only now it was no longer just a book to him but a sign. He knew the Lord had a purpose in leaving it with him, and the excitement of knowing that purpose spurred him on. The seal was broken and the sides no longer looked like bindings. In essence, it was almost the same as the article he carried with him the day before. Now he knew the message was for him.

He reverently opened the book and saw several pages of maps. He recognized them instantly, since many of them were places that *Koinonos* was starting as refuge areas. He could see Petra clearly marked and knew that God's message was clear for the ancient city: a last stand outpost. He gazed lovingly on the pages of cities marked clearly as places for the remnant to gather and escape the coming madness.

The last page of the book was blank except for a name written very carefully on it in bold script. David's heart felt a chill as he gazed upon the name and felt a momentary stab of panic. *Gregory A. Kavidas.*

His initial reaction was that the book belonged to Gregory, and perhaps he already knew the locations of their secret camps. But he quickly realized that Andy would have warned him differently—let him know that things are not always as safe as they seem.

No, he knew—he could *feel*—that this name was here for a different reason. Maybe only for confirmation of their suspicions or to let him know that they had not seen the last of this man. For whatever reason he was chosen, he knew that the other members of his group would also benefit from this knowledge. One of them would know what other message the angel sent this night.

With the book's message out—it was only an ordinary vessel again. Its divine purpose had been spent, so it was now nothing but pages bound with wax. David laughed as he threw the book in the air and caught it in his right hand. Flakes of wax chipped off in his hand, and he could smell the faint scent of coconut on them. *Surfer's wax!* He could see how creative God can be—wax as the holding tank of the information he had chosen to give to David.

Even so, Lord—use me!

"Are you saying Andy was an angelic being when all the while the church thought he was a homeless person?" Kathy exclaimed when David told her of his spiritual encounter. She plugged in the electric coffeepot and sat down at the table. It was obvious this would not be an ordinary breakfast event.

David nodded. "He had to be. Apart from invoking a wonderful spirit of peace upon me, he knew all about Kavidas, Stein, *Masterlink*, and all sorts of things."

Kathy's radar lit off. "What sort of things? Don't hide anything from me," she demanded.

"I'm not sure you can hear this now," he replied after a minute or so.

"Let's hear it, David."

"We'll wait for Matthew. I already called him—he's on his way."

By the time they finished their second cup of coffee, Matthew arrived. He went directly to a vacant chair as he waved consent for a cup of coffee and a toasted bran muffin. "What's happened, David?" he started impatiently.

David reached into his shirt pocket and pulled out a piece of paper. "I scribbled some quick notes after my visit with the...*new man* in our church last night."

Matthew shot a look at Kathy and blinked in wonder. "Would you repeat that, David?"

Fumbling with the note, David replied, "I had a visit from a mysterious man last night, or maybe I should say a *being* who looked like a man. Maybe he was an angel. I don't know, but he sure had a lot to say."

Matthew slugged down a mouthful of coffee. "Like what?"

David glanced at Kathy, then spread the note out on the table. "He said a terrible evil force—like during the time of the Babylonian King Nebuchadnezzar—is presently on the rise. It is going to be a dreadful scourge upon mankind, and Kavidas and Stein are the selected vessels to both initiate and carry on this work until the Holy One, Jesus Christ, puts an end to their reign."

"We're going into the *tribulation* period?" Matthew gulped.

"No. Not yet. This is just the *prelude* you might say. Like Noah's shipbuilding period before the Flood came. A grace period for people to turn to the Lord before the Tribulation period arrives, I guess."

"Oh, my!" Kathy blanched.

410

David extended his arm and clutched Kathy's hand and continued. "Soon Rainbow Pharmaceuticals and *Masterlink* will be sold off, and their financial holdings will be diversified worldwide so they cannot be traced. Then they will go into hiding, only to emerge elsewhere under assumed names so that God's purpose can be fulfilled. There is nothing anybody on earth can do to stop them. These events are fixed in God's timetable. *Masterlink* will be the worldwide financial system that will enable Kavidas to exercise ultimate control over everybody."

He held up a *Masterlink* card magazine advertisement. "This card will soon become obsolete. To avoid theft and unauthorized use, along with many other *promotional benefits*, it will be replaced by a microchip surgically inserted in the hand—" he patted his Bible—"as prophesied in the Book of Revelation. Right now we're reveling in the victory of ZOÉ." He shrugged toward Matthew. "But that will stop when the Kavidas-Stein partnership surfaces in the future under a new name. Then the AIDS virus will suddenly mutate one last time into an incurable strain that will touch every household on earth."

"You mean something like the death of the firstborn plague in Egypt?" Kathy noted somberly.

"Among other judgments and plagues, yes." David shot his eyes heavenward and said optimistically, "Hopefully the Lord will have come for us Christians before that happens. Within the next several years, the Kavidas-Stein Network will tenaciously seize and acquire control of the European Nations' economy, then branch out to influence their politics, their military, and ultimately their religion. By then, he will be fully united with the Arab-bloc states to do the same thing."

"Things will really be poppin' by then," Matthew noted dryly.

"In the meantime, the Lord will give us small victories, but we cannot win the war. But Jesus will return as the victor to set things right." He reached into his pocket, pulling out the small book. "He also left this book." David passed the book to Matthew, and he saw that Matthew understood the significance of it at once. Their eyes met and the men both nodded. Matthew turned to the end of the book and noticed Gregory's name.

"What about this?" asked Matthew as he glanced at it from all sides.

"I was hoping you could tell me," said David skeptically. "There must be a reason that this was included. Some kind of message?"

Matthew passed the book to Kathy, and she eyed it shrewdly. "Gregory Kavidas. The name sure does seem to come up a lot."

"Gregory *A.* Kavidas," David corrected.

Matthew's eyes lit up with surprise. "Gregory *A.* Kavidas—I didn't even notice that!" He took the book back and stared at it in awe. "I looked right at it and the *A.* said nothing. When you corrected her, I saw it!"

"Saw what?" asked David as Kathy looked on, just as perplexed.

"The missing number. David, don't you remember we couldn't figure out why Kavidas's name didn't add up to 666? Well, here it is!" He passed the book back triumphantly. "When we researched his name, we were told that he had no middle name. But you see, he does. He must have kept this secret, knowing himself what he is and what it means."

Understanding dawned on Kathy's face.

"You mean that one A—"

"Exactly. That one A. We were at 665. The A equals one. That puts us at 666 and we have our man." Matthew began to smile, but the smile faded as the sheer terror of the awesome truth set in to all of them. Knowing who the man was and having it confirmed. The group became suddenly quiet.

"Did he say anything else, David, anything personal?" Kathy asked predictably.

"I'm sure there'll be individual trials here and there, but then again, that's to be expected," David replied evasively. He was glad Matthew deciphered the message left in Gregory's name. It saved him the trouble of telling them that he couldn't divulge everything at this time. And for their sake, he didn't want to.

There was no dissonance between them, but Mort needed Gregory to reassure him when adversities came upon them. In his mind, the recalling of the vaccine, together with designs to relocate, were extremely disconcerting, casting shadows on the path for the future. Privately, Gregory's unobtrusive and peaceful nature often embraced Mort and enabled him to find comfort during stressful periods. Outwardly, Gregory became increasingly anxious and demanding as if he were on some kind of a schedule with a deadline nearing. Carefully controlled, the dichotomy resulted in a dynamic that Mort found to be magnetic, present in demigods only.

True to his own ethos, Mort forcefully dismissed any negative thoughts about Gregory, reminding himself of his calling to stay on with Gregory; there remained much work to accomplish.

It was early Saturday morning when Mort arrived at Gregory's estate in West Palm Beach. He walked across Route A1A, jumped up on the seawall, then sat and gazed off into the distance as the ocean waves splashed against the concrete barrier. Doubts were destructive—Mort knew that from his experiences with ventures in the corporate world—but when it came to the spiritual world, they were much more damaging. *I do have doubts about my life together with Gregory*, he thought, *doubts that have recently surfaced. Is it not human to doubt?*

Further contemplation seemed to extend his doubts to life after death, but instinct and faith advised otherwise. He believed his destiny was inextricably linked with Gregory's, so despite the battling of doubts, he resolved to go forward.

Clusters of flowering vines cascaded through the wrought-iron gate at Kavidas's estate, arresting Mort's attention. *Dwell on things of beauty—things that bring joy—not dismal thoughts. Joy brings strength*, he reminded himself. He leaned over, smelled the variegated bougainvillea blossoms, and smiled. *Things won't be so bad. Okay, so I'm adverse to change, but most changes are for the good*. He pushed the gate open and stepped lightly to the front door.

Surprisingly, Gregory answered the door himself. "You gave Walter the day off?" Mort asked as he stepped into the mansion. Taking notice of Gregory's peaceful demeanor brought on a welcome, calming effect.

"I anticipated your coming. I thought we could spend some quality time together without interruptions. Let's head up to my study."

They marched up the spiral staircase to the first landing, then entered Gregory's private sanctuary, his study, where few mortals have ever trespassed. Mort's discernment advised him that this was a special visit since no one, not even Gregory's cleaning lady, had ever been allowed to enter the study.

Despite the tropical weather in Florida, many homes sport a fireplace for such winter days when the temperature dips below 60 degrees. Today, there was no fire, but Mort's eyes were immediately drawn to the large oil painting above the mantel. "Your mother looks beautiful there," Mort commented as he approached the elegant lady replicated on canvas. Up close, he noticed the artist's signature on the canvas, with a date inscribed beneath it, and suddenly became flushed. The painting was dated 1946, yet she looked the same as when he had met her in Athens just a little over two years ago.

Gregory perceived his bewilderment. "Just doesn't seem to age, does she?"

"No, she does not," Mort replied as he studied the painting. "I'm really astonished, to say the least."

"It's the Greek bloodlines. Family legend has it that way back in antiquity, her ancestors made a pact with Pallas Athena, the goddess child who sprang from the forehead of Zeus. In addition to being the goddess of Greek cities, arts, and wisdom, she is also known for her long life. I guess you could say my mother inherited the gift."

"Immortal is more like it. And you?" Mort returned.

"I have it too," Gregory replied with a tight smile. He motioned for Mort to sit and relax in the overstuffed sofa that faced the fireplace, while he set a tray of tea and muffins before him. "Eat, eat," he urged.

With a shake of the head, Mort replied, "Not hungry."

Gregory sat in the chair opposite the sofa, looked up at his mother's portrait, then back at Mort. "I suspect you're troubled, Mort, and I wanted an opportunity to allay any fears or doubts you may have about our purpose."

Mort heard the operative word *doubt*, then turned and faced Gregory. "Are you a mind reader?" he replied in disbelief. "How did you know what I'm going through?"

"Let's just say that I know your nature, and I'd like to reassure you that our destiny together is secure." He stood up and walked in front of the wall adjacent to the fireplace where massive long shelves held ancient books and scrolls of maps. Books on Judaism and Christianity lined several shelves. One shelf contained the entire Talmud with Targums, the Kabbalah, and Encyclopedia Judaica. The Apocrypha, the Pseudepigrapha, and the Mishnah, along with Josephus and Philo on another. What looked like an original version of the Septuagint, along with many authoritative texts of the modern Bible on still another shelf.

414

Gregory dropped to his knees in front of the sacred books and began swaying as if entering an ecstatic rite.

Mort looked on in amazement, thinking he had never before seen Gregory display such effusive behavior.

Within minutes he stood erect, still captivated by a force that sought communion and started to gyrate to some kind of divine music that brought further release.

Somewhat familiar, Mort recalled reading in the Zohar, a mystical book, about something like this when he was in Hebrew school. It is called Kavvanah, a cleansing ritual of prayer, where a Zaddik, a priest, enters into deep meditation and is capable of descending into the realm of the dead and make a selection from among the kelippoth, where he can raise up fallen souls or even save his own.

As if he were dancing before a deity, Gregory continued in his unabashed devotion for nearly five minutes as Mort's heart raced in unexplained anticipation. Then, suddenly, an overpowering ray of light that fanned out into a swirling ball of fire appeared suspended in midair behind Gregory.

Startled, Mort covered his eyes until the flaming ball, which took on the shape of a burning torch, moved off into the corner like a sentry.

Seconds later, Gregory raised his arms in adulation, then quickly went limp as a figure began to materialize behind him.

Mort momentarily turned his head in fear until he recognized a voice calling him. "Mortimer, my son," the principality said as it became a distinct entity, "my journey is now complete."

"Rabbi Vital?" Mort replied in astonishment.

The visitor nodded, then poured oil over Gregory's head from a sparkling cruet he held in his hand. As the oil dripped down his face, another presence began to take shape behind him. The specter increased in energy until a tall shadowy image formed. Rabbi Vital quickly recognized the being and gave him obeisance as he reverently stepped aside, leaving Gregory standing alone with the magnificent spirit that came from nowhere.

Suddenly all electrical devices shut down, while outside noises abruptly deadened as a strange silence came over the room. Then an eerie darkness extinguished the morning light coming through the windows, isolating the room from the rest of the world.

A terrifying power took control as the awesome presence began generating luminosity and evolved into an incorporeal being that resembled a man with four wings, two for flying and two for covering his body, that extended from the floor to above his head.

Mort crumpled to the floor and began to cower when he realized who this visitor really was: the exalted angel who once dwelled with God and was now in charge of the world.

Oscillating between silhouette and image, features slowly began to delineate. Although his wings shielded his face somewhat, his eyes penetrated them, focusing on Mort as he lay on the floor. Mort felt the eyes invade his soul and search his heart for the doubts that he cursed himself for once having.

Peeking through his fingers as he shielded his face, Mort became entranced by what he saw. The creature lifted his wings, revealing heavy, massive features with hairless arms that he placed on top of Gregory's shoulders. Darkness radiated from his body that absorbed any light nearby, leaving the torch as the sole source of illumination. Shadows obscured the image, but Mort could make out that he had a mouth, yet the being never uttered a word. He spoke to his mind.

"Yes, true faith is dangerous, because it abandons all. True faith is trust. You can trust me, but you must abandon your doubts," the voice said.

"I want to, but my faith is—" Mort whispered in a lame defense.

"Weak, I know," the angelic being completed Mort's confession.

Mort rubbed his eyes in terror as his body began to lift off the floor and relocate over to the supernatural being that controlled the room. As he arrived, the deity held up a wing and embraced Mort, holding both Gregory and Mort together, side by side. Mort squeezed his eyes shut, not knowing what to expect. Then the revelatory vision appeared in his mind.

The vision brought him to the city of Jerusalem. Mort looked up and realized that Solomon's Temple had been rebuilt, erected in place of the Mosque of Omar, the Dome of the Rock. He found himself walking into the outer court of the Temple grounds and saw a crowd standing around a man lying on the ground. His heart pounded as he approached the crowd, thinking in his mind what he had read in the Bible, but nagging doubts caused his mind to reject the event.

The crowd parted as he approached, leaving Gregory on the sacred ground, dead from a gunshot wound to the head by some unknown assailant.

Mort collapsed on top of his fallen companion and wept bitterly until he could weep no more. He stood up and raised his fists to heaven in defiance, then knelt down by his friend and prayed for guidance as the crowd grew to a giant multitude.

Time stood still as Mort looked down on Gregory's contorted face on his lifeless body. Silently and methodically, as if directed by some divine force, Mort climbed on top of Gregory's body, placing his arms over Gregory's arms, his legs over Gregory's legs, and his lips over Gregory's lips. Both remained motionless until Mort placed a holy kiss on Gregory's mouth and breathed air into his lungs six times, then rose off the body and waited.

Lightning bolts struck the Temple Mount and thunder clapped in exultation as Gregory began to stir. At first his arm elevated as if in praise to the conqueror of death; then his eyes fluttered, and finally he sat up as the crowd gasped, "He lives!"

Mort reached over and helped Gregory to his feet as the gunshot wound miraculously closed up before their very eyes.

"Messiah! Israel's Messiah!" the people yelled. At first, only the crowd closest to Gregory fell to their knees; then the entire assembly followed, leaving Gregory and Mort standing as thousands chanted praises for their promised deliverer.

Reveling in the glory, Gregory stood as a towering, invincible god, receiving their worship. Mort looked up into Gregory's face and realized that this was the purpose for which he had been born.

Once the vision ended, Mort came to a semiconscious state; then he turned his head in reflexive alarm to focus on Gregory and started to tremble. The realization that Gregory was truly anointed brought him to whisper a hallowed pledge that he would never doubt again.

No sooner had that vow been made than the room began to brighten, and the torch disappeared. As Mort looked at Rabbi Vital, he saw him wave good-bye as if he had passed his authority off to a higher power. Within seconds, the supernatural grip relaxed, and the presence of their master began to fade. Mort and Gregory then stood alone, with their relationship forever bonded.

"You needed this," Gregory said as he put his arm around Mort and escorted him over to the sofa.

Mort was dumbfounded and sat down without saying a word.

After 10 minutes, he stood up and excused himself to use the bathroom, then quickly returned. Gregory soon learned that Mort's attitude adjustment would greatly impact on his performance. "Where are we in terms of our objectives?" Mort rebounded.

Gregory grinned in satisfaction, then opened a file on his desk containing several flow charts. The charts reflected his current and future assets transfers. Mort noted that the completion of the transfers to a host of European banks would occur within the next 12 months. Next he pulled out a bonafide offer for the sale of Rainbow Pharmaceuticals, followed by a diagram explaining the goals of *Masterlink*.

"We're going to sell Rainbow to El Magar, an organization that I set up with Omar Sidmaj who we met in Geneva. The Arabs will manage Rainbow since the records will show that they own it, but in reality, we will own it through Euro-Rainbow. My friends have seen to it that our interests cannot be traced. So we're safe there. Regarding *Masterlink*, is the data gathering complete?"

"Just about," Mort replied. "We now have full access to the American people. The European and Asian people will be taken care of after we relocate to our base abroad. Seventy-seven percent of the national census is now in our database. Probably 20 percent will remain recalcitrant, while the remainder will fall in line. Probably in just a matter of six months. The resistors can be dealt with in the future."

Gregory nodded, pleased with Mort's report. "We must take that information with us, so guard it with your life."

"All doubly protected on encrypted CDs, flash drives, and the like in secure depositories." He turned and asked, "How will you keep control of *Masterlink*?"

"The Dimakos Corporation. It's actually a dummy organization I've created in Athens, managed by a newly acquired friend, Anastasios Kokkoris, who formerly worked in the Athinai Bank. You will oversee the GDC and exercise complete authority over the operation. He will funnel all decisions through you. These changes will enable us to concentrate our efforts on the political changes we need. Of course, we will have an inexhaustible financial base that will expedite our conquests."

"Looks like all our ducks are in a row," Mort said confidently.

418

"Not quite. A *messenger* visited Douglas last week and disclosed some vital aspects of our future to him."

"Uh-oh," Mort interjected.

"We need to finish some business with Douglas. This guy is not going to leave us alone—we need him out of the way—he knows too much and will continue to be an adversary. When we are ready to relocate, we won't want him nosing around in our overseas operations."

"I'll take care of it," Mort assured.

Gregory clapped as he smiled and said, "Everything is falling into place. I'm excited about the future. Now let's finish up the loose ends."

Mort, restored and fired up for duty, gave Gregory a look of admiration and walked out.

The newly renovated sidewalks of the Fort Lauderdale Beach greatly renewed interest in the ocean front community. Tourist season brought bulging crowds while locals paraded up and down the walks as they enjoyed the ocean air. Girls on roller blades frequently zigzagged around gawkers as they inspected the sunbathers, while others dined at the various restaurants that afforded a splendid view of the Atlantic along the Avenue where many hotels provided a luxurious refuge from the frigid Canadian winter.

Kathy resolved to find a recreational outlet that would lessen the emotional trauma that never seemed to leave her family. She mandated they walk the one mile long sidewalk after church each week. Recognizing the therapeutic value of a family outing, the weekly event became a time where the children could frolic while David and Kathy caught up on each other's lives. After the third week, the family seemed to depend on the excursions.

While waving the children over to a sidewalk restaurant, David staked out a table on the esplanade nearest the ocean. Passersby flowed around the table as if it were a rock in a running river. Interestingly, it was private amidst the crowds since everyone was doing their own thing, paying no attention to any particular person or conversation.

Kathy took the orders, then went to the food counter as David watched over the children. As he sat relaxing and breathing in the refreshing salt air, an ominous feeling suddenly came over him. He felt they were being watched. He looked at the slow-moving traffic and saw nothing unusual. He stood up momentarily, scanned the crowds, but again saw nothing unusual. Nevertheless, his spirit was troubled as a mental flashback reminded him of Andy's warning.

"Dad, are we going to go swimming today?" Hillary asked as she fussed in her chair.

"'Don't know yet, darling," David replied with a tinge of impatience.

Alan and Paul turned up their noses in disappointment and shuffled their feet in protest.

As Kathy returned with the burgers and fries, she held up several dollar bills she'd received as change. "It won't be long before this stuff becomes extinct."

No matter where they went, reminders of the rapid changes in society surrounded them. David nodded, then said, "Let's pray and eat."

Hillary started on her fries, then casually asked while pointing to a creeping car passing by, "Daddy, why is that man looking at us?"

David shot upward to get a better look, but by then the vehicle moved out of view.

Kathy looked quizzically at David. "What's the matter? We're getting a little paranoid, aren't we?" Turning to Hillary she said, "Honey, with all these people around us, someone is bound to be looking at us."

Hillary shrugged and continued eating.

Shoving his plastic plate aside with the uneaten hamburger, David sat pensive with his arms crossed across his chest, watching the ocean through the passing traffic.

"What are you thinking about?" Kathy asked, reaching for his hand.

Deflecting his real worry, he reached into his wallet and retrieved a credit card. "I wonder how long we can hold out. One year? Two years? Unless the Lord provides us with a fantastic bartering system, the entire Christian lifestyle is going to dramatically change. I mean, who can survive today without using credit?"

"Our parents lived without credit. It can be done," Kathy asserted. "The real question is can we do without some of the goodies, toys, and frills that we're accustomed to—?"

"There he is again, Daddy!" Hillary blurted almost apologetically.

420

"Which one, honey?" David replied as he turned quickly toward the passing traffic.

"He was in the blue car with the window rolled down," Hillary said. Jumping up and running to the curb she added, "The one with the windows tinted."

David followed her and looked down the street, but the car turned into a hotel parking lot. "Rats," he muttered. "Okay, let's call it a day," he announced as he walked away, motioning for them to follow him back to the car.

Alan walked to dispose of the trash, then ran to catch up with his family waiting at the crosswalk. As he approached them, he thought he saw the blue car suddenly pull out into the street ahead of them. He stepped out into the street to get a clearer view, but a Broward County bus stopped to unload passengers at the crosswalk, blocking the line of sight between him and his family. From behind, a car came to a screeching halt as he dodged out of the way. Oncoming cars restricted his view, but he thought for sure that he saw the blue car racing toward the corner where his family stood.

"Dad, look out!" Alan screamed when he confirmed his fears, but the sound of the bus engines muffled his cry. As soon as the bus cleared the corner, the driver of the blue car floored the accelerator and pointed the vehicle for the Douglas family standing at the crosswalk.

The light changed, and the crowds began walking across the street, leaving David and his family isolated, waiting for Alan. By the time David caught sight of Alan running in terror toward them, it was too late.

Suddenly Alan froze with fear as he watched the speeding car about to kill his family. "No!" he shrieked as he covered his eyes.

David turned to meet the blue car head on, yelling and signaling in a vain attempt to shield his wife and children from the impending disaster. He grabbed them into a huddle and cried out, "Lord, save us!"

From across the street, a man dressed in a tropical business suit started running, then vaulted over two cars moving slowly in the opposite lane, and with lightning speed plowed into the would-be victims, shoving them clear of the menacing car.

The car crashed into a T-shirt shop, running over and injuring a visiting sailor before hitting a concrete fire wall and coming to a stop. The driver, wearing gloves and a motorcyclist's helmet, jumped out of the smashed vehicle and fled through the crowd.

Alan ran and threw himself on his family as they lay in a heap on the sidewalk.

Onlookers later attested that the Good Samaritan simply came from nowhere, and it was physically impossible for him to achieve the kind of speed he needed to intervene and prevent the calamity from happening, but David knew otherwise.

A huge crowd cheered as the family stood up off the ground and hugged each other, praising God for being alive.

After several minutes David cleared his eyes of the tears of anguish and looked for the rescuer, only to be told that the man simply vanished after performing the heroic deed.

Kathy went to his side and said, "The Lord protected us, David. He sent an angel to push us out of the way of that car."

David smiled. "My eyes were closed except for that last second before we were almost killed. It was my friend Andy."

Kathy fell onto his chest and sighed deeply as the thought of David knowing in advance about this would-be tragedy occurred to her, but she hadn't the strength to discuss it now.

Once the police and paramedic units arrived, it would be another 90 minutes before the family would be allowed to go home.

Only a vacuous mind could dismiss the incident as accidental. Three days after the near catastrophe at the beach, David continued to run the tapes in his head, replaying Alan's scream and seeing Hillary's face as the car raced to snuff out their lives. Thoughts of his family life being invaded by the enemy once again intensified, giving way to obsession. Everywhere he went, he saw the blue car coming at Kathy, ready to mow her down like a stray dog.

His work at school began to suffer immediately as his focus constantly shifted from the present back to the Sunday where his family was almost murdered. His ministry suffered as well. While he feared innocuous preaching, his heart could not grant forgiveness at this time. *Yes,* he thought, *it will negatively influence my homiletics.* But he held to his resolve and called in an itinerant preacher to temporarily solve the problem. Yes, Andy, the angelic edifier, had warned him to be prepared to face trials, but a life-threatening assault on his family was totally unexpected and unbearable.

Predictably, the police advised him that the car had been reported stolen, and there were no hostile fingerprints on it. Once again, no proof existed, but he didn't need it. He knew it was all Kavidas and Stein's work.

He knew that at times like this, he didn't want to be spiritual. He recalled the gas station fiasco when he admonished the youths for retaliating with violence, but that seemed so long ago, and besides, the action was not directed against *his* family.

"Vengeance is mine, saith the Lord." Yes, he remembered that verse, but divine justice took too long while jungle justice was swift and at times more fulfilling. In this frenetic environment, nothing made sense anyway. The world's value system was so chaotic that evil acts were heralded, while the Christian virtue was constantly attacked and ridiculed—if not branded as fanaticism. If he waited for the civil law to act, Kavidas would be long gone by then—safe and secure behind his impregnable demonic and financial barriers. So, David thought, he could be carnal for a while and repay Kavidas, then go and repent. The game worked for thousands of other Christians, so why not him? Convinced in his mind, he looked for an opportunity.

The Swains waited outside the Douglas home for one hour before they finally returned. The purpose of the meeting was to bring David up to date on the *Koinonos* program.

Eddie and Sydelle had invested huge amounts of time and energy personally contacting and soliciting subscribers until a makeshift network was in place. The directory now listed participating organizations that honored and discounted costs for *Koinonos* members, treating it like a fraternal club. Fortunately, there were still some Americans who believed in free enterprise and despised the *Masterlink* network, despite all its glory, and were willing to work with *Koinonos* to help them build a system independent of the assiduous, all-consuming monster.

Family members were sharing both their resources and their abilities to lessen dependence on non-member commercial artisans. Eddie and Sydelle devised a credit and debit system using points instead of currency. When the home of a member family required electrical work, that member would contact the network director who would assign a member electrician who would charge the discounted rate in points. The member who received the services would be debited the points and would work them off according to his profession elsewhere within the network. A monthly statement would apprise the member of their account status. By extension, the formula worked well with other services and suppliers also. This way, all members were receiving most of their services and merchandise through *Koinonos*. Utilities, insurance, and major purchases still remained outside *Koinonos*, but in time, Eddie and Sydelle hoped to formulate a plan to embrace them as well.

Waving to the Swains as they pulled in the driveway, the Douglas family apologized for their lateness and escorted Eddie and Sydelle into the kitchen, where they prepared a fresh pot of coffee and settled the children down.

Eddie noticed David's preoccupation immediately and signaled Kathy aside to ask what the problem was. When the phone rang for David and he took it in the adjoining room, Eddie seized the moment. "Kathy, what's with David? He's in another world."

Shaking her head in worry she replied, "He is ballistic over this running down with the car stuff. He thinks of nothing else. It's a fixation. He blames Kavidas and Stein and thinks about them day and night—I've never seen him like this before—he's half-crazed about it. Whatever you do, don't bring up the subject."

With a look of consternation, Eddie asked, "Can't you appeal to him in the spirit? I mean, after all..." He paused so as not to sound overly critical. "He is a pastor...eh, of course, we all have our moments, but—"

Kathy waved him off. "Don't be so hard on him, Eddie. He's been on overload for so long. He's a spiritual man, but he is still only a human being. I just pray he snaps out of this; that's all." She brought some cake to the table and added, "Just give him a little more time."

424

With that, David got off the phone.

"Everything all right, David?" Eddie asked, pointing to the phone.

David nodded and said gruffly, "Fort Lauderdale police. No leads on the assailant. Will keep me informed," he reported mechanically.

Eddie looked up at Kathy, remembering her warning, but David brought it up. He reached over and touched David's hand. "Time to let it go, David. Your family is safe; that's all that matters."

"They're not safe!" he retorted. "Rainbow and Kavidas/Stein is everywhere. My family is targeted, and they're not safe, believe me."

Unprepared for an argument, Eddie threw up his hands and in lame defense said, "David, you are consumed with this. You've got to leave this problem with the Lord. He'll protect your family—he proved that to you—you've told us that yourself."

Sydelle looked at David with sympathy.

Kathy simply considered her husband through stifled tears and said nothing.

"Bring me up to date on *Koinonos*," David grumped. Changing the subject was his way of saying the subject was closed.

Eddie shrugged in defeat, then reviewed the progress of *Koinonos*. Afterward, he solicited David's advice by presenting him with a current marketing problem. Eddie had contacted numerous food wholesalers and offered them services in exchange for payment, but it wasn't working. On a smaller scale, local shops throughout southeast Florida were engaging in the bartering system where their services were met in payment for purchases by *Koinonos* members, but the large food chains were controlled by corporate heads that refused the system. Eddie surmised that their national profits through the *Masterlink* network persuaded them. He believed David's gift of spiritual discernment could shed some light on the stalemate, but David was not concerned with *Koinonos* right now. Eddie easily recognized the dilemma.

Hoping the problem would dislodge David's preoccupation, Eddie persisted. "Do you have any ideas to help us, David?"

An inordinate silence ensued that reminded Eddie of the spiritual conflict that occurs within the heart of the Christian. He could see in David's eyes the battle between the flesh and the spirit. His flesh wanted only to retaliate, while the spirit wanted restoration—a renewing of the communion with God that inspires the Christian to do what is right.

425

"David?"

David had zoned out but quickly responded, "I suggest you re-contact the big suppliers and advise them that you are formulating a boycott list that will include all those corporations that decline to help out *Koinonos*, and that list will be circulated throughout our network. From there we will develop another avenue of leverage to force them to capitulate in our favor."

Eddie looked up at Kathy and hooted with his thumbs up, "He's back! That's a terrific idea! I would never have thought of that." Triggered by David's response, he pulled out his presentation folder and jotted down some notes, adding other concepts that popped up in his mind. He then chuckled and said, "We'd be lost without you, David. I hope you realize that."

Sydelle smiled at Kathy as David reached over to put his arm around Eddie. "I haven't been myself these past few days. Please forgive me."

Quick to forgive, Eddie replied, "Done. Now we need to get back to work."

Nodding, David resumed his advice on *Koinonos*.

But as soon as Eddie and Sydelle left, the ugly memories returned.

It was early Saturday afternoon when the doorbell rang several times, followed by successive loud, attention-getting raps on the door.

David jumped off the sofa and dashed to the front door. Recognizing his young neighbor through the peephole, he immediately released the security latches. "Mrs. Welch, what's the matter?"

His neighbor held her limp eight-year-old daughter in her arms. The unnerved woman managed to say, "She returned from her Little League practice and began losing her memory; then she fainted! My husband took the car to work. Can you take us to the hospital?"

David looked at the child and recognized trouble. Scampering for his hat and car keys, he quickly escorted them into his car and headed for the Coral Springs Medical Center Emergency Room.

Two hours later the blood test revealed the little girl had contracted AIDS from a mosquito bite during an evening baseball game six weeks ago.

The doctor was shocked at the short period of time to the onset of symptoms and speculated that the AIDS virus when spread by insect vectors was definitely mutating and probably brought on the amnesia.

His remarks that the virus was once again cycling and becoming more unstable and unpredictable elevated David's concerns to an even greater height. Everywhere he turned, the evil metastasis pointed to Kavidas and Stein.

By the time Kathy returned home from work, David was again lying on the sofa, brooding. After 25 minutes of probing and cajoling, David finally shared the incident with Kathy, but she was unable to persuade him from his inner resolve. Echoing in his mind were the words of the British police officer when quoting on the AIDS pandemic, "Everywhere I go I see increasing evidence of people swirling about in a human cesspool of their own making."

It was after eating his lunch when David tuned into CNN and saw a news clip on the recent trade agreements of the European Community, followed by an announcement that the EC's next series of meetings was to begin tomorrow at Orlando's Marriott Hotel in central Florida at the behest of Gregory Kavidas, their recently elected president. The broadcast added that Kavidas's attempt to woo the members was having a favorable effect.

Speculation further added that Kavidas's diplomatic endeavors to bridge European and American businessmen was a portent of his political designs to unify the world much like he attempted to unify the world through his AIDS vaccine. Although the vaccine went awry, nobody could deny that his heart to serve people wasn't pure.

After the news report David convinced himself that God providentially arranged the convention and that he should be there.

Rising at five o'clock the next morning, David took the Florida Turnpike from his home in Coral Springs north to Orlando. At seven he called Kathy from his cell phone while parked at the Yeehaw Junction rest stop, some 150 miles away, to wish her a pleasant day and disarm any inquiries of his whereabouts.

"How come you didn't mention to me last night that you were leaving so early?" Kathy asked over the phone.

"I forgot to explain that I needed to prepare for student consultations today," he replied, "but I should be home on schedule." His conscience troubled him for lying, and he hoped there would not be a need to call the school for any reason. Historically, anytime he lied, matters always got worse.

"Love you," Kathy replied as she clicked off and went about her morning.

"Love you back," he echoed reflexively as he clicked off and resumed his drive.

David knew that a force had overtaken him like a hypertrophic disease. The force of evil as it was, that which opposed God and his work, was now reigning and controlling him, with the proclivity to totally consume. In conscience, he couldn't blame Satan for his actions. Sure, Satan may have put the notions in his mind, but his own heart took up the ball and ran with it. *Lord, I've read where David rid the land of the Philistines— those evil agents who fought against your people Israel—all in your good name. Good against evil, God against Satan, Rainbow against the Christians, David against Kavidas.* It all made sense to him, filling him with a terrible resolve.

Arriving at 8:30 at the Marriott Hotel in Orlando, David sat in his car for 30 minutes to gather his thoughts and plan his moves. From there he went to the concierge's desk. "Excuse me," he started, "where is the EC conference being held?"

The welcoming official looked David up and down, paying particular attention to his Brooks Brothers suit, and decided to answer. "Sir, the delegates will be meeting in our Mahogany Room at 1 p.m."

Thanking him, David walked to the conference room area to survey the Mahogany Room closely.

He noticed a main foyer connecting a large room with two massive mahogany doors and a side door used by the service staff. Inside the mahogany-paneled room were at least 13 round tables, all with elegant dinner settings and signs denoting the countries of the EC emblazoned on them. A long table with floral pieces, flanked by a lectern, was placed at the head of the room.

From the front entrance, David walked around to the side to view the route from the Mahogany Room through to the kitchen area and onto the service exit that led to the parking lot. It looked like a passageway that would easily accommodate a quick escape, filling him with relief.

Outside the hotel, he checked his time, then looked around at the many signs directing traffic to the various tourist attractions in and around Orlando. His eye fell on Universal Studios Park. He drove east to the park, then spent the next two hours exploring exhibits and enjoying the rides as he carefully made his plans. Allowing himself plenty of time to prepare, he arrived on station at 12:30 p.m.

As he entered the lobby, he immediately sensed the highly charged environment. Several TV networks were positioned and interviewing the various emissaries as they emerged from their hotel rooms in anticipation of Gregory Kavidas's arrival. David looked everywhere, but Kavidas was conspicuously absent.

With only 20 minutes to spare, a sudden commotion erupted outside on the front lawn. David quickly learned that Kavidas and Stein had flown in by charter helicopter. Accompanied by an entourage of Rainbow VIPs and bank officials, Kavidas and Stein waved to the news reporters as they descended on the group like ants on a sugar cube. Kavidas stopped to make some introductory remarks, then continued on his way to the conference room as the media personnel followed in tow.

David continued to observe from a safe distance as hotel security concentrated their scouting efforts on unsavory looking characters while fastidiously dressed visitors were overlooked.

At the lectern, Kavidas and Stein smiled at the TV cameras as they prepared to make a public announcement before the EC and the world.

"Friends," Kavidas began, "before we begin our session on pertinent economic issues, Mr. Stein and I purpose to dispel any rumors you may have heard regarding Rainbow Pharmaceuticals." He turned to Mort and added, "Along with *Redisearch/Masterlink*. In order to give the European Community my full attention, I've decided to sell my interests here in the United States and relocate abroad, namely in Athens. Mr. Stein and I have instructed our attorneys to take the necessary steps to finalize the sale of

Rainbow to an organization that will maintain the integrity and vision of our firm—"

A hand shot up from a reporter.

"Yes?"

"Mr. Kavidas and Stein. Is the sale to foreign interests?"

Gregory answered immediately. "Yes, it is. Historically, many American firms have been sold to foreign investors. This is not new."

Seizing the break, another hand went up. "Mr. Kavidas, is this your way of saying that Toi-VAX was a flop, and you're bailing out?"

Gregory considered the reporter with a tolerant grin for several seconds, then answered, "What is your name?"

"Marty Lestor from the *Orlando Tribune*," he answered sheepishly.

Gregory cocked his head slightly and said with a twinkle in his eye that conveyed a threatening rebuttal, "Toi-VAX was never considered a flop, Mr. Lestor. The AIDS virus mutated, thus rendering the vaccine innocuous, but the vaccine was *never a flop,* and we are relocating to an European theater for the benefit of my newly appointed position with the EC."

Gregory paused out of sudden discomfort. He loosened his tie and scanned the audience carefully for someone that could harm him.

"What's the matter, Gregory?" Mort whispered into his ear.

The onlookers started mumbling as Gregory glared at the doorways in search of the enemy. "We have company," he replied, then regained his composure. "And so you know ahead of time, my partnership with Mr. Stein is being legally dissolved, and in fact, he is selling his interests in *Masterlink* so as to be a full-time assistant to me in Athens."

Suddenly a man pushed himself through the service entrance and rapidly snaked himself around the tables until he stood about 20 feet from Kavidas and Stein. The man pointed his finger at Kavidas and called out, "And pray tell, what else might you be doing in Athens, Mr. Kavidas? And you, Mr. Stein. Perhaps you could shed some light on what your real function is going to be."

With that all the cameras reoriented themselves to the live feed unfolding before them.

Two hundred and ten miles away, Kathy Douglas received a phone call at work from David's father.

"Kathy, get to a TV quick—David is on CNN— in Orlando in front of a crowd of people, and it looks very dangerous."

Kathy, panicked, ran to the nearest television set.

Hotel security started running to the front of the room when Gregory held his hand up in a halting gesture. "Everything is under control, gentlemen."

The security men froze with their eyes riveted on the intruder.

Gregory shot a look at Mort, instilling confidence and victory over the moment. He then nodded to the man and said diplomatically for the cameras to record, "Mr. Douglas, how good of you to join us. How can I help you?"

David pushed the tables aside to make a path for himself, then made his way up to the microphones with Kavidas and Stein. As he faced the audience he saw it grow to a large crowd from hotel guests and employees who rushed in to witness the drama. Once again he shook his finger at Kavidas and Stein as he nervously cleared his throat to launch a verbal assault.

Gregory, knowing the cameras were trained on David, gave Mort a smug look that signaled a sigh of relief.

David glanced at the crowd as he teetered back and forth momentarily to organize his thoughts, but a strange oppression inundated him like a tidal wave, sending his mind into a state of confusion. Perspiration dripped down his forehead as he began to lose control.

"You were about to say something, Mr. Douglas?" Gregory goaded.

With his eyes blazing, David began searching his jacket and pants pockets, then wiped the sweat off his brow. "I, eh, came to tell everybody who you really are—"

"Now, Mr. Douglas," Mort interjected, "everybody already knows who Mr. Kavidas really is." Mort put his arm around Gregory and grinned into the cameras. "The real question is, *who are you?*"

With that a thunderous applause followed.

When the clapping and hooting died down, Mort added, "I think Mr.

Kavidas has been very kind to allow you to break into our conference like this...."

Back at her office, Kathy broke out into tears as she watched the office TV. "Their diabolical powers are making him look like a blubbering idiot."

David continued to fumble in his pockets while muttering into the microphone, "I came to warn the public and stop you from taking over." He paused, then smiled in relief as he pulled a black object from his pocket.

Suddenly a shout came resounding through the room, "Gun!" Two security guards ran from behind and tackled him, knocking him to the floor as the crowd scattered immediately. One guard grabbed the smashed black object as the other held David down. The guard stood up and handed Gregory the object, a micro digital recorder.

"Hmm, well, I guess there's no threat here," Gregory quipped into the microphone. He turned to the guard and said, "Let him up."

Regaining his composure, David brushed off his suit and walked to the microphone as Gregory watched him carefully. "My intention was to play back testimonies of—"

"Please escort Mr. Douglas out of here," Gregory commanded the guards as the Orlando PD showed up to assist them.

With the cameras trained on David, the police removed him from the conference room as the people gathered around Gregory and Mort to console them.

SIXTEEN

-

A decadent civilization
compromises with its disease,
cherishes the virus infecting it,
loses its self-respect.
E. M. Cloran

If he stopped to search his heart for the real reason he wanted to castigate Douglas, Maurice Ryder probably would have settled on one particular incident where his youth pastor violated a confidence. Twenty-two years earlier when he was 11, he had gone to his youth pastor for help to overcome his obsession with pornography and had deeply regretted it ever since. In his mind, he was betrayed.

Curiously toying with one of his father's magazines—supposedly a one-time excursion to satisfy his emerging desire for lust—quickly grew to enslavement. Over a few years, not recognizing his bondage, he craved greater visual stimulation and so connived a system where he received adult videos through the mail. He had them sent to his friend's house where both parents worked days, enabling his friend to have complete access to the mail delivery. After several months of secret viewings he could no longer contain his fantasies, and asked the 12-year-old girl who lived next door for sex to satisfy his sexual imaginations. When the girl's mother demanded that he keep away from her, he realized that he may have a problem.

Troubled in his conscience, he sought advice from his youth pastor. Lacking experience and perspicacity in counseling, the young pastor suggested he destroy all pornographic material and serve the Lord. But he went beyond and divulged the confidence to Maurice's father as a monitoring safeguard. His father shamed him into apologizing to the girl and her mother, but the father continued to indulge himself in pornography, forfeiting his son's respect. Maurice shifted the blame from himself and his father to his youth pastor.

"Do we have any file images of David Douglas?" Ryder asked the archive department clerk. "I'm looking for photos of him with family or even while teaching to use with the photo of him on the floor in the Marriott."

The clerk raised an eyebrow. "He's been target material for the past year or so; we have plenty to work with." She looked at the monitor with David Douglas's name on index and added, "We have stills of him with Lane Pharmaceutical's owner, Matthew Lane, cameos entering and exiting the college where he teaches, a few you shot with him preaching at a meeting with other pastors. Also, videos of a rally at Rainbow and a clip from a local TV station that covered an incident where a runaway car nearly hit his family in Fort Lauderdale a couple of weeks ago."

Ryder looked at the screen and picked out four. "Let's see the stills of him with Lane, him preaching, and make a still of him right after that car incident. Finally, the one with him looking like a jerk on the floor of the Marriott in Orlando."

The clerk couldn't help but wonder why he had such a vendetta for Douglas. She had no choice but to retrieve the images he requested.

Once Ryder had the four images he wanted, he sat at his computer and composed the article that would change the future for the Douglas family. Although financial remuneration from Kavidas entered his mind, he was doing this for himself.

"'Preacher Goes Berserk...' The dirty dog," Matthew said as he read aloud the *Miami Star* headlines. "'A Chronicle of the Righteous Going Wrong.' This guy Ryder is just like a dog after a bone—he won't stop until he eats the thing up."

"I'm really surprised he didn't use the photo where the police dragged me out of the room. That was my best shot," David observed bleakly.

"He has an ax to grind," Kathy opined dryly.

David shook his head as a tear rolled down his cheek. He reached across the table and held one of Kathy's hands while at the same time latching onto one of Matthew's hands. "Thanks for using your clout and getting me off, Matt." Turning to Kathy he said, "Thanks for sticking by me, babe."

"This is really going to hurt us, David." Matthew groaned.

Looking sheepishly at them both, David lamented, "I really thought I could expose him in front of national TV."

Kathy looked at her husband sitting across from her at the breakfast table and wondered what really possesses a person to act irrationally at times. She had always viewed David as an impregnable spiritual fortress who continually made godly decisions where she could totally trust him. The incident with Maggie proved that. But this was an example and reminder that Christians are just saved sinners, capable of falling into sin under the right circumstances—David, along with countless others, not being immune from the condition. She squeezed his hand to reassure him during his battle. "We all make mistakes. Let's put it behind us."

He gazed out the window. "It's obvious that the Lord wasn't in it to begin with, or Kavidas never would have been able to control me like that—"

"No, he wasn't," Matthew concurred, "and I hate to remind you, but this is going to have some pretty ugly ramifications."

"Yes," David conceded as he tapped his fingers on the table in deep concentration, "and one of them is the terrible consequence that is to befall us since it's obvious Kavidas cannot be stopped—"

Banging at the front door silenced them.

The frantic knocking brought a burst of confusion as their three children ran to answer the call. They all looked at the security monitor and saw Eddie glancing at a newspaper while Sydelle stood impatiently bouncing their baby from hip to hip.

Kathy grinned at the children to dismiss them while she opened the door. "We really need you now," she said to Sydelle, half apologizing.

Eddie went directly to David without saying a word. "David, I know you're hurting right now, but I must give you a status report on *Koinonos*."

David shook his head and gave him a dismissive wave.

"Pull yourself together!" Eddie scolded frantically. "Our phones at home and at *Koinonos* are ringing off the hook! Sponsors who were honoring the system are threatening to withdraw; our members were horrified over *your* TV coverage. Remember, you are their hero and crusader."

Eddie dropped the newspaper on the kitchen table and continued, "But now they want to disown you." He pointed to the series of pictures in the tabloid. "This being the clincher. This Ryder is on a headhunt for your scalp, and he's not going to quit until he crushes the movement and everything connected with it. If you value your church and teaching ministry at the college, you'd better slip into a hole and park yourself somewhere for a while until this blows over, or we risk losing everything."

Matthew nodded. "I didn't have the heart to tell you like Eddie did, but it had to be said. We're losing public support very quickly." He picked up the paper. "Ryder has branded you as a volatile fanatic that can't be trusted. Christians or no, most people will stay with a crusade during the victories, but once you begin to lose battles, they fall away."

"And for the cause of Christ?" David argued.

"David," Sydelle entreated softly, "we're going into end times soon when people will be fighting for their survival. Don't expect them to choose you over their family. Of course Christians will always choose Christ, but we must wait for him to orchestrate the plan. It can't come from me—" she scanned everybody at the table—"or anybody here, not even you."

"'In the multitude of counselors there is safety,'" David quoted. "Okay, I get the message. If you're all in agreement—then it must be from the Lord. So then, we must stop all offensive action against Kavidas and let the Lord and his providence handle him." He nodded and smiled in acquiescence. "As for me, I'm done—my vigilante days are over."

Kathy returned the smile but wondered in her heart if he really meant what he said.

Amy looked up at the supermarket window and noticed the We Welcome the *Koinonos* Card sign. She grabbed a cart and headed for the produce section. Carefully inspecting the quality of the vegetables, Amy selected only what her family absolutely needed for the week. This was veggie week. Last week they had chicken for their main weekly meal, next week fish. Beef was scheduled for three weeks from now. She implemented her rotation system right after she received her *Koinonos* debit card, pledging austerity and frugality as her way of helping the cause.

The price of lettuce was down this week from $3.75 per head to $3.19, so she placed two heads into her basket. The carrots looked limp, so she passed them up. The cucumbers looked artificially grown, but the price was right. Broccoli was out of season, so she substituted romaine and treated the family to a tomato.

*Well, things could be worse,...*she thought. Many of her Christian girlfriends' husbands had government jobs that didn't allow them the trading benefits of *Koinonos* and were still dependent on *Masterlink*. Having an automobile mechanic for a husband guaranteed a meal and roof over the family's head, she reasoned gratefully.

The clerk passed the groceries through the product code scanning window while the bagger stuffed them into thin plastic carrying sacks and finally placed the bags back into the shopping cart. Then the checker totaled the order and held out her hand for payment.

Amy handed her a *Koinonos* card, confident in knowing her credits were well over $450 dollars.

The checker waved the card in the air, then threw it on the conveyor belt and yelled out, "Look what we have here—one of the followers of Douglas, the crazed preacher from Coral Springs!"

"Give her the boot!" one of the shoppers at the rear of the line shouted.

"That card is good," Amy said in meek defense.

"Not in this store," the clerk snickered.

"Oh, really," Amy protested as she pointed to the sign taped to the front window. "Then what does that welcome poster mean?"

The checker and the rest of the shoppers on the line looked up at the sign.

"I want to see the manager!" Amy cried out as the checker cringed.

"Feisty little thing, aren't you?" the checker replied as she snatched up the *Koinonos* card and ran it through the card reader.

"Just do your job, lady, and cut the comments," Amy retorted.

The lady looked at her with disdain and deliberately slowed the process down to irritate her.

"And you can be sure that I will register a complaint with the regional manager about the fine service I received here, sweetie," Amy added sarcastically. She was sick of Christians being picked on and abused but recognized that the incident signaled a much greater problem. Christians and *Koinonos* were being lumped together and identified with Douglas, and that spelled bad business.

Originally developed in 1983, the CD or compact disc is an optical disc with digital codes embedded beneath the surface of the disc that is read by a beam of light. A high precision laser beam burns microscopic pits into a thin metal (aluminum) layer on a master disc that in turn is used to produce copies. The pits are layered down into patterns and then the reflective surface is covered with a transparent plastic coating to form the CD-ROM (Read Only Memory).

The player contains a low-powered laser and special lenses and mirrors, along with a servo motor that positions the optical elements to a track on the optical system. The laser then directs a narrow beam of light onto the tracks of the spinning compact disc. Along the track, regions with pits scatter the light differently from regions without pits, and this sequence of regions represents the audio and optical information.

A photo detector picks up the scattered light from the pits and sends a signal to a microprocessor which converts the signal to sound and pictures. As an alternative to phonograph records and audiotape systems, the CD is virtually indestructible since nothing touches the encoded portion; the CD is not worn out in the playing process.

The CD-ROM has a very high information-packing density that typically can store in excess of 500 megabytes or 600 million characters of data. Converting that into words, one CD-ROM could contain almost two complete sets of encyclopedias.

But with the advent of the DVD, the CD-ROM became almost obsolete since the DVD capacity was in excess of four gigabytes.

Mort entered the command on the *Redisearch* super-computer to download all the *Masterlink* files from his project Renaissance directory onto DVD. His design was to personally transport the 15 disks needed to store the 225,000,000 million member names with their vital statistics to their Dimakos Corporation in Athens. This figure represented almost 90 percent of the American population. As a safeguard, portable hard drives would be sent priority Federal Express and kept in an underground vault.

Shortly after the transfer process began, Mort's cell phone rang.

"Mort, I just received a call from Kokkoris in Athens," Kavidas said. "When can he expect delivery of the *Masterlink* files? He has six American computer reps on contract over there, working all sorts of hours to set up the network system, and they're almost ready to load the names."

Mort checked his wristwatch. "I'm leaving on a flight out of Miami at eight tonight. He'll have them sometime tomorrow."

"Sounds good," Gregory replied. "Oh, and what about the other thing we talked about?"

"Already set in motion," Mort blurted, anticipating Gregory's question. "It will happen very soon." He couldn't see Gregory crack a smile, but having a kindred spirit meant you could sense when the other person felt relief.

Dressed in a Florida Power and Light employee uniform, he walked up the Douglas driveway, taking time to wave to a neighbor, and went into the backyard to the electric service meter box.

As usual, his surveillance paid off. Early afternoon proved to be the time when the house was unoccupied. *Not even a dog barking*, he thought. *Fantastic.*

First he snipped the meter lock and pulled the meter out of the housing, exposing the power terminals. Next he attached alligator clips from the cigarette pack size device to each of the two power yoke connectors, then snaked another, 10/3 gauge, three-wire cable down to the security alarm box, also fastened to the wall, beneath the meter. He removed the outside cover of the alarm box that revealed the telephone, video surveillance cameras, and alarm bell lines. Then he coiled the excess wire around the alarm lines and attached the thick gauged wires to each of the alarm lines with wire nuts.

Once the connections were made, he replaced the cover and the meter. The entire job took less then four minutes. He knew the break in electric service would require resetting the clocks and timers inside the house, but Florida Power and Light was notorious for power failures, so this interruption would not be unusual.

He whistled as he nonchalantly walked back to the stolen van, paused, and pretended to look at his work orders, then jumped in the van and drove away to disappear without a trace.

At 2:30 the following morning, the timer, encased in the small packet in the electric meter, fused the power terminals together, causing the electric lines embroidered throughout the walls in the house to heat up. At the same time, the alarm lines melted together, rendering them inoperative.

Within 60 seconds, all of the circuit breakers popped in rapid succession, stopping the current to the receptacles, light switches, and appliances, but the power to the circuit breaker box, located in the garage, continued to flow.

The 12 and 14 gauge wire, with 220 volts flowing through it, got hot enough to melt away the plastic shielding, causing the current to arc to the metal casing, where combustion took place. The circuit breaker box burst into flames. Wooden beams and shelves, situated above the breaker box, then caught fire, igniting storage boxes that rapidly spread throughout the garage.

The Douglas home was a single-story ranch with three bedrooms and a bath on the west wing, with the master bedroom and second bathroom on the east side, separated by the living quarters. Normally the air-conditioning ducts would circulate any smoke into the proximity of a smoke alarm, but that was factored into the plan, and the air-conditioning shut down.

David ordinarily slept very lightly, waking at the slightest noise, but lately things were not normal, and with him, high-anxiety levels brought sounder sleeping periods.

The recurrent scene was a favorite of his, where he seemed to return to it often, especially when fatigue and stress overpowered him. He envisioned himself lying in a hammock in his backyard, reading a theology book with one eye as he watched the children frolic with the other.

Kathy sat in a chaise longue nearby, reading her third book of the Zion Chronicles series, sipping a lemonade. Unique to this dream, Kathy turned to him and said, "Better flip the burgers on the barbecue. It smells like they're burning."

David glanced at her lazily and nodded but didn't move.

Seconds later, she raised her voice an octave and said, "David, something is burning."

He smiled at her, then yelled over to Alan, "Please turn the hamburgers over; I'll be right there!" But David simply turned over on his side.

Kathy stood up and shouted, "David, right now!"

David bounced out of the hammock but suddenly realized his feet wouldn't move. They were fastened to the ground.

"David, the barbecue is on fire!" Kathy screamed, but David stood frozen in time as the smoke swirled around him while he fell back into the hammock.

He started to drift off into sleep when suddenly a man appeared before him as he lay in the hammock. The man reached over and shook his shoulders and ordered, "David! Get up! Your house is on fire!" He recognized the specter of his friend Andy immediately.

David jumped out of his bed to the acrid smell of a sweeping electrical fire. He looked and saw a red glow with black and yellow smoke trickling in under the door. He turned to Kathy, asleep in the darkness, scooped her out of the bed, and carried her into the bathroom, knocking over the night table and lamp as he stumbled on his way. "The house is on fire!" he yelled. "You get out through this window and get help while I get the children."

Kathy was so dazed and confused that she only said, "Oh, help us, God!" as she wiggled out the small window.

David thought to close the window to keep the draft down, then fumbled his way to the bedroom door and dropped to the floor as he opened it. A blazing fire was carving a huge hole on the living room side of the circuit breaker box, pumping smoke into the house. He looked at the fire door to the garage and saw in the fire light that it was still secure. "The gas in the car," he cried out as he began crawling toward the children's rooms.

The bellowing smoke ascended to the vaulted ceilings until it had no place to go, then began to compress, pushing the hot gases from the burning plastic down to the floor. The caustic smoke burned so much that he could only squint through one eye as he slithered along the carpeting, coughing violently as his lungs rejected the hot vapors.

He paused in the middle of the living room to estimate his distance. *Just 25 more feet, Lord—help!*

"Daddy, help!" Hillary screamed from her room.

"Keep your door shut, honey. I'm coming!" he yelled back. He glanced at the garage fire door and saw the paint bubbling, knowing flames were consuming the other side. With his heart pounding, he crawled faster. He looked ahead through the smoke-filled darkness and saw Hillary standing 20 feet ahead of him, swaying erratically from smoke inhalation. "Get back to your room!" he shouted, but Hillary fell limp on the carpet.

Whoosh!

Turning toward the noise, David saw a great hole opened in the upper half of the fire door. The screws holding the metal panel to the fire door had burned out, and the metal panel was laying on the floor, smoldering. The opening acted as a tunnel for oxygen, fueling the contained fire through the garage. Plumes of black smoke shot through the doorway, followed by flames darting out over David's head. The temperature soared, searing the paint on the walls, igniting the furniture and carpet all around him.

Fear stricken and gulping for air, David dug his fingers into the carpet and pulled himself toward his daughter. Then without warning he heard glass shatter.

"We have the boys!" Kathy shrieked. "We have the boys—get Hillary!"

The distance to Hillary was now less than 18 feet, but to him it was like a mile.

"Hold on, Hilly. Daddy's coming!" he shouted with renewed strength.

Whomp! Crash!

The Sheetrock off the ceiling detached and fell on top of him. Incredibly, the Sheetrock insulated him from the flames and heat, cooling his body down. He broke off a section and held it over his body as he crept toward Hillary. "Hold on, honey. Daddy's coming!" he cried out again, hoping to hear her voice as the thought of the car's gas tank exploding propelled him forward.

When he reached her, she was unconscious. He lifted the Sheetrock off his head to determine distances, then clasped onto her pajama top and started carrying her toward the sliding glass door by the rear patio.

Bang! Swoosh! A tire on the car exploded.

"Lord, help!" he cried out again. He looked down at Hillary and couldn't see her breathing. He groaned in his spirit and stopped moving. *It's no use,* he thought. *It's too far, and I'm too tired.* He squeezed his eyes shut and clutched Hillary's head and held her to his chest.

Open your eyes, David, a voice said to his mind a second later.

One eye slowly lifted, focusing on their 50-gallon tropical fish tank before him. He blinked several times, then glared at the tank standing on a metal frame just two feet from him. Menacing flames reflected off the tank glass. "But how?" he gulped.

Suddenly a chunk of Sheetrock with a burning piece of a rafter attached to it fell on him.

In a burst of energy, he wrenched the section of rafter free and smashed the side of the tank with it.

Torrents of water poured out all over him and Hillary onto the floor, cooling and clearing a path ahead of him. Strengthened, he dragged himself and Hillary toward the sliding door as another tire blew up. *Just a few more feet, Lord,* he begged.

From behind he heard a loud metallic popping and knew it was the car gas tank expanding as flames enveloped it. Then a hissing sound followed, and he realized the tank was about to blow.

"Hold on, Hillary," he murmured as he frantically inched along the floor.

He reached the glass door, fogged from the steam of the fish tank water, but it was locked. He thought of banging on it but feared it would implode on them. "Help me, somebody!" he cried out. Listening for a second, he heard voices screaming in front of the house. "Back here!" he shouted. "Back here!"

He slumped against the sliding door and felt the moisture from the steam condensing on the door and closed his eyes once again. "So close..." He trailed off into a whisper as sleep began to overtake him. He shifted his body to cover Hillary up just seconds before the explosion.

The gas tank exploded, sending a shock wave that traveled like a rocket through the rooms, seeking the easiest escape route. The blast hit the tempered glass door with David leaning on it, shattering it into harmless fragments. The energy generated propelled him and Hillary safely out onto the lawn.

Kathy and several neighbors ran to their side as both David and Hillary gulped fresh air into their lungs. David looked down at Hillary as she fluttered her eyes and burst out with tears of joy.

Only a portion of the east wall remained standing. The charred concrete block wall, surrounded by smoldering debris, stood as a horrible memorial of the ghastly events that occurred a little more than 24 hours earlier. Mounds of partly burned clothing mixed with mattress springs and appliance components drenched with water from fire trucks reminded David of a battlefield scene during his Vietnam tour. Only the burned-out skeleton of his car told him where his garage used to be.

"It's a miracle you all survived this inferno," Matthew said as he surveyed the ruins.

"A house can be replaced, but my family's lives cannot," Kathy said somberly as a tear slowly rolled down her cheek. She clutched David's hand as he stared out the car window and smiled at him. "We'll be all right, darling."

David returned the smile, then stepped out of Matthew's car and walked around his property. Meandering and bending over to uncover random remnants of furnishings and decorations, he took the time to talk to God. Gratitude for his family's lives overwhelmed him. He refused to fall into the futile trap of asking why, but felt compelled to ask, what now?

His heart suggested an answer, but he needed confirmation to act. *Lord, I need to hear from you*, he thought while picking up a scorched letter from where his desk used to be. "Humph," he uttered as he read aloud the logo on the envelope, "'Institute of Holy Land Studies, Jerusalem.'" He recalled receiving it three months ago, then brushed it off and folded it to stuff it in his pocket. The Institute requested him to teach

Old Testament theology there for a semester, but he dismissed the notion at the time.

"David, time to go," Kathy shouted from the car, breaking up his thoughts.

He nodded, then took another look at the guttered remains of his home. "Coming."

The children fell in love with the Ambassador Motel of Coral Springs. The oversized swimming pool, the game room, and the fact that they didn't have to clean their rooms every day reminded them of a vacation. For David and Kathy, the temporary quarters, just two days after the fire, seemed inadequate for their needs.

"When we get the insurance settlement on the house, what do you think we should do?" David probed Kathy as he sipped a lemonade at the motel pool side.

"Undecided. Maybe we'll rent a home for a while until we make up our minds," she replied cautiously. She knew David long enough to know when he was waiting for the Lord to speak through her in response to a question he had asked. She was confident that when the time was right, it would come out.

"Keep in mind that our homeowner's policy will only pay for us to stay in a motel for 90 days. After that we'll need long-term housing," he advised.

After nodding in consent and a moment of contemplation she said, "Maybe we should leave Florida altogether."

David shrugged. "Perhaps."

"Do you have any leading from the Lord at all?"

He glanced at her suspiciously. "Yes, but I need to know that it is *of* the Lord before I discuss it."

Kathy gave him a thumbs-up and smiled.

"Dad, you're in the newspaper again!" Alan blurted out as he walked over from the motel lobby and tossed the paper on his father's wet bathing suit.

Thankfully the picture of the smoking remains of their home wasn't front-page material. Without reading a word of the article, David announced, "This Ryder is unremitting—getting on my last nerve—he just won't give up!"

Kathy walked around and sat on his chaise longue and read the story along with him.

David suddenly crunched the paper together and squeezed his eyes shut. "Do you believe he's insinuating that the burning of our house was a judgment from God? The dirty dog. He should be stoned, and his body eaten up by a flock of buzzards!"

Kathy gently removed the paper from his shaking hands and continued to read excerpts from the article aloud. "'After a disgraceful exhibition at Orlando's Marriott where Douglas, in an unsuccessful attempt to discredit the luminary Gregory Kavidas, was dragged out of suffering from humiliating setbacks as founder of the faltering *Koinonos* movement." She paused, then said, "It's all in here. All the garbage. What isn't here is the arson squad's opinion that the fire was suspicious and—"

"That I claim one of Kavidas's henchmen set the blaze." David completed the sentence while shaking his head in disgust. He began to tap his fingernails in cadence on the armrest as his thoughts wandered off, once again searching for answers.

Kathy set the paper down, pulled the scorched letter from the Institute of Holy Land Studies in Jerusalem out of her pocket, and held it up. "I found this in your jeans' pocket when I was doing the wash this morning. I read it four times, and each time I read it, the Lord spoke to my heart. If we look at this near tragedy as a punishment from God, we'll become bitter toward him. But if we look at this fire as an opportunity from God, where he has given us a change of direction, we'll have peace over any decision we agree on."

David's eyes lit up. "Go on."

"Well, let's face it. If you had asked me and the children to go to Israel to stay a year at the Biblical Institute when my house was still standing, I would have said you're crazy. We've given up too much in the last year already. But now—" she waved her hands in the air—"now that the obstacle of the house has been divinely removed and the fire insurance settlement after the mortgage is satisfied, we're mobile and liquid. We could go to Israel."

David clapped his hands in exultation and recited, "'Who is like unto thee, O Lord, among the gods? who is like thee, glorious in holiness, fearful in praises, doing wonders?'" He hugged her and added, "I prayed that the Lord would confirm my thinking, and he has."

Returning the hug and smiling she reminded, "We have a lot to tend to before we can go, and I anticipate Kavidas-Stein, et al, along with our *Koinonos* group, is going to get pretty sticky."

"Agreed," David conceded, looking heavenward. "We'll consider this an adventure for the family and an opportunity to watch..." He stopped himself to check Kathy's reaction. *Kavidas and Stein from another observation point,* he didn't say.

"To watch the world come to an end?" Kathy opined.

"Something like that."

Hillary popped out of the water with a broad grin. "What's all the clapping and hugging about?"

"Daddy and Mommy are showing their joy of the Lord," Kathy replied.

Matthew Lane considered the smiling faces of the Douglas children gathered around his dinner table and said, "Blessed is the man whose quiver is full of them." He reached over and pinched Hillary's cheek. "I'm going to miss this whole family."

"We're going to miss all our friends here, especially you, Matthew," Kathy replied, "but David and I are confident about our decision."

Matthew nodded. "I know we must obey our calling, but it can be hard on those left behind—"

"Eh, Mr. Lane, eh, can I see you for a moment?" a quavering voice from the kitchen interrupted.

Matthew turned to David and Kathy when he heard his maid's voice and said, "Excuse me a moment. Ellie needs me."

As soon as Matthew arrived in the kitchen, Ellie burst out crying.

"What is it, my dear?" he entreated.

The rotund, middle-aged woman who had tirelessly served him for the past 15 years was crumbling in front of his eyes. "I just received a phone call from my daughter at home." Her voice trailed off as she sobbed.

"What is it? What's wrong, Ellie?"

"My next door neighbor's daughter came down with AIDS last month, and now she's lost her memory."

"Yes, I've heard that the virus has altered," Matthew concurred somberly.

"But—"

"But what, Ellie? You can tell me. Come now," Lane cajoled softly.

"Now they're blaming us Christians! The girl's father just threw rocks through our windows—*my* daughter had to call the police just before she called me."

"What? Why are they blaming you?"

Stifling tears she added, "They say the Christians are to blame for the new virus mutations—the amnesia—that we've called a curse down on them. So now they're taking it out on us."

"But we have the serum now," Matthew reminded her, "so her condition will only be temporary."

"Maybe so, but they hate us anyway. This only gives them another reason to persecute us."

"Hmm, yes. Well, I want you to go home to your family now. We'll take care of things around here." He escorted her to the front door to see her out.

"Is everything all right?" David asked with concern as Matthew returned to the dining room. "She sounded pretty upset."

Lane exhaled deeply, then shook his head. "Not really. Ellie's daughter called to tell her that their next door neighbor's daughter came down with AIDS a while ago, then became an amnesiac. Now the new thing with the newspapers is that Christians are to blame—the father reacted by throwing rocks through their windows—a melee broke out. Called the police, the whole bit." He toyed with the remnant of his dinner as he finished relating the salient details.

"Uh-oh." David looked at Kathy. "Despite the serum, it seems like we can't get away from Kavidas and now Ryder's accusatory finger. Putting more pressure on the people of God."

"What do you make of the virus bringing on amnesia?" Kathy asked Matthew.

"My researchers tell me that this AIDS virus is the strongest they've ever encountered and that unless the population is inoculated with the

448

ZOÉ serum, anything can happen."

"Remember," David explained, "AIDS dramatically curbed the lifestyles and appetites of the homosexuals and drug abusers, but once Toi-VAX and then the serum became available, they've thrown off the restraints once again. So maybe this tenacious virus just worked its way around things. Altering the side effects as it travels. Don't you remember what the 'messenger' said: 'The virus will continue to mutate'?"

"Twenty-five years ago, AIDS was unheard of. Now the world is consumed with an intrusive, mutating virus that can even be transmitted by mosquitoes, AIDS victims with demons or amnesia, faulty vaccines, drug company wars, people hating Christians, a global financial network taking control. It just goes on and on—" Kathy pushed her plate away and added, "I just can't wait till we get out of the States." She stood up and left the table.

David and Matthew traded a knowing look. World conditions were only going to worsen.

The first formal international monetary system was the gold standard, placed in effect during the nineteenth and twentieth centuries, which successfully served as an instrument of exchange until the improved gold-bullion standard replaced it. But that system was abandoned in the 1930s. Then the gold-exchange standard was installed, and most nations fixed their currencies to the U.S. dollar.

In the 1960s, however, a severe drain on U.S. gold reserves led to the introduction of a tier system where the price of gold fluctuated according to supply and demand. In 1976 the International Monetary Fund (IMF) members, plagued by new troubles, accepted a system of controlled floating rates and took steps to diminish the importance of gold in international transactions, including elimination of the official price.

In the latter part of the 1980s, a dramatic increase in the number of credit cards issued by non-banks, including telephone companies and especially national retailers, pushed the credit card business to an all-time high.

By the early 1990s, consumer credit on revolving charge cards soared to over $267 billion. It became increasingly obvious that modern society was in need of a monetary system that eliminated the problem of gold fluctuations while simultaneously centralizing and simplifying its need for credit.

Mort ran his hands over the supercomputer console, then pulled a smart card out of his wallet. As he held the card up to see the hologram sparkle in the light, he marveled at the world's acceptance of *Masterlink*, the system he believed to be the natural successor.

While the computer chip with encoded information in the smart card enabled the holder to perform many transactions, including paying bills, purchasing goods, and services, and provided limited medical data without a telephone link to the card issuer, *Masterlink* would offer many other perks to the holder.

"Can you visualize everything that's on this card—" he ran the card through a make-believe scanner—"will be right here sometime in the next few years."

He placed the card over his right hand. "Surgically implanted to eliminate theft, unauthorized use." He smiled at the computer technician and added, "And who knows? Maybe in time we'll do something special so the microchip will become a status symbol...personalize it, you know, like the American Express Gold Card."

The computer rep appeared to be enchanted by the concept. She turned and glanced at the immense bank of computers behind him. "Is that what this is all about? The mushrooming new financial network *Masterlink*?"

Mort patted her on the back. "Do you think we would transport you and all these other techs over here to Dimakos Enterprises in Athens just to set up a company computer? My friend, this baby is going to handle the whole world!"

Clearly the young woman could not grasp the magnitude of the operation. She shot a look once again at the array of computer hardware. "Mister, that's a lot of ferrite!"

Mort grinned, knowing that the compound ferrite was used in computers to store data. "Yeah, and a lot of optics and laser beam connections—we sure have come a long way from the abacus."

"What's an abacus?"

It was only a soft tapping at the church door. Pastor Fred paused from preparing his sermon to investigate, only to find an aged woman holding a shopping bag, looking in the window. "Can I help you?" he asked warmly.

The elderly woman wore an old kerchief over her white hair and trembled as she buttoned her frayed coat. Stooped with age and having deep wrinkles etched in her face, she squinted at the minister. "I'm scared."

"Please come in," Pastor Fred replied as he opened the door wide. "Tell me, what are you scared about?"

She checked her surroundings carefully. "Is this a Christian church?"

"Yes." Feeling the need to qualify his statement, he added, "Well, we don't have a giant building or affiliate with any one particular denomination. This is a small ministry but still a Christian church."

"Are you the pastor?"

"Yes," he replied gently, "Pastor Fred."

She reached out and grabbed his arm. "Pastor Fred, I had a terrible nightmare last night, and I'm scared. Can you help me?"

He started escorting her over to a nearby chair. "Please sit down and tell me about it," he solicited.

The feeble woman continued to survey the building while walking and hummed the hymn "Amazing Grace."

"Everything is okay," the pastor said. "You needn't be worried. You're safe here."

Peace seemed to sweep over the lady. She smiled as the tension oozed out of her. "My name is Marilyn. When I was a teenager," she began with a quiver in her voice, "I followed the Lord. But after college I fell for this man who said he was a Christian. When we got married, I found out otherwise..."

Hearing that scenario before, Pastor Fred replied, "I'm terribly sorry to hear that. Please go on."

"After we divorced, I concentrated on my career; then 10 years later another man came into my life. We started dating, but I was afraid of marriage so we just lived together until I lost all respect for myself; then I gave him the boot and started living alone."

She paused to catch her breath as the pastor held her shaking hand. "Take your time," he assured.

"And that was over 35 years ago." She looked down at her clothes and continued, "I know I'm a mess now, but at one time I looked nice."

The minister's heart broke for the lady. "Tell me about your dream."

Age had not affected her mind because she sounded lucid. "Pastor Fred, I think this dream was in the future because I noticed the date on my sales receipt; it was three years from now. I was at a drugstore refilling a prescription, and when it came time to pay for it the pharmacist told me to place my hand under a machine that had two blinking lights—one red, one green. I looked at him queerly, wondering why he didn't take my cash I'd saved and be done with it. When I shrugged and put my left hand into the machine, he shook his head and placed my right hand in, but the red light flashed on and off. Then he took back the prescription, so I screamed that I needed it for my heart condition, and he just shook his head and waved on the next customer.

"In the dream I stood there looking at the other people all getting green lights on the machine and receiving their medicine, but I couldn't have mine. I cried until I woke up." She took a deep breath of relief once she told her dream and looked to Pastor Fred for an explanation. "Can you help me?"

Pastor Fred suspected that some form of divine revelation was occurring in these perilous days when he recognized the prophetic content in the dream. Perhaps a special outpouring of God's Spirit upon humanity to prepare them for the difficult times ahead.

"Yes, I can help you," he consoled. "You need not be frightened about this dream, and you can avoid it by receiving Christ as your Savior. Once Christ is in your heart he will protect you so you will not have to go through those things."

The woman looked askance at him, as if at first suspicious of his explanation, but nodded with simple understanding.

"The dream predicts a time when you will not be able to buy or sell anything unless you have the name of the *Masterlink* credit system encoded in a special device implanted in your hand," Pastor Fred explained. "It's the marking prophesied in the Bible."

She held up her right hand and examined it, then set her arms across her chest. "So what's the problem? What's the catch?"

"The problem is—" he quickly asked the Lord to open the woman's eyes—"if a person has the device implanted, they have sided with *Masterlink*. They have sided with the evil founder of that credit system, and they have sided with the forces of evil. No Christian will have the encoded device. By the way, the device is a microchip, and it's already been developed. It's waiting to be used."

She scratched her head. "It's been a long time since I've read a Bible. Is it too late for me?"

"It's never too late," Pastor Fred replied quickly.

A single tear appeared in her right eye. "I don't want to be afraid ever again. I want to be sure."

Pastor Fred sensed God's leading and clasped her hands and prayed with her to embrace God's forgiveness through Christ.

Brandon's heart raced as they traveled down Jordan's Red Rock Canyon that led to the ancient city of Petra. The bus they were in seemed almost as old as the weary sandstone around them. No air conditioning had left them hot and sweaty for hours. A far cry from the luxurious Triumph mega-bus they had traveled in while in Jerusalem. Still, this wreck of a Mercedes-Benz, which looked as if it were surplus from World War II, was doing its job. They were on their way through the narrow Sik, the mile long gorge that led them past the towering red granite cliffs of Petra.

It was easy for Brandon to see how the area was known as the most inaccessible place on earth. He couldn't count the number of times he had closed his eyes while they passed through the constricted artery that served as the only road to *Sela,* the ancient Hebrew name for the city of the Rock.

Brandon heard Pano gasp as they approached the Carved Rock Temple of El-Khazneh. The 150-foot high edifice was carved into the rock and was adorned with columns and pillars that surpassed even the Acropolis in its beauty. Brandon could see that Pano's eyes moved over the stone and knew that he was thinking of his own country; it was easy to see why. The Hellenistic influence on the carvings of Petra was unmistakable.

Brandon heard the group begin to shuffle and prepare to depart. He looked behind him and saw the convoy of trucks following in their wake. Amid the dust of the ancient road, he saw the supplies and equipment necessary to transform this barren rock into a refuge for these people.

He knew that it was going to be more than hard work. Under the auspices of an archaeological dig, and with the influence of Dr. Barrett and his father's money, they had been granted permission to begin the historical restoration of the city. Still, knowing the distrust that the Arabs have for Westerners, he knew that they would be watching. They had to make it look like a real dig and that restoration was taking place. Not just a renovation to make the place a livable refuge. And arming the place for defense, well, that bridge was one they still had to cross.

Brandon stared in awe at the beauty of the brilliantly colored granite and sandstone that surrounded them on both sides. *Here I am,* he thought. *I will make a stand here against the coming tide. I will help these people in their pursuit of their haven against the evil that is coming. And I do know that it is coming. But I am not one of them. I don't fit in. Neither does Pano.* He smiled quickly at the man at his side.

He was certain that Pano was not prepared for the feelings of revulsion that these Christians would feel toward them and their lifestyle. He was not entirely sure he was ready himself. Pano, however, had grown up in an entirely different culture. Greece's tolerance was on a completely different level than America.

As much as Brandon wanted to help, and as desperate as he wanted to make a difference, he wasn't sure it would work. *Still,* he thought, *I can always pave the way till David or someone else comes along. Then Pano and I can be on our way into the world. Wherever that takes us.* He stared at the approaching apex of the city and knew it was time to disembark. He gathered his things and moved out with Pano to see the city for the first time with his own eyes.

The international movers carefully encased Kavidas's antiques and books in bubble wrap and gently placed them in corrugated boxes along with the other cartons for ocean shipment. Most of his furniture, except the family's priceless pieces that would receive special handling, had already been removed to the marine piers at Port Everglades for loading aboard an Olympic Lines cargo ship heading for Athens.

Strolling the near-barren second floor of his estate, Kavidas mentally checked off his list of remaining items to be done before leaving the country. He couldn't help but revel in his accomplishments at the same time. *Everything is installed according to my master plan,* he thought. *Networks and assets are in place, Mort is in Greece setting up Masterlink, and Euro-Rainbow will be functioning when he officially relocates to Athens. Nice package, but then again, another glitch hit the system.* Kavidas's sources advised him of the failure to destroy Douglas and his subsequent plan to relocate to Israel.

He paused to reflect and realized that amidst his accomplishments, Douglas remained a thorn in his side that just couldn't be removed. *I will have to make him a priority when I get situated in Athens—need to totally eliminate the problem.*

The intercom beeped. "Mr. Kavidas, a phone call for you," his butler announced.

He walked to the telephone sitting on the floor where a table used to be. "Kavidas."

"Mr. Kavidas, Maurice Ryder here."

"Oh, hello, Ryder. Thanks for your support. I won't forget it."

Kavidas had already paid Ryder numerous bonus checks; the number was in the six figures. The man probably mentally added up another one every time they talked on the phone.

"I thought I might be able to put in one last word before you leave for Athens," Ryder said.

A man can be very resourceful when he's put on commission, Gregory thought. "Anything come to mind?"

Ryder snickered. "The *Koinonos* thing is old news. They're splintering even as we speak. What about working Douglas from the personal angle, like enlarging on his relationship with Lane's son?"

Gregory looked at the phone in surprise. "How do you mean that?"

"You know, a little flowery journalism."

His patience was wearing thin. "Spell out what you mean, Ryder."

"Well, to silence him for good, we need to brand him in such a way that no one would dare follow him again."

"Go on."

Gregory knew that Ryder had baited the hook; now he started reeling in the line. "Well, my sources advise me that his friend Brandon is gay, and I'm thinking that if we can link him—"

"By claiming that Douglas is having a homosexual relationship with him?" Kavidas put in.

"I know it will work."

Gregory had to admit that Ryder earned his money and the public was repulsed by gay ministers. It had good possibilities. "Let me think about it."

"My deadline for tomorrow is 2 p.m. today. I'll call you back after lunch."

"Fine." Gregory replaced the phone and thought about the timely suggestion. This kind of press could never be lived down, even if it were a bold lie and the paper had to print a retraction the following edition— weekly tabloids proved that. Most people were predisposed to believe evil or bad reports of someone, especially a celebrity who'd been in the media spotlight recently. Coupled with Douglas's fiasco in Orlando, the public would swallow the whole thing; he was sure of it.

The Taco Shack at Flagler and NW Third Avenue was Ryder's favorite place for lunch. A little over two miles from the *Miami Star*, he looked forward to taking his motorcycle, his new Harley Heritage Softtail 1580, down the sun-swept streets each day. The fully dressed out metallic blue bike with belt drive commanded respect. Even at idle, the tremolo from the Screaming Eagle pipes made his presence known. He loved coming up to a stoplight, then revving the engine as onlookers held their ears from the deafening roar. The motorcycle had cost him nearly $24,000, but happiness had no price tag and to him it was worth it.

Sudden thunderstorms and violent tornadoes were a part of South Florida's summer weather patterns. Often, a sun shower could bring rain on one side of the street while the other side remained sunny. Few people adjusted their lifestyle for the abrupt tropical rainstorms since they rarely lasted more than an hour.

Today was no different. After his lunch, Ryder looked out from the Taco Shack and saw the unexpected rain falling and shrugged it off as no big deal, knowing his rain gear was in his saddlebags and his big hog could easily navigate the wet terrain.

The traffic heading north on NW Third Avenue came to a standstill due to the rain, and when he checked his watch, he grunted when he realized his deadline was in 20 minutes. *I'll take an alternate down Miami Avenue*, he thought, *even though it's not my favorite route for the bike*. He hated the potholes and the small kids playing in that street; he had to drive too slow. *Tough it out*, he thought. *Take the challenge*.

The rain was falling heavily, but at least the traffic was moving. Half a mile down Miami Avenue he got caught in a downpour. "Great, just what I need," he sneered, as the rain hit his helmet shield.

He quickly wiped off the falling rain with one hand, but at this speed, the oncoming rain blurred his vision. He reduced his speed to a crawl and kept his eye on his watch when suddenly he hit a pothole. He cursed aloud but was relieved that no damage to his bike occurred. He accelerated to 35 mph to make up for the lost time.

His Harley was heavy but would still hydroplane under certain rainy conditions. Pushing the edge was Ryder's style, so he throttled up to 65 mph. He marveled at how well his Harley handled in rough weather but was upset with the helmet shield fogging.

On the adjacent street, lightning stuck a transformer atop a telephone pole, shutting off the power to the nearby vicinity, disabling the traffic signals.

Ryder raced through the intersection. He never saw the Sunbelt cab coming at him. He screamed violently through his helmet as the Harley slammed into the cab.

When the cab driver ran to aid the motorcyclist, the first thing he noticed was the rider's contorted neck somewhat still attached to his limp body.

"Who is this?" the voice on the phone said.

"Isn't this Mr. Ryder's private line?" Kavidas asked, surprised when a woman picked up the phone. He looked at his wristwatch and raised an eyebrow, irritated that press time was half an hour ago.

"Yes, this is his private line, but he's had an accident, and I'm covering his desk."

Startled by the news, Gregory asked, "Oh, is he okay? It wasn't serious, was it?"

"I'm afraid he was killed, sir. A fast-moving cab hit him as he rode his motorcycle during his lunch hour."

Gregory cringed. "I'm really sorry to hear about it." He paused; then a thought came to mind, "Has anybody been assigned his work yet?"

The lady was very cooperative. "It's a little too soon, but by tomorrow, the editor will have another journalist reviewing his work. Can you call back?"

"Perhaps. Thank you." Gregory clicked off. "Rats," he muttered, "and just when I was beginning to think he had a good idea."

Perplexed over the turn of events, he jumped on top of a wooden crate containing his heirloom sofa and carefully pondered his options. In a matter of minutes, a superior revelatory idea formed in his mind that would rid the earth of the irritants that blocked his path.

A full day spent in the hot Jordanian sun entitled anyone to some rest. Brandon and Pano had spent the last 11 days on the summit, where the ancient theater remains were located. They left their tents and supplies with the rest of the group and retired back to their main camp at Nabat Kibbutz, where they could more effectively control the restoration and ultimate re-provisioning of the ancient city. With Petra being the ancient capital of the Nabataeans, it seemed natural that the kibbutz would be named after that people. With the people long gone from the world, the monuments in the city and the small kibbutz were all that remained of this once great civilization.

With all the tour groups emerging on the city every day, the archaeological team was forced to be discreet. The huge amphitheater provided the perfect place for them to set up camp. The area easily sat

3,000 spectators, and the small camp did little to detract from the area's natural beauty.

Seeing a large group of archaeologists on a dig even gave the tourists something to talk about. All of Brandon's people were purposely friendly and helpful, letting each one of the tourists think that they were present while a great discovery was being uncovered. To a certain extent, this was true. With permission from Jordan's government, Brandon was able to go into ruins that had been closed to the public for decades. They were not only preparing the ancient buildings for a safe haven; they were actually uncovering many genuinely interesting artifacts. He was glad of that since the government expected some return for their generosity to the scholarly team. It certainly gave credence to their operation, since archaeology wa,s in truth, not their major concern.

"On second thought, Pano, maybe we probably should get some of these artifacts to Barrett," Brandon said. "He will want to catalog them for the museum before giving them to the authorities in Amman."

Brandon knew that Sam was not looking forward to going to Jordan's capital city and had even requested that the artifacts go through the Jerusalem museum prior to being taken deeper into Jordan. The government was being cooperative, but they were not taking any chances that the Jerusalem museum would end up with their goods. They agreed that Barrett could catalog them privately in Jerusalem, since he was working there. But they were not interested in having the pieces shown in Israel.

"When is he coming to Nabat, *file mou?*" Pano asked lazily. He didn't seem to want to break out of his reverie.

"I don't think he'll be here for a while, and I think we should let the Jordanian officials see that they made no mistake in allowing us to come here," Brandon added. "I'll have to take these pieces to Sam myself."

"But you are too important *here, Basili,*" Pano argued. "The group needs you here to, well, push them along."

"Yeah, but I need a bath." Brandon grinned. "Twelve days is a little long without one—even if this heat is dry and you hardly sweat before it evaporates. Besides, I wouldn't trust just anyone from the group to go. These items, even though they are small, are still too valuable." Brandon could see the look in Pano's eye, and he knew the man had not dropped the subject. He could tell Pano was thinking and waited patiently until he said what was on his mind.

"Would you trust me, *file mou*?" Pano asked seriously.

"You?" Brandon exclaimed, perplexed. "Of course I trust you," he said, almost laughing. "Why would you ask that?"

"Well, you didn't mention that I would come with you when you leave for Jerusalem," Pano began cautiously, looking down toward the floor, "and I know how important it is for you to be here. Much more important than me, since you bring the group together. I thought maybe you could send me in your place. This way the work here would continue. No delays."

"It simply never occurred to me to send you, but you're right. It would be better for me to stay and keep pushing on with the work."

"I will do this for you," Pano said excitedly. "Then I will know that you are safe."

He smiled at Brandon, searching his face as if he could read any hidden misgivings. When Brandon didn't offer any, Pano said he'd begin to plan his trip.

Raindrops dripped lazily down the airport windows while David watched the baggage handlers load the jumbo jet bound for Tel Aviv.

Thinking back, he was amazed how quickly the four weeks went since their home was destroyed and how God's mercy enabled him to get all the necessary documents and visas ready in such short notice.

He turned and smiled at Kathy, sitting contentedly with their children, reminding himself, despite the slow drizzle that seemed to cast a dreary light on the event, that they were determined to make this journey an adventure. No, they hadn't really taken the time to dwell upon the right or wrong of leaving their friends and family, not wanting that to influence their decision. What really mattered was the wonderful assurance they had in their hearts and spirits. In the main, it struck him as odd that *Koinonos* continued to scatter and weaken, especially when he believed the organization was orchestrated by God from the beginning. But then again, he also thought that stalking and confronting Kavidas was right, too.

He shook his head as he continued the diatribe. *No, that was different,* he thought. *That was an emotional reaction that God couldn't honor. But I really believed* Koinonos *was from the Lord. Perhaps the program was too soon. The idea is sound, but the time is not right yet.*

He motioned to Kathy and walked to the airport newsstand for the paper.

"Kathy, listen to this," he said aloud as he walked back to her. "Ryder was killed in a motorcycle accident three days ago." He pulled out the obituary section of the *Miami Star* and handed it to her.

Kathy read the piece silently, then handed the paper back to him. He knew her long enough to know what she was thinking, and he thought the same thing. He sat down next to her and gestured for the kids to move down a few seats.

"Interesting coincidence, wouldn't you say?" he said softly as he put his arm around her.

"We don't believe in coincidences, remember?"

"Of course," he agreed. "I also believe this is another sign that the Lord is going to protect and take care of us while we're in Israel."

The flight attendant announced boarding procedures as Kathy rubbed David's cheek with her finger. "May it be so."

Brandon watched as Pano gathered the last of the artifacts and readied himself for his trip. He felt as if his right arm were leaving, even though he knew that if he himself were making the trip, it would mean the same separation. There was still something different about being left behind.

He looked over the list in his hand for the last time and gave it to Pano. "Here is the list of supplies we will need from Jerusalem, after you have met with Sam. David will be in the city by the time you get there. Meet with him first at the Institute and let him know of our progress. It will be easier that way, since Kathy may be able to help secure the supplies while you travel to meet Sam. Someone at the Institute will be able to help you both get around.

"I know it seems like a long time," Brandon continued. "But you will be back in a few days. You'll see." He smiled.

Pano smiled. Then he walked away and got on the bus that would take him back to Beersheba and then to Jerusalem.

Brandon himself would be on a different bus in a few hours—one that would take him back through the Sik and up into the city again. So now he waved as Pano's bus drove away.

Come back to me soon, Pano, my friend.

SEVENTEEN

The view of Jerusalem
is the history of the world;
it is more,
it is the history of earth and heaven.
Benjamin Disraeli

The flight from Miami to the Holy Land was long, but in David and Kathy's minds, doing God's will, along with the prospect for the future made it all worthwhile.

The Holy Land, where God has directed the course of events since time began, would be their home for an interminable period. The Holy Land, a tiny piece of real estate in the Mideast, wherein lies the ruins of the world's ancient civilizations. The land that through the ages was the land of the prophets and of Christ, who with their immortal teachings and laws, superintended the course of humanity toward justice and law by producing the three monotheistic faiths. Judaism, Christianity, and Islam. A land of faith and love that has also been a land of war and misery. Babylonians, Greeks, Romans, Persians, Crusaders, Turks—even the British and Arab worlds—have fought to maintain control for over 2,500 years. Hopefully it would be a city of peace for the Douglas family. They longed for that special peace that comes by being in the will of God.

But God's will for David would postpone that peace until a later season.

Stringed together hand in hand, the Douglas family deplaned at the Ben Gurion Airport in Tel Aviv, united in their goal to start a new life amidst a

463

hostile land that has been occupied as early as 9,000 BC.

"*Shalom alechem,*" David greeted the sherut (station taxi) driver with his luggage cart.

"*Alechem shalom,*" the frail Israeli replied with a broad smile. "I can speak English. I used to live in New York."

"Seems I can't get away from those New Yorkers," David replied in jest. "We need to go to the American Institute on Mount Zion."

The driver nodded and smiled, displaying several missing teeth. "We will take the scenic route through Jaffa by the sea."

"That will be nice." David waved his family into the van as the driver loaded their luggage. The aura of Israel, with its nearness to God and its Chosen people, brought happiness to his heart.

The Jaffa Road, located northwest of Jerusalem, overlooked the beautiful Mediterranean on one side and the ancient city of Jaffa on the other. Staying on the road brought one into Jerusalem.

At the intersection of the Jaffa and Hebron Road, David tapped the shoulder of the driver and motioned for him to pull over. They couldn't pass up the view overlooking the sacred city Jerusalem, where, in 1,000 BC, King David built his home that would someday become the holiest city in all of Israel. From where they stood, the sun-drenched golden light shone on the old city where the Western (Wailing) Wall and the Temple compound were, signaling a divine welcome. *Lord, it sure is good to be here*, he thought.

Twenty minutes later they were at the American Institute, known to Americans as the Institute of Holy Land Studies.

Registering and unpacking took the entire afternoon, leaving David only a brief period to see the classroom where he would be teaching.

Exhaustion, however, gave way to excitement so that after dinner, he was revitalized. "Let's go to the wall!" he exclaimed to Kathy. "We can walk it from here, but the air is cool, so put jackets on the children."

Kathy held his arm and replied, "It's going to be good for us here."

Reveling in his newfound tranquility, he hugged her with one arm while mussing his son's hair, then reached down and scooped Hillary up in his arms and started singing in rhyme, "We're off to see not the wizard, but the wisest and not of Oz, but of God."

"Huh?" Hillary said.

"The Temple or what's left of it, silly, built by Solomon, the wisest man on earth." David skipped out of the institute's dining room with his three children following him as if he were Dorothy on the yellow brick road to Oz.

Once they passed through the security gate at the Temple site and gazed at the Wall, David walked over and sat down on a bench. The scene was far too overwhelming. He couldn't believe he was really here at the holiest shrine of the Jewish world—the last relic of the last Temple rebuilt by the Roman emperor Herod the Great in 20 BC. It was originally destroyed by the Babylonian King Nebuchadnezzar in 586 BC and rebuilt on a smaller scale by Zerubabel 70 years later. Herod refurbished the Zerubabel Temple as a token of friendship to the Jews in 20 BC. In 70 AD, the Roman general Titus destroyed it again for the last time. The Temple had represented the visible symbol of God's invisible presence.

"David, look at the Dome," Kathy said as she pointed to the Mosque of Omar—the Dome of the Rock. The dome on top of the mosque, made of plates of aluminum impregnated with gold, gleamed as the setting sun hit it.

"Beautiful." He sighed, then led Kathy by the hand to the Temple esplanade where the men and women separated into their own prayer quarters. He took his sons while Kathy took Hillary to the Wall.

When David stood before the wall, he leaned over and put his palm on the stone, then set his head on his hand and praised God for several moments.

To his immediate right were two Hasidim dahvening as they read their prayer books. Clothed in long black coats and bowler hats, with long side curls or peot emerging and dangling near their ears, the Orthodox Jews took no notice of David's arrival.

"Psst, Dad, what are those?" Alan asked, pointing to the thousands of small papers wedged in the crannies of the gigantic blocks of rock.

"They're prayer requests," David whispered. All slits, crevices, and holes in the rocks on the entire wall were stuffed with both tiny and large sheets of paper by unknown supplicants. Some of the petitions were faxed over from America and other points on the globe where their Israeli counterparts jammed them into place.

Alan nodded, then took one step back. "Why do they call it the Wailing Wall?"

David gestured for Alan to withdraw from the wall a short distance so they could confer. "Toward the end of the Roman occupation, the Jews were not allowed to come to Jerusalem. However, during the Byzantine period, they were permitted to come once a year on the anniversary of the destruction of the Temple to mourn the dispersion of their people and cry over the ruins of the Temple. After a while, this section of the wall became known as the Wailing Wall."

"Oh, that's cool."

Paul tugged on his father's arm and asked, "What do they call those weeds growing out of the Wall?"

David looked up to the wall. "Hyssop."

The shrub was an aromatic plant dating back to antiquity. Growing in rocky crevices, the plant was bunched and used to sprinkle blood on the doorpost in Egypt on Passover, and in purification ceremonies. At Christ's crucifixion it was used to relieve his thirst. *Even the weeds are part of history*, David thought.

Sensing his sons had enough of Bible class, he escorted them back to the courtyard to leave them with Kathy and Hillary. "I'll be just a few minutes," he said to them as he walked back to the Wall.

The Wall represented the last vestige of God's working in Israel. The meeting place where millions of pilgrims have journeyed to worship. He couldn't leave just yet.

It was hardly the moment for ruminations, but David took the time to square his thoughts before the Wall. *After all,* he thought, *the Wall is a place to pray and organize your thoughts before God, to clear your conscience before your Maker. Lord, if you have a job for me to do over here....*

The airport limousine stopped abruptly at the front entrance of the Dimakos Corporation where a man dressed in a uniform courteously opened the car door for Shlomo Shoen, a handsome, middle-aged Israeli, smartly dressed in an expensive European suit. Athletic-looking and sporting an American hairstyle, Shoen's expertise and vicious nature engendered respect throughout the Zionist community.

"Welcome to Athens, Mr. Shoen. May I escort you to the

receptionist?" the security guard asked.

Shoen nodded as he emerged from the car and shook his head in bewilderment. He stood on the sidewalk for several minutes, enthralled with the mammoth size of the Kavidas and Stein building. As a man who prided himself on being of few words, Shoen motioned for the man to lead the way up to the corporate offices.

Shoen looked around in amazement. *Such opulence,* he thought. *Do not my people deserve an opportunity to live like this?*

Equivalent in square footage to the *Redisearch* building back in the States, the Dimakos building had one major structural difference—a subterranean section that housed all the *Masterlink* computers. Both Kavidas's and Stein's stately offices were on the first floor, while a host of clerical offices, fitted with the state-of-the-art electronics, occupied the second story. A hidden elevator from both Kavidas's and Stein's floor provided quick access to the underground supercomputer room. This was the one area guests like Shoen would never see.

"Please sit down," the pretty Greek receptionist advised Shoen as she pointed to a Grecian-style love seat outside Mort's office. To celebrate his relocation to Greece, Gregory had his offices furnished in Grecian antiques from the sixteenth century.

"Mr. Stein will see you now, Mr. Shoen," the young woman said a short time later.

Effusive as ever, Mort clasped Shoen's hands. "Welcome, Mr. Shoen." He walked him over to an elegant stuffed chair and gestured for him to sit down. "As you know, our representative in Tel Aviv arranged for you to meet me based on your association with Zionism and in particular the Atara L' yoshna organization. You are hailed as a mighty warrior who fights with his mind, not with his fists."

"You are very kind," Shoen replied modestly.

Mort pointed toward the basement and continued, "We have access to great amounts of information through our *Masterlink* system, and with the aid of our Israeli network, we developed a list of candidates for an important mission. Your name came up on the top of the list." Mort could discern that Shoen was flattered but reserved.

A knock on the door arrested their attention.

The receptionist opened the door and stood still as she waved in a short-bearded man.

"Mr. Shoen, I'd like you to meet Mr. Kokkoris of the Athinai Bank. He handles our finances here in Greece," Mort announced.

Shoen motioned for a handshake and said, "My pleasure, Mr. Kokkoris." There was something about the banking business that commanded respect.

The men settled in their chairs with a high degree of apprehension since Mort had kept the agenda of the meeting secret. "In my mind, Zionism is an important tool," Mort began. "One that I plan to support well."

Shoen grinned and interjected, "God will bless you."

Mort ignored the blessing and continued, "It is a fact of political science that Israel is a time bomb, and certain strategic sites, holy if you will, are detonators. I'm thinking of so-called sacred buildings and memorials that have been standing for centuries where worshippers from around the world come to pay homage. These places are magnets that draw followers and are extremely volatile and important playing cards in the game of political and military poker in Israel. Specifically, the Temple Mount area that includes the Wailing Wall and the Dome of the Rock."

Shoen's physiognomy revealed his state of perplexity. He shot a look at Kokkoris and shrugged, as if to imply, *Where are you going with this? What do you want, Mr. Stein?*

"A brief kaleidoscope back in time will serve as background," Mort continued. "Back in the year 1187, the Crusaders were dislodged by the Moslem leader Saladin, and Jerusalem was confirmed as the third holiest place in Islam. Mecca and Medina in Saudi Arabia are numbers one and two. But prior to that year, the Moslems weren't even interested in Jerusalem.

"In the year 1990, violence broke out on the Temple Mount between Moslems and Jews over the issue of ownership, providing recent evidence that the Moslems believe that Jerusalem is AL-QUDS, 'the Holy One,' and that the Jews have no right to it. On the other side, today, we know that the Atara L' yoshna militant organization is determined to restore Jewish life to its former state with complete Jewish sovereignty that includes a rebuilt Temple. In their minds, there is no justifiable basis that would historically support Jerusalem or the Temple Mount to be a holy place in Islam."

He paused and winked at Shoen. "Of course, the Moslem presence has divinely preserved the holy sites for the Jews," he added.

Shoen curled his lip in disgust at the mention of the Arabs.

"This is where I need your help, Shlomo, since you're a part of that group. Now we know that these two hostile forces are presently in neutral, waiting with baited breath for God to move in some supernatural way to show who he wants to win out in the contest—the Moslems or the Jews."

Mort continued to build his case. "Jewish authorities have approached the Islamic Council and proposed a plan to dismantle the Dome of the Rock and other sacred sites, then reassemble them in Mecca—their holy place—in an attempt to diffuse the age-old, ongoing conflict, to no avail. Even during the Desert Storm War of 1991, many Israelis were praying a misguided Scud missile would accidentally land on the Dome and destroy it. Of course extremists are always on the prowl to help any cause that threatens to blow one of the sites up, but they are neither organized nor adequately funded, or perhaps the timing was not right."

He turned to Shoen, carefully watching his reaction. Shoen and Kokkoris simply remained silent to allow Mort's dissertation to sink into their minds.

"As a Jew," Mort said, "I know that when Messiah comes, he will make all things right..."

Shoen shot up his clenched fist in a gesture of triumph at Mort's words.

Mort continued, "And while that event is unpredictable, what's wrong with helping God usher in the Messianic reign by—" he dramatically halted his presentation, hoping Shoen would fill in the blanks.

"Are you suggesting that we help God along somehow?" Shoen asked, flushed as if with sudden revelation. "Don't you realize that Moslems know that if Israel rebuilds the Temple, it will be impossible for Islam to regain jurisdiction of the Mount area? There would be a cry of the Jihad that would not stop until the blood bath ran high enough to reach—"

"'The bridle of a horse,'" Mort quoted somberly.

Shoen blinked and nodded.

"Well, not really. That game doesn't happen for a long time yet and with a different set of players," Mort corrected, "but we are thinking in the same direction." He walked over to Shoen and placed his hand on his shoulder. "Soon after World War II, after the UN sanction of Israel's independence, the Mufti of Jerusalem declared, 'The entire Jewish population in Palestine must be destroyed or driven into the sea. Allah has bestowed upon us the rare privilege of finishing what Hitler only began. Let the Jihad begin. Murder the Jews. Murder them all.'"

He stepped in front of Shoen and asked, "Has that changed?"

Shoen shook his head, then squeezed his eyes shut and chanted, "They will not stop until they have complete domination of all non-Moslem land—it is commanded by their god, Allah." Then he recited like a foreign creed, "The late Mr. Arafat has said that Palestine is the cement that holds the Arab world together, or it is the explosive that blows it apart."

Recognized by the UN and the Arab states since 1974 as the government of the Palestinians, the Palestine Liberation Organization was founded in 1964 and dominated by the Al Fatah guerrilla squads under the leadership of Yasir Arafat until his death. The position of the PLO is that Israel is an illegal country that should be displaced by Palestinianism, using guerrilla warfare and terrorism to achieve its goals.

He opened his eyes slowly and added, "It is as you say."

"Then I've given you some ideas?" Mort prompted. "Remember," he added slyly, "if you refuse, the blessing and glory will go to someone else."

That last phrase got to Shoen. His eyes blazed with the prospective glory that incites rabid extremists. "'Love, friendship, and respect do not unite people as much as a common hatred for something.' The words of the great Russian Anton Chekhov. Fits here, doesn't it? Hate will reign bigtime after this goes down."

Mort saw the dirty look that Kokkoris gave Shoen. Mort knew that, down deep, Kokkoris really hated Americans and Jews—especially Jews who idolized and mimicked Americans. "You will be a champion among your people," he asserted, "and a wealthy one at that."

Mort knew that Kokkoris was adding something else too, but he didn't say it: *And hopefully get killed along the way.*

"What's needed here, Mr. Stein," Shoen said, "is a committed Israeli who is not concerned with Islamic reprisals—but *is* concerned with making Israel a homeland for Jews only."

470

Mort pointed to Kokkoris. "We have all the assets we need to accomplish that part of the goal, and, I hasten to add, to rebuild the Temple. Remember, Shlomo, Zionism is only a dream—a theory—without the Temple. With the Temple standing, Zionism *is* a reality. Do you believe the task of rebuilding the Temple will better your people while at the same time acclaiming you as a hero for helping it all come about?"

Shoen smiled. "The Lord, blessed be his Name, is capable of working through Atara L' yoshna." He gazed out the window. "My parents were killed by the PLO in Beirut in 1981. They were living in a Jewish settlement near the buffer zone." He shook his head as his eyes filled with rage. "Very unfortunate for them; very unfortunate for the PLO. That's one more reason why I'm a so-called fanatical Zionist."

"You're a good choice," Mort affirmed. He turned to Kokkoris. "Take Mr. Shoen out to dinner and discuss our payment schedule, making sure that his needs are met."

Shoen smiled in triumph because the realization of a dream was coming true today. The opportunity for him to be instrumental in bringing on the Messiah and to become wealthy and live in opulence had finally presented itself. *Maybe I'll leave this mess afterward and go live in Beverly Hills*, he thought with a chuckle.

The thought that this plan could backfire and begin the destruction of Israel never entered his mind.

Later Kavidas congratulated Mort in doing his homework. To recruit and sell Shoen on the plan to help God along by destroying the sacred mosque was nothing short of supernatural.

An hour north of Jerusalem, a little over 52 miles, lies the city of Scythopolis. Near the junction of the Jezreel and Jordan valleys, the historic city attracts archaeologists from around the world. Known in biblical times as Beth Shan, diggers have unearthed 18 separate levels of occupation, dating back to prehistoric times. Contributing to the continuous occupation were the natural and geographic factors, the many natural springs and intense heat, making Beth Shan a garden paradise. Because the city was located at the crossroads of Palestine's two great valleys meant that all traffic, from Egypt to Damascus and from the Mediterranean coast to the east, had to pass by the city.

Moses' predecessor, Joshua, was unable to capture Beth Shan since his troops could not cope with the iron chariots of the Egyptians. The Philistines, however, occupied the city and after killing King Saul in battle cut off his head and placed it along with his body and armor in the temple of Dagon. One of their pagan gods.

From the entranceway leading into the ruins, David and Kathy's eyes fell upon the giant Tel that fills the horizon as one comes into the region of Beth Shan. With layer upon layer of forgotten civilizations, the Tel rises over 100 feet above the latest victor's architecture.

Kathy stood in a corner as David walked over to the man wearing a time-worn safari hat and jacket. The man was measuring one of the many arches in the Roman amphitheater. David tapped him on the shoulder. "Sir, could you direct me to the men's room?"

The aging man turned with a befuddled look. "Direct you to where?" he said gruffly. "David!" he exclaimed as he dropped his tape measure to the ground upon seeing his face. They hugged each other for several moments as Kathy walked over to them.

"It sure is good to see you, Sam! We found out from Matthew what your itinerary was. How is your research going over here?"

"Very well. And how are your accommodations at the Institute?"

"Couldn't ask for better."

Dr. Barrett turned to Kathy and said somberly, "Real sorry to hear about your home burning down."

"A blessing in disguise," she replied as she gave him a big hug. "If it weren't for that incident, we wouldn't be here with you."

Barrett nodded in appreciation. "Children all right?"

"They're fine," Kathy replied. "Staying with a fellow professor from the Institute while we visit with you."

"Let's go for a walk," Dr. Barrett suggested as he picked up his tape measure and motioned for them to follow him into the giant bowl of the amphitheater.

They wandered over to the remains of the stage area and sat down. After a few moments of contemplation he asked, "Have you thought about your purpose in being here, David?"

David nodded toward Kathy. "We believe the Lord sent us here, but he hasn't revealed his plan for us yet. So we're simply going about our task of teaching at the Institute—keeping a low profile, you might say."

"Certainly a worthy vocation," he observed, "but I believe it's no accident you are here now…in these unfolding of events. This is a divine appointment. The Lord has sent you here for a purpose."

"Has the Lord spoken to *you* about us?" David asked.

"No," Sam replied, "but I feel intensely within my spirit that your being here is for a reason.You're a star that the Lord has destined to guide others to himself, especially in the events that are occurring here in Israel. You must believe that."

David grimaced. "Did you hear about my fiasco back in the States up in Orlando over Kavidas? I crashed and burned bigtime."

Barrett smiled. "All part of God's plan to launch you into orbit so you would land here in Israel."

Hearing a homily from an archeologist—acting as one of his mentors—reminded David of how easy it was to become desensitized to spiritual things. He was taken aback when faced with the revelation that he had been disappointed with God. "You're reminding me of God's sovereignty and that everything in life is connected to God's purpose."

"Everything," Dr. Barrett replied. "In fact, I believe that group you started, the *Koinonos,* will play an important part of future events. Right now the group is scattering in the U.S. because of the persecution generated by Kavidas and his cohorts. But I have a hunch that the day will come when that organization will be mightily used of the Lord, and you and Brandon will probably be one of the key figures of leadership that is used to regroup them."

David shrugged, ashamed of his secular reasoning. "Right now I'm not really thinking of leading anything anymore except my classroom at the institute," he added humbly.

"It will happen in God's time, David, and not one second before," Dr. Barrett reminded him. He reached into a deep pocket in his safari jacket and pulled out a notebook with diagrams of the ruins. "Now let me show you some artifacts that date back to the time of another David, the King of

Israel." He stood up and motioned for them to follow him into the site.

Later, as he looked out his classroom window into the Valley of Hinnom, David tried to imagine where the ancient high places of Baal used to be. The wicked pagans, along with Kings Ahaz and Manasseh of Judah, were guilty of sacrificing their children as burnt offerings to the god Molech. The prophet Jeremiah prophesied that God would judge the horrific abominations and would cause such a destruction that the Valley of Hinnom would become the "Valley of Slaughter." Hinnom was used as the garbage dump for the city of Jerusalem where refuse, waste materials, and dead animals were burned. Continuous smoldering fires and smoke produced a wretched stench that rose day and night so the place became a symbol of woe, judgment, and the place of punishment. Translated into Greek, the Hebrew *Hinnom* becomes *gehenna* or *hell*. It was easy to see why.

"Mr. Douglas, do you have your field trip itinerary yet?" a soft voice from behind asked.

Snapping out of his concentration David turned around. "Hi, Ilyana. How are you?"

The young, attractive Sabra had started as a student at the Institute last year. "I'm fine, thank you," she replied in fragmented English. She repeated her request. "Do you have your field trip itinerary prepared yet? We are ready to print it for your students."

David reached into his attaché case and pulled out a two-page schedule and reviewed it with her. "Monday, the 15th we'll tour the Old City of Jerusalem. Tuesday the 16th, Jerusalem and Bethlehem, which includes the Mount of Olives, Gethsemane, the Garden Tomb, and the Holocaust museum Yad Vashyem. And Wednesday, the 17th, The Wailing Wall, the Temple Mount, the Dome of the Rock, and the Al-Aqsa mosque." The schedule included the approximate arrival and departure times. The Institute would provide the transportation by bus.

"Very good, Mr. Douglas," she replied. "The programs should be completed by 2 p.m. tomorrow."

474

"We're going along with you," Kathy declared after David announced his upcoming tour at dinner that evening. "The children have never seen any of those holy sites, and it's been years since I've been to them. It won't be a problem with the Institute, will it?"

"No. It will be fine. The class is only 12 students, so with our family, the group is still very manageable. In fact, you can help chaperone—it will be like it was back in the States when we used to go camping." David grinned as Kathy grunted.

To avoid suspicion he dressed in a custom kaffiyeh and caftan and waited on the steps of the mosque until a burst of tourists arrived. After 35 minutes, several bus loads of Americans and Europeans filled the courtyard, triggering in his mind the go-ahead to enter the holy site. The tourists stripped off their forbidden accessories (cameras, shoes, pocketbooks, etc.) and laid them in a pile. Careful to appoint a watch person, Shoen made his way to the main entrance where an armed guard looked him over, nodded his approval, and let him in.

Once inside the Dome of the Rock, Shoen methodically and religiously walked around the octagonal sanctuary noting every entrance, exit, and window necessary to complete his mission. His eyes were like a video camera, capturing in his mind every column, vestibule, and all the security personnel, particularly noting the times of their patrol.

Since this was only his third visit to the shrine, Shoen couldn't help but be overwhelmed by its beauty. For several moments, he set aside his mission and gazed in wonder at the house of worship. As one of the most striking monuments in all of Jerusalem, the Byzantine design, along with the Oriental decoration, including Persian tiles and marble slabs, set it apart from all the sacred places in Israel. Rising above the floor of the Temple is a dome that reaches a height of 108 feet, with a diameter of 78 feet. Beneath the dome lies the rock of Mount Moriah. The rock is 15 yards long by 12 yards wide and said to be the very rock where the patriarch Abraham prepared to sacrifice his son Isaac in the second millennium BC. Moslems maintain that Abraham took his other son, Ishmael, to sacrifice, not Isaac. Some Christians purport that it was the Mount where Christ was offered on Calvary. For both Jews and Arabs, the site is holy.

He walked to the wooden balustrade barrier that kept pilgrims and tourists from snatching a piece of the rock, pretended to pray, then disguisedly paced off the distance to the outside wall. Confidently, he decided on the location, then made the necessary mental calculations for the size of the charge and quietly moved along with the crowds out of the building.

Stopping off at a service station to change back to European clothes, Shoen arrived at the Grand Hotel on Hayarkon Street in Tel Aviv, exactly 45 minutes after leaving the mosque. Using a pseudonym, Mort had rented the room by phone in Athens that would serve as a short-term shelter and, more importantly, a laboratory. With a degree in engineering from Haifa University, Shoen worked as a land surveyor for the Israeli Department of Transportation by day and as the chief ordnance technician for the Atara L' yoshna by night.

As he stepped in, he noticed an an overnight express envelope purposely slipped under the door. He set down his briefcase, opened the envelope, and read the message. It was from Stein in Athens.

The day of your visit must be Wednesday, the 17th, at 2 p.m. I just discovered that someone who has done me much harm will be there at that time. Snapshot enclosed.
—M.S.

He shrugged. The date and photo meant nothing to him, but he would happily comply. He checked the calendar on his wristwatch. *That's two days from now.* He smiled. *No problem.*

After closing the drapes and putting on the overhead light, he cleared an area on the hardwood floor to use as a stable surface. It was time to prepare the device.

Next he opened the briefcase and removed three small plastic jars containing nitrocellulose, a pulpy polymer derived from cellulose treated with sulfuric and nitric acids, nitroglycerin, and petrolatum that had been dissolved in acetone and dried. Then he took out a small vial containing fulminate of mercury powder encased in bubble wrap and placed it carefully on the floor next to the other items. The fulminate of mercury would act as the detonator when exposed to heat.

He spooned the fulminate of mercury, a gray crystalline compound, into a small perfume tube and kept it separate from the other ingredients for assembly just before transport. The nitrocellulose and nitroglycerin were mixed into a moldable doughlike solid and then rolled on the floor into a one-half inch strand that resembled licorice. Once covered with black cloth, it would look like an agal, the cordlike binding on top of the Arab headdress. He determined that the common agal length was three feet—providing sufficient corditelike explosive rope that would yield the required blast.

When the explosive cord dried, he wrapped it in black cloth, then sat down on the sofa and sewed the cloth with the explosive inside with black thread to form the agal to wind around his kaffiyeh. The two components were then set inside the briefcase for safekeeping. In two days he would sew in the detonator tube to complete the bomb.

On a hilltop in south Ramat Gan, located adjacent to Tel Aviv, Shoen calibrated the theodolite, then telephoned the adjustment in to his partner, Itzak, 200 yards down the road. The Department of Transportation needed a new survey of the suburban city streets near the diamond exchange in order to begin remodeling by next spring. Routinely he rotated the telescope on its tripod, then signaled his young assistant to move the measurement stick. He recorded the height and waved him in.

It won't be like this after tomorrow, he thought. *Pretty soon we start a new life. No more will I have to be subjugated to this department or their bureaucracy. I'll be my own boss.*

When Itzak returned, he put the stick in the van and shot a look at Shoen's clipboard. "Shlomo, are you sure about that entry? I thought the degree of declination was more than 18 degrees."

Shoen shrugged. "Close enough."

Itzak laughed. "Close enough? In this line of work, close enough is not enough. We wouldn't want to build the new road through somebody's store, would we? What's come over you?"

Shoen couldn't help himself. The dichotomy was getting to him today. His profession was in the building business. Roads, structures, bridges. His avocation was destruction. But the thrill of malicious mischief always appealed to his dark side—that was where he got his kick. "Not feeling good today, probably coming down with something. I'm not sure I'll be working the rest of the week. We can finish this up another time." He checked his watch and thought about the mission. "Let's quit early."

"Okay, with me," the novice said. Then he did a double take. "Shlomo, when did you get that new Rolex?"

"Came into some money recently. Thought I'd treat myself."

Itzak reached over and glanced at the precision timepiece. "Nice."

Itzak was trained to be alert. He was trained to think about variables and possibilities well beyond appearances. He was trained to be suspicious and trust no one except his higher command. He was trained to deny reason, logic, and the romantic ideology that posits the good of humanity. To him, everybody was a potential criminal if conditions are right. To Itzak, that was the very fiber of the real enemies of Israel. That was why he'd joined the Mossad, Israel's intelligence agency and reputed secret arm of justice, six years ago.

Pretending to nod off on the drive back to Tel Aviv, Itzak closed his eyes and pointedly recalled several heated debates he'd had with Shlomo over the past year that were now suspect. Shoen continuously championed Vladimir Jabotinsky, the militant Zionist leader who worked toward creating a Jewish state and demanded unrestricted immigration throughout Palestine after World War II. He also denounced the UN-sponsored truce that halted the war of 1948 to 1949 where the Arab states, made up of Egypt, Syria, Transjordan, Lebanon, and Iraq invaded Israel in protest for the planned statehood—Shoen believed Israel could have defeated them totally—avoiding UN interference.

Then he remembered when Shoen agreed with Theodore Herzl, the Austrian Jewish journalist, when he asserted that anti-Semitism would be cured when a totally Jewish state was established. Shoen had made it clear that any accommodation with the Arabs could come only from a position of Jewish strength. To prove his point one day, Shoen had brought in a pile of newspaper articles he had begun pasting in a scrapbook and looked to pick an argument with some of the "apolitical" surveyors before they left for their field assignments.

One article in particular that Itzak remembered was when the Arab world ridiculed Zionism as a "tool of imperialism" in 1975, followed by the UN adopting a resolution equating Zionism with racism. Shoen was furious. Looking back, Itzak recognized Shoen's penchant for extremism. Could Shoen have been working for Atara L' yosh*na* all along? he wondered.

Soon after Shoen dropped Itzak off at his home, Itzak made a phone call to meet with his team leader. Caution had dictated it.

Israeli intelligence boasts of being the best in the world. In the spirit of Ariel Sharon, Israel's celebrated Minister of Defense and politician, their mind-set is: "Jerusalem is not negotiable. It will never be negotiable. Jerusalem is the heart of the Jews. It has been the capital of the Jews for the last 3,000 years. We will accept no other arrangement."

For Israel, any state of emergency is a national crisis. With only 7,992 square miles of land (excluding Arab territories), which is about the size of the state New Jersey, Israel cannot afford to take any threat against its national security lightly.

"Give me your best guess. What do you think he's up to and who do you think he's working for?" Moshie Lenz asked Itzak.

Lenz was a highly disciplined man in his 50s who had family that worked in the Haganah, an early paramilitary organization, and knew the intelligence business like Arabs know sand. The Mossad had an anti-terrorist network that extended throughout the world. The network orchestrated the lightning raid on Entebbe, Uganda, in 1976, where Israeli commandos rescued 103 hostages seized by Arab and German terrorists. After the Oklahoma City Government Center bombing in 1995, Israeli officials offered their help to ferret out and bring the perpetrators to justice. Consistently, Israeli intelligence has preserved their title as a force to be reckoned with. "Whatever it is, I suspect he's making a lot of money off it. He acted like he wasn't coming back to the job ever again. That's what made me start thinking."

Lenz looked at the fax brief he just received on Shoen. "Hmm, seen in New York with the radical American Zionist leaders and their supporters, suspected of affiliation with Atara L' yoshna, parents killed by PLO in Lebanon, still single, good work record with Israeli government—but keeps to himself. Obviously he's a misguided Israeli with real allegiance to his homeland."

Itzak nodded. "If I had to make the call, I'd say he would go ballistic with the right motivation—like money. He often spoke about the Arabs killing his parents and his disagreement with government policy." He scratched his head and concluded, "He's a fanatic."

Lenz nodded and motioned that the meeting was over for now. "We're having him followed as we speak. You keep in touch."

The twelve o'clock sun was very hot. Shoen set a black cloth tube with a thermometer inside on his windowsill and observed the mercury's rate of climb. He had to test the detonator beforehand. Experience and knowledge of explosives, together with basic scientific know-how, qualified him to approximate the amount of fulminate of mercury to use, but he would get only one chance at this, so he had to time it just right.

In five and a half minutes, the temperature soared inside the cloth sleeve to 170 degrees and ignited the sampling of fulminate of mercury. *Perfect!* The sun for the next two hours would be hot enough to set off the charge while allowing him enough time to vacate the premises and be out of the Arab sector to fade into oblivion.

Satisfied that the device was operable, he donned his Arab garb, then attached the detonator to the agal on the kaffiyeh and fastened the entire headpiece securely to his hair with several bobby pins. He checked the room to ensure he took everything he needed, then grabbed his umbrella to keep the unwanted sun off his head and hailed a cab to take him to Jerusalem.

Pano arrived in Jerusalem without incident. He felt somewhat alone, since his English was still not perfected. Brandon had always been on hand to translate for him if he didn't understand. Now he needed to do this by himself. He wanted to be an integral part of what was going on.

Jerusalem was a city that he was not prepared for. Greece had its share of antiquity, but it was not the same as the Holy City. Greece was a country in decline and an antiquity that told only of yesteryear. Jerusalem was a city of tomorrow and of today. The monuments and the holy sites spoke of things that were alive. He could still feel a presence as he approached the city, unlike Athens, whose patron goddess Athena was long ago forgotten.

He could hear the guttural sound of the Hebrew language, and it reminded him of his native Greek. Mixed in was a fair amount of English, and he realized that America had a much larger influence here than in his country. Very few people spoke English in Greece anymore. The American tourists had long since stopped coming in large numbers. English still had a presence, but people only learned the language to be able to serve in the resort areas. In Israel, he noticed many people who looked like native Sabras speaking English with ease. He found himself admiring these people who had a spirit that spoke so vibrantly of life. It was as if the country were young again.

He wished something so wonderful could happen to his country. Greece was just so old, and he didn't see anything on the horizon that was going to give it the appearance of youth. The country, like its gods, was fading into history. Israel and its God would never be forgotten.

Pano paid the taxi driver to take him to the Institute and asked for David Douglas. When he was told that David was not in his office, he was left with little alternative but to wait. Having nothing but the Institute address and the Douglases apartment number, his second choice was to call. However, with no one at the Douglas home he decided to take a tour of the Institute itself.

Weaving in and out of the halls was not a problem. He had some difficulty in reading the signs and the exhibits, which were posted in Hebrew and in English, but he continued along, wishing he had taken Dr.

Barrett's number and address.

He realized, however, that Dr. Barrett would most likely be out on a site, and therefore Pano contented himself with the surroundings, the extensive collections of the institute, and the importance of his mission. He could see the look of pride on Brandon's face as he returned to Nabat or to Petra itself after completing his task. It made him smile to think of it, and he lost himself for a few minutes thinking of this small pleasure.

He was jolted out of his musing when he noticed a large display case. He could see that there were photos and small pieces that served as examples of several different kinds of scroll work. Recognizing some of the writing to be in Greek arrested his attention. He began to stare at the writings and compared them in his mind to the scrolls of the *Genesis Apocryphon* that they had found and translated. Although the scrolls were obviously of minor importance, being that they only talked of mundane daily living and didn't provide any life giving secrets as theirs had, he was still so engrossed that he didn't hear the young lady talking to him until she tapped his shoulder.

"I said, excuse me, sir. Can I help you?" The young woman was attractive and slender, and he could see from her large brown eyes that she was sincerely trying to be of assistance.

He tried his best to use his English and hoped it would be enough.

"I am waiting for friend," he said simply, knowing how easy it is to complicate matters and lose something in the translation when using complex ideas.

"What is his name?" the girl said succinctly, enunciating each syllable.

Pano inwardly smiled, knowing that the girl could see he had difficulty but savoring the fact that he was not as bad off as she thought.

"His name is David Douglas," he said clearly, proud of his efforts and sure that she had understood everything so far.

A perplexed look came across the girl's face. "You're not waiting for him here, are you?" she asked.

Pano had to ask himself the question several times, sure that he was getting it wrong. He simply couldn't understand why she would ask if he was waiting for David here. Maybe she felt he should wait by his office?

"I do not understand. I should wait someplace else? Can you show me his office?"

The girl smiled, as if finally understanding. She walked him over to the aerial map of the city on the opposite wall and pointed toward the center. "Mr. Douglas is going here today. He's taking a tour of the city with a group from the Institute. He isn't coming back today."

Pano frowned as he made the connection. Without Dr. Barrett's number or the Douglases' address, there was little he could do.

"I'm sorry. I did not know," he said slowly. Mentally, he calculated his options and asked the only thing he could think of. "Does he come here tomorrow?"

The girl smiled and beckoned to Pano as she walked across the hall.

"Come into my office. I may be able to help you. This is a nice place to visit, but I'm not sure you'd want to sleep here." She motioned to the chair in front of her desk.

He quickly sat down, amazed that this stranger would take the time and effort to assist him. At the same time, relief was washing over him as he realized he was not quite as prepared for this solo mission as he had thought.

"Here is a copy of Mr. Douglas's itinerary for today." She passed him the paper, and he looked at her quizzically. He didn't recognize the word. "Itinerary," she repeated, "like a schedule."

At this Pano nodded and smiled. One thing he had learned a great deal about since he arrived was keeping a schedule.

He looked at the time on his watch and saw that he was already too late to catch up with the tour at Hezekiah's Tunnel. He had no choice but to meet them by the Wailing Wall. He pointed to the entry on the paper and read it back to her. "Wailing Wall. I could meet him here, no?"

The girl lifted her hands in the air and clicked her tongue. "You see, you're on your way again, and you don't have to sleep on a chair." She seemed triumphant in her achievement and moved Pano back into the hallway. "Not that I would mind if you hung around. But I'm sure you'd rather join your friends."

Pano recognized the word *friends* easily enough. In fact, he felt as if he had just made another one.

"Yes, I will go see my friends, and I thank you for being my friend today. I will find the Wailing Wall." He looked over again to the map on the far wall and hoped it was marked.

"Well, if you get there early, there are plenty of other things to see. Look around. I'm sure you'll see the group and you'll find your friends.

And I'll see you tomorrow, yes, with your friend Mr. Douglas?"

Pano nodded and waved as she walked away. "Yes, tomorrow."

With the first obstacle out of the way, he tackled his next job. Finding the Wailing Wall. Fortunately the map was marked, and he found the Wall right away. He tried to figure out how he was going to get there without getting lost when he noticed that the large golden dome of the building marked the mosque was right next to the Wailing Wall.

If I get lost, I will look to the sky. You cannot miss this golden dome anywhere in the city.

He walked outside again and was greeted with the noise of the streets and the heat of the day. He laughed out loud as he realized his worry was for nothing. Directly in front of him was a line of taxis, waiting for their next fare.

Without looking back, he stepped into the car and closed his eyes. He was back on the right track, and he was going to do this. He patted the precious cargo he carried with him and visualized the artifacts as he leaned forward and spoke to the driver.

"Wailing Wall, please."

The driver took off without a word, and Pano was glad. He didn't want to have to explain a thing.

Sol, the senior member of a surveillance team, trained in long-range visual and audio acuity, took off the headphones attached to the parabolic antenna aimed at Shoen's room. They were across the street from the Grand Hotel. Together with his 1200 mm telephoto video lens, he could listen and record spiders weaving webs over 1,000 feet away.

He hit the speed dial on his special network cellular phone. "This is Sol. We just lost visual and audio on the subject. He left disguised like an Arab."

"I want you in his room now!" Lenz ordered over the wireless instrument.

The two men dropped everything and dashed across the street into Shoen's room.

Within four minutes, Sol was combing the room for clues. He went to the corner and knelt down, then smelled his finger after wiping it on the hardwood floor. His finger had traces of a gray powder on it. "Smells and looks like fulminate of mercury. I think we have a bomber on our hands," he advised Lenz on his phone.

"That Arab-looking person is our man, gentlemen, and I have a suspicion that he's on his way to make the drop."

"One more thing," Sol's partner added as he held up a snapshot, "I just found a wallet-size photo next to the cushion on the sofa. Looks like an ID shot of a white Caucasian—looks American."

"Bring it with you to the holy sites." The phone line went dead.

Since Israel has lived with terrorism for decades, intelligence officers like Lenz were trained to quickly recognize terrorist patterns. All the historic and sacred sites in the vicinity are continually watched, knowing they are prime targets for political aspirants. Accordingly, Sol knew that Lenz was giving the command to double the security at all the holy sites in Tel Aviv and Jerusalem. Everyone in the Mossad was on alert.

David's students and family filed out of the bus and regrouped in front of the entrance booths leading into the Wailing Wall compound. Despite the incident where a young student from the Netherlands fell and sustained a minor injury in the water shaft at Hezekiah's Tunnel, they arrived on schedule.

"Forty minutes to take notes and photographs at the Wall and Mount," David announced to the assembly. "Then meet me at the entrance to the Dome of the Rock so we can all go in together." He waved them away, and they dispersed into the crowds in seconds.

"We've already seen the Wall, David. Let's go up and wait in the courtyard by the Dome," Kathy suggested.

David latched onto Hillary as Kathy motioned for her sons to fall in line. "Let's do it," he said.

Pano arrived at the Wailing Wall a little early, according to the schedule he received at the institute. He began to walk around and found that the entire area was a mixture of culture, people, and religion. He was happy to find that the Church of the Holy Sepulcher had a strong Greek influence. There were inscriptions everywhere, and it inspired him to do some reading while he bided his time.

> In 638 AD Islam invaded the Holy Land and after subjugating the non-Moslem population began erecting buildings on their sacred sites. During the reign of Umar, the second caliph after Mohammed, Jerusalem was captured. Fifty-eight years later, the Umayyad caliph Adbed El Malik Ben Marwan built the Qubbat as-Sakhra, Arabic for the Dome of the Rock, a shrine to contain the Holy Rock.
>
> At first the Rock had no religious significance for Islam, but in time, perhaps to attract tourism to Jerusalem, stories of Jerusalem being the location where Mohammed's resurrection and journey into night were fabricated. Ironically, according to the Koran, Islam is the original religion of the Middle East from which all other religions, including Judaism and Christianity, sprouted.

Pano was unconvinced, but he was willing to go along with it since he was in such close proximity to the Dome. He decided to go and see for himself what the controversy was about. He had only another five minutes before the scheduled arrival of the tour, and he wanted to be back by the Wall early enough to spot the whole group.

He moved over to the mosque and was crestfallen when he saw the sign in English that said he could not bring anything into the building itself. He was very disappointed, but knew he could not leave his artifacts unguarded. He took a brief look around and moved toward the Wailing Wall to meet with his friends.

It was 2:05 p.m. when the entire group of students finally arrived. David checked his watch and shook his head—they were running a little late, and with the huge crowd touring the site, movement would be extremely slow. "We need a volunteer to stay outside and watch our shoes and camera equipment while we're inside; then we'll rotate and let that person tour the mosque."

A student from England raised her hand as the rest of the group set their belongings into a pile a short distance from the main entrance. With David and Kathy in the lead, the group marched toward the holy place.

Just then Kathy spotted a man she thought she knew outside the doors. She nudged David and edged closer. "Pano!" she exclaimed. "What in the world are you doing here?"

David looked up in surprise.

"I'm here for Basili—for Brandon. We have the first shipment of artifacts for Dr. Barrett. That, and to get supplies. To see you as well." He politely tried to shake hands with David and Kathy and awkwardly waved a hello to the remainder of the group.

"We were just going up to the Dome of the Rock," David said. "Come with us and tell us some news. The tour is almost over."

"I cannot go in, unless I leave my things," Pano said slowly, "and I do not want to leave them outside. They are very important." This last part was said slowly and quietly, as if he guarded a big secret.

"No problem," said David affably. "We've got someone watching our things. Leave your bag with her. She'll watch it carefully till we come out. You really should see it. It's worth it."

Seeing that David trusted this arrangement, and knowing that Brandon trusted David, Pano agreed. He placed his possessions in the hands of the English girl and moved with the rest of the group toward the top of the Temple Mount. He tried to relay the latest information from Petra, but he was hard pressed in so little time. The walk was not long, and the entrance not far away.

Lenz arrived on the Mount and signaled his plainclothes agents circling the mosque to form up with him in a huddle. "As I told you over your phones," he said, "we're looking for an Israeli carrying an explosive device, who is probably dressed like an Arab."

The agents looked in dismay at each other. There had to be over 200 Arabs there that fit that description.

"I know that doesn't narrow it down too much, but we'll have to wait till he makes a move. So half of the team works the outside, and the other half goes inside with me."

The outside team quickly started checking the identification of suspicious men fitting the description as the inside team flashed their IDs to the Arab guards. They walked in and rapidly fanned out inside the mosque. Despite the mosque being in Islamic jurisdiction, Lenz was confident the Arab officials would waive their objections in view of the crisis.

Inside, hundreds of Moslems silently walked around the circular path, many pausing and touching their foreheads to the ground in prayer. Others were clasping their hands on their stomachs and patting their knees in adulation. A large percentage of the men had removed their headdresses as they moved through the mosque.

As he strolled around the rock, Shoen checked the time as he checked the crowds, then spotted Douglas at the rail or balustrade that fenced off the rock. The rail somewhat encircled the rock. He reached for the photo and realized he misplaced it somewhere. "I'm sure that's him," he whispered to himself.

A glimmer of a smile of victory came across his face as he made his way toward the west window to set the device. He pretended to pay homage to the rock while looking around, then took off the kaffiyeh and laid it on the sill. Suddenly he realized the window was in shade. He muttered an expletive, then looked up and saw the weather had changed abruptly. It was now overcast. *Never planned on this*, he thought as he cursed. He scanned the building for an alternative location.

"This is the actual rock that Abraham offered Isaac on," David said over the noise of the crowds as he looked over the rail at the massive rock. "Can you believe that?"

Kathy nodded and reverently kneeled on one of the Persian carpets meticulously placed in front of the rail to allow worshippers and onlookers a close-up view. She grabbed David's hand to cherish the moment.

Suddenly an observant Moslem touched them on the shoulders and shook his finger in their face. "No, no," he whispered in English.

"I guess we're not allowed to hold hands in here," Kathy noted with a grin.

David looked across the Rock to the west side and saw a man take off his kaffiyeh and place it on top of one of the obscure corner lamps that shone light on the Rock. He gave the man a quizzical look, scratched his moustache, and dismissed it. Then he motioned for his children to join him at the rail for firsthand instruction.

"Do you think they'll ever be peace in this city, David?" Kathy asked. The aura of thousands of years of religious pilgrimage to these sacred memorials triggered the tear that now trickled down her cheek.

He leaned over to whisper in her ear, "The *Koran* says, 'The true Umma—the community of Islam—must fight in the way of Allah; all infidels in the way of idols. So true Moslem, fight the friends of Satan.' Only when Jesus returns will there be peace."

Two more tears rolled down her face before she stood up.

As he walked away from the rail, Shoen shot a look over at Douglas to check his movement. He turned to exit and realized he was in trouble. Israeli men dressed in European suits were stopping and asking the Arabs questions. Whether that would spark an international incident or not, he didn't care. He knew it was time to get out. He double-checked his time. He had just over four minutes to flee the building. *Idiots. They better not stop me.*

Lenz pulled one of his agents aside. "How many have you checked?"

"About 40 to 50. So far—nothing."

Sol hurriedly walked up to Lenz amidst the throngs and said quietly as he flashed the photograph, "Look—there's the man in the photo we found at the apartment. He's on the other side of the Rock!"

Lenz looked at the photo, then peered at David. "You're right." He assessed the distance and factored in the multitudes. "I'll get to him; you alert the others that this must be the location. On my signal, we announce an emergency to their security and clear the mosque."

At the doorway, Shoen checked the time, then turned to get a visual on the device. "I'll be—" he hissed. A Gentile teenager had knelt down near the kaffiyeh, spotted it laying on a lamp, and started toying with it. "Fool kid!" he rasped. He started making his way back to the railing.

A man walked up to David, popped a photo in his face, and said calmly, "Sir, I'm Moshie Lenz from Israeli intelligence. What is your name?"

David peered at the photograph, then back at Lenz. "David Douglas."

"I don't mean to frighten you, but this photo of you was found in a terrorist's apartment just one hour ago, and we believe your group and others are in danger—you must leave here right now!"

Discerning the threat to be genuine, David silently grabbed Kathy and his children by the hands, then called, "All Institute students outside

490

immediately!" He looked toward the exits and thought it impossible. Oceans of people were all around them. "We'll never get out of here," he groaned.

"Follow me, David," a young man commanded as he grabbed hold of David while waving his arm to plow through the people.

David squinted and gaped into the man's face as they marched out, thinking that he knew him from somewhere. *Could this be my guardian, Andy?* he thought in all the confusion.

Time seemed to stand still as the stranger spearheaded a path through the crowds to the door. Within 30 seconds, David's family and group were standing outside the mosque in front of their belongings, completely bewildered. He looked around for the mysterious guide and found nothing. Strangely enough, Pano was also missing.

As Shoen neared the railing, he saw the teenager tire of the novelty item and flip the kaffiyeh on top of the rail by the Rock. Shoen froze as his heart jumped. He reached for the kaffiyeh and gingerly placed it back on the light and checked his watch for the last time. *Two minutes. Phew! I'll just make it.*

Signaling his agents, Lenz shouted in Hebrew, Arabic, and English, "Bomb! Everybody out!"

Panic ensued and the four sets of double doors of the mosque flew open, allowing the masses of people to run out.

Pano only vaguely understood the words being shouted and looked around desperately to find David and the others. They were nowhere to be found.

The fulminate of mercury reached its unstable temperature 1.5 minutes earlier than Shoen expected, detonating the nitrocellulose and nitroglycerin compound. It produced a blast that would have blown the building apart had the doors been closed with the mosque filled with people. But the early warning minimized the casualties and structural damage.

As soon as David heard the thunderous report from the bomb, he yelled out, "Everybody hit the deck!" and dived for the ground.

Onlookers who heard the warning took cover where possible. The force of the bomb rebounded off the Rock and projected outward toward the walls of the mosque, catapulting many of the worshippers and tourists through the air and out the doors to safety. Only those within the close proximity of the bomb were killed. The concussion ripped chunks of rock from the sacred stone and splintered the railing, turning them into missiles that pummeled and tore flesh like fragmentary grenades. Three of the interior support pillars, situated five feet from the blast, toppled, crushing the bodies of escaping pilgrims.

Shoen was one of them.

EIGHTEEN

We have always said
that in our war with the Arabs
we had a secret weapon—
no alternative.
Golda Meir

Pano felt the initial blast hit him in the chest, and he was thrown across the room and onto a hard surface. He was not sure where he was but could not feel anything below his neck. He was certain the impact had severed his spinal cord, and he knew that the numbness that he felt throughout his body would soon spread to his head, ending his life forever. He tried to move his head and saw the lights around him that had shone on the stone itself, along with the balustrade that surrounded the Rock.

He knew that he was on the Shetiyyah Stone (the Foundation) itself and closed his eyes. *Am I the sacrifice today, God? He who would not believe in you and rejected all that you said—all that you would tell me?* He heard and felt a cough come from his throat and could taste the salt of his own blood as it spilled from his mouth on to the sacrificial stone.

His mind raced toward Petra and the man he loved, the man he knew he would not see again. Tears came to his eyes—not just as he thought of Brandon, but as he thought of the finality of his days and of the darkness that lay ahead. He tried to call out to David, the one person he knew in the area, but could not.

He lay still and tried to pray, but his mind went blank. He didn't know who to pray to. In all the years he could remember, he had never sought his name. Now, he feared, it was too late.

"Everybody okay?" David asked while his people began to stand and brush debris off their clothes. His entire group was unharmed. As he surveyed the compound, hundreds of people were still lying prostrate on the ground, covering their heads with their arms.

The Mossad and Arab guards, somewhat in control, welcomed the newly arriving police, who were frantically running in and out of the mosque, deciding what to do next.

"What happened?" Kathy asked David. She held her three children close to her as the turmoil unfolded.

"Somebody set off a bomb," David replied somberly, shaking his head. "Apart from any deaths inside, this is the one place, a sacred Moslem mosque, where a bomb explosion will reverberate around the world. This is going to cause big trouble."

"Mr. Douglas!" Lenz shouted. He was limping out of the mosque, holding a piece of someone's caftan as a bandage on his wound. "Can you come inside with me for a moment, please?"

David nodded at Lenz. "Coming."

Weaving his way among the dead and wounded, Lenz led him over to the place where the bomb exploded. He reached down and turned over a body trapped under a fallen pillar. Half the man's torso was torn away, and only one side of his face remained. "Recognize what's left of this man?"

"Never saw him before."

"My man Sol identified him as the bomber. He was placed by our surveillance team as the man renting an apartment in Tel Aviv. We had it staked out based on a tip."

David shrugged. "Don't know him."

He looked David straight in the eye and followed up his initial question. "We did find this picture of you in his place. Are you sure you didn't know him?"

Suddenly David became very uncomfortable. "Never saw him before."

Lenz opened up a small canvas evidence bag he was holding and pulled out a partially melted plastic card. "Does this mean anything to you?"

His eyes couldn't believe what they saw. It was a *Koinonos* ID card, but the subscriber's name was illegible. "Where did you get this?" David gulped in astonishment as he was about to reach for his wallet.

Lenz pointed to Shoen. "We found it near his body, but we're not sure what it means yet. We have to check it out with Interpol to see if there's any connection to Shoen or somebody else."

Chills ran up and down David's spine. Discretion was the better part of valor, and while he really wanted to keep his mouth shut, he had to answer. "I've seen those in the States. It's a new independent financial system for credit purchasing." His mind whirred with the implications of finding the card at this bombing site.

Lenz stuffed the card back in the bag and began to limp away. "Somebody is going to pay seven kinds of torture for this; that's for sure."

David was aghast as he looked around at the devastation, knowing that he was seeing only a fraction of the decimation that could have occurred. His body was seized in a momentary panic as he thought about the implications of the meeting with Lenz but forced himself to put it out of his mind. As he trained his mind to forget the encounter, at least for now, he scanned the chamber and moved toward the focal point of the room—the Shetiyyah Stone. Then he saw Pano.

Within seconds he was at the man's side. Security, long since moved away from the sacred stone itself to calm the hysterical crowd, did not interfere as he breached the barrier and put his hand on Pano's forehead. "Pano," he said sympathetically, "can you hear me?"

The man did not respond, and David quickly looked Pano over. There was evidence of massive bleeding and obvious trauma. Hesitant to move him, he stroked the man's temples and called desperately, "Pano, speak to me. Talk to me—it's David!" As the events of the day sunk in, he realized that the devastation had now hit home, and David had a flash of foresight. He could see that Pano's body was crushed beyond repair. He knew that Pano would die. The only question in his mind was whether Pano was ready to go.

As if in answer to that question, Pano's eyes flickered open and focused on David. They appeared glazed and weak, and David saw that the pupils were almost nonexistent. But he had a mission now, and he wanted to fulfill it.

"Pano, can you hear me? It's David. I'm here!" He could feel the tears surging up inside and wondered if they were for Brandon, Pano, or himself. He had never shown the man in front of him any particular kindness in life and was now grieved to see him die, not knowing if he knew Jesus as his Savior or not. The question nagged at his soul as he saw Pano's eyes dilate, and he could see partial recognition in the man's eyes. *I promised myself to tell Brandon. Can I do less to Pano?*

"David," he whispered, as the life slipped away, "tell me what to do." The command was open-ended, and David was surprised and taken off guard. "I know it's over. I know he's there. Tell me how to know him."

David smiled as he realized the mercy of God and the gift that the Father had given through his Son. A free gift, open to all who asked. He looked down upon the shell of the man who had walked in less than an hour ago. As life slipped away out of his broken body, David knew that it was not too late to call out to God.

"Pano, listen to me. Call on the name of Jesus. If you believe on him, that he died for you, you will be saved." He wiped the sweat off the dying man's brow and closed his eyes briefly in prayer. *Please, Jesus, let him believe!*

He was greeted with a stare more coherent than he had expected. Pano looked him squarely in the eyes. He blinked twice and closed his eyes. "I understand. And I know. I know who he is, and I call out to him to save me and take away my sin." Pano smiled as he leaned his head back against David's outstretched arm.

David moved to bring the head more comfortably toward him as he saw the life escape from this man.

"David, do something for me," Pano gasped as he opened his mouth, laboring to breathe. "Tell Brandon what happened."

David nodded and pushed the hair off Pano's brow. "I will, Pano. I will." David did not trust himself to say anymore. He just sat and waited. With his free hand he grabbed Pano's wrist and put his hand in his own.

"David," he said weakly, "let him know that it's okay to trust Jesus to forgive our sins. Tell him it's okay. Tell him I said so, and that I did. While I thought of him."

David nodded in response and watched as the man's eyes twitched, then closed for the last time. He felt pressure in his palm as Pano squeezed his hand to emphasize his last words, and then the hand fell limp.

Time seemed motionless as Pano's spirit departed and David watched. No one came to ask what he was doing there or who the man was who had been laid to rest on the sacrificial stone. But David knew. And he knew Jesus did, too.

Kavidas joined Stein in his office to watch the telecast of the Israeli military evacuating the wounded from the Temple Mount using giant Sikorsky helicopters, while the dead were wheeled by carts into trucks waiting outside the compound. Glimpses of victims being lifted out of the mosque's debris and put onto stretchers, along with mourning survivors and family members, provided the backdrop for interviews. Reporters were questioning Israeli and Moslem officials separately, avoiding any spokesperson from the Mossad for the present. Speculating on what terrorist group would claim responsibility for the bombing consumed a great deal of the conversations, but no hard information was released over the airwaves.

"Make some phone calls—find out what's going on," Gregory ordered Mort after a period of silence.

After Mort left he room, Gregory returned to his contemplation. He knew what had to occur in order for his plan to unfold in the Holy Land, the place where destiny would ultimately place him. That's why the outcome of this mission was an important factor in the fulfillment of his objective. *It's not the right time yet, is it?* he reasoned as he continued to watch the broadcast.

There was elation on Mort's face as he returned.

"Things went well?" Gregory asked.

Mort gave him a 50-50 gesture. "Bad and good. The Dome of the Rock monument was only slightly damaged, mostly the interior. Our intelligence suspects something went wrong with the placing of the device, and perhaps somebody, maybe the police, got there and warned the worshippers since the doors were all opened. Dissipated the blast—maybe 30 fatalities. Our man Shoen was killed in the operation—"

Gregory always interrupted when he became impatient. "And the good?"

"Douglas was uninjured, but it looks like he'll be implicated in the attack. The *Koinonos* card you told Shoen to plant was found, and since it's an American organization founded by Douglas, there's a good chance Israeli and Arab police will embroil him in this."

Gregory smiled. "It's not exactly what I wanted, but it will do for now. Society will demand a scapegoat, and they can no longer take it out on Shoen, so make sure they incriminate Douglas, and that will be the end of him."

Mort nodded obediently and walked out. He had more phone calls to make.

At 5:30 p.m. the same day, the Israeli police were at the Institute to question David under suspicion of complicity in the planting of an explosive device in a religious monument. The Institute's president, Dr. Edward Slantz, formerly of Detroit, and his staff attempted unsuccessfully to dissuade the American and European media from televising the police visit to minimize the bad publicity. Their tenacity convinced him that they were on a mission to exploit and ruin both David and the Institute.

Since 1948 when Israel declared its statehood, Israeli police had a reputation of being extremely thorough and unrelenting. With the nation living in a constant state of military readiness due to continuous border disputes, the military and police authorities could not afford to be slipshod.

Born in a refuge camp to returning Soviet Jews after World War II, Jacob Mergenthal, a nimble man of average build, resided over the position of inspector of police for the past five years. He had a history for preserving the integrity of Eretz Israel, the Land of Israel, at any cost. He viewed any person or entity that affronted his country or its peace as a personal enemy.

Inspector Mergenthal politely directed David into a well-lit room. "Mr. Douglas," he began respectfully, "could you summarize your affiliation with a group that had its origin in Florida, a group called *Koinonos?*"

Returning the question with a smile, David replied, "I was one of the founders of that organization. It was merely a financial network designed to operate as an independent system from the newly created *Masterlink* credit card system."

"And would you define their political aspirations?"

David sensed the direction the inspector was headed and carefully chose his words. "None. The group was simply a bartering, buy-and-sell type of network to help out others in our fraternal organization."

The inspector opened a file he was holding, then said gruffly, "We have an Interpol report on you that documents your being involved in considerable trouble back in America." He flipped through several pages as David sat confidently assured. "Things like organizing protests to march on a Rainbow Pharmaceuticals, their corporate headquarters; harassing a drug company's sale of an AIDS vaccine; obstruction of a national company's right to free enterprise through a credit system—"

"You have that all blown out of proportion," David interrupted dispassionately. "Rainbow is up to a colossal world-wide conspiracy—"

"Is that why you attacked Gregory Kavidas, the owner of Rainbow Pharmaceuticals, at a symposium in Jacksonville, because you believe he's heading up a conspiracy?"

Suddenly David realized he was unwittingly incriminating himself, which he had set out not to. "No comment."

Inspector Mergenthal was only getting started. He pulled out fax copies from Interpol of David's picture on the front page of the *Miami Star* along with other news articles and danced them in front of him. "No comment on this, Mr. Douglas? Is it pure coincidence that you bailed out of Florida after all this ruckus and relocated in Israel—or did you have a plan to form a new political party over here?"

He closed the file and continued, "Because of the high regard we have for the Biblical Institute and your association with Dr. Samuel Barrett, who contributes greatly to our culture by his studies in antiquities, we are not going to press charges at this time. However, it is my duty to advise you that you cannot leave Israel until the investigation is completed, since you are named as a possible co-conspirator to the bombing. You have a history of being a troublemaker, but because we lack probable cause, we are releasing you into the recognizance of Dr. Barrett."

He opened the door and let Dr. Barrett in while pronouncing his decree, "Please be sure to keep me informed of your daily whereabouts until further notice."

Once outside the police headquarters, Dr. Barrett attempted to discuss the interrogation with David, but David fell sullen and refused to talk. He knew he was in a grave predicament.

Dr. Slantz peered over the rim of his eyeglasses at David. "Don't you think you should retain an attorney? This may turn into an international incident that could impact on your life and career, not to mention it could seriously jeopardize the Institute's position here in Jerusalem."

David and Sam exchanged glances. "I'm innocent!" David exclaimed. "Why in the world should I engage a lawyer when I didn't do anything except take my class and family on a tour of the Dome at the same time of the bombing?"

"The wrong place at the wrong time, David," Slantz observed bleakly.

The phone on Dr. Slantz's desk rang. After a moment of listening, Slantz stood up and went to the window.

"Something wrong, Dr. Slantz?" Dr. Barrett intuitively asked.

"A group of Arabs, possibly a delegation from the PLO and undoubtedly Hamas, are forming a protest line outside our gate."

David and Barrett walked to the window.

Slantz looked down at the crowd and added, "I have a friend in the police department; that was him on the phone, and he told me that you've been branded a *Christian Zionist*—one who will do anything to rid Jerusalem of the Arabs to usher in the Christian era here in Israel. One who will sacrifice Moslems if need be to achieve your goals, with the same determination you portrayed back in the States. It doesn't look good."

"The closer you get to the consuming fire, the more dangerous it is," David paraphrased. "I cross the Atlantic Ocean to begin a new life in obedience to the Lord here in Israel, and now I'm being framed."

"By who?" Slantz asked.

David waved him off as he shook his head. "You wouldn't understand."

Barrett assisted. "David and I believe that Gregory Kavidas, the Greek-American pharmaceutical magnate—"

500

"I know who he is, Dr. Barrett," Slantz grumped. "One of the most influential men in the world. Don't tell me you think *he* is behind this?"

"He has been trying to destroy me and my family for nearly two years now," David asserted as he twisted his moustache, "and he apparently is not going to stop until he achieves his goal."

Futility and desperation swept over David like a squall. He began, for the first time since leaving the States, to calculate his chances of survival.

"We at the Institute are very satisfied with you, Mr. Douglas, but we need to protect ourselves, so you must clear yourself of any connection with this disaster." He reached over for his Rolodex. "Shall I call the Institute's attorney for you?"

David contemplated his answer for several seconds. "Not just yet. I want to pray with Kathy for direction. I'll let you know tomorrow."

At 8:30 in the morning, under armed escort, David made his way through the crowds that lined the entranceway into police headquarters, where Mergenthal ushered him into his office. He asked him to sit down in a chair. "I hate to say this, but conditions have worsened, Mr. Douglas. Not only is the Arab sector turning up the heat, but we have new reports that could lead to you having a probable motive in the bombing." He walked over and looked out the window at the burgeoning horde. "Over here, if the Arabs get stirred up, we must take immediate action to prevent rioting that could lead to war. Their Grand Mufti is calling me every three hours for answers."

David dropped his face into his hands. "I told you before, I'm innocent."

"That doesn't fly, Mr. Douglas. Our data-gathering network now tells us that you have an affiliation with Zionism. Are you in any way connected with the Atara L' yoshna—the extremist group?"

"I've never even heard of them."

"You do believe in Zionism, don't you?" he demanded. "Then—"

"Yes," David interrupted, "I believe Israel is the homeland of the Jews. That's what the Bible teaches. What's wrong with that?" he argued.

"I believe that too, Mr. Douglas, but I don't go around planting bombs in Arab mosques to force the Moslems out so the Messiah can come in. There's a big difference. Now if we link that unstable Zionist mentality with your Christian fundamentalism and then top it off with your radical *Koinonos* group, we have the makings of a political faction that may *very well* have hired an explosives expert like this fanatic Shoen."

His intimation about Zionism worried David.

"But I don't even know the man nor am I concerned with Zionism," David maintained. "And even if I did, would I willingly remain on location during the bombing and be blown to bits?"

"A diversionary tactic to throw us off perhaps. You knew you would be safe," he temporized. "At this point, your connection to Shoen is the missing link. But we do have that photo of you that we're still working on." He lifted the phone and pressed the intercom button. "Send in an escort to see Mr. Douglas home."

David stood up and with piercing eyes attempted to appeal to Mergenthal's better nature. "You're doing your job; I know that. But again, I had nothing to do with this bombing, believe me. I only came to Israel to teach at the Institute and live in peace; that's all."

"Mr. Douglas, the public outcry for this heinous crime will continue until the guilty party or parties is charged and brought to justice. The Jewish and Moslem communities will demand retribution for this, short and simple." He pointed to another file on his desk. "Although Shoen was certainly guilty, our investigation shows that the people, and I say this unofficially, in a land where substitutionary atonement was a way of life, will demand a living sacrifice to satisfy the transgression." He bit his lip as he opened the door and warned, "Stay close."

Brandon wasn't sure he was happy about coming back to Nabat Kibbutz. He was glad to get the chance to shower and be more in touch with civilization. He just hated leaving Petra when things were going so well. He was more than a little annoyed when the runner came into camp and told him he had to go back to the kibbutz for an important phone call. He was hoping to have made the trip after the kibbutz had received word that Pano was on his way back. Now it looked like he would have to make another trip within the next few days. An unwanted delay.

He spent the rest of the day trying to get a hold of his father back in the States but had very little success. Between the time change and his father's schedule, he was better off writing. He tried to get in touch with Dr. Barrett, but he knew how hard he was to reach in the middle of a dig.

He was somewhat confused as to why the important phone call was from the Institute. He thought that David would have called himself with any information that the Institute would have considered vital. His curiosity began to get the better of him when the phone finally rang. He pushed any anxiety into the back of his mind, attributing it to the fact that he was not at the camp, where he felt he should be.

"Hello?" he answered simply in English, not knowing what to expect on the other end.

"Brandon, is this Brandon Lane?" came an unfamiliar voice. "This is Dr. Slantz, president of the Institute."

"This is Brandon Lane. How do you do, Doctor? It's nice of you to ring me. How is everything going at the Institute?" Brandon paused and waited for a reply. When no answer was forthcoming, Brandon pressed the issue. "Doctor, are you there?" He felt suddenly disquieted by such a purposeful silence. He sat up fully erect and braced himself for whatever news the doctor had.

"Brandon, I wish I didn't have to be the one to tell you this. I know we've never met, and I wish that David or Kathy could have been the one to break this to you. However, they can't contact you right now."

"Why? Has something happened to them?" Brandon felt his anxiety well up into a panic as he thought of his friends being in trouble. Suddenly the fact that he was no longer in Petra seemed meaningless. If a friend was in trouble, he was going to be there and help him out of it.

"They're in a big mess with the explosion at the mosque, but that's not what I called about."

"Doctor, I've been up in an archaeological dig for some time. I'm not sure I know what you're talking about. What mosque? What explosion?" Brandon's fear was now causing him to sweat and begin to tremble. He could feel the adrenaline begin to course through his body.

"There was an explosion at the Dome of the Rock. For some reason, David is being implicated. We are trying to get him extricated, of course, but the entire incident is beginning to mushroom. It's turning into quite a political event."

Brandon, even in his excited state, could tell that the man was understating the true and current climate in Jerusalem. He knew all too well the shock waves that an explosion at the Dome of the Rock could cause. World politics, however, was not one of his priorities at the time. He was more concerned with the well being of his friends.

"Doctor, has David or Kathy been hurt? Have they been arrested?" He was beginning to feel exasperated as he continued to pull the story from the reluctant doctor.

"No, the authorities have not placed them in custody. They are continuing to investigate. We should know soon. David and Kathy are both cooperating with the various agencies working on the problem. As to being hurt, neither of them were injured in the blast."

Brandon breathed a sigh of relief. "I'm glad to hear that. Can you get someone out to Dr. Barrett and notify him? He'll want to be nearby to help out. If you think it would help, I'll be glad to come to Jerusalem and stand up for David."

"No, Brandon. I don't think you should come to the city for now. And Dr. Barrett's already been notified. He was here right away. He came immediately after the bombing. In fact, he was going to be the one to call you. But he has been so busy coordinating things with David and helping him out. The job kind of fell to me."

"Well, if Sam is back in Jerusalem, my friend should be there, too. I sent him down to meet with David and then Sam on some business that we're conducting from here." Brandon felt his demeanor begin to slip back into his normal business mode. He relaxed on his bed and started to flip through some of the itinerary papers he had brought with him from camp.

"Yes, Brandon. Pano is here as well."

From the second that Dr. Slantz spoke Pano's name, Brandon felt an icy finger wrap itself around his heart. With dread, he stood up and walked over to the table, bracing himself against the wall as he formulated his next question.

"Is he there with you? Can I speak to him?" Brandon closed his eyes tightly as he waited for the answer. Hundreds of ideas and pictures began to run through his mind as he pleaded with his own thoughts. *Please pick up the phone, file mou! Please!* He began to rock back and forth as he stood at the table, and his foot tapped wildly against the floor in

504

desperation.

"No, Brandon. He's not here. That's the reason I called. Pano is dead. He was killed in the explosion at the mosque."

Brandon had steeled himself for the answer and had braced his entire body for the impact of the words. It did no good. His muscles went limp, and his entire body pitched toward the wall. His forehead struck the doorframe as his body hit the table, swinging him around so that his back hit the door. His legs gave out, and he slid to the floor, still clutching the phone in his hand. He could hear the man's voice coming from the receiver but couldn't respond. The reality set in and took on the form of a numbness that spread from his head, where he had hit the wall, to his arms that now could not lift the phone to his lips. His eyes, now open, just blankly stared straight ahead, seeing nothing, just drinking in the surroundings.

How? Why? Things were starting to go so well. Images of Pano flashed before his eyes, and with almost no emotion, he let them go by, unable to focus on any single picture. Not knowing how long had gone by, he let out a sigh, allowed his head to lean back against the door, and closed his eyes.

He concentrated on the phone in his hand, long since gone silent, and raised it again to his ear. "Doctor," he croaked out weakly, "are you still there?" His voice already felt raspy, as if he'd been crying, when in fact he had not yet shed a tear. He knew that was coming, but he was not yet ready.

"Yes, Brandon, I'm still here. And I am sorry." Having had to deliver such news many times, it was obvious Dr. Slantz was accustomed to the initial grief and was both courteous and wise enough to know that the less said the better.

"Thank you for telling me, Doctor. I suppose I will have to go to Jerusalem after all." He took a deep breath and let it out as slow as he could.

"I know you want to, but I think you should wait where you are. At least until we know what is happening with David."

Accepting this in his mind and pushing it aside, Brandon moved on to his principal concern. "Did he suffer?" The thought of Pano lying there, bleeding and in agony, was more than he could bear. He could wait a little, if he knew that Pano had not been tortured.

"No, he didn't suffer. And David was with him till the end, holding his hand. Giving him comfort and urging him to reach out to Jesus. To take peace in his hand."

Brandon smiled slightly, knowing that David would do just that. "Thank you for that news. It does bring comfort to know that he's with Jesus now," Brandon answered wearily.

"He wanted you to know that Jesus gave him peace, and he wanted you to have it, too."

"Well, I'm sure David will give me the rundown when I see him," he answered shortly, his nerves starting to fray, "but I'm sure you'll understand that I don't feel very much at peace right now. I can't help but feel that God is somewhat capricious in his giving. Peace to Pano but misery to me." He felt guilty about the tone of his voice, but couldn't help his anger. If he didn't share some of it with this kind doctor, his emotions would burst, and that barrier, once down, would not be put up again that easily.

"I can understand how you would feel that way, Brandon. Let me know if you want to talk or if there is anything I can do." The man's sympathy was genuine, and Brandon tried to take it as such.

"Thank you. I'll remember that." He hung up the phone, then put his head in his hands and waited for the tears to come. When they didn't, he pulled his knees into his chest and grabbed his legs with his arms and tried to curl up as tightly as possible. He began to rock again, moving his body back and forth with an unconscious rhythm that provided just enough distraction that he didn't have to think.

The paneled van pulled up to the Institute's rear exit and flashed its headlights twice. "He's here," Kathy announced while peeking out the window.

"Just a few more minutes," David advised as he continued to highlight the maps before him. He glanced up at her and asked, "All packed?"

Kathy nodded, then started pacing up and down the apartment floor.

Sam sensed her anxiety and embraced her softly. "You'll be all right. Don't worry. Once you're over the frontier, your family will be safe."

Kathy sobbed profusely. "I thought we were going to be safe here in Israel, but that wasn't meant to be." The children walked in and saw their mother crying and went to her aid. They clutched her legs in silence.

Barrett attempted to console her. "The day will come when you and your family will be vindicated and you can return; you'll see."

"Paul, help your brother bring the suitcases to the front door," David directed calmly.

His sons quietly obeyed. Hillary went and sat on the sofa, combing the hair on her doll. David recognized the heightened level of apprehension in his family and forcibly commanded his will to be strong.

David stuffed the maps into his attaché case and signaled to Sam that the time for departure had arrived. "I should be in contact with Brandon within two days."

"I'll contact him and let him know," Sam replied. He walked to the window, then said, "Hershel will guide you well. He has been a faithful assistant of mine."

"As soon as I get near Jordan, I'll send him back."

"They'll brand you an outlaw and consider you a fugitive, David. Just like King David was when Saul chased after him in the wilderness 3,000 years ago. But as our God watched over King David, so too will he watch over you."

David fell on his neck and gave him a holy kiss. "Thanks for the prayer, Sam, and for Hershel. May the Lord watch between you and I until we are able to meet again in peace." He looked once more at his apartment, then turned off the light as they picked up their suitcases and walked into the night.

Mergenthal stood on the steps of the Biblical Institute, flanked by news reporters, angry Moslems, and Jews.

An arrogant newswoman shoved a microphone near his face. "Inspector, are you going to hold the Institute responsible for Douglas's escape?"

"No, the Institute knew nothing about it."

"Do you know where he fled to?"

"That's privileged information. I'll just tell you that we are now adding more men to the investigation."

The reporter directed her cameraman to pan the unruly crowds while asking, "Do you anticipate any trouble due to this development, like rioting?"

"I prefer to think there will be a peaceful, civil reaction to this." He waved the rest of the reporters off as he walked into the Institute.

Mergenthal had a very high regard for the Biblical Institute because it promoted American-Israeli diplomatic relations. He would make it his business not to implicate the Institute in their manhunt. "Did Douglas give you any hints that he planned to flee?" he asked Dr. Slantz.

"None," Slantz replied. "He is a man of integrity, and my guess is that this business just pushed him over." He gestured toward the outdoors and asked, "Is it any wonder that he took off? With that mob forming, do you think he would be treated fairly?"

"He would be given the full protection of the law, like anybody else."

"Well, that's debatable," Slantz argued. "With the pressure you're under from your superiors and the Arab League to nail somebody, I seriously question the legal process." He cocked his head. "By the way, whatever became of your investigation of Shoen?"

The inspector debated whether or not to divulge any information about Shoen, then opted to be open and friendly. "Off the record, I'll tell you that we haven't been able to link him with any outsiders—he probably was a loner operating from within Israel—but that's not to say that Douglas is not an accessory to the crime. We hope to find out conclusively in the next few days."

Slantz pointed outside again. "Things could get pretty hot around here until then."

"We have assigned extra personnel and have the military standing by if need be." Inspector Mergenthal and stood up to leave, then as a feigned afterthought asked, "Any speculation as to where Douglas might be heading?"

Eyes met eyes in a steely test of character. "Like I told your detective, I haven't the slightest idea, and that's the truth."

Mergenthal mused for a moment, then said, "Well, he left all his belongings, taking only clothes and some personal things. Obviously it was a quick decision." He opened the door and politely said, "Thanks for your

508

time. I'll be in touch." He took a step and paused for one more imperative. "If you should hear from him, it's your Christian and civil duty to advise me."

"I will, Inspector," Slantz promised.

Mergenthal replaced the phone and turned to one of his veteran detectives, Abraham Yalom. "That was my contact in Miami with the Federal Bureau of Investigation. He doubts Douglas would return to the U.S.—there's nothing there for him. He has his family with him, and he's severed any ties with his college and church. The *Koinonos* thing is dying off over there, and his buddies are all here in the Mideast."

"Narrows it down for us," Yalom observed.

"Yes, and I suppose I'll have to get his mentor, Dr. Barrett, involved in this now. I really didn't want to. Casting aspersions on a man with his reputation and political clout can only mean trouble for us when you look closely at our case."

"You were hoping this would all go away, weren't you?" Yalom asked intuitively.

"If the truth be known," Mergenthal confided, "we really don't have a case. The thread of evidence linking Douglas to Shoen is so thin—just a photograph and conjecture on our part. Any good attorney could get him off. Makes us look like jerks for implicating him."

"But because of the political outcry, we need to have somebody to blame," Yalom proffered.

Mergenthal nodded. "That's the pitiful part of this whole thing. Shoen's dead body isn't good enough because this is a *religious* thing, and the zealots will want live blood. Blood to appease their god for the blood shed at the Rock."

"Blood shedding begets more blood shedding," Yalom observed bleakly. His mind flashed back to the 1989 Israeli military occupation of the West Bank and Gaza Strip where Palestinian protesters and Israeli troops clashed, culminating in the October 8, 1990, uprising around the Al-Aqsa mosque on the Temple Mount were 20 Palestinians died and 150 were injured. *Americans could be trouble too*, he thought.

He recalled the incident at the Hebron mosque that halted the Israeli-Palestinian peace talks. A New York–born Jewish extremist opened fire with an automatic rifle on hundreds of praying Moslems. The physician-turned-terrorist left his home in the West Bank settlement of Qiryat Arba, entered the mosque at the Cave of the Patriarchs, and killed 29 worshippers, wounding 98—three more being trampled to death in the stampede to escape. The perpetrator was pummeled to death by the horrified Moslems.

As an afterthought he said, "Why don't you just let the investigation and search for Douglas 'run out of gas' so to speak. He's probably left Israel and you'll never find him, so why not cut your losses now and move on?"

"And focus on the culprit we do have. Shoen?" Mergenthal conceded.

Yalom nodded. "Then we can bring some closure to this and move on." He stroked his chin in contemplation. "Make a public statement that infers that Shoen *may or may not* have had Douglas as an accomplice—our evidence is inconclusive—and that the investigation is ongoing. Then emphasize that at this point, people should get on with their lives—to get beyond it. Of course you'll have to restrict the media or they'll nurse this thing along for months."

"Hmm, yes, it makes sense." After Yalom left his office, Mergenthal made up his mind to bring in Barrett as a perfunctory measure to placate the Jewish and Moslem officials. Giving the order to slow down the search for Douglas would follow.

The black Rolls-Royce pulled up to the base of the Acropolis; then the chauffeur stepped out and opened the door for Gregory and Mort. Mort suggested that the weather was ideal for a walk of the ruins, providing both physical and mental therapy. Citing the urgent need to revise his strategy now that Douglas had escaped, Gregory reluctantly agreed.

The uphill walk to the mount invigorated them both, temporarily ameliorating Gregory's anxiety. They walked through the Parthenon into the Erechtheum ruins, a temple built between 421 BC and 405 BC and sat down on a fallen pillar of the southern portico.

Gregory's spirit brighten slightly as he looked around at the tourists enjoying the remains of the ancient city. "The word from Sidmaj about Douglas's skipping out confirmed my hunch that the time is still not right for us to advance religiously. If our plan for Shoen and Douglas had been successful, that would have been the go-ahead for the next step to begin relocating to Israel to begin our work. As it stands, that is yet future."

Mort stood up and held his hand on one of the columns still standing. "When Mnesicles, the architect for this temple, designed this monument, he anticipated it would take a while for the plans to leave the drawing board and become a real-life building. But it took 16 years before his masterpiece would be complete." He pointed to one of the Caryatid supports, named after the girls of the town of Caryae, and continued, "And after 2,000 years, his handiwork still shows." Mostly for his own clarification he summarized, "Obviously we must be patient and wait in order for all the members of this colossal chess board to be put in their proper place. When our work is complete, it will stand until the end of time."

"Agreed." Gregory sighed. "Meanwhile, we will concentrate on developing the final stages of *Masterlink* and maneuvering the political figures through the EC until we are able to infiltrate the religious realm."

Gregory knew that historically the only true way to control the masses was through a religion, and the day would come when he would be the central figure in global worship.

"And Douglas?" Mort asked.

Gregory looked Mort in the eyes and with a tolerant smile said, "He'll show up again; you can count on it. And when he does, the world will be totally different."

Brandon left Nabat Kibbutz almost immediately after hearing the news of Pano's death. He told no one and arrived back at the camp very sullen, again erecting barriers between himself and most of the team, who didn't know the reason for his melancholy.

They will soon know the source of my grief, he thought.

He suddenly found himself in a period of intense meditation. *Maybe I've been wrong all along. I've been trying to look either out or in when I should have been looking to see who was at my side.* He sat down again and stared at a picture of him and Pano before they left America only a short while ago. But this time, it was without anger. He knew that Jesus would be there for him, too. He realized that now would be a good time to look and see just what God was offering.

Three days of hiding at Hershel's brother's house in Beersheba gave David's family a time to rest. Situated only 44 miles south of Jerusalem, midway between the Mediterranean Sea and the southern end of the Dead Sea, Beersheba was considered the southern extremity of the Promised Land. It was at Beersheba that the patriarch Abraham made a pact with Abimelech, king of Gerar, pledging seven ewe lambs to bear witness to the sincerity of his oath of mutual assistance, hence the name *Beersheba*—"the well of the seven." Abraham returned to this city after God prevented him from offering up his son Isaac as a human sacrifice on Mount Moriah.

In the early morning of the fourth day of their journey, David climbed up the ladder leading to the roof of Hershel's brother's house with his two sons to view the Negev. He walked over and sat on top of the solar water heater drum and gazed into the horizon. In the Negev, barrenness was everywhere. Only intermittent vegetation and an occasional bedouin dotted the hostile wilderness.

"We're not going out there, are we, Dad?" Alan asked.

David turned the opposite direction, to the east, and pointed. "No, we're going out there instead."

"But that's a desert, too," Paul remarked.

"Well, we're not going to live in it; we're just going to travel through it on our way into Jordan where Uncle Brandon is."

"Mom said we're going to live in a kibbutz about 20 miles from a place called Petra. Will that be fun?" Paul asked while grimacing at his brother.

David cracked a smile when he thought about God's sense of humor. "Yeah, that'll be fun. Don't you remember when we were in Florida I told you that living in the Mideast would be an adventure? Well, tell me this hasn't been an adventure so far."

Alan glanced at his brother. "Sure, it's been an *adventure*, but are we running away?"

David put his arm around Alan. "No, we're not running away from anything or anybody, but we must wait for the Lord to open the door before we can return." He stood up and faced Jerusalem with confidence. "The Lord will give us another chance at another time."

Bibliography

This novel is a fabrication of the author's interpretation of Bible prophecy. It is completely fictitious, but the support research is real. The following reference works may assist the avid reader of prophetic fiction and eschatology to learn more about the events that may soon come upon the earth.

BOOKS

Archer, Gleason L. *The Rapture: Pre-, Mid-, or Post-Tribulational?* Grand Rapids, MI: Zondervan Publishing House, 1984.

Backhouse, Robert. *The Kregel Pictorial Guide to the Temple.* Grand Rapids, MI: Kregel Publications, 1996.

Baer, Robert. *Sleeping with the Devil.* New York: Crown Publishers, 2003.

Biblical Archaeology Society. *The Origins of Things.* Washington, DC, 2002.

Brickner, David. *Future Hope: A Jewish Christian's Look at the End of the World.* San Francisco: Purple Pomegranate Productions, 1999.

Bullinger, E. W. *Number in Scripture.* Grand Rapids, MI: Kregel Publications, 1996.

Chapman, Colin. *Whose Promised Land?* Grand Rapids, MI: Baker Books, 2002.

Cohen, Gary. *Understanding Revelation.* Chattanooga, TN: AMG Publishers, 1987.

Cooper, David L. *An Exposition of the Book of Revelation.* Los Angeles: Biblical Research Society, 1972.

Crichton, Michael. *State of Fear.* New York: Avon Books, 2004.

Dickason, C. Fred. *Angels, Elect & Evil.* Chicago: Moody Press, 1995.

Edersheim, Alfred. *The Life and Times of Jesus the Messiah.* McLean VA: MacDonald Publishing Co., circa 1979.

Evans, Michael D. *Beyond Iraq, The Next Move.* Lakeland, FL: Whitestone Books, 2003.

Folger, Janet. *The Criminalization of Christianity.* Sisters, OR: Multnomah Publishers, 2005.

Friends of Israel Gospel Ministry. *Eye on the Middle East.* Bellmawr, NJ: The Friends of Israel Gospel Ministry Publication, 2001.

Fruchtenbaum, Arnold. *The Nationality of the Anti-Christ.* New Jersey: American Board of Mission to the Jews, Inc., circa 1978.

Gold, Dore. *Hatred's Kingdom.* Washington, DC: Regnery Publishing, 2003.

Grant, George. *The Blood of the Moon: The Roots of the Middle East Crisis.* Brentwood, TN: Wolgemuth & Hyatt, Publishers, 1991.

Guiley, Rosemary Ellen. *Encyclopedia of Angels.* New York: Checkmark Books, 2004.

Hagee, John. *Jerusalem Countdown.* Lake Mary, FL: Front Line Publishers, 2006.

Hamada, Louis Bahjat. *Understanding the Arab World.* Nashville, TN: Thomas Nelson Publishers, 1990.
Hislop, Alexander. *The Two Babylons or the Papal Worship.* Neptune, NJ: Loizeaux Brothers, 1959.

Ice, Thomas, Randall Price. *Ready to Rebuild.* Eugene, OR: Harvest House Publishers, 1992.

Kennedy, D. James. *The Real Meaning of the Zodiac.* Ft. Lauderdale, FL: TCRM Publishing, 1997.

Kent, Phil. *The Dark Side of Liberalism.* Augusta, GA: Harbor House Publishers, 2003.

Koch, Kurt. *Occult Bondage and Deliverance.* Grand Rapids, MI: Kregel Publications, 1976.

LaHaye, Tim. *No Fear of the Storm.* Sisters, OR: Multnomah Press, 1992.

LaHaye, Tim, Thomas Ice. *Charting the End Times.* Eugene, OR: Harvest House Publishers, 2001.

Lindsey, Hal. *Apocalypse Code.* Palos Verdes, CA: Western Front Ltd., 1997.

Missler, Chuck. *Prophecy 20/20.* Nashville, TN: Nelson Books, 2006.

Netanyahu, Benjamin. *Fighting Terrorism.* New York: Farrar, Straus, and Giroux, 2001.

Patterson, Lt. Col. Robert. *Dereliction of Duty.* Washington, DC: Regnery Publishing, 2003.

Pentecost, J. Dwight. *Things to Come.* Grand Rapids, MI: Zondervan Publishing House, 1975.

Posner, Gerald. *Why America Slept: The Failure to Prevent 9/11.* New York: Random House, 2003.

Price, Randall. *Fast Facts on the Middle East Conflict.* Eugene, OR: Harvest House Publishers, 2003.

Price, Randall. *Jerusalem in Prophecy.* Eugene, OR: Harvest House Publishers, 1998.

Price, Randall. *Unholy War.* Eugene, OR: Harvest House Publishers, 2001.

Ritmeyer, Leen and Kathleen. *Secrets of Jerusalem's Temple Mount.* Washington, DC: Biblical Archaeology Society, 1998.

Sears, Alan and Craig Osten. *The ACLU vs. America.* Nashville, TN: Broadman and Holman Publishers, 2005.

Shoebat, Walid. *Why I Left Jihad.* Top Executive Media, 2005.

Shorrosh, Anis A. *Islam Revealed.* Nashville, TN: Thomas Nelson Publishers, 1988.

Spencer, Robert. *The Politically Incorrect Guide to Islam.* Washington, DC: Regnery Publishing, Inc., 2005.

Steadman, Ray C. *Waiting tor the Second Coming.* Grand Rapids, MI: Discovery House Publishing, 2007.

Walvoord, John F. *Daniel: The Key to Prophetic Revelation.* Chicago: Moody Press, 1989.

Walvoord, John F. *The Revelation of Jesus Christ.* Chicago: Moody Press, 1966.

White, John Wesley. *WW III: Signs of the Impending Battle of Armageddon.* Grand Rapids, MI: Zondervan Publishing House, 1977.

Woodrow, Ralph. *Babylon Mystery Religion.* Self-Published, 1966.

PERIODICALS

Discerning the Times Digest. *The Global Environment Agenda to World Government and Religion.* www.discerningtoday.org. 2001.

Biblical Archaeology Society. *The Origin of Things.* Washington, DC: 2002.

THE TRIBULATION SERIES
Book Two

The
Lights of God

Ralph D. Curtin

**How much would you pay
to know the mind of God?**

In 31 B.C., the Temple high priest, Amariah, flees to the ancient Essene fortification at Qumram, on the shore of the Dead Sea, to avoid Roman persecution. Hidden in his saddle bags is the Urim and Thummim, the revelatory device used to ask and receive answers from God, which hasn't been seen since the Babylonian captivity in 586 B.C. When Amariah is murdered, the Urim and Thummim are buried with his body in a cave-vault, later sealed by an earthquake that strikes Judea in 32 B.C. There they remain until the present day, when they are discovered by Ishmael, a treasure-hunting young Arab Bedouin, then are passed to Rehavam Krasnoff, an unscrupulous chief investigator for the Israeli Antiquities Authority.

When two masterminds in Athens, Gregory Kavidas and Mortimer Stein (who've developed the global financial network *Masterlink*—the precursor to a cashless world economy) become alerted of the stones' discovery, they set out to seize the stones for themselves...before their evil agenda is exposed.

THE TRIBULATION SERIES
Book Three

The
Seven Seals

Ralph D. Curtin

A sinister plot advances.
But who will believe the shocking truth?

When the Arab-bloc nations begin to encroach on the land of Israel, Israel's Prime Minister Zeman makes a deal with Gregory Kavidas, head of the European Union (formerly the European Economic Commonwealth) to ensure Israel's defense. But is all as it seems? Is the heralded Kavidas really the savior of Israel—or the prophesied Antichrist, out to destroy God's people and their land?

As PLO/Hamas sympathizers seize a nuclear power plant in Israel, Russia is set to invade. On the Mount of Olives, two strangers appear out of nowhere, with a special message for the *Koinonos* resistance group. But can such a small contingent make a difference against the supernatural, evil forces marshalling their efforts in a campaign of death?

Coming Soon…

THE TRIBULATION SERIES
Book Four

The
Seven Trumpets

Ralph D. Curtin

**Earth is in its final days…
and God is displaying His wrath
against everything unholy.**

Meteor showers blanket the earth. Volcanoes erupt. God's wrath consumes one-third of all trees and grass on the planet. Demonic forces are unleashed to torment unrepentant man. The world is in chaos.

Paul Douglas, son of Bible college professor David Douglas and his wife, Kathy, remains in Jerusalem while Simon and Jonathan Landau, newly acquired members of the Christian resistance group *Koinonos,* join forces with other K-groups in America and Rome to war against the infamous duo, Gregory Kavidas and Mortimer Stein, the masterminds behind the evil plot to take countless souls with them in the Lake of Fire for all eternity.

About the Author

DR. RALPH D. CURTIN is a family man, pastor, and counselor in a large Christian denomination and a college professor at Trinity College, where he teaches Biblical Studies. When he's not preaching or teaching, he's either writing a book or riding his big Harley.

Other interests include a passion for nature photography, of which he has had many of his images published by a stock agent in national magazines. Photo-graphing his grand-children and making DVDs for the family gives him great pleasure as well.

"Through many years of Bible research and being a bit of a news junkie," says Dr. Curtin, "I arrived at the place where I earnestly desired to transform Bible prophecy into reality so that it would be believable. Many people don't read the Bible, but will read biblical fiction. This is my way of educating the public in a non-preaching manner, while giving them a taste of my interpretation of what we may expect in the future. I don't like fluff, so my writing is designed to intrigue the reader, give them facts that interest them, as well as raise their level of understanding on a particular subject. Readers are fascinated with science fiction, so prophetic fiction—which has a great degree of the supernatural—will only excite the reader who craves suspense, yet knows that our Good God will win in the end."

You may write Dr. Curtin at: **drrcurtin@bellsouth.net**